Against All Odds

Russian Nobility in the Crucible of War and Revolution

Copyright © 2016 Kyra Petrovskaya Wayne

The views expressed in this work are solely those of the author and do not necessarily reflect the views of the publisher, and the publisher hereby disclaims any responsibility for them.

This is a work of fiction. All of the characters, names, incidents, organizations, and dialogue in this novel are either the products of the author's imagination or are used fictitiously.

Bennett & Hastings titles may be ordered through booksellers or by contacting: sales@bennetthastings.com.

ISBN: 978-1-934733-88-2 paperback
ISBN: 978-1-934733-90-5 hardcover
Also available in eBook format.

Edited by Adam Finley and Celeste Bennett
Intern: Ciara Caya
Cover design by Kyra Alexandra Wayne

Please visit kyrapetrovskayawayne.com.

Against All Odds

Russian Nobility in the Crucible of War and Revolution

To Natalie,

with all my love.

Grandma *Kyra*

Kyra Petrovskaya Wayne

Bennett & Hastings Publishing
2016

Other Publications by Kyra Petrovskaya Wayne

Kyra
An Autobiography, Prentice Hall, 1959

The Quest for the Golden Fleece
Lothrop, Lee & Shepard, 1960

Kyra's Secrets of Russian Cooking
Prentice Hall, 1961

Shurik: A WWII Saga of the Siege of Leningrad
Grosset & Dunlap, 1970

The Awakening
Grosset & Dunlap, 1973

The Witches of Barguzin
Thomas Nelson, 1975

Rekindle the Dreams
Dell, 1977

Max: The Dog that Refused to Die
Alpine Publications, 1979

Quest for Empire: A Saga of Russian America
Hancock House Publishers, 1986

Lil' Ol' Charlie
Alpine Publications, 1989

Quest for Bigfoot
Hancock House Publishers, 1996

Pepper's Ordeal
Hancock House Publishers, 2000

The Chaperone
Trafford Publishing, 2006

Memoirs of a Piano
Xlibris, 2007

Contents

From the Author

It took me almost four years to write this book. I dedicate it to the memory of my father, who was one of the Russian pilots during the First World War and the Russian Civil War that followed.

I don't remember my father. I was a toddler when the Bolsheviks executed him. However, my mother, a beautiful and talented young woman, kept his memory alive by reminiscing about him.

Years later, my young son became fascinated with aviation. In time, he became a pilot in addition to being a physician. My son seemed to have inherited his maternal grandfather's love of flying. He urged me to write a book about my father.

I did not have any tangible materials such as letters or photographs. My mother had destroyed all of them in order to hide her noble background and survive the years of Red Terror. I had only my mother's memories. Thus, I decided to write a *novel* set during the years when my parents were young—the years of the Russian Revolution and Civil War—as well as the first years under Soviet rule, which I lived through as a young child and can still recall.

This book is a work of fiction. I plunged into research about military aviation and the monumental changes the revolution brought to Russia and, indeed, to countries around the world. During my research, I came upon photographs of Tsarist military medals. Something about the Order of St. Anne looked familiar to me, even though I had never seen it before. Then it dawned on me: I *had* seen the red ribbon with gold edges from which the medal was suspended. I had that ribbon!

For seventy years, it had been nestling at the bottom of my sewing basket!

My first memory of it dated back to when it had been at the bottom of my mother's sewing basket. As a child, I had tried to expropriate it for use as a hair bow. It was useless as a hair bow: too stiff and too short, impossible to make into a bow. The ribbon went back into my mother's basket, and I forgot about it.

Then, when the Second World War engulfed Russia, I found myself in the Red Army, along with millions of other Russians. While preparing to join my unit in the defense of Leningrad, I raided my mother's sewing basket to prepare my own sewing kit with emergency needles and basic threads of black and white. For no conscious reason, I placed the folded piece of red ribbon into my kit, and it stayed there through the Siege of Leningrad and beyond.

After the war, when I married my American husband and was getting ready to leave Russia, the red ribbon landed in my new sewing kit and traveled with me to America. Why did I keep it? That is a bit of a mystery, even to me.

I still have it. Now, I know that it belonged to my father. It now rests with my own military medals.

I consider it my "message in a bottle," for it seems as ancient and romantic a medium of communication as those sealed bottles set adrift by mariners. In this case, the ocean was time, and the message was one of love and encouragement, from my father to me.

Kyra Petrovskaya Wayne
Poulsbo, Washington U.S.A.
January 2016

Particularities of Russian Names and Forms of Address

The Russian language, if spoken correctly, is very expressive. However the complexity of Russian names and forms of address is confusing. I shall try to explain some rules using the most popular names as examples.

Every Russian name, male or female, must have a patronymic following the given name. Thus every Ivan, the most popular name through the centuries, will be Ivan plus his father's name, like Ivan Petróvich or Ivan Vasílievich or Ivan Nikolayevich. The same rule applies for females: Maria will be called Maria Petróvna, or Maria Vasílievna or Maria Nikoláyevna, like my grandmother. Note the ending of every patronymic name: for males is *vich* and for females it is *vna*.

This is the polite form of address and it is used in official documents with the addition of a family name, such as Ivan Petróvich Ivánov, or Ivan Vasílievich Petróv or whatever it may be. The same rule applies for females except with different endings: Maria would be Maria Ivánovna plus her husband's last name but with a feminine ending of *va*, like Maria Nikoláyevna Ivanova.

The same structure is used for last names with different endings: Ivan Ivánovich Ivanóvsky or Maria Nikoláyevna Ivanóvskaya. My own name Kyra (pronounced kee-ra) Vasílievna Petróvskaya is a good example.

The third group of Russian names has its roots in the Ukrainian language. Names such as Savchenko or Kovalchuk have no female forms and usually belong to the lower classes.

In my grandmother's time the formal way of address was strict and the family name was never used in a private conversation. It was considered impolite. Thus General Ivanovsky should be addressed just as General or Your Excellency. His wife would be called Madame and sometimes also Your Excellency without mentioning the family name. If the general and his wife knew the person with whom they were conversing and if they had given permission to be called by their names, they would be called by their first name with the patronymic, simply Ivan Petrovich, not mentioning his official title of General.

In the XVIII century after the French Revolution, Russian nobility chose French as their first language. Hundreds of French exiles poured into the country and began to turn Russians into Europeans. Children of the nobility began to learn French as toddlers, speaking in their own native tongue only to the servants. Even family dogs and riding horses were trained using the French language. The upper classes from the Tsar down, adopted the manners and the rules of French politesse.

In my time, after the Communist Revolution, forms of address became standardized to become simply Comrades. Generals became Comrade Generals without using their family name. Their wives would be also addressed as Comrades, without their personal names. In case of a close relationship between parties, they addressed each other by their personal names, often without using the patronymics. There were no more "Excellencies" and "Madames", nor were people addressed by their ranks or titles. All titles were abolished. Everyone became a "Comrade" and in official conversations the family name was added, such as Comrade General Ivanovsky, or his wife Comrade Ivanovskaya, without mentioning their personal names. All military ranks were renamed and the word "General" was changed into Comrade Commander, without mentioning his personal name. Women were allowed to keep their maiden names if they wished, but always with feminine endings. Russians were ordered to speak Russian.

A new specification entered the language adopted from the French Revolution, that of a Grazhdanín and Grazhdánka, meaning citizen for both genders, and the Civil War that followed the Soviet Revolution became known in Russia as Grazhdánskaya Voiná.

During the Second World War Stalin reverted to the old military ranks, from generals down to several grades of lieutenants, returned the epaulettes and gold embroidered tunics and ordered the old word "Officer" back into circulation.

To encourage millions of Soviet soldiers to fight the invading German forces, new medals were created to commemorate their valor and victories, including the medal For Defense of Leningrad. I am one of the honored recipients of that medal.

I hope I have not confused you with all these explanations. Reading my book I think it all becomes quite simple and logical and perhaps even interesting. If not, ignore the details and enjoy the story!

Cast of Characters

This is a fictional story of two great Russian military families based partially on my own family during the first World War, the following Revolution, the Civil War, and finally the first few years of Communist rule.

Historical characters, such as Tsar Nicholas II or Grigory Rasputin or Vladímir Lenin and others, are mentioned in fictional form. This allowed me to include them as characters in my story, while adhering to their historical backgrounds.

In Petrograd

General Vladímir Ivanovich Rezanov
Varvara Michailovna Rezanova, his wife
Andrei Vladímirovich Rezanov, a pilot and a hero, their son

General Sergei Petrovich Orlov an old friend of General Rezanov
Maria Nikoláyevna Orlova, his widow
Larissa Sergéyevna Orlova, (Lara) their daughter, later wife of
    Andrei Rezanov

Ksusha, Maria Nikoláyevna's old servant, later her confidante
Natasha, Larissa's maid, later her best friend
Olga Nekrasova, piano teacher at Smólny Institute, Larissa's teacher
    and Maid of Honor at her wedding
Anna Vyrubova, close friend and confidante of the Tsarina, liaison
    between Rasputin and the Tsarina

Rasputin (Grigory Efimovich), confidant of the Tsarina, murdered
    by a group of conspirators
Prince Felix Youssoupov, one of the richest men in Russia, an
    assassin of Rasputin
Vladímir Purishkevich, reactionary member of the Duma, (Russian
    Parliament), an assassin of Rasputin
Grand Duke Dimitri Pavlovich, nephew of the Tsar, a conspirator
    against Rasputin
Stanislaus Lazavert, doctor at a hospital train financed by
    Purishkevich, a conspirator against Rasputin
Captain Ivan Sukhotin of Preobrazhensky Regiment, friend of
    Youssoupov, conspirator against Rasputin

Gátchina Flight School

Colonel Gorshkov, Commanding Officer of the Gátchina Flight School

Captain Sergei Rublev, one-legged instructor and Andrei Rezanov's mentor, a Best Man at his wedding

Lieutenant Philip Shilov, one of the cadets at the Flight School and Andrei's roommate

Petrovich, an old mechanic, a former mechanic on Igor Sikorsky's six-engine planes, the largest planes in the world at that time

Lieutenant Nicholai Borisov, aide-de-camp of General Rezanov

Lieutenant Alexander Seversky, Andrei's main trainer and mentor, one of the Best Men at his wedding

At the Front Lines

Captain Vassily Egórov, (Egórka) an ace pilot, best friend of Andrei

Captain Alexander Kozakov, famous Russian ace, Andrei's commanding officer

Igor Kóshkin, Commissar of Kozakov's Flight Detachment, Andrei's and Egórov's enemy. Later, benefactor to Larissa and her child

Colonel Barsky, Chief Surgeon at the field hospital

Captain Vyacheslav Tkachev, famous ace, assistant to Grand Duke Alexander, the Commander of Russian Air Forces

In Odessa

Doctor Shubin, Chief Surgeon at Odessa Memorial Military Hospital

Veronica, Scottish Chief Nurse

Glafíra Ivánovna, Chief Castellansha of hospital supplies, later Commissar of Memorial Hospital

Madame Juliette, (Julia) proprietress of a fashionable dress salon, a friend of Larissa

Yasha, Julia's son, an eleven-year-old genius, Odessa chess champion

Isaak Cohen, Julia's father, a thief and a member of Mischka Yaponchik's criminal gang

Minna Solomonovna, his wife

Arthur Antonovich Anatra, owner of airplane factories in Odessa and the Crimea

Akim, horse carriage driver, later a godfather of Larissa's daughter

Nina (Nínochka), Larissa's and Andrei's daughter, born during the Civil War

After the War

Vladímir Klimov, chief musical representative at the Mariinsky Opera House

Alicia Eduardovna Bolshakova, a famous mezzo-soprano at the Mariinsky Opera House

Colonel Bolshakov, Alicia's husband, old friend of General Rezanov

Nikolaí Svirsky, an officer at the Imperial Guards, later an artist at the Mariinsky Opera, groomed for the leading baritone roles, in love with Larissa

Fatima, a young Armenian soprano, groomed for leading roles at the Opera House

Doctor Kline, Medical Chief of Women's Hospital

Commissar Gavrilko, Bolshevik's Chief of Women's Hospital

Dimka, a Commissar at a rubber boot factory, Natasha's lover, friend and benefactor to Larissa's family

Historical Characters

Tsar Nicholas II

Tsarina Alexandra Feodorovna, his wife

Tsarevich Alexis, their son, heir to the throne, suffering from hemophilia

General Mikhail Alexeyev, Chief-of-Staff of Russian forces, later a leading person in promoting the Tsar's abdication

Alexander Kerensky, the head of the Provisional government

Vladímir Ilyich Lenin, (*Ulianov*), popularly known as *Ilyich*, political and ideological leader of the Bolsheviks (the Reds)

Leon Trotsky, Lenin's chief political deputy, later an organizer of the Red Army that won the Civil War

Mishka Yaponchik, a colorful Jewish gangster, for a short while fighting with the Reds in the Civil War, but assassinated by them for desertion with his "army"

General Baron Peter Vrangel, progressive and talented final Commander of the Whites who successfully arranged the evacuation of over 150.000 Russian troops and civilians from five ports in the Crimea

1

"Tell me how my first Papa disconnected the bomb." Nina pulled the blanket up to her chin. It was cold in their room.

"You must know it by heart, I've told it to you so many times," chided her mother.

"Tell me again!" Nina wriggled closer to her mother. Their hard iron bed, too narrow for two people, felt cozy and safe to her.

"It's too late." An image of her young husband clinging to an airplane's wing streaked across Larissa's mind, followed by a shiver of painful recollection. "Go to sleep."

"I'm not sleepy. Tell me at least how Papa proposed to you—the funny part about the horses. I like that part!"

Larissa smiled and ruffled the girl's golden hair, which reminded her so much of Andrei. "Well, all right. I was about seventeen, in my last year at school, when I first noticed your father. He had just graduated from the military academy and was assigned as an aide-de-camp to your grandfather's regiment—"

"I know, I know that," Nina interrupted impatiently. "I want to hear about the horses."

"Yes, the horses ..." Larissa resumed, "The first time your father captured my attention, we were at a Grand Ball at the Nobleman Assembly. He was a duty officer that day. Being 'on duty' meant—"

"I know. He wasn't allowed to dance and had to stay next to the flag," Nina said quickly. "You've told me that before. I want to hear about the horses."

"I was smitten," Larissa continued dreamily, ignoring her daughter's petulant tone. "Your father was so handsome in his Cavalier Guards dress uniform, standing there under a portrait of the Tsar ..." She smiled at her memory of Andrei.

"It wasn't 'love at first sight.' Our fathers were old friends and our families had often spent time together, but your papa and I had only met during the holidays—when both of us were home from our boarding schools. When we were children, I never liked your papa. He was too noisy and rough, or so I thought then. To be fair, when I was about your age I did not like *any* boys."

"You're right, they are too rough! I don't like boys either," Nina said.

"The first time I *really* noticed your papa was at that ball."

"I want to hear about the horses. I mean, when you were riding together and his horse farted!"

Larissa felt uncomfortable and then laughed at herself. Mention of a bodily function was always unpleasant, but a fart seemed innocuous compared to all she had survived. "Well, yes … anyway," she continued, "several months after that ball, our parents invited friends for a country picnic. Your grandmothers and the other ladies rode in carriages with the children, but the young women rode on horseback with the men."

"You too?"

"Certainly! I was a good rider and had my own horse since I was ten. Her name was Lucinda."

"I wish I had a horse … or at least, a cat!" Nina sighed. "How were you dressed?"

"All the young ladies wore elegant Amazon habits. Mine was made of midnight blue velvet. It had a lace *jabot* and was set off by a chic little top hat with a veil and an ostrich plume." Larissa sketched the line of the feather with a graceful wave of her hand. "I had on black leather gloves with deep cuffs, like the Three Musketeers would have worn, and shiny black boots."

"Did you ride sidesaddle?"

"Of course! Ladies never rode astride."

"So, what happened?" Nina prodded, even though she knew what was to follow.

"Well, your father and I found ourselves riding behind the others …"

Nina giggled. "You did it on purpose! You were *in love*!" She pressed closer to her mother, her imagination alive with the image of a handsome young couple riding side by side.

"So, there we were, the horses going *clip-clop, clip-clop*, the dogs running ahead, then waiting for us, then running again."

"What dogs? You never told me about the dogs."

"Well, we always had dogs."

"What were their names?"

Larissa smiled at the memory of their clumsy St. Bernard, a stable mate for the horses, and elegant Irish Setters, whose shiny, feathery coats were brushed daily by her father's orderlies. "The St. Bernard was named Caesar, and the Setters were Brutus and Diana."

"The horses," Nina reminded.

"Yes. Well, there we were, riding side by side, your papa's horse practically touching mine. Suddenly, your papa reached out for my hand and …"

"He said, 'I love you.'" Nina savored the familiar story.

"Not quite yet. First, he said 'I must ask you something very important, Mademoiselle Lara.' I blushed, my ears burned, and my heart beat faster. I just *knew* that he was going to tell me he loved me. I had been madly in love with him ever since that ball, and I felt certain that he was in love with me. We had used every chance to meet. We'd gone to the opera, not alone of course, but with our parents. We had been to several balls where he had placed his name on every line in my dance book, so we danced only with each other, which would not have been proper if he had not intended to propose. And when he was not on duty at the regiment, he came to our house for tea on Thursdays, when your grandmother received visitors."

"The horses," reminded the child.

"Yes. So, your father reached for my gloved hand and—"

"And at that moment his horse farted!" Nina finished the sentence, laughing in delight.

Larissa laughed with her. "Yes, my dear Nínochka, the horse—. Loudly!"

"Say it! Say the word!" Nina insisted.

"Well, all right …" Larissa hesitated. "The horse *farted,*" she whispered.

Nina happily kicked her feet under the blanket and kissed her mother. "There! You said it! What happened next?"

"We pretended that nothing had happened. Of course, we were mortified, but we pretended that we had not heard a thing."

"So, Papa tried again."

"Yes. He tried again." Larissa lowered her voice in imitation of a man. "'Dear Mademoiselle Lara, I wanted to tell you that I am—.' At that moment his horse began to," Larissa paused, "to empty itself."

Nina pealed with laughter. "It went *flop-flop*, instead of *clip-clop!*"

"I could have *died* with embarrassment. Your father turned red as a beet, and his orderly, a Cossack, who rode behind us, broke out in loud laughter. Do you know what 'an orderly' is?"

"Oh, yes. It means a soldier who shined Papa's boots and took care of him. Sort of a military servant."

"Exactly. So, the orderly shouted—"

"'Tell the lady that you love her!'" Nina cried, quoting the familiar phrase.

"Yes, that's exactly what the orderly shouted. So, in a way, your papa's orderly proposed to me on behalf of your papa!"

"What did *you* say?"

"What do you think?"

"You said 'I love you too, and yes, I'll marry you.'"

"That's right. That's exactly what I said." She kissed her daughter's smooth brow. "Now, go to sleep."

"Tell me more. Tell me about Papa flying an airplane. And about the bomb, how he—"

"Some other time. Go to sleep."

"I'm not sleepy. Tell me at least how you played piano for the Tsarina," Nina kept stalling.

"Next time."

"Then, tell me something else. I'm not sleepy yet. Just for five minutes, please! Tell me something else about Papa. Tell me how he learned to fly an airplane."

"Your papa learned to fly the same way you are learning to write," Larissa said, running a finger along the curve of her daughter's chin. "He went to school."

"He went to school? Like me?" Nina imagined her father as a student in short pants, a satchel of books bobbing upon his back. She giggled. "Was he a good student?"

"Of course he was a good student. Now go to sleep, darling ... I am exhausted."

"Oh, all right. Don't talk. Go to sleep," Nina said with grown-up benevolence, patting her mother's shoulder, "you must be *really* tired." Her imagination was occupied by visions of her father as a schoolboy. "Mama, what was the name of his school?"

"Gátchina, darling," Larissa yawned. "Gátchina Flight School."

"Gátchina," Nina said, sleepily as she rolled onto her side. "Good night, Mama."

Larissa kissed her. "Good night, Nínochka." Nina plumped up her pillow and in a moment was asleep.

"I wish you'd stop filling her head with romantic stories," Nina's grandmother grumbled from her bed. "The less she knows about the past, the safer it is for all of us. Our lives are over, Larissa."

Larissa did not reply. Telling Nina about the family's past was a bittersweet pleasure. Her mother was right. Although memories of her youth were lovely, they were dangerous. She would talk with Nina in the morning and tell her to keep those stories secret ... but how could she explain their past to a seven-year-old without unleashing a flood of questions?

Perhaps she could tell her that all the stories were really fairy tales and that she used the family names to make it more interesting ... No that would never do. Nina was too smart, she would never believe it. The best thing would be to tell her the truth and explain *why* their conversations were so dangerous. She hated to bring *fear* into her daughter's innocent life.

Larissa got out of bed, kissed Nina's warm cheek, and tucked the blanket around the little girl's slim body. It was cold in their room and would grow colder by morning. Their allotment of firewood had run out two days before. She would have to barter something on the black market for fuel, a thought that worried her.

Larissa gathered Nina's underwear and stockings for laundering. She left their room and shuffled down the dark corridor, its solitary light bulb having burned out long ago.

At the threshold of the cheerless communal kitchen, Larissa waited patiently while her neighbor Ivan Vassilich performed his nightly rituals, pressing his nostrils with a thick finger and dislodging a huge amount of green mucus. Ivan Vassilich suffered from chronic sinus infection.

"I am sorry to have made you wait, Comrade Larissa," Ivan Vassilich said as he gathered his soap, toothbrush, and tin box of tooth powder. He grinned at her, showing yellowed teeth.

"It's quite all right, Ivan Vassilich, I'm in no hurry." Larissa waited for the old man to leave the kitchen before she scrubbed the sink with her own soap, erasing the vestiges of his toilette as well as whatever remained from other neighbors who shared the same cold water flat. She had trained herself to focus on other things while she worked on unpleasant tasks.

"I must convince Mother to part with one of her rings," Larissa told herself, as she ran frigid water over Nina's small garments. Maria Nikoláyevna was reluctant to sell anything from her dwindling supply of jewelry. "And rightly so," Larissa thought as she applied soap and scrubbed at a mud stain on Nina's clothing. Ration cards issued to two unemployed females and a child provided barely enough food coupons to last a month. They were fortunate to receive occasional food packages from Nina's other "Papa," but how much longer he would be in their lives? They needed so much in addition to food! They needed shoes, but there were no coupons for shoes. Nina was outgrowing her winter coat, and winter—that long, bitter Leningrad winter—was just around the corner.

Whatever they needed could be obtained through the black market. It meant risking arrest, but Larissa felt there was no choice. "But how long will our 'savings' last?" she wondered as she rinsed the garments and noticed how red her own hands had become.

"These hands," she thought wryly, "that once played piano for the Empress." She chuckled bitterly.

The refined education Larissa had received at the Smólny Institute for Noble Girls failed to prepare her for the new, Soviet reality. In the brutal days of the new society, her knowledge of foreign languages or ability to play the piano marked her as being from the wrong social class. She was of the *nobility*. She and her mother were of the *former people*, and as such, they were marked for extinction. *The Dictatorship of the Proletariat* was in power and clearly written into official government policy.

Larissa had been trained as a nurse but work was scarce. She had gladly taken menial jobs but been fired because of her *family's past*. Refusing to be discouraged, she registered at the Leningrad Department of Unemployment. She went there every day to check the lists of available jobs, but there was no future in the Soviet Union for non-proletarians.

She and her mother had all but abandoned their hopes for a better life. The only pleasure in their lives was little effervescent Nina. Subconsciously, they competed for her love. Larissa fueled the child's imagination with siren songs of the past, while Maria Nikoláyevna made her rag dolls with exquisitely embroidered features. Nina was like a golden thread winding its way through the dark tapestry of their lives.

Unaware of their rivalry, Nina loved them both with the innocence of a much-adored child.

Larissa felt tears gathering and made an effort to stop them. What was the use of crying? Her mother was right; their lives and the lives of their friends were over. "Friends? What friends?" she thought bitterly as she wrung her daughter's garments. Their friends from before, the people who really knew them, had either been *liquidated* or had emigrated from Russia, and the world seemed to be uninterested in the fate of those who had failed to escape Russia and were now left to drown in the treacherous waters of the Soviet regime.

For a moment, Larissa stood paralyzed by the enormity of all she had witnessed. A whole class of people, obliterated—their homes and property, confiscated, their families destroyed—by that horrendous cyclone, the Revolution. She closed her eyes and recalled the beloved men who had died too soon: fathers, husbands, brothers, and sons—all gone. Some had fallen on the battlefields of World War I. Others devoured by Russia's desperate Civil War … and then there had been the Bolshevik firing squads.

She shuddered. Perhaps she should marry Igor Kóshkin, after all … He was in love with her and he adored Nínochka. Igor, a Red Commissar of Andrei's Detachment would provide a safe life for them, even though he was Andrei's mortal enemy. No! She could not betray her husband's memory.

Larissa forced herself back to the present. She reminded herself that she was but one among millions of widows made destitute by war. She gathered her daughter's damp clothes into a fraying towel and returned to the room that housed her mother, her daughter, and herself—all that remained of the once-great families Rezánov and Orlov. She hung her daughter's damp clothes over a line to dry. Then she made the sign of the cross and joined Nina in their bed, asking herself the same old question: how had it all happened? How had proud, powerful Russia devolved into a conglomeration of men and women who were eager to destroy everything for this new ideology? How did it happen?

2

It happened slowly, starting in the previous century with the assassinations of the Tsar and other ruling figures of Russian government. It swelled into a revolution in 1905, which became a dress rehearsal for *two* revolutions in 1917 that ended three hundred years of the Romanov's empire and saw the word "Russia" almost completely displaced by a new word, "Soviet."

However, before it happened there were a few peaceful years before the First World War when Russians of the upper, educated classes enjoyed their lives and the working classes, given certain guarantees, found their lives a little easier.

In 1909, an exciting event occupied the world's attention. A young Frenchman, Louis Blériot, a daredevil pilot, had crossed the English Channel in a plane of his own invention, instantly becoming the world's hero. Thousands of young men of all nationalities were afflicted with the desire to become pilots, while their governments, recognizing the military possibilities of flying machines, hurried to order new machines for their military forces. France became the first country promoting the new craze—aviation!

Russia, unwilling to lag behind, ordered a couple dozen flying machines from France and sent a group of young cavalry officers to French flight schools.

This was good news. Russia needed something positive on which to focus. Here was a new technology that would allow men to fly! The high commands of the Imperial Army and Navy decided to promote the birth of aviation by creating a special new branch of military service. They declared 1911 to be the year of the All-Russian Aeronautical Exhibition, at which there would be demonstrations of machines flown by Russia's first military pilots.

Invitations went to all commanding officers of the Army and the Navy, along with the diplomatic corps, members of the Cabinet, some delegates of the Duma, (Russian Parliament) and members of the nobility. The aeronautical exhibition became *comme il faut,* an affair one must be seen attending. General Vladímir Petrovich Rezánov invited his wife and his fifteen-year-old son Andrei, a cadet at the Cavalier Guards Academy, to accompany him to the exhibition.

General Vladímir Petrovich Rezánov and his wife, Varvara Mikháilovna, sat across from their son, Andrei, in an open carriage. It was sunny on the first day of the exhibition. The sky, after several days of that monotonous gray peculiar to St. Petersburg, was a dome of pale blue, sun rays periodically breaking through thin clouds. A crowd of high military officials and their guests was assembling at a weed-choked field on the city's outskirts. Young Andrei observed the colorful tableau with growing excitement, as dozens of carriages carrying dignitaries and guests formed a giant horseshoe around the field's edges.

Ladies in light summer costumes hid themselves from the sun under white parasols, chatting and flirting with the men. The air buzzed with subdued, polite conversations in several languages, peppered with occasional bursts of laughter and the neighing of carriage horses as they greeted arriving groups of cavalry officers. The riders dismounting to mingle among the guests threw reins to their orderlies, who led the horses away. Everyone was intrigued by the "heavier than air flying machines," as the new invention had been described in the newspapers.

Andrei felt exultant simply being present. He worshiped the young pilots who stood frozen at attention next to the flying machines. Dressed in black leather jackets and helmets, with white silk scarves around their necks and their faces all but hidden by goggles, the pilots had recently returned from flight training in France. Now, they were about to demonstrate their skills before Grand Duke Alexander Micháilovich, the head of the new Imperial Russian Air Service, and the admiring public. Andrei saw them as gods about to exercise their powers.

A military band played patriotic marches as Grand Duke Alexander and his three young sons, with an entourage of aides-de-camp and French, British, and German military attachés, inspected the strange machines. Photographers took pictures of the Grand Duke and his sons at the controls of airplanes as the spectators waited, hiding their impatience. After what felt like hours to Andrei, the Grand Duke and his party returned to a special viewing platform decorated with flowers and the Russian imperial eagles. The music stopped. The flying demonstration was about to begin.

"What silly contraptions! They look as if some capricious child made them of sticks! And look at all those young fools in their leather garb, ready to risk their lives," General Rezánov grumbled under his breath, making sure that Grand Duke Alexander could not hear him.

Young Andrei said nothing. More than anything, he wanted to be one of those "young fools in their leather garb."

The Grand Duke gave a signal and the pilots climbed into the new machines, French Blériots and Farmans. Beneath each plane, mechanics dressed in crisp overalls hurried to remove the ropes that tethered each plane to short posts. There were five mechanics to each plane. Four mechanics held tight to each plane's wings while the fifth stood in front of the propeller and awaited the pilot's command. At the shout, "Contact!" the fifth mechanic grabbed the propeller with both hands and gave it a mighty pull.

Not all the planes started at once. Some in the viewing crowd smirked, as if to say, *"Machines cannot fly, and here is proof!"* The men at the propellers repeated their maneuver until the propellers were turning on their own, whirling faster and faster, with an accompanying increase in noise. The men who held the planes down released their hold on the wings and stepped aside. The planes began to roll. The crowd applauded.

The noise of the engines grew to a deafening roar. On the field's periphery, the cavalry horses grew nervous. Carriage horses trembled and whinnied, straining at their harnesses. Coachmen comforted the animals but were frightened themselves. No one, except the pilots, had ever seen flying machines before.

The wind blast from the propellers flattened grass and tore hats off men's heads. Frilly parasols were snatched from women's hands and floated in the wake of the planes like gigantic white chrysanthemums tossed by the wind.

One by one, the aircraft wobbled and bounced across the field, gaining speed until all of them lifted off the ground. The deafening noise subsided. Servants hastily retrieved men's hats and ladies' parasols and then ran back to the safety of the crowd, fearful that the flying machines would start falling all over the field.

Andrei was transfixed. He knew, *he felt in his bones,* that the planes would fly and land safely. He only wondered how long they could stay aloft. They looked so delicate, like dragonflies, circling the field, fragile and unsteady, wings dipping in one direction then another, as if at the will of the wind.

The airplanes climbed until they looked like tiny specks in the sky. Then they grouped into pairs and circled the field, gradually descending.

Throwing back their heads, spectators followed the maneuvers with various degrees of alarm or skepticism. Women made the sign of the cross as they watched the fliers through elegant opera glasses, while men followed the flimsy objects through powerful field binoculars, many still thinking that flying machines were another folly of the High Command.

As the planes began to descend, the noise grew louder and the horses grew nervous. Members of the crowd held their breath and then sighed with relief when the planes touched down on the field and tumbled to a stop in front of the reviewing stand. No plane had failed to land safely. No pilot had been killed.

The military band launched into a triumphal march from *Aida.* The age of Russian aviation had been born.

Riding back home in his mother's new English carriage, Andrei happily chattered about his impressions. "Imagine, how wonderful it must be flying high up in the sky, looking down at cities and rivers and forests and feeling free as a bird!"

His parents exchanged amused smiles. They adored their only son. "Next, you'll be saying that you want to become a pilot yourself!" his father said with an indulging smile, knowing that such an idea would never enter his son's mind. The Rezánovs were always cavalrymen. It was in their blood to ride and to fight on horseback.

"Yes, Papa. I would like to transfer from the Cavalier Guards Academy to a flight school," Andrei replied, misreading his father's good-natured remark.

The expression on the general's face changed immediately. "You must be joking, young man," he said icily. "No son of mine would ever become a greasy mechanic hopping over the air in some, some ..." The general's face turned red in his search for a devastating epithet, "... in some fangle-dangle contraption!"

Andrei's mother placed her gloved hand on her husband's knee. "Don't irritate yourself, Volódya, think of your heart. Andrei was only joking."

"No, Madame. Such 'jokes' must be squashed at once, before they become ideas," the general replied, glaring at his son. "I *never* want to hear such nonsense again!"

"Yes, Papa," Andrei made an effort to sound sincere, but to himself he promised that as soon as he graduated from the academy he would apply for admission to a flight school.

When Germany declared war on Russia, August 1, 1914, Andrei Rezánov thought it meant his opportunity to apply for pilot training; however, his father was quick to pull strings and have his son, still a cadet, assigned as a junior aide-de-camp "with specific duties" to his old friend, General Sergei Orlov. In exchange, General Rezánov took Orlov's young son, Peter, as *his* aide-de camp. Neither of the generals wished to risk losing their sons in the mobilization. Both declared that at present the main duties of their sons involved graduating from the officer's academy.

Andrei and Peter felt humiliated. While thousands of young men were fighting the enemy at the front, they spent their days safely ensconced at military headquarters in Petrograd, the capital's newly Russified name for St. Petersburg.

The shift from "St. Petersburg" to "Petrograd" was part of a cultural defense. Under the circumstances, a Germanic version of their capital city's name was intolerable! Andrei supported the idea, and he longed to be active in the fight against the Kaiser.

Meanwhile, high society continued its rarefied life. The elite patronized the opera and ballet, and attended charity balls and concerts in pursuit of the noble cause of raising funds for Mother Russia's heroic soldiers.

Andrei hated his "specific duties" of accompanying General Orlov to various soirées put on by the Ladies' Volunteer Society. He felt pricks of guilt attending the ballet, seated in the loge behind General Orlov and his family, while thousands of young men his age were risking their lives. Yet, he had to admit to himself, it was pleasant to dance at the balls, flirt with young women, and finally, to fall in love with Larissa, the daughter of General Orlov.

In 1915, Andrei graduated with honors from the Cavalier Guards Academy. He was immediately assigned to his own father's command. He became a junior liaison officer trailing after his father, carrying official documents to meetings between Russia and her allies, France and Great Britain. General Rezánov was one of the military strategists who, like his friend General Orlov, had remained in the capital.

Andrei's dreams of learning to fly had to be postponed. Andrei promised himself that as soon as he attained legal age the following year, he would enroll in flight school. He would find a way, he told himself. Meanwhile, he intended to have a good time courting Larissa!

Andrei and Larissa's blossoming romance was encouraged by their parents. It would be a good match. Both families had impeccable ancestry and substantial inherited wealth. Their fathers had been friends for decades, dating back to when they were cadets at the same Cavalier Guards Academy.

Andrei was confident that Larissa would accept his proposal of marriage. She was madly in love with him! There wasn't a trace of nervousness as the moment approached, which made it all the more appalling when his flatulent horse nearly ruined their perfect moment. They both suffered embarrassment, but good manners prevailed. They pretended that nothing had happened, and Andrei finished his declaration of love as they rode side by side to the family picnic.

Larissa accepted.

They both knew there would be no objections from their parents. Still, tradition required that Andrei ask Larissa's father for her hand in marriage. Despite his confidence in the outcome, Andrei was nervous as he requested an audience with Larissa's father.

General Orlov met him in his study. The general was suffering a nasty cold, shuffling around the house in his pajamas and Siberian fur slippers, his beefy shoulders covered with one of his wife's knitted shawls. "Please excuse my appearance, but I have an influenza," he said hoarsely. "What is so important that I must see you at once?" He sneezed.

"I am sorry, Your Excellency, I had not realized that you were ill."

"Never mind. Tell me what is on your mind. The way you are dressed, in your formal uniform, it must be something very important."

"It is, Your Excellency," Andrei bowed and clicked his heels. "May I have your permission to marry your daughter, Larissa?" He bowed again.

The general had suspected that Andrei's visit concerned a proposal of marriage. He stared at Andrei through his gold-rimmed spectacles, saying nothing, enjoying the young man's growing discomfort. The general paced the floor, pretending to think, his brows gathered in wrinkles as if in deep thought. Then he stopped in front of the burning fireplace to warm his behind and ask gruffly, "Does Larissa know your intentions?"

"Yes, Your Excellency. Larissa Sergéyevna accepted my proposal of marriage."

"She did, did she?" He looked at Andrei quizzically, then laughed and embraced him in a bear hug. "Nothing would please me more, Andrúsha, than to have you as my son-in-law! Sit down, sit down, and take off your gloves! Let's call my wife and Larissa and tell them the news!"

Larissa burst into the room, followed by her mother. "You don't need to tell us!" she cried as she threw her arms around her father's neck. "We were listening at the door!"

And so, they were engaged. Andrei presented Larissa with a pearl and sapphire ring to which he would add a diamond solitaire at their marriage, and Larissa gave her fiancé a gold onion-shaped repeater Breguet pocket watch with the entwined monogram of their initials engraved on its cover.

The wedding was to be in a year, when, they all predicted, the war would be over. Andrei easily convinced Larissa that his secret plan of becoming a pilot would not upset their plans for the future, nor that flying was dangerous, and Larissa, being under the spell of love, was ready to agree to anything he suggested. Shortly after their engagement was announced, Andrei sent his application to the flight school along with the endorsement he had secretly obtained from Grand Duke Alexander.

🎇 3 🎇

Gátchina Military Flight School was located in the suburbs of the capital.

"How convenient! I can sneak up to the city on Sundays and be back before anyone notices my absence," Andrei thought, as he rode toward Gátchina in the smoking car of the commuter train.

He could hardly believe he was on his way to the famous flight school! After months of anxious waiting, his application had been accepted. It had taken the intervention of the Grand Duke himself, but here Andrei was, on his way to Gátchina! His father was furious, but General Rezánov was helpless—as Andrei had known he would be—against the Grand Duke's order.

Through his compartment's window, Andrei viewed a passing landscape of thin forests, neat country dachas—each with a small flower garden—and churches boasting bright blue cupolas topped with golden crosses. It all looked familiar: the same modest landscape, peaceful and comforting, Andrei remembered from his childhood, when an amiable tutor used to take him for a day in the country. Their destination had often been a huge park adjacent to the Gátchina Royal Palace.

Andrei recalled his tutor's lessons: the Royal Palace was once the residence of Tsarevich Paul, despised heir to the throne, whom his mother, Catherine the Great, had exiled from her court. In the decades following his death, various members of the extended Romanov family had lived there. Presently, the palace was unoccupied, and the park and surrounding flat fields—where the Tsarevich used to drill his personal troops—had become training grounds for the Gátchina Flight School.

Andrei extinguished his half-smoked cigarette and stood. Smoking was new to him and gave him a headache, but he stubbornly cultivated the habit, believing it made him look sophisticated. He glanced at his reflection in the window and liked what he saw: a tall, well-muscled young man with bright blue eyes, a straight nose, and slightly wavy blond hair. He smiled, showing brilliantly white teeth, and touched his upper lip to check the progress of what he hoped would be a fine moustache. "Ah well, perhaps one more week ..." Squaring his shoulders, he picked up his cap with its oval insignia, the mark of a cavalry officer, and thought, "Starting tomorrow, I'll be wearing a pilot's leather helmet!" He saluted his reflection.

"And, here I am in Gátchina!" Andrei thought as he jumped down onto the wooden platform.

A number of young officers had stepped down from the train. They gathered around the stationmaster, an old man holding red and green signal flags, and Andrei heard one ask the stationmaster to show them the way to the flight school.

The old man shook his head. "I can't leave. I am the only one here." He waved his green flag and the train moved forward.

Andrei joined the group. "I know where it is," he said. "Next to the palace. It's not too far. Let's go."

The young men introduced themselves to one another. They were junior commissioned officers in various branches of the Russian military, united by their obsession with aviation. An airplane buzzed overhead and, as one, they looked up and grinned. Soon they too would be up there, flying, flying, *flying!*

Andrei led his new friends along the railway tracks and through the old park to a large field. Two well-worn airstrips crossed the field, allowing for simultaneous takeoffs and landings. Barns and stables, once belonging to the palace complex, served as hangars and repair shops. Several airplanes were tied down nearby. A short distance away was a row of empty tent hangars awaiting the delivery of new French-designed but Russian-manufactured aircraft.

"Well, this must be headquarters!" Andrei said.

The group headed toward a long building with the double-headed eagle emblem on display above its entrance.

The duty officer, Captain Sergei Rublev, a man in his early forties, greeted the new recruits in the large central hall, apologizing for not meeting them at the station. "We are short of staff here," he explained, shaking hands with them in the civilian way. "We are short of everything here. We don't have enough planes or instructors. I hope you all speak German, because some of our instructors are Austrian prisoners of war."

"What? Our *enemies* are teaching us how to destroy them?" Andrei thought.

The captain continued. "You probably think that is crazy, but we rely on their sense of honor. In return, we treat our POWs as gentlemen. We are, after all, officers and gentlemen, despite our nationalities." He paused. "I also hope that at the end of your training some of you will choose to become instructors and stay with us. It would save you from going to the front!"

The young men looked at one another, uncertain whether they should laugh. To be safe, they chose silence.

Andrei began to raise his hand like a schoolboy but quickly changed it to a salute. "Where will we be quartered, sir?"

"Ah, yes, quarters. What's your name, Cornet?"

"Andrei Rezánov, sir."

"Well, Cornet Rezánov, I will show you gentlemen to your quarters. I expect all of you to change into the flight school uniforms that the quartermaster has waiting for you. We want our cadets to look dashing," he said and winked.

The young men felt free to laugh.

"Follow me," the captain said. He had a noticeable limp, and Andrei wondered whether he had been wounded while flying. He decided that he liked the man even though the captain seemed a little too informal, his manner almost civilian. Even his looks were unconventional: Captain Rublev reminded Andrei more of the headmaster at a boys' school than a military authority.

Captain Sergei Rublev did look a bit unusual. His face and hands were covered with ginger-colored freckles, a few muted steps down the color spectrum from his flaming-red hair and moustache, a huge monstrosity he often touched as he spoke. He was broad-shouldered but short, and secretly convinced his stature didn't represent his authority to the cadets, all of whom were at least a head taller. To minimize this disadvantage, Rublev fashioned himself "one of the boys," an older brother who spoke their language, laughed at the authorities, and occasionally dared to bend the rules.

All cadets loved him. He hoped the new recruits would soon learn to love him also.

The new men were billeted in a large guesthouse expropriated from Baron Theodore Von Hafenberg. It stood within the park in its own small enclosure surrounded by a tall wrought-iron fence. It had been built by a German architect in the contemporary style known as Art Nouveau, with huge horizontal windows and unexpected protuberances in its façade. All ten elegantly furnished suites faced the park. But the most desirable modern feature of the building was the presence of a bathroom with hot and cold running water attached to every bedroom.

The young cadets, accustomed to spartan living at their academies, had never expected the Gátchina quarters would be so luxurious.

Andrei suggested drawing lots to choose their roommates. He drew the name of Second Lieutenant Philip Shilov, a boyish, sunburned artillerist from the Urals, who looked even younger than the rest of them. They liked one another immediately.

Captain Rublev led the new cadets to the formal dining room, which was to be their mess hall. Long dining tables were covered with stacks of canvas overalls and boots in different sizes. Nowhere could Andrei see any leather jackets or helmets.

"Choose your uniforms and boots, men," the captain ordered briskly, as he twisted his magnificent moustache, which he obviously tended as a gardener would tend a rare ornamental bush.

"But these are *overalls*, sir," Philip Shilov objected loudly.

"Yes, and they are your *uniforms* until you learn how to fly," Captain Rublev replied, enjoying their disappointment. Every group of cadets had the same reaction to the overalls; they always arrived imagining themselves in the traditional pilots' attire of leather and goggles. The overalls were always their first disappointment.

Captain Rublev grinned. "Change, and be back down here in half an hour for assignment to flight groups." He saluted and limped out of the room, still grinning.

"Well, it looks like we won't see leather jackets for a while," Andrei said sarcastically. "That could be, what? A month or two? Or three?" The men laughed uneasily and hurried to their rooms to change.

Thirty minutes later, dressed in baggy overalls and knee-high boots, they were back in the mess hall. The tables were cleared of clothes and set for dinner *á la fourchette*. The men served themselves, unnerved by the lack of military formality. Andrei observed the proceedings with amusement; so far, the flight school felt more like an English sports club than a military installation. "It probably will change tomorrow," he thought.

Captain Rublev returned to the mess hall. The cadets jumped to their feet. "Save the saluting for tomorrow, when you will meet Colonel Gorshkov." He looked them up and down. "You all look splendidly efficient, as if you were a brigade of street cleaners behind a cavalry parade," he said, chuckling wickedly. "You'll have the rest of today to yourselves. Unpack, go for a walk, look at the sunset, become acquainted with each other. Sleep well ..." He left, still chuckling.

The next morning, the cadets awoke to a six o'clock bugle call. They hurried to wash and don their stiff overalls, and then proceeded to the mess hall for a breakfast of fried eggs, hot oat porridge, black peasant bread, butter, milk, and tea.

Colonel Gorshkov and Captain Rublev entered the hall. The cadets sprang to attention.

"At ease," Gorshkov ordered. The cadets remained standing.

"Sit down," the colonel raised his voice slightly. "We, the commanding officers of the Gátchina Flight School welcome you into our flying family. As you must have noticed, we are not strict disciplinarians. We know that each of you is already a fully commissioned officer, trained to lead. You don't need basic indoctrination. You know how to behave like an officer. We also know that each of you, as an officer in the service of our Emperor, will serve with honor. Our code of behavior will become obvious to you very quickly. As military pilots, you will depend upon each other, more so than officers in any other branch of service will. Your motto will be *Honor and Loyalty*." He stopped and looked into their eager faces.

"I want to make it clear, gentlemen, that you must also have a special respect for your mechanics, most of whom are privates. They are *not* your orderlies. Think of them as your equals. Your lives will depend upon the experience and knowledge of your mechanics. Respect that knowledge! Your lives will be in more danger than they would be in any other branch of service. But you have chosen to be in the elite company of fliers. So, prove to yourselves that you deserve to be Russian military pilots!" he concluded solemnly.

The young men jumped to their feet and enthusiastically yelled "Hurrah!"

The colonel continued, "I will mention, briefly, something about the airplanes you'll be flying. They are obsolete, pre-war Farman IVs. Senior cadets, men who have already made their solo flights, are flying newer models. However, you must learn a lot before you fly better machines. You must learn aerial photography and radio signal communications. You must learn to shoot several types of machine guns, including the Lewis, the Maxim and the Vickers, *while flying the aircraft*. You must learn certain emergency repairs, and perhaps even restore some aircraft. Your hands will get greasy with castor oil and your bodies will be in pain. Your teachers will include educated engineers and half-literate mechanics. I repeat: do not look down on the mechanics. What they teach you about airplanes may save your lives."

As Andrei listened, he recalled the proverb *pride goeth before a fall.* Class distinctions could ruin a pilot, he thought, and he added becoming a good mechanic to his list of personal goals.

"You will be divided into small flight groups, constantly rotated," the colonel continued. "In the end, you will be equally well trained. That is all. Carry on." He turned to Captain Rublev.

Captain Rublev stood and touched his moustache, as was his habit. "We want you, future pilots, to be aware of certain small rules. Everyone must always be clean-shaven. You may have moustaches, but no beards. Smoking is not allowed, for obvious reasons: you'll always be close to fuel. Drinking is not allowed. Our discipline is rigid when it comes to flying. You are military men, and we expect total obedience to your commanders." He paused. "We will start at once, with blueprints of the Farman IV. Please, follow me."

The cadets crowded into a lecture hall full of flat desks, its walls covered with enlarged photographs of the Farman IV.

Captain Rublev began his explanation of the aircraft's basic characteristics. "Gentlemen, the Farman IV. The design is French, but we build it here in Russia at Dux, the factory near Moscow. It is a biplane that rests on four wheels, set in pairs. Fabric covers its wings on one side. The aircraft has a *pusher* type construction; that is to say that the engine, a seven-cylinder Gnome rotary type, is behind the pilot. It has a triangular boom assembly joined at the tail. The pilot's seat is located on the leading edge of the lower wing," he indicated the photograph with a wooden pointer. "This construction allows the pilot to see the ground when he looks down, between his feet. The plane's light frame extends forward from the lower wing. It carries the pivoted crossbar, which operates the rudder at the very end of the aircraft. Please note that the crossbar of the rudder is operated by the pilot's feet: the pilot must press with his right foot for turning right, and with the left for turning left. Simple, isn't it?" The cadets agreed.

"The stick is connected to the ailerons, which are used to roll the machine right or left." Captain Rublev moved his body, illustrating the movement. "It is also connected to the elevators. Pushing it forward or backward, the pilot can move the nose of the aircraft up or down. As I said, this Farman IV is obsolete, and our new Farman XVI will be more advanced, but for student pilots, the Farman IV is just right. It has everything necessary to understanding the rudiments of aircraft. Any questions, so far?"

"Yes, sir," Andrei raised his voice. "How powerful is the Farman IV engine?"

"Fifty-horsepower."

"And it's capable of how high a speed?"

"It can reach a top speed of about thirty-five miles per hour. Of course, when we get our new Farman XVIs, you will see many improvements. It will have an enclosed fuselage with an open cockpit for the pilot. It will have a top speed of about sixty miles per hour, and its eighty-horsepower engine will make it easier to fly. Now gentlemen, let's go to the field and meet our Farman IVs!"

Captain Rublev led the way. The cadets eagerly crowded behind him. Andrei's throat was dry with excitement.

※ 4 ※

Andrei found his first lessons surprisingly dull. His flight group learned how to taxi a Farman IV along the airstrip. Back and forth they went, day in, day out, each cadet seated in the fuselage of a dismantled and wingless aircraft pushed around the field by soldiers. Soon, they seemed to know every bump on the strip. Boring though it was, Andrei had to admit it was not easy. Crosswinds often pushed the machines off course and the students had to figure out how to correct the situation. Their best help came from windsocks at each end of the runway. Primitive as they were in terms of technology, windsocks were reliable.

Despite these anti-climactic first experiences, Andrei's first week at Gátchina Flight School passed quickly. There were so many things happening at once that Andrei worried he might miss an opportunity to learn more about aviation. He ran from lesson to lesson and rationed his time spent on sleep and food so he would have more time to study. He was especially fascinated with the varieties of aircraft. He wanted to master them all, but that was out of the question: the ever-expanding war was in constant need of new aircraft, and flight schools had to make do with obsolete or rebuilt machines. When a four-engine Sikorsky *Ilya Murometz* bomber arrived at Gátchina, Andrei jumped at the chance to study it. He spent all of his free hours under the tutelage of an old mechanic named Petrovich.

Petrovich was one of the few dedicated mechanics who had worked with Sikorsky on the original four-engine *Ilya Murometz* bomber. Petrovich worshipped the young designer, Igor Sikorsky, and was fiercely proud of being part of the team that had built "the first in the world four-engine airplane." When the flight school requested Petrovich transfer to Gátchina to train cadets in the mechanisms of the *Ilya Murometz*, the senior mechanic felt it was a demotion. He grew depressed and, in the Russian peasant tradition, went on a binge, drinking without stop for several days. It took Igor Sikorsky himself to convince the old man that the request from Gátchina represented a promotion and well-deserved recognition of the mechanic's abilities. Petrovich felt unworthy of such an honor; however, he stopped drinking, went to a steam bath and sweated for an hour. Then he went to church, lit a candle, and fell on his knees. Bowing low before an icon of St. Nikolaí, he touched the stone floor with his forehead. He prayed that none of his future pupils should suffer death because of his teaching. Feeling somewhat better, he boarded a train for Gátchina.

Petrovich taught Andrei everything about the huge aircraft's workings, but Andrei found that his heart was not in the bulky Sikorsky giant. He preferred a maneuverable, light craft. He imagined himself at the controls of a small, fast airplane, like the Nieuport IV that legendary pilot Peter Nesterov had flown in performing the first "death loop." Nesterov's photograph stood on Andrei's desk next to a picture of Larissa.

A shipment of Farman XVI two-seater trainers arrived, but the cadets of Andrei's flight group could only look at them. The new models were for the advanced cadets.

"How do you like these new machines?" Captain Rublev asked the cadets. He leaned against a wing. The plane tilted slightly under his weight. "Looks rather fragile, don't you think? And yet, it will support any two of you. Look at this plane and imagine you are in it, way up there in the blue sky … lovely, isn't it? Now, imagine yourself under enemy fire, dodging bursting shells or maneuvering this plane in a dogfight. Technical skills will not be enough to see you through. You must develop a special *feeling* for the machine, almost as if it were human. You must *love* your airplane!" He paused dramatically, twisting his moustache as he looked at their eager faces.

"The best I can describe the relationship between you and your machine is to portray the airplane as a demanding mistress. Her allure will seduce you into feeling superior and all-powerful. She will purr and follow your every command. She will enclose you within herself until you believe that you are invincible. Like a clever mistress, the machine will betray and punish you for any mistake or neglect, perhaps even *taking your very life* in revenge. So, think of it that way. Flying is a dangerous business."

Andrei felt uneasy. "Of course flying is dangerous!" he thought. "Why tell us something we already know? Does he think some of us might quit?" Andrei's determination strengthened under the weight of the potential insult. He felt certain he would be flying one of the Farman XVIs within a month.

Andrei's first flight was with instructor Senior Lieutenant Nikolaí Seversky, a middle-aged man whose two sons were also at Gátchina, one already an instructor and the other a cadet. Scion of an aristocratic family, tall and good-looking with an elegant dark moustache and courtly manners, Nikolaí Seversky owned his own airplane as early as 1908. He had trained his sons to follow his passion for flying when they were still boys. By the time they were of legal age, they already knew how to fly and were ready to train as military pilots.

Lieutenant Seversky liked Andrei, recognizing in him the same burning ambition that drove his own sons.

"Let's go!" he said climbing in the front seat of the Farman IV, pointing Andrei to the narrow bench behind him. "Tie the altimeter onto your leg, where you can easily see it. It is a nuisance, but when you progress to flying modern aircraft, you'll find the altimeter in front of you on an instrument panel, where it belongs, but that is far too logical for this old bucket."

"At last!" Andrei thought, securing the round, pocket-watch-sized altimeter above his knee. He felt calm, though his palms were moist inside his leather gloves.

Seversky eyed him steadily, satisfied with the young cadet's serious mien. "To start with, I'll demonstrate the basic rules of moving the aircraft along the airstrip. I realize you have been doing it for days, with men pushing and pulling it around the field, but now we'll use the engine to do it." He motioned to a mechanic to untie the plane.

Andrei shifted on his narrow seat and the plane creaked. Seversky smiled but said nothing.

Another mechanic hand-propped the machine. It choked and coughed. The mechanic swore under his breath and tried again. Seversky sighed. "They are a curse for all of us, these obsolete aircraft!"

The machine finally caught. Nearby dusty weeds prostrated themselves, submitting to the force of wind created by the propeller.

"Watch what I do," Seversky shouted over the engine, "and then describe how you would do the same procedure." He started to move. The plane taxied, skipping and dipping on the uneven ground, until it reached the flight strip and the instructor stopped. "Well, do you know what I did?" he said turning around.

"Yes, sir." Andrei easily described the exercise.

"Good. Now, we'll go up!" Seversky gunned the engine and gently pushed on the stick. The plane surged forward. Andrei felt its tail rising, then, as the plane leveled off, he experienced the long-awaited sensations of gathering speed and ascent.

Seversky shouted instructions over his shoulder, reinforcing them with primitive sign language. They circled over the field several times, Seversky demonstrating a modest climb to an altitude of three hundred meters. After a few turns, he prepared for landing.

"Landing is the most important part of flying," he shouted. "Nose your plane down and then cut off the motor, keeping her going down at a steady, steep angle. It's very tricky. You'll be almost at ground level when you level off. Watch!" He landed easily on the field.

Once on the ground, he turned in his seat and smiled at Andrei. "Do you think you can repeat *verbally* the procedures of your first flight?" Andrei complied, faultlessly.

Seversky was impressed. He had recognized a kindred spirit. "Good!" he said. "Ready to try?"

"Yes, sir!" Andrei saluted and grinned, unable to conceal his excitement.

"Fine. Let's exchange seats." Andrei climbed into the pilot's seat.

"Before we start, tell me what you are going to do," Seversky said, close to his ear. Andrei recited the protocol, drawing upon what he had learned from his textbooks, what he had picked up in discussions with older cadets, and what he had witnessed a few minutes before.

"You got it. Now, let's go!" The mechanic hand-propped the warmed-up machine and it instantly roared.

Andrei advanced the throttle and the plane rolled forward. Gently, almost before he realized it, the plane rose into the air. Andrei felt as if he was on fire. The excitement was almost painful. He wished he could yell. Seversky, having experienced the same on his maiden voyage, leaned forward and shouted, "Go ahead. Yell!"

Andrei let out a great whoop. He looked down at the airfield with its parked aircraft and tiny figures of men and shouted, "Look at me! I am flying!" He made a turn and flew over the railroad tracks where he saw a toy train puffing along, far below. Descending a few feet, he flew over a meadow and stampeded a herd of cows. He yelled exuberantly, again and again.

"All right my friend, enough," Seversky shouted. He touched Andrei's shoulder and with a gesture signaled that he wanted Andrei to land the plane.

"Yes, sir!" Andrei nosed the plane down, cut the engine and began his first successful descent.

Two weeks later, Andrei completed his first solo flight and received clearance to fly Farman XVIs and other makes of aircraft, such as Blériots and Nieuports.

Proud of his achievement, Andrei sat down to write his fiancée and his mother. He had accumulated stacks of their letters, which he had promised himself he would answer, but had postponed the task from day to day. He had always been a poor correspondent. Besides, there had been nothing to write. They wouldn't be interested in his descriptions of pilot training. As for his father … well, he was still angry that his son had gone against his wishes and over his head in appealing to the Grand Duke for help. No, his father would not appreciate tales of his training or his victory; they would only make him angrier. The women, however, would rejoice at his success! Even if they could not comprehend the magnificence of his achievement, they would be impressed by his bravery and pray to God for his safety.

He seated himself at the desk in his room, ready to write, but nothing would come to mind. He could think only of how he felt during flight, which was impossible to express. He had to write *something*. Finally, he used the official Gátchina Flight School stationery for two quickly composed, almost identical notes.

Greetings, my dearest! I have only a few minutes before I must fly again, so I cannot write a proper letter. I have completed the most important test in my life: the solo flight. In a few weeks, I will be graduating from flight school. Because of military security, I cannot tell you more. I miss you very much and look forward to seeing you for a few days during my furlough.

He had lied about military security to excuse writing such a short note. To his mother he added, "give my love to father," and to Larissa he wrote that he was counting the days until he could lock her in his embrace, another white lie. Frankly, he had not missed any them. He had been preoccupied with training, caught up in the excitement of it. He thought of Larissa, of course, but without real yearning. She was safe in the city, waiting to marry him when the war ended. What else was there to say?

Before sealing each note in an envelope, he included a photograph of himself at the controls of a Farman IV. "That will do it!" he thought.

News from the front failed to interest Andrei. He knew the war was going badly for all the belligerents, not just the Russians. The whole of Europe had become one bloody battleground over which millions of men fought and died. Huge armies were moving back and forth, taking or losing the same territories several times, without decisive victory by anyone. Like most cadets, Andrei was interested only in news about aviation. He eagerly searched the papers for stories about the aces Kozakov and Kruten and the famous German fighter pilot Baron Manfred von Richthoven. These men fought their enemies one-to-one, far above the earth, and Andrei secretly thought that only pilots, the pilots of *all* the warring nations, embodied the true warrior's spirit.

He ignored articles on political issues affecting civilian life. Political fights among the fractured Russian government confused him. The flood of proclamations by political parties battling for control, the constant changes in the High Command, the rumors about the "Mad Monk," Grigory Rasputin and his influence over the Empress—all of them disgusted Andrei, and he shut his mind to the disturbing reality behind those pieces of news. He knew that strikes and food shortages often besieged the big cities, that university students held anti-government protest meetings and paraded with red flags, that in some instances Cossacks dispersed crowds and drew blood, but none of those things alarmed him. There was only one piece of news that would have disturbed him if he had thought it was true.

Andrei did not believe there would be a serious attempt to remove the Russian royal family. Coming from generations of loyal military elite, he never questioned the validity or political meaning of the monarchy. He believed what he had since early childhood: that a man's character was measured by his commitment to honor, and honor demanded he pledge his life to his country and the Tsar.

He would become a *great* pilot, like Kozakov or Kruten, and serve his country with honor.

To celebrate his solo flight, Andrei decided to give a formal dinner for his comrades. They all needed a little relaxation, he thought, to forget for a few hours that the war was going badly, that the front demanded constant replacements of men and machines, and that they were entering the last phase of their training and would soon be sent to the front, perhaps never to return.

Andrei rented a large private room at *Chez Bertrand* and invited his flight group to the restaurant, with his trainer Lieutenant Nikolaí Seversky to attend as a guest of honor.

Chez Bertrand was a grand place, located in the park and not far from the palace compound. Two Frenchmen, formerly in charge of the palace kitchen, owned the fine restaurant. While the palace was unoccupied, they remained as overseers of its stored equipment, with permission to open an exclusive dining establishment in one of the empty buildings. The Frenchmen had access to the palace storerooms of porcelain, silver, crystal, and fine linens, and they took advantage of that privilege by using the royal silver and china for some of their restaurant's special occasions. Andrei's banquet was to be one such event. It was to be a men's gathering. However, Andrei's roommate, Philip Shilov, thought that the banquet needed something livelier than traditional congratulatory speeches. It needed *women!* As a surprise for everyone, Philip hired a band of Gypsies to sing and dance for the guests and, perhaps, perform something more intimate afterwards. Philip secretly hoped the Gypsies would also give him something to listen to other than his friends bragging about their accomplishments.

Philip Shilov had nothing to celebrate. He had not done well in his training. He still labored over takeoffs and landings under the tutelage of an instructor while the other cadets in his group had already progressed to solo flights. He often thought that perhaps he should give up pilot training and return to his artillery unit. Only his pride drove him to climb every day into the worn-out seat of the Farman IV, struggle with acrophobia, and suffer the humiliation of nausea and retching. He finally had to admit to himself that he hated airplanes. Why had he ever volunteered to enter flight school?

The cadets of Andrei's flying group gathered at *Chez Bertrand*. For the first time they wore their new, shiny, black leather jackets, visual proof that they belonged to the flying fraternity. Only Philip Shilov still wore the uniform of an artillery officer. He felt out of place among his comrades who boasted about their adventures and laughed at their mistakes, calling their airplanes "dear old crates." They already felt superior. They were *pilots!* Well, *almost* pilots!

Philip laughed along with them, slapped them on their backs, pretending to be one of them, while the poisonous snake of jealousy coiled in his heart. He was *not* one of them. He was an outsider. He was a failure.

The party started with a line of waiters, stiff white aprons tied high under their armpits, trooping into the room with trays of vodka in small, cheap glasses the guests could smash after the toast.

Lieutenant Nikolaí Seversky, the senior instructor, offered the first toast: to the health of the Emperor. The cadets rose to their feet with a shout of "Hurrah!", emptied their glasses in one gulp, and smashed them against the marble fireplace. The waiters brought a second round. Andrei, as host, offered a toast to all of them, the *almost* fighter pilots. "Hurrah!" the young men shouted. They gulped their vodka and smashed the second set of glasses. One more toast followed "To our ladies!" and a third set of broken glasses followed.

Lieutenant Seversky raised his voice. "No more!"

The cadets settled around the banquet table, its expanse covered by snowy white linen set with fine cobalt blue and gold porcelain from the palace collection. A stiffly starched, fan-folded napkin rested atop each plate, and silver knives, forks, and spoons elaborately embossed with the royal crest completed each setting. The young celebrants were impressed.

While servants cleared thousands of shards of broken glass from the floor, waiters placed delicate champagne goblets before each guest and poured wine. The restaurant owners hovered in the doorway, praying there would be no more breakage.

"My friends and future comrades-in-arms," Lieutenant Seversky stood and raised his goblet of champagne. "I wish to congratulate you on completing the most important task of your training—your first solo flight. You will execute tasks that are more crucial in your careers but nothing will be as meaningful to you neophytes as *your first solo flight*. I salute you, my young friends!"

"He is not talking about me," Philip Shilov thought bitterly. Full of self-hatred, he dutifully lifted his glass and yelled, "Hurrah!"

Waiters began serving dinner. They filed out of the kitchen carrying trays of tulip-shaped glasses for white wine to go with the fish and taller, rounded glasses for red wine to accompany the main course. The servers' demeanor was solemn, their way of reminding the cadets that this was a formal occasion and the cadets were to behave like gentlemen. The cadets quieted down. Although dressed like pilots, they resembled the well-mannered boys of their childhood as they awaited their supper.

Waiters returned with plates of delicate fish with tiny red potatoes, then a tangy salad Olivier followed by roast beef with white asparagus and cauliflower under béchamel sauce, all accompanied by different wines. The young men tried to maintain their decorum, but it was not easy. Little by little, their faces reddened and their voices and laughter grew louder as the alcohol, forbidden during training, took hold.

During the dessert course of soufflé and strawberries, the double doors of the room flew open, and a band of Gypsies rushed into the room. The cadets jumped to their feet, greeting the Gypsies with applause and shouts of approval.

First in were seven young women dressed in voluminous skirts and colorful blouses worn low, off bare shoulders. Unrestrained breasts bobbed under thin cotton blouses, riveting the attention of all the young men. The dancers were young and olive-skinned, with shiny black hair left loose over their supple backs. They came in a swirl of color, shaking their soft, round shoulders. Every motion beckoned to the men, tempted them, proclaimed the women available. Dozens of coin necklaces tinkled and bounced around their necks, disappearing for a moment among their bobbing breasts, reappearing again over their blouses. Their red-painted lips promised passionate kisses, and their tongues, darting out to moisten bright lips, teased the young pilots.

Five Gypsy men crowded at the door, aggressively strumming guitars. They scowled at the cadets, lupine teeth gleaming against their swarthy complexions. They wore red and green silk shirts that exposed hirsute chests, and black trousers tucked into shiny black boots of soft, pleated leather. Stuck in their corded belts were long daggers sheathed in intricately chased silver. Smaller blades were concealed in their boot tops. The men exuded hostility, playing their guitars as if attacking the instruments. The tipsy cadets missed the intended threat. Their eyes were on the women.

An old Gypsy woman entered the room last. Covered in black with a colorful shawl over her bent shoulders, her white hair stood out from her wizened face as if she were the source of some electrical current. She looked menacing, like Baba Yaga come forth from some ancient fairy tale.

She sat down on a chair in the corner and began to sing in a surprisingly strong but hoarse contralto. She sang of fearless hawks gliding high above the earth, in command of the world below. The women stopped their wild gyrations and crowded on the floor at her feet, humming in harmony, and the men began strumming their guitars almost gently.

"The old woman is singing about us," the cadets thought. "We are the hawks who dominate the sky."

The Gypsy finished her song and hobbled around the table shaking her tambourine before each guest. The men dropped coins into the tambourine. If the singer thought that it was not enough, she continued to shake her tambourine until the man gave her more coins amidst the laughter of his pals.

Lieutenant Seversky leaned toward Andrei. "Thank you for inviting me," he said quietly. "I must leave now. I had not realized that there would be ... *entertainment*. Enjoy yourselves, but remember tomorrow is another flight day. No exceptions for hangovers," he added meaningfully. He was sorry now that he had accepted Andrei's invitation and worried about how the evening might end; whenever there were Gypsies, one could expect trouble. "Don't get up," he said seeing that the cadets were about to spring to attention.

"Yes, sir." Andrei saluted without standing up.

With the departure of the senior officer, the party grew wild. The women drank champagne from the cadets' glasses, climbed on their laps, kissed their lips, unbuttoned the tight collars of their shirts, unhooked their belts, and toyed with the buttons of their trousers. They pulled some of the cadets to the dance floor, clinging and rubbing their bodies against them.

"Did you notice the women have nothing under their skirts?" shouted one cadet, hiccupping with laughter.

"Truly?"

"Truly! Look closely!"

"Ten rubles if you show us what's under your skirts!" the cadet yelled drunkenly.

"Ten rubles to *each* girl," replied the old Gypsy in her booming contralto.

"It's a deal! Hey, fellows, contribute to the fund!" The cadets hooted, reaching into their pockets.

In no time, the money was raised and so were the skirts. Assisted by their men, the young women jumped on the table and danced, clicking the heels of their red boots and shamelessly swiveling their hips. Their skirts flared and rose like blossoming flowers, and every cadet could glimpse the dark triangle pointing towards the junction between their bare olive-skinned legs.

The proprietors of *Chez Bertrand*, followed by waiters, rushed into the room to save the precious china and crystal at risk of being shattered by dancers' flying feet. Some plates and glasses already lay in pieces, and dirty boots prints degraded the once-pristine tablecloths.

Andrei, stupefied, watched the destruction. "Who is going to pay for this?" he thought, vaguely remembering that he had nothing to do with inviting the Gypsies. But then ... maybe he did? Maybe he'd asked Philip to engage the group. He was too drunk to remember. He must ask Philip ...

The cadets lost control of themselves. Some tried to grab women, but the Gypsy men pulled the women off the table and formed a tight knot in front of them, pulling their daggers. They glared, ready to take on the drunken pilots. The cadets retreated.

The old crone tugged at Andrei's sleeve. "If you want the girls, it will cost. They'll come to your rooms. But you pay me first!"

"No!" Andrei cried, realizing that the party was on the verge of becoming a brawl. He felt unsteady, his vision blurry. He leaned against the table and looked for Philip ... Philip, who had hired the Gypsies. Let him deal with them! Philip was nowhere to be seen.

"Get out!" He shouted at the old Gypsy witch.

"Not until you pay me. Pay me now!"

"How much?" Pulling himself together, Andrei reached into his pocket. He did not know whether Philip had already paid the Gypsies, but this was no time to argue. At any moment, the insulted cadets might challenge the Gypsies and a brawl would ensue. That much he could still understand.

"A hundred rubles."

"A hundred rubles!" Andrei swallowed hard. He felt in his pockets and pulled out a bunch of bills. Without counting, he handed them to the old crone. "Here! Get out of here! Now!" The Gypsies did not need urging. The women cursed and the men spat at the cadets' feet. In a moment, they were gone.

Andrei glared at his humiliated comrades. "Let's go home," he announced, his tongue feeling as if it did not belong to him.

Trying to preserve some dignity, the cadets staggered out, helping one another remain upright.

The waiters began to pick up the debris.

Andrei made his way into his room. He felt sick. He did not bother to look for Philip. Holding to the wall for support, he shuffled to the bathroom, stuck two fingers into his throat, and retched. Still nauseous, he tumbled into bed without undressing.

Philip Shilov had been quite sober when he left the party. Vodka did not touch him, but he felt drunk with hatred. The envy that he felt toward his comrades consumed him. It burned his soul. He needed to prove that he was competent to fly. He slouched toward the tents where his Farman IV stood parked for the night. "It's your fault," he muttered, kicking viciously at the airplane's tires. "You ugly old piece of shit ... you wait and see! I will fly you even if it kills me!" He gulped for air and tore at his collar.

A plane parked next to the Farman IV caught his attention. It was a new trainer: the single-seater biplane Nieuport X. Philip felt an irresistible desire to fly the Nieuport. "I want this one," he told himself, without realizing he was talking aloud. He circled around the plane, noting that the engine was in front and the aircraft rested on two wheels that made the old four-wheeled Farman look like a child's clumsy wagon. His heart beating in his chest like a bumblebee in a covered jar, he imagined himself at the controls of the sleek Nieuport. "I must do it," he said aloud. "I *will* do it!" An intoxicating fog of invincibility enveloped him.

He went mentally through the steps necessary to launch the aircraft. The absence of a ground crew complicated his task, but he was fueled by a mixture of pride and senseless bravado. There were no thoughts about consequences.

Philip was unaware his hands were shaking as he removed the heavy wooden blocks that held the plane's wheels in place. Knowing that it would begin to move as soon as the engine started, Philip tied a length of rope around the tailskid, wrapped it around the base of a tent pole and tied the other end to a wing strut within easy reach of the cockpit. He climbed into the cockpit, the words of his instructor echoing in his mind as he opened the fuel valve, set the throttle, and turned on the ignition switch. The plane stood quiet and motionless, watching him as if challenging him, looking *hostile*, Philip thought.

He wished that he had the help of the ground crew. Never mind, he thought, he would do every step of preparation himself.

Jumping out of the cockpit, Philip turned to face his adversary. He grabbed the propeller and gave it a mighty pull. With a clank and a huff, the prop stopped after a quarter turn. Philip tried again and again. The plane refused to obey. Cursing, the young cadet threw his full weight into the next attempt. With a bang and a puff of gray smoke, the engine sprang to life. Philip stumbled backwards and fell directly in the path of the slashing propeller blades. The plane lurched forward, but yanked to a stop and stood trembling at the end of its restraining rope.

Philip rolled to the side, beyond the deadly propeller's reach, then stood and limped around the wing. "You, shit!" he cursed. The Nieuport vibrated, mocking him.

Once again, Philip climbed into the cockpit. He started to signal for release of the tether, but remembered he had no ground crew. He desperately tried to think of some solution.

"My dagger!" he suddenly thought. Dress uniforms for all branches of the armed services included decorative daggers with elaborate handles. The daggers were useless as weapons—the men often substituted the short blades for penknives—but Philip thought it might do. He pulled the dagger from its burnished silver sheath and began to saw at the rope.

The plane sprang forward. Philip advanced the throttle and felt a thrill as the power surged. The blast from the prop caused the tent behind him to inflate and tear. A large section of canvas caught on the plane's vertical tail, but Philip stared wildly ahead, unaware. At a distance, he could vaguely see the palace surrounded by a grove of trees.

A crescent moon dimly lit the airfield where several airplanes stood parked in a row. Darkness obliterated the thin rims of red and blue painted around each plane's roundels, but the large white centers stared at Philip. For a moment, he thought they were eyes on some otherworldly thing threatening him with disaster. Then a nightmarish vision from childhood flashed through Philip's mind. There had been an old, blind beggar with white cataracts; to the little boy it had seemed like the old man had two white bottomless holes instead of eyes. "You won't scare me this time!" Philip shouted at the airplanes. He threw his cap on the ground, as if challenging his opponent to a duel.

The Nieuport X bounced across the field, but something was wrong, and Philip knew it. He pushed on the throttle, but it was already wide open. "Fly, you son of a bitch!" he screamed, cold with sweat but certain he could subject the machine to his will and take her skyward.

His will was no match for the physics of what trailed behind. The plane became airborne and wobbled. "I'm flying!" Philip shouted triumphantly a moment before the aircraft drilled into the grove of trees at the edge of the field. As fuel from the fractured tank hit the hot cylinder heads, a ball of fire erupted. Philip's solo flight was over.

5

The sound of the engine and then the explosive crash brought security men running to the field. A fire battalion followed, but it was too late. Firemen were able to stop the inferno from spreading to the buildings and parked aircraft, but nothing could be done for the unknown pilot. There was nothing left but a few charred bones.

Philip's old artillery cap, found along the runway, solved the mystery. Everyone presumed that he was drunk. All training flights were cancelled for a day to clear the airfield of debris and let the cadets settle their nerves, badly shaken by the accident.

Colonel Gorshkov conducted the preliminary investigation. There was an obvious break in discipline. Apparently, there had been a drunken party with Gypsies. Moreover, one of the senior instructors had been a guest at the unauthorized party. Gypsies, women, and drinking—all that spelled *scandal*.

The colonel reported the incident to the headquarters of the Imperial Russian Air Service.

The whole school, from Colonel Gorshkov to the youngest cadet, waited with trepidation for the reaction from headquarters. The careers of all of them were at stake. Andrei and his pals faced expulsion from Gátchina. Even worse, they could be court-martialed: their country was engaged in the Great War, and such a vagrant break in discipline was bordering on sabotage.

The reply came back swiftly in a telephone call from headquarters. "Stop the investigation. This was an unfortunate incident, but nothing must interrupt the training of new pilots. Your establishment is a *military* school, and in any military training accidental deaths may occur. The destruction of a new aircraft is a pity, but this too is a risk in training. Reprimand participants in the unauthorized celebration, but do not enter the event in their dossiers. Continue your fine work, training pilots in the service of our fatherland. The Grand Duke sends his regrets."

The inquiry ended, but the cadets remained stunned by Philip's death. "What a stupid waste of life," they said as they talked amongst themselves, each one wondering whether his own life was on the cusp of extinction the moment he sat down in a cockpit. "No, no, no!" each cadet thought, "it could not happen to me!"

The entire school staff attended Philip's requiem in Gátchina Palace's church. The cadets carried the coffin to the catafalque and followed it to the cemetery, marching in formation as a military band played Chopin's funeral march.

Andrei blamed himself. He had known for some time that Philip was afraid of flying and was considering resignation from flight school. Instead of being sympathetic to his roommate's confession, Andrei had dismissed it as a minor annoyance. "Philip wanted to prove that he wasn't a coward. That 'accident' was a gesture to prove it to me. How could I be so callous and not realize that the man was suffering?" These thoughts tormented him as he accompanied his friend's coffin to the graveyard. He recalled that he had even made a joke about some cadet who had soiled his pants during his first solo flight. "It's all in the game," he remembered saying. "That cadet wasn't a coward. He was just scared shitless. We all get scared, but we don't give into it!"

The cortege moved slowly along the dusty country road. Two black horses pulled the catafalque, elaborate black ostrich plumes atop their heads moving up and down. Andrei marched along with the cadets, his mouth set in a bitter line, his gaze fixed ahead.

At the cemetery, the cadets saluted the coffin, then, one after another, dropped small clumps of earth on top of the sealed casket. Each clump made a dull sound, the sound of no motion. The cadets crossed themselves and stepped back, many fighting tears. The vainglorious death of their friend was the first one among their squadron. Many of them wondered who would follow.

Priests chanted prayers, mourners chanted prescribed replies, and soon the service was over. There were no speeches. Cemetery workers filled the grave with earth and placed a few wreaths on top of the small mound that marked Philip's final resting place.

A week later, Captain Rublev invited Andrei to his house. "I must talk to you, Cadet Rezánov," he said gruffly. "It will be a private talk."

Andrei walked through the park toward a cluster of small dachas. "He is going to tell me that I am expelled," he thought gloomily.

Captain Rublev's wooden dacha was the last one on the short un-paved road. It was built in the traditional Russian peasant style with three windows facing the street, their frames and the front door decorated with intricately carved flowers and roosters painted in faded primary colors. There was a small garden in the front of the house and a crooked fence supporting huge sunflowers forever turning their bright heads toward the sun. "This must be his wife's garden," Andrei thought.

He knocked at the door and heard the barking of a large dog. "Come in, come in Rezánov!" Captain Rublev opened the door. "Down Ka-zbeck!" he called off his Doberman. "My dog doesn't bite, he is just noisy."

"I am used to dogs. I love them. I grew up with them." Andrei smiled and proffered his hand to the dog. Kazbeck sniffed it and then gave it a quick lick.

"Sit down. This is not an official meeting." Rublev pointed to a deep leather chair in his small study. The dog jumped on another chair as Rublev placed himself behind a desk covered with rolled maps and text-books with embroidered bookmarks wedged between pages. The femi-nine bookmarks with embroidered kittens and puppies looked incon-gruous inside military aviation manuals, and Andrei must have had an amused expression on his face. Rublev smiled. "Every Christmas, my grandmother sends me an embroidered bookmark. She is almost ninety now and half blind, but she still makes her bookmarks. I honor her by using her creations."

"They are charming," Andrei said.

"Yes, they are pretty," Rublev agreed. "Vodka?"

"No, thank you. I think I disgraced myself enough already."

"Yes, you did. You all did. And that is what I want to talk to you about. I fully understand your desire to celebrate your solo flight with a good dinner. But to create a drunken orgy—with precious china and crystal broken, and Gypsy whores and thieves who stole three silver forks right off the table—that I cannot comprehend! Did *you* hire the whores?"

Andrei hesitated. He did not want to betray Philip's memory any further. "No, sir, I did not," he finally said.

"Who did?"

"I would rather not say."

"I was told that you paid the Gypsies."

"I did. The old woman demanded to be paid on the spot. To avoid confrontation with her men, who pulled knives on us, I had no choice."

"How much?"

"I think, a hundred rubles. I am not sure ..."

"A hundred rubles! Did any of our men ... fornicate with the Gypsy women?"

"No, sir."

"Then you paid for *nothing!* They *robbed* you!" Rublev laughed and twisted his red moustache.

Andrei grinned. "Well, they *did* dance for us, and sang. And they showed us that they wore no underwear. I suppose that was worth something. As for the forks, I knew nothing about that."

"Anyway, you were overcharged," the captain insisted, still laughing. "Who is going to pay for the destruction? I was told that the table was set with Imperial china and silver."

"Yes. I didn't request Imperial settings, but I suppose I will be charged. After all, it was my 'special banquet.'"

"Too bad. It will cost you a lot. With your pilot's salary, it will take you a lifetime to pay for those plates and glasses. Fortunately, your family is wealthy." In a more serious tone, Rublev continued. "In any case, I wanted to let you know that there will be no mention of that whole embarrassing episode in the cadets' private dossiers. However," he raised his index finger, "tell the others to keep their mouths shut about it. No bragging about escaping punishment. I am telling this to you in confidence, because we feel that you are a born leader. Do you understand? *No bragging!*"

Andrei nodded. "I understand. No bragging."

"Good. We want you to remind everyone that carousing and flying don't mix. *'Those who hoot with the owls by night do not fly with the eagles by day.'* That proverb ought to be stamped on every pilot's license. A cup of tea?" Rublev changed the subject.

"Yes, that would be nice."

"I'll be right back. I must tell Trofimovna to bring us the samovar." Rublev limped out of the room. The dog followed him.

"Perhaps there is no wife," Andrei thought. He looked around the study. It was a small room. The dark green wallpaper was covered with enlarged photographs of hot-air balloons, airplanes, and aerial landscapes. On the desk were two photographs in Fabergé frames, one of an old lady with a small dog on her lap (Rublev's grandmother, Andrei presumed) and one of the Emperor. On top of a bookcase between the windows were two bronze sculptures of racehorses and a statuette of a jockey.

Rublev returned, followed by his dog. "I was looking at the aerial photographs," Andrei said. "Are they your work?"

"Yes, most of them. I was a balloonist some years ago."

Presently Rublev's servant, an old peasant woman dressed in the traditional *sarafan*, shuffled into the room, bending over a large tray with a puffing silver samovar, a sugar dish, a cream pitcher, two china cups, and a small plate of biscuits. She tried to place her load on the desk.

"Let me do that. It's too heavy for you," Rublev said, taking the tray. "Thank you, Nyanushka. You go now. I can manage."

Seeing his commanding officer help a servant perform her humble tasks impressed Andrei. It showed a sensitivity Andrei hadn't expected, and he felt a new tenderness toward Rublev. He could never imagine his own father helping a servant.

The dog gave a single bark and wagged his behind, which had been cropped of a tail. Rublev gave him a biscuit, then took a small teapot off the top of the samovar, poured a little strong black tea into their cups, and filled them to the top with boiling water from the samovar. "Cream?"

"No, thank you. Just two lumps of sugar."

Rublev handed him the cup. The tea was too hot to drink, so they observed one another silently, the dog drooling for another biscuit.

"Tell me about yourself," Rublev said. "Do you have a girl?"

"Yes, sir. I am engaged to Mademoiselle Larissa Orlova, the daughter of my former commanding officer."

"When is the wedding?"

"As soon as the war is over."

"If I were you, I would marry her as soon as I graduate. This war is going to last for years. And you are going to the front. I hate to say it, but ..."

"I know, I may not return."

"Yes, or you may end up crippled, like me. Marry her *now* and enjoy whatever time is given you by our Good Lord. If you don't marry her now, you may end up an old bachelor living with your childhood nurse and a dog."

"So there is no wife," Andrei thought. He did not want to discuss his wedding plans. Pointing to one of the photographs on the wall, he said, "I have never flown in a balloon but was always curious about them. Did you like the aeronautic service?"

"Yes, I did. Our Colonel Gorshkov—he was a staff captain then— and I shared a fondness for balloon flights. It is true the progress was slow, but it was peaceful and relaxing. Of course, that was before the war; there was no need to hurry anywhere. I loved the total silence of balloon flight. It was also much easier to take aerial photographs because the flights were so much smoother."

"So you and Colonel Gorshkov are old comrades-in-arms?"

"Oh, yes. We trained together at the Officer's School of Aeronautics. Colonel Gorshkov is a great man. A famous man. A great pilot. Did you know that he flew Sikorsky's original *Ilya Murometz*, the so-called IM-V? His Majesty himself christened the airplane *'Kievsky.'*"

"The same airplane that flew from Petersburg to Kiev and back?"

"The same airplane," Rublev smiled. "Unfortunately, I was unable to participate in any of the flights of the great four engine giant. By that time I had lost my leg and become useless."

Andrei wanted to ask Rublev how he had lost his leg but thought better of it; perhaps that was too personal.

"Yes, I was totally useless for a time. I started drinking heavily, but Colonel Gorshkov recommended me for a position at Gátchina Flight School and here I am, playing teacher to my boys," he continued without bitterness. "I am happy here," he added. "I think if I were a civilian I would have been a teacher at a boys' school."

Andrei couldn't resist. "How did you lose your leg?"

"Oh, it was nothing dramatic, nothing heroic. I wasn't shot down, or anything like that. It was a stupid accident. I fell off a horse. I always loved horses, a fondness you can appreciate, being a cavalryman yourself. I was a good steeplechaser. Built like an amateur jockey: light and wiry. Well, at some inter-Army steeplechase competition, my horse failed to clear the barrier, threw me over and fell on me. I broke my leg at the hip. There were some complications with the surgery, and the leg could not be saved. That was years ago, before the war. Colonel Gorshkov was in France, learning how to fly fighter planes. But there was no flying for me. When Gorshkov came back, he rescued me. He saved me by inviting me to work here, to train you young devils; to teach you aerial photography and some other things. It turns out, I was lucky."

"It was lucky for us too," Andrei said sincerely. "We all like and respect you."

"That's good to know." Rublev smiled crookedly and twisted his moustache. "You know, Rezánov, I should have known that Shilov was not a good candidate for military flying. He should have stayed in the artillery service."

"I thought the same. Shilov actually told me that he was thinking of leaving Gátchina, and I, like a fool, tried to convince him that with a little will power he could overcome his fear of flying."

"Don't blame yourself. It was a tragic accident. Or, if one is religious, it was God's will, which is always mysterious." He glanced down at his leg. "Anyway, it was good to talk to you, Rezánov. For all I know about your record, you are on your way to becoming one of our best students. Keep up the good work, and marry your girl the moment you are free to do so!" He stood.

Andrei also stood and saluted. "Thank you, sir. Thanks for the tea." He put his teacup on the side table. "I enjoyed our conversation."

"So did I, although I did most of the talking," Rublev said with a chuckle. "Goodbye, now."

Andrei saluted again. Captain Rublev and his dog escorted him to the door.

6

Two telegrams were waiting for Andrei when he returned from Captain Rublev's house.

My father died STOP doctors said heart attack STOP please come STOP Larissa.

The other was from his father:

General Orlov died STOP doctors suspect heart attack STOP come home at once STOP Father

Andrei rushed to Colonel Gorshkov's office with both telegrams in his hand.

Gorshkov's aide-de camp already had the documents necessary for his leave. "We received a telephone call from your father, requesting a week's furlough for you," he said. "I used to serve under General Orlov before the war, when I was still in the cavalry. I am very sorry."

"Thank you. When may I leave?"

"Right away. Colonel Gorshkov authorized the use of his staff automobile to take you to the city. It will be much faster that way."

"Thank you, Lieutenant." They saluted one another and Andrei hurried to his quarters to pack.

Andrei arrived at his parents' residence on the Fontánka Canal after midnight. The Nevsky Prospect was dark, its elaborate lampposts turned off as a precaution against German aircraft, which, it was rumored, might attack the city. Across the canal, the northern sky illuminated things just enough that the Anichkov Bridge with its four gigantic equestrian sculptures was silhouetted dimly through the fog. It was an eerie impression. The huge rearing horses rising over the parapets of the bridge looked like mythical beasts ready to trample anyone, including their own nude riders.

It was too late to go to the Orlovs' house; however, both families had recently installed telephones. Andrei picked up the receiver.

An aide-de-camp answered. "The ladies have retired for the night. Should I wake up Mademoiselle Larissa and let her know that you have arrived?"

"No, no. But leave a message with her maid that I'll be at their house tomorrow morning about … about nine o'clock."

"I'll do so. I am so sorry for your loss."

"Yes. Thank you."

General Orlov's residence was an elaborate mansion on the embankment of the Nevá. Servants placed a thick layer of straw atop the semicircular drive leading to the main entrance to soften the noise of arriving and departing carriages. The late general's young aides-de-camp managed the flow of traffic, the dismounting of cavalry detachments at the back garden, and the movement of mourners through the formal section of the house.

A line of florists' vans had formed at the service entrance to deliver memorials from friends, military units, and the Emperor himself, who sent a grand wreath of red and white roses and blue fleur-de-lis, entwined with black silk ribbons. A servant immediately took the tricolored, patriotic wreath into the house for placement at the feet of the late general, who lay in an open coffin atop a catafalque in the center of the Orlov's colonnaded ballroom. At the head of the coffin stood two many-branched floor candelabras with lighted wax candles. They cast a glow over the general as he lay in repose, clad in his court uniform covered with medals, his arms crossed over his chest and a small icon of the Savior beneath his folded hands. Four cavalry officers in full dress uniform stood motionlessly, one at each corner of the catafalque. Every two hours the honor guard changed.

The grand ballroom where so many brilliant gatherings had taken place was somber now, hushed in the presence of death. Its mirrors were covered with white sheaths. An old, hirsute priest in stiff golden robes mumbled prayers at a lectern that supported an ancient Church-Slavonic Bible encased in heavy gold covers. Two younger priests in black robes and skullcaps swung smoky censers that filled the air with nauseatingly sweet incense.

A long line of visitors filed past the general's bier. Making the sign of the cross, they stared briefly at his peaceful countenance and proceeded to an adjacent sitting room to pay their respects to the grieving family.

General Vladímir Rezánov and his family, as the Orlov's oldest friends and future in-laws, joined the widow Maria Nikoláyevna and Larissa in the sitting room.

Andrei embraced Larissa. She felt small and fragile in his arms. Instead of being inflamed by her nearness, Andrei felt only tenderness and sadness. He lifted her face and kissed her eyes, tasting her salty tears.

Like her mother, Larissa was enveloped in black, her bountiful chestnut hair plaited in a single thick braid that fell down her back, in a peasant manner. Her huge eyes, usually so radiant, were swollen and encircled in red. "I am devastated," Andrei whispered softly. "I truly loved my godfather."

"I know … He loved you too," she nodded.

Maria Nikoláyevna beckoned him to her chair. She embraced and kissed him. "Andrúsha, take Larissa to the winter garden. She is exhausted. She has been up all night crying, and now, with all these people …"

"I'll do that," Andrei said, kissing her hand, his own eyes misting. He glanced at Larissa and, with a slight movement of his head, pointed to the door. Like a child, she obediently followed his signal.

General Orlov's winter garden was deserted. Sun shone through the double-story beveled windows and stained glass of the vaulted ceiling, creating kaleidoscopic reflections among the exotic plants. The air felt slightly humid and smelled of orange blossoms. Immaculately raked pathways curved and beckoned among the greenery.

When he was a boy, Andrei liked to visit his godfather's winter garden and pretend he was Caliph Harun al-Rashid from *The Arabian Nights*, who dwelt in a secret palace hidden among magical perfumed gardens, far from foggy St. Petersburg. The rest of the city might be immobilized by swirling snow and icy winds from the Baltic Sea, but the garden remained vibrant year-round, famous for General Orlov's collection of rare orchids. Hidden pipes circulated warm water to keep the imposing glass structure free from frost and snow. There was also an intricate temperature control system, imported from England, which had allowed the general to propagate and create unusual hybrids of his beloved plants.

"The gardens are still magical," Andrei thought. Tiny hummingbirds hovered above, alighting on flowers then dashing away, and canaries filled the air with their trills from cages hidden among the dwarf trees.

Andrei and Larissa embraced. They covered each other's eyes, cheeks, and mouths with tiny, chaste kisses as Larissa sobbed. She wanted to tell Andrei how much she had missed him, but no words came out.

Andrei led her to a bench in front of an elegant marble fountain portraying Flora, the goddess of flowers. The goddess stood in the midst of a low circle of flowing water as if hesitating to cross a forest stream. Her arms were filled with flowers and her short tunic had slipped, exposing a shoulder and breast. A coy smile curved her cupid's bow lips. The resemblance to Larissa was unmistakable. General Orlov had commissioned an Italian sculptor to create a statue of the goddess using his young daughter as a model.

Seated on the cold marble bench in front of the fountain, Andrei held Larissa against his chest as if she were a small child. He stroked her hair, murmured sweet words of love, and kissed her tears away, though they continued to flow.

At the sound of crunching sand, they quickly drew apart and Larissa wiped her face with his handkerchief. Her eyes were puffy, and her nose was red. "She looks adorable," Andrei thought, his heart overflowing with tender sorrow.

Andrei's parents approached. Andrei stood.

"Maria Nikoláyevna wants me to take Larissa to her room," his mother said. "I'll stay with you, my dear," she put her arm around Larissa's waist. "You must rest now." She led her away.

"I'll be back tomorrow," Andrei said. Larissa nodded but did not look at him.

Andrei's father lowered himself heavily to the marble bench. "All in God's hands," he sighed and made the sign of the cross. "Sergei Orlov and I were friends since we were young boys. I loved him so ..." He cleared his throat loudly. He took off his glasses and wiped his eyes with a handkerchief.

Andrei had never seen his father weep. He wanted to say something encouraging, something that would make his father stop grieving, but nothing except banalities came to mind. What could one say to someone who has lost a beloved friend? He squeezed his father's hand. "I loved him too," he said quietly. "And ... I love you, Papa." He said awkwardly, unaccustomed to expressing his feelings to his father.

"I know, son, I know. I love you too, and I am proud of you. I worry about you, flying up there. Though now, of course, there is no safe place for anyone. Infantry, cavalry, aviators, this cruel war is going to get us all." He embraced his son tightly, his fringed gold epaulette scratching against Andrei's cheek. "I have more bad news, and I don't know how to deal with it."

"What bad news, Papa?"

The general took a deep breath and said almost in a whisper, "I don't know how to tell Maria Nikoláyevna ... Peter Orlov has been seriously wounded at the Polish front, near Warsaw. How does one tell a woman who just lost her beloved husband that her son is on the threshold of death as well?"

"Dear Lord! It will kill her," Andrei said. "And Lara, too. They are totally spent by grief. We shouldn't tell them anything until we know the severity of Peter's situation."

"Yes, I thought so, too. Don't say anything to your mother, either, or to anyone."

"I won't." Andrei squeezed his father's hand, stunned by death's appearance in his own life.

The death of an important military leader required a public service, and General Orlov's *panikhida* was held the following day in Kazan Cathedral. Built in the first decade of the nineteenth century, it was designed to resemble St. Peter's Basilica in Rome and was an architectural jewel. Many of the city's public religious services were performed in the central church building, its two great colonnaded wings able to accommodate huge crowds.

Hundreds of people filled the cathedral. Standing shoulder to shoulder holding lighted candles, they prayed for an old man whom they did not know. Candlelight illuminated the frescos of saints that covered the walls and made the gilt *rizas* shimmer, their icons gazing benevolently upon the gathered crowd. From marble floor to the ceiling six-stories above, the cathedral looked like a huge, golden vault. The church choir supplemented by the Imperial Chorale Capella, filled the great space with solemn hymns and chants of the sacred requiem. Their voices rose thunderously to the vaulted ceiling or fell to bare whispers, stirring listeners' souls.

Andrei stood between Larissa and her mother, both women swaddled in deep mourning, their faces hidden by thick black veils. The widow, Maria Nikoláyevna, after attending the vigil for two nights, was unsteady on her feet. She trembled and clung to Andrei's arm. Larissa sobbed quietly. Andrei could not comfort either of them while holding the lighted candle. He glanced at his parents for help and they stepped forward. His father put a supporting arm under the widow's elbow. His mother embraced Larissa's waist and kissed her over the veil.

The *panikhida* lasted well over two hours and the mourners were exhausted. Flames seemed to have consumed all the oxygen. Andrei silently cursed the orthodox customs. "We should have pews in our churches, instead of forcing everyone to stand or kneel."

Maria Nikoláyevna and Larissa, together with Andrei and his parents, were finally escorted to the carriage that would transport them to the cemetery. Maria Nikoláyevna collapsed on the soft cushions of the carriage and lifted her veil. Andrei was aghast at the change in her face: when he'd left for Gátchina, she was a handsome fifty-year-old coquette who did not look her age. She had suddenly become a wilted, worn-out old woman. Her eyelids and cheeks sagged, her mouth turned down at the corners, and her nose was red and swollen from constant weeping. Her beauty was gone.

Clergy led the procession on foot, carrying heavy golden crosses and church banners. The catafalque followed, pulled by four black horses under black and gold blankets. Dozens of carriages followed, after which a battalion of General Orlov's Cossacks mounted on beautifully groomed bays rode in close formation. At the end of the cortege marched the regimental band, announcing their presence with muffled drums and mournful music. The group crawled along the Nevsky Prospect, past the Admiralty and Winter Palace and over the Palace Bridge, headed toward the small island that housed Smolensky Cemetery with its classical monuments and elaborate family vaults. People along the streets stopped to watch the solemn pageant. Men removed their hats and women crossed themselves, wondering whose death occasioned such an impressive farewell.

Smolensky Cemetery's chapel bell tolled once as the procession approached its elaborate iron gates. The bell continued to toll at regular intervals throughout the short ceremony at the grave. Maria Nikoláyevna dropped the first fistful of earth into the grave, immediately followed by Larissa. Andrei and his parents were next, then the officers of General Orlov's staff. Priests performed last rites over the grave, and then cemetery employees filled it with earth and piled on wreaths and flowers. A mountain of flowers rose above it, soon spilling onto surrounding paths and nearby graves.

Maria Nikoláyevna could barely stay on her feet to receive the condolences of departing mourners. Stoically, she let her cheek be kissed by women and her hand by men. She felt dizzy. She leaned heavily on Andrei's arm, already assigning him the duties of her son-in-law.

General Rezánov said, "Maria, you must stay with us for a few days! You shouldn't be alone."

"We won't be alone. We have all the servants ..." Maria Nikoláyevna objected weakly.

"You know what we mean, Maria. You need to be with your family, and *we* are your family. Well, almost ..." Andrei's mother smiled through her gathering tears.

"Yes, Mama," Larissa said. "Let's not go home yet ... I don't know how I could face the house without Papa being there."

"Well ... all right ... for a few days, all right. Thank you." Maria Nikoláyevna turned to Andrei, "*Mon cher,* please tell the servants that we won't be home for a few days. They are here ... somewhere ... they were riding in carriages ... I don't know where they have gone ... the servants, I mean ..." She looked around wildly, and Andrei laid his hand gently on her arm.

"Don't worry, Maria Nikoláyevna, I will find them and tell them."

The last few days of Andrei's furlough were laden with grief. Larissa and her mother constantly wept, and his mother's tears often spilled over as well. His father became even more taciturn, secluding himself in his study, burdened with the terrible secret of Peter's ordeal.

Andrei was left to deal with the grieving women. He suggested to Larissa that they visit the Manège for a little horseback riding, but she rejected it with indignation: "I am in *mourning!* How can you even think of it?" Chastised, he offered a walk in the park instead. Larissa became hysterical.

She seemed removed from reality and, he thought, cold. She would allow him to kiss her but would not return his kisses. In exasperation, he finally cried, "Don't you love me anymore?"

Surprised by his outburst, she said with a hurt look, "Why do you ask? Of course I love you!"

"Then kiss me! Kiss me as you used to!"

She came close to him and they embraced. She kissed him with a lingering kiss that made his loins stiffen with desire, and he released her from his embrace in embarrassment.

"I love you with all my heart," she said. "But it seems that nothing matters to me anymore, not even our wedding plans. Be patient with me. Don't get angry, Andrúsha. I love you, but I feel so miserable. I miss Father … I loved him so much …" She started sobbing again. "And I am worried about Peter. Why haven't we heard from him? Oh, why does God punish me so?"

Andrei blanched. He led her to a chair. "Sit down, dear. I too am full of sorrow. We can talk about our wedding plans and happier things, later. We have plenty of time."

"Yes," she nodded and tried to smile.

"Would you like me to tell you about my solo flight?" He was eager to tell someone about his great victory.

"Yes, tell me." She wiped her tears. "Were you scared?"

"Yes and no." He sat on the carpet at her feet and began to describe with relish the most wonderful experience of his life.

7

Andrei was eager to leave the city and the depressing atmosphere that pervaded his family. The women were constantly in tears, and his father hid in his study. Bent under his own sorrow, the general could not bring himself to deliver another blow to Maria Nikoláyevna and Larissa.

Peter was General Rezánov's godson, and the general loved him like a son. He was proud that Peter served in the cavalry, as was tradition in both families, a fact the general reminded Andrei of at every opportunity.

Peter had died in the field hospital, never regaining consciousness. The general read the official telegram repeatedly, taking his glasses off and then putting them back on, his eyes clouded with tears. "I can't do it," he kept repeating. "How can I tell them about Peter? It will kill them!"

Andrei had no answer. He searched his heart and mind for some heroic way to deal with this new tragedy. "We must let Mother know about it," he finally suggested. "Maria Nikoláyevna is her best friend: Mother will know how to tell her."

"Yes, yes, that's a good idea! Let your mother do it," the old man exclaimed with relief. "She will know how to deal with it." Both men avoided each other's eyes, ashamed of their cowardice.

"Call your mother," the general said gruffly, but no sooner had Andrei's hand touched the doorknob than they heard a scream and a thud from the adjacent drawing room. Another scream followed and Larissa burst through the door. "Mother fainted ... Petya is killed!" she cried, her face distorted. The general and Andrei hurried with Larissa to the drawing room, where Varvara Mikháilovna had just arrived, her face a mask of confused concern.

A boyish-looking aide-de-camp was kneeling on the carpet over the prostrate body of Maria Nikoláyevna. He jumped to his feet and saluted the general. "I was ordered to deliver the telegram to Madame Orlova. I arrived at her house but learned that she was at your residence, Your Excellency, so I rushed here and handed the telegram to Her Excellency. She read it and fainted." He handed the crumpled telegram to the general. "The telegram was sealed ... I am so terribly sorry. I did not know what it was." He was trembling.

Andrei put his arm around the shaking young man. "It is not your fault, Cornet, that you brought such terrible news. Go now." The young man made a salute to the general and, in his confusion, to Andrei, who was also a cornet, before he departed.

Servants, alerted by the commotion, hovered over Larissa's mother, holding smelling salts under her nose, massaging her hands, and gently wiping her face with a damp towel.

Andrei's mother took command. Maria Nikoláyevna was carried to her bed, a footman was dispatched to bring the doctor, and Andrei was left to take care of Larissa, who seemed to have become catatonic. Andrei felt helpless. He could find no proper words to ease Larissa's pain. He kissed her wet face and murmured words of love, but she remained indifferent.

Unnoticed in the commotion of the new tragedy, Andrei's father slipped back into his study.

That night, his furlough over, Andrei bid goodbye to his family and Larissa. His father rode with him to the railroad station. They kept silent during the ride, unaccustomed to small talk with one another. On the platform, the old man embraced his son in a bear hug and made the sign of the cross over Andrei's chest. "Be safe my son," he said, his voice trembling. "You'll be going to the front, in a couple of weeks … God save you …" His eyes welled as he hugged Andrei again.

"I'll be fine, Papa." Andrei felt his own eyes misting. "I'll come back, you'll see. I'll be fine! I promise!" He climbed the steps of the smoking car and turned to wave to his father. The general was walking away from the train, his back bent, his broad shoulders slack, his usually proud bearing gone.

"I love you, Papa!" Andrei shouted toward the receding figure. His father did not hear him.

Gátchina Station was in total darkness as a precaution against possible German air attacks. Andrei was the only passenger to disembark. The moon was rising and the black sky was sprinkled with twinkling stars, a sight seldom seen in the city. Andrei took the longer road through the park.

It was very quiet. He walked slowly under a canopy of old chestnut trees, their long limbs intertwined across the path, creating an aromatic tunnel. The chestnut flowers, in their last days of blooming, looked like hundreds of ghostly conical candles. Here and there, where the tree branches failed to touch one another across the path, Andrei could see the starry sky.

He sat down on a wooden bench and lit a cigarette, his mind full of thoughts of his family and his own emotions. His father … this was the first time in his adult life that he felt tenderness for his gruff father. "I love him," he thought. "I truly love the old coot." Larissa … it bothered him that she was so distant, even cold, during his stay. "I am her fiancé, the man who will soon be her husband, yet she treated me as if I were merely a family friend. Where is her passion, which once allowed me to kiss her breasts? Doesn't she care for me anymore? No," he thought, "that's impossible! She loves me." He thought about the loss of her father, and then the shock of Peter's death. "To be fair, even if we were already married, she probably would not let me make love to her while she was in deep mourning. It just isn't done."

Andrei's sexual experience was limited to a few visits to Madam Elsa's, an expensive brothel patronized by Guards officers. Mme. Elsa was well known for her subtlety in initiating young gentlemen into the pleasures of copulation. His first visit to the infamous madam's house was to celebrate his graduation from the academy; he and four of his friends had pooled their resources to rent a private room and five young women.

Madam Elsa warmly greeted her new customers, introducing them to the "young ladies" as if they were indeed women of their own class. The young women's behavior outside the bedroom supported this illusion. They behaved modestly and exhibited proper ways of eating, drinking, and even conversing. Only during coitus were they encouraged to use vulgar language and shamelessly compliment inexperienced young men for their sexual prowess. Through this thoughtful approach to introducing very young men to sex, Mme. Elsa had assured their devotion to her establishment.

Andrei and his friends saved their money for repeat visits to Mme. Elsa's mansion on Morskoi Prospect. There were plenty of cheaper brothels in the city, but Mme. Elsa guaranteed the absence of venereal disease among her women. Scions of the best Russian families patronized only the best and safest house.

Andrei felt no guilt, no sense of betraying his fiancée. He was a young man, and he craved sex. Society understood. Once he married, he would stop going to Mme Elsa's … unless his domestic sex life proved inadequate. Most young men of his acquaintance already had mistresses. He knew that, at one time, his own father had kept a mistress. Having sex with a prostitute didn't mean that one did not love his wife; prostitutes were available to squelch man's need for sex, as a glass of water was there to satisfy his thirst. It was as simple as that.

Andrei extinguished his cigarette and stood. "I will write Lara at least once a week," he said to himself as he resumed his walk toward the school.

A light breeze touched the trees, and they whispered in their secret language. A nightingale broke out with a long passionate trill, and Andrei stopped to listen. "Everything will be alright," he suddenly thought. "Lara loves me and I love her. Everything will be alright."

The last, exciting phase of training—aerial pursuit and attack—was already in progress when Andrei rejoined his flight group the next morning. English and French pilots called air battles "dogfights," and the Russians adopted the sobriquet.

The cadets were eager to participate in *faux* dogfights. It was great fun to outsmart one another, to fly higher and turn sharper, to escape being "shot down" by a daring maneuver, or to "shoot down" an opponent. Like a band of adolescents on a playfield, the cadets chased one another across the sky. They yelled exuberantly, laughed as if they were insane, and saluted one another for a well-executed maneuver, giving no thought to the grim reasons their country needed fighter pilots. Sobriety would come later, after they landed and learned how many times they had been "shot down." Then, their instructors would remind them that in a few weeks, they would be at the front and facing the real test of their abilities.

With the fun of practicing dogfights thus greatly reduced, the young men concentrated on the strict routine developed by the famous ace Evgraf Kruten, one of their heroes.

Kruten had written several textbooks about basic flight theory. He described how to deal with malfunctions while in the air and, in the most popular book among young pilots, explained tactics for winning air battles. Kruten simplified an aggressor's role into four parts: *altitude, speed, maneuver,* and *fire*. First, the aggressor must reach an altitude above his adversary with the utmost speed. Next, he must place himself behind the enemy, firing from that advantageous position. Then, immediately he must maneuver his own craft right or left by diving sharply or climbing steeply and getting behind the enemy as soon as possible to repeat the assault. It was essential to pay close attention and avoid the reverse situation, when the enemy was behind one's back. Dive fast, or go up sharply while making a turn, but *shake him off your tail,* Kruten advised. If making an approach in good weather, have the sun behind your back, to blind the enemy to your approaching craft.

Andrei absorbed every bit of information. He tried to solve every hypothetical situation, be it heroic or mundane, picturing a solution for every occurrence.

"The excitement of a dogfight might impede your thinking," Captain Rublev addressed Andrei's flight group as they relaxed in the drawing room after the evening meal. "In the heat of battle, a pilot feels invincible. But that is the time when most young pilots commit their fatal error: they fail to quit when they are ahead." The captain twisted his moustache, looking from one cadet to another. "Imagine, gentlemen, that you are in a *multi-fight,* with several aircraft on both sides. The British have a good name for it: *furball.* Think of a fight involving several dogs and imagine the fur flying around. Amidst the swirl of a furball, with everyone maneuvering and shooting at one another, it will be impossible to keep your eyes on every plane involved. Therefore, the smartest way to win is to avoid being in the center of the furball. Shoot down a couple of planes if you have a chance, but get to the side of the battle and stay there to catch the enemy not by direct pursuit, but by *stealth*, getting him when he is coming out of a turn or going into a dive."

"Isn't that cowardly?" asked one of the cadets.

"No," Rublev replied seriously. "It is smart. You are not hiding; you are in full sight, firing and maneuvering. You are not just a pilot, you are a tactician. You must think about saving your life and your machine. Rushing blindly into the midst of a furball is suicide. Your duty is not only to kill the enemy but also to stay alive. Remember that!"

"What about Nesterov?" Andrei asked. "He rammed a German with his own plane and they both went down. He was a hero."

"Yes, Nesterov was a hero. He was also the first pilot in the world to complete the death loop; he was a highly skilled pilot, in addition to being a smart man and a patriot. Nesterov rammed an enemy plane only after knowing he had been mortally wounded and that his own plane was going down. He had no chance of surviving, so he made his machine a battering ram and took the German aircraft down with him."

"What a glorious way to die!" Andrei exclaimed.

"Yes, but I urge you, gentlemen, not to try that maneuver."

Rublev lit a cigarette and continued in a lighter tone, "Now, I want to share a bit of airmen's wisdom." He smiled wickedly. "I know you all admire the beautiful silk scarves worn by our well-dressed French colleagues. Most of you, I am sure, think our French brothers-in-arms are typical dandies, wearing white silk opera scarves to impress the ladies. The scarves look so elegant! So, *je ne sais quoi!* Well … have you noticed that the English, the Germans, and the Austrians are all sporting silk scarves? Why might that be?" he said with mock gravity. "Because their necks are *raw!* Yes, gentlemen, you have flown only short distances, once or twice each day. But what of flying for hours at a time, day after day? Our stiff uniform collars rub our necks into a bloody mess. No one thought of designing comfortable clothes for pilots, and nobody thought that pilots would be constantly turning their heads. This sad condition is universal among the belligerent nations. *Ergo,* the solution: scarves! Make sure that you wind these soft silk scarves around your necks, or you will look as if you had a rendezvous with the blade of a drunken executioner."

The cadets laughed.

"And don't worry about the ladies. They will *adore* you! They'll put balm on your chafed necks and wash your bloody opera scarves," Rublev chuckled. "You'll look dashing to them. The newspapers call you 'the knights of the sky.' Well, enjoy your knighthood, my friends!"

"Are there other words of wisdom we should take to heart?" asked one of the pilots once the laughter had subsided.

"Yes," Rublev replied. "Watch your fuel gauge. In the heat of battle, new pilots often fail to think about the returning flight. It is especially important if one is flying over enemy territory. Lack of fuel might mean a forced landing and internment or, even worse, a crash. So, watch your fuel gauge, and make sure you have enough fuel to bring you home!"

Andrei spoke up. "I read that Louis Blériot said that if his plane was disabled and he knew he was going to crash, he would throw his body onto the wing because the canvas would protect his body. Is it true that the wing's canvas might help a pilot survive a crash?"

Rublev smiled. "I have read the same story," he said, "and I don't know if it is true. Any group of people with mutual interests creates their own myths and legends. Pilots are no exception. Blériot is a great hero to the French. He was the first to cross Pas de Calais. He designed the airplanes that bear his name, but as to his method of surviving a crash—it sounds a bit improbable to me."

"What *is* the best way of surviving a crash?" asked one of the young men. The cadets laughed.

"Don't laugh. It is a logical question," Rublev replied seriously. "Aim for the trees. A canopy may protect you, somewhat. Otherwise, it's a question of luck."

Andrei's work with Petrovich confirmed that he did not want to fly Sikorsky's four-engine bombers. The Squadron of Air Ships, a newly established branch of the Air Service, required a crew of four or six for each of its giant planes, and that did not interest him. He wanted to be his own man. He wanted to be an ace: fly a fighter plane, be a top shooter, and be a reconnaissance man, all in one. This meant additional training in aerial photography and machine guns.

Firing machine guns was not new to Andrei. He had learned to use them while at the academy, even though the instructors had sneered at the training program. No one expected cavalry officers to flop on their bellies and shoot machine guns! That was for the infantry! But times were changing. Warfare was becoming more complicated, weapons more deadly, and the cavalry all but obsolete. Ground forces were being mechanized, with tanks and trucks replacing horses. Airplane reconnaissance was proving more accurate and efficient than that of cavalry scouts. Machine guns were becoming more important than ever.

Despite his earlier training, Andrei found the task difficult. A pilot had to shoot while simultaneously flying his aircraft. "How can one work the controls, watch the sky the full 360 degrees, maneuver the plane, and shoot accurately at the enemy? And, oh yes, photograph the terrain," Andrei wondered.

Instructors warned that armaments constantly improved with the introduction of new aircraft models, and pilots had to adapt instantly to the improvements. The mounting of a machine gun on the airplane was most important. On some planes, the so-called "pushers," the engine and propeller were behind the pilot but the machine gun was in front of him, eliminating the need to avoid the propeller's blades. However, on the "tractor" type airplanes, where the engine with its propeller was in front, it became necessary to calibrate the arc of the fire *above* the propeller. On some tractor type airplanes, cutting a V-shaped indentation in the upper wing of the craft allowed a gun muzzle to protrude above the engine. On two-seater models, the gun was placed over the upper wing entirely, which allowed the observer to shoot while standing.

Andrei quickly adapted himself to the various aircraft and their armaments. He always had been an expert shooter, and mastering a machine gun while flying proved simpler than he had anticipated. Reconnaissance photography, however, proved more complicated. The cameras were cumbersome and difficult to focus. A bouncing, dipping, and soaring airplane provided no stability, and photography required stability. At the beginning of training, the cadets learned the rudiments of operating cameras while being pushed around the grounds in the wingless fuselages. Later, while flying with instructors, they practiced by photographing the terrain of Gátchina and the palace grounds. "That was easy!" the cadets declared. Instructors were quick to remind them that in combat they would simultaneously be dodging gunfire from the ground and enemies in the air, and be maneuvering their own plane. Then, the task of reconnaissance photography would be extremely challenging.

Reconnaissance was becoming the most important aspect of military aviation. Germany seemed to possess the best photography equipment, while Russians suffered the usual shortages of inventory and spare parts. Andrei decided to sharpen his skills by buying a camera and photographing whatever happened to be within radius of his sight. Rather than bother his father with a request for a camera, he decided to enlist Larissa's help.

Larissa and her mother still resided at the Rezánovs' house. Maria Nikoláyevna was suffering an undiagnosed illness, and Andrei's parents persuaded her to stay with them until she could recover her health. Larissa readily agreed; to stay at their empty house was beyond her endurance. Her mother needed gentle care and Andrei's mother lovingly provided it.

Andrei approved. *"My dearest one"* he wrote to Larissa, *"I am so glad that you are staying with my parents for a few weeks! I'll be home soon myself, for a week of furlough. Meanwhile, I would like you to do me a favor: go to the Gostinny Dvor and find a photography shop. I need a good photo camera, for practice. Send one to me as soon as possible. When I come home, I'll take pictures of you, my sweet one!"* He added a few more words of love and mailed the letter. He hoped the task would provide Larissa a positive thing to do amidst what he imagined were days and nights lived in grief.

His graduation was fast approaching, and Andrei suddenly became apprehensive. While before he had hardly given a thought to his forthcoming assignment to the front, he now faced the fact that in a very short time he would be under enemy fire and perhaps fighting for his very life.

It struck him with the force of a blow. All his life he had trained for battle, but this was the first time he faced the possibility that he might *die* in battle. He thought of Larissa's brother. "Peter was only a year older than I," he thought. "Was he afraid? He must have been … how did he cope with it?"

Andrei's feeling of invincibility was gone, replaced with a cold-sweat anxiety that he would not be able to hide his fear from the others. He suspected that all his classmates had similar feelings hidden beneath adolescent bravado, but there was no one in whom he could confide. His trainers might understand his feelings, but it was their responsibility to nourish the spirit of invincibility. "Am I a coward?" Andrei asked himself, painfully aware that he was terrified of the possible answer.

From his early youth he had been prepared to serve Russia in battle, as his father and grandfather had done before him. "How did they cope with their fears? They must have been afraid to die," he tormented himself. He could not talk to his father. The old general would accuse him of being a coward. He would give him a long lecture about the honor and duty of a Russian officer. No, his father would not help him. The old warrior would never accept that his son suffered deep doubts and fears that were tearing him apart. No, not *his* son!

Andrei suffered in silence.

The graduation ceremony took place on the airfield, which was a break from the tradition of holding ceremonies at the huge and ugly Engineers' Castle, a red brick fortress Tsar Paul had built and in which he was murdered. Usually, members of the Imperial Family attended the ceremony and the Tsar himself signed the diplomas. This time, the hastily conducted graduation ceremony involved only a few invited guests. No member of the Imperial Family attended, all being at Stavka, the Russian headquarters in Mogilev.

The mood of the small crowd was somber, made so by rumor that a huge new offensive was in progress. The fledgling pilots would be given their assignments and depart for the front immediately. Only the families of cadets who lived in the capital were invited to the celebration; there was not enough time to await families from other parts of the country.

The cadets demonstrated their newly acquired skills in flying, staged several faux dogfights, and then landed on the strip one after another. Mechanics moved the airplanes into a parade line, ready for inspection, and the cadets stood stiffly next to their machines, waiting to be awarded their accreditations as military pilots.

Andrei was assigned to the air group on the southwestern front. It was an honor for a novice pilot to be sent to the most active front, and Andrei knew that, but he felt only dread. The survival statistics for a new pilot on the western front were four to six weeks. "What am I doing?" he thought, looking at his assignment order. "I don't want to be killed ... and I don't want to kill anybody!"

Captain Rublev came to congratulate him for graduating at the head of the class. "How does it feel to have wings on your breast?"

"I must talk to you, Captain," Andrei blurted. "Confidentially."

Rublev scrutinized him. He suspected that Andrei was undergoing an experience common among young graduates: the shattering discovery that they were capable of real fear. "Come to my house after the reception. We'll talk," he said quietly.

After the official procedure of presentations of diplomas, there was a brief reception. Andrei's father and Larissa were his only guests, his mother being indispensable to Larissa's mother. Maria Nikoláyevna's grief still ruled her life.

Andrei introduced Larissa to his friends, and she charmed them all despite being dressed head-to-toe in mourning black. She looked composed and sophisticated, as if beneath the veil and ostrich feather-trimmed hat was a woman of the world rather than an eighteen-year-old girl.

Andrei's father, who used to say, "In my estimation, a pilot is nothing more than a chauffeur," charmed as well. He seemed to have reconciled himself to the fact that his only son had become a pilot, for he was cordial to everybody and seemed proud that Andrei had graduated at the head of his class. He chatted amicably with Colonel Gorshkov and other senior officers. And although he was disappointed that Grand Duke Alexander was absent, being himself one of the summer offensive's strategists, General Rezánov understood.

The guests toasted the graduates, nibbled on hors d'oeuvres, and departed early, uneasy in their hearts. They knew that these brave young men, who had so proudly demonstrated their flying skills only an hour before, would likely be dead within a few months. Insatiable Mars, the god of war, would gladly devour them all.

"I'll be home tomorrow," Andrei whispered to Larissa as he kissed her goodbye. She clung to him for a moment, her eyes welling with tears that she furiously blinked away.

"I am looking forward to it," she said. She took General Rezánov's arm.

"See you tomorrow, Son," his father said. "Your mother is planning a family celebration." He steered Larissa towards a new Packard.

"I didn't know you'd bought an automobile, Father," Andrei said. "Have you learned how to drive?"

"Don't be silly. I don't need to drive. Driving is for chauffeurs."

Despite himself, Andrei grinned. "Well, I hope, you won't mind if I take a spin in your new machine. After all, I *am* a qualified chauffeur myself now!"

The general laughed. "That you are, my son. That you are!"

Later that evening Andrei knocked at Captain Rublev's door. The immediate response was a loud bark from Rublev's Doberman, which joyfully jumped at Andrei's chest as the door opened.

"Down, down Kazbeck," Rublev commanded. "This damn dog has no manners. The only thing that I've been able to teach him is not to shit in the house. But I love the devil," he said ruffling the dog's short hair.

"He's a fine dog," Andrei said.

"Well my friend, before you tell me what is bothering you, let us celebrate your graduation with a drink. Vodka?"

"Yes sir, thank you."

"Nyanushka," Rublev called toward the kitchen, "bring us *vodochka* and a few of your pickled mushrooms. And might as well bring us some of that bread you baked this morning." Then, to Andrei, "Trofímovna, my childhood nurse. God bless her, my nyanushka, she still takes care of me."

A few minutes later, the old woman entered the study balancing a loaded tray. *"Serezhen'ka,* I have added some of the little pickled cucumbers. I thought the young officer might like some."

"Oh, you are a treasure," Rublev kissed her on her withered cheek. The old woman smiled and patted his shoulder. "Do you want me to take the dog with me?"

"No, Kazbeck can stay. My young friend likes him."

The nurse shuffled out of the study.

Rublev poured vodka into two small silver goblets. "To you, our new military pilot!" he said, touching Andrei's goblet. "May you be a *great* pilot. Someone like Kozakov ... who will be your commanding officer."

"Kozakov! My commanding officer? How do you know?" Andrei blushed at the stupidity of his question. Of course, Rublev would know! It might have been Rublev himself who had proposed the assignment.

Rublev only smiled. "We thought that our best graduate ought to go to our best ace, who is very particular. Kozakov was recently elevated into his own command and is in the process of selecting his pilots. He demands that his officers be in love with flying, as he is. He demands candidates with a wide knowledge of aircraft and machine guns. He expects his young pilots to be well disciplined and not reckless, but ..." Rublev raised his index finger, "he also wants them to be *aggressive!* Above all, he wants honorable men. We thought we had such a candidate—you!" He twisted his moustache and winked.

Andrei gulped his vodka.

"Were we wrong?" Rublev asked. He knew exactly why Andrei had come to him. It was not the first time a young pilot on the cusp of departure for the front had sought his reassurance.

Andrei stared silently at the floor. He finally said, feeling miserable, "I ... I don't know, anymore. I am suddenly thinking of ... of death. I don't want to die ... I don't know if I could kill anyone either, even though I know how to do it ... Am I a coward? I don't know anymore ..."

Rublev waited for him to continue.

"I *love* flying," Andrei continued, "I enjoyed every aspect of my training, including the messy jobs at the repair shops. Flying is fun; an adventure, a challenge! Flying is freedom ... Flying, to me, has never meant death." He kept talking fast, repeating himself, searching for the right words. "I never thought, *really thought,* that I might die. I mean, I know eventually I will die ... like everyone, but not yet ... not *me.*"

Rublev let him talk. He wanted Andrei to empty his mind and heart of the pain behind his debilitating doubts.

"I know I contradict myself," Andrei continued with great agitation. "I have been training to destroy the enemy, but somehow I never gave a thought to what it really meant. To kill a human being ... a person I have never met. A person—"

Rublev interrupted, "This is no time to be a humanitarian. We are at war with a country that has coveted our lands from time immemorial. That country has its troops on *Russian* soil! That country's pilots are shooting down our *Russian* pilots! Those persons whom you have never met, do you want them to conquer our land?"

Andrei was shocked by the question. "Of course not!"

"Well then, all *Russians,* including you, must stop them!"

"I know, I know ... but ... would I, Andrei Rezánov, fire a gun at another human being?"

"There are no legitimate excuses for doubting your ability," Rublev said quietly. "You are a fine pilot and you'll fulfill your duties with honor. Instinct will take over the moment you see your first enemy plane. You are not a coward, Andrei. I guarantee it. You'll fire at him and try to down him, and perhaps you will. You are a fine marksman. You will bring your plane home and go up again and again. You'll be as aggressive as Kozakov, or Kruten, or Nesterov."

"What if I am not?"

"If you are not, you'll be shot down on your first mission and join the angels." He paused and refilled their glasses. "Lieutenant, we all fear death, and we live with this fear all our lives." Put your doubts away, my friend. You are not a coward. You are going to be a great pilot because you learned well. You will enjoy flying, which you love so much, and as for killing … I am sure that you hunted with your father when you were a boy, didn't you?"

"Yes, I have."

"And, being a good-hearted young man, you felt sorry for the deer or duck, didn't you?"

"Yes."

"And you shot them anyway?"

"Yes," Andrei had to smile as he said it.

"Well, you will do the same now, only from your airplane. Think of it as self-defense. After all, the enemy's fine pilots will be trying to shoot you down the moment they see you. Your actions will be justified and your conscience clear."

"You make it sound so simple."

"It is simple. How is it in that aria in Tchaikovsky's *The Queen of Spades* where Gehrman sings *'Today it's you, tomorrow, it's me!'* He sang the phrase in a fine, ringing tenor.

"Gehrman was talking about winning or losing in gambling," Andrei said, smiling.

"War is the greatest gamble of them all," Rublev replied.

They touched goblets. "Thank you for listening to me," Andrei gulped his vodka and stood. "Somehow, I feel better."

"Good. You are a fine person, Andrei," Rublev said. "You are not a coward. If you were, it would have demonstrated itself long ago. Fly, you Russian falcon! Enjoy your 'freedom,' as you call it, and do not think of death. It will come in due time. Meanwhile, fly my boy, fly!"

He escorted Andrei to the door, Kazbeck following.

"Thank you for your help," Andrei said, shaking his hand.

"It was my pleasure. Have a splendid furlough with your fiancée and family!" He closed the door.

Twisting the end of his long moustache, he limped back to his study. "All those clichés! All that pontificating!" he thought cynically. "How gullible the young are! They can be persuaded to believe *anything.*"

Andrei bade goodbye to his comrades and instructors and collected their addresses, promising to write about Kozakov, whom they all greatly admired. Then he paid a final visit to Petrovich, the old mechanic at the airstrip shops.

"Well, Lieutenant Rezánov, I see that you are ready to fly the coop," Petrovich said, wiping his greasy hands on his greasy pants. "Let me shake your hand and wish you good luck."

Andrei embraced the old man in a hug. "I am sorry, Petrovich, that I did not follow your advice and concentrate on the *Ilya Murometz* bombers," he said. "But I really think that I am more of a small plane man. The Murometz frightens me," he smiled.

"Yea, the Murometz will do that," the old man cackled. "Like the *real Ilya Murometz*, the great warrior knight of our fairy tales! You know, Sikorsky named his great airplane after our Russian hero! It is the biggest airplane in the world, and I helped build it!" The old man was ready to tell the tale of its building once more.

Andrei interrupted, having heard the story several times. "I brought you a little farewell present." He presented the old man with a large tin of English tobacco.

"Oh, where did you get it? This is the best tobacco in the world! Thank you, thank you, Lieutenant! And I have nothing to give you ..."

"You gave me more than you know. You taught me how to fix an airplane if it is hit. You taught me how to fix a jammed machine gun. You showed me how to take care of an engine, and so many other things that I cannot even count them. If I ever have trouble with a plane, I will know where to look for the trouble because you, Petrovich, have taught me. Thank you!"

"God bless you, boy," the old man said, his voice trembling. "May God keep you safe." They shook hands and Andrei left the repair shop.

He made a short stop at Captain Rublev's house. "I wished to say a special goodbye to you before I leave," he said sheepishly, seeing that Rublev was already wearing his pajamas. "You helped me tremendously the other night."

Rublev leaned on a cane to balance his body. The left leg of his pajamas hung loose without the prosthesis. Andrei tried to avoid looking at it.

"Come in, come in, Lieutenant. Excuse my *déshabillé*. I was about to go to bed. Won't you sit down?"

"No, sir, thank you. I don't want to disturb you. I only wanted to thank you for listening to me and helping me to come to my senses." Kazbeck came to his side and Andrei stroked his silky head. "Of all the people that I have met, you were the one who understood my concerns."

"You grossly exaggerate, my friend," Rublev said, flattered nevertheless. "All pilots have the same fears, only some of them are able to hide them better than others. I always liked you. As a matter of fact, I would like to keep in touch with you, from time to time. Will you write to me?"

"I will be happy to!" Andrei exclaimed. "Although I am not a good correspondent, as my family can confirm."

Rublev laughed. "Give me a hug, my boy. I can't shake your hand because of this damn cane, so give me a hug." Andrei's words touched him deeply. Of all the young men who came through Gátchina Flight School and sought his advice, few truly seemed to appreciate it.

Andrei stepped forward and awkwardly embraced Rublev. "I must be going," he said. "I'll write to you from the front."

"Write to me about Kozakov. He is one of my own heroes, you know!"

"I will," Andrei smiled. "Goodbye, now."

"May God save you," Rublev said and made the sign of the cross over Andrei's chest.

⁘ 8 ⁘

Andrei arrived in Petrograd in early afternoon. The sky hung low and drizzled rain over the city. Eager not to waste a minute of his furlough, Andrei hired a one-horse carriage at the station square and ordered the driver to hurry. The drizzle turned to rain, and Andrei arrived at the Fontánka house thoroughly drenched.

He ran up the marble staircase to his family's private quarters on the second floor. "Mother, I'm home!"

Larissa met him at the door to his mother's sitting room, her finger to her lips in a shushing gesture. "They are napping," she whispered as she closed the door and embraced him, paying no attention to his dripping leather coat. "At last!" she breathed into his neck, "I missed you so much!"

Andrei kissed her then held her face between his palms, staring as if he had never seen her before. She no longer had the look of a young, unperturbed, pretty girl. Still sheathed in black mourning silks, her grief seemed to have given bloom to maturity and mystery. "By God, you are lovely!" he exclaimed.

She shrugged, dismissing his compliment. "You sound as if you are seeing me for the first time," she said, pleased nevertheless. "I am the same."

"No! You are more beautiful than ever!"

She smiled a little. "Let's go downstairs. I don't want to wake Mother. Today is the first day she has been able to sleep in the afternoon."

Stepan, the general's orderly, greeted Andrei at the base of the stairs. "Welcome home, young master," he said, and a slow grin spread across his bearded face. Stepan had served the general since Andrei was a boy. Andrei could grow a moustache, become a lieutenant, and earn his pilot's wings, but Stepan would still call him "young master." It was a mark of his privileged familiarity, and Andrei did not mind it at all.

"Hello, Stepan," Andrei said, cordially. "Can you help me out of this wet jacket?"

"Yes, young master. I will take care of it. It is good to see you!"

Larissa led Andrei to the music room. "I must practice. I may be invited to play the piano at the Empress's benefit for wounded soldiers."

"Oh? When?"

"A month from now."

Andrei was impressed. He knew that Larissa was a talented pianist, but to play at a concert sponsored by the Empress was a great honor.

"I was supposed to play last month, but mourning forbade it. Your father explained the situation to the Imperial Secretariat, and they understood. Unless they have already invited someone else to play at the next charity concert, I will be re-invited. So, I must be ready."

They entered the Rezánov's formal music salon. Fashioned after eighteenth-century chamber music salons in Vienna and Salzburg, its ornate decor was to the eye what its architecture was to the ear: it provided perfect acoustics. The high ceiling was festooned with painted garlands, cupids, and muses. Tall windows separated by mirrors gave the illusion of infinite space. Tall bronze candelabras recently wired for electricity and placed at equal intervals around the salon bathed the room in golden hues, gently reflecting off marble busts of famous composers set atop pedestals along the walls. Three rows of delicate, gilded chairs formed a semi-circle near a low platform dominated by a Bechstein grand piano. On each side of it stood a golden concert harp, in ornate contrast to the severe lines of the black concert piano.

"You sit in your papa's chair while I practice."

Andrei took a seat in the general's throne-like armchair at the center of the room.

As a small boy, Andrei often had sat on one of those fragile chairs, forced to listen to Bach or Scarlatti. All those fugues and canons! He recalled his boredom and smiled to himself. As an adult, he had learned to enjoy music, especially opera. Under Larissa's influence, he had even become fond of Bach and Scarlatti.

"I must warm up first," Larissa said, running her fingers lightly over the keys.

"Go ahead. I'll be quiet."

She ran through a set of arpeggios and then a couple of furious chromatic scales.

"I am ready," she finally announced. "I'll play Nocturne no. 2 in E-flat Major. I was scheduled to play Sonata no. 2 in B-flat minor, the one with the funeral march, but I cannot bring myself to play it. I want something more cheerful, and Olga Petrovna, my teacher, suggests Nocturne no.2. What do you think?"

"I am sure that whatever you play will be wonderful," Andrei said, unaware of the merits of either.

Larissa bent her head over the keyboard in concentration, poising her hands over the keys. In a moment, the luscious sounds of Chopin filled the room.

Andrei watched her, his heart full of tenderness. "I am a lucky man," he thought. Larissa's chestnut hair, gathered in a loose knot, was coming undone, and a few strands fell to her chest. Her lovely, porcelain skin was accentuated by her somber dress, and her pink full lips, the softness of which he knew so well, were slightly apart. He saw her in profile, but if he looked at one of the several mirrors, he could see her reflected *en face*, and himself, watching her. They could not have been more different. She was delicate and dark-eyed, he broad-shouldered, blue-eyed, tall, and fair. "I wonder whom our children will resemble," he reflected,

"Will I live long enough to have children?" he thought, suddenly numbed by fear. He ordered himself to concentrate on the music, but he could not shake an image of himself at the controls of a burning airplane. With trembling hands, he reached for a cigarette, but a sudden shortness of breath caused him to gasp and the unlit cigarette fell from his mouth. "What's the matter with me," he thought, near panic. His heart palpitated wildly. "Am I going to faint?" He stood and wove his way between the fragile golden chairs, towards the door.

"What happened?" Larissa called, stopping the music abruptly. She stood, ready to help, but Andrei waved her back to the piano bench and staggered out of the room.

He ascended the broad staircase two steps at a time and locked himself in his room. Without undressing, he threw himself on the bed. Feeling suffocated, he tore open his collar. His heart was beating rapidly, and that frightened him even more than the vision of a burning airplane. "Am I losing my mind?" he thought, wiping sweat from his brow. He shivered then pulled the cover over his head. He heard Larissa knock and, finding the door locked, go away.

He must have fallen asleep. When he opened his eyes, it was dark outside. He felt weak, but his mind was clear of terror and the image that had haunted him seemed abstract; it had become *a* burning airplane, not *his* airplane.

He washed his face, brushed his teeth, and changed into a clean uniform. "What happened to me?" he wondered. He recalled how beautiful Larissa had looked at the piano, how pleasant the music of Chopin had made him feel, and how his thoughts had turned to their … The uncertainties of their future were best left unattended, he decided.

Andrei examined himself in the mirror. "I look the same," he thought. "In any case, I feel all right now." He combed his hair and twisted the ends of his moustache. Then he unlocked the door and went downstairs.

Larissa looked at him inquiringly. "Don't say anything," he whispered to her as he kissed her cheek. "I'll tell you later."

Andrei kissed Maria Nikoláyevna's hand, as she joined the family downstairs for the first time in weeks. She looked pitifully thin. "I am so glad that you are feeling better," he said.

"I wanted to see you before you departed for the front," she replied, kissing his forehead.

Andrei blanched. "She thinks I will be killed," he thought. Afraid to say anything, he smiled crookedly at her.

Maria Nikoláyevna wobbled, and Andrei's father stepped forward to escort her into the dining room. Andrei followed and led his mother and Larissa to their chairs.

There were no guests. The presence of Maria Nikoláyevna, as well as their own mourning, had led Andrei's parents to curtail their formal dinners; guests and the white-gloved footmen who served them had all but disappeared. Since the deaths of General and Peter Orlov, the entire Rezánov household had operated in a strangely informal manner. Often, Andrei's mother had gone around the house without a corset, dressed in her peignoir, her hair still in wrappers. The general had neglected his handsome beard, allowing it to lose its shape. Larissa had stayed in her room when she was not tending to her mother. And Maria Nikoláyevna had wailed like a peasant woman, frightening the servants. A doctor had attended Larissa's mother several times a week, prescribing ever-increasing doses of laudanum.

Tonight, however, everyone was well groomed and Maria Nikoláyevna had made a brave effort to rejoin the family. Larissa and Andrei were her only remaining pleasure in life. She gazed at them, so young, and wondered what kind of future they could hope for, with Andrei at the front. She had a vision of Larissa always in black, waiting for Andrei and never becoming his wife. Maria Nikoláyevna felt tears gathering in her eyes and made an effort to hide them behind her starched napkin.

The general tried to vitalize the mood by loudly proposing a toast for Andrei's success, but it fell flat. Everyone knew that success at the front meant killing or avoiding being killed. Andrei and his father touched glasses and gulped vodka, but the women took only tiny sips of wine.

They ate their borscht in silence. When the maids brought in *pozharsky cutlets,* savory chicken patties with mushroom sauce, the general tried again. "Ah, my favorite dish!" he exclaimed heartily. "Does anyone know why these tasty little cutlets are called *pozharsky?* What do they have in common with *'pozhar,'* a firestorm?"

No one volunteered an answer. The general carried on. "Perhaps it was the favorite dish of Prince Pozharsky?" He paused, and then charged once again into the quiet. "Perhaps it is like no one knowing why Prince Stroganoff's name became associated with *beef á la stroganoff.* Some learned professor should do scientific research on these things," the general joked.

No one laughed. The general gave up.

When the last fork and spoon had been placed back on the plates, Larissa asked, "Would you like to hear me play some Chopin?"

"Yes, yes, we would!" the general exclaimed with relief, exasperated by the morbid atmosphere in his house. The presence of Orlov's lachrymose widow was getting on his nerves. He loved the Orlovs dearly. He missed his old pal and his godson, but enough was enough. Those men had been *soldiers,* and they were gone—but he, a voluptuary who loved life, was alive and ready to live it in full.

He offered his arm to Maria Nikoláyevna and led her to the music room, where he settled her in his own chair. Andrei brought her a fur lap throw and tucked it around her bony knees then joined his parents, already seated on the small gilded chairs.

Larissa began to play.

An hour later, when the impromptu concert was over, the family exchanged goodnight kisses. Everyone was relieved that the day was over.

Andrei, disturbed by memories of his panic attack, undressed and stepped into the bathtub under a recently installed hot shower. What would he do if panic gripped him while on assignment? He let water pour over his head until it began to turn cold. He wondered whether any of his Gátchina cohort were experiencing similar fears. He moved mechanically through his mundane nightly tasks, drying his body with a thick Turkish towel, donning clean pajamas, brushing his teeth, and finally getting into his bed, its thick covers already turned down by a maid. He turned off the lamp and slowly drifted towards sleep.

There was a light knock and the door opened slowly. Andrei sat up. "Who's there?" he called.

"It's me … May I come in?" Larissa whispered. "Don't get up." She walked in and locked the door, her white, high-necked nightdress visible in the dark. "I couldn't sleep. I was suddenly seized by fear, afraid that I might lose you. I had to be with you." She was trembling. "I am cold. I want to lie down next to you. I am cold," she repeated.

Andrei was speechless, stunned by her sudden appearance.

"Andrúsha, let me lie down next to you," she said.

Andrei lifted his blanket and she slipped into his bed. She clung to him along the length of his body, kissing his neck. Andrei ran his hands along her, feeling her body warm to his touch, though she continued to tremble.

"What are you doing!" he whispered hoarsely. He felt aroused. "Lara, you shouldn't be here …"

"Kiss me," she whispered, "I want you to make love to me … I want to be yours and you to be mine."

"What are you saying … we cannot … we are not married, and you are in mourning," he breathed into her breasts.

"I don't care. We may never be together again. I want to belong to you and you to me …" She helped him remove her nightdress and shed his own pajamas. They entwined their bodies, kissing and caressing, Andrei still hesitant to take the final step. They were breaking old traditions.

"Take me, my love," Larissa whispered, reaching toward his loins. "Make love to me!"

"It will hurt you," he said with a last, weak attempt at chivalry.

"I don't care." She opened herself to him.

Hungrily, he entered her.

They lay in an embrace, breathing heavily, Larissa's head on his damp chest.

"I did hurt you, my darling ... I am sorry," he whispered, touching her face.

"It wasn't bad ... Now we are *one*. I love you, Andrúsha."

"I love you, too ... I adore you ..."

They rested and then, still embracing, fell asleep.

The sun was barely rising over the city when Andrei awoke. Larissa was breathing quietly, her hair spread wildly over his pillow, her pink-tipped breasts beautiful to behold. He felt himself stir with arousal.

"Darling, wake up. You must go back to your room," he said, running a finger along her neck.

She opened her huge eyes and stretched luxuriously. "I don't want to go to my room," she said. "I am staying here, with you."

"You can—cannot," he stuttered. "Your mother ... My parents ..."

"We are married before God. We are married, in our own way. Who knows when we will see one another again? They will understand," she said with conviction. "The loss of my father and brother makes it even more important for me to be loved. I want *you* to love me!" She threw the blanket off, inviting him into her outstretched arms.

Andrei was amazed. This Larissa was passionate and bold, a woman whom he did not recognize. He responded to her invitation.

They slept again, sated this time in their passion.

Sunlight awoke Andrei, and he slipped from the bed and went silently to the windows. The sun's rays caressed the giant equestrian sculptures on the bridge across the Fontánka. Since childhood, Andrei had begun most days at that window, admiring the magnificent bronzes. Their character changed with the weather. In sunshine, the men and horses looked alive and virile. In fog, they presented frightening apparitions. In winter, covered with snow, they looked mysterious, as if they might burst forth at any moment. And every spring, they shone brightly, freed from winter's grime by soap and polish and looking as if they were ready to lead a parade. He stood at the open window now and contemplated how he might best rein in the powerful consequences of his new relationship with Larissa.

She woke and came to him, embracing him from behind. "Are you happy, my darling?" she whispered in his ear.

"Yes," he turned and enclosed her in his arms, feeling his desire for her swell. "I am very happy. We must get married. *Legally*, I mean. Before I leave."

"Yes. We should elope." She glanced out the window and realized that their parents would soon be out of their rooms. Hurriedly, she pulled her nightdress over her head and braided her disheveled hair into a long plait. "I feel so happy! I love you." She clung to him again. "We made a mess of your bed!" she laughed. "It looks as if you murdered me! Where are my slippers? Oh, dear, I came here barefoot!" She chatted nervously.

Andrei felt that it was time to put her mind at ease. "Don't worry my darling. We will face them together with the *fait accompli*. We will get married today, or at the latest, tomorrow. They may be angry, at first, but they love us, so they will forgive us. We'll go to Gátchina. There is a small church there, where we can be married. I have a friend there who can be our witness," he said, thinking of Captain Rublev. "Meanwhile, hurry. Go to your room."

They kissed, and she slipped into the corridor.

Andrei glanced at the tousled bed and bloody sheets. "Ah, what the hell," he thought. "Once everyone knows we are married, it won't make any difference."

He heard Larissa scream. His heart in his throat, he pulled on his pajamas pants and rushed into the corridor. There, facing Larissa, was his father. Larissa was pressed against the wall, her face buried in her hands.

"What's going on?" his father thundered. "What did you do, you scoundrel!" he shouted at his son. The general's face was red with fury. "And you, young lady, why didn't you call for help? You son-of-a-bitch!" He advanced on Andrei and struck him with a hard slap across the face.

Larissa ran into her room and locked the door.

The commotion brought Andrei's mother to the corridor. "What happened?" she cried in alarm.

"*Your* son *raped* Larissa! That's what happened!" the general roared.

"What's going on?" Maria Nikoláyevna, also in her nightclothes, appeared at the door to her room.

"Disaster!" cried Andrei's mother hysterically. "I don't know what to say. I can't believe it … I am going to faint."

"Tell me, what happened?" Maria Nikoláyevna turned to the general.

"Our son, the scoundrel, dishonored your daughter!" the general shouted.

Andrei stood unable to talk, unwilling to lie, his face burning. Larissa, in a robe now, opened her door and faced the outraged general.

"Vladímir Petrovich," she raised her voice almost to a shout. "No one has raped me," she said more calmly. "I went to Andrei's room last night and told him that I wanted to be his wife before he leaves for the front. I love him. I have given myself to him as he has given himself to me. He did not force me."

"I am going to faint," Andrei's mother whispered dramatically. "How could you do such a thing?"

Andrei put his arm protectively around Larissa. They stood together, boldly challenging their family traditions.

"Well, what is done is done," Maria Nikoláyevna said quietly. "Let's all get dressed, and then we can discuss the situation calmly. No one has raped anybody. Our children were engaged to be married. They have hastened the occasion, but there is no real tragedy."

The general collected himself. He tied the belt of his robe, which had become undone in his agitation, and made a small bow to Maria Nikoláyevna. "Let us meet in my study in an hour. All of us," he emphasized. "I am sorry, son, for accusing you," he apologized gruffly, not looking at Andrei, "and for striking you."

An hour later, the family gathered in the general's walnut-paneled study. In contrast to the rest of the mansion, which emulated the gilded style of Louis XVI, the general's study was in an English style, with dark brown, deep leather chairs, mahogany bookcases, and a large desk. A matching refectory table, used only for studying military maps, occupied the center of the room. A map of the Western Front was spread across the table, bristling with miniature colored flags that represented troop movements. A large painting of Peter the Great in battle armor hung above the mantel of a carved stone fireplace. A portrait of Tsar Nikolaí II dominated the opposite wall. It was a handsome room, with a thick, deep-red Persian carpet to soften the sounds of cavalry spurs.

"What shall we do?" The general looked sternly at the older women, as if it was their fault the young people had misbehaved. He ignored Andrei and Larissa, who had chosen a spot distant from their parents. Larissa sat in a deep chair against the wall and Andrei perched himself on its broad armrest, his arm wrapped protectively around her shoulders. It seemed they were subconsciously flaunting their newfound unity.

Andrei's mother sighed dramatically and dabbed at her eyes with a perfumed handkerchief.

The general cleared his throat. "With Andrei going to the front next week, what shall we do? What if he has made Larissa pregnant?"

"Oh, dear Lord! Don't say such awful things!" Andrei's mother began to cry.

Andrei felt a cold blast of fear. Clearly, his father thought it likely he would not return from the war.

Maria Nikoláyevna said quietly, "They must be married at once, before Andrei leaves. The Church will dispense with its rules on mourning. Our blessed departed would certainly forgive Andrei and Larissa their digression. Andrei is leaving. God knows what he will have to endure ... Larissa gave him something that only she could have given him under the circumstances: *herself.* Willingly. I don't condemn them. Let them be married at home and enjoy a few days together."

Andrei's father frowned. "I never suspected that you were such a libertine, Maria. How can you condone their behavior?"

She smiled faintly. "Have you forgotten how it felt to be young—"

"But what will people think when they hear that our children were married secretly while Lara was still in mourning?" Andrei's mother interrupted.

"Do you really *care* what people would think, Varvara? I don't. As for mourning, I'll continue to wear my widow's weeds and mourn my husband and my son, but I want my daughter and my godson to have some happiness. Larissa will mourn her father and brother in her heart for the rest of her life, but now she deserves to be with her beloved. Let them be married, today or tomorrow, married at home, without a big formal wedding, which is nothing, really, but a costly spectacle."

The general took off his glasses, wiped them with his handkerchief, steamed them with his breath, then polished them again.

Andrei felt he had to take a lead in the discussion. "Larissa and I want to be married at once. Our respect for her father and brother could not be greater. If things were different—if I were not scheduled to leave for the front—we would have delayed our ... our *action*," he felt himself blushing, "and honored our traditions. But, because we did not, and because I must leave, we do not want to delay our official marriage."

Larissa spoke. "We thought that we would go to Gátchina. There is a small church, and Andrei has friends who could stand up with him."

"People we don't even know!" exclaimed Andrei's mother.

"They are my *friends*, Mother," Andrei said without hiding his irritation at her constant insistence on protocol. He blamed it on her pride at having once served the Dowager Empress as a lady-in-waiting.

"We will settle the details later," Maria Nikoláyevna said. Her voice was firm, without a trace of tearfulness. "I will talk to Father Afonasii and ask him to perform the ceremony and arrange the legal papers. And you, Varvara," she turned to Andrei's mother, "order your staff to prepare a simple reception. Under the circumstances, I don't think that Larissa will want to invite her friends—"

"Only one," Larissa interrupted. "My music teacher, Olga Petrovna Nekrasova."

"A good choice," Maria Nikoláyevna said.

Andrei watched Maria Nikoláyevna with curiosity. She seemed rejuvenated. Unlike his mother, who had collapsed, Larissa's mother had taken control of the situation and stood up for them. "She has real *guts!*" he thought in admiration, recalling the pilots' vulgar expression.

Andrei's mother touched her swollen eyes with her handkerchief. "I don't know if I can do anything right now. I am too upset," she sobbed. "You take over, Maria, and do what you think must be done ... I must lie down or I'll faint."

Normally, Andrei, a dutiful son, would be expected to comfort his mother in a time of distress, but he remained at Larissa's side. Everyone understood this to be a declaration of his independence. He was a man now, whose responsibility was to take care of his wife—Larissa.

A slight smile of approval played on Maria Nikoláyevna's face. "Andrei will protect my girl," she thought briefly. "All right, dear," she said to Varvara Mikháilovna, "you go and lie down. When you feel better, you and Larissa select a suitable gown for the occasion."

"She can't wear white! She is not a virgin anymore!" Andrei's mother objected.

"Varvara!" the general and Maria Nikoláyevna cried in one voice, shocked by her insensitivity.

"Larissa will wear whatever she wants," Andrei raised his voice. "You behave as if Larissa is a marked woman, someone guilty of a crime rather than the girl you could hardly wait to call your daughter-in-law!"

"I will wear my cream-colored lace tea party dress," Larissa said quietly. There was nothing more to discuss.

9

Late that morning, the family finally called for breakfast. Andrei and Larissa were served on the garden terrace, and Maria Nikoláyevna joined them. The general ordered his breakfast brought to his study. Andrei's mother refused to eat anything and locked herself in her room.

Maria Nikoláyevna, after weeks of barely touching food, felt ravenous. Cracking the top of her soft-boiled egg, she spoke of the future. "Well, my children, you must decide where you are going to spend your honeymoon, or to be realistic, your four days before Andrei must leave."

"Can't we stay where we are?" Larissa asked.

"I would not recommend it. The atmosphere here is a little tense, as you know. I think you should be by yourselves. Go to one of the hotels. The Astoria, perhaps."

"We can stay at the inn in Gátchina," Andrei said. "It is right in the park and quite nice. If we get married in Gátchina's church, we won't even have to return to the city."

"That will give us more time to ourselves! I like it!" Larissa exclaimed.

Maria Nikoláyevna nodded slowly. "I think staying in Gátchina for a few days is a good idea; it will give your parents time to cool down. So make your arrangements, my boy. Now, I advise you not to repeat your … ah … your action of last night until you are officially married. Don't flaunt your exception to tradition!"

Andrei kissed her hand. "Thank you," he said looking deep into her eyes. "Thank you for your understanding." He embraced Larissa. "I'll be right back. I must face Jupiter now and request permission to use his telephone."

Captain Rublev readily agreed to be the best man and promised to make reservations at the inn.

"When are you arriving?"

"Tomorrow afternoon. The priest suggests a four o'clock wedding, a short one, without the choir. I would like Lieutenant Seversky to be my other best man, but I have not been able to reach him."

"Not to worry. I have a meeting with him tonight and I can ask him on your behalf. I am sure he will be honored."

"Thank you! You were right, sir, when you suggested that we should marry as soon as possible!"

"I won't ask why you took my advice," Rublev replied with a smile. "See you tomorrow."

Olga Nekrasova, Larissa's piano teacher, wasted no time opening the envelope bearing a hastily written note from Larissa. The maid who had delivered it stood by, awaiting a reply.

Dear Olga Petrovna,

My fiancé leaves for the front in six days, and we will be married tomorrow in Gátchina.

I would like you to be my Matron of Honor. Please, say yes! If it is "yes," simply send word with the maid who delivered this note and come to the Rezánovs' residence on Fontánka tonight. My mother and I are still at General Rezánov's residence. Spend the night with us, so that we all can go to Gátchina together in the morning. Please, please, say "yes!"

Larissa

Olga Nekrasova read the note twice and then said to the maid, "Tell your mistress that I am happy to accept her invitation. I will come to the house tonight, after dinner."

"The young mistress told me to ask that you come before dinner. They will be discussing wedding plans during dinner, and she wants you there."

"So, you know about the wedding?"

"Yes, Ma'am, we all know." The maid grinned. "We are so happy for them!"

"Well, all right," Olga said. "What's your name?"

"Natasha."

"All right, Natasha, tell your mistress that I will be there about four o'clock."

"Yes, Ma'am." Natasha curtsied and left.

Olga Petrovna Nekrasova, now in her forties, had taught piano since she was a young woman. Her youthful dreams of glory as a concert artist had been shattered when she was denied entry into a piano competition because she was female. Shortly afterwards, she was offered a teaching position at the Smólny Institute for Noble Girls. It was a prestigious position that paid very well.

Olga was from a family of modest means, and she was glad to have a position that afforded them some ease. She established her reputation as a remarkable teacher and soon afterwards, Olga's father, a piano tuner, joined the staff at the Smólny. His good work there led to side jobs servicing pianos in the homes of most Smólny students, and that allowed the family to buy a dacha in the suburbs of the capital city.

Olga Petrovna was a serious musician who had never married. She bottled her affections, then carefully measured and dispensed them to her students and her cat, who was usually present during lessons, curled up in a small basket.

Olga chose her students carefully; no amount of money offered by ambitious parents could make her accept a student without musical talent. Among her chosen were one or two whom she favored and groomed. Larissa Orlova was one of them, and she continued to coach Larissa after Larissa graduated from Smólny.

When Larissa received an invitation to play at a fundraising concert patronized by Empress Alexandra Feodorovna, Olga felt triumphant. The occasion would be a fashionable affair, and Olga felt her own talent would be on display at that concert! When Larissa cancelled her concert appearance because she was in mourning, Olga Nekrasova was devastated.

Disappointed, she channeled her efforts toward arranging for Larissa to play at the next concert. When Olga learned that someone else had already been invited—a *male* conservatory student, who was to play his own composition—Olga was livid. This time, she would not meekly allow a male to usurp her time in the spotlight! She wrote a letter to the Empress' social secretary. She explained why Larissa Orlova, who had graduated from Smólny with the diamond *chiffre*, a special trophy established by Catherine the Great for outstanding graduates, had withdrawn from the earlier concert. She wrote that Larissa was a Christian girl, subtly enforcing rumors that the proposed male pianist was a Jew. Every member of the Smólny faculty signed the letter.

The reply came within a few days. The Empress expressed her sympathy to Mademoiselle Orlova on the loss of her father and brother, and her wish to have Mademoiselle Orlova play at the next concert, with the program of her choice.

Olga Nekrasova was jubilant! She decided on Chopin's music. She had heard that the Empress loved Chopin. It wouldn't hurt if the Empress were pleased, she thought. She chose the delicate Nocturne no. 2 in E-flat Major as a main piece and then something very different for an encore, the thunderous Polonaise Militaire no. 1 in A-Major. The Polonaise, with it heroic mood and technical brilliance, would be uplifting for the wounded soldiers.

Olga packed a small valise with her toiletries and a change of clothes and sent her housekeeper for a *drozhki*, a one-horse carriage for hire.

"What a strange message," she thought. "A sudden wedding, while Larissa is still in mourning!"

Ensconced in the jolting *drozhki*, Olga pondered why the Orlovs and Rezánovs, two highly traditional families, would suddenly abandon their mourning traditions. "Is it because Larissa's fiancé is departing for the front? Perhaps they fear he will be killed and, with him, the Rezánov progeny. If Larissa were pregnant, his seed would not be lost. However, if that were their motivation, they could have planned a traditional wedding while he was still with the Cavalry Guards. *A rapid wedding in Gátchina?* Is Larissa *already* pregnant?" She thought of her pupil and dismissed the idea. "The girl seems prim and innocent, except when she is immersed in music. No, she is a good girl who would not flaunt tradition."

Dinner was served in the informal dining room. Andrei's mother came to the table wrapped in a downy woolen shawl, complaining of the cold while the rest of the company enjoyed the unusually balmy evening.

The general made an effort to be congenial. "No use crying over spilt milk," he told his wife, but she preferred to act miserable. Her dreams of a huge wedding, a grand ball, and perhaps even attendance by a member of the Imperial Family, had to be abandoned because of Larissa's shameless behavior.

"I don't blame Andrei," she thought. "He is a *man*, and no man can resist the temptation of a woman giving herself freely. Larissa seduced him. She came to his bed as if she were some low-class chambermaid!"

Maria Nikoláyevna, by contrast, would not dwell upon what had happened; she was planning what was *going* to happen. A wedding!

"Did you order the flowers?" she inquired, suspecting that Andrei had not given it a thought.

"I forgot," he confessed sheepishly.

Maria Nikoláyevna frowned. "It's too late now. Flower shops are closed for the night. And we won't have time tomorrow morning …"

"Why don't we get flowers from Father's winter garden?" Larissa said. "Send someone to our house with a note for the head gardener, and he will make a bouquet for me and boutonnieres for the men."

"Of course!" Maria Nikoláyevna exclaimed, giving Lara a kiss.

Andrei's mother felt shaken by Maria Nikoláyevna's enthusiastic response. Her best friend was rallying after having lost the two most important men in her life, even blessing the young couple's wedding with a gift from her husband's beloved garden! Suddenly, Varvara Mikháilovna felt ashamed of herself. Perhaps, given the circumstances, the young couple's indiscretion had been something forgivable. She dropped her hostility. "Lara can have my Brussels lace veil," she said. "It was a wedding present to me from the Dowager Empress when I was her lady-in-waiting. I always dreamt I would give it to my daughter at *her* wedding, but my only child is a son. I would like you to wear it, dear," she said, turning to Larissa.

Larissa jumped to her feet and smothered Varvara Mikháilovna with kisses. "Oh, thank you, thank you," she cried. "When I have *my* daughter, I will give it to *her*, for her wedding! It will always stay in the family!"

"Hear, hear! Good show!" the general, forever the Anglophile, declared.

The hostility of the elders and the embarrassment of the young seemed to vanish as quickly as Varvara Mikháilovna's tears. The family reunited, planning a modest wedding in the little town of Gátchina.

Olga Nekrasova observed the goings on around the table with fascination. Covertly, she glanced at Larissa's waistline. There was no obvious bump ... but *something* unusual was pushing these two families beyond the usual customs of their class. Olga watched Andrei and Larissa, so well matched, so obviously in love, and she wondered if her first guess had not been correct after all. Perhaps both families simply wanted the Rezánov line to continue and feared that would never happen if they postponed the wedding because of Andrei's deployment. She had read the statistics: among all the men serving at the front, pilots had the shortest life expectancy. Olga realized with sadness that the handsome, vibrant young man might never see his first child.

The general and the two mothers awaited the young couple in the general's study. It was time to bestow the parental blessing.

Andrei and Larissa entered the study together and knelt before their parents. They had spent the night in their separate bedrooms, but both blushed and felt ill at ease, Lara shy in front of Andrei's parents and Andrei unable to look Larissa's mother in the eye.

The general took an icon of the Savior from the family's holy corner and held it over the young couple's bowed heads. Their mothers stood on either side of the general, holding lighted candles. "May our Lord bless you and keep you," Andrei's father said in a solemn voice. "May He keep you safe and well. May you, Andrei and Larissa, be true to one another and happy in your union." He raised the icon three times over their heads and then replaced it on its stand. Everyone made the sign of the cross, and the parents kissed the young couple three times. Following tradition, they all bowed their heads for a minute of silent prayer. Then, making the sign of the cross again, they were ready to go.

Carriages took them to the railroad station, where the general's aide-de camp, Lieutenant Sergei Borisov, was waiting with first class tickets for the group. Two maids carrying luggage and flowers would travel in second class, along with household staff members of both families, whom Larissa had invited as her guests.

Captain Rublev met them at the station in Gátchina, dapper in his dress uniform. He saluted the general and gallantly kissed the older women's hands. Andrei was surprised to see a Cross of St. George among the medals pinned on the captain's tunic; Rublev had never mentioned receiving such a prestigious military honor.

Rublev led them to the four carriages he had hired to transport the wedding party to the inn.

The inn was located on the shore of a picturesque little lake within the Palace Park. The wedding party had reserved the whole building for a day and its best suite of two rooms with a bath for four additional nights.

"How charming!" exclaimed Maria Nikoláyevna. "It reminds me of the inn at Baden Baden, where my husband and I often stayed!"

"How much time do we have before the ceremony?" General Rezánov inquired.

Rublev replied. "A little over an hour. Lieutenant Seversky will meet us at the church, Your Excellency. I wasn't sure if you wished to follow the Russian tradition of the parents waiting for the newlyweds to return from the church, or the European custom of attending the wedding."

"We've had no time to discuss details, because of my son's leaving so soon," the general said stiffly, a bit embarrassed. "What do you think, Maria?" He turned to Larissa's mother, who seemed to be in charge of all decisions.

"In the European way," she replied without hesitation. "Staying at home to welcome the newlyweds would seem a bit silly here," she gestured around the inn. "We all will go to the church with the bride. And you, Volódya," Maria Nikoláyevna looked at Andrei's father, "you can escort Larissa to the altar, in the European way, in place of her own father."

"Couldn't I walk with Andrei, in our *Russian* way?" Larissa asked. "After all, there are certain sweet things in our native ceremony, not just archaic ones."

"It's fine with me." The general looked at Maria Nikoláyevna. She nodded.

"Yes, that's how it will be," the general said. He directed Lieutenant Borisov to accompany Andrei to the church.

Andrei marched across the park toward the church, alongside Lieutenant Borisov and Captain Rublev. There was an absence of small talk, and Andrei imagined both men were musing on the probable cause for a quick wedding.

"Captain," he said, turning to Rublev, "some time ago, you suggested that I marry *before* the end of the war. You can see I am following your advice!"

"You will not regret it!" Rublev grinned. He slapped Andrei on the shoulder. "The way the war is going, you would have remained a bachelor for a few years! God forbid!" He twisted his red moustache.

"I think, I'll take that advice myself," Borisov said. "I am engaged to be married in November, but why should we wait? By November, I may be at the front myself, and if I died, my fiancée would have to start all over, searching for another victim!"

Andrei and Rublev both laughed at the joke, pretending that it was a good one.

Silence descended again. Andrei thought of his classmates, already gone from Gátchina. New cadets, strangers to him, were now training there. The wedding would be devoid of many familiar faces, but Andrei had asked Rublev to invite some of the flight school instructors and several mechanics, including old Petrovich.

A small group of flight school mechanics awaited them in the church vestibule. They wore clean white shirts and trousers tucked into polished boots, their hair shiny with brilliantine and neatly divided with a center part. The little vestibule reeked of eau de cologne.

The mechanics greeted Andrei with broad smiles. "*Mnogy leta*, Lieutenant! Many years of happiness!" They all liked him. Andrei had always listened to them with the same eager attitude he had displayed towards his officer-instructors, and they knew that Andrei respected their knowledge and experience. His standing as an officer and a nobleman had not been an issue. Now, they liked him even more: he had invited them to his wedding!

"Thank you, thank you my friends," Andrei shook hands all around as he and his escorts entered the church. The mechanics crowded in behind them.

The modest little church was lavishly decorated with flowers. Andrei had secretly telegraphed Rublev a hundred rubles for decorating the church, and Rublev did not disappoint. In addition to the flowers, wax candles in tall silver candelabras lined the narrow red carpet leading to the altar. Their flickering flames made the church walls shimmer as they reflected off silver *rizas* hung floor-to-ceiling on the church walls. Andrei tried not to think of the grim saints' portraits. As a child, he had felt terrified by the suffering saints, especially St. Sebastian, whose blood flowed from around dozens of arrows embedded in his flesh. "Church images are always so forbidding," Andrei thought. "No one smiles except the Madonnas …"

Lieutenant Seversky greeted him near the candle box in the nave. "Congratulations!" He shook Andrei's hand. "I am deeply honored to be your best man." Like Rublev, he wore his dress uniform, handsomely adorned with medals and aiguillettes. A miniature white rose was pinned above his pilot's insignia.

"Let me help you with your boutonniere," he said, pinning one on Andrei's chest. Rublev and Borisov helped each other with their little roses. Together, the four men presented themselves to the old priest, Father Alexii.

"Now, we wait," Andrei thought.

The sound of horses' hooves announced two carriages bearing the rest of the wedding party. Borisov went outside to greet them.

Larissa looked radiant dressed in a cream-colored batiste dress edged in lace, her shiny chestnut hair crowned with a wreath of small white roses and a fine Brussels lace veil. She exuded happiness as she walked through the door on the arm of Andrei's father. Their mothers followed, Maria Nikoláyevna still in black silks but having added a white lace collar to ease her dress's severity, and Varvara Mikháilovna in her chic pale gray suit. Olga Nekrasova walked behind the mothers, carrying the bridal bouquet. At the end of the little procession came members of the two households: maids, valets, cooks, and gardeners.

Old Petrovich, clutching a bunch of daisies, squeezed himself through the crowd and joined the group of mechanics. "I was afraid that I might miss the wedding," he declared in a loud whisper. "I wanted to bring flowers to the bride. I had to run to the village and raid someone's garden!" He was still breathing hard.

The priest was confused. He had never performed a wedding in the European style. By Russian tradition, the young couple would walk forward together with their godparents behind. The parents would be at the bride's home, awaiting the newlyweds with front door open wide to indicate that the bride was always welcome to return should something go wrong with the marriage. Also, the little carpet at the end of the runner was missing. Tradition had it that the first to step on the carpet, bride or groom, would be the dominant one in their marriage. The priest had heard many mothers encourage their daughters to put their foot on the rug first! Andrei and Larissa, however, were a modern young couple who felt they could be equal in their marriage. The priest was too old to care.

A familiar and joyful sound burst forth from the choir gallery in the narthex, startling the wedding party. Unbeknownst to anyone, Captain Rublev had hired a choir. *"Mnogy Leta,"* the choir intoned, filling the church with the ancient chant, repeating the words with beautiful harmonies.

The general felt his eyes misting. He glanced at Larissa and then at his wife and Maria Nikoláyevna. *"Mnogy Leta,"* he whispered to Larissa as he took her hand and passed it on to Andrei. *"Mnogy Leta,* my children!" He stepped back to his wife and Maria Nikoláyevna. A young assistant to the priest handed them lighted wax candles.

Andrei and Larissa stepped onto the long red runner. Followed by their two best men and Olga, they walked up the aisle with measured steps then bowed their heads before Father Alexii. The old priest blessed them with an icon and nodded to his assistant to pass the wedding crowns to the best men.

Lieutenant Seversky and Captain Rublev raised the gilded crowns over Andrei and Larissa. Captain Rublev, whose balance depended on his cane, stretched to lift the crown above Larissa's head and wobbled on his prosthesis. He felt the crown slipping. He knew he would not be able to maintain his stance throughout the long service, and glanced at Borisov. "Help me," he mouthed. The tall Borisov quickly exchanged places with Rublev. The old priest did not notice.

The lengthy ritual continued. After awhile, the couple sipped ceremonial wine from a chalice, and the choir responded joyfully. The priest took Andrei's and Lara's hands and lightly bound them together with an embroidered cloth. With the symbolic binding in place, he led them three times around the pulpit, murmuring prayers. The best men followed closely behind, holding the crowns above the bride and groom's heads while trying to avoid stepping on Larissa's long veil.

The assisting priest presented Father Alexii with a small velvet cushion atop which were two plain gold rings. The priest chanted a blessing over the rings and directed Andrei and Larissa to place the rings on each other's fingers. The choir burst out in a triumphant wedding song. The priest continued to chant in Church-Slavonic, but no one was able to hear him. The happy refrain, *"Mnogy Leta,"* filled the church, amplified by the guests, who spontaneously added their voices to those of the choir.

A crowd of well-wishers surrounded the newlyweds in the small yard outside the church. Petrovich squeezed through the throng and stuck his bunch of daisies before the bride's face. "I got them for you, Madame Rezánova," he bowed before her with a flourish.

"Thank you! What is your name?" she said, smiling.

"Everybody calls me Petrovich, Madame. I am a mechanic at the school. I taught your husband."

"Of course! I have heard Andrei speak highly of you." She passed her bridal bouquet to Olga and took the daisies from Petrovich. "Thank you so much!"

Petrovich beamed. *"Mnogy Leta!"*

"Thank you, Petrovich," Andrei said. "And here is something for you and the men." He handed Petrovich four ten-ruble gold coins and looked at the mechanics. "Have a drink in our honor!"

"Hurray!" they shouted. *"Kacha't!"* They surrounded Andrei, ready to foist him over their heads and carry him away in their exuberance, as was customary at peasants' weddings.

"Oh, no," Larissa begged. "Don't do that, please!"

"Bratsy, brothers," Petrovich interceded. "Let Their Excellencies go to their celebration. And we'll go to our tavern and have a drink to their health!"

"Ladies and gentlemen," said the general, helping his wife and Maria Nikoláyevna into a waiting carriage, "we have a small reception at the inn and then we must catch the 8:30 train back to the city." He turned to Petrovich and handed him two more gold coins. "Perhaps, Petrovich, your friends won't mind entertaining our people in your tavern. Just make sure that they are sober enough to be on the 8:30 train."

"With pleasure, Your Excellency!" Petrovich stretched his old soldier's body, sucked in his stomach, and saluted smartly.

The crowd began to disperse. The officers and Olga Nekrasova settled in the second carriage, while Andrei and Larissa joined their parents.

"Ah, it was such a beautiful wedding!" Larissa sighed as she put her head on Andrei's shoulder. "I am so happy!" She twisted the wedding ring on her finger and admired it with a demure smile.

"Mnogy Leta!" Smiling strangers on the street shouted and waved as the wedding carriages, festooned with floral garlands, passed by on the way to the inn.

They had a short reception with champagne and caviar and then a wedding cake. The wedding guests enjoyed these things at their leisure, while the bridal party allowed a photographer and his assistants to herd and pose them amongst artificial shrubbery set before a canvas painted to resemble Greek ruins.

In the formal family portrait, the general sat on a throne-like chair, his left arm resting on the hilt of his ceremonial sword while the mothers, one on each side, rested their hands on the back of his chair. Behind the general stood the bridal couple, slightly elevated on a small platform. Everyone looked at the camera, unsmiling. The photographer's head kept disappearing under a little curtain attached to his camera as he set up the shot. At last, an explosion of lights and puff of smoke from the long T-shaped pole his assistant was holding indicated the image had been captured. The group was rearranged and more photos taken. Finally, the photographer took a portrait of the *smiling* bridal couple standing alone, next to each other. The assistants began to pack their paraphernalia. The session for posterity was over.

While the family was preoccupied with having their pictures taken, several more officers had joined the celebration. They were flight instructors who had been on duty at the school and unable to attend the wedding. All of them liked Andrei and saluted his marriage with champagne, silently hoping his life would extend long enough to see many anniversaries. The party was becoming lively when General Rezánov announced that it was time to leave. They had only half an hour to make it to the station.

"Well goodbye, my children," the general kissed Larissa on her brow. "Enjoy each other, while you can." His voice trembled. He cleared his throat and embraced his son. "Be well, my boy ... We'll see you both before you must leave," he whispered into Andrei's ear, not knowing how to express his love and worry.

"Yes, Papa, we'll be back in four days ..." Andrei replied, also unable to say anything of real importance.

The mothers broke out in tears, kissing Andrei and Larissa, blessing them, kissing them again, smiling at them through their tears, and holding tight to their hands, unwilling to let them go. The young couple felt the significance of their mothers' tears and, for a moment, forgot their newfound bliss. Larissa clung to her mother, suddenly realizing that Maria Nikoláyevna would be completely alone in their large, empty home. Andrei looked deeply into his mother's wet eyes.

"We'll be back in four days, Mámochka," he kept repeating, using his childhood name for her.

The best men and Olga Nekrasova felt awkward witnessing the family's leave-taking. They stood at the window, looking at the darkening park and the serene lake beyond. They did not talk. It would have been impolite.

Finally, Borisov helped the general with his overcoat. Olga kissed Larissa and whispered in her ear, "I'll be in touch with you about the concert. Be happy!" Captain Rublev and Lieutenant Seversky kissed the older ladies' hands and saluted the general, then slapped Andrei on his back and respectfully kissed Larissa's hand. She was a married lady now, and that was proper.

Then, everyone was gone. Andrei and Larissa were suddenly alone.

10

They felt shy with one another. "Are you hungry?" Andrei asked stupidly.

"No," she replied, seeing nothing stupid in his question. "Are you?"

"No."

They stood in a chaste embrace.

Larissa was the first to speak. "What now?" she asked, not expecting an answer. There was none, so she said, "Let's go to our rooms, Andrúsha. I am exhausted."

"Yes. Let's." He kissed her smooth pink cheek, as if she were his sister.

"Do you love me?" she asked, looking deep into his eyes.

"Why do you ask? I *adore* you!" He still felt shy.

"Then let's go to bed. But let's just *sleep* together and not … you know. So much has happened in such a short time that I must gather my thoughts." She entwined her fingers with his. "No," she corrected herself. "I don't need to gather my thoughts. Everything is as I want it to be … I am tired, that's all."

"Of course, my darling. I am tired too. We'll sleep in each other's arms. We don't need to hurry anything. We have our entire lives ahead of us," he said, thinking, "only four days … who knows if there will be any more."

Moonlight bathed the bedroom in its ghostly light, making sharp silhouettes of every object in the room. A summer breeze fluttered the window's lace curtains, almost imperceptibly. A nightingale trilled passionately under their window, but they did not hear it. They were asleep atop a high old-fashioned sleigh bed. Larissa's hair lay strewn across a pillow, partially covering Andrei's face. Her head rested on Andrei's broad chest, and his arm encircled her waist. Both were naked, partially covered by a sheet, all other covers having been tossed to the floor. Despite their agreement, they had made love half the night.

A clock in the drawing room chimed nine times and Andrei awoke. He lay quietly for a few minutes, watching his sleeping wife. He was amazed at the perfection of her skin and form. "My wife," he thought. "This perfect creature is *my wife!*"

Larissa moved and opened her eyes. "What time is it?" she asked sleepily.

"Nine.

"I don't want to get up."

"You don't have to. We can stay in bed all day, if we like."

"I'd like that! Let's order in good café au lait and brioche, and some soft boiled eggs … and of course, fresh butter and maybe, a little strawberry jam. I am not very hungry."

Andrei laughed. "What else would you order if you *were* hungry? I must know your appetites."

"I don't know," she smiled and stretched luxuriously. "It was so-o-o good last night."

"It's another day." He winked.

Andrei jumped from the bed and pulled on his pajamas. "I'll tell you what I think we should do. We'll have *un petit dejeuner*, and then we'll take a bath together, and then we'll nap. Then … we'll have lunch in our room, and if we like, we'll go for a walk in the park, or take another nap, and have dinner served in our room, and then—"

"When you say 'nap', do you mean 'sleep' or 'go to bed and make love'?" Larissa interrupted.

"Whichever you prefer, Madame, as long as we are *together*." He bowed to her ceremoniously. "That's our schedule for today. And if it pleases us, we shall do it all over again tomorrow and the next day and—"

"And we know that it pleases us greatly! We'll do it to the end of our honeymoon. And forever, *together*."

"All right. I'll go now and make arrangements with the owner. I'll request that food and wine, and whatever we might want, be left outside our door. No one is to bother us. *No one*. Only in case of fire, and then they will have to break down our door!"

Larissa giggled. "What will they think of us?"

"Who cares? I know one thing: they will be very envious." He put on his velvet robe and combed his hair. "I'll be right back."

Larissa brushed her teeth and braided her hair. Then she put on her silk peignoir and stared at herself in a mirror. "I look the same, but I know that I am not the same. I have been *penetrated*," she thought. She and her friends at school had discussed such things in whispers, when the idea had simultaneously frightened, teased, and excited them. Now, it had happened, and she liked it! "And I am going to be penetrated again!" she told her reflection.

"Everything is arranged," Andrei declared, entering the room. "I told them to change the linens and towels only while we are taking a walk. Otherwise, we can manage without. Do you mind?"

"Not in the least. Who cares about linens? As a matter of fact, I am not going to get dressed at all. I hate my corset and petticoats and high-buttoned shoes. Today, I'll wear my peignoir or nothing at all."

"I prefer 'nothing at all,'" Andrei said. "I'll do the same. I hate my high boots and starched collars and all these leather belts and epaulettes. I'll wear my robe, or nothing at all!" They laughed. "I'd better wash up," Andrei said, "our breakfast will be at the door in a few minutes."

They were ravenous. "This is our first breakfast together as a married couple," Larissa said. "Let's celebrate with a little champagne! We do have champagne, don't we?"

"Of course, my love. What kind of a bridal breakfast would it be without champagne? I also ordered some Westfallen ham." He reached into the covered basket and retrieved a bottle of chilled Perrier-Jouët. "Now, we'll *really* celebrate our wedding," he said, uncorking the bottle with a loud bang. He poured the wine into two glasses. "To us. Forever," he said, handing one glass to Larissa.

"To us. And forever," she repeated. They wolfed their food and finished the wine. They danced around the room, humming Tchaikovsky's *Waltz of the Flowers,* Larissa's body half-covered by her unbuttoned peignoir. Feeling tipsy, she finally collapsed on the bed.

"*Penetrate* me," she said, her tongue feeling thick in her mouth, her head spinning.

"What?" Andrei was stunned. "What did you say?"

"That is what the girls used to call *it* when I was at the Smólny," she giggled. "We knew the vulgar word for it, but we were all well-brought-up young ladies. I like it, I mean the word, 'penetrate.' It is very descriptive. I also like the action very much. It makes me feel that we are … that the two of us, are one," she explained, seeing a look of incredulity on Andrei's face. "Come to me, my darling!" She opened her legs.

Sated, they slept. When they awoke, their room was warm and sunlit. Birds chirped in the old chestnut tree under the window, and they could hear children's voices from the park.

"What did you say we should do after our nap? Take a bath?" Lara asked with a mischievous smile.

"Yes. Are you willing?"

"Of course! Let me run the bath for us," she jumped out of bed and ran to the bathroom, her pink firm bottom looking like a perfect Crimean peach. He heard the water splash into the huge marble tub and Larissa humming.

"What a treasure she is!' he thought. "What a high spirit! And where did she get that sensuality? I am a lucky man."

"Come on," she called.

Andrei stepped into the tub. Lara was already in, her firm round breasts and erect nipples visible above the water.

"Don't sit down yet. Stand like that! I want to look at you," she said. "Before this, I've never really *seen* a man's organ. I've seen it on statues or in paintings, of course, but not on a real man. I mean, I have seen yours, but briefly. It was almost always *inside* of me!" She laughed.

Andrei felt embarrassed by her innocently lewd talk. "She talks as if she were one of Madam Elsa's whores," he thought briefly. "Where did she get that!" He blushed as if he were an adolescent and plunged himself in, splashing water over the marble floor.

"I've embarrassed you!" she exclaimed. "You are blushing! I am sorry. I did not mean to make you uncomfortable. But we are married! I only wanted to look at your … member. Or *organ*? I don't know what to call it. I know the vulgar name for it, the one that people write on walls, but I don't want to call yours by that name."

Andrei cleared his throat, a self-conscious habit he had inherited from his father and one that served him well whenever he felt unable to properly reply. Lara moved her hips and legs to the side to let him stretch his legs in the tub. They sat facing one another. Lara observed his penis.

"I just love it!" she declared. "I never imagined that it could have such dramatic transformations. Right now, it is floating, you see? On statues it is always pointing down, looking soft and gentle. I remember before the war, when I was about thirteen, my parents took me on the Grand Tour of Europe. We were in Florence and I saw that gigantic statue of David by Michelangelo. I was fascinated by the sculpture and intrigued by David's … *je ne sais quoi*. So, I stared at it. My Papa put his hand over my eyes and turned me around." She laughed and Andrei finally joined her.

"You are a very, very unusual girl," he said, laughing self-consciously. "I would have never suspected that you, of all people, were so interested in male anatomy and could talk in such a naughty way."

"Well, *I am* interested," she replied simply. "I am curious: does it hurt when you sit on it? And how can you ride a horse? It must *hurt*. Do you have to wear something soft in your breeches, like we do when we have our monthlies? That night I came to your room, I thought that it looked … sort of *threatening*, standing up. You know, *aggressive*. But it didn't scare me. I loved it already, even though it hurt when you penetrated me for the first time. The girls used to say they had heard it was painful and dirty and shameful to do it. But I *love* it! We are married now, and it's so good that we can talk about everything, and we can touch and do all kinds of pleasurable things to each other. Don't you think?"

Andrei had finally regained his composure. "Yes, my love. I am very glad we are married and can do all kinds of 'pleasurable things to each other.' And, no, I don't sit on my *thing*, as you call it." He smiled, "It is in front of me." He stood in the tub. "Be my guest. Examine my thing in all its transformations!"

They spent the rest of their four days as they had planned, in their room, mostly in bed. Only once did they go for a walk in the park and watch the training airplanes soaring in the cloudless sky. The buzz of the planes was constant, sounding like a swarm of angry insects. "Is it always so noisy around the airplanes?" Larissa asked.

"Yes," Andrei smiled. "It is always noisy."

"And you don't mind it?"

"No. I love it!"

"Well, here is something new I have learned about you. You are *in love* with airplanes!" she pouted.

"Yes, I love them!"

"More than me?"

"Silly girl!" He kissed her.

She refused to be mollified. "I hate them … I am afraid of them." She did not say that she was thinking of him and the danger the airplanes represented, but he understood.

"I'll be careful. I have a feeling that luck will be with me. Not everyone gets shot down … Lara, even if I had stayed in the cavalry, I would have to go to the front. You know that. I would have been in action for more than two years by now. And far more men are killed on the ground than in the air," he said, hiding the percentages in the white lie.

"Yes. I know. Like Peter …" she whispered.

Andrei tried to comfort her, but she was already thinking of their broken lives, tears clouding her eyes.

The general surprised the couple by extending their time at the inn by one night. He knew that, under the circumstances, Andrei's presence would be hard on everyone. The women would prematurely weep and mourn for him. The men would pretend to be strong and, although the general loved British culture, he did not want to keep a *stiff upper lip*. Rather than bringing the couple back to the Rezánov mansion the night before Andrei's departure, he sent his Packard to Gátchina, instructing the chauffeur to pick up Andrei and Larissa in the morning and take them straight to the railroad station. The general and both mothers would meet them there, to say their goodbyes.

As they rode to the station, Andrei and Larissa were oblivious of the automobile's luxury. Lara wept all the way, and Andrei, his jaw set firmly, tried not to succumb to tears himself. For Larissa's sake, he professed invincibility, but his heart felt cold tendrils of terror reaching for it and his body felt heavy with grief.

They held hands tightly, afraid to let go of one another. As the automobile entered the city and rolled along the Nevsky Prospect, Larissa's quiet weeping became a hysterical outburst. "Don't go! Let's run away, Andrúsha! Let's go to America ... to Brazil ... somewhere away from the war, where no one knows us," she sobbed. He kissed her clutched fists and murmured words of comfort, but she was beyond reason. Disheveled, her hat askew and her hair spilling over her shoulders, Larissa buried her blotchy, tear-stained face in Andrei's shoulder. "She looks wild," Andrei thought, full of love. "My poor little wife ..."

The automobile stopped at the wide steps leading into the terminal, and the chauffeur opened the passenger door. "Here we are, Lieutenant. Madame," he bowed to them. "Have a safe journey," he saluted.

"Thank you," Andrei said. He offered his arm to Larissa. She appeared near collapse.

Staggering on the broad steps, they walked into one of the smoke-filled first class waiting rooms. Their mothers and the general were already there, along with several other mothers and fathers sending their sons to the front. Men, young and old, fidgeted and smoked. Several young officers, torn between affection for their suffering parents and a desire to be on their way, wherever it might lead, stood in little groups, laughed a little too loud, and glanced often at the station's round wall clock. A few men wept quietly in the arms of their beloved.

Andrei and his father stood at the window facing the platform, watching the commotion outside while Maria Nikoláyevna and Varvara Mikháilovna hovered over Larissa, who was beyond reasoning. Maria Nikoláyevna tried to fix Larissa's ragged hairdo, but Larissa angrily waved her away. Larissa's handkerchief became a wet ball, and she furiously threw it into a waste bin then wiped her eyes and nose with her sleeve, like a peasant. Andrei's mother sobbed quietly. She was accustomed to sending her men to war. First, it had been her own father, when she was young, then, three of her brothers, and finally, her husband, for the war with Japan. Now, it was her only son, Andrei. She cried silently, desperately, her face hidden by a veil.

The general and Andrei watched as two hundred Cossacks boarded the third class passenger cars and their horses were led up special ramps into cattle cars at the end of the long train. The well-groomed animals were skittish. They neighed and kicked, and their handlers filled the air with curses, pushing and pulling and lashing the horses until they entered through the cattle cars' wide sliding doors.

"It is a mistake to send the Cossacks away from the city at this time," the general said, watching the loading. "There is a lot of unrest here. All those damned strikes!" He lowered his voice conspiratorially, "Vandals have begun looting the stores. A few days ago, the manager of your godfather's residence came to see me. Men on strike—men carrying red flags—broke some glass in his Winter Garden. The manager wanted to know what should be done. I told him to replace the broken glass immediately and say nothing to Maria Nikoláyevna. Fortunately, she is still staying with us. The poor dear has had enough grief already."

"Is the garden okay?" Andrei asked, glad that Maria Nikoláyevna was unaware of the disturbing episode.

"Yes. It is lucky that it is summer and the weather is warm, so the plants did not suffer. But you see what I mean? We *need* the Cossacks in the city. God knows we need them to keep order. It is the wrong time to send them away."

"We still have several Cossack regiments in the city, I am sure. Stavka needs some fresh troops, I suppose."

"Stavka! They keep changing top commanders and no one knows anything. They always need fresh troops, but they should not waste the *Cossacks!* We need the Cossacks in the capital!"

"Somebody, please, open the window!" Andrei's mother cried. "I am suffocating in this smoke! Andrei, open the window!" Her voice was shrill. Andrei hastily tried to open the filthy window, but it would not budge.

"Let's go to the platform," the general said. He helped his wife stand and whispered in her ear, "Behave yourself, Varvara. No hysterics, please. Let the boy leave in peace."

The officers in the waiting room sprang to attention as the general led his family to the platform.

The air there was not much better. In addition to smoke and steam from the locomotive, the air carried the smell of two hundred horses whose manure was being scraped off the platform's wooden planks. It did not bother the general, being a cavalryman, but the women covered their noses with their handkerchiefs.

Andrei and Larissa walked with their arms around each other, unable to say anything. All the words had been said. Their parents let them walk by themselves, issuing silent prayers for Andrei's safety.

A shrill whistle startled everyone. All the Cossacks and horses had boarded. The train was ready to leave. The departing officers and their families poured out of the waiting rooms. There were dozens of them, ranging from eighteen-year-olds just out of the military academies to grizzled colonels returning from furlough. Relatives swarmed around the men. Women of good breeding publicly lamented their loved one's departure, their manners overcome by dark premonitions.

The general and the mothers gathered around Andrei. "God save you, my boy," the general whispered, making the sign of the cross over Andrei's chest. Not caring anymore for the dignity of his rank, the general wept on Andrei's shoulder, his tears falling on his son's new insignia of pilot's wings. Both mothers clutched Andrei's hands, kissing them, whispering words of love, making the sign of the cross over him, temporarily oblivious of Larissa, who stood alone, her tears all wept. She waited for the elders to let her come closer, but their grief was selfish. No one thought of her.

A shrill second whistle ordered the men into the cars. Andrei shook off the embraces of the general and the mothers and reached for Larissa. They clung to each other wordlessly. Then Andrei tore himself away from her, picked up his two valises, and jumped on the train.

The train slowly pulled out. Larissa, as if suddenly awakened, broke away from the family and followed Andrei's car. As the train began to gather speed, so did she. In a few moments, she was at a run, her hat lost, her hair totally undone and streaming down her back. She fought through the crowd on the platform, breaking open a path for herself. She heard Andrei shout, "Go back, go back," but she paid no attention. Larissa ran after the train.

She reached the end of the high platform and had to stop. "Andrúsha!" she screamed. Her voice was drowned out by the train's final parting whistle. Andrei was gone.

11

Andrei stretched out on the upper berth of the four-man compartment. He knew that during the day a steward would convert the lower berths into sofas to serve as shared space. If a man took a lower berth and wished to have a little privacy during the day, he was out of luck; but the upper berth would belong only to him, and that suited Andrei very well for the present.

Arms folded behind his head, he stared at the dirty window, neither seeing nor caring to see the monotonously flat country the train passed through as it moved westward, toward Poland. In his mind's eye he saw Larissa's disheveled figure pursue the departing train, but his thoughts were turning toward the deep vortex that was about to suck him in—the war.

He felt suddenly cold, as if a wave of winter air had entered the compartment. His head split with a fleeting sharp pain. A single thought quivered in his mind like a captured bird. "I don't want to die."

Three artillery officers sprawled on the lower berths laughed loudly at some joke. They were in their early thirties, men who had already spent two years at the front and apparently felt no fear as they headed back there. Andrei hated their dauntless air. They were *veterans*. He, a just-hatched pilot without any experience, was obviously not one of them.

"Hey, Lieutenant, come down from your perch and have a little vodka with us," one of the artillerists called him. "Stop bawling over your sweetheart! You'll find plenty of them in Poland!"

"Not like that one," another man joined. "I saw her as she ran after the train ... I wouldn't mind if one like that ran after *me!* She was a real peach!"

"After you? You old dog! No decent woman would ever run after you!" They all laughed drunkenly.

"How do you know that she was a *decent* woman?" the third man challenged. "No decent woman I've ever met would make a spectacle of herself."

"Believe me, even decent women can lose their proper manners and become mewling peasant *babas*. My wife always does. That's why I didn't let her see me off," said the officer who had invited Andrei to join the group. "It's bad enough that I must go back to hell. No sense adding a wailing woman to my troubles!"

The men laughed uneasily. The one who had not permitted his wife to come to the station took out a large handkerchief and wiped his eyes. "This *stupid* war," he said, "it changes everything. Who knows whether my wife and I will see each other again? Perhaps I should have let her come to the station and run after the train, like that girl ..."

Andrei jumped down from his berth. "My name is Andrei Rezánov." The officers shook hands and introduced themselves. The one with the handkerchief was Captain Sidorov.

Andrei continued, "The 'girl' who ran after the train is my wife, Larissa. We have been married for five days."

The men were embarrassed. "I am sorry that we spoke about your wife with disrespect," said Captain Sidorov, as he pocketed his damp handkerchief. "We meant no harm."

"Of course. You didn't know that she was my wife," Andrei said, grateful for their conversation. His panic attack had vanished as he'd listened to the captain admit his own anxieties.

"Join us," Sidorov said. "Let's get happily drunk. We have a couple of days of freedom before we enter the fiery realms. Have a drink!" the captain uncorked a new bottle and filled their glasses.

The artillerists were too drunk to go to dinner. Andrei, who had drunk very little, made his way to the dining car alone.

The restaurant was full, except for one table at the end of the long car. Seated there was a man with a pilot's insignia and a Cross of St. George on his tunic. Andrei made his way straight there.

"May I join you, Lieutenant?" he inquired, saluting.

"By all means, Lieutenant. It's good to see another pilot among this crowd of infantrymen and artillerists! My name is Vassily Egórov. And yours?"

"I am Andrei Rezánov." They shook hands and Andrei took the seat opposite Lieutenant Egórov.

Vassily Egórov was a handsome man with dark hair and a neat moustache trimmed in the English style. He was older than Andrei. His well-worn leather coat hung on the back of his chair, his breeches with cavalry stripes—everything about him—proclaimed competence and experience. Andrei imagined Egórov at the controls of a Nieuport and keenly felt his own inexperience.

"Is this your first trip to the front?" Egórov asked pleasantly.

"Yes. I graduated from Gátchina two weeks ago. And you, Lieutenant?"

"I am returning to my unit, after a month of recuperation. I was wounded, but I'm back in the saddle."

Andrei smiled. "You were a cavalryman before, weren't you? So was I."

Egórov nodded. "So I presumed. I saw your family at the station in Petrograd. You are General Rezánov's son?"

"Yes. Do you know my father?"

"Not personally, but I have seen him. I served under General Orlov's command, before he retired."

"It's a small world, indeed! I am *married* to General Orlov's daughter!"

"You? Already married?"

"Yes, sir!"

"Any children? Probably not."

Andrei laughed. He suddenly felt at ease with his new acquaintance. "No, I have no children. The wedding was only five days ago."

"Five days! Well! In that case, let's drink to you and your bride! Let's drink that you come back to her. Let's drink that this damned war ends before it kills us all!" He signalled the waiter and ordered a bottle of champagne. Noticing the surprise on Andrei's face, Egórov shrugged. "I have traveled enough to know that it is wise to look after one's own little pleasures on these military trains. I bring a few bottles of cognac or champagne and, for a small bribe, have them stored in the dining car's ice chest. I am a sybarite and like to indulge my vices. Besides, it is usually the last time that I can enjoy a good drink. As you know, we can't drink if we fly."

"I wish I had thought of something like that! Instead, I have a bag of cookies that my wife's nurse made for me, as if I were still a boy."

Egórov laughed. "Never mind. We'll eat your cookies. Which unit are you assigned to?"

"First Combat Air Group under Alexander Kozakov. In Lutsk."

"Kozakov! He is my own commander! I am also going to Lutsk!"

"Terrific!" Andrei exclaimed. "Kozakov is my hero. You must tell me about him!"

Andrei realized that he probably sounded like an excitable young boy, but he did not care. Here he was, in the company of a veteran pilot, a Cavalier of St. George, who had served under his hero and was returning to serve with him again. "How lucky one can be!" he thought. Andrei felt invincible again.

"Yes, our captain is a true patriot, deservedly the most famous Russian ace."

The champagne arrived. The waiter poured it into the goblets. "Here's to you and your bride!" Egórov raised his goblet and looked straight into

Andrei's eyes as the proper etiquette of toasting required. They both took a sip. "What would you like to know about Kozakov?"

"Everything!"

"That's a tall order. There is a lot to say about his flying career, but not much, I am afraid, about the man himself. Kozakov is a taciturn man. I met him when he was assigned to the 4th Detachment Air Unit. I was already there. We were flying Morane-Saulnier Type-G monoplanes in support of the First Army. Are you familiar with that type?"

"I flew it a couple of times during training, but mostly I have flown Voisins and Farmans."

"Good training machines. I did the same at the Katchinsky Flight School in the Crimea. Kozakov is a brilliant man. He introduced several improvements in aggressive flying techniques and airplane equipment."

"I heard he invented some kind of a hook to grab an enemy plane," Andrei said.

"Yes, he tried it himself and it almost killed him. His idea was to attach a small sea anchor on a long cable connected to his plane's fuselage, maneuver above enemy aircraft, ensnare it with the anchor, and then release flammable material along the cable to explode the enemy's plane." Egórov gesticulated, demonstrating the maneuvering action of both planes. "Do you follow me?"

"Yes. So, what happened?"

"The anchor somehow got caught and was dangling *under* the enemy plane. Kozakov tried to dislodge it by striking the German craft with his own undercarriage. It didn't work."

"What did he do?"

Egórov clipped and lit a cigar. "It was a German Albatros, a good plane. Kozakov's landing wheels collapsed when he struck it, but he destroyed the Albatros. Unfortunately, Kozakov wrecked his own plane as well. His propeller was broken and there was serious damage to one of his wings and landing gear. But being the great pilot he is, Kozakov managed to land on our own airfield, even though he was seriously wounded."

Andrei was so caught up in the story that he forgot his drink. It fizzled in his glass.

Egórov took a sip. "And we have Kozakov to thank for seat restraints. During one air battle, he lost his mechanic, who fell out of the plane when Kozakov had to make a steep dive. Since then, Kozakov has engaged in a campaign for safety. All planes are supposed to have seat restraints now. *And he wants us to use them!* The belts are very uncomfortable, as you well know."

"Yes, I know. At school we often sat *on* our belts!"

Egórov laughed. "I understand, but Kozakov has insisted on enforcement of the rule, particularly in two-seaters."

"I studied some British manuals. It was mandatory for them to use seat restraints a long time ago. The same for the French, and I think for the Germans."

"Yes, but not for us, the *Russians!*" Egórov hissed. "One would think that the simple idea of providing something to prevent a man falling out of a plane would present itself to our leadership, but apparently our Russian High Command never thought of it until Kozakov made the necessity clear. Anyway, let's refill our glasses. You'll meet Captain Kozakov soon enough and form your own opinion. He is an interesting man. Very honest, and he cares about his pilots. He accepted his current position on the condition that he be assigned pilots who are *la crème de la crème*. So we pilots, the chosen ones, feel privileged to serve under him. He takes good care of us, even though none of us has ever succeeded in becoming his personal pal. It is better that way. There are no favorites."

"How old is he?"

"About my age. Maybe a year or two older. I am twenty-eight. As you know, there are no *old* pilots in our service," he smiled crookedly.

Andrei sighed. "I hope I will be able to fulfill his expectations," he said. "I *love* flying!" he exclaimed and blushed.

Egórov smiled. "We all do. That's what makes us so special."

Andrei drank, his imagination fired by Kozakov's adventures. "What else do you know about Kozakov's collision with the German Albatros?"

"Kozakov managed to switch his engine off at the moment of collision. Ironically, he was struck and wounded by his own plane's wing as it collapsed. He glided to our own lines and managed to land. The commanding officer wrote a glowing report, calling him *'the pride of Russian aviation,'* and he received an Order of St. Anne, for bravery."

"To Kozakov, the pride of Russian aviation!" Andrei cried, jumping to his feet and raising his glass.

Officers at other tables turned toward them, smiling at the young pilot's enthusiasm. Egórov raised his own glass. "I will drink to that any time!" They emptied their glasses. The waiter refilled them.

"Have *you* flown with Kozakov?" Andrei was insatiable.

"Oh, yes. The last time I flew with him was when I was wounded. So was he. It happened in the most terrible dogfight I have ever encountered. There were eleven Germans and eleven of us."

"You were evenly matched!"

"Not by design; by chance. I went up as Kozakov's wingman on a reconnaissance of the Austro-Hungarian trenches. There were several of our planes in the air on assignments of reconnaissance and photography, all of us feeling rather peaceful, going about our business, bothering no one. Suddenly, Kozakov noticed a group of enemy planes flying in formation toward their own lines. We found out later that they were returning to their home base after dropping over forty bombs on our Fifth Army near Dvinsk. Kozakov immediately attacked one of them, flying right into their midst. I followed and engaged another. We were in a good position for the attack. The sun was behind us and the Germans did not see us at first. They were totally surprised." Egórov was gesticulating again, demonstrating with his hands and the cigar how the planes dived or climbed steeply.

Officers at surrounding tables, attracted by his voice and gestures, turned toward them with interest.

"Yes, it was a *fierce* battle," Egórov said, noticing his new audience. "Eleven of us and eleven of them, all trying to outsmart one another, shooting our machine guns in short bursts and trying to avoid colliding with our own planes while getting in close contact with the enemy. They had better machines, but we were more aggressive. I think we were better pilots."

"Did you shoot down any of them?" one of the listeners asked.

"Oh, yes, we surely did. Kozakov shot one down almost at once. Then I sent another one down in smoke, then—"

"Did we lose any of our own?"

"Yes, sir, we lost two, but they lost *four* and had to retreat. We could not follow them, for none of us had enough fuel, but we certainly won that dogfight. Four of our men died and several were wounded, including Kozakov and me. I am returning now, after spending two weeks in the hospital."

"And you, Lieutenant?" the same listener asked Andrei.

Andrei blushed. "I recently graduated from flight school. I have never been in a dogfight ... Or, in any fight," he added.

"Don't hurry, son. Your time too, will come," the man said, rising."Goodnight, now. It was a pleasure to meet both of you," he saluted the pilots.

The dining car emptied as officers returned to their compartments.

The train rattled along toward the front.

"Well, it was such a pleasure meeting you," Andrei said, also rising. "I enjoyed our conversation. Thank you for the champagne. I hope in Lutsk I'll have a chance to reciprocate."

"I also enjoyed meeting you, Lieutenant. I was talking so much that I learned nothing about you! Why don't you join me in my compartment? I am all by myself. We can continue to drink and talk. Move in with me! There are at least two more days of travel at this pace."

"You mean it? That is, moving in with you?"

"Of course! I like you. Perhaps we can share quarters in Lutsk, as well."

"I'd be delighted! I have so much to ask you! I feel like an idiot, with no combat experience! I need to learn more about these planes and techniques, and—"

"Hey, hey, slow down!" Egórov laughed. "Let's go to your compartment and get your things. As for being an idiot, we all are idiots. The war itself is idiotic, but that is something we can discuss later!"

The artillerymen in Andrei's compartment were fast asleep, still wearing their clothes and boots. The air was heavy with tobacco smoke, the peculiar smell of leather boots, and the sharp odor of men's sweat. Several empty vodka bottles rolled on the floor with every lurch of the train.

"Disgusting!" Egórov wrinkled his nose. "One of the things that I detest about our Russian brothers, noblemen or peasants, is that they become swine when they are drunk! Get your stuff and let's go to my place."

"I must leave a note for them," Andrei said. "They might think that I fell off the train," he joked, scribbling a note on paper from his pocket notebook.

"What do you care?"

"I think, just to be polite …" Andrei said sheepishly. He placed the note on a folding table between the berths.

Egórov laughed. "You are a nice young man." He slapped Andrei on his shoulder.

Egórov's compartment was cool and clean, the lower berths already turned into beds by the porter.

"Here we are." Egórov tossed Andrei's luggage on one of the upper berths, the other being occupied by his own things.

"You were lucky to get a private compartment," Andrei said.

"No luck was involved. I announced to the train's dispatcher that I represent the pilots of the 19th Detachment and that we share our compartment only with other pilots. Later, I put my things on all four berths. Anyone who looked for an empty berth presumed that my compartment was already full." He looked at Andrei with the sly expression of a naughty boy who had gotten away with his prank.

Andrei laughed.

"Anyway," Egórov continued, "let's have a good rest. I feel a bit light-headed after all this champagne. We will talk more tomorrow." He began to pull off his boots.

Andrei followed his example, even though he would rather have continued their conversation. He lay on his berth and fell asleep at once.

12

"Let's have breakfast in our compartment," Egórov said the next morning.

"I don't think they will allow room service on a military train," Andrei said, stretching luxuriously. He had slept surprisingly well.

"Oh, they will allow it for *us*!" Egórov pressed a button at the side of his berth. Within a few minutes, a porter arrived.

"Your Excellency, what would you like?" Egórov sat up and reached for his wallet.

"First of all, bring us some good hot tea, and whatever else there is for breakfast. How much champagne is left?"

"Three bottles, sir."

"Bring us one. We'll have the others for dinner."

"There is not much for breakfast, sir, only hot oatmeal."

"Well, perhaps you can find something more exciting," Egórov said, proffering the porter ten rubles.

The porter took the money and bowed. "Maybe I can find a few eggs for omelets."

"Yes, that would be fine. Omelets and bread and butter. But no oatmeal. Perhaps, instead, you can find a few sausages? Or ham?" He smiled at the porter.

"Yes, Your Excellency. I am sure I can find some sausages," the porter bowed and left the compartment.

Egórov glanced at Andrei with a look of self-satisfaction. "Here, my friend, is your first lesson on how to survive. If one has money, which I know you have, and if you like comfort, as I know everyone does, then spread your money around. Never be stingy. What is money for?" he asked rhetorically and then answered, "but to be spent for one's comfort and pleasure!"

Andrei grinned. "I had not realized that you were a philosopher, in addition to being a pilot and a raconteur!"

"Oh, yes, my friend! I have many talents: I am a fantastic lover, a dutiful son, a champion chess player and what else? Oh yes, I am also a poet."

"Anything else?"

"Yes. I am a loyal friend. I offer you my friendship. Will you accept my offer?" His tone was humorous, but Andrei felt that he was serious.

"I am honored. If you had not offered it, I would have tried to follow you everywhere, like a puppy, seeking your friendship," Andrei replied sincerely.

"Well then, let's seal our friendship with some Veuve Clicquot as soon as the porter brings it. We'll call one another by our first names! What does your wife call you? Andrúsha or Andrei?"

"She calls me Andrúsha. My mother calls me Andrei."

"And your father? What does he call you? Don't tell me! I bet I know! He calls you *son*."

Andrei laughed. "How did you know?"

"It is one of the traditions of our Russian nobility: our mothers talk to us in French and our fathers ignore us when we are children and then they continue to stay distant by calling us *son*. Only our nurses and lovers call us by sweet diminutive names … but only for a while. Within a short time, our lovers begin to call us *fool* or *beast* or whatever else. Only our old, old childhood nurses remain loyal. To them we are forever Andrúsha or Vasyutka, as in my case. But I should not be talking like this! You are a newlywed, and if you are lucky, your wife will call you Andrúsha for the rest of your life."

Andrei felt uncertain how to respond. His friend seemed embittered by the topic. Andrei decided to put off asking whether Egórov, too, was a married man.

A knock on the door put an end to their conversation. Their porter proved his worth, setting their table with plates of hot omelets and sausages and a chilled bottle of champagne.

They drank to their new friendship, linking arms at the elbows and looking into each other's eyes before draining their glasses. They shook hands, calling each other *"brat,"* the Russian for "brother," and then concluded the ceremony by kissing each other on the cheek three times— right, left, right. They were brothers now.

The closer their train moved toward Lutsk, the slower its progress became along a route jammed with stock cars carrying troops. Every junction was a showcase of trains that had been side-railed to let more important trains pass, but always trains moving west, towards the front. It looked as though no trains were able to move east.

"How are wounded men being evacuated?" Andrei wondered. Where were the hospital cars? He had seen thousands of cars but not one with a red cross painted on its side. Who was taking care of the hundreds of thousands of wounded? And why was his train, a train carrying Cossacks and horses and infantry, moved to a sidetrack even though they were going to the front? While their own train was stopped, he spotted a passenger train parked on another sidetrack, its passengers obviously stranded. They had set up camp alongside the rails. Why was there so much disorganization, and why did it seem that no one was in charge?

He was distracted from his thoughts by a train zipping through, its locomotive whistling loudly. Its cargo consisted of partly-crated aircraft loaded atop several long, open platforms.

"Look Vassily, new planes!"

"At last!" Egórov exclaimed, joining him at the window. "Those must be the planes Kruten negotiated for in France. We've been waiting for them for months! Now we'll really start flying!"

With the fast train and its aircraft cargo gone, the troop trains began to crawl out of the sidetracks. Andrei's train slowly backed up to the main track and resumed its journey toward the front.

They arrived in Lutsk the next day, at a railroad station clogged with troops. Hundreds of soldiers sweated in the summer heat, their heavy military coats neatly rolled into fat gray sausages strapped to their torsos from left shoulder to right hip. They also carried knapsacks, metal mugs, spoons stuck into the stiff upper portion of their boots, rifles, leather boxes of ammunition, and portable shovels to dig foxholes—the equipment of a Russian foot soldier. Though they came from all parts of the country, they had one purpose: to replace regiments that had suffered heavy losses during the offensive. They stood in loose formations, dull expressions on their tired faces. Among the vast aggregation were scattered a few officers who occasionally shouted commands that marched small groups from one place to another with no visible purpose.

Andrei and Egórov awaited the pilots' escort, biding their time in the first class waiting room and glancing through windows plastered with criss-crossed paper strips supposed to prevent glass from shattering in case of bombardment.

"Let's wait for half an hour," said Egórov. "If no one's come for us, then—"

"Then perhaps we can join the crew that came with the new aircraft," interrupted Andrei, eager to see the new planes. "They're probably going to the same airfield as we are, don't you think?"

Egórov slapped him on the back. "We'll do just that!"

Cossacks were unloading from a train, moving their horses into the already overcrowded square. Through the glass, Andrei heard hooves clattering on stone, horses neighing, and tired men cursing. Exhausted by their long journey, the horses snorted and tossed their heads. The Cossacks, sour and angry, whipped them viciously, forcing the horses into a four-chest formation. When the horses protested the rough treatment by rearing up, the Cossacks whipped them even more.

"Brutes!" Egórov exclaimed furiously. "I would like to use a whip on *them!*"

Andrei shifted his gaze and saw, on the periphery of the square, several medical carts filled with wounded. Women in white, nurses or nuns, were carrying large pitchers, apparently dispensing water among the men. One young woman was sitting quietly at a stretcher, holding a wounded man's hand. Her lips were moving as if in prayer or quiet conversation, and the sight of her gentle behavior filled him with longing for Larissa. It was four days since they parted … an eternity. He felt his eyes moisten and made an effort to squelch his thoughts. "Let's go see the planes," he said abruptly.

They made their way back to the main platform and to the flat cars carrying the new aircraft. Several pilots were crowded around the planes. A group of mechanics was already moving some of them to lorries. The fuselages of the planes resembled giant insects with their wings torn off by some cruel gargantuan child.

"Nieuport XIs! Spad VIIs! "Aren't they beautiful?" Andrei exclaimed.

Egórov smiled, remembering his own similar reaction to new aircraft. "One of them may be yours."

"Egórov!" They heard someone call. "Welcome back, you son-of-a-bitch!" A pilot dressed in a cavalry officer's summer tunic and sporting wings on his epaulettes waved to them from the crowd.

"Hey, Platonov! Still around, eh?" Egórov responded. "Sashka Platonov, my roommate," he explained to Andrei. "You'll like him. He is a great chap, who sings like a …" Egórov paused, searching for the right word.

"Like an angel?" Andrei volunteered.

"Well, you could say that if he was to sing in church, but Sashka sings the best lewd songs you would ever want to hear. He is very popular with our mechanics: they take especially good care of *our* planes!"

They made their way through a crowd of mechanics and pilots who all welcomed Egórov. He shook many hands and slapped many backs, introducing Andrei to everybody as "our new fighter pilot Lieutenant Rezánov, my good friend" as they made their way forward.

Platonov and Egórov embraced. They kissed one another on their cheeks.

"And who is your friend?" Platonov asked.

"This is Andrei Rezánov, who just graduated from Gátchina. Like us, he is a cavalryman. But he is a newlywed, so don't corrupt him with your visits to the Polish whorehouses."

They all laughed. "Welcome to our family," Platonov said. "As for the visits to the fair ladies of the best whorehouse in Lutsk, I am afraid there will be no time for that. As you probably have heard, we are in the midst of an offensive, which is turning into a *defensive*, I am afraid. Until now, we have been pushing the enemy back. After all those months of retreat, we were finally advancing! But … the lines of the front have changed. The Germans brought in fresh troops to help their Austro-Hungarian allies. All of us must fly several times a day now. The planes have no time to cool down! And the pilots …"

"Are there many losses?" Egórov grew serious.

"Yes. In our command, four pilots and three planes in the last few days," Platonov replied, and a visible nervous tic suddenly twisted his face. "Komarov crashed."

"My God!" Egórov said softly. "Not Komarov!"

Platonov nodded. He turned to Andrei. "Komarov was our latest replacement. He was shot down on his very first flight. He was only twenty."

Andrei felt as if a stream of icy water had run down his spine.

"I see Kozakov is here," Egórov said. "Let me introduce Andrei to our commander."

Andrei saw a tall man talking to a group of mechanics. He was dressed in a blue military jacket, riding breeches, and knee-high black riding boots with spurs. Like most officers of the Imperial Russian Air Service, Alexander Kozakov had been a cavalryman, and like most of them, Kozakov still cherished his cavalry traditions and wore his former uniform, with pilots' wings added to his epaulettes. The Air Service had not yet designed its own uniform. Only while flying would pilots wear their trademark silk scarves, leather jackets, helmets, and goggles. As for boots—most pilots did not bother to remove the spurs. Unlike officers in other branches of service, Air Service officers were without orderlies.

Kozakov turned around and Andrei had his first look at his commanding officer's face. Partially hidden by the visor of his cavalry cap, what Andrei could see was a narrow, bony face with a straight nose and prominent cheekbones that created dark shadows in hollow cheeks. From a distance, Kozakov's face looked like a skull.

Kozakov waved to them. "Welcome back, Egórov!" he shouted. "We missed you!"

"I missed you too, Captain. A hospital bed is no place to be. I see you've finally got your new planes!" Egórov said, approaching the lorry and saluting the captain.

"Yes, you should be testing them in a couple of days."

"I look forward to it. Allow me to introduce our new pilot, Andrei Rezánov," Egórov said formally.

Andrei stretched at attention. Kozakov looked him over slowly. Then he smiled, and his wheat-colored moustache lifted to reveal a set of huge white teeth. "We have received impressive reports about you, Lieutenant Rezánov. Welcome to our First Combat Air Group. Be in my office tonight for your assignment to a squadron. For a few flights, you'll be allowed no action; you'll be observing the action. Of course, you'll be flying with one of our veteran pilots watching over you."

"Yes, sir," Andrei saluted.

"If I may, Captain … Would you mind if I be that 'veteran pilot' for Lieutenant Rezánov? We are friends, and I would like to be of help during his neophyte flights," Egórov said.

Kozakov nodded. "I have no objection. Perhaps later, I too, will fly with you," he said to Andrei.

"It would be a privilege, sir! Flying with *you!*" Andrei exclaimed.

Kozakov looked embarrassed. "Good!" he said dryly. "See you at the airfield." He turned his attention back to the airplanes.

The new pals hitched a ride on a lorry that was ready to depart. From the back of the lorry Andrei watched the turmoil along the streets saturated with the troops, horses, and vehicles. Lutsk, once a neat Polish town, was now a hub of the Russian offensive. The town went through the German onslaught and now it was in Russian hands, both armies contributing to its ruination.

The soldiers withdrawn from the trenches, waiting to be moved to the reserves, stood out easily. Dirty, tired, and footsore, they were barely able to keep plodding ahead. In contrast, the newly arrived troops marched with vigor, their banners unfurled, and the men singing lustily. There were several Cossack regiments riding their superb battle-trained horses, the men wearing high lambskin hats, *papákhas,* with dashing allure. And then there were primitive, two-wheeled carts drawn by exhausted horses that carried the wounded. The carts, under canvas covers with huge red crosses, were stuck among the moving troops, unable to deliver the suffering men to the aid stations.

There were hardly any civilians in the streets. Several shops had doors gaping open, windows blown out, and shelves empty. The trees, once shading the streets, stood forlornly, their crowns shorn off by the furious bombardment of both adversaries.

Andrei, under the spell of meeting his hero, was not going to dwell upon the tragedy of war. He was going to take part in the glorious fight for his country! He was going to be a great pilot! He was going to fly with Kozakov!

The lorry finally made its way out of town and into the country road, but its progress was not any easier. The road was blistered with huge craters from the heavy shells that had rained on the town and the surrounding countryside for weeks. The exhausted earth looked as if its face was disfigured by smallpox. The lorry groaned under the heavy weight. The mechanics encircled the aircraft with their own bodies, lest the ropes would not be strong enough to protect the planes from the damage along the perilous way.

The pilots joined the men in placing their body weight in support of the shifting cargo.

"I didn't realize that Lutsk was so badly shelled," Egórov said, his shoulder against the fuselage.

Any damage to our airfield?"

"No. So far, we are lucky. Aside from losing our men who were shot down, we had no damage."

Andrei listened to their conversation, sounding so ordinary even though they were talking about death and destruction. "Will I be like them?" he thought briefly, admiring them, and yet, feeling uneasy about their lack of emotion. His shoulder began to hurt from the pressure of the aircraft. Andrei tried to ignore it, concentrating on his surroundings.

He saw a river in the distance that looked like a burnished silver ribbon. "It must be the Styr," he thought, recalling the map that he had studied when he had received his orders. As he remembered, there was a cobweb of smaller rivers on the map that all seemed to concentrate at the Pripyat Marshes, the huge wetlands north of Lutsk. There were several villages spread along the river, their bright white-washed houses looking from a distance neat and untouched, but probably ruined and deserted. He turned his attention toward a forest looming ahead of them.

It was a pitiful sight. Once it must have been a majestic ship-timber forest; it was charred now, broken trees sticking up like blackened, rotten teeth in the mouth of a dead animal. The greenery was all gone. Not a blade of grass was left to gladden the heart, only gray and black stumps of the dead forest.

"The birds and animals," Andrei thought. "Where did they go? Could they escape the bombardment?"

As if to answer his question, he heard a whistling, growing louder. There was a resounding thump and an Austrian shell hit the ravished forest. A huge spurt of earth disgorged from the new crater.

"We'd better get under the truck," Egórov said, jumping off the lorry. "Less chance to be hit by shrapnel."

"What about the planes?" Andrei asked and immediately felt foolish. Obviously nothing could be done about the planes.

Andrei and Platonov crawled under the truck. The driver and the mechanics were already there.

"Now we'll wait. If we are lucky, we won't be hit," Egórov said.

"At least, we won't become pincushions for the shrapnel," Platonov tried to joke. "These so-called 'light wounds' are nasty. They are the bane of our existence: too light to be serious enough to be sent to the rear!" The men laughed nervously. They all knew the truth behind the joke.

Andrei thought that being under a vehicle loaded with fuel was just as dangerous. Answering his unspoken question, Egórov said, "of course there is no real safety anywhere. Just pure luck if one survives. But to protect oneself from being wounded, that's always a wise move."

Another whistling sound was approaching, growing louder by the second, and another explosion shook the ground. The mechanics made the signs of the cross. Andrei glanced at his brother-officers. Their faces were blanched. Platonov made the sign of the cross and Andrei followed.

"Thank God!" Egórov said. Turning to Andrei, he continued with nonchalance, "I am an old agnostic, so I don't make the sign of the cross, but I do thank the Higher Power. And I don't mean our *brilliant* leaders!" he added. Platonov and Andrei chuckled despite themselves.

The artillery attack continued for almost half an hour, shaking the earth with each explosion, all shells landing way ahead of them. Obviously, whatever the target was, it was not Lutsk, but some territory southeast, beyond the forest. Perhaps the enemy was softening the Russian positions in preparation for its offensive? Andrei wanted to ask his friends about it, but decided against it. They probably knew as much about it as he did, that is, they knew nothing.

They arrived at their destination in the evening. The airfield was nothing but a large empty field. Two long rows of tents at the far end of the field housed repair shops, fuel, and supply sheds. Several huge tents, extra wide and empty, were the hangars for the new airplanes. Behind them stood the regular army tents for the support troops, mechanics, artillerists from the anti-aircraft battery, and the serving personnel, and still further back was a small field hospital with a red cross on its roof.

The lorry stopped at the tall gates of a large manor house abandoned by a Polish nobleman. It was surrounded by an ornate iron fence with gilded medallions and the owner's crest of arms. It faced the airfield, which must have been at one time a spacious meadow. It appeared that neither the airfield nor the house with the small garden around it had suffered any damage. The slate roof of the house looked intact, the windows unbroken, and the trees in the garden voluptuous in their greenery.

"I like it!" Egórov exclaimed. "Our quarters before we took Lutsk were atrocious. When did you move here?"

"About a week ago. It used to be an enemy airfield. The house is still full of furniture," Platonov said. "Obviously, the owner's family had to leave in great haste."

"Were they afraid of the Germans or of us?" Egórov asked sarcastically. "Let's drop our things at the door. I am sure the house can wait. Let's go to the flight line. I want to show Andrei our machines! I missed them!"

They walked through the garden and into the field.

There they were, the airplanes, standing wing to wing in the flight line, about twenty of them, making an impressive display. They were of different makes, but they all bore the insignia of the First Command Air Group on their rudders—black skulls and crossed bones on an oval white background. Some airplanes had the insignias in reverse: white skulls on a black background, flaunting their belonging to the original 19th Corps Detachment under Kozakov. The planes were lined up with military precision and looked resplendent to Andrei.

"That one is Kozakov's Nieuport 10," Egórov pointed to the first plane in the line, a fighter with the Imperial double-headed eagle emblem on its cowling.

"The aces are allowed to select their own insignias," Platonov explained to Andrei. "How many kills did you have, Vassily, before you were wounded?"

"Three confirmed, and two unconfirmed," Egórov replied.

"Only two more confirmations to get your ace status. Then you could have your own insignia."

Egórov nodded. "I must start thinking of something suitable. How many kills do you have, Sashka?"

"I have two. I had one while flying with Kozakov. We both were credited. But of course, he is well ahead of both of us. He turned to Andrei. "Kozakov is a terrific pilot. So fearless, so aggressive! He flies as if he owns the sky. And he has his own method of attack that he likes to teach new pilots."

"I would love to learn it," Andrei said.

"Not everybody likes it," Platonov continued. "I have my own way of attack, but other men swear by Kozakov's method. He will show it to you, I am sure, and then it will be up to you to decide which you prefer."

"How about you?" Andrei asked Egórov.

"I admire Kozakov's aggressive approach. But I don't like aerobatics. I prefer my own way of attack. Some years ago I thought that I was cowardly being so ... so cautious, but now, I know that it is just my way of doing things."

"You? You thought that *you* were a coward?" Platonov laughed. "You, one of Russia's best pilots?"

"Yes. And I am sure every man, be he a pilot or a cavalryman or a cook at the field kitchen has had the same thought. No one wants to die, especially when we are young. I am sure you too, Sashka, thought at times that you were so scared that you wanted to cry. Admit it!"

"Of course. I was scared an hour ago, hiding under a truck! And I will be scared in the next five minutes if the Germans start their bombardment again. But do you know, I am *not* scared when I fly! When I fly, I don't think of the danger. I think only of flying and how great it feels, just ... flying!"

Egórov grinned. "I am not ashamed to admit that I have had moments of fear, but fortunately not in the midst of a dogfight. I am too busy trying to outsmart the German farts up there! But to tell you the truth, I was *really* scared six weeks ago, when I got wounded. Stuck under the crashed plane, I felt that I was going to die, and nobody would even know it. I felt the breath of death on my face, I was so *cold* ... but I wasn't ready for death!"

"How did they find you? And who found you?" Andrei, as usual, wanted to know more.

"Andrúshka, you are like a bulldog! You never let go once you got your teeth into a story!" Egórov laughed, flattered by Andrei's interest. "I was lucky, I was hit close to our territory. I was able to glide over the lines and crash near our trenches. The infantry saw me plunging and sent scouts to find me."

"Actually, we thought that you were gone," Platonov said. "You had lost so much blood that the doctor thought you would not survive the night."

"But I surprised you, no?"

"You surely did!"

"All right *bratzi*, let's get our things into the house," Egórov said. "Are there enough rooms for individual use? Or are we supposed to double?"

"Neither. We'll quadruple. That is, the three of us and one more man, probably Klembovsky, when he gets back from the hospital. It is a great room, second only to Kozakov's. It faces the garden, has a balcony, and best of all, it has a huge bathroom with a real shower! Unfortunately, there is no running water. However, our mechanics are fixing up some

123

kind of a pump to connect water pipes with the fish pond. They've already fixed the water heaters. So if the Germans don't shell us to hell, we might enjoy hot baths and showers, as if we were at the Grande Hotel de Paris!"

"Or, we'll have fish from the pond in our bathtub!" Egórov joked. "But what about the Germans? Haven't they bombed or strafed the airfield?"

"They tried, but we have a brand new anti-aircraft battery set up on the other side of the field. So far, so good. Austrian scouts came to reconnoiter a couple of times, but our artillerists gave them such a scare that they haven't been back."

"They'll be back," Egórov said.

The room was as good as Platonov had described. A thick Persian carpet covered the floor and a huge oil painting of cavorting nymphs hung over the fireplace. A wide, luxurious bed under a red velvet cover dominated the room. Several red velvet chairs and small tables with ornate oil lamps completed the furnishings. The three camp beds standing against the walls were incongruous.

"It looks like a baronial brothel," Egórov said. "It makes me feel at home!" He winked at Andrei.

"Shall we flip a coin for the bed?" Platonov suggested.

"I have a better idea," Egórov said. "Let's designate the bed for the one who has just returned from a hospital. That chap will need all the comforts of a decent bed. And, since I have just been released from the hospital, I'll take it! However, I promise, *parole d'honneur,* when Klembovsky returns, I'll surrender the bed to him." There was a sly expression on his face.

Platonov shook his head. "I don't like it. What if Klembovsky doesn't return? Or, what if one of *us* gets wounded, but not seriously enough to be sent to the hospital? Would he qualify for the bed?"

"Well, I guess I did not think of everything ..." Egórov said. "All right then, let's flip a coin for the bed." He fished in his pocket and produced a ten-ruble gold coin. "Andrúsha, you're the least corrupt of us, so, go ahead, call it."

"Heads!" Andrei said. It came up heads.

"We have a winner!" Egórov lifted Andrei's arm as if he were a boxer.

Andrei blushed. "No. No I cannot accept it. I am taking a cot," he said and plunged himself on the nearest cot.

"Ah, what the hell," Platonov said. "You take the bed, Vaska! You *are* our recuperating hero, so take the damn bed!"

"I cannot disobey the decision of the majority. I am *forced* to take the bed," Egórov said with comical solemnity. "Thank you gentlemen." He bowed in the best style of a Louis XVI courtier. They all laughed.

13

About forty pilots gathered in the briefing room, nine or ten men from each of the four squadrons. They greeted Egórov with slaps on his back, congratulating him on his St. George Cross, all genuinely happy to see him back and in good health.

The pilots were all young, none over thirty. Some just returning from missions were still unwashed, their faces chafed from wind and splattered with oil. The pale skin that had been beneath their goggles formed a comical mask. All the pilots were in high spirits, their adrenaline still pumping. They talked loudly and laughed loudly. No one had been shot down, everyone had come home. It had been a good day!

Captain Kozakov and Lieutenant Tomsky, his deputy, entered the briefing room, and the pilots sprung to attention.

"At ease," Kozakov said. "Please sit down." The men took their seats.

"First, I would like to make a couple of announcements. We have a new pilot, Andrei Rezánov, sent to us from Gátchina." Andrei stood and saluted. "Some of you must have met him already. Tomorrow, he will fly as Vassily Egórov's observer. Rezánov was trained as a fighter pilot, but for a couple of weeks he will concentrate on reconnaissance. I also wish to welcome back our Egórov, who was awarded the Cross of St. George. Congratulations, Lieutenant. Welcome back."

Egórov also stood and saluted. "Thank you, Captain. It's good to be back!"

"Now, all of you know that we have finally received sixteen new aircraft," Kozakov said. The pilots jumped to their feet and yelled "Hurrah!" like a bunch of schoolboys. Kozakov waved his hand to settle them down. "You all will have a chance to fly the new planes. I am as eager as you are to try them," he added with a smile. "Our mechanics and engineers are busy assembling the new machines. In a couple of days we can start testing them. Now, listen carefully. Starting tomorrow at dawn, we'll be sending a couple of two-seaters on contact patrols along our front line. Egórov and Platonov will lead the first group. As you know, our offensive was halted, and it looks as though the enemy is preparing for a breakthrough. The contact patrols will take photographs of the terrain, but the main object of the mission is to prevent enemy scouts from snooping. The fighters, including myself, will stay at the alert, next to our machines. In case of penetration, we will be in the air the moment we receive a message from the ground troops. Any questions?" There were none. "Lieutenant Tomsky will debrief those of you who have flown today. Have your reports ready. The rest of you, study your maps. If the enemy is going to move, there will be a lot of confusion. We must know the terrain like the back of our hands. Be back after supper to get your assignments for tomorrow. Dismissed."

The pilots, subdued now, left the briefing room.

Andrei could not sleep. His mind was churning with images: ruined Lutsk inundated by troops, charred remnants of forest, trees blasted and split, roads and fields mottled by yawning craters, sounds of an approaching shell and then a volcanic eruption of noise and motion.

He tried to think of Larissa, but his mind supplied him only with the disturbing image of her running after the train. He willed himself to think of her luscious body, but the picture of her distress persisted in his mind's eye.

He imagined enemy airplanes coming toward him from all directions and tried to conjure up how he would deal with them. He saw himself at the controls, maneuvering, diving steeply, banking sharply, or rising vertically. He imagined seeing his foe in his gun's sights and firing at short range. He knew what had to be done, theoretically. But would he be able to do it when the time came?

Andrei jerked violently at the sound of the alarm. In the darkness, he did not know where he was until he heard the hoarse voice of Egórov swearing juicily at the stubborn matches that kept breaking.

"Is it already four o'clock?" Andrei asked.

"It must be. You had better hurry and get to the bathroom. We have fifteen minutes to get ready. We'll have tea and a quick breakfast at the field."

Egórov finally succeeded in lighting a match and reached for a candle on his bedside table. "Oh, to have electricity!" he sighed. "I have become soft in the Empress's hospital ... electric lights, soft blankets ... even telephones!"

"I know what you mean. My parents had telephones installed a month ago," Andrei said pulling on his breeches. "Such a convenience!"

"Stop talking and get to the bathroom or you'll have no time to brush your teeth," Egórov grumbled through a yawn. "Platonov is still sleeping! Hey, Sashka, get up, it's after four!" He pulled the blanket off Platonov.

Platonov gathered his body into a tight fetal position and continued to sleep. Andrei laughed.

Egórov did not think it was funny. "Help me push this son-of-a-bitch off the bed. He never wakes up by himself!" Together, they pushed Platonov off the bed.

He woke, sat on the floor for a moment, and then said in surprise, "I must have fallen off the bed ..."

"Yes, you must have," Egórov finally laughed.

Platonov's observer met them at the officers' mess tent, near the table with a puffing samovar. He was holding a glass of hot tea in its silver holder, and he chewed a sweet roll. He was a new pilot who had arrived at the front from Kiev a week before Andrei. His name was Ivan Mironov. He was a curly-headed Cossack from the Don region, with a friendly boyish face covered with freckles and a thick *tchoob*, a forelock of hair brushed to one side above his ear in a Cossack fashion. He cocked his service cap over his *tchoob* with a special panache. Mironov spoke with a soft Don regional accent. His French was hilariously atrocious, and he knew it. He often spoke it to entertain his friends. When they joked about his French, he joked along, never feeling offended. The pilots liked him, treating him like a mischievous younger brother.

Mironov introduced himself to Andrei and Egórov. "It looks like we'll have an easy time today," he said pleasantly.

"One can hope," Egórov grumbled, still not quite awake. "Unless we run into the artillery barrage. Or, our own infantrymen mistake us for the enemy and start shooting. It has happened to me," he said, pouring hot water from the samovar into his glass over a splash of strong black tea. "Any milk?"

"Not today, Lieutenant," the regimental cook presiding over the samovar replied. "Our cow was killed two days ago by our own anti-aircraft artillery. One of the cooks left yesterday to try and requisition another one."

"You see what I mean? Our own Russian men killed our own Russian cow!"

Holding a plate and napkin, Andrei walked around the table and filled his plate with fried potatoes, scrambled eggs, and sausages, along with some freshly baked black bread, still warm, and cheese.

Egórov handed him a glass of strong tea with a spoonful of strawberry jam. "Hurry. I want to be in the air before the sun," he said, blowing on his tea. The elegant sybarite, whom Andrei had met on the train only three days ago, was gone. In his place there was an unshaven pilot slurping his tea and licking his fingers smudged with strawberry jam.

The men ate fast, watching the field where the crews were moving two Voisin L planes into the takeoff positions.

"Voisins," Andrei said with a hint of despair. "We had a couple of those at Gátchina. I was hoping that we would fly something faster."

The Voisin L was a French machine widely used by the Imperial Air Service. A pusher-type biplane, it had its engine behind the cockpit. Its nacelle, containing two seats in tandem, protruded forward from the lower wing, and its nose rested on a pair of fragile-looking wheels. Two larger, sturdier wheels under the wings supported the rest of the machine. Two radiators in the shape of an inverted V were mounted behind the crew. The Voisin had two swivel-mounted machine guns. One, facing forward, was on an arch above the pilots head, the other facing to the rear, was on the leading edge of the upper wing. The observer would have to stand to operate either gun.

Andrei knew the construction of the Voisin L, thanks to the teachings of old Petrovich. He was familiar with its armament, too. He had regularly scored a hundred percent at machine gun practice, but of course it was *practice*, firing at the targets without any danger of being shot down. Now it was going to be different. The fate of Kozakov's mechanic, who had fallen out of the plane during a fast turn, was on Andrei's mind.

"Well, brothers, time to go!" Egórov announced, suddenly looking bright. "Check your scarves, boys, make sure that your tender necks are well protected!" he joked. "Does everybody have his personal pistol?"

Andrei, Platonov, and Mironov checked their holsters and nodded. They gobbled the rest of their food and followed Egórov to the waiting airplanes. The mechanics helped them don bulky flight jackets and handed out the peculiar-looking helmets of cork and leather.

Andrei felt his hands turn sweaty in his leather gloves, but he was calm. He was about to make his first flight as a military pilot, his dream becoming reality. He made the sign of the cross, his hand grazing the binoculars that hung over his chest. "I am ready," he said.

"Good!" Egórov slapped him on his back. "Let's go, Andrúshka!"

The pilots climbed into the machines and settled in seats made of wicker, like garden furniture. The observer's seat was even worse; it was a narrow wooden shelf. Someone had placed a cushion on it, thinking of the observer's comfort.

They buckled the protective harnesses and signaled the mechanics to start the engines. The mechanics grabbed the propellers and gave them powerful twirls. The engines caught on at once, having been already warmed-up.

"Clear!" Egórov shouted over the noise of his machine.

"Clear!" Platonov joined.

The crew quickly removed the wooden chocks from under the wheels, setting the airplanes free.

Egórov, followed by Platonov, began to move along the two lines of lanterns set to illuminate the takeoff strip. Hopping along the uneven field and gathering speed, the two Voisins rose up toward the sky.

Myriads of twinkling stars carpeted the black sky, but the eastern horizon beyond the River Styr was beginning to show a narrow crimson line of sunrise.

Andrei squirmed in his narrow seat, trying to find a comfortable position for his long legs. He looked at the dark airfield below. Tents on the outskirts looked like smudgy blots, and the line of parked airplanes was a thick thread on a dark velvet cloak.

The Voisins took a northwest course at an altitude of fifteen hundred feet.

Cold wind rushed at Andrei's face. He hunched his shoulders and lowered his chin into the scarf around his neck. The scarf was getting loose, its fringed ends flapping in the wind, and the thought flashed through his mind that he should have copied Egórov's way of wearing the scarf; it seemed to stay in place. "I really don't know the simplest things about flying!" Andrei thought briefly.

The planes moved languidly side by side. The even hum of the engines made the men feel comfortable in their machines. All four of them scanned the sky. The sun was still hidden, but the horizon was ablaze with color. Andrei removed the goggles and adjusted his binoculars. He swept the skies around him and then looked at the ground below.

It was a sad, devastated land torn apart by merciless bombardments, with zigzagging trenches disfiguring its face. The silvery snake of the river meandered through the valley, reflecting the reddening sky. Andrei centered his binoculars on the eastern horizon. Far in the distance there seemed to be a peaceful land of fields and pastures, spread like a peasant quilt of yellow, green, and brown fragments. There were clusters of homes, too far away for Andrei to see whether they were still intact. Beyond them, melting with the horizon, was a dark line of forest.

The Voisins climbed another five hundred feet. The sky was still empty of enemy aircraft. Andrei began to wonder if there were enemy planes in the area at all. Perhaps this was Kozakov's tactful way of testing his two new young pilots and easing the recuperating pilot, Egórov, back into service.

Egórov and Platonov circled over Russian artillery positions while Andrei and Mironov took photographs. It was soon time to go back. Andrei had hoped that they would discover at least one Austrian scout sneaking over the front line and perhaps exchange a few shots, but of course, the order was *not* to get into a fight. "Oh, well," he thought, "Perhaps tomorrow ..."

"We are done. Ready to go home?" Egórov shouted over the noise of the machine.

"Yes!" he shouted, suddenly exuberantly happy. He was a *pilot* returning home from an accomplished mission!

After three more observation flights over Russian territory, when Andrei's duty was to photograph the terrain around Lutsk, Kozakov announced at a briefing that Andrei would be his observer on a mission over *enemy* territory. "Tomorrow we'll fly in formation following the British method. I will fly the Morane-Saulnier Parasol. Egórov, Platonov, and Rybakov will accompany me as my escorts flying the Nieuport XI."

"The new ones?" Egórov asked eagerly.

Kozakov smiled into his moustache. "No. Not yet. Our new *Bébé* are still being tested. We will use our old aircraft. I understand your impatience Vassily, but we must thoroughly test our new planes before we use them. You know that. Be patient!"

Kozakov shuffled some papers on his desk. "For the benefit of our new pilots, I want to reiterate the British rules of formation flying that we have adapted. We follow the 'face of the clock' rule. I, as leader, am at twelve o'clock. The escorts are at three and nine o'clock, and the most important escort machine is at six o'clock to protect our tails. We will be staggered as well. I will be at the lowest altitude. The two quarter fighters will be five hundred feet higher and the tail fighter at least a thousand feet higher. This type of formation has proven to be the most winning. So stay within the combination, unless we are involved in a fight. Then, of course, you know what to do." Kozakov smiled and unrolled a new big map.

Orderlies pinned the map to the wall.

"Study the map," he said to the pilots. "It is the most current of the front line."

Andrei could think only of the Morane-Saulnier, which he would fly in with Kozakov. Andrei had never flown in the Morane-Saulnier, but he knew that it was a monoplane with a wing mounted over the fuselage. A large cutout in the wing provided good visibility for spotting enemy aircraft. It had two machine guns: the forward one was mounted on top of the wing, in front of the pilot. The observer's gun was on the fuselage deck. Both guns were synchronized with the propeller's arc. The most unusual part of the Morane-Saulnier was a web of supporting wires over its upper wing that looked like the under structure of an umbrella. Thus, its name, "Parasol."

It was to be a very important mission. Kozakov informed the pilots that Stavka, the general headquarters under the command of the Tsar himself, had sent specific orders for new, detailed photographs of the Austro-Hungarian trench topography.

"We know that the Austrians have moved their heavy artillery closer to Lutsk. It could mean that they are preparing the ground for a break-through," Kozakov said. "It could also mean that the next weeks will be very busy for us. We will participate in night bombing raids against the artillery positions, in addition to our usual duties of reconnaissance and patrol. So, be ready, everybody!"

Andrei felt good: he was to fly with Kozakov! He was well aware of the inherent risks. In addition to the obvious danger of an aerial fight, they would be flying through a barrage of anti-aircraft batteries, which the British called "Archies." Should they fly low over the enemy trenches for more clear photography, they could become the targets of the smaller arms of the infantry. Andrei willed himself *not* to think about the odds.

They took off at dawn. Kozakov circled the field, gathering speed. His plane had two bright red stripes on each side of the fuselage: during the fury of a dogfight, his pilots could follow his lead with more ease. Of course, the stripes also identified him as a leader to his enemies, making him the most desired target.

Andrei looked up and down, right and left, testing the comforts of his silk scarf that he had wound around his neck according to Egórov's directions. The scarf felt comfortable, tight to protect his neck from chafing but loose enough to allow free movement of his head. Waiting for Kozakov to give him a signal to start taking photographs, Andrei observed the terrain. They were flying over the Russian fortifications, a mass of zigzagging long holes that looked like the passages of ants in a disturbed anthill. The trenches seemed to be never-ending and from the air they looked empty, the soldiers' gray uniforms dissolving in the labyrinths of gray earth and barbwire.

In a short time the four airplanes crossed the front line and began their gradual descent over enemy territory. Kozakov signaled to Andrei. Below them were the Austrian trenches.

Andrei noticed a startling difference between the Russian and Austrian fortifications: the latter were just as numerous as the former, but they seemed to be reinforced by wood and constructed with precision. "A good example of Germanic exactitude," Andrei thought sarcastically. "Everything must be neat and in good order, even the holes where they die."

Kozakov and his escorts stayed on course. So far, so good, they all thought. No one wanted to get involved in a fight over enemy lines. Perhaps if they were lucky, they could slip back to Russian territory without being noticed.

Suddenly the sky became filled with small black puffs of exploding shrapnel from an anti-aircraft battery. They were discovered, after all. The Archies' barrage would shortly bring on German fighters.

Kozakov turned toward Andrei. "How many photographs?" he shouted.

"Ten," Andrei spread his fingers. Kozakov nodded, made a sharp turn to the left and pointed the nose of his machine upward to begin the steep ascent. The escorts followed.

Andrei scanned the sky through binoculars, his perception made keener through the knowledge of an imminent menace. High above, against a large cumulous cloud, he discerned three dark dots. .

Kozakov also noticed the enemy. He rolled his wings briefly, signaling his change of course to the escorts, and made a sharp southeastern turn. The point of order was to reach home territory without getting into a fight.

The enemy airplanes changed their course as well, obviously in pursuit. Andrei placed his hands on the machine gun controls, ready and calm. He thought of nothing.

The Germans were gaining on Kozakov's group. Andrei thought that they were Pfalz machines, which Russian Nieuports could outrun, but the Morane-Saulnier was a much slower craft. "There will be a fight," he thought, his throat tight.

Kozakov also realized that he could not outrun the Pfalz. He decided to accept the inevitable and began another steep climb. His three escort planes followed, ready for the fight.

Andrei glanced at the trenches below. In the full light of morning he could see that they had a confusing pattern, not the neat geometrical design of Austrian fortifications. His group was back over Russian territory. He was sure that Kozakov had noticed it also, for his commander had leveled his climb and maneuvered his plane into a position with the sun behind him.

Andrei understood his intentions: Kozakov did not want to risk getting into a fight, yet he was ready to do so should the enemy attack.

The Austrians decided to attack. They went after Kozakov.

Egórov, Platonov, and Rybakov intercepted the Austrians. Boldly they dived under the rising planes, destroying their formation, positioning themselves behind their enemies, giving them short bursts from their machine guns, then quickly rising again to dive once more in a repeat maneuver. The Austrians, in defensive mode now, tried to rise ever higher, to swoop down on the Russians coming out of their maneuvers.

Andrei could see the sparks of fire as both adversaries fired at one another. Kozakov made a sharp turn and the Morane-Saulnier was suddenly behind the tail of one of the Pfalzen. Without hesitation Andrei pressed the button of his machine gun. A short blast of tracer bullets hit the fuselage of the Austrian. Andrei quickly readjusted his aim and pressed the trigger again. A row of bullet holes appeared on the fuselage.

Kozakov was also firing. The Pfalz began to lose height. Andrei could see the enemy pilot slumped in his seat, obviously wounded but still trying to control his damaged machine. Kozakov moved his plane near to the Austrian's and pointed to the ground, inviting the wounded pilot to land.

The Austrian nodded and raised his hands in surrender. He went into a vertical spiral dive, his plane emitting dark smoke. The other two Pfalzen gave up the fight, turning west toward their territory.

Kozakov dived and circled almost at tree level, watching the enemy plane crash-land. Andrei saw a group of soldiers scurrying at the site, pulling the pilot out of the plane that had landed on its nose, its propeller broken. A motorcycle with a red cross on its side carriage sped toward the crash site. He hoped that the pilot was still alive.

Kozakov turned toward him, raising his gloved thumb in a salute. "Congratulations!" he yelled, a smile crinkling the skin on his sharp cheekbones. "Well done, Rezánov!"

Kozakov pitched his plane upwards and resumed his course toward their base, the Nieuports taking their places in formation.

14

The downing of the Pfalz was credited to Kozakov and Rezánov. The infantry unit that had witnessed the dogfight confirmed their victory. The wounded Austrian pilot was given medical help and sent to a hospital in Lutsk.

Still glowing in the illumination of his sudden celebrity, Andrei felt the need to share it with Larissa.

He had thought very little of her in the past six weeks. She was still a stranger to him after only four days of marriage filled with sexual intoxication. His life was brimming with the excitement of his masculine camaraderie and the heady stimulus of flying. He had easily fitted into the brotherhood of pilots, who all shared the same infatuation with flying.

He did not think of himself as a husband. He loved Larissa, of course, and he recalled with pleasure their four days at the Gátchina Inn, but he felt no special obligation toward her as his wife. Subconsciously he relegated her to 'the family,' the people whom he loved dearly but did not need to be with all the time.

He realized that he really did not know Larissa. What was there to know? He felt proud when his friends admired Larissa's photograph that stood on his night table, but he had nothing to tell them about her, except that she was beautiful and a wonderful pianist. Wasn't that enough? But then, his complacent mind would suddenly be shaken by an image of her running like a mad Fury, her hair undone, her face distorted, running, running after his train. It occurred to him that perhaps he did not deserve her. There was more to her, something that he had never seen.

Perhaps he was still too young to be married. The responsibilities of an *adult man* were still ahead of him even though he was extremely capable of performing his duties as an officer and a fighter pilot.

The need to tell his family about his first victory was overwhelming. He tore a page from his flight log notebook and began to write.

"My dear darling wife, the love of my life! I miss you so!" he wrote. *"I could not write to you any sooner because our group was in constant action. Yesterday, my commanding officer Captain Kozakov and I had a great victory: we forced an Austrian pilot to crash land on our territory!"* He proceeded to describe the dogfight in dramatic detail, not thinking of how it could affect Larissa. He concluded with a request that she should share the letter with the other members of the family. He promised to write individual letters to all of them as soon as the postal authorities removed the restrictions on correspondence from the front. He exaggerated the role of the restrictions, but it served him well as an excuse for not having written before.

Larissa was disappointed by his letter. There was no warmth in it, nothing about his feelings, except a short sentence about "missing" her, a cliché. He did not ask about her life nor did he inquire about his parents or her mother. She could understand his need for sharing his excitement with her, but she made an effort to dismiss her disappointment, finding excuses for the flippancy of his letter. "He must be exhausted by the constant tension of flying," she thought. "He probably cannot sleep with all those guns blasting away, with the airplanes making noise, with all this flying and with the Germans trying to shoot him down ..."

Larissa cried as she read the letter again trying to unlock some hidden sweetness in it, but finding nothing but his pride at downing an airplane. She thanked God that he was spared, but she was unable to rejoice in his victory.

The general had a different reaction to the letter. He slapped himself on his knee, laughed heartily, and exclaimed, "That's my boy! I *knew* that he would prove himself up there! He is of the *Rezánov* stock! *All* the Rezánovs were heroes! In *all* Russian wars! I bet anyone ten gold rubles that Andrei will get the Cross of St. George! And to think, this was his *first* dogfight! That's my boy!"

The mothers' reaction was predictable. They embraced each other, crying and laughing like young girls. They were so proud! Then they cried again, consoling one another, and finally, they complained: Andrei was telling nothing about his everyday life. Where did he live, what did he eat, had he made any friends? They treated his letter as if from a young boy on his first vacation away from home.

The general, tired of their tears and chatter, called for champagne. He distributed silver rubles among the servants and ordered the chief butler to give them a big bottle of vodka, the sale of which was prohibited during the war.

"Andrei mentioned nothing about my letters," Larissa thought. "Did he receive any of them? Probably not." Everybody was complaining about the postal service between the front lines and the rear of the country. "My letters probably sit in some provincial post office. Or, maybe even in some *German* post office, with all these retreats at the front. One of these days Andrúsha will receive a whole lot of my letters, all at once!" she thought, trying to perk herself up.

She sat at the large desk in her father's study, staring at the photograph of herself and Andrei taken at the time of their engagement. It was barely two years ago, she thought, but how much had happened: she had lost her father, then her brother Peter. A bit of happiness came her way with her marriage to Andrei, only to be snatched away by Andrei's leaving for the front.

She picked up a pen and began to write.

> *My dear Andrúsha,*
>
> *First of all, let me congratulate you upon your great victory. Your father, our mothers and I celebrated it with all of your father's aides-de-camp, at a big dinner at your house. My mother and I are still staying with your parents, for Mother hates our house now, without Father and Peter in it. But that's another story.*
>
> *We drank champagne in your honor and later, I played the piano, something from Tchaikovsky.*
>
> *Speaking of playing the piano: I played at the Benefit for Wounded Heroes, the big concert sponsored by the Empress. It was held at the Great Hall of the Noblemen Assembly. The Grand Duchesses were there, the three older girls sitting in the Tsar's Loge, but the Empress was absent, and of course, His Majesty was at Stavka. The Grand Duchesses Maria, Tatiana and Olga, all very pretty, were dressed in nurses' uniforms but without the head coverings, as were many ladies in the audience. All of Petrograd seems to be wearing some kind of a uniform these days.*
>
> *Your family and my mother were there, of course. Our mothers wore their Red Cross uniforms. All three of us volunteer twice a week to roll*

bandages at the Empress Hospital. Sometimes I am allowed into the officers' ward to read to someone or to write a letter for someone. But I am not allowed any real nursing duties: the young women of our class are protected from seeing naked men. Even though I am a married woman, they treat me as if I were a girl.

Your father donated ten thousand rubles for medical services, specifically designated for the wounded pilots of the Imperial Russian Air Service. I think it was the highest donation at the benefit, and he received an ovation. My mother donated five thousand in memory of Peter, to be used for wounded cavalrymen, and altogether, I think the benefit raised over two hundred thousand rubles!

There is very little in my life without you. Your father took me to the Manège for a little bit of horseback riding. I did not know that he was such a good dressage rider! He told me that you too were trained in dressage when you were a boy. Well, what else? Oh, yes, our mothers and I went with Olga Nekrasova to a new exhibit of modern art at the Artists Corner. Everyone talks about it and we wanted to see what the fuss is all about. We saw some strange, ugly paintings. Portraits of people with their eyes inside their ears or noses on their foreheads! And such garish colors! It was awful! The nudes, so distorted that one could not guess what was an arm or a leg, a breast or a buttock. Awful! Awful!

Our mothers are always together now, like twin sisters. They left the exhibit in disgust after looking at only one painting, but Olga and I stayed, fascinated by the ugliness, wondering what was on the painter's mind when he produced such nightmarish paintings? Did he think that anyone would buy such rubbish? Oh, well. Chacun à son goût!

Anyway my darling husband, I miss you terribly, I pray day and night for your safety. This stupid war seems to go on and on without end. I sympathize with the crowds that march down the street demanding the end of the war. But I must not express my opinion about the war: I may be accused of being unpatriotic. Oh, well. There is a lot going on that we are advised not to talk about, like this monk Rasputin. People gossip about him: apparently he has some mysterious power over the Empress.

Well, that is about all I can report about my life. Please, darling, write to me about yourself, write about how you feel, write about your new friends, about everything, everything!

With all my prayers, my sweetheart, be safe,

Your loving wife, Larissa.

P.S. I am not pregnant.

She folded the letter and included several photographs taken at their wedding. She decided to send the packet through General Rezánov's military channels, rather than regular mail.

Andrei received Lara's packet within a week. It was waiting for him as he and Egórov arrived in the briefing room after an uneventful reconnaissance patrol. Andrei still performed the duties of observer, growing steadily impatient with his assignments. He envied the pilots who reported exciting encounters with the enemy, describing fights or their escapes, while he had to report only locations and the number of photographs he had taken. It was too dull.

Egórov teased him about his impatience. "You are already a *hero*, Andrúshka, after your first dogfight! Seriously, don't be a fool. If you are seeking danger, you already have it! Each time you get into an airplane, you are in danger!"

"That is the point! I can be killed doing *nothing!*" Andrei complained.

"Stop itching about getting into a fight! Perhaps tomorrow or the day after, Kozakov will send you up there as a fighter. Right now, he is apparently impressed with the quality of your photographs, and he wants you to continue supplying him with superior reconnaissance."

Andrei was not convinced. "If I continue to fly as an observer, I'll forget all that I have learned about aggressive flying."

"Nonsense!" Egórov was losing his patience. "Get your mail and let's wash up and then go to dinner. I am starved."

Andrei read Larissa's letter while Egórov was shaving in the bathroom.

"Anything interesting?" Egórov shouted.

"She writes that there are citizen demonstrations demanding the end of war ... that she played the piano at the Empress' benefit concert ... some rumors about Rasputin ..."

"Did you say, Rasputin?"

"Yes.

"I met him ... when I was at the hospital." Egórov came into the room, wiping his face with a towel. "What did she say about him?"

"Nothing much, except she was warned not to discuss him."

Egórov chuckled. "Of course! We cannot *discuss* His Holiness! We must worship him. I met him when he visited the officers' ward with the Empress and her entourage. He blessed us and the Empress looked at him adoringly, as if he were God Almighty. He talked to us, urging us to fight to death for our Fatherland. He looked and talked like an illiterate peasant, which of course he is. He looked unkempt, dressed in some dirty peasant shirt. He had bright penetrating eyes, I should say *hypnotic* eyes. When he stared at you, he made you feel … well, uncomfortable. It was funny to see *the Russian Empress* looking at that dirty *mouzhik* with such devotion and humility. Of course, funny though it was, no one laughed."

"I understand that Grigory Rasputin is becoming a real power in Petrograd," Platonov said from his bed where he was reading his mail. "My father is an official at the Ministry of Foreign Affairs. He writes that while the Emperor is at Stavka, the Empress is apparently our regent. They say that she consults Rasputin about *every* detail, including the appointment of cabinet ministers, even the changes of generals at the front! Rasputin advises the Empress, and she, in turn, tells the Emperor what should be done. And the Emperor does it. Voilà! That's how our Russia is being governed now!"

"Watch out, Sashka, don't talk that way," Egórov said. "You may be accused of being subversive."

"Incredible!" Andrei raised his voice. "Who is this Rasputin, anyway?"

"Nobody, and that is the point!" Platonov declared. "He is an illiterate Siberian *mouzhik* who is supposed to be a holy man. They say he is able to cast a spell that protects our heir to the throne from some mysterious bleeding disease. My father has heard that the Empress fired the doctors upon his advice and listens only to Rasputin."

"Whether it's true or not, let's not talk about it. It's not safe," Egórov said.

Andrei changed the subject. "My wife sent me our wedding pictures. Do you want to take a look?"

"Of course!"

Andrei spread the photographs on the table.

15

Kozakov announced that the new airplanes were ready to be flown. The pilots were to fly them one by one in short flights over the base. They were to check the accuracy of the new machine guns at the firing range away from the field, using cut-up plywood silhouettes. The general atmosphere around the airfield suddenly became almost carefree, as if indeed the pilots were still cadets having great fun flying, with no disturbing thoughts about death.

Egórov and Andrei were to test a two-seater Spad A.2, a new French-designed biplane. It was a strange-looking machine: the observer's pulpit was way out in front of the craft with the propeller and the engine *behind* him. The pilot's seat, on the other hand was *facing* the engine, which was in the middle of the plane. The aircraft looked more like a 'contraption' than an airplane. The French did not like the Spad. They unloaded the unwanted machines on the Russians, who were forever in need of aircraft.

Egórov complained. "This design is crazy! The engine and the propeller are right in the middle of the craft, as if slicing it in two parts!"

"Maybe it should be called the *slicer,*" Andrei joked.

Egórov grinned.

Despite Egórov's dislike of the Spad, Andrei found the new machine more accommodating for the observer. The observer-gunner's view was unobstructed and the machine gun placed in a position so that the gunner could easily point it in all directions. The same applied to the photo camera. No part of the airplane interfered with a clear view of the sky or terrain.

"Well, brother, hop in and let's try our new *'slicer,'*" Egórov said.

They flew over the field several times, Egórov trying sharp turns and pitches, almost-vertical rises and steep diving and gliding. The machine responded faultlessly, but Egórov complained that it was awkward to fly.

Andrei checked the Madsen machine gun, which was on a flexible mount. It moved easily. The camera was well-placed, giving the observer more work space, and to Andrei's delight, a little more leg room.

"Well, what do you think?" he asked Egórov. "Do you still dislike the slicer?"

"Not bad. Of course, as the English say, *'the proof of a pudding is in the eating.'* We'll see how it performs in a dogfight."

They did not have to wait long. At dawn, they were up in the air on their way to Lutsk, with Kozakov flying the Nieuport XI, the *Bébé,* as their escort.

It should have been an easy mission flying over Russian territory toward Lutsk, but almost as soon as they had left the periphery of the airfield, Andrei spotted an enemy scout on its way toward their base. He motioned to Egórov and pointed up to three o'clock.

Egórov raised his arm and signaled Kozakov in the direction of the enemy. Kozakov at once changed his course, rising steeply, Egórov following.

The German pilot of the Albatros continued on his course.

Andrei's pulse was racing. He watched Kozakov reach the proper height against the sun, then bank sharply in the direction of the Albatros and dive under, coming out behind his tail. Andrei saw several sparks of tracer bullets as Kozakov fired at close range at the unsuspecting pilot. Egórov repeated Kozakov's maneuver, and he and Andrei simultaneously fired their new machine guns at the unfortunate Albatros. Andrei clearly saw their bullets tearing a row of holes in the fuselage and the wings of the German machine.

The pilot slumped, wounded or dead. Egórov maneuvered the Spad for a repeat attack, but the fight was over. Kozakov wagged his wings, pointing to the Albatros that was falling down in a screw pattern, trailing thick black smoke.

"He never knew what hit him," Andrei thought. "It all happened so quickly. Did I participate? I must have. I fired my gun … I saw the holes made by my bullets …" He turned toward Egórov, who was beaming.

"Did we do it?" he shouted. Egórov raised his thumb.

Kozakov wagged his wings and pointed north. They were to continue with their mission as if nothing had happened. They had not suffered even one bullet hole.

Everyone already knew, when they returned to their airfield some two hours later, the news about their victory. The infantry units below had seen the falling aircraft and confirmed the kill.

"You were born under a lucky star, Andrúshka!" Egórov yelled even before they climbed out of the Spad. "Two victories in less than a month!" He grabbed Andrei in a bear hug and kissed him on both cheeks. "It took me three months before I got my first kill!"

"I don't even know what I did," Andrei stammered.

"You did what you were supposed to do. You fired at the son-of-a-bitch and so did I, and so did Kozakov, and we three sent him down!"

"Good work, Rezánov!" Kozakov shook his hand.

"Thank you, Captain. I was just lucky!"

"Don't be so modest," Kozakov smiled, his strange bony face suddenly looking almost handsome. "Tonight we'll celebrate our victories with a splendid dinner. We have been so busy fighting these last few weeks that we've had no time for fun. I think we deserve a special dinner, don't you? Besides, our infantry friends have sent us a gift. Fortunately, there is a storm coming tonight so no one needs to go on patrol."

"What kind of a gift?" Egórov asked.

"It is a surprise. You'll see it tonight," Kozakov said slyly.

Later that day, a huge storm enveloped the airfield. The soldiers secured the aircraft with additional ties and tucked canvas tarpaulins over the cockpits. It was raining hard as the pilots gathered in the officers' mess tent, all freshly shaven and in dress uniforms, some wearing decorations.

"There is Lieutenant Bashinsky. Hello there!" Egórov greeted a round-faced officer with three medals: two on his chest and one over his neck. "He is a great pilot," he said to Andrei in a low voice. "He shot down an enemy fighter with his hand gun!"

"What do you mean?"

"His machine gun jammed, so he shot the pilot with his Mauser. Bashinsky got his St. Anne for it!"

Andrei looked at the Order of St. Anne dangling on its scarlet ribbon under the pilot's chin.

"Incredible! I don't think that I could've done anything like that!"

"Oh, yes, you could. I saw you firing the machine gun without hesitation. Your instincts are immediate, I saw it."

"Well, thanks, but I don't believe that I could have used my *personal* hand gun to kill a pilot."

"You would do what must be done. We are killers. Don't you know that? We were raised to be killers, like our fathers, Andrúshka! All soldiers are killers!"

"All right, gentlemen, please take your seats," Kozakov called above the noise of conversations and laughter. Chairs scraped on the plywood covering the earthen floor as the young men settled around two long tables. Fine china, crystal, and silver settings from the cupboards of the evacuated Polish nobleman decorated the snowy tablecloths. Andrei noted the incongruities: the formal tables under the sagging, leaking canvas roof, the pilots' dress uniforms and colorful decorations and the earthen floor beginning to turn to mud.

The soldiers of the kitchen platoon, wearing white aprons over their drab uniforms, brought in trays of small glasses filled with *nastoika,* vodka flavored with ash berries.

"I must warn you, gentlemen, there will be no smashing of glasses after the toasts," Kozakov said. "We are still on alert, and our consumption of spirits is going to be limited. So, let me offer the first toast to His Imperial Majesty, the Emperor!"

"To the Emperor!" yelled the pilots jumping to their feet, throwing back their heads and emptying their vodka serving in a single gulp.

Andrei recalled the similar toast and the shower of shattered glass at the celebration of his solo flight in Gátchina. "That was only a few months ago, yet it seems like something I only read about!" he thought.

The soldiers from the kitchen staff wheeled in a cart covered with fresh fir branches, atop which rested a wooden platter bearing a huge roasted pig. The pig, juicy fat dribbling onto the platter, lay among piles of peeled roasted potatoes and chestnuts, little mounds of pickled cucumbers and fried mushrooms. A large red apple protruded from its mouth. The enticing aroma of roasted meat spread throughout the tent, and the pilots laughed and applauded.

"Gentlemen!" Kozakov tapped on his glass. "This pig is a gift from our brother officers of the infantry, who came upon it by chance they say, and we won't ask. They thank us for our patrols over their trenches, which they say make them feel safer. They have also been enjoying watching our dogfights. Apparently they find them entertaining." Kozakov grinned, adding, "I hope that they don't bet *against* us!"

The head cook began to carve the pig with a knife that looked more like a saber. Soldiers passed plates of meat and vegetables to the pilots, as more soldiers entered the tent pushing a cart loaded with a dozen bottles of French champagne. The pilots applauded enthusiastically. French wine!

Kozakov motioned the soldiers to uncork the wine. With the corks popping up like small arms fire, the soldiers went around the tables, pouring.

"We have had heavy losses in our squadrons during this last offensive," Kozakov said in a serious tone, a glass of champagne in his hand. "Not one of us escaped being wounded! Many of our friends paid the ultimate price for our victories: they sacrificed their lives. We have received replacements from several flight schools and, I must say, we have been lucky. But there will be hard days ahead. As you have probably noticed, there is increased activity around the front. The enemy is moving its armies. Everything points to the Germans preparing for a new offensive. For us it means more reconnaissance behind enemy lines, more dogfights, and more night bombing of their forward positions. It means that we are required to stay on high alert with no days off for rest. Winter is coming. As we Russians know, in all our wars winter has been our ally. The French, the Austrians, the Turks, they all succumbed to our winters, and they will succumb again! We'll put our airplanes on skis and continue our strafing and bombing, while they'll be shivering in their trenches! And come spring—we'll be on the offensive again and, we hope, the war will be over!" The pilots applauded wildly and yelled "Hurrah!"

Kozakov took a sip of wine and continued, "I have received some information that our friend and fellow pilot Captain Tkachev has been appointed a temporary inspector of aviation for the southwest front. We should expect him to visit us shortly. I think he will find our group performing above all others. He may present some awards. Just look how many aces we have! And how many of you are about to become aces!" he smiled and his cheekbones protruded even more sharply. "Now, enjoy your dinner and one more glass of wine. Remember: *'Those who hoot with the owls by night do not fly with the eagles by day.'*

Kozakov waited until all glasses were filled and then offered a final toast: "To our brave squadrons! To us and to our lost friends," he said with obvious emotion. "To the pilots!"

"To the pilots!" the young men yelled ebulliently, emptying their glasses.

Egórov sipped and savored his wine, thinking that someone ought to teach pilots *not* to gulp champagne as if it were vodka.

"I wonder how Kozakov was able to get French champagne at the front," Andrei said.

Egórov had a sly expression on his face. "Well, there are always ways," he said evasively.

Andrei slapped himself on his forehead. "*You* got it! But *where* did you get it? You didn't carry it all the way from Petrograd."

"Well, with a bit of curiosity and the inborn tendency for larceny, I discovered that our Polish mansion has a fine wine cellar. The owner of our mansion had no time to evacuate his wine cellar. So, I decided to take care of his collection of fine wines and other spirits. Now, if *we* start to retreat, we'll have the same problem: what to do with the wine cellar? Obviously, we don't want to leave it to our enemies. So, I'll have to figure out how we can save the poor, dear Veuve Clicquot and Dom Pèrignon and what else might be in that magic cellar. Any ideas?"

"Oh, you rascal! I am sure you'll think of something!"

"Yes, I guess I'll have to think of something."

On the day of Aviation Inspector Tkachev's visit, the weather was perfect. Service crews washed the aircraft and polished the propellers. The pilots, wearing their dress uniforms, lined up in two formations along the flight line. The mechanics and soldiers of the service crew, in clean and ironed shirts, were stationed next to the service and repair shops.

Two long tables laden with champagne bottles and wine glasses stood on the grass. Sun rays winked from the cut crystal, creating a joyful palette of colorful jewels. Even Kozakov's pet dog, Barboss, a large boxer, the mascot of the Air Group, was given a bath and a new collar with the Group's insignia.

A photographer and reporters from Petrograd and Moscow were at the base, having arrived from Lutsk by automobile. While waiting for the arrival of the Inspector, they were ensconced in the officers mess tent. Kozakov promised that, after the ceremony, they would be free to have short interviews with some of the pilots, but no photographs showing the airfield would be allowed for security reasons.

To make the visit of the Inspector festive, Kozakov bribed an infantry unit to lend him a marching brass band. Egórov provided the bribe: ten bottles of English brandy for the officers and fifty rubles, donated by Andrei, to be divided among the musicians.

The ten bandsmen arrived by lorry early in the morning. They were placed on the grass near the runway to greet the Aviation Inspector with music the moment he touched down.

At promptly noon, Captain Vyatcheslav Tkachev, accompanied by his aide-de-camp, arrived piloting his favorite two-seater, the Morane-Saulnier Parasol.

The band met him with a thunderous rendition of Tchaikovsky's Overture *Marche Slav* rewritten into a form suitable for marching troops. As Tkachev taxied his plane to a stop and the soldiers placed wooden chocks under its wheels, the marching tempo of the Overture changed to a majestic melody of *"God Save the Tsar."*

Protocol required all personnel to stop and freeze in a salute. Tkachev and his aide-de-camp, still in the Morane-Saulnier, raised their hands at a proper angle to their heads. Kozakov and the pilots, the mechanics and the soldiers of the serving crews did the same, all looking like rows of military mannequins.

Tkachev was visibly embarrassed. *"God Save the Tsar"* was a national anthem; he was certainly not entitled to have it played in *his* honor. Kozakov too, was embarrassed. He did not want to appear to be groveling before the new authority. The pilots, standing stiffly at attention, hid their smirks, enjoying the awkward moment while the band continued to play, finishing the anthem with a vigorous drum roll.

Andrei observed Tkachev. He knew that the new Inspector was a famous pilot, much respected by the High Command and the regular pilots. He was originally an *Esaul,* a Cossack Captain of cavalry, and an author of military manuals on aerial engagements. Rumor had it that he was a personal friend of Grand Duke Nikolaí Nikolayevich, the former Supreme Commander of Russian Forces, who respected Tkachev's opinions and advice.

Tkachev was of medium height and appeared to be in his early forties. As he took off his goggles and changed the helmet for a military forage cap, Andrei noticed that his dark hair was cut very short, standing like a bristle over his round head. His thick, dark moustache was twisted into stiff points. He was wearing cavalry boots with spurs and a handsome brown leather coat that snuggly fitted his well-proportioned body.

He jumped down to the ground like an adolescent and saluted the waiting Kozakov. Kozakov returned the salute, and then both men embraced. They were old friends, glad to see one another.

Tkachev turned to his aide-de-camp. "Let me have the names. You hold on to the boxes." The young man proffered him a small leather notebook from the top of three velvet boxes.

"My visit with you, gentlemen, will be very short today. I must be back at HQ within two hours," Tkachev began, facing the pilots. "At ease. I would like to start by acknowledging the brave pilots of the First Combat Air Group. Knowing that many of you must leave on patrol soon, your commander and I have decided to shorten our meeting by avoiding the lengthy reading of individual battle histories for which pilots are going to be honored. Descriptions of their victories are included on the awards certificates. We also must forgo the traditional luncheon, but we will at least toast our heroes. That I promise," he smiled. "If Captain Kozakov doesn't object, we'll start without further ado."

"Go ahead, Captain," Kozakov said.

Photographer and reporters took their places, ready to record the occasion.

"We have three pilots this month who have confirmed victories, and five pilots whose victories unfortunately cannot be confirmed. We congratulate all of you. As a pilot myself, I know very well how frustrating it is to win a fight and yet to remain unconfirmed. Actually, I have more *unconfirmed* victories than confirmed ones, three to four," he chuckled. "So we all are in the same boat, so to speak." The pilots laughed.

"May I have the box?" Tkachev resumed. The aide-the-camp proffered him the first velvet box. "Among those three pilots that I have mentioned, there is one very young man, a neophyte, who had two *confirmed* victories in less than a month! And this is in his very first month of service!"

Andrei felt hot blood rush to his face.

"Flying as an observer, this young man not only produced superb photographs for the High Command, but he has proven himself to be an excellent sniper. Lieutenant Andrei Rezánov, please step forward!"

Andrei made three steps forward, stretched into a stiff posture, and saluted.

"Are you related to General Vladímir Rezánov of the Preobrazensky Regiment?"

"Yes, sir. He is my father."

"Well! What do you know! I served under him when I was a cornet. Is he retired?"

"No, sir. But he is now in the Strategic Cavalry Service."

"And he let you become a pilot?" Turning to Kozakov, he said with a smile, "General Rezánov always believed that the cavalry was the one and only honorable service."

"He still does," Andrei said with a smile of his own.

"Well, he will be proud of you, now. In the name of His Imperial Majesty, you, Andrei Rezánov, are awarded the Order of St. George, Fourth Degree. Wear it with pride. Congratulations!" He took out of the box a white enameled cross on black and orange ribbon and pinned it to Andrei's tunic.

Andrei saluted crisply and replied, "I serve my Emperor and my Fatherland," the soldiers' required reply to praise. He stepped back into the ranks. The drummer of the band made a show with the drumsticks as he saluted Andrei in his noisy way.

"Vassily Egórov," Tkachev called. Egórov stepped forward.

"I understand that you, Lieutenant Egórov, were seriously wounded during the last offensive. Are you well, now? You must be, since you have had another confirmed victory!"

"Thank you, Captain. Yes, I am quite well again!"

"Good. In the name of His Imperial Majesty, you, Lieutenant Vassily Egórov are awarded the Order of St. George, Third Degree. Wear it with pride. Congratulations!" Tkachev opened the second box.

Egórov saluted and replied, "I serve my Emperor and my Fatherland." Tkachev pinned the new St. George Cross next to Egórov's first one. The drummer again exploded with virtuosity.

"The last but not least on our list is the Commanding Officer of the First Combat Air Group, Captain Alexander Kozakov. How many confirmed kills do *you* have, Captain? Seven? Eight?"

"Nine."

"How many unconfirmed?"

"Six or seven … I try not to think of it." Kozakov's moustache spread over a hidden smile.

"In the name of His Imperial Majesty, you, Captain Alexander Kozakov are awarded the Order of St. Anne, with swords, Second Degree. Wear it with honor. Congratulations!" From the third box, Tkachev took out and carefully unfolded a scarlet silk ribbon of the Cross of St. Anne and slipped it over Kozakov's neck.

"Thank you, sir." Kozakov repeated the procedure of reply and saluting, while the drummer used this last chance to exhibit his skills.

The reporters scribbled in their notebooks. The photographer placed his tripod in front of the regimental banner and posed Tkachev under it, with the decorated pilots around him, all standing stiff with their left hands resting on the hilts of their ceremonial daggers, with the dog sitting at Kozakov's feet. The photographer dived under the curtains of his cumbersome camera and from underneath yelled to his helper to explode the little puffs of illumination from a T-shaped pole.

The official part of the Inspector's visit was over. Tkachev did not mention the names of the pilots with unconfirmed kills. "It is better that way. No use in rubbing it in," many thought.

Kozakov motioned the Inspector and his aide to join the pilots for a glass of champagne.

"To the pilots!" Tkachev exclaimed raising his glass high and draining it in two swallows.

"To the pilots!" repeated the pilots.

"Well, I must be on my way," he said. "Congratulations to all of you. You gentlemen, all of you, are the pride and joy of our Fatherland. God save you all! *Au revoir!*" He embraced Kozakov and climbed into the Morane-Saulnier, his aide-de-camp following. The band exploded with the sounds of *"God Save the Tsar"* again as Tkachev waved to the pilots and sped along the runway.

16

Larissa and the family learned about Andrei's decoration before the arrival of his letters: a long story with the photographs of the award presentation was on every newsstand. Larissa and the family eagerly read and re-read the article. They bought a stack of newspapers and cut out the article to send the clippings to all their friends. The mothers complained that the photograph was too small and one could not *really* see Andrei's face. The general promised to have the photograph enlarged so they could frame it and place it on the wall. The whole Rezánov household celebrated. The stablemen nailed the clipping to a wall in the tack room, the kitchen staff pasted it on the kitchen window, and the maids carried it in their pockets. Andrei's childhood nurse stuck it to her icon of the Savior.

Larissa kept the clipping under her pillow. She was proud of Andrei, but she was disturbed by the circumstances. Andrei was involved in dogfights, where his victories could just as well have been defeats. Larissa deeply suffered her separation from Andrei. Even though she was raised in the tradition of a military family, where all males had to serve under the Tsar's banner, she took it badly. She was furious: frustrated that nothing could be done to change the situation, angry that everyone took it for granted that the men of their class had to fight in all the wars. It was their duty. They called it their *sacred* duty.

"I see nothing *sacred* in going to war," she thought angrily. "Especially this stupid war. Why should we care that some Austrian Archduke was assassinated? Why should Russians die because of it? Why do *I* have to spend my youth without my husband? Why did I have to lose my brother in some stupid cavalry attack that was called *heroic?* What's so heroic in dying young?"

She tried to talk about it with her mother, thinking that she would be sympathetic after losing her son, but Maria Nikoláyevna replied that it was God's will. "It's our national duty to serve the Tsar."

"Damn the Tsar! The Tsar!" Larissa thought angrily. "That wet rag who is under the foot of his wife who is bewitched by that *mouzhik* Rasputin! People say that he is her lover. I don't believe it, of course, but simple people, they *do* believe it …" Larissa had heard the rumor from her maid, Natasha. She warned Natasha not to repeat the gossip. It was too dangerous. The rumor was that Rasputin had spies everywhere, and that he himself was a German spy.

Larissa did not realize that before long she would meet the monster.

In early October, it felt that the sunshine had forever abandoned Petrograd. Wide boulevards stood naked, the trees having lost their colorful garments in September. It was an annual occurrence. People suffered from gloom that would last for several weeks, until the first snows. Their spirits would perk-up by the end of November when the gray waters of the Nevá froze and the long winter began its rule.

Small children with sleds would suddenly appear on the ice, watched over by *bábushkas*, and the older children would build snow forts and stage fierce snowball battles. Horse-driven troikas would race along the ice and platoons of soldiers practice cross-country skiing. People would cross the river by foot, plowing their way through hip-high drifts rather than going over the bridges—it was simply more fun. People were invigorated by frosty air and sparkling snow. Russians knew how to enjoy their winters.

In early October, Larissa received a letter with Prince Felix Youssoupov's crest on the envelope.

It was a request to appear at a benefit concert for the wounded soldiers at the residence of Prince Youssoupov. The Prince's secretary wrote that His Excellency, having heard Mademoiselle Orlova play the piano at the Empress' Benefit, was so much impressed by her artistry that he hoped she would agree to perform again at his residence. The Prince added a handwritten note to the invitation: "Please, do say 'yes,' I beg of you!"

Larissa consulted with her family. "Should I?" In her mind, she had already accepted the invitation. Prince Youssoupov was a fabulously wealthy young man married to the favorite niece of the Tsar, the beautiful Grand Duchess Irina.

"Of course, you must accept Youssoupov's invitation," was the collective decision of the family. "It will be good for you to get acquainted with the upper crust of the Russian Court!"

Andrei's mother sighed deeply. "I still miss my days at Court when I was a young Maiden of Honor to the Dowager Empress. All those brilliant balls ... I fell in love with Andrei's father at one of them."

"Just like I fell in love with Andrei at the ball," Larissa said. But Varvara Mikháilovna was not interested in Larissa's recollections; she had her own.

"He was a Lieutenant of the Horse Guards, on duty that day at the Winter Palace. I don't remember who introduced us, but we fell in love instantly. Lieutenant Rezánov paid us a visit on my mother's visiting day, which happened to be on the day after the ball, and from then on *every* week on her visiting day. Finally, my parents started joking about it and decided to help him. They gave a big ball at Christmas so that we would have a chance to dance and talk to one another. So we danced and I flirted with him and he was shy, but at the end of the evening, after the great supper, he pulled himself together and proposed to me. Then he asked my permission to talk to my father. Of course, I said yes to both his requests. But I too had to get permission—from the Dowager Empress."

"Really?" Despite herself, Larissa grew interested in the recollections.

"Oh, yes. In those days, the protocol of our society was very strict, especially at Court. The Empress always liked me and she knew that Lieutenant Rezánov's family was one of the oldest hereditary noble families, like mine, so our marriage would not be *mésalliance*. She gave me her blessing. And later, she gave me the most beautiful wedding gift—the veil of Brussels lace."

"The one that you gave me, for *my* wedding," Larissa said, embracing her mother-in-law.

"Yes," Varvara Mikháilovna said, her eyes misting as always when she felt sentimental. "We had a beautiful wedding in the Kazan Cathedral. One of our best men was Grand Duke ... I don't recall his name, there were so many of them!" She giggled like a young girl and wiped her eyes.

"Quite a difference from my wedding," Larissa said.

"Yes, don't remind me," Varvara Mikháilovna's mood instantly changed from gay into sorrowful. "I can never forget my disappointment. My *only* son married in *Gátchina!*"

Larissa's pride was stung. "Well, we both thought that it was a lovely wedding. We were very happy," she said dryly.

"Oh, I did not mean to upset you!" Varvara Mikháilovna exclaimed, but it was too late. Larissa left the room, holding her head high.

Larissa wrote a short note thanking the Prince for his invitation and asking whether he had any preferences as to the program. She ended by signing the note "Larissa Rezánova, née Orlova." She was no more a young girl; she was a married woman and she wanted everyone to know it.

Larissa felt that she needed Olga Nekrasova to prepare her for the concert. She asked her mother for the use of her carriage and told the driver to take her to the Smólny.

It was a pleasant ride. The day was crisp and the sky pale blue, so unusual in Petrograd in the autumn. So far, there was not much snow and the city traffic still moved on wheels and not on sleds. Swathed in her new sable coat, a wedding present from Andrei's parents, Larissa relaxed in the velvet luxury of her mother's carriage as it rolled almost soundlessly on rubber tires along the Nevsky Prospect.

Unexpectedly fair weather brought out prosperous crowds to the Nevsky Prospect. People enjoyed leisurely strolls along the sidewalks. Nannies pushed baby carriages, older children walked with their governesses, and it looked like everything was right with the world; there was no war, and no poor or hungry people anywhere. The shops were full of goods, their windows displaying the latest fashions or the most enticing arrays of caviar, huge sturgeons, and voluminous hams. Who had said that Petrograd was suffering a lack of food?

Given the beguiling scenery, Larissa was startled by the sight of a small crowd approaching the Nevsky Prospect from one of the side streets. Poorly dressed men and women carried red flags and slogans printed on long sections of red cloth demanding "Bread and Freedom." Some of them carried hand-printed placards announcing that they were on strike. Some women carried babies or dragged older children by their hands.

Instinctively, Lara moved back, deeper into the shadows of her carriage. The old driver reined the horse to a stop to let the marching crowd pass.

Six Cossacks on matching Don-region horses followed the demonstration at some distance. The mounted Cossacks looked as if they might have been escorting the marchers, but the citizens of Petrograd knew better. The Cossacks were there in case the demonstration turned violent. Ever since the disturbances of 1905, the Cossacks had many calls for suppression, until they were placed on permanent alert.

As the demonstrators and the Cossacks crossed the Nevsky Prospect, foot traffic on the sidewalks resumed and carriages began to roll again. The ragged crowd did not invade the Nevsky Prospect.

Larissa was relieved. Like most of the people of her social class, she had no knowledge of the lower classes. She loved her family servants, and she thought that they loved her also. But she knew nothing about them and had no interest in knowing anything. The servants lived in the same house with their masters, entrusted with the family's comfort and welfare. It was so for generations and continued after serfdom was eliminated and the servants became salaried employees. As for the new and growing industrial working class, Larissa had developed an uneasy feeling of … *distrust*. The more she read the newspapers, the more she became aware that workers were different from servants. They were independent, rough and demanding, while servants seemed to be content to live in the security of their masters' benevolence. The newspapers often discussed the possibility of a revolution. What if the workers, thousands of them, united and …? *"Bread and Freedom."* The words refused to leave her.

The golden cupolas of the Smólny Cathedral loomed ahead, bright and reassuring.

Olga Petrovna was not at the School. Larissa was told that she was in Gátchina for a few days.

"In Gátchina? What is she doing there?" Larissa thought, as she wrote her a short note. "I need your help again. I was invited to play at another benefit concert. What should I play? My mother and I are back at our own house, so you and I won't need to worry anymore about giving headaches to Varvara Mikháilovna with our practicing the piano!"

For several days, there was no reply.

"I wish I could telephone her," Larissa thought. "But why is she in Gátchina? I should've kept up with her after the Empress' concert … perhaps she is angry with me. She probably thinks that I am an ungrateful girl, still in constant need of help. First with my sudden wedding, then with two benefit concerts!"

Olga's reply came the following week. *"I'll be delighted to help,"* she wrote. *"However, I have only one week to be with you before I go back to Gátchina. I am engaged!"*

Engaged? It seemed impossible. "She is old, at least forty! And she is not pretty … And she can be very sarcastic. One has to know her *really* well to like her," Larissa thought with the cruelty of the young and the beautiful. "Her fiancé must be in Gátchina. But who is he? Why have I never heard about him?"

It was snowing lightly when Olga Petrovna arrived at the Orlov's residence. She paid the driver of the hired carriage and walked under the porte-cochère supported by two half-nude caryatids to the high, carved door encrusted with bronze. She pulled on a heavy bronze bell.

An old butler in black breeches and white silk stockings opened the door. "Whom do you wish to see, Madame?" he asked.

"I would like to see Mademoiselle Orlova, I mean, Madame Rezáno-va ..."

"Yes, Madame." He opened the door widely, inviting her in. "May I have your coat?"

"Please."

The butler helped her to take off her coat. "The young Madame is in the Music Room. Whom should I announce?"

"You don't need to. I know where the Music Room is. I am her music teacher."

"Yes, Madame." The old man made a small bow and stood aside.

Larissa was sitting at the piano, diligently running her fingers in the dull exercises that Olga insisted her students play before the lesson. Olga smiled. She always knew that Larissa took her music seriously. She stood at the door, watching. The young woman's back was turned toward the door, but she could see Larissa's profile reflected in one of the tall mirrors.

"She is so lovely," Olga thought. "And, so vulnerable."

Larissa continued to practice the scales, changing soon to more interesting arpeggios, unaware of Olga standing at the door.

Finally, Olga clapped her hands. "Enough!" she said in her dry authoritative teacher's tone.

"Olga Petrovna!" Larissa cried happily, jumping from her piano stool and running to Olga. "I did not hear you come in!" They embraced. "I am dying to know about your engagement! Who is he? When did it happen?"

"Later, later," Olga laughed.

"No, now, now! Please let's sit down and you tell me about your fiancé." Larissa led Olga to a small banquette and all but pushed her down to the seat. "Tell me!' she cried

"Well, all right. Actually, you know him," Olga looked embarrassed.

"Do I? Who is he?" Larissa insisted, taking her place next to Olga. "Is he one of the teachers from the Smólny?"

"No. He is one of your best men. Captain Sergei Rublev."

"No! Oh, I am so sorry," she added, quickly remembering Rublev's disability.

"It's all right. It doesn't bother me. I mean, it doesn't bother me that he is a cripple, and short. He is a wonderful man and I am truly in love, for the first time in my life!" She blushed.

"I am so glad for you!" Larissa grabbed her hands and pressed them to her chest. "Do you feel my heart? It is beating extra fast in my happiness for you! Andrei will be so excited to hear the news. He *loved* Captain Rublev. When is the wedding?"

"There will be no wedding. Sergei is married, even though he hasn't lived with his wife for more than ten years. She is in Samara. But we don't mind. In our hearts, we will be married. Are you shocked?"

"Well, I don't know ... I've never met anyone who lived together without being married ..."

"Does it shock you?" Olga repeated.

Larissa hesitated and then said firmly, "No, it doesn't shock me. If Andrei and I couldn't be married, I would still want to live with him!"

"Well, it's settled then. Anyway, how is your mother?" Olga asked. "How is she coping with her losses?"

"She is much better now. I never suspected that she was so strong. After Andrei left and I was like a zombie in my grief, she took care of me and pulled me through. She resumed her duties running the house and my father's financial affairs. She is a remarkable woman, my mother. I am glad that I know it now. As a girl, I often resented her decisions. But tell me about you and Captain Rublev!"

"His name is Sergei," Olga corrected.

"All right, tell me about Sergei. Did you know him before our wedding?"

"No, I met him for the first time at your wedding. It was quite funny how we met again. As you know, your mother took over ordering your 'thank-you' gifts to the best men and to me. They all were from the Fabergé store, since you and Andrei were on your honeymoon and she did not want to bother you."

"Yes, I was very grateful to Mother that she took care of everything. I hope you liked your gift? I haven't seen it. I told Mother to use her own taste."

"Oh, yes. The Fabergé picture frame is very elegant. I placed your wedding picture in it, the one with all of us around you. It is charming. It sits on the top of my piano. However, when I received my gift, which came directly from the Fabergé store, I opened it and was surprised to find a beautiful gold cigarette case! But I don't smoke! Then, I saw a little note inside, which said 'Captain R.' Some clerk at the store must have mixed up the gifts. So, I wrote to Captain Rublev, saying that I had his gift delivered to me by mistake. He wrote back that he had my gold and blue enamel picture frame delivered to him!"

"Oh, how embarrassing!" Larissa was humiliated.

"No ... How *wonderful!* If this mix-up hadn't occurred, Sergei and I would have never met again. Sergei asked in his letter if he could come to the Smólny to exchange our gifts. Of course I said yes, so he came and we had some tea, and then we took a walk in the garden and we laughed and talked and had a great time. He told me about the Flight School, and I said that it sounded fascinating, and then he asked me if I would like to see the school. We made a date for the following Sunday, and I took a train to Gátchina. He met me at the station, and we spent the whole day talking, walking in the park, and watching the cadets practice flying. I had a marvelous time. We had dinner at the inn and I thought of you. He told me that he admired Andrei, and he thought that Andrei was one of the very best young men he had ever met."

"And—then?"

"Then I went back to the city."

"Did you make another date to meet?"

Olga laughed happily. "Yes, we did. He came to the Smólny the following Sunday, and we spent the whole day in the city. We went to a matinee at the Mariinsky Theatre to hear *The Barber of Seville,* and we laughed when we saw the great Fabergé store nearby on Morskaya Street. By that time, we both knew that we liked one another very much!"

"So? Larissa prompted.

"We visited each other every Sunday for about two months. On one of my turns to go to Gátchina, he invited me to his house. I met his old nurse, Trofímovna, and his dog, Kazbeck. He told me all about his childhood, and I told him about mine. Trofímovna cooked a great dinner for us and Sergei played some music on his gramophone."

"And?" Larissa was smiling.

"And then he said, 'Neither of us are in our first bloom of youth and it is foolish to waste time on a long courtship. I would like you to marry me. Will you have me?' Without hesitation, I said, yes." She smiled gently. She looked almost pretty.

"Then, he told me that our 'marriage' could not be sanctioned by the Church, for he was already married. And I said that it did not matter to me. He called in his old nurse Trofímovna and told her that he and I will be living together as man and wife. Trofímovna embraced me and kissed me and she cried a little, and then she said that she was so happy that her boy had finally found himself a real wife! Then, she said 'I'll go and make your bridal bed' ... I was so embarrassed! But Sergei just kissed me and said, *You are my wife.*' So I've moved in with him and his Trofímovna!" she laughed happily. "And you know, even our dogs, his huge Doberman and my tiny Yorkie, like each other!"

Larissa was dying to know whether Olga was a virgin, but she did not ask. "I am so happy for you," she said. "Andrei told me that the Captain was the one who had recommended that he not wait for the end of the war to marry me. He advised Andrei not to waste time on the old tradition of long engagement."

"Well, he obviously believes what he was preaching!" They both laughed. "Anyway, tell me about that benefit concert. What are you planning to play? And where will it be?"

"I was thinking of *Rondo Capriccioso in E Major*, by Mendelssohn. It is both melodic and, in the second movement, quite technical, so it will give me a chance to show-off a little. What do you think?"

"It is a good choice. And what will you play for an encore?"

"I suppose some Chopin."

"Everybody plays Chopin. Be adventurous. Be *modern!* If only you could play Scriabin, but he is not for the Russian Court. All those Grand Dukes and Duchesses would crucify you for playing such revolutionary music, even if he is Russian."

"What about Ravel? I adore his *Pavane pour une infante défunte*. Or, Debussy's *Clair de Lune?* Or, *Poissons d'Or?*'"

"Any of them. But don't worry yourself. You will likely play only one song, so pick your favorite and keep one in reserve in case they ask for more."

"And what if they want even more than that?"

Olga laughed. "You are a greedy little thing! What makes you think you are so great that your listeners would not let you go? Work on whatever you wish, but plan on only one for the concert."

"Well, Ravel or Debussy it will be. When you visit me, we'll work on it."

"You didn't tell me where the benefit concert will take place. At the Noblemen Assembly Grand Hall again?"

"No! At the Youssoupov's Moika palace."

"Oh! I always wondered about that infamous place!"

"Why infamous?"

"Well, mainly because of Prince Youssoupov's reputation. He is known for his extravagance and strange … shall we say, *habits?*"

"I don't know anything about his habits. I know that he is one of the richest men in Russia, married to the Grand Duchess Irina, and that's about all. My mother-in-law used to know his parents when she was at Court herself. The Prince is very handsome, although not to my taste."

"And that is partially the problem. The pretty Prince is a pederast and a transvestite."

"I can't believe it!" Larissa said. "He is married!"

"Grow up, my girl. Marriage has nothing to do with it," Olga laughed cynically.

They heard footsteps and Maria Nikoláyevna entered the drawing room. "Ah, Olga Petrovna!" she greeted Nekrasova. "Whose marriage has nothing to do with what?" she asked.

"We were talking about Prince Felix Youssoupov, Maria Nikoláyevna," Olga said.

"Oh, that pederast," the old woman said with contempt.

"You … you know about him, Mama?" Lara was greatly surprised.

"I don't know *for sure*, but the rumor about him has been circulating for years," she shrugged.

"Anyway, I am intrigued by him and I look forward to meeting him and his wife and I feel honored that they had asked me to play at their benefit!" Larissa declared.

"By all means," her mother said. "What are you planning to wear?"

"I don't know. I don't want to wear any of my white ball gowns and I don't have any adult theatre gowns. All my theatre gowns are too juvenile …. I would like to wear something dark, and in velvet, something sophisticated, like one of your theatre gowns, Mama, the dark green velvet one. It is my favorite."

"Well," her mother said slowly, "We don't have enough time to have a new gown made, so why don't we have mine remodeled for you? My *modiste* Georgette surely can do it in no time. And you can wear my emeralds."

"Oh, Mama! Thank you!" She rushed at her mother, smothering her with kisses.

"I must be going," Olga said. "I'll see you next week. Learn your new pieces." She bade them goodbye and left.

The green velvet gown looked perfect on Larissa. With long narrow sleeves and a deep décolleté, it bared Larissa shoulders and slightly exposed the tops of her breasts. It fitted her lithe body closely, falling in soft folds down her back to the floor as a small train.

Maria Nikoláyevna encircled Larissa's neck with a collier of huge emeralds surrounded by diamonds and attached the matching dangling earrings to her earlobes.

"But what about shoes?" Larissa suddenly exclaimed. "We forgot about the shoes!"

"My shoes will be too small for you," Maria Nikoláyevna said. "You were raised as an athletic child, while in my time we were not supposed to do anything more energetic than embroidery or playing piano. Your generation of girls has much larger feet and hands."

The maid brought in the green velvet shoes. "I don't even have to try them on. They are too small." Larissa was disappointed.

"Well, do you have any suitable shoes at all?"

"No. But wait a minute. Yes, I do have a pair of *gold* slippers! They are embroidered with some colored threads. Let's take a look!" They went to Lara's dressing room where her maid Natasha climbed up the stepladder to retrieve the box with the gold slippers. They were indeed embroidered in some intricate pseudo-oriental design.

"Too garish," Larissa sighed. "The gold is not bad; it's burnished, but the embroidery!" She wrinkled her nose in disgust as she put on the shoes.

"What if you dye them green?" the maid suggested. "I know a shoemaker. He dyed my black boots red and you can't tell the difference."

Larissa and Maria Nikoláyevna looked at each other. "Should we try? Do you have your red boots here?" Maria Nikoláyevna asked.

"Yes, Madame, they are in my room."

"Why did you need *red* boots, Natasha?" Larissa asked.

Natasha blushed. "There was a costume party last spring at the Narodny Dom and I went dressed as a Ukrainian girl."

"Let's see your boots," Maria Nikoláyevna said. The girl jumped down from the ladder and hurried to her room in the servants' quarters.

"We must take care of your 'adult wardrobe,' as you called it," Maria Nikoláyevna said. "Even though we are at war, you must have proper clothes. We'll go to Anna Indus Atelier tomorrow and order you a new wardrobe."

Natasha returned carrying a pair of bright red boots. "Here they are, Madame."

Lara and Maria Nikoláyevna examined the boots closely. The boots were certainly red.

"They look very good," Maria Nikoláyevna said. "I think it is worth trying. Let's get a small sample of color from the inside of the gown and send it with Natasha to her shoemaker."

Larissa was ecstatic when Natasha brought back the shoes two days later. They were of the exact color of the gown, the garish embroidery now looking elegant.

"Just right!" exclaimed Maria Nikoláyevna. "You are a smart girl, Natasha!" The maid blushed. It wasn't often that the old lady paid compliments to her servants.

Lara tried on her concert outfit again. The shoes and the gown matched perfectly.

17

The week passed quickly, devoted only to music. Larissa hoped that Olga would tell her more about her romance, but Olga avoided any personal revelations. Larissa gave up. She had other things on her mind.

Prince Youssoupov's secretary sent her a note. On October 20, at seven o'clock in the evening, she would be picked up by a motorcar to take her to Youssoupov's Palace. The prince hoped that she could stay for an intimate champagne reception 'for a few friends' after the concert; she would be delivered back to her residence afterwards. The prince regretted she could not bring anyone, since his private theatre would accommodate no more than two hundred guests.

The note was very dry and efficient and left an unpleasant taste in her mouth. It was almost like a summons to appear before some potentate, she thought. But then—the Youssoupovs *were* potentates!

She was relieved that her mother would not accompany her. It was time that everyone, including her mother, realized that she was a married woman and not a young girl in need of a chaperone.

On the day of the concert, Maria Nikoláyevna's own *coiffeur* Monsieur Jean-Paul and a manicurist, Mademoiselle Solange, arrived at the Orlov's residence. Jean-Paul washed Larissa's hair in fragrant water and then made her wear a Turkish towel turban perfumed with a Jean Patou fragrance, while Solange began to file her nails into an elegant almond shape.

"No, no, don't shape my nails. I play the piano and one can't play well with long nails. Don't look so disappointed," she laughed seeing the young woman's bewildered face. "You may buff them!"

Jean-Paul teased Larissa's hair until it stood from its root. "I look like Medusa," Lara thought. He started arranging it, strand by strand, into an elaborate knot at the back of her head, letting several long strands curl loosely down her back.

"I think we need some decorations among the strands at the top and in back," he said to Maria Nikoláyevna, who was supervising Larissa preparations for the evening. "The young Madame will be wearing the emeralds. No?"

"Yes."

"Well, some emeralds will be perfect. Not a tiara, but something small, just peeking out from among her hair. Perhaps some beaded necklace, which we can open and wind around with Madame's hair?"

"We have two bracelets from the same set."

"Perfect!"

Maria Nikoláyevna sent her maid to bring the bracelets.

Jean-Paul braided the flattened bracelets with Lara's hair, securing them with invisible hairpins, creating an intricate and elegant coiffure.

"It is beautiful!" Maria Nikoláyevna exclaimed. "You are a real artist, Monsieur!"

"Merci! The young Madame has the most beautiful hair. It was easy!"

At seven o'clock exactly, a big black and yellow Rolls-Royce Silver Ghost stopped at the Orlov residence. The chauffeur rang the bell.

As the old butler opened the door, the chauffeur said with a strong British accent, "I am to drive Madame Rezánov to Prince Youssoupov's residence. I'll wait at the machine."

"Yes, sir," the butler replied, in awe of the splendid automobile. "She will be down in a minute."

Larissa came down wrapped in her sable coat, her hands in heavy woolen mittens hidden inside an enormous sable muff to keep them warm. Maria Nikoláyevna and the maids came after her, all making the sign of the cross, all proud of her beauty. "Good luck!" her mother said and kissed her cheek. "Have fun!"

Larissa smiled, her mind already far away. She was nervous. She knew that she would play well, but the prospect of meeting the notorious Prince Youssoupov and the Tsar's niece unnerved her.

She had never ridden in a Rolls-Royce. She admired the soft tufted leather upholstery, noticing its little touches of indulgence and beauty, such as special supports for the passengers' feet and a fresh yellow rose in a small crystal vase attached to the window.

It was a short ride to the Palace, which was one of the largest buildings along the narrow Moika Canal.

The long façade of the eighteenth century Youssoupov Palace was a dull structure, painted in pale yellow with white columns and cornices, looking more suitable to a government building than a palace.

A narrow strip of bare pavement between the building and the canal's granite embankment prevented easy access to the entrance. Carriages and automobiles had to drive into the inner court through one of two high arches at each end of the building.

However, once inside the entrance one could see the famed elegance of Italian architecture. There was a summer garden, and a winter garden under a dome of stained and beveled glass. Beautiful marble sculptures, fountains, and other marvels were hidden behind the dull façade.

"I wonder whether his Winter Garden is better than Papa's," Larissa thought. "Probably bigger, but not necessarily better. Papa's orchids were famous!"

The chauffeur stopped the automobile. "Here we are, Madame," he said, opening the door. "I will escort you to the theatre." He helped her down and led her to a modest side door. "It is the Artists Entrance," he explained.

"Oh … But of course, *I am not a guest*. I am only a performer," Larissa thought in disappointment.

The large room she entered was the artists' waiting room. It was furnished with small sofas and chairs. Against one wall were small tables separated from one another by partitions to allow a certain amount of privacy. Atop each sat a mirror.

Three doors at the farther end of the large room were marked Ladies, Gentlemen, and Stage.

The chauffeur grinned. "I'll take you back after *the party*," he said with a touch of impudence.

"What does he mean?" She was suddenly alarmed. "I was invited to a champagne reception, not a *party*," she thought. The chauffeur bowed slightly and left.

Larissa took off her coat and checked herself in a full-length mirror. She looked very good, she thought. She kept her mittens on and her hands inside the muff.

"What now?" she thought, feeling ill at ease.

There were fast footsteps behind the door leading to the stage and a young man in evening clothes entered the room. Larissa recognized him at once, even though she had never met him before.

"I am so sorry, Madame, that my chauffeur brought you here instead of the Grand Foyer," he apologized. "I am Felix Youssoupov." He extended his hand.

"I know," she said, "I am Larissa Rezánova."

"I know," he said, smiling. They both laughed.

"I am not giving you my hand because I am wearing mittens to keep my hands warm," Larissa explained.

He smiled. "I can wait. I will kiss your hand *after* the concert. Let's go!" He offered her his arm and led her through the empty stage with a huge concert piano in the center. The heavy stage curtain was still drawn, but Larissa could hear the buzz of voices from the other side of it.

"The first few rows in our theatre are for wounded officers," the Prince explained. "We have a small hospital, sixty beds, and most of our patients are ambulatory now. Our wounded guests are already being seated."

"You mean the hospital is right here, at your palace?"

"Yes, Madame."

"My mother and my husband's mother and I volunteer at Her Majesty's hospital twice a week."

"Is your husband at the front?"

"Yes, Prince. He is a pilot with the First Combat Air Group. He has just been awarded the St. George Cross!" She could not resist bragging.

Youssoupov smiled gently. "My wife also volunteers," he said. "She is not here tonight. She is in the Crimea. She will miss your performance, but we'll have some other occasions, and I hope you will honor us again. It was my wife who recommended you for our benefit after hearing you at Her Majesty's concert."

"Thank you," Larissa said, but she was disappointed. She looked forward to meeting the fabulous Princess Irina.

They entered the Grand Foyer full of military men in dress uniforms, their chests covered with rows of medals, and women in dazzling gowns and priceless jewels. A few men wore civilian evening clothes, like Prince Youssoupov, who apparently was not associated with any of the military branches.

Servants attired in eighteenth century dress moved among the guests, serving champagne. Their knee breeches, white silk stockings, and powdered wigs remained fashionable for servants at court and in the homes of nobility.

The guests greeted the prince with familiarity, looking with interest at Larissa. No one knew her. "Who is this young beauty?" many whispered.

The women noticed her emeralds. "Is she Youssoupov's mistress?"

Larissa began to feel uncomfortable under their stares. Finally, she saw a familiar face: her schoolmate, the young Princess Zinaida Volkonskaya, who graduated from the Smólny a year ahead of her.

"Zina!" she called.

Zina turned around. "Larissa! I had heard that you were going to play tonight! I also heard that you were married!" she came to Larissa with outstretched arms. They embraced and kissed.

"So, you know each other," Youssoupov smiled.

"Yes, we went to school together," Zina replied.

"I bet I know which school!" They all laughed.

Youssoupov said, "I beg your pardon, Princess, but I must take Madame Rezánova away from you. The concert is about to start. Let me have your muff ... and your mittens," he smiled conspiratorially as he passed the muff to a servant.

Youssoupov led Larissa back to the stage.

"Don't be upset when you see some of the wounded. Two or three have severe head wounds: they look as if half of their heads were blown off. There is also one pilot who was badly burned."

"A pilot?" Larissa's hand resting on his arm trembled.

"Oh, I shouldn't have mentioned that he was burned! Are you all right?"

"I am fine. Just a little nervous before my performance," she said, trying to divert her thoughts.

"Would you like to dedicate this concert in honor of your husband and his decoration for valor?"

"Yes, I would. It would give me great pleasure," she exclaimed readily. "How can I do it?"

"Not to worry. I'll do it for you," Youssoupov said, kissing her hand. "It is my privilege to introduce you to your audience. Good luck!" he smiled as he went to the massive velvet curtain and, parting it slightly, stepped in front of it.

A resounding rumble of applause greeted him. *"Bonsoir, messieurs, et mesdames,"* he began, and switching into Russian, continued, "It gives me the greatest pleasure to introduce our talented young pianist Madame Larissa Rezánova at our first benefit concert. Madame Rezánova's husband is a pilot and a recent Cavalier of the Order of St. George. Madame Rezánova would like to consider her performance to be in his honor." The audience burst into applause. "So, be generous ladies and gentlemen. Donate your money or jewels to the welfare of our wounded heroes. Many of them are here with us tonight, and we want to thank them for their sacrifice to our Fatherland." More applause followed.

Larissa stood alone in the wings. She flexed her fingers, nervously waiting for the heavy crimson curtain fringed in gold to part. The great shiny black piano was beckoning to her, its lid opened, its keys awaiting her touch.

She heard Youssoupov's footsteps as he walked off the stage. The curtain parted, and the audience applauded again, welcoming her.

Larissa walked onto the stage, blinded by the footlights. She walked slowly, with her head held high as Olga had taught her, and stopped at the curvature of the piano. She took a deep breath and then made three small bows—to her right, to her left, and to the center of the hall. She noticed that the first three rows were filled with wounded men, some in bandages and even in robes. Behind them were waves of titled and wealthy men, sparkling with their gold epaulettes and decorations, and women with their bare shoulders and jewels.

The hall hushed as she adjusted her piano stool and announced in a clear voice, looking at the wounded men, "I would like to play for you *Rondo Capriccioso* by Felix Mendelssohn."

She began to play.

After the first chords, she surrendered herself to the music, her whole being becoming ephemeral, as if her physical self had dissolved in the melody.

The audience rewarded her with an ovation as she finished the rondo and stood.

"Brava! Brava! *Bis! Bis!*" the men shouted as the ladies applauded with dainty enthusiasm. Now, they accepted Larissa. They had discovered that she was the daughter of a famous general, the daughter-in-law of the former maiden-in-waiting of the Dowager Empress. She was one of them. Her emeralds were justified.

"Play some more!" she heard someone yell rudely. She turned toward the voice. A strange hirsute man, looking out of place in the brilliant crowd, stood and yelled again, "Play some more!" He was dressed in a dark peasant shirt belted with a braided cord. A huge gold cross hung on his broad chest.

"This must be Rasputin," Lara thought, fascinated.

Larissa finally smiled and sat down at the piano again. "I shall play Claude Debussy's *Clair de Lune*," she announced.

She placed her hands on the keys and concentrated before she struck the first notes of the exquisite melody. Debussy's music was not yet well known in Russian concert halls, even though he had spent several years in Moscow as a teacher and an accompanist in the household of Madame von Meck.

His elegant short piece was approved by the audience. They demanded more.

Again, Rasputin yelled, "Play more!" Again, the men shouted *"Bis!"*

Larissa did not let them beg for long. "I'll play Maurice Ravel's *Pavane Pour Une Infante Dèfunte*," she said.

She played with deep concentration, her lovely mien enhancing the melancholy theme of the composition. When she finished, there was a pause before the audience, as if enchanted by the unusual music, demanded more. "Play something *lively!*" Rasputin yelled, jumping up, the cross on his chest jumping also.

Lara thought as she sat down again. She had not expected to play so many pieces. She hesitated. "Something lively? All right. I'll play one of my husband's favorites. *Poissons d'Or*, by Debussy.

The fast and joyous melody, technically brilliant, filled the theatre. It was a very short piece, perfect for an encore. She finished it with a flourish, stood, and made a deep bow toward the wounded men. "Thank you," she mouthed.

"We want more!" Rasputin yelled again. "Play something Russian!" She bowed in his direction and folded her hands as if in prayer, indicating that was all. Then she bowed again to the whole audience and left the stage.

Youssoupov appeared behind the stage, beaming. "You conquered them all!" he exclaimed. "Listen to that applause. Can you play just one more piece? You must be tired, but maybe one short piece more?"

"Rasputin wanted something 'Russian," she said.

"Oh, you recognized him?"

"I have never seen him before, but he is a unique figure. It was easy to presume that it was Rasputin!"

Youssoupov laughed. "How right you are! Will you play? Just one more!"

"Well, all right. I will play Tchaikovsky's *Troika*. Will you announce it?"

"With pleasure." Youssoupov returned to the stage. "Madame Rezánova has graciously agreed to play one more piece, but before she does, the secretaries of the Benefit Committee will collect your donations," he announced. "Afterwards, Madame Rezánova will perform *Troika* by Tchaikovsky."

The curtain closed and several of Youssoupov's secretaries went from one row to another among the invited guests collecting their pledges written on little pieces of paper.

Lara rested in an armchair in the wings. She could hear small explosions of laughter as people made their pledges. She was tired but exalted by her obvious success. "I wish Olga were here!" she thought.

The curtain was parted again and Larissa walked to the waiting piano, smiling as she walked. She loved that little bagatelle of Tchaikovsky's, which she had learned when she was twelve years old and played every Christmas at the Smólny's winter concerts. It was a 'descriptive' piece, expressing the joy of riding in a troika sleigh through snow.

Larissa played it with the zest of youth, smiling coquettishly at the wounded men. They loved that. When she finished, she stood and replied to enchanted men's applause with several air kisses.

"Charmante," was the judgment passed upon her by the highest crust of society. Larissa became instantly *en vogue*.

Larissa and several other guests, her friend Zina among them, were invited to proceed to the red drawing room for the intimate champagne reception.

"You were wonderful!" Zina whispered. "I was sitting next to Grand Duke Dimitri Pavlovich and he was *enchanted* by you! 'Why haven't we seen her before?' he kept saying. There he is!" she exclaimed, leading Lara to a tall, blond, handsome young man in the dress uniform of the Cavalry Regiment of the Imperial Life Guards.

"Madame!" the young Grand Duke exclaimed, bending over Larissa's hand. "You captivated us!"

"Thank you, Your Highness," Larissa blushed. "You are too kind."

"No, no, I mean it! Your interpretation of Impressionist music was fabulous! I never heard anyone who could master Debussy or Ravel with such delicacy and feeling. You made it live for me!"

"You are too kind, Your Highness!" Larissa repeated.

"Sit next to me. I want to talk to you about the Impressionists," he said, leading her to a low table with only two chairs. There was a large crystal bowl on the table filled with caviar and a tray with small round crackers. Two spreading knives with gold handles and two folded napkins rested next to two small plates with the Youssoupov's crest. Zina melted back into the crowd.

The Grand Duke held the chair as Larissa sat down. "You must be tired after that long program," he said.

"Not really. I am still buoyed by it. But I agree that it was long. Perhaps, too long. My teacher told me that no program should be longer than three selections, but I played five!"

"It meant that we had the pleasure of hearing you play two more times!" the Grand Duke said, looking above her head. She noticed that he avoided looking directly at anyone; he gazed at the ceiling or at the floor or some other object, avoiding meeting people's eyes. Was he too shy, or too arrogant?

"Tell me, Madame, what made you interested in *impressionism?* Are you interested in modern art in general?"

"I know very little about *modern art*. I went to the Exhibition at the Artists Corner not long ago and I was appalled. Why is everything so distorted? So unreal?"

The Grand Duke smiled, a little patronizingly, Lara thought.

"Let me explain it to you," he said looking at the tip of his polished boot. "When you look at a *traditional* painting, what do you see?"

"A picture."

"Right. Whether it is a landscape or a nude or a horse, you immediately recognize it as such. But when you see a *modern* painting, you ask yourself—How? That is, *how* was it painted? Do you see what I mean?"

"Not really. When I see a *modern* painting, I ask myself—*Why?* Why something so ugly had to be painted, and *why* can't I recognize whether it is a landscape or a nude or a horse?"

He chortled. A footman brought two tall crystal glasses and poured the champagne. "You are very clever, Madame. To tell you the truth, I have often asked myself the same questions."

A raucous voice interrupted their conversation. "What's so funny?" Rasputin said moving a chair to join them. "You played that piano beautifully, young lady," he said to Larissa. "So, your hubby is at the front, eh?"

Larissa was surprised at his sudden appearance and intrusion into her conversation with the Grand Duke.

She answered, "Yes, he is at the front." The notorious monk sat uncomfortably near her, so close that his knees almost touched hers. She waited for the Grand Duke to say something, but he kept silent. He twirled the stem of the champagne glass in his fingers, staring at his boot.

"Well, it must be hard for a young woman like yourself to be alone," Rasputin continued. "No wonder you make love to your piano!" he cackled, enjoying his joke.

Larissa watched him in morbid fascination, as if he were an intriguing but dangerous creature, like a cobra, that could strike out at her without provocation.

Rasputin was of average height, yet he gave the impression of being a much taller man because of his wide shoulders and broad chest. He parted his oily long hair in the middle, in the peasant fashion. His long beard and moustache were unkempt and there were a few crumbs of food stuck in his beard. His hands were broad and the stubby fingers had crescents of dirt under the fingernails. He smelled of old sweat and something else unpleasant, like boiled cabbage.

The footman offered him champagne, but Rasputin waved him away."I don't touch champagne. It gives me gas," he said for all to hear. "Bring me some good Madeira wine!"

The Grand Duke kept silent. His hand holding the glass trembled slightly.

Rasputin turned his attention to Larissa again. "Do you believe in God?" he demanded loudly.

"I do," Larissa replied.

"Look into my eyes," he ordered. Larissa stared into his eyes, set under a bush of thick eyebrows. His eyes were piercing. They seemed to be dark, yet they were blue and intense, full of magnetic attraction.

"Do you believe in salvation and the forgiveness of sin?"

Larissa did not know whether it was a serious question or some kind of uncouth joke.

"Well, do you?" Rasputin insisted.

"Yes, I do believe in the forgiveness of sin," she said in a small voice.

"All right," he said, apparently satisfied with her answer. "But in order to forgive sin, sin must be committed. Without the sin—there is nothing to forgive, am I right?"

"I don't know ..." Lara was frightened. "What does he want of me?" she thought.

"Let me explain. Let's take you, for example, a young woman whose husband is away for a long time. You are lonely. You want to make love, you want to be kissed and caressed, but your husband is not with you. What should you do?" he stared at Larissa with his penetrating eyes. "I'll tell you what you should do. Get a lover! Commit *the sin* of adultery! Then, confess and your sin will be forgiven! That is the way to your final salvation!" He immobilized her with his hypnotic eyes.

The footman brought a glass of Madeira and Rasputin gulped it as if it were water.

"Think of it," Rasputin said. "Let me know if you want me to pray for your husband." He stood and left, walking a little unsteadily.

"I thought he would never leave," the Grand Duke shuddered. "I can't understand why some people find him inspiring ... he is nothing but a dirty *mouzhik*. I despise him." For a moment, he glanced at Larissa's face, but only for a moment.

She pulled herself together. She wanted to go home, to be safe, with her mother and the photographs of Andrei.

"Your Highness, do you think we could find our host and arrange to take me home?"

"That scoundrel upset you?"

"Yes, Your Highness. He ruined my happy feeling."

"I am sorry. He has that ability. Many people hate him ..."

Larissa wanted to ask him more about Rasputin, but she did not dare.

He stood and offered her his arm. "Let's go and search for Prince Felix."

Grand Duke Dimitri escorted Lara through an enfilade of drawing rooms and music rooms connected to one another with carved and decorated doors. All were overflowing with golden chairs and sofas, ormolu tables and crystal chandeliers, old master paintings or Gobelin tapestries. One drawing room seemed to melt into another, even though the walls and draperies of each were of different colors of silk.

There was the red drawing room, where Lara had sat with the Grand Duke, the green music room with two golden harps, the yellow room with several canary cages, and the blue room with crystal and cobalt chandeliers. There was a severe-looking game room with several chess tables and then a Persian-style drawing room with low divans and colorful cushions, soft carpets and hookahs. It looked as if that room had arrived on a magic carpet from *One Thousand and One Nights*.

The wide open doors between all these rooms provided a long vista in both directions from the upper landing of the two-winged white marble staircase. It embraced the foyer like the wings of a trumpeter swan. A huge ceiling chandelier illuminated the staircase and the Grand Foyer below.

The Imperial Drawing Room encased in red damask was reserved for receiving the Royal Family. It was adorned with intricately carved and gilded furnishings with numerous double-headed eagles, the Romanov's emblem. "But of course! There is not enough grandeur without the eagles!" Larissa thought cynically. It was empty now, its doors crossed by velvet ropes like in a museum.

Larissa felt like she was walking through a stage set. Everything around her was so rich that it looked unreal. She recalled how as a little girl she had gobbled too much cake at her birthday party and then vomited all over her party dress.

"Too much, too much," she thought. For a split second, her mind played a joke on her: she saw in a quick flash a dark crowd of people invading the fabulous rooms, moving toward her, demanding "Bread and Freedom."

"Where is Prince Felix?"she cried impatiently..

"Perhaps the Prince has retired to his private quarters. It is in another part of the palace. But, before we give up let's visit the Music Rotunda," the Grand Duke said, leading her through the rooms on the other side of the grand ballroom. Almost every room held several small clusters of guests, drinking, gossiping and flirting. In one room, Larissa spotted Rasputin seated in a large winged chair and surrounded by a cluster of women.

"Don't stop here," Lara whispered. She pointed with her eyes to the relaxed figure of Rasputin.

"Yes, I see him," the Grand Duke murmured from the corner of his mouth.

They reached the Music Rotunda, a large round hall surrounded by eight columns supporting a domed ceiling painted to represent the sky and the nine muses.

The Prince was there, talking intimately with a stout, middle-aged gentleman. Both men were so preoccupied by their conversation that they did not hear the approach of Larissa and her royal escort.

The Grand Duke coughed politely. Youssoupov turned around. "Ah, it's you Dimitri! Thank you for taking care of our guest of honor! Madame, may I introduce to you Monsieur Purishkevich, illustrious member of our Duma and leader of the Union of the Russian People."

"Monsieur," Larissa bowed slightly as she offered him her hand.

"Madame," he bent over her hand. His head was as bald and shiny as the proverbial billiard ball, but as if to compensate, his face was overgrown with a bushy beard and moustache.

The Grand Duke shook hands with Purishkevich and said, staring at Youssoupov's bow tie, "Madame Rezánova is ready to depart. Would you like me to take her home?"

"No, no! I will take her home myself, but you can come with us, if you wish. Monsieur Purishkevich and I are finished with our discussion. I'll see you in a few days," he said turning to Purishkevich.

"Yes, Prince. I have been invited to dine with His Majesty at Stavka. I'll see you when I come back. Goodbye, Madame," he bowed and left the Rotunda, his footsteps resounding on the parquet floor.

"Well, shall we go?" Youssoupov asked gaily. He was obviously in good spirits.

"Yes, as soon as I get my coat and muff," Larissa said.

He laughed. "But of course! And the mittens! Let's not forget the mittens!"

The Rolls-Royce was waiting at the main entrance. Youssoupov and Grand Duke Dimitri helped Lara into the automobile, taking their places on each side of her.

"It's such a beautiful night!" Youssoupov sighed. "Look at that moon! Would you like to take a little ride along the Winter Palace Embankment before we take you home? It's just too beautiful to go to bed!"

Larissa smiled in the darkness. She felt good being out of that intimidating palace. "Yes, the night is beautiful! Let's ride along the embankment!"

"Fletcher!" Youssoupov lifted the tube of an internal telephone. "Take us for a ride along the Winter Palace Embankment."

"Yes, Prince. Do you want a fast ride or a crawling one?"

"How do you want it, Madame?" Youssoupov asked.

"Fast!"

"Go fast!" The prince said into the tube. The chauffeur revved the engine and the machine surged forward. They circled around St. Isaak's Cathedral, sped along Morskaya Street, and dashed under the Grand Arch and into Palace Square with its tall Alexander Column. The Winter Palace looked grim in its somber color, its windows dark because the Tsar's family preferred to stay at the Alexander Palace in Tsárskoye Selo.

They raced around the column at breakneck speed several times, blaring the horn, which reverberated on the empty square. Then, passing the Hermitage with its four giant malachite caryatides, they turned toward the Nevá at the Troitsky Bridge. Making a sharp left turn, Fletcher raced along the Palace Embankment, passed the Winter Palace on its river side, passed the Admiralty then the Senate Square and the famous sculpture of Peter the Great, and finally continued along the embankment to Larissa's residence.

"That was wonderful!" she exclaimed when the automobile finally stopped at her house. "Thank you! I can't invite you in because it is too late, but I would not mind if you visit us sometime on my mother's receiving day. It is on Thursdays."

Both men bowed, "It will be a pleasure," Youssoupov said. "Yes, indeed," the Grand Duke joined. They kissed her hand and accompanied her to the door, waiting until the old butler opened it.

Maria Nikoláyevna was waiting for her, curled up in her late husband's favorite armchair, wrapped in a warm shawl, her little dog on her lap.

"What time is it?" she yawned.

"Almost two."

"Did you enjoy yourself?"

"Yes and no. I enjoyed performing. I played four encores! I saw Zina Volkonskaya, remember her? I had champagne with the Grand Duke Dimitri Pavlovich. And of course, I met Prince Youssoupov. Princess Irina was not there, but I did meet *Rasputin!*"

"No!"

"Yes! And I talked to him, or rather, *he* talked to me. I'll tell you about it tomorrow. I am dead tired now and my feet hurt." She kissed her mother, kicked off her shoes, and pulling up the hem of her dress, ran to her room. "Good night, Mama," she called from the door.

Tired as she was, sleep evaded Larissa. She decided to write a quick letter to Andrei.

"My dearest beloved husband," she wrote, *"It gives me such pleasure to write 'husband'! I am full of interesting news that I am dying to tell you. Last night I met Rasputin!"* She described the concert, her success, the richness of the palace, and her meeting with Prince Youssoupov and the Grand Duke. *"Both of them are very good looking, especially the Prince. Actually, one could call him beautiful. He is very effeminate. They were very kind to me and after the reception they took me for a crazy drive in the Rolls-Royce! What an automobile! When you come back, we must buy one! Anyway, Grand Duke Dimitri Pavlovich confessed to me that he hates Rasputin."* She described Rasputin's theory of forgiveness and salvation, making fun of his logic, not mentioning Rasputin's advice that she ought to take a lover. *"The Grand Duke showed me quite a lot of the Palace. Bozhe Moi! What indescribable riches! I really felt that it was wrong for any one family to be so rich. And I am not saying it out of envy, my darling. I really mean it! I send you, my dear one, a million kisses and blessings. I hate this horrid war that separates us. I'll write you a long, long letter in a few days. I love you and I miss you terribly. Oh, yes! A surprise! Your friend Captain Rublev and my music teacher Olga Nekrasova are lovers and are living 'in sin' in his house! Good for them!"*

18

Andrei carried his new mail into the bedroom. He had three hours before his next flight. He was still flying as an observer: Kozakov liked his work as a photographer, but Andrei chafed at being a mere 'picture taker.'

Egórov tried to reason with him, reminding him that reconnaissance was the primary duty of the Air Detachments, but Andrei was deaf to his arguments. He wanted to fly as a fighter pilot! Alone! In the single-seater!

Andrei had three letters: from Larissa, from his mother, and from Captain Rublev.

He opened Rublev's letter first, saving Lara's letter 'for dessert', as he used to say about something special when he was a boy.

Rublev's letter was humorous. "What do you know, my boy: I am in love! What's more, with someone that you know: your wife's Maid of Honor!" He described the mix-up of the Fabergé gifts and the Sunday visits between Smólny and Gátchina. "Olga will move in with me, but she will continue to teach at the Smólny two days a week. We cannot marry, but that is another story. Congratulations upon your St. George Cross! I read about your awards ceremony in the New Russian Times and placed the clipping on our bulletin board for all to see. Old Petrovich had his own clipping, which he nailed above his workstation. He brags about you to all our new cadets, saying that he taught you everything that you know."

Rublev finished his letter by wishing Andrei more victories and the Good Lord's protection, even though he himself was an agnostic.

Andrei smiled as he read this letter. "Read this," he said to Egórov. "It is from my old trainer and friend in Gátchina."

Egórov was subdued. He had only one letter. "And you read that," he proffered Andrei the official looking letter. "The bitch is asking for a divorce!"

Andrei knew nothing about Egórov's private life; none of the pilots did. For all of his libertine attitudes, Egórov was tight-lipped about his love life. Andrei suspected that it was not a happy one. He guessed that Egórov was married, or at least had been, but Egórov always refused to talk about it, so after a time Andrei had stopped asking.

"What are you going to do?"

"Nothing. Let her have her divorce."

"But, the Church ... You must have the permission of the Church for a divorce."

"To hell with the Church. I don't give a damn anymore. I'll sign anything, including that I have been keeping a harem at the front if she names me as an offending party."

Andrei was stunned. Divorces were rare in his social circles. It carried a large stigma. "I am so sorry."

"Don't be. Anyway, what did you want me to read?" Egórov closed the door to a further discussion.

"Well, nothing important, just a funny letter from one of my former trainers at Gátchina. He is in love!"

A cynical grimace contorted Egórov's face. "One's out, one's in!"

Andrei did not know how to react. He was still too inexperienced in life to give advice, and not knowing anything about Egórov's wife, not having even seen her photograph, he did not know whether he should be sympathetic or cynical. He remained silent. He opened his mother's letter.

The faint aroma of her favorite perfume, *Rose de Bois*, reminded him of home. He read the letter smiling, not caring for the contents. Whatever his mother had to tell him was of no interest to him, just gossip, the usual expressions of worry about him, and complaints about her health.

He was stalling with opening Larissa's letter, anticipating the pleasure of holding it, of seeing her handwriting and finally, rewarding himself by reading it.

Within the first paragraphs, his senses sharpened. Something was wrong; Larissa was having a wonderful time with the young Grand Duke Dimitri Pavlovich and Prince Youssoupov, riding with them *at midnight* in a Rolls-Royce, while Youssoupov's wife was away! Larissa's meeting Rasputin did not impress him as much as her riding through the sleeping city with two well-known rakes and seducers.

He re-read that section of the letter in rising anger. What had she been doing there? Why hadn't she gone home after the concert? Why had she accepted the invitation to ride so late at night? Had she ever thought of her husband? Andrei was overcome by jealousy.

"Bad news?" Egórov asked. Andrei shook his head, not looking at his friend.

"No. Nothing." He crushed the letter in his fist. "It's time to go," he said, as he stuck the letter into his pocket.

"Yes, something is wrong," Egórov thought. "I hope this bride of his is not following in my wife's footsteps. They are all whores, every one of them! Even our Empress with that *mouzhik* Rasputin!"

They walked to the aircraft line, Andrei buttoning his leather jacket. The crumpled letter in his pocket felt like it weighed a ton.

The mechanics greeted them cheerfully, busy with attaching bombs to the Voisin LA for their mission.

"You must tell me what's eating you," Egórov said. "We are going on a mission and we can't fly safely if one of us is upset."

"I am not upset," Andrei protested, trying to pull himself together.

"Don't be a prick. I know that your wife's letter upset you. Tell me. I told you about my problems, now you tell me about yours. There is nothing that can't be solved."

Andrei hesitated, then told him all.

Egórov chuckled. "Is that all?"

"They drank champagne and the Grand Duke showed her the palace."

"Is that all?" Egórov repeated, raising his voice.

"Well, basically it is all."

"When we get back, let me read that letter. Meanwhile, think *logically*. First, how old is your Larissa?"

"She will be nineteen next spring."

"She is still a young girl. For the first time in her life she is free from parental control. Going for a midnight drive with *two* men of royal blood would seem like a lark for a young girl. Don't be a fool and kill yourself with jealousy. Would a nice young girl, properly brought up, deeply in love with her young husband do anything so stupid as to allow two known *pederasts* to do anything improper with her? Where is your respect for your bride? Think of it! I bet you ten gold rubles, you will realize how stupid you are!"

"You don't understand—"

Egórov interrupted. "Let's go!"

Annoyed with one another, they walked toward the waiting Voisin, its nose already into the wind.

The object of the mission was the destruction of a railroad junction in enemy territory. The Austro-Hungarians had been moving their reserves closer to the front line. The enemy was preparing for an offensive.

Egórov was the leader of a three-airplane group.

The mechanics completed attaching four small caliber bombs to a special rack on the side of the nacelle. Platonov and his observer were already waiting in their craft as were Klembovsky and his observer.

Egórov gave the signal to start the engines and within minutes the three airplanes were up in the air.

Their course was northwest over the familiar Russian fortifications that were still visible in the autumnal evening. Then, crossing the front line, they would go north, toward the railroad junction.

Andrei made an effort to dismiss Larissa's letter from his mind and concentrate on the task ahead. He had no experience in dropping bombs aside from some practice with sandbags at Gátchina. Now, for the first time he was to release live bombs from a low altitude.

He felt nervous. He went over in his mind what had to be done: estimate wind velocity, the speed of the airplane, and altitude to make sure that the bombs hit their target. Theoretically, each bomb had to follow another like the dots in an ellipses, and all this must be done while flying into anti-aircraft fire. Those infamous Archies! There was no way of avoiding their murderous gray puffs. One had to ignore them, pray for good luck, and fly through.

Andrei turned his head toward Egórov and pointed down. They were crossing the front line. Egórov nodded. They knew there soon would be two or three bursts of red or white rockets in the dark sky as enemy ground troops signaled their air command of the approach of Russian planes.

In about ten more minutes they should be over their target, Andrei thought, his mouth dry. The landscape below was camouflaged by the night, as if the sky had spread its ink-black mantle over the land to hide it. It felt preternatural to fly through the void toward nothingness, surrounded by nothingness.

Egórov began his descent to a bombing altitude. Andrei hoped that the wingmen saw his maneuver and would follow. "Who had the asinine idea that bombing could be done in the dark? How in the hell can anyone see anything?" he thought, full of resentment.

As if in answer, the clouds parted and a moon, almost full, lazily floated into the sky.

He could see the curvaceous river, some buildings, and clusters of woods below. They were approaching their target.

Egórov raised his arm in a signal. Andrei pulled one bomb out of its rack and made it ready. He was calm now.

The anti-aircraft batteries crews had also benefited from the emergence of the moon. An immediate barrage of shrapnel surrounded the Russian airplanes, and deafening explosions filled the air.

A wedge of fierce light sliced the sky, then another one, then still another one. They united in a single spot, catching and following the planes in their brutal illumination. The searchlight blinded Andrei for a few seconds, but it also allowed him to see the silvery web of rails down below. The Voisin was over the target.

Egórov sharply jerked his arm down and Andrei let the first bomb go, followed immediately by another. Two explosions indicated that the bombs had hit the target. A momentary blast of hot air surrounded the plane.

Egórov touched Andrei's shoulder and grinned, "Well done!" he yelled. He pulled the plane up and out of the way to let his wingmen make their drops, while he maneuvered for his second approach.

Andrei could see the explosions from the bombs of the wingmen. "They got it!" he thought.

The barrage of the Archies seemed to subside. "Did the boys hit the battery?" Andrei wondered as he pulled the next bomb out of its rack. "Oh, I hope so!"

Egórov was descending again. Andrei waited, ready for the signal to toss the next load. Down came Egórov's arm and Andrei tossed another bomb. But something was wrong: the bomb did not go straight down. It wedged itself among the struts and wires supporting the wheels of their Voisin.

Andrei was seized with a debilitating terror. He saw Egórov look down, the pilot's face contorting as he saw the rogue bomb. Egórov rocked the Voisin wings violently trying to dislodge it.

Platonov and Klembovsky saw his unusual action and knew something was wrong. They took their positions on each side of the endangered Voisin. They also had problems: the left wing of Platonov's machine was severely damaged, and Klembovsky's observer was seriously wounded. He was slumped in his seat, perhaps already dead.

Egórov motioned the wingmen to take the course south, back to home base. He banked the plane sharply again, hoping that it would cut loose the bomb, but without success.

Andrei instinctively knew that it was up to him now. He swung one leg over the edge of the cockpit, bumping his forehead on the inverted V of the radiator. Balancing on one leg over the lower wing, he grabbed the strut supporting the upper wing and brought his other leg down.

He was standing on the wing, clinging to the strut for support. A few feet below him was the bomb.

Egórov, his face tense, flew as straight as possible, praying that there would be no sudden blast of wind, or, God forbid, an enemy aircraft.

The wingmen understood that something horrific must have happened. They could not see the bomb, but they saw Andrei on the wing and watched him helplessly, expecting any moment to see him plunge to his death.

Andrei stood motionless, trying to acclimate himself to the rush of freezing wind that threatened to tear him off the wing. The cold air invaded his lungs, making breathing difficult. Slowly, he shuffled his legs into a better position. He was not thinking of what he was doing or what he must do next. His actions were strictly instinctive.

Slowly, *very slowly,* Andrei lowered himself down into a squatting position, clutching the strut with one hand and probing along the wing with the other.

Egórov was flying low now, just above the tree line. They were close to Russian territory, but another danger loomed ahead. Egórov feared that, in the darkness, Russian infantry in the trenches might mistake them for an Austrian patrol and open fire.

Andrei slowly changed his squatting position to a prone one. He probed with his feet, very slowly, along the wing surface until he felt some wires. He braced his feet against that support. Clutching tightly to the strut and the edge of the wing Andrei began to change his position until he was lying stretched across the wing, his head hanging down. He could see the bomb. He pulled himself further toward the edge of the wing. He could just reach the bomb, but his leather gloves were too thick for the delicate operation.

By increments of millimeters, he raised his left hand to his mouth and with his teeth began to remove the glove. The wind was furious. It attacked him, pulling his hand away from his face, numbing his cheeks and lips, ripping off his scarf, threatening to tear off his goggles.

It was a tedious process trying to take off the glove, but Andrei's mind was empty of thoughts and he had no sense of time. With one glove finally removed, Andrei was exhausted. "I should rest," flashed through his mind, but his body rejected the thought. He was prostrate atop the wing, holding tight to the strut with his right hand, inching his left hand along the wing, toward the wedged bomb. The wind attacked him mercilessly, freezing his bare hand into a useless appendage.

Andrei was becoming hypothermic, though he was not aware of it. He moved his hand slowly along the wing until he reached the vertical wires that imprisoned the bomb. He tried to dislodge it, but his frozen fingers disobeyed him. He stuck them into his mouth as he used to do when he was a boy with hands frozen from building a snowman. The wind whistled past, and it sounded to Andrei as if it were laughing at his feeble attempts.

Doggedly, Andrei resumed his attempts to free the bomb. Finally, he felt a slight movement under his fingers. He held his breath. With a surge of adrenaline, he wiggled the bomb out of its trap. It plunged straight down, exploding on contact with the ground.

Andrei was exhausted, freezing. He cleaved desperately to the wing and the strut, his grave situation becoming obvious to him. He had no strength to climb back into the cockpit. He breathed shallowly with his mouth open, the vicious wind tearing at him, thrusting itself into his mouth and down to his lungs.

Egórov kept going, keeping the Voisin from tipping its wings. He prayed that Andrei had enough strength left to hold on.

The sun was up when they reached their base. The airfield was already alerted by a telephone call from an infantry unit that a group of Russian planes had been seen carrying a man on the wing.

A siren's high-pitched whine sent pilots scrambling to their machines. Medical unit men rushed out with stretchers, not knowing what kind of emergency it was but ready for anything. As the planes approached the airfield, the ground crew saw Andrei prone on the wing of the leading Voisin.

Egórov landed gently in the middle of a grassy meadow next to the bumpy runways, and rolled to a stop. Kozakov and a crowd of pilots raced toward the plane.

It took them a couple of minutes to unbend Andrei's frozen fingers from his grasp of the strut and the edge of the wing. He seemed unaware of anything around him. Pilots lifted him off the wing and placed him on a stretcher. At a trot they carried him to the field hospital, the elderly doctor hurrying behind.

In half an hour Egórov, Platonov, Klembovsky and Mironov, the young Cossack observer, were in the briefing room. The room was full of their brothers-in-arms, all waiting to hear the horrific story. Kozakov entered, smiling widely, his cheekbones looking more prominent than ever. "Our new hero is going to be fine. He is badly bruised and battered, and he is hypothermic and exhausted. Otherwise he is all right. The doctor has medicated him, surrounded him with hot water bags and swaddled him in blankets, so he looks like a mummy," Kozakov chuckled. "I think he is aware that he is home, but so far he has not talked. We will not ask him any questions for a while, but of course, this doesn't apply to you. So, Egórov, start from the beginning, what happened?"

When Egórov and then Platonov and Klembovsky finished their oral reports, Kozakov requested written reports as well. "There has never been such a thing as someone climbing out of the plane *while flying*, and surviving," he said. "It is not only the bravery of Lieutenant Rezánov we are facing here, but we also are verifying the abilities of our aircraft. There are many lessons that we can learn from this episode. I want it described in minute detail in your reports. You will be excused today from further missions. Start writing!"

Andrei dozed, his body occasionally shaken by spasms in his hands, arms, and legs. He was unaware of his surroundings, but the sensations of warmth and comfort were pleasant. He felt as if he were a tiny child in his cozy and clean little bed. There were kind people around him, who moved and talked quietly. Andrei felt that he was safe with them.

He finally drifted into sleep but it was not a restorative sleep. He was back on the wing of the Voisin. The plane was diving into a void, and his hands had nothing to cling to. He must have screamed. The doctor was instantly there with soothing words, warm hands, and something bitter to drink.

He heard the loud sounds of engines as airplanes were taking off or landing, and little by little he regained his awareness. He recognized the doctor, silver-headed and bearded Colonel Barsky. Andrei realized now that he was at the airfield hospital. He did not want to think of *why* he was there. He *knew* why, but he was not going to think of it. Yet, his mind was bringing back to him the ferocious wind, the icy surface of the wing, the bottomless void under him, and the terror he must have had but did not realize at the time. There was something else, even more disturbing. Something else that he had forbidden himself to think about. It was Larissa's letter.

Kozakov and several pilots visited Andrei after the funeral for Klembovsky's observer. They were in a subdued mood. The death of a comrade was always a reminder of one's own mortality. Among the aviation community it was almost a daily occurrence; Klembovsky's observer was simply the most recent one. A new grave was added to the ever-growing cemetery behind the service tents.

Following tradition, the carpenters made a cross out of propeller blades and then stenciled the dead pilot's name on it.

Kozakov wanted to boost his men's morale. "We must celebrate Rezánov's daring act," he thought. He was going to elevate Andrei's achievement to new heights: there would be stories in the newspapers with Andrei's photographs, and a special celebration when he would be awarded the Order of St. George and perhaps even a personal letter of congratulations from the Tsar. Kozakov would make Andrei into a national hero, like Nesterov. It would be good for the morale of everybody.

"Well, how do you feel, Andrúsha?" he asked, calling Andrei by his diminutive name.

"Much better, Captain, thank you. They have finally thawed me," Andrei smiled crookedly, his face hurting from the windburn.

"Do you need anything?"

"No, sir. Dr. Barsky and his staff are very kind ..."

"Well, good. You rest. Don't worry about anything. I'll check on you tonight."

"Thank you, Captain."

Kozakov left. He had to write a letter of condolence to the family of the fallen pilot, a grim duty that he hated.

The pilots moved several chairs closer to the bed. They were *dying* to ask Andrei about his ordeal but felt shy in the somber ambiance of a hospital..

Finally one of them, Junior Lieutenant Mischa Korobov, volunteered, "I would have *peed* my pants if I had to climb out on that wing!" The pilots roared with laughter. The ice was broken.

"Vaska Egórov thought that he was having a bad dream, seeing you climb out," said another pilot.

"He probably thought that you went crazy!" someone cried.

"Were you scared?" someone else asked.

"Were you airsick, standing there on that wing?" asked Korobov.

"Yes, he was airsick and he threw up all over the Austrians!" laughed another pilot. The men howled. Andrei laughed weakly with them. "I wanted to pee on them from up there, but my hands were grabbing the struts and I could not unbutton my pants," he said. The pilots loved it.

Dr. Barsky entered and the pilots jumped to attention.

"At ease," he said, looking at their young faces. Some of them had been his patients already; the others, sooner or later, would be his patients, unless of course, they would be dead. The old doctor passionately hated the war and what it was doing to a whole generation of young men. He had paid heavily for that war: his own two sons were among the dead.

"You had better go now, gentlemen, and let the Lieutenant gather his strength. He'll be back at his billets tomorrow, so you'll have plenty of time to talk to him."

"Yes, sir," they saluted and one by one left the room.

Andrei closed his eyes. He was exhausted.

"Good," the doctor said. "You rest now."

Andrei awoke in the middle of the night. He sat up, holding tight to the edges of the bed. For a moment, he thought that he was still on the wing, but there was no vicious wind and he was warm.

His body hurt all over. Andrei tried to stand, groping the floor near the bed with his feet as he had done on the wing. Every move was painful, but he was fully awake now. "I am at the hospital," he told himself. He fell back into the bed.

He tried to gather his thoughts. Now that he felt safe, he did not want to think about his ordeal. He knew that he would be talking about it for many days to come. Besides, he had something more important to think about: Larissa's letter.

"Where is it?" He recalled that he had crumpled it and shoved it into his pocket, but where were his clothes? Could it be that the orderlies emptied his pockets when they undressed him? Had they thrown out that wrinkled ball of paper?

He groped around the night table next to his bed until he touched a bell. He rang, and a sleepy orderly appeared shortly, a lantern in his hands.

"What can I do for you, Lieutenant?"

"Do you know where they put my clothes?"

"No, sir. You can't leave here until the doctor permits," the soldier said firmly.

"I am not trying to get out. I want something I had in my pocket. It is a letter from back home. Could you bring it to me?"

"Oh, of course, Lieutenant! Right away!"

Andrei gave a sigh of relief. "Before you go, can you help me to go to the toilet? I am wobbly, and I don't know where it is," he explained, feeling embarrassed.

"Certainly, Lieutenant." The soldier helped Andrei to his feet, placed a robe around his shoulders and slippers on his feet, then supporting him with an arm around his waist, the orderly led Andrei to the toilet. "The fellows around the base say that you are a hero, Lieutenant. No one can believe that a man could ride on the wing of the airplane!"

"I had no choice," Andrei said. "Please hurry, I must pee."

"Sorry, Lieutenant, down the corridor, just a few steps. I'll wait at the door."

"Thank you."

With a great feeling of relief, Andrei allowed the orderly to lead him back to his room. "All right my friend, now please go and get me my letter."

"Right away, Lieutenant."

In a few minutes, he was back. "There was no letter, sir; only your wallet, a cigarette case and a lighter. There were broken biscuit crumbs in your other pocket and some crumbled paper. Nothing else." He put the items from Andrei's pockets on the night table.

"What did you do with the crumbled paper?" Andrei cried.

"Nothing sir. I just threw it in a waste basket with the crumbs."

Andrei took a deep breath, which hurt his chest. "Please, go back and get that crumbled paper for me. It was the letter."

"Sorry, Lieutenant … I did not know …" The soldier hurried out.

"Good Lord, let me have her letter!" Andrei prayed. Nothing was more important to him at that moment than to have Larissa's letter in his hands.

"Is that it?" The orderly was holding a ball of paper in his hand.

"Yes, yes, give it to me! Thank you! Leave the lantern here," Andrei said. "What's your name?"

"Grigory, sir."

Andrei reached for his wallet and took out a ruble. "Here, Grigory. Thank you for your help."

Grigory shook his head. "No, Lieutenant. I am honored to help the hero. If I survive the war, I'll be telling my children that I knew you!" He saluted and left the room.

Andrei smoothed out the letter on his knees and began to read. The more he read, the more he saw the wisdom of Egórov's opinion: Larissa was still an immature girl, enjoying sudden privileges of adulthood that had never been allowed to her before. He was a fool being jealous. If there were anything improper between her and the two royal playboys, she wouldn't have written to him so innocently. She, like any woman, would have kept quiet about it.

But ... He imagined Larissa riding in the luxurious automobile, laughing, a glass of champagne in her hand, and two handsome royal men vying for her attention. He could not stand it. He crumbled the letter again. "I almost died 'for my Tsar and my country', God damn it, while those royal scoundrels are safe in Petrograd, drinking champagne and taking midnight drives with *my* wife!" he thought, full of toxic fury again.

Next morning Dr. Barsky allowed Andrei to return to his billet on condition that he would stay in bed for two days.

Andrei's friends came to collect him. Klembovsky, whose turn it was to sleep in the 'baronial bed,' surrendered the bed to Andrei. "You are our hero and the bed is yours!" he declared. The others agreed.

"No, no, I cannot accept it. I am not wounded," Andrei protested.

"But you are 'recuperating,'" Egórov said. "When the doctor releases you, we shall draw lots for the bed again. Agreed?"

"Agreed," the pilots declared.

Egórov drove Andrei to their quarters in the carriage of a three-wheeled motorcycle, the other two pilots perched behind. Egórov proceeded with a victory ride around the airfield, yelling "*Vivat* to our hero!" The pilots around the planes hooted and yelled "*Vivat!*" The aircraft crews, mechanics, anti-aircraft battery crews, and the kitchen staff greeted them with the shouts of "*Vivat!*" throwing their caps in the air.

Andrei was embarrassed. He wiggled himself deeper into his seat, pulling his head into the collar of his leather flight jacket as if he were a turtle.

"Come on, Vaska, don't do that to me!" he shouted to Egórov over the noise of the motorcycle.

Egórov ignored him. He took another tour around the field and finally brought the motorcycle to the massive doors of their quarters.

They helped Andrei inside and deposited him on the baronial bed. Egórov glanced at his young friend surreptitiously. "We had better go, fellows. Let our Andrúshka rest, as he is supposed to," he said to the others.

"No. Wait. I want to talk to you, Vaska!" Andrei said quickly. "Please, stay."

"We'll go to the mess," Platonov said. "See you later."

"Well, what did you want to talk to me about?" Egórov knew perfectly well what it was about.

"It is about Larissa. What you told me before makes sense, but I can't help getting upset by imagining her with those men, enjoying herself, drinking and …"

"Let me see that letter," Egórov interrupted him calmly.

Andrei proffered him the crumpled letter. Egórov pulled a chair to the window and began to read. Andrei watched him anxiously, trying to guess his impression, but Egórov's face was inscrutable.

Finally, he put the letter down. "It is a lovely letter from a young woman who adores and misses her husband. She wants to amuse her husband, to tell him about what's going on, while he is away. For God's sake, she met Rasputin! It is a fantastic story!" he exclaimed. "You are a lucky man, Andrúshka."

"What about the Grand Duke and the Prince? She went riding with them! At night! She might have been *drunk!*"

Egórov looked at Andrei for a moment, and then said in a dry voice, "So, you say, her letter made you angry. You are jealous. Let me tell you about *my* wife." He stood and pulled a chair to the bed.

"Tatiana is what they call 'gorgeous,' and I fell for her the moment I laid my eyes on her. She was a singer at the Cabaret *Letuchaya Mysh*. Perhaps you know the place."

"I have been there only once, but it was lots of fun."

"Yes. It was always full of fun. Well, Tatiana was their leading *chanteuse*. My regiment was quartered in Petersburg, so whenever I was off duty I was at the Cabaret, ogling her. Soon she noticed me and started coming to my table. I knew that she was not a lady, but it did not matter to me. I was smitten by her. I knew that she was being kept by some rich old man, a merchant of some sort. Perhaps she was sleeping around as well, but it did not matter to me. I wanted her! And it wasn't as difficult as I had imagined. I did not need to court her, all I had to do was to invite her for a ride to the islands in a hired carriage, after which she went to my flat."

As he said it he noticed that Andrei blanched. "I am a fool! Why did I mention the *ride?*" Egórov thought, but he continued, "So, Tatiana and I became lovers. God, oh God, I had never thought that fucking could be so fantastic! I did have women before, of course, at Madam Elsa's, when I could afford it, but it had never been as great as it was with Tatiana. At one time I asked her, where she learned all those tricks, and she answered, quite honestly, that a French whore in Paris had taught her everything! Apparently, her 'protector,' the old man, took her to Paris so that she could learn *'how to please a man'*, as she called it!" Egórov snorted sarcastically. "It should have been a warning for me, but it wasn't. I truly loved her, God knows why. She certainly was not an interesting woman. She was crudely opinionated about everything, but she knew nothing. She read only cheap novels, 'chambermaid literature.' But it did not matter to me. All I wanted was to make love to her and she was superb at that. Then, one day she announced that she was pregnant and that I was the one who had placed her in that condition. She cried and threatened to kill herself. She had said that she loved me, and I was the only one for her. Well, I believed her. Like the fool that I was, I said that I would marry her. At that time I had already finished my fighter pilot training and had my wings. She was excited about it. She was proud of me. The war had just started and I was about to be assigned to the front. Well, Tatiana moved in with me and we were married. I worried of course, how I could afford to have a wife and a child on my lieutenant's salary, but within a week, Tatiana announced that there would be no child: she had had a miscarriage while I was away. She showed me her pantaloons with the streaks of blood. Like a fool, I believed her. I think of it now and I can't believe that I was such an idiot!" Egórov laughed bitterly, shaking his head.

Andrei watched his friend with compassion. He could not comprehend how such a sophisticated man could have been so foolish. "So, what happened?" he prodded.

"Well, I was sent to the front and began to post my money to her. I missed her terribly, and I waited for her letters, ignoring her non-existent grammar. Soon I heard from a friend, an officer from my former regiment who did not know that I had been married to Tatiana. He wrote about some news and mentioned that Tatiana had returned to the Cabaret and was sleeping around. He mentioned that he had been lucky enough to be on her list. I wouldn't believe it. It was just gossip, I told myself. When I was wounded and sent to the hospital in Petersburg, she came to visit me a couple of times, dressed in the latest fashion, wearing a diamond brooch. I did not ask her about the brooch. I told myself that she must have had it before we were married. I was afraid to ask. Anyway, just before I was released from the hospital, she came to see me again. She told me that she was going to be a cinema actress. She had met someone who was making films and he had offered her a part. She was going to be famous. She had already given up our flat and rented a better one, near the Nevsky Prospect. She gave me her new address so I could send her money. We parted rather coldly: she was late for a rehearsal, and I was too stunned to say anything. The rest you know."

Andrei did not know what to say. Egórov studied his face for a moment and then said quietly, "One thing I can tell you Andrúsha, don't destroy your and Larissa's happiness by some stupid jealousy. Larissa loves you! I envy you that kind of love." He paused and inhaled deeply. "I bet, you have your own intimate proofs of her love, deep in your heart." he continued. "Think of it and you'll realize how stupid you were." With a crooked smile, he stood and left the room.

Andrei felt tears welling in his eyes. He saw in his mind's eye again how Larissa, her hair wild, had run after his train. He thought of how lovingly she gave herself to him for the first time and how passionately she loved him during those four short days. He felt ashamed of himself for thinking badly of her.

He was going to write Larissa a long, long letter, telling her how much he loved her. He was going to write to all of them, however, not about the bomb. He was not going to tell them about it. Perhaps he would write about it to his father and beg him to keep it a secret from the women. His father would understand.

He closed his eyes and finally relaxed. He was very lucky, he thought. *His woman loved him!*

❧ 19 ❧

Despite Andrei's attempt to protect the women of his family from the knowledge of his nearly fatal experience, it became known throughout the country. Within days, Andrei's photograph appeared in every newspaper in Russia and even in the Allied press. Florid descriptions of his heroic deed, accompanied by dramatic drawings of him on the wing of an airplane, excited the imaginations of millions. Since there were no photographs of Andrei on the wing, the artists went wild with their own renditions of the story. In some drawings he was depicted hanging under the airplane holding on to the wing with one hand, with a smoking bomb in another.

Andrei was quickly awarded the Order of St. George accompanied by a letter of commendation from the Tsar.

General Rezánov received a letter from the Tsar as well, congratulating him upon his son's bravery. Andrei's mother was rewarded by a sweet letter from the Dowager Empress, saying that it takes an honorable family to raise such an honorable young man.

The country was seized in hysterical adulation. It took no more than a week for the name 'Andrei' to become the most popular name given to newborn males. His photographs were printed as postal cards, along with those of famous singers and ballerinas. The merchants who had made his clothes or equipped his horses placed his picture on their walls with hastily made plaques proclaiming their establishments to be "The Suppliers of Lieutenant Andrei Rezánov."

The country torn by one military defeat after another, by the unsteady government and ugly rumors about the Imperial family, needed a hero, and Andrei Rezánov seemed to fill that need.

Andrei felt embarrassed before his comrades-at-arms about that adulation. Some, undoubtedly envious, teased him about it mercilessly, while the others defended him, knowing that he was not guilty of self-promotion. Tension arose between the two groups. Kozakov began to think that perhaps it was not such a good idea to publicize Andrei's heroic deed.

Larissa was torn between admiration for her husband and debilitating fear for his life. She prayed for his safety, knowing that each day could be his last. She became ill after reading in the newspapers about his ordeal. "Why didn't he write me about it?" she complained to her mother, choking with tears.

"You know why. He didn't want to worry you. He did not write about it to his mother, either. Be reasonable."

Larissa was beyond reason. She couldn't eat, could barely sleep, and when she did sleep, she was tormented by nightmares about Andrei.

Maria Nikoláyevna decided to act. Before going to bed, she called Larissa into her room. "I think, dear, that you are not doing too well being a 'straw widow.' I don't blame you. I was that way myself, when I was a young wife and my husband was fighting somewhere. But I had you and Peter. I couldn't afford to cry. I had to appear cheerful for your sake. But here, with you and Andrei, I think there may be a practical solution." She paused. Larissa waited.

"What if you enroll in the Red Cross nursing courses? What if you seriously study nursing as a profession? What if you become a *nurse* and not just a volunteer rolling bandages while gossiping? If you become a nurse, you can go to the front yourself. With our connections, I am sure we could place you in the field hospital near Andrei's aviation unit. What do you think of it?"

"Mama, it's a brilliant idea!" Lara cried. "And, you will let me go to the front?"

"I will hate it. I have lost a son at the front, and I lost my brothers and my father in the previous war, but we are a *military* family, Lara. All of us, the Orlovs and the Rezánovs. Losing sons and husbands, brothers and fathers, is our mutual bitter lot to bear. It has been so for generations. And it will continue, for as long as there are wars. Watching you suffer tears out my heart. But I know that if you and Andrei are together, or at least, *close* to each other, it will make *your* lives more tolerable. I am willing to take a chance for the sake of your happiness, if you think that you can do it!"

"Mama ... you understand everything!" Lara clasped her mother in her arms. "I'll do it!" she exclaimed, her eyes shiny.

"You have a jewel of a wife!" Egórov cried when Andrei told him that Larissa had enrolled in nursing training. "What woman of our class would ever think of *actual* nursing, taking care of ordinary soldiers, working with their blood and piss and shit? Sure, your mother and the other ladies volunteer to roll bandages, but I bet they don't *wash* those bandages. No! Their *servants* wash them. But your girl is different! I take my hat off to your wife!"

"Larissa writes that it was her mother's idea. I can't imagine why Maria Nikoláyevna is allowing Larissa to go to the front! She lost her son a few months ago, about the same time that her husband died of a heart attack. Why would she allow Larissa to go to the front? Larissa is the only one left for her!"

"It's for *you,* you fool! It is because they love you and probably think that you need Larissa so much that they are ready to sacrifice their own lives *for you,* you lucky prick!"

Andrei had nothing to say to his friend's argument.

December had arrived at the front near Lutsk with crisp and sunny weather. There was not much snow, and the planes were not yet fitted with skis. The threat of the Austro-Hungarian offensive still hung in the air, and the pilots were flying reconnaissance missions several times a day taking advantage of the clear weather.

Despite his celebrity status, Andrei was still a pilot of the First Combat Air Detachment, and he had to fly, too. However, one of the rewards of Andrei's new popularity was that Kozakov had allowed him to fly a Nieuport XI fighter, nicknamed *Bébé*.

Kozakov had misgivings about it. Not that he doubted Andrei's ability as a pilot; he was tormented about sending him into the cauldron of action. He liked the young man. He wanted him to stay alive. "Perhaps we can send him back to Gátchina and make him an instructor," he thought. "But of course, the boy would consider it an insult. He wants to be an ace! Besides, the High Command would never permit it. We've made Rezánov a *hero*. His life is not his own anymore." He pondered the problem. Then, a new idea came to his mind. "What if we recommend him for the *Advanced Flight School of Aerobatics*?" Kozakov thought. "The High Command would presume that we are trying to *boost* Rezánov's flying expertise with aerobatics. They might like the idea," Kozakov thought as he walked toward his Nieuport, pulling on his new tight gloves.

The pilots were finally issued winter flight suits, helmets and gloves, all lined with fur and warm leg coverings. A general from the High Command had taken a ride in a Voisin at 12,000 feet and then responded to the pilots' numerous requests for winter flight clothing.

Two dozen pilots were getting ready to go on patrols. Kozakov watched them. Biting winter air was filled with the smell of fuel and the noise of engines as the airplanes taxied to the runway and one by one soared into the pale sky of early morning. Finally, he gave a signal to his own patrol group and climbed into his Nieuport. His men followed.

Andrei's nerves were tight, but not by fear. He was exuberant. He was flying as a wingman with *Kozakov*, in a fighter plane! The mission was to fly at a low altitude and strafe the concentrations of enemy transports and troops as they moved toward the front lines.

Some pilots liked strafing missions. Flying so low that they could see the terror on the faces of the men, the pilots would be out of reach before the enemy could return fire.

A few sensitive flyers hated strafing. They dreaded seeing the distorted faces of the foot soldiers, who would throw themselves on the ground as if trying to disappear in it, as a stream of bullets rained on them and ripped their flesh apart. Those faces haunted the pilots' dreams.

Andrei was one of that small group. His colleagues were undisturbed by '*seeing the faces*,' as Andrei called it. They considered strafing an easy sport. He could predict Egórov's reaction should he confide his distaste for strafing. Egórov would probably ask, "How do you feel about *'seeing the face'* of an enemy pilot with whom you had been *dueling?*" "That's the point," Andrei would counter, "You've been dueling! That means placing myself in *equal* danger. While strafing I am relatively safe. It makes me a mass murderer, killing people who can't defend themselves."

That imagined conversation bothered Andrei. Ever since his traumatic experience with the bomb, he had become more critical toward many aspects of his life. Thanks to Egórov's interpretation of Larissa's letter and the revelations about his own life, Andrei was able to squelch his nascent feelings of jealousy. But new and even more disturbing sensibilities replaced his previous mental torment. Andrei did not want to discuss it even with Egórov, but he had lost his feeling of invincibility and developed instead some bitterly fatalistic attitude. The ever-expanding cemetery behind the tents of the aerodrome was a grim reminder that only pure luck thwarted the horrors that awaited him with every mission.

Despite the sobering thoughts that clogged Andrei's mind, he was still in love with flying, even more so now that Kozakov had finally allowed him to fly scout missions with Egórov, each of them in the single-seater Nieuport Bébé.

Egórov took time to explain to Andrei his method of attack in a one-seater. "I like to meet the enemy head on. I fly in the same direction, but of course, I'll try to be much, much higher. As I fly above him, I make a rapid wingover and dive, still going in the same direction." He demonstrated the maneuver with his hands. "If it the enemy is a two-seater, the gunner has to swing his gun all the way around before he can fire at me, and that gives me a few seconds to fire at him at very close range. As soon as he has turned his gun, I sideslip and fall below him."

"What about the danger of colliding with him during your wingover?"

"Only if I am too close. The two-seater is much slower, so I can always escape from the reach of the gunner."

"What about fighting single-seaters?"

"Oh, that's my favorite. It is more sporty. We both have only forward shooting guns, so our fight is basically in *outmaneuvering* one another. And, that's where the fun is! One time, a German pilot and I were flying almost side by side, as if we were one another's wingman. He attacked me. We both were good, but I felt that he had an advantage over me: I was on my way home and I was low on fuel. I knew that I could not fight for long. So, there we were, both trying to gain altitude, both climbing or diving, banking and doing all kinds of acrobatics, exchanging a few shots whenever one of us had a better position, until I knew that I had to quit. I had barely enough fuel to get home. Suddenly, I saw the German wigging his wings, and with a salute, diving steeply down. Apparently, the chap was also low on fuel!" Egórov laughed. "Of course, it was in the beginning of the war, while we still believed in chivalry. Nowadays, instead of saluting, he probably would have shot my head off with his hand gun!"

They walked to the field where the mechanics prepared the planes for the mission. It was to be their fourth mission as a team. So far, they had not been able to advance their score of confirmed kills. Egórov was indifferent, but Andrei was impatient to fight.

The odors of the aerodrome assaulted Andrei. Castor oil, used for lubrication, revolted him, reminding him of his childhood illnesses. However, the overwhelming smell of gasoline he found somehow exhilarating. The planes, mostly several models of Nieuports, a couple of new Spads, and slow, but still efficient Voisins, were lined up wing to wing at a slight angle to the runway.

The mechanics primed the machines, and the engines snorted. The planes throbbed as if alive, eager to spring forward, impatient to be in the crisp blue sky. The pilots waited, ready to board their craft.

One by one the mechanics stepped back from the planes, and for a moment the field grew quiet.

The pilots climbed into their deep cockpits, with only their heads protruding. Once again the mechanics crowded around the aircraft. They twirled the propellers and, as the engines caught on, pulled the chocks that were holding the wheels. Two soldiers held the tails of each machine slightly elevated to prevent it from 'plowing' the ground as the pilots taxied for lift-off, while two more soldiers held on to the wings, turning the planes to the starting positions on the runway.

Small pebbles and sand disturbed by wind from the propellers danced under the planes. The crews released their holds and the planes taxied to the starting positions. One after another, gaining speed with every second, the airplanes lifted into the wind.

The sun was slowly overtaking the horizon. Another day of fighting was about to begin.

Andrei and Egórov, flying side by side, watched the sky. Two large groups of enemy aircraft had been seen moving along the front line. Was the enemy patrol the forerunner of the anticipated advance? Or—was it the first wave of the advance itself? Everyone's nerves were tight.

Egórov gave his machine gun a two-second-burst to check it. Andrei did the same. Both guns fired perfectly.

The sky was crowded with thin feathery clouds, their edges touched with the pink of sunrise. The wind was murderous at 9,000 feet. Andrei tugged at his scarf to cover his nose and chin. He had heard that the engineers at the Dux Aircraft factory in Moscow were designing an airplane with an enclosed cockpit. He hoped that it was true.

He glanced at the ground below. It was a tight mass of evergreen trees under a thin cover of the first snow that looked to Andrei as if it were bunches of broccoli sprinkled with grated cheese.

Egórov rocked his Nieuport gently and zoomed upward, toward a bank of clouds. Andrei followed. Forget the broccoli, he thought. It is time to hunt for the enemy.

The enemy was there, stacked behind the clouds, as if waiting for them. There were three of them, the Albatroses, flying in tight formation, the black medieval crosses on their wings sharply outlined, the sun behind them. They saw the Russians and, having the advantage of the sun and altitude, instantly attacked.

The words of Kozakov flashed through Andrei's mind: *the best defense is offense!* He quickly went into a roll and then started to climb as fast as his Nieuport would take him. He briefly saw Egórov coming out of a loop and pursuing an Albatros that looked like a falcon in flight.

Andrei had two planes to deal with: one below him, bumping a pattern of tracing bullet holes into Andrei's machine. He could see splinters of wood and shreds of linen from his wings floating in the air. The other plane was in his sights. Andrei gave it a full blast from his machine gun as he felt a sudden sharp pain high in his right thigh. "Am I hit?" he reflected. He pressed the trigger again and saw the plane ahead of him bursting in a ball of brilliant fire. He had hit the fuel tank.

For a moment, Andrei was blinded. In moments the Albatros was falling in a plume of black smoke and fire. Andrei banked sharply and started to climb. He could not see his second attacker. He searched the sky for Egórov, but his vision was blurred.

Andrei touched his thigh and his glove came away smeared with blood. "Dear God, don't let me bleed to death …" he prayed as he pulled off his scarf and tried to wrap it around his thigh, using his hand to apply pressure, trying to stop the flow of blood.

"Where is that Albatros?" he searched the sky with his watering eyes. The sun was behind him. He was in an advantageous position for an attack. Where was that damned Albatros? He started to climb again. "Ah, there he is, the Albatros! Is it the same one? No, that one exploded …"Andrei was confused, his mind getting cloudy. He fired his machine gun at the second Albatros, but maybe he did not. He wasn't sure. Maybe there was no Albatros … He suddenly felt that he was out of his body. He felt like he had when he was on the wing of the Voisin.

His Nieuport was losing altitude. Through the veil of diminishing consciousness Andrei was vaguely aware that he must land … Right away … Land … Somewhere … Fast … *"Aim for the trees …"* came Captain Rublev's voice in his mind. *"The trees will support the wings and may prevent the plane from crashing."*

He could not see any trees. *There is only broccoli,* he thought. He could not see anything at all. He had slipped out of consciousness. Blood was seeping through his scarf.

Andrei's airplane crashed over Russian barbwire defense fortifications. It became entangled, its tail up in the air. Andrei's limp body hung over the edge of the cockpit, still attached to the plane by the seatbelt, dripping blood onto the dark soil.

Egórov saw Andrei's plane streaking to the ground. Furiously, he attacked the Albatros that had shot down his friend, but the enemy pilot was as sagacious as he. They battled one another with acrobatic skills, banking and looping, diving and soaring, rolling and stalling, until Egórov gained a brief advantage, hanging on the tail of the Albatros. With hate bursting his heart he emptied the entire drum of his machine gun. He saw the pilot sag, and the Albatros began its final descent, turning and turning in a falling leaf pattern. There was no sight of the third Albatros. Egórov did not care to search for him. He pummeled his bullet-ridden Nieuport with his fists, yelling obscenities and letting tears blur his vision. Finally he took control of his emotions and urged his wounded aircraft toward home base.

He landed roughly and rushed to the telephone shack. By now the infantry unit should have already notified the Air Detachment about Andrei, he thought.

"Lieutenant Rezánov is alive," the sergeant on duty yelled the moment he saw Egórov running from his plane. "They've just called. They also confirmed your two kills. Congratulations!"

Egórov was wild-eyed. "I need the motorcycle," he shouted. The sergeant quickly tossed him keys to the emergency machine. Egórov dashed out of the shack and leapt onto the saddle of the motorcycle as if it were a waiting horse.

He did not give a damn that he had achieved the magic number of confirmed victories. He was officially an ace now, but it failed to excite him. He raced along the road torn up by constant artillery barrages, paying no attention to the flashes from distant heavy guns.

20

Larissa did not want to attract attention to herself as the wife of a national hero. She registered for the Botkinsky Hospital Nursing Courses under her maiden name of Larissa Orlova. It was a long way from her house, and each day she took a *konka,* a horse-driven mass transportation wagon that wound its ways through the main districts of Petrograd. She could have used her mother's carriage, but the hospital was located in the poor section of the city, and she did not want to call attention to herself

A new world opened for her. Just by riding back and forth between the hospital and her home, she learned more about the mood of the city than by reading the newspapers or talking to her family and friends.

The mood of the city was explosive. She listened to the talk of her fellow-passengers, mostly factory workers and peasants, amazed at the freedom of their talk: no one seemed to be 'watching their tongue.' The traditional complaisance of the lower classes was gone, replaced by open discontent and hostility.

People blamed all calamities on the Tsaritza and the nobles. Larissa was dismayed by their unabashed hatred of the Tsaritza. They called her, "that German woman, *nemka,*" alluding to her German ancestry, saying that she was a German spy who was sending trainloads of food to Germany and caused famine in Russia. They called the Empress a slut and insisted that she slept with Rasputin. Larissa was surprised that they hated Rasputin as well. She thought that Rasputin, being a peasant, would be a hero to them. Instead, they blamed him, along with the nobles, for all the ills in the country. They called him the Antichrist, a false monk. They were saying that it was a *known fact* that the Germans paid Rasputin a million rubles every month. They prattled about wild orgies at the Winter Palace where Rasputin allegedly copulated with princesses and countesses, and even with the young Grand Duchesses. It was salacious talk, and the passengers savored it. The men guffawed, the women giggled, covering their mouths with their hands.

Larissa felt nervous among them. She did her best to blend with the crowd. She bought a cheap coat and felt boots, *válenki,* and she covered her head with a thick shawl and braided her hair in a single braid, in the peasant style. She looked like a young factory girl.

But Larissa was *not* a factory girl. She was offended by passengers who used crude language as naturally as Larissa and her friends used French. Many times she was tempted to object to some statement, but wisely resisted the temptation; her cultured Russian language would have given her away.

"Why am I afraid of them?" she asked herself. "They are good, God-fearing, Russian people. They are probably kind and full of simple wisdom, like in Tolstoy's novels. I shouldn't be afraid of them. I am not judging them. I would only like to correct some outrageous rumors," she kept telling herself. "But I won't. I must be only an observer."

There was much to observe from the slow-moving *konka:* long queues of poorly dressed people shivering in front of food stores, waiting for distribution of their ever-decreasing rations, tired, pale-faced and bedraggled women, many of them with small children, waiting in the snow for a loaf of bread.

Those were sad pictures of quiet desperation. Winter progressed, and severe storms brought more snow and misery to the exhausted people. Larissa noticed that the crowds were becoming more aggressive. They did not stand patiently in queues anymore, waiting for the stores to open, but gathered in large crowds shouting and pushing, even throwing stones and breaking windows.

Konka drivers whipped their horses to pass such crowds as quickly as the exhausted animals could make it, but one early morning the konka that Larissa was riding became involved in a dangerous incident.

The konka was approaching a small picturesque square buried under snow. It was tucked in the midst of a poor section of Petrograd and contained a miniscule cluster of trees. Four benches piled with puffy pillows of snow rested under the trees. The square was bordered by several small shops: a toy store, a Chinese laundry, a samovar repair shop, and a bakery, all of them still locked up so early in the morning.

"It must be a pleasant little island of tranquility during the summer," Larissa thought. But not that morning. That morning the shops' doors were torn off their hinges, their windows smashed, their contents scattered on the snow as dozens of men and women dashed around looting or destroying the shops.

The riot apparently had started at the bakery, but the destruction quickly spread to the other shops. Soon the snow was carpeted with shards of broken glass, torn papers, and pieces of broken furniture. Looters dashed between shops in a frenzy. Some carried doll houses, children's sleds, or toy bears, others embraced dented and broken samovars, or dragged shirts and pants from the laundry, hiding torn boxes of sweet rolls or loaves of bread under their coats. People fought each other for possession of a loaf of bread or a torn bed sheet with equal ferocity. They hit and pushed one another, yelled and cursed, trying to snatch as much as possible of *anything*. They were not choosy: everything had some value and could be sold or bartered for food.

Larissa watched the riotous mob with fearful fascination. She glanced at her companions on the konka. They sat stony-faced, with chins inside the collars of their coats.

The driver did not try to break through the mob. He guided his horses into a small alley. "We'll wait here … Stay on the sled. Don't get mixed up with them," he warned his passengers. "The poor souls must have been really desperate. Let's pray that the Cossacks won't come!"

But the Cossacks were coming. A detachment astride well-groomed matching bays trotted into the square. The mob met them with a barrage of stones and chunks of broken furniture. The horses, hit by stones, neighed.

"Sup-press!" sounded the command. The Cossacks aimed their horses into the crowd, scourging the rioters with their leather whips. The mob broke apart and some people ran. Clutching their loot, dropping it, picking it up, looters tried to escape from the square. The infuriated Cossacks spurred their horses to jump over the benches in the square as if they were barriers at a steeple-chase competition. They whipped the rioters furiously.

"*Zakol'lu!*" the Cossacks yelled, their faces distorted, "Cut you to pieces, you scum!" They knocked people off their feet and soon the dirty snow was clustered with fallen and bleeding bodies.

Larissa watched the confrontation, numb with horror. She had never imagined that Cossacks could be so brutal. She had always thought of them as brave and honorable horsemen. Her father had several Cossack officers as friends. Of course, they were senior officers who were educated at the best military academies, cultured like her own father, but … Would these cultured colonels and generals teach their men to be so brutal with their own Russian brethren? She could not believe it. "What's happening to us?" she thought.

Several people fell under the horses' hooves. The horses reared up snorting and trampled the fallen people. Lara covered her eyes with her hands.

It was over quickly. A police wagon appeared and two policemen went inside the looted bakery. Several others rounded up the looters who were hiding within the shops. With great efficiency, which obviously came from practice, they loaded the arrested rioters into the wagon, ignoring those on the ground. Order was restored. The police wagon left. The Cossack officer shouted a command and the Cossacks trotted away, and lined up again in neat formation, as if on parade.

Scores of injured people were left bleeding in the dirty snow. No ambulances came for them.

The konka driver pulled his horses out of the alley. "That was something!" he made the sign of the cross, wiping sweat off his face with a dirty mitten. "We'd better go."

"Wait!" Larissa ordered sharply. "What about the injured people? We must help them! We must take them to the hospital." She turned to the passengers. "Please, get off the sled. We must take the wounded to Botkinsky Hospital."

"Who are *you* to order us around?" one man objected.

"I am a nurse," she raised her voice. "It is my duty to help the injured."

"Well, it isn't *my* duty. I've paid for the ride," the man snorted.

"So did I. We all have paid for the ride," a woman joined him.

"You can take the next konka. It should be here shortly," Larissa said. "I'll reimburse you," She reached into her inside pocket for a small wallet and took out two and a half rubles. "At twenty-five kopeks a ticket, this ought to do it. There are ten of you," she said, counting them. "Now, please help me to load the wounded on the sled."

"What about me?" the driver demanded.

"I'll pay you extra, don't worry. Just help me load these people and take them to the hospital." She did not care anymore what they might think of her. For a few seconds she felt guilty that she had expropriated the title of nurse, but she would think of it later, she told herself. Now - she had to finish what she had started.

"Help me," she addressed the men. There was authority in her voice. She was not afraid of them anymore. She talked to them as she had been taught to talk to servants—with authority but always *polite*. "Please?"

"Yes, *báryn'ya*," a burly man said, calling her 'lady.' "I'll help you."

"We all will help," a stout elderly woman joined him. "It is the godly thing to do." They stepped off the sled and followed Larissa.

"Oh, well, we all will help." The driver pulled the konka closer to the slaughter ground. "God bless you, *báryn'ya*," he said quietly.

There were twenty victims with serious head and face wounds. Their twisted and helpless bodies were strewn over the dirty and bloody snow. Several dazed people managed to get up and wobble around, picking up loaves of trampled bread, the reason for it all.

Lara assessed the situation. It seemed that no one was killed, but the injuries were serious. One woman's eye was out of its socket, hanging over her cheekbone. Lara took out her handkerchief, filled it with clean snow from the top of a bench and pressed it against the woman's injured eye. "Hold it like that."

"It stings," the woman mumbled.

"It is supposed to sting," Lara replied, surprised at her authoritative tone. She did not know if it was supposed to sting or not, but she had assumed the voice of authority. She was *the nurse*.

"All right, let's move the wounded," she turned to the people still sitting in the konka. They helped the injured, supporting them as they shuffled toward the sled. The men carried those who could not walk. Soon all the injured were settled on the sled. They looked dazed, most of them bleeding profusely.

"What now?" Lara thought. She knew that she had to stop the bleeding. But how? She had no bandages … Suddenly, she recalled a patriotic picture of a nurse in the Crimean War, who was shredding her petticoat to bandage the head of a young and handsome officer, both of them smiling at each other. The picture was in her history book and as a young girl she used to love it, thinking that it was so romantic!

"Help me with my petticoat," Larissa touched a stout elderly woman on her shoulder. The woman looked at her, not understanding. "I'll unhook it from under my coat, and you pull it down, all right?" Lara explained.

"Why?" the woman asked, stupefied.

"Because we need to bandage those who are bleeding. We'll make the bandages out of my underskirt." She turned her back to the men and began to grope around her waist for the buttons of her skirts. It was hard to do with her heavy coat on, but she finally located a small button that held up her petticoat. "All right, pull it down!" she commanded. The woman reached under her skirt and gave a mighty tug to the undergarment. It came down in a billowing white cloud at Lara's feet, covering her ugly válenki. "Now, start tearing it into strips," Lara said.

"It's too pretty, *báryn'ya,*" the woman said, admiring the lace-edged petticoat.

"Nonsense," Lara said coldly," We need to bandage these people."

The woman began to tear the petticoat."Can I keep the lace? It is no good for a bandage. I have a young granddaughter …"

"Help yourself," Larissa interrupted, "But hurry up, *Bábushka!*"

The other women joined them. Being mothers, they did not need to be shown how to bandage the heads: they had plenty of practice in their lives bandaging heads of their hard-drinking husbands and hard-fighting sons. Soon, everyone was bandaged.

"Let's go!" Larissa said. "Thank you so much for your help! God bless you all!" She turned to her erstwhile fellow-travelers and smiled.

"God bless you, *sestritza,*" an injured man sprawled on the bench grabbed her hand. He called her "little sister," a nickname given by grateful patients to nurses.

It began to snow. The sled moved slowly, crunching new snow under its runners, leaving the bloodied and trampled square behind, the displaced passengers scavenging around for whatever had been overlooked by the looters.

Larissa decided not to tell her mother about the experience or the ugly information that she had been picking up from her fellow passengers. "It would only upset her," she thought, not knowing that Maria Nikoláyevna had her own sources of ugly information that she withheld from her daughter for the same reason.

Ksusha had been Maria Nikoláyevna's maid before Lara was born and then became the little girl's loving nurse. When Ksusha had finally retired on a good pension, she bought a little house on Petrovsky Island and moved there with her sister.

They did not get along. The sister was quarrelsome, and Ksusha found herself traveling across the city to the Orlov's residence almost daily, until Maria Nikoláyevna suggested that she should move back. Ksusha boarded up her little house, her sister returned to her village, and Ksusha moved back to where she had lived for twenty-five years.

Ksusha knew everything that was going on in the city. She had friends "in service" at the best Petrograd families, and she passed gossip about them to Maria Nikoláyevna, who had professed to dislike gossip but listened to it rather eagerly.

Lately, the gossip had become very juicy and even tinged with danger: one of Ksusha's close friends was working as a maid at Rasputin's household.

"Can you imagine who came for a visit with Rasputin the other day?" Ksusha announced one day.

"No. Who? The Empress?"

"No, no, the Empress hardly ever leaves Alexandrovsky Palace. Grigory Efimovich visits her there, everybody knows that."

"Are you now on intimate terms with Rasputin? You call him by his name and patronymic!" Maria Nikoláyevna interrupted. She liked to tease Ksusha.

"No, *báryn'ya*, but my friend Pasha, who works for him, calls him that. Anyway, can you guess who came to see Rasputin?"

"No. The Kaiser Wilhelm?"

"Don't make fun of me ... It was *Prince Youssoupov* who came for a visit! But Rasputin wasn't home."

"Prince Youssoupov, you say?"

"Yes!" Ksusha paused dramatically. "Well, Rasputin's seventeen-year-old daughter, Maria, was home from school and she offered the Prince a cup of tea. My friend Pasha brought it to him. The Prince seemed very nervous and hardly spoke to the young Maria Raspútina."

"Is she pretty, that Maria Raspútina?"

"No. My friend says that both Rasputin girls are very homely."

"Well, that's the reason why the Prince did not speak to her. He probably likes only pretty girls. He liked our Larissa. Remember?"

"I remember. My friend heard that he likes pretty boys better," Ksusha said with a wink.

"Your friend seems to be very knowledgeable. Anyway, what happened between Prince Youssoupov and Maria Rasplútina?"

"Nothing. He told her to let her father know that he had called."

"Is that all? How disappointing!" Maria Nikoláyevna exclaimed, still in her sarcastic manner.

"Well, I thought you would find it interesting that a Siberian *mouzhik* has reached such power that people like Prince Youssoupov call on him," Ksusha pursed her lips, pretending hurt feelings. "I won't tell you anything anymore …"

"Oh, Ksusha, I did not mean to hurt your feelings. Don't be angry with me!"

"Well, all right. Just don't make fun of my stories."

"I won't, I promise!"

It was part of a game they both enjoyed: Maria Nikoláyevna ridiculed the information, Ksusha acted insulted, the former begged forgiveness, the latter accepted it, until the next time, when the game would be played again.

A few days later Ksusha knocked on Maria Nikoláyevna's bedroom door.

"Dear Lord, do I have something to tell you!" she wiggled her large bottom into a chair near the bed. "My friend Pasha told me that Prince Youssoupov had become a regular visitor with *you know who!*" She had a smug expression on her round face. "Want to hear about it?"

Maria Nikoláyevna shrugged, pretending indifference. She was still in bed, her hair curled in *papillots*. "Wait till Luba brings my breakfast."

Luba, a new maid, brought in a tray with a silver pot of coffee, cream and sugar, and a soft-boiled duck egg in a delicate eggcup. Under a starched napkin there were two small brioches, a slice of butter, and a small dish of apricot jam. There were also two Meissen cups and saucers with matching small plates and silver spoons and knives for two. The servants knew that whenever Ksusha visited their mistress early in the morning, they shared their coffee. Ksusha was a privileged person in the Orlov's household.

"Well, all right, tell me about the mysterious visits of our handsome Prince to the notorious Rasputin," Maria Nikoláyevna said after Luba left the room. "Well, out with it!"

"Pasha told me that the Prince comes to Rasputin by the back door, with his sable hat low over his brow and the sable collar of his coat standing up, as if trying to hide his face."

"Your Pasha has sharp eyes. Are you sure that she said 'sable' hat and collar? Could it have been 'beaver' or maybe even 'rabbit'?"

"It was sable," Ksusha said primly. The game was on.

"Yes, it probably was sable. Prince Youssoupov can well afford it."

"Well ... Pasha says that each time they meet, the two of them go into Rasputin's study and the Prince lies down on the couch. Then they close the door."

"No!"

"Yes! And Rasputin starts waving his arms above the Prince, mumbling something. One time, Pasha said, the Prince was weeping. And Rasputin said to him that it was no sin to love men. He said, 'your confession will win you redemption.'"

"How does your Pasha know so much?"

"Oh, she is clever! She waits at the door, holding a tray with wine and biscuits, so if anybody passes by, or opens the door, she pretends that she is about to bring the tray into the study. She can hear everything."

"What do you suppose they talk about that requires such secrecy? And, why is Rasputin waving his arms over the Prince?" Maria Nikoláyevna chuckled. "Is this some new form of 'blessing'?"

"It's not funny! Pasha says that Rasputin's waving reminded her of a magician she saw at the People's Park some years ago. He made people go to sleep or do strange things. Pasha said that the Prince always acts strange after that, as if in a daze."

"How peculiar! What else?"

"Nothing else. But Pasha invited me to visit her and if you wish, I can go there today. Rasputin is at Tsárskoye Selo, with the Empress. Would you like me to?"

"It's up to you," Maria Nikoláyevna shrugged. "But if you are close friends, you should be polite and accept her invitation."

Ksusha returned from her visit in great excitement. "Oh, what a story!" she exclaimed, barging into the late general's study where Maria Nikoláyevna was working on the accounts. "Pasha told me so much! I don't know where to start!"

"Start from the beginning. Describe Rasputin's house," Maria Nikoláyevna said, taking off her spectacles and closing a ledger.

"There was no house. I mean, Rasputin lives in a large apartment building on Gorokhovaya Ulitza. There is no lift in the building. Fortunately, his flat is on the first floor."

"Tell me about his flat," Maria Nikoláyevna interrupted impatiently. "Is it well-furnished and rich looking?"

"Not by *your* standards," Ksusha replied, pretending to be offended by her mistress' tone of voice. "He has several rooms and a large kitchen. The dining room is big and he holds his prayer meetings there. The furniture is all big and heavy, made of oak. He has a large *iconostas* with many, many rich icons. Pasha told me that several of them were presents from the Tsaritza. Rasputin's own room is the smallest of all. It has a narrow iron bed covered with a red fox blanket. There is also a huge chest of drawers and a chair. Of course, there are several more icons. Nothing else. Oh, yes, all over the flat he has many pictures of the Tsaritza and her children and a couple of big pictures of the Tsar."

"Like portraits? You know, painted on canvas by some artist?"

"No, the pictures are photographs, printed on paper and colored to look pretty."

"What else? Is it a handsome building that he lives in?"

"No, just the usual apartment house. I was not impressed with his building, nor with his flat. It smelled of cabbage and fried onions. Anyway, forget the building. I wanted to tell you what Pasha *heard!*"

"Go ahead. I am listening."

"Well ... apparently, Rasputin is angling for an invitation to the Youssoupov's Palace to meet Princess Irina! He told the Prince that he had heard that the young Princess was the most beautiful woman in Russia and he wanted to give her his blessings!"

"The nerve! What did the Prince say?"

"According to Pasha, they made a date for next week, the 16th of December, for *after midnight!* Why, do you think?"

"I have no idea. What happened next?"

"Nothing much. They were served some tea and biscuits by Pasha, and the Prince left."

"Too bad your friend cannot be at Youssoupov's palace! We won't know anything about Rasputin's secret meeting with the Grand Duchess Irina!"

"Oh, but we might!" Ksusha exclaimed with a sly smile on her wrinkled face. "We just might! Pasha's young nephew is on staff at Youssoupov's palace, working as a footman! Pasha said that she will tell him to keep his eyes and ears open to whatever will be going on at the palace on the night of the sixteenth."

"Your Pasha is resourceful."

"She is interested in what is going on with that man, Rasputin. She says that she has seen him *fornicating* with high class women. Women, like you, *báryn'ya!* And after he finishes with them, he blesses them and they kneel together before the icons. She says when he is drunk, which is often, he exposes himself before the women in his household, walking around without his trousers, with his thing dangling. Can you imagine such crudeness? And he calls himself a *holy man!*"

"It is not for nothing that his name comes from the word *'rasputnick'*, which means 'libertine' and 'sinful.' He is well named," Maria Nikoláyevna laughed.

"Pasha hates his guts. She thinks that Russia would be better off without him."

"Who doesn't?" Maria Nikoláyevna shrugged. "But warn your Pasha not to talk like that. It is dangerous."

"I know. But, I wanted to tell you about the Tsarevich, our heir to the throne. Rasputin is good friends with Anna Vyroubova, a lady-in-waiting to the Empress," Ksusha continued. "Pasha has overheard several conversations between them about the illness of the Tsarevich. Anna Vyroubova visits Rasputin's flat quite often, and Pasha saw her kissing Rasputin's hands as if he were Archimandrite!"

"Tell me about the Tsarevich." Maria Nikoláyevna was intrigued, dropping all pretense of their game for a moment. Like everyone else in the capital, she had heard rumors that the young boy suffered from some incurable illness that had never been publicly disclosed. The Imperial family succeeded in drawing a curtain of secrecy over their lives in isolated Tsárskoye Selo.

"Apparently, the Tsarevich has something wrong with his blood," Ksusha continued, lowering her voice. "If he hurts himself, like all children do sometimes, he continues to bleed. And no one, not even the doctors, can stop the bleeding. No one but the *staretz*, the holy man, as they call Rasputin. He knows how to cast a spell, and it stops the bleeding. Very few people know about it. The Tsaritza threatened the servants with exile to Siberia and made them swear on the Bible that they would not discuss the Tsarevich's illness. Pasha heard Vyroubova brag that the *staretz* can stop the bleeding even by telephone!"

"By telephone? Incredible! Your Pasha must be a great storyteller."

"No, *báryn'ya*. She is an honest Christian woman who tells the truth. It is the *truth* that is incredible!"

"All right, Ksusha. That's enough for one day. Even the best of magicians cannot perform their magic by telephone. You made my head spin. You go, now. I must finish my work," Maria Nikoláyevna said, putting her spectacles on again, pretending that she was returning to the ledgers.

"All right, *báryn'ya*, I am also tired. I'll go and take a nap."

Maria Nikoláyevna remained at her husband's desk, staring at his photograph. She felt especially lonely and vulnerable. If only Sergei were alive! "What's happening to our country?" she thought. "Why did the Tsar replace Grand Duke Nikolái Nikolayevich as Supreme Commander? Why had he named *himself* Supreme Commander? What does *he* know about running the war? And the Empress … Could it be true what Ksusha said about Rasputin's influence over her? Perhaps I should go and talk with the Rezánovs. Vladímir would certainly know more about that Rasputin than some 'Pasha', whoever she is." With sudden determination, she picked up the telephone and asked the operator to connect her with General Rezánov's residence.

As usual, there were guests at the Rezánovs' dinner—two of his young aides and a Cossack general with his wife.

General Melekhov was on leave from the front after being wounded in action. His Japanese wife, Suzume, a beautiful bird-like woman, felt uneasy in the Rezánov's grand house. The rumor was that the Cossack general had abducted her from a geisha house at the end of his assignment in the Russo-Japanese war. Many of the aristocratic homes closed their doors to him, but General Rezánov continued his friendship with Melekhov, refusing to abandon him, even though Varvara Mikháilovna made no efforts to befriend his wife. Suzume was an exotic decoration in her drawing room, muted by her inability to speak French and her bare knowledge of a few Russian words. But she was exquisite in her beauty, and the eyes of all men were often concentrated on her.

The men crowded around the side table with vodkas in the anteroom of the dining salon, while the ladies remained in the drawing room sipping *jerez*. The conversation in both groups was about Rasputin.

"I am telling you, if I hadn't seen it with my own eyes I would have never believed it!" General Melekhov said loudly. "There we were, in Moscow, a group of Cossack officers celebrating the promotion of one of our men. The Gypsies sing and dance and we all are having a good time. Suddenly, we hear a commotion in one of the private rooms along the gallery. We hear a woman scream, then a man yelling obscenities, then dishes being broken, and a wild-looking bearded man *without trousers* appears on the gallery with his penis in full view. Women start screaming, men jump to their feet, someone calls the police and finally they subdue the man. By now, everyone recognizes Rasputin!" The general piled a dollop of caviar on a cracker. "I could not believe my eyes!"

"I've heard about that episode, but I thought it was just ugly gossip," General Rezánov said. "And to think: that person has become our *de facto* ruler!"

"Someone ought to shoot him, like a mad dog," one of the aides-de-camp said.

"Whom do you want to shoot, Captain?" Varvara Mikháilovna said, entering the room. "I bet, I know! Rasputin!"

"Yes, Madame," the young Captain said. "I beg your pardon."

"Don't apologize. I fully share your sentiment. Anyway, gentlemen, dinner is waiting. Please, follow me." The men followed her into the dining salon.

The joint conversation about Rasputin resumed, but in French. *"Pas devant les domestiques,"* warned Varvara Mikháilovna, nodding surreptitiously toward the maids.

"I have heard that Grand Duke Nikolaí Nikolayevich was relieved of his duties because of Rasputin," Maria Nikoláyevna began. "Is it true?"

"Oh, yes, Madame," the Cossack General Melekhov was ready with an answer. "One of my friends was on duty at Stavka at the time. Rasputin apparently wanted to visit the troops at the front 'to bless' them. The Empress telegraphed the Grand Duke, asking when Rasputin should arrive. The Grand Duke replied, 'let him come any time so that I can hang him!' The Empress demanded that His Majesty fire his Supreme Commander immediately and take over command of the army himself."

Throughout the first course of clear soup with croutons they discussed General Brusílov's vainglorious campaign against Austria, not blaming the general for its failure but rather saying that Stavka, with its constant changing of commanding generals, was at fault.

During the fish course, aside from the comments in Russian praising the delicately prepared fish with white asparagus in Hollandaise sauce, the conversation continued in French about Rasputin and his influence on the Imperial family.

"I had a visit from Deputy Interior Minister Dzhunkovsky," General Rezánov said. "General Dzhunkovsky is a distinguished man who had always been respected by the Tsar. He begged His Majesty to remove Rasputin from Petrograd. Well, the Empress heard about it, and Vladímir Dzhunkovsky was forced to resign."

The servants changed the plates and exchanged slim white wine glasses for rounded glasses for red wine, in preparation for serving wild game. They brought in the main course, wild pheasant under lingonberry sauce, with tiny roasted potatoes and sweet green peas.

The conversation switched back to Russian. General Melekhov described pheasant hunts with his hunting dogs on his estate in the Ukraine, before the war.

Maria Nikoláyevna was not interested in his recollections; she wanted to talk more about the political situation in Petrograd. The mood of the people was nasty, she could *feel* it.

Dessert was served, a hot, chocolate soufflé with coffee, after which the ladies retired to a small drawing room while the men remained in the dining salon, in the English manner. The dishes were cleared away, and a butler brought the gentlemen cognac and cigars.

The conversation turned to politics. General Rezánov recalled his visit to the Duma, where he'd had the privilege to hear a speech by Purishkevich, a conservative member. "It was in November and Purishkevich had just returned from Mogilev, where he dined with the Emperor. Purishkevich is a patriotic philanthropist, who had built a special hospital train that could be sent anywhere at the front. Some deputies at the Duma had hoped to use his *private* dinner with the Tsar as an opportunity to inform him about the growing discontent in the country. We all know that our Tsar is becoming more and more isolated from his ministers; they are fired or exchanged in their positions constantly. The ministers, who used to be able to speak and advise the Tsar, are hardly ever allowed to see him now. So, they beseeched Purishkevich to tell the Tsar the truth about the general unrest. I don't know whether Purishkevich dared to speak so boldly to the Tsar, but I do know that he did so at the Duma."

"What did he say?" General Melekhov asked.

"He described the situation in Petrograd as 'desperate'; strikes at the factories, food riots, growing signs of starvation among the lower classes. He talked about hundreds of locomotives disabled by the lack of spare parts, thus making food deliveries to the city impossible. He said that it appeared no one is in charge of Petrograd. He referred to the ancient tradition of ringing a village church bell to raise an alarm. He said that the peeling of the village bell was not enough anymore. The alarm must be sounded by the great bell in the Kremlin. But what moved me most was his impassioned call to all the ministers to go, *en masse*, to Stavka, to fall on their knees before the Tsar like in the ancient times, and beg him to get rid of that vile person, Rasputin, who was causing such a desperate state of affairs." The general paused and took a sip of cognac. "The deputies gave him a standing ovation. Of course, everyone was surprised that he spoke so openly against Rasputin."

"Well? Has anything changed?" General Melekhov asked sarcastically. "With all this talk and wringing of hands, I can't understand why no one has tried to shoot the devil and be done with it!"

"Rasputin is well protected by the *Okhrana*," said one of the young aides. "I have a friend who is an officer of the gendarmes, and he says that by the personal order of the Empress, Rasputin is under twenty-four hour protection by the secret police."

"Well, gentlemen, unfortunately it is not for us to solve the problem," General Rezánov said. "It's all in the hands of our Emperor. But he makes it impossible to reach him: when we come to Stavka with our reports, he looks ... well, he looks distracted. Sometimes I wonder if he *hears* our reports, even though he *listens* to them. The last time when we saw him, about three weeks ago, he had Tsarevich Alexei with him. The boy was dressed in a uniform, like a miniature soldier. I thought the child looked quite well, but the Emperor looked ghastly. I don't envy our Tsar ... The war is going badly, the Duma, our Parliament, is quarrelsome, millions of people are on the cusp of a revolt, all that resting on his frail shoulders! And, don't forget his wife and Rasputin! No wonder the poor man looks sick."

"I have heard that Rasputin gives the Tsar narcotics," General Melekhov said. "Could it be that he is addicted to narcotics?"

"I haven't heard about that. But who knows? There is so much gossip circulating that one doesn't know what to believe," General Rezánov concluded with resignation.

"Have you heard from your son?" General Melekhov asked, changing the subject.

"Not lately. Andrei is a very poor correspondent. The last letter from him was when he had received his second Order of St. George. Nothing since, not even to his wife."

When Maria Nikoláyevna returned home from the Rezánovs' dinner, Larissa was already asleep, her sixteen hour shift at the hospital having exhausted her.

Ksusha waited for her mistress, dozing in a chair in front of the flickering fireplace in Maria Nikoláyevna's bedroom.

"Do I have some news for you!" she exclaimed, instantly awake.

"All right, tell me your news, but first, help me to unbutton my shoes. My feet are killing me!" Maria Nikoláyevna plunged herself into a chair and stretched her legs toward Ksusha. Groaning, Ksusha knelt on the carpet and began to unhook the row of small buttons on her mistress' fashionable shoes.

"Well," Ksusha began as she pulled the tight shoes off, "Pasha's nephew at the Youssoupov Palace told her that he was ordered by the Prince to move some furniture to a basement room. So, Nikita, that's Pasha's nephew, and the other servants were moving carpets and tables and chairs into a basement, making it look like a cozy sitting room. They even put a white polar bear rug there!"

"So?"

"So, Nikita asked the Prince why he needed another dining room when he had so many rooms in the palace. The nerve of him!" she exclaimed with admiration, beginning to massage her mistress's feet.

"What did the Prince say? Did he tell him that it was none of his business?"

"No. The Prince was very nice and said that he was expecting some special guest and told Nikita to keep his mouth shut and say nothing to anyone."

"It is probably some new love affair that the Prince wants to keep secret from his wife!"

"Could be. But it isn't!" Ksusha exclaimed. "The Prince said that 'the special guest' would be arriving very late, on *the sixteenth of December!*"

21

For months, Russians of all classes had agreed that *"something must be done!"* From the salons of the nobility to the book-filled flats of the *intelligencia* to the humble hovels of working people, the cry was *"Something must be done!"* The call was so urgent that even the extended Imperial family of Grand Dukes and Princes was saying *something must be done* to end Rasputin's poisonous influence over the Empress.

Prince Felix Youssoupov, after hearing Purishkevich's impassioned plea for ministers to throw themselves at the Tsar's feet, was frustrated with the government's impotence. The ministers seemed incapable of doing anything about Rasputin, so Youssoupov decided that it was up to him, as a Russian patriot, to liberate his country. He, the hereditary Prince, would murder Rasputin.

He needed co-conspirators: the project was too complicated for a single person. He contacted Purishkevich after the benefit concert at his palace.

"I have taken some preliminary steps," the Prince confided to him. "I've befriended the scoundrel, pretending that I was suffering from headaches, and asked him to cure me. I believe he trusts me now. He expressed his wish to meet my wife, and I have said that I can arrange it. We chose a tentative date of December the sixteenth."

"That is next week!'

"Yes. We need to *eliminate* him."

"Who would dare to take such a drastic step?"

"I would," Youssoupov said calmly. "I will kill the son-of-a-bitch."

Purishkevich stared at him, saying nothing. Steely resolve stared back from the handsome face of the pampered young nobleman, and Purishkevich thought, "By God, he is serious!"

He exclaimed, "You'll be the savior of our wretched country, Your Grace!" There were tears in his eyes. "I pledge my life and honor to you."

"Thank you. I knew that I could count on your support. Obviously, we have to be very cautious. I have spoken about it only to my best friend, Grand Duke Dimitri Pavlovich, and he is with me," Youssoupov said. "He told me he is astonished by the change in our gentle Empress since she came under the spell of Rasputin. He said that she expressed vicious delight at news of the assassination of Prime Minister Peter Stolypin when he was conducting an investigation of Rasputin's activities."

"Yes. Stolypin had plans to send Rasputin back to Siberia, in exile," Purishkevich said. "I was present during the discussions."

"Yes. Well, Dimitri Pavlovich told me that when the Empress heard of Stolypin's assassination, she clapped her hands and proclaimed that it was God's retribution for offending '*Our Friend.*' Anyway, I have made some arrangements for receiving Rasputin at my home. I have already prepared a special room where we will meet. If you don't mind, come with me now, I'll show it to you."

"It will be my honor," Purishkevich bowed.

The 'basement room' was one of several similar rooms within the palace's formidable foundation. Built with vaulted ceilings and thick walls of solid granite that ran the length of the palace, some of the basement rooms were used as wine cellars, while others stood mostly empty.

The room chosen by the Prince was isolated and almost soundproof. It had a huge granite fireplace and was located directly under Youssoupov's own study, far from the servants' quarters. A narrow spiral staircase connected it to the study above and a hidden door on the side led to a small courtyard, making it convenient to slip in and out of the basement without going through the main house. The servants had cleaned the room, washed the stone floor and walls, and then filled the room with items of Prince Felix's choosing.

It was an intimate room, just big enough for two or three couples, divided by a ceiling arch that created two sections—one for dining, the other for lounging on a couple of low divans among silky cushions.

A polar bearskin rug was spread on the floor, the bear's head skillfully reconstructed by taxidermists, its muzzle threatening with long, sharp teeth, the glass eyes shiny even in the darkened room. The Prince had chosen some Arabic silver vessels and decorative porcelain figurines to be placed on the mantelpiece and a heavy Persian carpet to be spread on the stone floor. He ordered heavy hangings in dark brocade to block two small windows at ground level, making the room look as if it were Scheherazade's tent.

Youssoupov had placed his seven-string Gypsy guitar near one of the divans: it was well known that he was a talented singer. The presence of the guitar would create a certain atmosphere of informality, he thought.

The dining section of the room was less exotic. A small round table of Karelian birch wood and four chairs upholstered in red velvet stood in its center, facing an intricate ebony cabinet with many tiny drawers inlaid with mother-of-pearl. For some reason, as if seeking benediction, Youssoupov had placed a large rock crystal crucifix on its top.

The conspirators gathered in the salon of Purishkevich's hospital train. There were four of them now. The Grand Duke had invited Lieutenant Ivan Sukhotin, an old friend, to be included as a representative of the military.

Sprawled on comfortable lounge chairs, the conspirators sipped French cognac and puffed on Argentinean cigars, leisurely discussing the murder that was to take place within a few days. They felt good. They were not bothered by conscience.

Although Youssoupov and Purishkevich had agreed that their plans must be kept secret, they both were guilty of having dropped hints among their friends. Within days, Petrograd salons buzzed with rumors.

Youssoupov cleared his throat. "One thing I want to make clear, gentlemen: no servants must be involved in our plan. Whatever must be done, we'll do it ourselves. We cannot rely on the servants' loyalty. They can always be bought." The conspirators agreed.

Purishkevich spoke. "I would suggest that we use my personal physician, Doctor Lazovert, to acquire the poison. He is a patriot, like the rest of us, and I have total confidence in him."

"Splendid!" Youssoupov nodded. "The doctor will obtain the poison. One less thing to worry about!"

"Now, let's invite Doctor Lazovert to our meeting. We ought to hear his ideas about our plan. He is on the train, waiting." Purishkevich pressed a button on his internal telephone. "Doctor," he said into the horn, "please join us in the salon."

In a few minutes, Doctor Lazovert entered, rubbing his hands.

"Your Highness," he bowed to the Grand Duke. "Your Grace," he bowed to the Prince. "Gentlemen," he bowed to Purishkevich and Sukhotin. "I am at your disposal."

Lazovert was tall and fair complected, with thinning blond hair combed across his skull in an attempt to hide creeping baldness. His fine features were typical of Polish men—thin nose and lips, sharp chin, and light-colored eyes. He was about fifty and was already losing his military posture and acquiring a little round belly. His nervous habit of rubbing his hands made people uncomfortable.

Youssoupov did not like him, which was mutual. "A Polish quack!" Youssoupov thought with derision.

"A pampered pederast!" Lazovert thought with equal vitriol.

"Doctor, we urgently need your advice," Purishkevich began at once. "We have decided to use poison instead of a gun, for obvious reasons: guns are too loud, though, of course, we will have our personal guns handy. One never knows!" He laughed with exaggerated gaiety, joined by the others. "So, our idea is to place some fast acting poison into the wine and the pastries that will be served to our ... Let's call him, *our guest.* What would you recommend, Doctor?"

"Potassium cyanide is the best. It is fast-acting."

"Are you sure that you can obtain it without raising suspicion?" the Grand Duke asked, looking at the tips of his polished boots.

"Certainly. I am a *doctor*." Lazovert smiled with condescension.

Youssoupov caught his innuendo." Do you know how to drive an automobile, doctor?" he asked with icy politeness. "I need a chauffeur to drive me when I pick up 'our guest.' For obvious reasons, we don't want to involve servants in this particular enterprise."

"Yes, Your Grace. I know how to drive. I will be glad to drive, if you don't know how," the doctor bowed slightly to Youssoupov. "Touché!" he thought briefly. "Have you made any plans for disposing of the body?" the doctor inquired.

"Of course!" Purishkevich exclaimed heartily. "We have made thorough plans for everything! We shall take the body to the Malaya Nevka and drop it off the bridge into a hole in the ice. The local citizens have many ice fishing holes around there. Finding one won't be a problem. We shall place heavy weights on the body so that it sinks to the bottom of the river. Then, we shall burn his clothes and boots in this train's furnace. We will even call that popular Gypsy night spot Villa Rode and ask to talk to him!"

"Why?" asked Doctor Lazovert.

"To divert suspicion! In the following investigation it will be established that 'our guest' was expected to meet with the Prince at Villa Rode. Instead, he disappeared!" Purishkevich raised his glass. "And no suspicion will fall upon the good Prince. To the success of our plans!" The conspirators joined him, toasting their plan.

"Fine, gentlemen," Youssoupov said, standing. "We shall meet for lunch on the sixteenth at my residence to check on last minute details. With God's help, we shall liberate our suffering country from the evil influence of Gríshka Rasputin!"

Purishkevich made a wide sign of the cross over his broad chest. "Until then, God's blessing be with us all!"

The morning of December 16 was crisp and bright. It had snowed all night, and the city was buried under a carpet of fresh, sparkling snow.

The golden spire of the Admiralty pierced the brilliant blue sky. Only a few feathery clouds floated above the city.

Felix Youssoupov wrapped himself in his fur-lined overcoat, pulled his sable hat over his brow and walked along the canal the short distance to Kazan Cathedral. "Petrograd is so beautiful under snow," he thought, enjoying the invigorating air. His breath soon turned the fur collar around his chin into tiny spikes of icicles.

His mind was clear. He had no fear or doubt. He was a Russian Prince, a patriot, a man on the cusp of performing a great deed for his country. All he needed now was Divine confirmation! He was going to get it through prayer.

He passed under the colonnaded wing of the Cathedral and into its large reception hall hung with hundreds of colorful banners captured from Napoleon's defeated army in the glorious year of 1812. As a young boy, Felix knew all the banners by heart and had taken great pride in naming each regiment and its general to his indulgent father. He smiled as he recalled memories of those days.

"Russia was heroic then. Look at us now: defeat after defeat in battle, chaos in the cities, and grand treason within the ranks of the Imperial Family! But I shall change it! I shall change it, even if I have to give my own life in the process. Russia will be great again!"

He went directly to the Youssoupov family's chapel and dropped to his knees before a large icon of the suffering Savior. He prayed fervently, with the innocence of a child, promising the Lord to deliver Russia from the Devil. The ugly reality of the forthcoming murder was nowhere in his thoughts, a euphoric feeling of religious hysteria dominating him. Like Russian patriots of yore who had liberated Holy Russia from Teutonic knights, from Mongol hordes, and from Napoleon's Grande Armée, he would free Russia from her present scourge!

He asked the priest to give him a special blessing, for a warrior about to face the enemy. The old priest assumed that Felix was an officer on his way to the front and gladly blessed him, adding a little prayer of dispensation for all sins without taking a confession. The young man's earnestness and sincerity had impressed him.

Later that day the conspirators gathered in the basement room for lunch.

Everything was in good order. The pastry chef had prepared a variety of *petits fours* with chocolate and rose-colored cream, artistically displayed on two round platters, a Sèvres and a Meissen. One platter would contain the poisoned pastries. It was up to Prince Felix to remember which platter was which.

A dozen bottles of Madeira wine were lined up on the mantelpiece along with a few cranberry-colored crystal glasses.

"I suggest that the poisoned wine be placed on the right side. Prince Felix is right-handed. It will be easier for him to remember which group of bottles is poisoned," Purishkevich proposed.

"As long as the Prince remembers that the bottles will be on his right side when *facing* the mantel. In the excitement of the moment he could become confused," the doctor said with a disdainful smile.

Youssoupov, still under the spell of his religious exaltation was not offended by the doctor's remark.

Lunch was served but no one had any appetite. Despite their brave mien, all but Felix were nervous. They picked at their *Cotelletes à la Kiev*, toasted one another with Veuve Clicquot and agreed to gather again at ten o'clock in the evening in Youssoupov's study, directly above the basement room. The doctor, wearing a chauffeur's cap, would drive Felix to Rasputin's flat. The Grand Duke, Purishkevich, and Sukhotin would remain in the study above the basement room. As soon as they heard the arrival of Lazovert's automobile, they would start playing the gramophone, to pretend that Princess Irina was entertaining friends. Unfortunately, Felix had only one gramophone record, which was totally inappropriate: it was an American marching song "Yankee Doodle."

"Have we thought of everything?" asked the Grand Duke. He was nervous.

"I think so, Dimitri Pavlovich," Purishkevich replied. "We covered every detail."

"I hope nothing goes wrong," the Grand Duke said, his voice slightly trembling.

"Nothing will go wrong," Youssoupov reassured him. "God is with us!"

While the collaborators checked the last details of their plot, Rasputin was attending to his own preparations for the visit with Princess Irina.

He went to church, as was his habit every morning, and then to the *banya*, a public steam bath, where he flagellated himself with a birch besom, its leaves sticking to his wet buttocks. He had always felt rejuvenated after a trip to the banya, but that morning he felt especially good: in honor of his visit with Princess Irina, he let a barber trim his unkempt beard and whiskers. He even trimmed his fingernails, which usually carried a crescent of dirt under them.

He walked home, the snow pleasantly crunching under his felt válenki. Life was good, he thought. He smiled at three young boys throwing snowballs at each other. Scooping a handful of snow, he hurled it at the children. He missed and winked at the boys, spreading his arms wide, palms up, in a gesture of disappointment. The children laughed and ran away.

On the stairs to his apartment he gave a blessing to the soldier standing on guard. "Keep my enemies away from me, *bratishka*," he joked, using the Russian term for "little brother."

"Will do, Holy Father," the soldier replied.

His secretary, Simanovich, opened the door. "Anna Alexandrovna Vyroubova has been waiting for you," he said. "At least an hour."

Rasputin was not in the mood to see her. "What does she want?" he asked rudely.

"She said that she has something to give you. From Her Majesty."

"Oh, all right," he said, his good mood gone. That Anna! A stupid fat cow, always on the verge of sentimental tears, always grabbing his hands to kiss, always asking for his blessing … She annoyed him to no end, but she was a powerful person, being the confidante of the Tsaritza. He had to be cordial to her.

"Your Holiness!" Anna Vyroubova dashed out of the dining room like a young girl, her arms outstretched. "Give me your blessing, Holy Father!" She bent her head toward her ample bosom as he made the sign of the cross over her and mumbled a few words.

"Thank you, Your Holiness," she breathed. "I have a gift for you from our Matushka Tsaritza." She reached into her large handbag. "This is for you, with Her Majesty's devotion." Reverently, she handed him a small icon wrapped in a crisp linen handkerchief. It was the icon of the *Bogoroditza*, the Holy Mother.

"Thank you, it is beautiful," Rasputin said, kissing the icon as was the custom. "Tell our Matushka Tsaritza that I am grateful. Would you like a glass of wine before you leave, Anna Alexandrovna?"

"Yes, Grigory Efimovich, I would love it!"

"Hey, Pasha, bring us a couple of glasses and my new Madeira," he shouted into the kitchen.

"Yes, Grigory Efimovich!" Pasha shouted back cheerfully, foreseeing some new morsels of gossip for her good friend Ksusha.

'Sit down, Anna Alexandrovna," Rasputin pointed to a chair at the table covered with a white tablecloth, a puffing samovar at one end. "Tell me how things are at Tsárskoye Selo? How is the Tsarevich?"

"The heir is still with the Tsar at Stavka. He loves going there! He is doing well. He visited the wounded soldiers in Klevan. They adored him! The Council of St. George awarded him the silver medal for his visit, and he was issued lance corporal epaulettes! He is very proud about it. He wrote to his mother that he is the youngest corporal in the Russian army! He also wrote that he sleeps on a cot, like a real soldier, next to his father's cot," she related breathlessly.

"How old is he now? I keep forgetting."

"He is eleven, Your Holiness."

"Eleven …" Rasputin repeated slowly, thinking, "the poor child, with his illness he will be lucky to live to eighteen."

Pasha entered, carrying a tray with two wine glasses and an opened bottle of Madeira. "Here you are, Grigory Efimovich," she said smiling. She left, swinging her wide hips, knowing that he was watching her. She professed that she hated Rasputin, and she did, but it flattered her nevertheless when he would slap her behind: it showed that at forty-five she was still desirable.

Rasputin poured the wine. "Prince Youssoupov brought me this wine. It's from his vineyards in the Crimea. I like it very much. He has invited me to visit his vineyards next fall when they will be harvesting the grapes. He says it is very interesting to watch: local women stomp the grapes with their *bare* feet. Can you believe that?" he laughed, downing the wine in two thirsty gulps and refilling his glass.

Vyroubova giggled, taking a dainty sip. "It sounds very unsanitary."

"It is the dirt and the sweat of their feet that makes the wine taste so good!" he joked, savoring the wine. "I am going to Youssoupov's palace tonight to see Princess Irina, and I'm going to ask her if she has ever tried stomping grapes!"

"No!" Vyroubova cried in horror. "You can't do that! She is the Tsar's *niece!*"

He laughed. "Of course I would never ask her such a thing. I was only joking. I am invited to meet her tonight, after midnight."

"Why so late?"

"Who knows? She is entertaining some of her friends earlier. You know how those Royal Highnesses are: we have to obey them," he shrugged.

"Not you, Your Holiness!"

"Yes, even I! Who am I? I am just a simple Siberian peasant," he was suddenly very pious as he made the sign of the cross and bowed toward the icons. Then he downed another glass and refilled it.

"I had better go," Vyroubova stood. "Bless me, Holy Father."

He did not insist that she stay. He gave her his blessings without getting up, and watched as she left.

Later that evening Anna Vyroubova took a train to Tsárskoye Seló and then telephoned the Empress at the Alexandrovsky Palace. "I am back home now. This morning I visited *'our friend'*. He was very pleased with your gift. He kissed it."

"Good. How is he feeling? I had a terrible dream last night that he had died ..."

"Oh, he is fine! He is going to see Princess Youssoupova tonight. And he had his beard trimmed!" she laughed.

"Irina Youssoupova?" the Empress said. "But she is in the Crimea!"

"Well, that is what he said. He joked about the wine that Prince Youssoupov had sent him, saying that he would ask Princess Irina whether she stomped on the grapes ..."

"How strange," the Empress thought, no longer listening. "I know that Irina is still in the Crimea."

▌22▐

Doctor Lazovert personally prepared the poisons and placed them inside the *petits fours*. No one could tell the difference between the poisoned pastries and those that were safe.

"Don't forget Felix: everything on *your right side* will be poisoned," the Grand Duke said.

Youssoupov was annoyed. "Stop treating me as if I were a child! I remember! *Everything on the right will be poisoned!* How could I forget?"

The doctor said, "The four bottles of wine on your *extreme right* are heavily poisoned. I think it will be sufficient even for a heavy drinker. I replaced the corks, so you'll have to use the corkscrew."

"Thank you, Doctor! It's time we go. Here is your chauffeur's cap. Where is the automobile?"

"I left it on the other side of the foot bridge. We should go in my Ford. It is less conspicuous than your Rolls Royce."

"Good. Bring it into the inner court. We will depart from there. Less chance of being observed," Youssoupov replied calmly. However, he noticed that his hands were slightly trembling. He stuck them into his pockets.

"Courage, mon ami," the Grand Duke whispered. "I know how you feel."

"We all know," Purishkevich said. "None of us has any experience with murder."

"Let's not talk about *murder*," Youssoupov grimaced. "What we are doing is a noble deed. With God's help, it soon will be over." They embraced each other.

Doctor Lazovert drove the Prince through a darkened city toward Gorokhovaya Street, both of them silent. The sky, so bright during the day, was covered with low dark clouds, forecasting another snowfall. The moon tried to peek out of the clouds but finally gave up and retired behind them, leaving Petrograd in darkness. Because of the war, street illumination was reduced to every fourth lamplight.

There was no traffic. The doctor drove in the middle of the street, the Ford's headlights showing the way.

"Stop at the back entrance," Youssoupov said as they reached Rasputin's apartment building. "We'll come out through the back door." The doctor parked the machine next to a small iron gate leading to the back yard and turned off the headlights. Felix quickly entered the yard and proceeded to Rasputin's staircase.

"Where are you going?" challenged a voice from the dark cave of the entrance.

"To Grigory Efimovich," he replied without stopping, although his heart gave a skip. He heard a door open, and in its dim light he saw the silhouette of Rasputin standing in its frame.

"Come in, come in, my friend!" Rasputin exclaimed, then he shouted toward his invisible guard, "You may go home now. My friend has arrived, so you may go home!"

"Spasibo! Good night!" came the reply, and then the sound of a closing gate announced that the guard was gone.

Youssoupov came into the darkened kitchen, and the sour smell of rising dough and boiled cabbage assaulted him. Rasputin walked ahead of him toward the dining room, where a kerosene lamp threw a circle of dim light around the room.

Rasputin turned the wick to increase the light. "Let's have a drink before we go," he said.

"Why not!" Felix exclaimed. "You look good, Grigory Efimovich!" he added gaily.

Rasputin's long hair was neatly trimmed, parted in the middle, and slicked down with oil. His beard was combed and he exuded a strong scent of cheap eau-de-cologne.

He was dressed in a long white silk shirt embroidered with blue cornflowers at the high neck, along the hem, and around the edges of the sleeves. The shirt was gathered around his waist with a twisted wine-colored cord with tassels, and his roomy dark blue velvet trousers were stuffed into rough woolen socks.

"I can't find my boots," he said. "My girls must have hidden them again. They don't like when I go out at night. Would it be all right if I wear my válenki?"

"Of course!"

"Good!" He reached under the table for his felt boots and with a groan pulled them on. "Let's have that drink!" He poured Madeira from a half-empty bottle into two glasses.

"I have already started," he laughed. "To your wife! How is she today?"

"She is fine." They touched glasses. "She is looking forward to meeting you," Felix said, taking a sip, the sweet liquid slipping down his esophagus. He had never liked Madeira. "Shall we go?"

"One more drink, and then we go!"

"No more for me. Thank you," Felix said, covering the unfinished glass with his palm. Rasputin tilted the bottle and looked at it against the light. Seeing that it was almost empty, he did not bother with the glass: he lifted the bottle to his lips and emptied it in three gulps.

"Now I am ready! Let's go!" He grabbed his huge peasants' coat off its hook, slapped a fur hat on his head, and led Felix out the back door. The automobile was waiting at the curb. Doctor Lazovert, playing chauffeur, bowed and opened the passenger door. Rasputin and Youssoupov climbed in, and the doctor started the engine.

When the conspirators in Youssoupov's study heard the arriving automobile, they turned on the phonograph. A jaunty melody of "Yankee Doodle," softened by the thick walls, filled the air.

"What's that?" asked Rasputin. "Are you having a party?"

"Oh, no," Youssoupov laughed. "It's just my wife, entertaining a couple of her friends. I thought that they would be gone by now. Never mind. She will be down shortly."

Rasputin took off his coat and looked around. His attention was immediately caught by the ebony cabinet.

"What's that?" He came closer to the cabinet and began to open its various tiny drawers and doors, enjoying himself as if he were a child.

"It is a Chinese puzzle cabinet. Some doors have concealed springs that open secret chambers. I have not mastered all its secrets, even though I've had it since I was a boy."

Rasputin continued to play with the cabinet, opening and closing its many doors, hoping to find secret chambers. "I've never seen anything like it, not even at Alexandrovsky Palace!" he exclaimed.

"Would you like a drink?" Felix reached for a bottle on the far right of the fireplace mantel.

"Of course!" Rasputin replied, still engrossed with the cabinet.

Willing himself to stop his hands from trembling, Felix uncorked the bottle and poured the wine into a cranberry-red crystal glass. He placed the bottle back in its place on the mantel.

"What about you?" Rasputin asked, turning around.

"I don't really like sweet wines," Felix replied, reaching for a bottle on the opposite side of the mantelpiece. "I would rather have a Burgundy."

"Not me. I like everything sweet. Sweet wine, sweet women, sweet pastries … Everything *sweet*. Life is bitter enough," Rasputin said, taking his glass. "Here is to sweetness!" Rasputin emptied his glass at once.

"He drinks wine as if it were vodka," Felix thought with contempt. "A true *mouzhik!*"

"Good!" Rasputin grunted and wiped his mouth with the back of his hand. The muted sounds of jolly music continued to seep into the basement room. "They must be having fun, up there," Rasputin said. "Should we join them?"

"I think, they are leaving," Felix said, covertly observing him, waiting to detect some signs of reaction to the poison. There were none.

"Give me some more of your marvelous wine," Rasputin said, proffering Felix his glass.

"Gladly!" Felix refilled the glass almost to the top. "Have some pastry."

Rasputin concentrated his attention on the Sèvres platter of non-poisoned pastries, choosing a chocolate one. "Such a tiny one," he commented. "Just two bites!"

"Have more, as you can see, we have plenty." Felix picked up the Meissen platter and offered it to his guest.

"Don't mind if I do," Rasputin picked up one with rose cream. He chomped on it, smacking his lips. "Delicious. I like it even better than a chocolate one." He picked another rose-creamed pastry and devoured it.

"Have some more!" Felix exclaimed, moving the platter under his guest's elbow. He watched nervously as Rasputin ate two more little cakes and drank all his wine. He showed no signs of discomfort.

"If you don't mind, I'll go upstairs and see what's holding up my wife," Felix said. "I'll be back in a minute!" He ran up the winding staircase to his waiting collaborators.

"Is the beast dead?" Purishkevich greeted him at the door, stopping the gramophone.

"No! He drinks and eats like a pig and nothing touches him. He is inhuman!" Felix breathed out, not trying anymore to hide his shaking hands. "He is the Devil!"

"Pull yourself together," Purishkevich said, placing his arm on Youssoupov's shoulder. "Go back. Give him more wine. It must work!" He glanced at his watch. "It's getting late. It's almost one. We must get rid of the body before morning."

Youssoupov nodded. He collected himself. With new determination, he began descending the spiral staircase. "Yankee Doodle" filled the air again.

Rasputin was reclining on one of the divans. "I feel a bit dizzy," he said.

"Have a little more wine," Felix said. "Nothing is better for dizziness," he joked, filling the cranberry-colored glass with more poisoned wine.

Rasputin accepted the glass. "Is she coming?"

"Yes, in a few minutes. She wants to freshen herself up. You know how women are."

Rasputin sipped his wine this time, like a connoisseur. "It is really good! So light and sweet!"

"I'll send you a case, if you like it so much," Felix promised. "Another pastry?"

"I feel a little dizzy. Sing something for me. I like when you sing Gypsy songs. Sing something lively ... Sing *'Guy-da troika!'"*

Youssoupov picked up his guitar. "The poison must be working." He plucked the strings and began to sing a popular cabaret song about two lovers riding in a troika through the snow. He had a pleasant baritone voice, and Rasputin closed his eyes as if enchanted.

Felix watched Rasputin closely. Hatred mixed with fear was overflowing his heart. A painting of the devil by the famous Symbolist artist Mikhail Vrubel came to mind. Rasputin was absolutely still through the last chorus and final notes of the song. Youssoupov finished and stared at his lifeless guest, not knowing what to think. He had never seen anyone die.

"Don't stop. Sing it again," Rasputin murmured. "I like your voice."

Youssoupov was startled, but then picked up the guitar again and bellowed the same song. His nerves were stressed to the point of snapping. "Die, you Demon!" he cried in his mind. Rasputin's eyes were closed, but he moved his finger over his knee in time with the music.

Felix jumped to his feet and rushed again up the winding staircase. He was out of control.

"Is it done?" Purishkevich cried.

"No!" Youssoupov yelled. "He doesn't die! The poison doesn't even touch him!" Felix's beliefs in the supernatural were beginning to take over his mind. "I am telling you, he *is* the Devil!"

The Grand Duke put a comforting arm around his shoulder. "Calm down ..." he said, looking straight at Felix for once. "Perhaps we should forget the poison. We should use the gun."

"But, of course! We should use the gun!" Felix exclaimed with the sudden outburst of new energy. He glared at doctor Lazovert. "Your poison is worthless! He must be shot! Give me your gun, Dimitri," he turned to the Grand Duke.

Dimitri Pavlovich reached for his holster and retrieved his revolver. "Be careful, it's cocked," he warned.

"Maybe we all should go down and strangle him?" Purishkevich suggested.

"No. I'll do it." Felix was calm again. With the gun in his pocket, Felix once again went down the stairs.

Rasputin was sitting at the table now, breathing laboriously, his head hung low."I am not feeling too well," he complained. "My gut is burning. Give me some wine, I am thirsty."

"The poison is working!" Felix thought as he filled the glass to the rim and handed it to Rasputin, who began to drink thirstily. To Youssoupov's horror, the wine seemed to revive him.

"I want to go to the Gypsies," Rasputin suddenly announced, trying to stand. "To hell with your wife. She doesn't want to see me. And I don't want to see her. Who is she anyway? I see the Empress of Russia! Anytime! Whenever I want to!" He stood, wobbling and grabbing the table for support. "I am good and drunk!" he declared happily, a silly smile spreading over his face. "Let's go to the Gypsies! I love you, Felix! Come here, let me kiss you."

"He is the Devil," Felix thought, backing away. Rasputin wobbled to the ebony cabinet and for the first time noticed the crucifix on top of it.

"Where did you get that?" he mumbled, his tongue refusing to obey him. "Is it also Chinese?"

"No, it is not Chinese, and you should recognize it, Satan, and fall on your knees before it!" Felix screamed hysterically, raising the gun. "Pray for your soul, if you know how, you Demon!" he shouted as he pressed the trigger, hitting Rasputin in the back. "Burn in Hell where you belong!"

With a wild scream Rasputin fell on the white bearskin rug.

The rock crystal crucifix fell to the stone floor, a large crack disfiguring its carved face.

The conspirators heard the shot and the scream. Crowding one another on the narrow staircase, they rushed into the basement.

Rasputin was sprawled on the floor face down, blood spreading across his white shirt in a widening dark red blot.

"At last!" Purishkevich cried, both hands clasped over his head as if he were a winning boxer.

The doctor bent down to check Rasputin's pulse. He felt none. "Congratulations!" he vigorously shook Youssoupov's hand. The Grand Duke embraced Felix and kissed him on both cheeks.

They dragged the body by its legs to the stone part of the floor to save the bearskin from staining with blood and then danced up the staircase to Youssoupov's study. Laughing like idiots, slapping one another on their backs, gulping cognac as if it were water, their hysterical relief was bordering on insanity.

Finally, Purishkevich reminded everyone that they still had a lot to do. It was almost three o'clock, and they still had to dispose of the body, burn the clothes, and clean up the mess. Once again they filed down along the stairs to the basement room.

Rasputin was not there. The side door to the small courtyard gaped open and they could see a figure limping over the white snow toward the gate leading to the canal.

"The Devil is still alive!" Youssoupov screamed like a peasant baba. "Somebody, shoot him!"

Purishkevich drew out his heavy pistol and a loud shot fractured the night. He missed.

Rasputin was almost at the gate. One moment more and he would be out on the street. Purishkevich pulled the trigger again. He missed again. Rasputin was shaking the rusty gate, trying to open it. Supporting his trembling right hand with his equally trembling left one, Purishkevich shot again, this time hitting Rasputin's broad back. The man stopped, his body sagging, one of his hands still clutching at the gate. He tried to turn around.

Purishkevich aimed at his head and released the trigger. This time, Rasputin fell.

For a moment the conspirators froze, reality suddenly overwhelming them. They stared at the bleeding body, still twitching on the snow, and a new disturbing emotion grasped each of them: they could not remember why they hated that man so much that they had to murder him. They were suddenly unable to look at one another.

They dragged the body back to the basement, leaving a long bloody trail in the snow. Once inside, their original hatred returned. They kicked the still warm body with their boots. Purishkevich spat in his face, the sputum sliding slowly down into the murdered man's beard.

Finally, Sukhotin regained his composure. "We still have things to do, gentlemen! Let's wrap the body and get it into the Malaya Nevka!"

They rolled the body into a heavy curtain and tied it with a rope. It took four of them to carry the body to the automobile. The Grand Duke drove, with Sukhotin sitting next to him, while Purishkevich and Youssoupov sat in the back seat with the dead body between them. Lazovert departed for the train, carrying along the pastries and Rasputin's coat to burn. The doctor's nerves were shattered. He was unable to deal with the ghastly affair anymore.

The men drove through dark Petrograd toward their chosen spot between Petrovsky and Krestovsky Islands, where several fishing holes were cut through the ice.

Felix felt like screaming. He bit his lower lip and clasped his hands between his knees. The automobile rocked on the bumpy road, each bump shifting the dead body toward one or the other passenger. Felix moved a little farther away from the corpse, but the small gap made it even worse: the corpse leaned toward him.

"Can't you drive more carefully?" he yelled at the Grand Duke.

Dimitri Pavlovich ignored him. He, too, was at the limit of his mental endurance.

Finally, they arrived at their destination: a small wooden bridge joining the islands. Both islands were dark and spooky. The frozen Malaya Nevka, a tributary of the Nevá, stretched like a derelict narrow road, full of bumps and potholes. Like most city canals and Nevá tributaries, it was a dumping ground for snow from central parts of the city. Dirty snow was piled along the edges, while the center of the frozen river was disfigured by round fishing holes.

"Stop here," Purishkevich ordered. He took over the leadership of the operation. Felix was useless in the throes of his hysterical mysticism. He trembled and mumbled to himself, making the sign of the cross, his eyes periodically clouding with tears.

"Take hold of yourself," Purishkevich told him. "In a few hours we'll be proclaimed the saviors of our country."

They got out of the automobile and stood at the railing, listening. Everything was dead quiet. Purishkevich lit a lantern and lowered it over the bridge railing, searching for a suitable fishing hole. "Here," he pointed down. "It looks wide enough. Hurry!" The Grand Duke and Sukhotin pulled the body out of the motorcar and lowered it over the rail and into the hole. They heard the thin ice break under the weight of the body.

"Let's go, let's go! It's almost morning!" Purishkevich hurried them from the car, where he was waiting with Youssoupov. Shivering and wet, Dimitri Pavlovich and Sukhotin joined them.

The Grand Duke started the engine. Felix was shaking in the back seat. "You have forgotten the chains," he muttered, his teeth chattering. "To weigh the body ... The chains are still here, on the floor ... I can't think straight ... I am scared."

"My God! How could we do that! The body may surface ..." Purishkevich said, touching the forgotten chains with his foot. "We must stay calm. There is nothing we can do about it now. We must finish what we started in the name of our Lord and our Fatherland! Pull yourselves together, gentlemen. Dimitri, let's go!"

Dimitri Pavlovich backed up the machine, its bumper striking a snowdrift. Cursing loudly he turned and began the long drive back to the city. Left behind on the wooden bridge, near the railing, was one of Rasputin's boots, overlooked by his assassins.

By noon many people in Petrograd knew that Rasputin had disappeared. By mid-afternoon, many more had become aware that he was murdered, and by the evening the authorities knew who had killed him.

The clues were easy to follow: Youssoupov Palace was located directly across the canal from the police Home Office. Officers on duty had heard shots coming from the palace and noted it in their log book. Later, officers sent to investigate the shooting were met by the disheveled Prince himself, who at first refused to let them in. When they insisted, he said that some drunken guest had shot his dog.

The investigating officers, who by now included several high ranking generals, were skeptical. Then suddenly, Youssoupov's frayed nerves snapped completely. He disclosed the truth: he and Purishkevich were the ones who had killed the public enemy, the Devil, Grigory Rasputin.

With obvious relief, Felix excused himself and drove to his father-in-law's palace. He went to bed in utter exhaustion.

The newspapers, under strict censorship, were muted about the incident. Only one of them mentioned Rasputin's disappearance. In small print, without mentioning Rasputin or Youssoupov by name, the paper announced that "a certain person, disappeared after visiting another certain person."

The next day one newspaper decided to challenge the censorship. It printed a short announcement that Rasputin had been killed at a party in "one of the aristocratic homes in Petrograd." This news was picked up by other papers. Within twenty-four hours the whole country knew that Rasputin had been murdered.

Upon learning the identity of the assassins from the police Home Office, the Empress immediately ordered that Felix Youssoupov and Grand Duke Dimitri Pavlovich be placed under house arrest.

Purishkevich, full of pride for his part in the conspiracy, nevertheless found it wise to leave Petrograd: he took Doctor Lazovert and Lieutenant Sukhotin on his train directly to the front, where they were greeted as heroes.

Petrograd's salons buzzed with excitement. Rumors passed back and forth among friends who had heard something from their servants, who had friends working for one or the other of the participants. Everyone gossiped, sifting and analyzing scant information, trying to imagine the details of the crime.

On December 18, a trail of blood and a lone felt boot were discovered by an ice fisherman on Petrovsky Bridge. This led to the discovery of a body, identified as that of Grigory Efimovich Rasputin. The right arm of the corpse was outside of its binds, as if Rasputin had tried to set himself free. Was he still *alive* when he was shoved under the ice? A partial autopsy showed that Rasputin's lungs contained water, which could have meant that he had died of drowning.

The Empress ordered a stop to any further autopsy, and no official report was issued. The Emperor hurried back from Stavka to be with his grieving wife and to attend the funeral. "Who is going to help our son should he become ill again?" the Empress asked him when he entered her boudoir. The Tsar had no answer.

23

The Homeric proportions of Rasputin's murder and its aftermath were dwarfed in General Rezánov's household by news received from Alexander Kozakov.

> *Your High Excellency, the Esteemed General Rezánov,*
>
> *Your son, Lieutenant Andrei Vladímirovich Rezánov, is recovering from wounds after being shot down near Hutanova. We are sending him to Odessa's military hospital since our field facilities are not able to care for such severe injuries. I am proud to report that Lieutenant Rezánov again has proven himself to be one of our bravest pilots: despite being seriously wounded, he succeeded in shooting down an enemy Albatros. His name has been submitted to the St. George Committee for an award of the Cross of St. George.*
>
> *Congratulations to you and your family.*
> *With respect,*
> *Staff Captain Alexander Kozakov*
> *Commander, First Combat Air Detachment*

General Rezánov read the letter again, tears clouding his eyes. "My boy ... shot down ... seriously wounded ..." He thought of calling his wife, but decided to wait. He could not deal with the hysterics that he knew would follow this devastating news.

He paced the floor of his study and then summoned his aide-de-camp. "Read that," he said to Captain Borisov, giving him the letter. "I want more information. I'll try to reach the Grand Duke and get the details. We must keep the news away from the ladies until we know more, do you understand?"

"Yes, sir, I understand."

The general sank into his chair, his stately military posture collapsing under the weight of his sorrow. He was suddenly an aging man, his shoulders sagging, his face blanched and his vision clouded with tears.

The civilian telephone on his desk rang sharply. Maria Nikoláyevna's familiar voice sounded unusually strident. "Volódya, we have a letter from Andrei's friend Captain Egórov," she began without preliminary greetings.

The general could hear she had been crying. "I know," he interrupted. "I have just received a letter from the commander of his squadron. Does Larissa know?"

"Yes. She wants to go to Odessa. She is graduating next month, but she wants to go to Odessa immediately. What are we to do?"

"Come to my house. Now. With Larissa. Don't panic: he is alive, and that's what is important. I did not tell his mother yet … You know how she is, so you and I must do it together. I am sending my automobile to pick you up." He replaced the receiver.

Within an hour Maria Nikoláyevna and Larissa had arrived. Larissa ran into the house without waiting for her mother to get out of the car. She rushed up the marble staircase, two steps at the time, to her father-in-law's study.

"Larissa! What are you doing here?" Varvara Mikháilovna, who was about to descend the stairs, exclaimed from the landing. "Why such a hurry?"

One look at Larissa's face twisted with pain told her everything. "It's Andrei!" she cried.

"He's alive, he is only wounded," Maria Nikoláyevna shouted from the bottom of the stairs.

"No!" Varvara screamed, clutching at her heart.

"Not now!" Larissa growled, slapping her mother-in-law's cheek. Torn apart with her pain, she had no pity for her mother-in-law.

232

"Control yourself," Maria Nikoláyevna said sternly to Larissa. She turned to a maid. "Help me take her into her room. Bring me some water and valerian drops," she ordered briskly.

Together they helped Varvara Mikháilovna to her feet. "Andrei is alive. He is wounded and has been sent to Odessa," Maria Nikoláyevna said soothingly. With the help of the maid, she unlaced and took off her friend's corset and shoes and led her to her bed.

Larissa felt guilty for having slapped her mother-in-law. She realized that she had expressed her own despair in that slap. She kissed her mother-in-law's hands and they both dissolved in tears.

"Stop it!" Maria Nikoláyevna shouted. "It's no time for crying. We must make some important decisions now …" She counted out the valerian drops into a glass of water and made Varvara Mikháilovna drink it. "Ask the General to come to Madame's room," she ordered the maid.

"Yes, Ma'am," the maid said, wiping her own tears with her apron. She too adored Andrei.

Wearing a velvet smoking jacket over his military breeches, the general entered his wife's boudoir braced for the torrent of tears he knew would greet him. He was surprised that his wife was reasonably calm, although her eyes were rimmed in red and her nose swollen. So were Larissa's, and even the maid's. Only Maria Nikoláyevna seemed to be in full possession of her senses.

"Sit down, Volódya," she said, indicating a chair near the bed. She and Larissa settled on a small settee in the embrasure of the bay window. "We must decide what has to be done. You told me that you were seeking some details about Andrei." At the mention of Andrei's name, Varvara Mikháilovna and Larissa began to sob again.

"Stop it!" Maria Nikoláyevna raised her voice. "Enough of these hysterics!"

General Rezánov glanced at the maid. "You may go, Glásha, we will tell you later about the young master," he said kindly. He knew that she was eager to hear the news, but he did not want his information spread in the servants' quarters and beyond.

"Yes, *barin*," Glásha said, wiping her tears with the back of her hand as she left the room.

"Well?" Maria Nikoláyevna prodded.

The general cleared his throat, lowering his voice in case Glásha was listening at the door, he said, "There is a lot of action right now at the southwestern front. Austro-Hungarian forces are on the offensive, and

233

our positions are seriously threatened. An enemy breakthrough is eminent. Our troops will have to retreat. As a precaution, we must evacuate our wounded further inland, to keep them safe."

"But what about our Andrúsha?" Larissa interrupted, not interested in the overall strategy.

"That I don't know. So far I could get no specific information about Andrei."

"I'll go to Odessa tomorrow!" Larissa declared, jumping up. "Please arrange for my train tickets."

"Don't be so rushed," the general said. "You still have to graduate."

"I don't give a damn about graduation! I'll go to Odessa and volunteer at the military hospital. You write me a letter of introduction, and I am sure they will accept me, the daughter-in-law of the famous general! If not—I'll bribe my way into the hospital. I have enough money to do so."

She spoke brashly, wishing to shock them, and she succeeded. Her crying was over: she was the daughter of Maria Nikoláyevna Orlova, ready to face reality and take action.

"Slow down," the general said. "We don't know yet whether Andrei is already in Odessa or if he is still in transit. You don't need to be there immediately." He had already mentally surrendered himself to her will: she would go to Odessa, with his permission or without it. "Before you go we need to make arrangements for your lodgings."

"I can find lodgings when I get there."

"No," the general said firmly. "Enough of this female assertiveness," he thought, his face reddening.

Larissa wanted to object, but her mother put a restraining hand on her knee. "No one has asked for my opinion," she said, "but as Larissa's mother and Andrei's godmother, I am entitled to one. I am going to allow her to go to Odessa as soon as possible, even if it means that she must miss her graduation. Graduations are just a formality. She needs to be with Andrei if his wounds are serious, as the letter said."

"What letter?" Varvara Mikháilovna and Larissa exclaimed almost in one voice. The general sighed. He reached into his pocket. "I did not want to upset you, my dear, until I knew more about the situation," he said sheepishly, looking at his wife.

"You did not want to *upset me!*" she shrieked like a fishwife. *"Read it to me now!"*

The general obeyed. When he finished, Varvara Mikháilovna dissolved into sobs.

"Stop it!" Maria Nikoláyevna raised her voice again. "Stop your hysterics!" She turned to Larissa. "I'll go with you to Odessa and see you settled. I'll bring back all the information and, if possible, arrange for transferring Andrei to a Petrograd hospital, where we all can take care of him. That is my decision. Volódya, please arrange for our tickets."

"What about me? I want to go, too! He is *my son!*" Varvara Mikháilovna pleaded in a teary voice.

"Your health is too fragile," Maria Nikoláyevna said in a gentler tone. "Your duty will be to make sure that when we bring Andrúsha back home, everything will be ready for him."

"Yes, my dear, I think that is an excellent idea," the general said, looking with gratitude at Maria Nikoláyevna.

And so it was done. Three days later, Maria Nikoláyevna and Larissa boarded the train bound for Moscow-Kursk-Kiev, where their wagon-lit would be reattached to the train going to Odessa.

They were comfortably settled in a two-berth compartment with its own toilet. Upon Maria Nikoláyevna's suggestion they were dressed in simple clothing, wearing no jewelry except their wedding rings and carrying sparse luggage. "Whatever else we might need, we can buy in Odessa," Maria Nikoláyevna declared. They looked like two school teachers from a Women's Gymnasium.

To their surprise, Larissa received her diploma a few days ahead of time, and the Chief Surgeon wrote a letter of introduction to his colleague in Odessa, recommending her as a nurse. With the additional letter of introduction from General Vladímir Rezánov, Larissa was assured a welcome reception in Odessa.

The general accompanied them to the railroad station. "Go with God's blessing," he said, kissing them both and making the sign of the cross over them. "Let's hope that you will be able to bring our boy home."

"We'll telegraph you the news as soon as we know what's going on," Maria Nikoláyevna said. They all sat down for a minute of prayer, as the tradition prescribed, then the general kissed them both twice on their cheeks, and left the compartment.

The train began to move away, slowly gathering speed.

It was to be a journey of three or four days, perhaps even longer because military trains would be given priority. "We might as well unpack our night clothes and put on our robes," Maria Nikoláyevna said. "I have no desire to go to the dining car. We shall order food to be brought in, do you agree?"

"Oh, yes. I am in no mood to be around strangers." They unpacked their toiletries, neatly arranging their hair brushes, combs, toothbrushes and tins of tooth powder on each side of the mirror in their tiny lavatory. Then, changing into bulky terry cloth bathrobes and slippers, they sat on their beds across from one another, staring at the large window filmed over with delicate tracings of hoarfrost.

"Well, here we are, on our way to sunny Odessa!" Maria Nikoláyevna said. "I have had enough of sleet and blizzards! It will be nice to walk under leafy trees in the warm sun ... By the way, do you know what we all have forgotten?"

Larissa shrugged her shoulders.

"It's almost Christmas!"

Larissa smiled sadly. "So it is ... You are right."

"We all did. Even the servants. Everybody was too preoccupied with Rasputin's murder first, and now Andrei. Anyway, in a few days you will see your husband, whom you haven't seen for several months. So, tell me, how do you feel?"

"I don't know, Mama. Of course, I am happy that I'll see him. But I am worried, also. I try to prepare myself for seeing a terribly mangled man, who is my husband, whom I adore. But, *I don't know him*, Mama. He is a stranger to me, even though we *knew* one another all our lives. We saw each other during the holidays when we were children, we played together at Christmas, we exchanged Easter eggs and kisses at Easter ... And when we grew up, we danced at the balls, fell in love and married. But we had only *four* days to learn about each other as persons! ... And then Andrei was taken away from me by this stupid, horrid war. We have never learned anything about one another ... I don't even know his favorite color! And now ..." she did not finish.

Her mother observed her closely. Larissa was calm, but oh, so sad. "Come here," she said. "Sit next to me."

Larissa sat next to her mother. Maria Nikoláyevna put her arms around her and kissed her. "You'll learn a lot about him while you'll be taking care of him. Men, when they are disabled, become little boys again and open up to women, their wives or mothers or even their childhood nurses. You'll know him in no time, rest assured. And you could find out what is his favorite color!" she smiled and brushed a strand of loosened hair off her daughter's face.

"But will he know *who I am?*"

"That will come a little later, when he is well again. One day he will suddenly realize that he knows you only as his lover and caregiver. He will want to know you as a person. And he will fall in love with you all over again when he discovers who you are, and what is *your* favorite color."

Larissa smiled. "It sounds so wonderful! Is that how it was with you and Papa? I know that your marriage was arranged by your parents and you did not meet one another until you were engaged."

"With us it was different. It took many years before we finally knew one another. We already had you and Petya. Frankly, it was only *then* that we realized that we truly loved each other."

"But what about … passion? When you were first married? Haven't you been in love?"

Maria Nikoláyevna smiled, somewhat ruefully. "Passion, my dear, has nothing to do with love. When people are very young, as you and Andrúsha, passion dominates your feelings for one another. As you grow older, love begins to dominate your passion. Anyway, let's have some tea! I brought along a box of French chocolates," she cut short their discussion. She realized that perhaps she had confused Larissa more than she had intended.

She pressed the button above her bed to summon the porter.

They sipped tea from tall glasses in silver *podstakanniki* and savored chocolates from a red velvet coffer. "Yesterday, when I stopped at the Elyseev's for the chocolates, I saw a large group of factory workers marching along the Nevsky prospect carrying slogans," Maria Nikoláyevna began, opening a new conversation. "I must confess, I was frightened. I ducked back into the store, actually feeling ashamed that there I was, with the most expensive box of chocolates, while those marching people had nothing, not even bread! It's *awful* what is happening in our country! I don't think that the assassination of Rasputin has changed anything. I think that the Emperor is a good but weak man who is surrounded by men incapable of doing anything positive under the present system."

"What should they do? What do you mean?"

"I mean, first, we must get out of this war. Then, Russia should be governed by the Parliament, like in England. The Tsar should be like the

King of England, a titular ruler, with limited power. They call it a *constitutional monarchy*."

"Who would rule Russia, if not the Tsar?"

"The Duma. Representatives would be elected by the citizens to serve as deputies for all of us, rich or poor. They would make the laws under a constitution. The *absolute* monarchy, the Tsar as autocrat, *'anointed by God'*, would be abolished!"

"Mama, you are a revolutionary!" Larissa exclaimed, not knowing whether to laugh or take her seriously.

"No, I am not. But you can't deny that the English have it right! I'll go a little further: I like what the *Americans* have done—no kings, no tsars to govern them. Just a smart constitution with reasonable laws applied to all equally!"

"Mama, you have created a new problem for me: not only do I not know my husband's favorite color, but now, I don't know *you* either! Did Papa think the same way?"

"Yes, my dear. He was always a *"respublicanets"* in his heart, which of course is quite dangerous to be in an absolute monarchy. He did not belong to any subversive organizations, nor did he ever talk about his beliefs to anyone but to Andrei's father and me. He was a loyal Russian officer who would have died for his Tsar, but his thoughts were subversive, by our standards. And, I may add, Andrei's father shared his beliefs." She picked up a piece of chocolate and continued, "I don't approve of *a revolution*. All revolutions are brutal. But I do believe in parliamentary rule. I believe in the Republic."

"I don't know what to say," Larissa said slowly. "I am totally confused."

"You are a smart girl. Say nothing about it to anyone. What I have been saying is a *subversive* thing in Russia, under present circumstances."

Larissa looked pensive. "You know, Mama, I had a very disturbing experience a couple of weeks ago when I was riding in the konka, going to my courses. I haven't told you about it because I was afraid that you might forbid me going to the courses, but now, I'll tell you what happened."

Maria Nikoláyevna listened to her daughter's recollection, thinking "my little girl is finally facing real life ... her protected, happy existence is over ... how sad!"

Larissa finished her story. "You know, Mama, at first, I was disgusted by the looting and the fighting and all that senseless destruction. But then, I thought, what would I have done if I were desperate, if I had a child and nothing to feed it? Would I break a window to grab a loaf of bread? Yes, I would. Then, when the Cossacks came and started to whip these people, I suddenly began to hate the Cossacks, the soldiers whom we always venerated as the most noble. So, who were the criminals? The rioters or the Cossacks?"

Maria Nikoláyevna shook her head sadly. "The barbaric times we live in make everybody a criminal. As the war continues, we'll see more riots, more beatings and more killings on both sides … I shudder when I think of it," she said and actually shuddered.

The next day, they arrived in Moscow. The wagon-lit was immediately attached to another train and within an hour they were well on their way toward Kiev.

"I hope the rest of our trip will be as smooth as this," Larissa said. "I don't want to be delayed in Kursk or even in Kiev. I want to go to Odessa without delay!"

"I brought along a travel brochure about Odessa. I was there only once with my parents when I was a little girl and all that I remember about it was the amazing long and wide expanse of stairs that led from some statue at the top, all the way down to the sea. It was so huge, that I was frightened. I remember, I had a new red ball and I had dropped it. I watched it as it kept rolling and rolling from one step to another, all the way to the sea, finally disappearing!" She laughed. "Of course that was my impression as a child; now, the stairs may not look so grandiose."

"But they may be still dangerous should one fall and roll down, like your ball," Larissa said, smiling.

"That's true. Anyway, let's take a look at this brochure and learn some facts about the city." She opened the gaudy pamphlet with a bright blue-colored sea and an armada of sailboats on the cover. She began to read.

Larissa stared at the frosted window. The rhythmic sound of the train, instead of soothing her, made her nervous, and the frost-covered windows that precluded any chance of viewing the landscape made her feel claustrophobic. She yearned for Andrei. Her body craved him, her desire starting in her loins and spreading like a warm wave enveloping her whole body. It was a sharp, pleasurable feeling and she enjoyed it. She had it mostly in her sleep, but she could invoke it almost any time by thinking of him. Lately however, her imagination supplied her only with images of his broken body, her pleasurable memories becoming abstract.

"Here it is, the famous Steps," Maria Nikoláyevna said, pointing to a photograph. "It says here that the staircase is 142 meters long. I wonder, how many *actual* steps are there? They don't mention it. Oh, here is the monument to Duc de Richelieu. Our Tsar Alexander I appointed him as the Governor-General of Odessa in 1803."

"A Frenchman as Russian Governor?"

"It says here, that the Duc had escaped from the French Revolution and served under Catherine the Great. It is left to the readers' imagination as to *how* he served *under* her. She was quite hefty!" She giggled.

"Mother!" Larissa cried, shocked.

"There is the Opera house! It says here that it is the most beautiful baroque opera house after the Vienna Opera. So, as soon as Andrei becomes ambulatory you could have some pleasure by going to the Opera!"

"That would be nice," Larissa said without much enthusiasm.

"Cheer up, darling girl! You'll like it in Odessa. It will be warm and beautiful, and as I read somewhere, Odessa is now the only Russian city where food is plentiful! Do you want me to read you some facts about the city?"

"If you wish."

"Oh, here is something very interesting! There are *catacombs* under the city! Let's see what they say here. *The Odessa catacombs are the largest in the world. They consist of more than 2,500 versts, about 3,500 feet.'* That's hard to believe!" she put the brochure down. "2,500 versts? That must be a mistake—a typographical error."

"Let me see," Larissa took the brochure. "Well, that's what it says. It also says, 'the population of Odessa is polyglot, and its languages and dialects are many. The largest block of population is Jewish, with their own dialect called Yiddish. But the official language of Odessa is Russian.'"

"What about the Navy?" her mother asked. "Odessa is known as a naval base. As a matter of fact, do you know anything about the mutiny on the *Potemkin?*"

"No. I have never heard of it."

"It was an infamous episode in our history when a group of sailors mutinied on the battleship *Prince Potemkin* in the Odessa Harbor. It was in 1905. You and Peter were still young children then. There was a lot of unrest in the cities, strikes and demonstrations, not as bad as it is now, but bad enough. The sailors on the *Prince Potemkin* apparently demanded better food. There was a rumor that they were served some rotten meat. The captain did not believe it and ordered them to eat it. They refused, demanding that a doctor be sent to verify that the meat was *rotten*. The doctor egregiously certified the meat suitable for human consumption. The captain once more ordered the sailors to eat it. Again, they refused. The marines were called on the top deck, but I think they refused to shoot at the sailors. The sailors overpowered their officers, threw many of them overboard, executed the captain and the doctor, and took command of the ship. They raised the red flag of the revolution and sent signals to other ships of the fleet inviting them to join the revolt. The Commander of the Black Sea Fleet feared that the other ships might join the mutineers, so he permitted the *Potemkin* to leave Odessa harbor. It sailed to Rumania, where it was immediately impounded and its crew repatriated back to Russia. The leaders of the mutiny were executed. The *Potemkin* was eventually returned to the Black Sea Fleet. There were rumors that the divers who were examining the ship's hull upon its return saw the skeletons of the dead officers standing upright and swaying under the water, their feet weighted down with chains. I don't know if it is true, but that's what people were saying in those days."

"How awful … I have never thought of us, Russians, as brutal people …" Larissa said pensively. "But lately, all I am hearing about or seeing are examples of our brutality."

"It is not just us, darling. Think of the Crusades, or of the Inquisition! Think of the cannibals in Africa! And what about Henry VIII and his unfortunate wives? And, what about the French Revolution and its guillotine? It is not only Russians. It's the whole of *humanity* that lacks humanity, if you excuse my unintended pun," her mother exclaimed.

Larissa leafed absentmindedly through the travel brochure, thinking, "Yes, even my Andrúsha killed some unknown men, who in their turn tried to kill him … Is there any end to this madness?"

The train kept going toward Odessa without interruption by military traffic. Soon the windows were clear of frost, an indication they had entered the more hospitable climate. After they passed Kursk, they began to enjoy typical views of Central Russia and Malorossia with its endless forests and rivers, and picturesque Cossack towns and villages.

The closer they came to their destination, the more nervous they both became. They assumed that Andrei was already at Memorial Hospital, but had no idea as to his condition. Larissa imagined the most horrible wounds and injuries, questioning her newly acquired medical knowledge: would she be able to take care of him? What if he had a leg or an arm amputated? Her beautiful golden boy … His beautiful body torn and disfigured … how would he live as a cripple, God forbid. What if he were wounded in his genitals … "I would love him, no matter what, but what about him? Would he still love me? Or, would he hate me for being whole and healthy, while he …" She was afraid to let her imagination to go any further.

24

Andrei, unconscious most of the time, was moved from the field facility at the air base. Egórov accompanied his stretcher to the train station, but Andrei did not recognize him. His thoughts, if he had any, were dominated by nightmares of burning airplanes.

His machine gun-inflicted wound was actually three wounds running into one, continuing from his right hip down to his knee, creating a long and deep cavity along his right thigh. By the time he arrived in Odessa after several days on the military transport train, he had developed an acute myonecrosis, damage to muscle tissue.

Surgeons at Odessa's Memorial Hospital were of the opinion that it was frivolous of the field hospital medical staff to risk sending such a seriously wounded man on a long trip. But there he was, a young pilot, a national hero, dumped on them with orders from Stavka that he should be afforded special attention and care.

The doctors gathered at an emergency *concilium* to decide on a suitable therapy for their new patient. Were he an ordinary man, there would be no problem: his leg would be amputated. But this was no ordinary man. They all had admired him after reading about his heroic deed on the wing of the Voisin. His photograph had been pinned on their own bulletin board, for God's sake!

The unanimous decision was to try maggot debridement therapy, the best available therapy under the circumstances. Tiny maggots, the larvae of green blow flies, would feed on the necrotic tissue, ignoring the healthy flesh. Within several days, the maggots would have grown many times their original size and, hopefully, would have thoroughly cleansed the wounds. Should the maggots fail to take care of the infection, the only remaining action would be immediate amputation. There were no other alternatives.

Doctors applied a colony of tiny maggots imprisoned in moist gauze to Andrei's gaping, foul-smelling wounds. Nurses covered his torn and grotesquely swollen leg with a loose bandage.

"I suppose we should move Lieutenant Rezánov into a private room," the Chief Surgeon Colonel Shubin said. "Considering his fame and the obvious interest of Stavka in his welfare, we must make him as comfortable as we can."

"Besides, we would confine the effluvium to a smaller space and liberate other patients from the awful stink," joked his assistant.

Andrei, lapsed in amnesic blankness, was ignorant of the decisions made about him. Once in a while he would suddenly open his eyes and seem to concentrate on some spot of light, only to fall back into oblivion.

Larissa and her mother arrived in Odessa at eleven o'clock in the evening. Their train had been detained in Kiev for three hours while waiting for some Grand Duchess to board. Larissa fumed. It was too late to go to the hospital. Obviously the Grand Duchess hadn't given a damn about the needs of other passengers on the train.

"Settle down, my dear. We'll go to the hospital first thing in the morning. Meanwhile, we have time to unpack and have a good night's sleep in proper beds," Maria Nikoláyevna said.

They had reservations for a suite of two bedrooms and a sitting room in one of the two best hotels in the city. It was called *Otrada* ("delight") and was located near the seashore on quiet *Ouyutnaya* ("cozy") Street. Maria Nikoláyevna liked the names; they sounded charming and suggested peaceful surroundings. To Larissa the names meant nothing, but to be polite, she agreed with her mother that the place was charming.

Larissa could not sleep. She tossed in her bed, plumped her pillows in search of a cool spot for her feverish face, and when she had finally succumbed to physical and mental exhaustion, she was tormented by nightmares that Andrei was dead. She awoke with a start, her heart beating wildly, for a moment not knowing where she was. Like a little girl, she grabbed her pillow and tip-toed to her mother's room. She climbed into her bed and clung to her as she used to do as a child. Her mother put a reassuring arm around her. "Sh-sh," she whispered "It was just a bad dream ..."

The four-story Memorial Hospital stood large and imposing on a cliff overlooking the Black Sea. It was built in a U-shape with a garden between the wings and an elaborate fountain surrounded by benches in the center. One wing was allocated for officers. The wards in that wing were as large as in the soldiers' wing, but each ward accommodated fewer patients, and there were several private rooms facing the sea.

Andrei was in one of the private rooms. His arms were securely tied to the sides of his bed to prevent him from scratching at the bandage as the maggots did their job. He was covered with a light-weight woolen blanket, arranged to leave his wounded leg uncovered. That leg was bandaged from knee to pelvis, the cloth wrapping around his hips to anchor the bandage. The exposed part of the grotesque, beet-colored leg was supported by a pillow, its crisp whiteness intensifying the wound's ugly colors.

Larissa and her mother froze at the entrance to Andrei's room. The man on the bed hardly looked like Andrei. This was a stranger, his face covered with blond stubble, his hair overgrown and plastered around his damp brow. He looked very thin, almost emaciated, his eyes shut, his mouth hidden by an overgrown moustache.

"Andrúsha!" Larissa shrieked. She dashed toward the bed and knelt, kissing Andrei's tied hand. "My love, my love, I am here, I am with you, I'll make you well!" she kept saying, kissing his hand, wetting it with her tears. Andrei remained silent, oblivious to her presence.

Maria Nikoláyevna, torn by grief, watched her daughter silently.

"I am sorry, Madame! We have not prepared the Lieutenant for your visit," said Colonel Shubin, standing at the door behind her. "We should have shaved him and trimmed his hair, and so forth. We'll send the barber to his room at once."

"That would be nice," Maria Nikoláyevna nodded. "How is he doing?" she asked fighting her own gathering tears.

"The lieutenant is a strong young man. The fact that he is so thin is not very important. As soon as his wounds begin to heal, we'll fatten him up. He is in a coma and badly dehydrated by fever, and we have to feed him only very small amounts of clear chicken broth and purified water, but as soon as he regains consciousness, we'll place him on a more substantial diet. I understand his wife is a trained nurse. Is she familiar with maggot therapy?"

"I don't know. She has just graduated from nursing courses and has never mentioned it. *Maggots*, did you say?"

"Yes, maggots. It is an ancient way of cleansing wounds. Right now, he has three colonies of maggots removing dead tissues from his wounds. We have high hopes that it will work."

"And if it doesn't?"

The colonel glanced at Larissa, who was still kneeling at Andrei's side. "If it doesn't, we'll have to amputate his leg, or we lose him," he said lowering his voice.

Maria Nikoláyevna made the sign of the cross. "Dear Lord!" she sighed.

"However, don't despair. This is only his second day of therapy, and we have already noticed an improvement in the appearance of his wounds. We may avoid gangrene setting in." He smiled. "The Lieutenant is fortunate that his wife is a nurse. With such a huge influx of wounded, we acutely feel the need for more nurses. But not to worry. Since your daughter will be working here as a *volunteer*, I have already ordered that she will be in charge of only one patient—her own husband."

"Thank you, Doctor."

"Don't mention it. Madame Rezánova." He addressed Larissa, "Would you be so kind as to join your mother and me in my study to discuss the details of your duties?"

Larissa stood and wiped her tear-stained face with her handkerchief. She composed herself. "I'll be glad to," she said, trying to keep the tremor out of her voice. "I am eager to start."

Colonel Shubin opened the door to his study. It was furnished in the traditional style of a gentleman's study, with handsome leather-upholstered furniture, a large desk, and tall bookcases with leather-bound books. But instead of Russian, German, French, and English classics, the bookcases contained medical books in all four languages. And Latin.

There was a large fireplace encased in dark green marble with an equestrian painting of the Tsar over it. Every other piece of décor had a medical purpose. The mahogany-paneled walls were practically concealed behind huge multi-colored diagrams of the human body. A full-sized skeleton stood in the corner, its teeth in a ghoulish grin.

With a gesture Colonel Shubin invited his guests to be seated on the leather sofa with a small table in front of it. A tea set for three was laid out on the table. "I thought we should have a bit of tea while we are getting acquainted," he said pleasantly. The colonel pressed a button on his desk and an old, bewhiskered soldier appeared shortly. He stretched out at attention and saluted the doctor. He reminded Larissa of Petrovich: he too, used to stretch out with great pomposity.

"Bring us some good hot tea, Stepanich, and some freshly baked rolls and butter and strawberry jam. Oh, yes, and a few slices of our famous Odessa lemons," the colonel said.

"Yes, Your Excellency," the old man saluted again and left to fill the order.

"Stepanich has been with me for more than twenty-five years," the doctor said. "He used to be the best medical orderly, but in the last couple of years he developed certain health problems, and we decided that for safety sake, it would be better if he became my personal orderly. But his knowledge of the practical care for the wounded never diminished. You may find him helpful," he said to Larissa.

She smiled. "No wonder he reminded me of someone. My husband's flight school had an old mechanic who was like your Stepanich. He was very knowledgeable and kind, even fatherly, to the young pilots. My husband loved him!"

"Sounds like our Stepanich. Anyway, let me tell you about the medical condition of your husband. I hope you are not a *fainting* kind of a woman. Since you are a nurse, even though you are very young, you must have seen and maybe even taken care of all kinds of wounds. How old are you?"

"Almost nineteen."

"Almost nineteen ... how soon will you turn nineteen?"

"In March."

Shubin smiled gently. She was even younger than his own daughter. "How long have you been married?"

Lara did not want him to know that she was with Andrei only four days. "Since August."

"And when was your husband sent to the front?"

Larissa hesitated. "Also in August," she replied, blushing.

Shubin reached for her hand and kissed it. "You poor dear child," he said kindly.

"Thank you," Larissa's eyes filled with tears.

"You have told me, Doctor, that Andrei's conditions are improving," Maria Nikoláyevna said quickly. She did not want Larissa to fall apart again.

"Well, yes. The Lieutenant was brought to us about a week ago. I won't hide the truth from you, he was in a very bad shape after that long trip in the hospital train. He was badly dehydrated and his wounds were infected. We decided to take an aggressive approach. That's why we immediately started the maggot treatment." Shubin watched Larissa's face for a grimace of disgust. There was none. The young woman was very composed, listening with deep attention.

"We are doing everything we can to save his life and his leg," he said to Larissa. "Since you'll be taking care of him as his nurse, I'll treat you as a nurse, and not as a charming young woman. Our Chief nurse, Sister Veronica, is English. She will introduce you to our protocols. She doesn't speak much Russian, but she speaks pretty good French, so you shouldn't have any trouble."

"I speak English," Larissa said.

"Splendid! Then you'll have no problem at all! After we finish our tea, we'll go back and observe Sister Veronica changing the bandage. Sister Veronica will be supervising your work, which I must tell you, will be exhausting. You will be working twelve-hour shifts."

"Who would be watching my husband when I am off?"

"Why, one of the other nurses, of course."

"Then, I have a request, Doctor. Could I be assigned special *no time limit* duties and have an extra bed placed in my husband's room for me to sleep in? Since I'll be only *his* nurse, I could easily fulfill my duties no matter the time."

"Well, let me think ... Oh, here is our tea!" he exclaimed, glad that he had a bit more time to consider her request. He liked the young woman. She was obviously spunky and very much in love with her husband, but she was still *a girl*, barely out of school! Even though she had a diploma, how much did she actually know about nursing, at her age? How could she be allowed to be in full charge of a patient? And what impact might her constant presence in the hospital have on the rest of the staff and patients? These thoughts rushed through his mind as he watched Stepanich place a tray with the small silver samovar and the little basket of warm rolls and jam on the table in front of the visitors.

"Would you mind pouring?" Shubin asked Maria Nikoláyevna distractedly.

"I'll be glad to," she said. She recognized he was stalling as he considered Larissa's request. She understood his reticence.

Maria Nikoláyevna proffered him the tea. "If you have any doubts whether my daughter would be able to fulfill her duties as a nurse, have no fear," she said. "This young woman has nerves of steel and a sense of honor worthy of a Roman senator. She may lack experience, that's true, but under your guidance and the supervision of the Chief Nurse, she will acquire it promptly. She will not quit. She will not complain. She will not be a bother in any way. She will do all the grim tasks assigned to her, and she will help you to save her man!"

The doctor nodded decisively. "I'll have no objections to allowing you to share the room with your husband," he said. "If the Chief Nurse approves, that is. However, if she says 'no,' it will be 'no.' Sister Veronica is the true Chief of Nursing here and her decisions are rarely questioned. Everyone at Memorial, including me, obeys Sister Veronica when it comes to care of our patients. She is priceless in her dedication to her duty, and she demands it from the others. Keep that in mind," he said, staring at Larissa.

"I will," she said, feeling uncomfortable under his stare. "Is he warning me about this woman? Should I fear her?" she thought.

"Meanwhile," he continued, "our linen manager will outfit you with your uniform and your mother with a doctor's robe." He pressed the bell and Stepanich immediately appeared at the door. "Please send Glafíra Ivánovna to my study," he said.

"Right away, Your Excellency. Should I remove the samovar?"

Professor Shubin looked at the ladies."A little more tea?"

"No, thank you," Maria Nikoláyevna said. "It was delicious. I have never tasted such juicy lemons!"

Shubin looked pleased. "It's right from our lemon trees in the garden," he said. "You Petersburgians know nothing about real *fresh* lemons!" he exclaimed with childlike pride. "All right, Stepanich, you may remove the samovar."

Glafíra Ivánovna was a short round woman with a jolly round face and fat little hands with fingers that looked like German sausages. Everything about her looked round, including her coiffure of many small, round curls. She exuded friendliness. She appeared to be perpetually smiling, even when she wasn't smiling: her dark eyes were mere slits lost in her pink cheeks.

"Glafíra Ivánovna, this young lady is our new nurse, Sister Larissa Rezánova. Please outfit her and find a proper visitors' robe for Madame Orlova."

"Yes, Arkady Petrovich," she beamed. "Come with me, my dear," she said to Larissa. "We'll find something for you in no time!"

They gathered in the hall in front of Andrei's room about an hour later. Larissa was now unrecognizable. Attired in a long, dark-blue muslin dress with white cuffs up to her elbows and a broad white apron, her head was surrounded by a white coif, which left only her face visible in its oval opening. She looked like a serene medieval maiden except for the large red cross embroidered on the chest of her apron, an emblem repeated in a smaller version on her coif.

"You look splendid, Sister Larissa!" Shubin exclaimed.

"Very impressive!" her mother agreed, buttoning a white doctors' coat that Glafíra Ivánovna had given her.

"Thank you," Larissa said, her eyes on a tall, angular woman in similar nursing attire but with her sleeves rolled over her elbows. "She must be Sister Veronica," she thought.

"Hello," Veronica said. "I understand, you speak English?"

"I do, but perhaps not ..."

"I am sure, it will be sufficient," Veronica interrupted in a rich low voice. "I am your supervisor, and my name is Veronica. We'll talk with each other in English, agreed?"

"Yes, Ma'am." Larissa was already intimidated by Sister Veronica.

"I recommend that you roll your sleeves up, like mine. Whoever designed the nurses' uniforms obviously knew nothing about what nurses do." She looked sternly at the colonel, as if it were his fault that she was uncomfortable.

"We have requested modern uniforms again," he said apologetically. "Whoever is in charge of uniforms in our Ministries apparently doesn't care about such a small matter as the sleeve length on nurses' uniforms. Perhaps we should take the matter into our own hands and shorten the sleeves ourselves!"

"Why not?" Veronica said. "No one would send us to Siberia for doing that. Or, would they?" she laughed with a short, hawking outburst. "I should think we can find a seamstress to shorten the sleeves."

"I can do it," Maria Nikoláyevna offered. "I am sure you have a sewing machine somewhere, so I can easily do it!"

"Mother! I did not know that you could sew!" Larissa exclaimed.

Her mother smiled slyly. "Ksusha taught me how."

Shubin was as surprised as Larissa. A lady of high social rank was not expected to know a *trade*. It was as if a Grand Duke knew how to repair boots!

"It will give me an excuse to stay longer in Odessa and watch my son-in-law's progress, while doing something useful," Maria Nikoláyevna said.

"I think it is a great idea, Doctor," Veronica said. "Let's chop off our sleeves! Meanwhile, Sister Larissa, roll-up your sleeves, your patient is waiting."

The putrid odor in Andrei's room was overwhelming. Sister Veronica quickly distributed face masks. One after another, they washed their hands with soap and hot water, dusted the insides of the rubber gloves with talcum powder, and then pulled the gloves on.

Andrei was still in a coma. A young military surgeon, Doctor Popov, was writing notes on Andrei's chart.

"Well, let's see now what we have under the dressing …" Dr. Shubin said. "Please, Sister, remove the bandaging."

Sister Veronica picked up the scissors and cut the bandage along the length of Andrei's leg, peeling the wrapping off gently as if she were peeling an Easter egg. The deep ugly wound teeming with fat wiggly larvae was exposed.

Larissa suppressed a cry at the sight of it. Dr. Shubin was right: she had *never* seen such wounds. Maria Nikoláyevna made the sign of the cross.

Doctor Popov picked up a small surgical forceps and lifted a patch of *tulle gras* dressing from one section of the wound.

"Beautiful!" Shubin exclaimed. "Just look how much cleaner it is already! And look how fat they are!" he cried joyously, turning to Maria Nikoláyevna. "I have read that the maggots increase their weight a hundredfold within a day!"

Sister Veronica and Larissa bent over the sphacelated wound. A terrible odor had risen from it, and Larissa tried to breathe though her mouth. Veronica seemed to ignore the odor as she removed two more wound coverings.

"Hold that basin for me," she said, looking toward a small kidney-shaped enameled basin. A bloody patch with maggots removed by Doctor Popov was already there. As Larissa held the basin, Veronica dropped the rest of the patches containing colonies of wiggling creatures into it. "Cover it so they don't crawl out." Larissa covered the basin with its tightly-fitting cover. "Now, we'll irrigate the wounds," Veronica said.

"We use water purified with chlorine," Shubin explained to Maria Nikoláyevna as they watched Sister Veronica and Larissa gently dribble water into the wounds. "Later, when all the necrotic tissue has been removed by the maggots, we shall irrigate the wounds with a special solution and pack the wounds with *tulle gras* dressings soaked in that solution. It creates antisepsis and prevents gangrene and tetanus."

"How long does it take for such deep wounds to heal?" Maria Nikoláyevna asked.

"It is hard to say. But knowing that he was a very healthy young man, I would say two or three months for it to basically heal, that is if we *save* his leg."

"We are ready, Doctor," Sister Veronica said.

"Good." He peered into the wound through his glasses. "Beautiful!" he exclaimed, assessing the maggots' work as if it were a demonstration of some artistic achievement. "Just look at that wound! It is almost debrided!" Maria Nikoláyevna stared at the long ugly hole of red, purple, and almost-black flesh along which lay a few fat maggots that had fallen out of their "cages," as the doctor called the patches of *tulle gras*.

They watched as Veronica folded fresh circles of *tulle gras* into the palm of her cupped hand and squeezed them. When she reopened her hand, the circles took the shape of a cup into which Doctor Popov quickly emptied a small vial of white blowfly eggs that looked like kernels of rice. Veronica placed the filled cups over a part of the wound, as if she were trying to catch a bug under a glass, and held it down firmly. Doctor Popov smeared a small amount of medicinal glue over the edges to keep the cups directly over the wound. They repeated the procedure until the whole wound was covered.

"Are you observing the procedures, Sister Larissa?" asked Shubin. "Tomorrow we expect *you* to assist Sister Veronica."

"Yes, Doctor," Larissa replied.

"All right. You may re-bandage the wound *lightly*," he said. "The maggots must have oxygen. By the way, my name is Arkady Petrovich."

"Yes, Arkady Petrovich." Larissa began to re-bandage Andrei's leg, her hands touching it as gently as she could, willing herself not to panic under the critical stares of Sister Veronica and the doctors and the loving watch of her mother. The putrescent odor made her reel, and she felt nauseated to the point of fainting. *"I am not the fainting kind,"* she told herself now. "I am not the fainting kind!"

She finished bandaging the leg. Sister Veronica watched closely as Larissa took off her contaminated gloves, threw them into a special container, washed her hands and then pulled new gloves on. "Jolly good," Veronica said.

Larissa blushed under her mask. Apparently, she had passed her first test.

Days passed, but Andrei remained in a comatose state. Sister Veronica and Larissa changed his dressings regularly and fed teaspoonfuls of chicken broth in the corner of his mouth, but he was unaware of their efforts.

Larissa left his room only to go to the toilet. She willed herself to ignore the odor of the wound and tried to take her meals in his room, but it proved impossible: she gagged and retched painfully.

"Don't be a fool," Veronica admonished her. "Your love and devotion to your husband will not be questioned if you eat or drink a cup of tea in the mess hall."

"I am not worried about anyone questioning my 'love and devotion,'" Larissa replied tersely, "I just want to be with my husband the moment he regains his consciousness."

"When it happens, he won't recognize you anyway," Veronica said, refusing to be compassionate. "He might even be scared of you!"

"Not my Andrúsha!"

"Have you ever seen anyone coming out of a coma?"

"No," Lara had to admit.

"Well, it's not a pretty sight. Anyhow, you'll soon witness it yourself. Your husband's temperature is at last falling."

"Check his pulse," Maria Nikoláyevna commanded. Veronica raised her eyebrow but said nothing as Larissa lifted Andrei's arm. She counted the pulse and her eyes crinkled in a smile under her mask. "It is *steady!*" *she announced.*

"Marvelous!" Maria Nikoláyevna exclaimed. "I am sure that our boy is on the mend! Now I can join Glafíra Ivánovna and finish the alterations. We have only about twenty uniforms left. I'll leave Andrei to your ministrations!"

"Good," Larissa said. She wished that her mother would go back to Petrograd. Maria Nikoláyevna had become a domineering force around Andrei's room, giving commands and dispensing advice despite her lack of training. She brought fresh flowers into the room every morning. She read some of Pushkin's poetry to Andrei in the hope that he might be able to hear it. Larissa felt annoyed. "Why does she behave as if *she* is the one who takes care of my Andrei? What about Veronica and me? I am a nurse, for God's sakes! She made Glafíra Ivánovna her handmaiden in that sewing room. Before long, she will be running the whole hospital! Let her go home!" Larissa thought in childish rage.

Maria Nikoláyevna was not ready to leave Odessa. She wished to be present when Andrei regained consciousness. Once in a while he mumbled something that no one could decipher, but most of the time he seemed to be asleep, his pulse slow but regular.

The year 1916 was ending. Many hoped that Rasputin's death would return stability to the country's governance. Those hopes proved false.

The Empress continued to meddle in affairs of state, and the Tsar followed her recommendations. The paranoid influence of the Empress began to dominate every aspect of Russian life. She hated the former Supreme Commander, Grand Duke Nikolaí Nikolayevich, and insisted on his exile to the Caucasus. The constant re-shuffling of commanding generals and Cabinet members allowed Brusílov's successful offensive on the Southwestern Front to fizzle out.

The new Supreme Commander, the Tsar, was incapable of stopping the onslaught of the Central Powers. He knew nothing about commanding troops. The phlegmatic Tsar watched as his aides moved little color-coded flags on a huge map of the war theatre to mark the movements of troops. Almost every day the flags with black German crosses moved deeper into Russian territory.

The Tsar did not know how to stop the disaster. "What should I do?" he asked his Chief-of-Staff. "Do I have enough troops?"

General Alexeyev reported that there had been more than seven and a half million Russians fighting on all fronts since the beginning of the war with another two and a half million in ready reserves. The Tsar looked pleased. "My brave Russian people!" he exclaimed, making the sign of the cross. "God, grant them victory!" The general mentioned other statistics: Russian forces had suffered three and a half million casualties, but the Tsar did not seem to hear him.

Wearing no decorations, the Tsar played the role of a humble soldier by leading a Spartan life. He had himself photographed wearing a soldier's uniform, carrying a rifle and the full equipment of a private, including a portable shovel for digging foxholes. He slept on an army camp bed, ate simple meals, and took pills that the Empress sent him to fight his chronic headaches and gastric disorders. Those who observed him on a regular basis thought that he was over-medicated. He looked ill. He was listless, often smiling politely but appearing as if he did not know what was going on around him. He liked to walk in the woods with his aides tagging along a few paces behind, and he enjoyed playing dominos.

Occasionally, the young Tsarevich joined his father at Stavka. Alexei would also wear a private's uniform, and sleep on a camp bed. Father and son played the roles of disciplined soldiers who shared the burdens of war with the rest of the troops. The Tsar allowed his son to attend briefings, where the boy was permitted to move the little flags on the map. The eleven-year-old looked forward to the briefings; he often asked more pertinent questions than his father.

The war was going badly. Turkey signed an agreement with Germany and entered the war on the side of the Central Powers. This closed the Black Sea ports to Allied nations and effectively cut off the foreign aid and supplies that had been reaching Russia via that route. Further north, the Baltic Sea ports became unavailable as well due to the German Navy's U-boats, and to frozen harbors during winter months. Winter, that powerful force, caused delays and cancellation of heavy equipment, guns, ammunition, and aircraft deliveries.

Deliveries of food and fuel from the interior of Russia to her cities were irregular and insufficient; the break-up of the Russian railroad system immobilized hundreds of locomotives, which were broken and abandoned, lacking spare parts. When Romania joined the Allies and the Russian troops were moved to fight in the Carpathian Mountains, the situation grew even worse.

Romania desperately needed help. Germans occupied Bucharest in the winter of 1916, and the Romanian Government moved to Yassy. The Romanians urgently requested more Russian troops. The Tsar obliged his new ally and ordered the reorganization of Russian forces, sending large quantities of troops and equipment to Romania at the expense of his own troops.

Alexander Kozakov's First Combat Air Detachment, renamed KAO-19, was ordered to depart for Romania with their pilots, mechanics, airplanes, and all their equipment. Vassily Egórov was one of the pilots among them. He was due for a month's leave, and he decided to go to Odessa. There was nothing waiting for him in Petrograd. His wife was in the process of divorcing him and he wasn't even sure whether he still had his flat there. Tatiana had most likely helped herself to his belongings.

Egórov hitched a ride with an artillery unit going to Romania and at the border joined a cavalry battalion going to Russia on rotation. It felt good, he thought, to be back in the saddle! The horse was of a sour disposition, but Egórov was a good horseman and enjoyed the challenge. The cavalry officers complained that all their horses were poorly trained. The horses were underfed, and so were their riders. The daily rations of horses' fodder, which was supposed to be twenty pounds of oats per horse daily, were cut in half. As to the soldiers' rations, the officers would not even talk about them. They joked that the Russian soldiers were trained from their cradles to suffer from hunger: *suffering* was what a Russian soldier knew best.

Egórov became aware of a slow burn of discontent among the ranks, from the commanding officers to the ordinary privates. He had not felt it among the officers of his elite group of pilots, but he suspected that the mechanics and the soldiers of the service units were beginning to feel the growing restlessness. Alarming rumors circulated that there were over two thousand strikes in the country. Over a hundred uprisings were recorded in Petrograd alone. Each had to be put down by Cossack troops. Blood had been shed.

"What is happening to our Holy Russia?" everyone seemed to be asking but no one was able to answer.

Egórov arrived in the city in the evening. Odessa met him with a soft, salty breeze from the sea and a velvety darkening sky full of early stars. At the horizon, the thin line of a crimson sunset was reflected by calm blue waters. After the dismal rains and blinding blizzards of Lutsk, after the bone-chilling flights in an open cockpit, it felt as if he were at some health resort. The sounds of music floated toward him from somewhere close to the shore. His spirits soared; he had three weeks to enjoy life again, listening to music, walking along the sea shore, paying a visit or two to the best whorehouses, and of course, seeing Andrei.

It was too late to go to the hospital. He hired a carriage and ordered the driver to take him to the hotel Morskoi, a small, luxurious hotel of well-appointed suites. It was expensive, but Egórov never regretted spending money on comforts. He surrendered his traveling clothes and wrinkled formal uniform to the porter to be cleaned and pressed, with instructions that his boots be shined and the spurs removed.

He took a long bath in a large marble tub, adding hot water from time to time, his first tub bath in many months. He called a barber to shave him, cut his hair, and trim his moustache in the English style. Then he had an epicurean dinner and cognac on the balcony overlooking the sea.

He went to bed, a wide comfortable bed with fine linen sheets and crisp, cool pillowcases.

Egórov awoke the next morning feeling vigorous. He lit a cigarette and watched its smoke curl toward the ceiling. It felt good not to jump out of bed, splash some icy water on his face, and rush to the mess hall for a platter of cold eggs and lumpy oatmeal. It felt good not to climb into the cockpit and rise into hostile skies where death hid behind every cloud. Here, the skies were friendly, wispy clouds were edged with the pink of sunrise, and the sea shone calm and blue. Egórov got up and stepped out on the balcony, stretching, every inch of his body relaxed and ready for the new day. The distant sonorous sound of church bells resonated through the air and Egórov, an agnostic, made the sign of the cross, a habit from his childhood.

The acacia trees under the balcony swarmed with chirping birds; they took off in a noisy cloud at the sight of him. He smiled. At the airfield the birds would be a dangerous nuisance. Here, they were a delight.

He rang for the porter. "I would like to have plenty of hot coffee with cream, a large omelet with ham, a couple of brioches and some jam, and a bottle of chilled Veuve Clicquot." he said.

"Yes, Captain, right away!"

Shortly, the porter was back with Egórov's order while the bellboy brought in his clothes and boots.

"Good. Set the table on the balcony," Egórov said. "I can't get enough of this warm fresh air."

"Yes, Captain, I understand," the old man smiled. "You must be a flyer!"

"Yes, I am."

"God bless you, sir. Enjoy your breakfast!" He closed the door with reverence.

Egórov, still in the bathrobe, settled himself at a small table on the balcony. Several pigeons appeared on the railing of the balcony, promenading back and forth, cooing and ogling him in expectation of sharing his breakfast. Egórov grinned. He had forgotten how pleasurable it used to be to feed the pigeons, he thought. He crumbled some of his brioche and shared it with the greedy birds, his soul at peace.

The dramatic process of debridement of Andrei's wounds was over. A tedious process of healing was about to begin. As the fever subsided, Andrei's lucidity began to return. His hallucinations resembled reality: he saw

Larissa's visage and Maria Nikoláyevna's kind face floating over him. There were voices, but he did not recognize them. A thought flashed through his mind that he was in the falling airplane. "No!" he cried in his mind. "Not again!" he struggled to get up, but there was no strength in his body, only the agonizing pain in his hip. He could not move. His right leg felt as if it was a telegraph pole. Or, maybe it was not even there ... Only the huge pain was there. "It hurts," he whimpered as if he were a child.

A woman in white bent over him. "I know," he thought that he heard her say. She had soft hands and a familiar face.

"Lara," he said and closed his eyes. "No, it can't be Lara ... I want to go home ..."

"It is Lara ... darling, it is Lara ..." She touched his face. "I love you ..." He did not hear her. He was again in the netherworlds of semi-consciousness.

Egórov arrived at Memorial Hospital and presented his documents to the duty officer, a young medical resident who was duly impressed with Egórov's three Orders of St. George. He accompanied him to Colonel Shubin's study.

"I am Captain Vassily Egórov. I was the leader of the patrol when Lieutenant Rezánov was shot down," Egórov introduced himself to the old doctor. "How is he? I know he is seriously wounded, but may I see him? We are best friends."

"Of course, Captain Egórov," the doctor smiled. "Lieutenant Rezánov is much better. We succeeded in saving him from the amputation of his leg. We promised his wife that the Lieutenant will dance the mazurka one of these days!" he chuckled.

"His wife?"

"Yes. Larissa Sergéyevna Rezánova is here, and so is her mother. Do you know them?"

"No, sir, I met the Lieutenant a few months ago, in the service. I have never met his family, but of course I know about them and I have seen their photographs. So, Larissa is here! I am delighted! Now, our Andrúshka will fight like hell to get well again! When can I see him?"

"Right now. Let me get you a white coat ..." He pressed a button on his desk and shortly an orderly appeared at the door. "Stepanich, bring a visitors' coat for the Captain, he is the friend of our famous hero."

"Right away, Your Excellency. May I ask the Captain a question?" Stepanich asked, eyeing Egórov's medals.

"Certainly."

"Were you with our Lieutenant when he climbed on the airplane wing?"

Egórov was amused by the orderly's referral to Andrei as *'our Lieutenant.'* "Yes, I was there. I was flying that plane."

"Oh, God bless you, sir!" Stepanich was full of boyish exaltation as he saluted.

"Thank you," Egórov returned the salute.

Colonel Shubin led Egórov to Andrei's room. "Look whom I have just found!" he exclaimed, opening the door. "Captain Egórov! Our famous patient's flying partner, on leave to visit his friend!"

Two nurses were bent over Andrei. They stopped their work for a moment and stared at the visitor.

"I am Vassily Egórov," he said to the younger nurse. "You must be Larissa!"

"I am," she smiled under her mask and several laughing creases appeared at the corners of her eyes.

"She's lovely!" Egórov thought, although he could see only her large brown eyes with long curving lashes. "How is Andrei?"

"Captain, I am sorry, but Sister Larissa can't talk to you right now. Please leave. In a few minutes we'll be through," the older nurse said sternly. She spoke with a foreign accent, but apparently she was in charge, for Doctor Shubin sheepishly apologized, "Sorry, Sister Veronica, we'll come back in half an hour."

Larissa smiled at them. "Andrúsha is much better," she said to Egórov. "I am so glad to have met you!"

"Sister Larissa!" the older nurse raised her voice. "We don't talk during procedures!"

Shubin closed the door. "Sister Veronica is a tough disciplinarian, and we all obey her," he said to Egórov apologetically. "She is English. But she is priceless when it comes to taking care of the hard cases."

"She looks and sounds quite *formidable*," Egórov said.

"That she is. *Very* formidable, in the English way."

In a while they were back in Andrei's room. Sister Veronica was gone and Larissa, without her mask, was sitting at Andrei's bed, trimming his fingernails with her curved manicure scissors.

Shubin picked up the daily chart hanging on Andrei's bed. "I see our boy has a normal temperature. A few more days, and he'll be talking to us! Well, I'll leave you now, so you two can get acquainted. But tonight, I want both of you, and Maria Nikoláyevna, to have dinner with me. This is *an official order*, Madame Rezánova," he shook his finger at her as if she were a little girl. "You don't have to spend every minute with your husband now. And tonight you don't need to wear your uniform. So, seven o'clock, at my quarters." He made a slight bow toward them and left the room.

"Well!" Larissa exclaimed. "Vassily Sergeyevich, I am so glad that you are here!" She took his hand into both of hers as she stared into his face with her radiant eyes. "Andrúsha wrote so much about you that I feel as if I have known you all my life!"

"I too feel that I have known you for a long time! I admired your photographs and enjoyed whatever Andrei told me about you. So, tell me how he is doing? Does he know that you are here, with him?"

"I don't think so. A couple of times I thought that he had recognized me, but he was delirious and burning with fever. Last night, he called my name, but I know that he did not see me. I must have been in his dreams. Tell me about that terrible ordeal you both went through, that is, when Andrúsha was on the wing of that plane. He wrote nothing about it. All I know about it came from the newspapers and what he wrote to his father."

"Well ... I'll tell you exactly what happened ..." Egórov moved two chairs to the bay window away from Andrei's bed. "It was one of those awe-inspiring, unbelievable situations ..." he said as he brought back in his mind that terrifying flight.

There was a knock at the door. Maria Nikoláyevna hesitated at the partially opened door. "May I come in?" she asked.

"Oh, Mama, come in! This is Captain Egórov, Andrúsha's best friend!" Larissa exclaimed, jumping up. "Vassily Sergeyevich is on leave and he came to see Andrúsha. He was just about to tell me about that terrible flight when Andrúsha climbed on the wing!"

Maria Nikoláyevna opened her arms. As spontaneously as if he were her own son, Egórov walked into her arms.

⁙ 25 ⁙

No one witnessed Andrei regain consciousness. He came out of the stupor suddenly, during the night, when Larissa was asleep on her cot and only a dim nightlight illuminated the room.

Andrei opened his eyes and slowly looked around him. It was a strange room, with a wide bay window and total darkness beyond it. He tried to lift himself but was too weak. He felt that his body below his waist was not there. He could move only his hands and arms but his legs were asleep, or were they gone? He panicked and quickly reached down. He could feel his legs.

With a sigh of relief, Andrei tried to sit up. He felt deep, continuous pain in his right hip and leg. He touched the leg again and his fingers recognized the thick bandages encircling it. He made an effort to concentrate his thoughts on ... what? He could not remember. Andrei looked around the room again. In its dim light he saw a bed, no, it was more like a cot, and someone sleeping on it. It looked like a woman, for there was long, half-braided hair on the pillow. "Lara has hair like that," he thought. "Is it Lara? No, Lara is in Petrograd and I must be ... That's it! I have been wounded ... I remember now! I must be in the hospital! Yes, I was flying, and I fought with the Albatros. I shot him down. No ... *He* shot me down ... and I was wounded ... Yes, I remember it now ... There was a lot of blood on my glove ..." He tried again to sit up but the sharp pain in his leg made him groan.

The woman on the cot lifted her head and stared at him. "Andrúsha!" she cried as she jumped up. She was fully dressed except for her shoes, which were neatly stowed away under the cot. "Andrúsha, my love!" she dashed toward him.

He stared at her and a wide silly smile spread over his gaunt face. "I see my Lara! Don't mind me nurse ... I am delirious again," he said, and closed his eyes.

"I am here, my darling. Your Lara is here. You are not delirious!" She covered his face with small quick kisses, his carbolic soap-smelling hands, his chest covered with a hospital shirt, and then his face again, crying and laughing and kissing him again and again.

He looked helpless under her stormy onslaught. He tried to gather his thoughts. "Lara ... is it really you?" he finally asked. "I am not dreaming? My leg hurts. Where am I?"

"My sweet darling! You are at the hospital, in Odessa ... You have been wounded, but you are getting well! I am here to care for you. And my mother is here and Vasya Egórov is here. We all are here, to take care of you, my sweet love!"

"Egórov? Is he back? I did not hear him landing."

"He is still delirious," Larissa thought. Aloud she said, "Yes, he is going to see you shortly. But now, rest. I'll be here with you. Hold my hand.

Just rest." Like an obedient child, he took her hand into his and closed his eyes. He was safe now, his instinct told him.

Sister Veronica entered the room early in the morning to see Larissa sitting in a chair next to Andrei's bed and holding his hand. Veronica noticed that Larissa was disheveled, her hair uncombed and uncovered by the required coif. She was in her stocking feet. She was asleep.

Veronica glanced at the patient. His eyes were open wide.

"Sh—sh—she is my wife," he whispered.

Veronica smiled, exposing long, yellowing teeth. "I know. Welcome back, Lieutenant," she said in English.

"I haven't been anywhere," he replied in the same language.

"It's a figure of speech," she said."I am glad you speak English."

"Do I? Say something in English," he replied.

Veronica smiled again. "We are speaking English. I'm afraid I don't speak Russian very well. I am Veronica, and I am your nurse. Now tell me, how do you feel?"

"I think I feel good, except that I can't move my legs and I have severe pain along my whole right side. I also don't understand how my wife happened to be here. Do you know, Miss Veronica?

"Call me *Sister* Veronica. This is a military hospital. I'll talk to you later. Your wife and I must change your bandages, so you wake her while I prepare the instruments."

Larissa was embarrassed that she had fallen asleep. "Never mind," Veronica said. She smiled. "I know you are in seventh heaven, but we must be ready for the doctors' inspection."

"Yes, Sister Veronica." She kissed Andrei on his stubby cheek and mouthed "I love you" in Russian.

"I love you, too," he replied with the same happy, idiotic smile that seemed etched on his face ever since he had opened his eyes.

He watched with interest, as if he had never seen it before, how Larissa combed and braided her hair and wriggled her feet into her shoes. She placed a white coif with its red cross on her head and all he was able to see was her pink face in the oval opening.

"I think I want something to eat," Andrei said in Russian.

"We shall give you your breakfast after the doctors leave," Veronica replied, also in Russian. "Can you say that in English?"

"Why?"

"Can you? And in French?" Veronica insisted.

Larissa watched Andrei's face lose its smile as he concentrated on Veronica's request. Then, with a smile, he repeated that he was hungry, first in English and then in French.

"Bravo!" Veronica exclaimed. "Your brain is working fine, Lieutenant! We'll feed you as soon as the doctors examine you. Meanwhile, Sister Larissa, please get ready to remove the bandages."

Andrei watched them, but the pain in his leg was excruciating. His body stiffened. With all of his re-awakened willpower, he tried not to cry out. Veronica noticed it with approval. "He is trying to control himself," she thought. "He is a strong young man."

With the smelly, bloody bandages removed, Andrei saw his gaping wound. "Gracious Lord!" he exclaimed. "I have never seen anything so ugly!"

Veronica suppressed a smile. Larissa placed an elongated basin near Andrei's exposed leg and began to drip tepid solution into the long fleshy canyon of the wound. Andrei grimaced. The color faded from his face.

"Hold on, Andrúsha, it will be better in a few minutes," Larissa said through her mask. It pained her to watch his efforts not to groan.

Sister Veronica dabbed at the wound's edges with soft balls of cotton dressing. *"Courage, mon ami,* we are almost finished," she said in French.

There was a knock on the door and Doctors Shubin and Popov entered.

"Well, how are we doing today?" Dr. Shubin exclaimed heartily, seeing that Andrei was awake. "Are we lucid?"

"Not only lucid, but lucid in three languages!" Veronica replied as if she were the proud governess of a smart child.

"What is *your* report, Sister Larissa? Does your patient know who you are?"

"Yes, Doctor, he does. And he is hungry!"

"Good show! Now, let's see what's going on in that wound of his." The doctors bent over Andrei's leg.

"Excellent!" Shubin exclaimed. "The granulation tissue looks healthy."

Doctor Popov prodded gently around the edges of the wound with a cotton ball and showed it to Shubin. "Healthy looking," he said, pointing to the yellowish stains on the cotton.

"Excellent! Continue the treatment. You are in good hands, Lieutenant! "

"Thank you, Doctor," Andrei said. "Have you met my wife?"

Shubin laughed. "Not only have I met your wife, but I met your mother-in-law and your best friend, Captain Egórov! They are all here, in Odessa, eager to be with you! You had better hurry up and get well quickly so that we can drink champagne to celebrate your recovery! Carry on!" he said, closing the door.

Popov remained. He listened to Andrei's heart and lungs, making notations on his chart. He moved the injured leg up and down, but the pain was so great that Andrei cried out.

"He is not ready to exercise his leg," Sister Veronica said dryly. "His wife and I will take care of it."

"You are doing well, Lieutenant!" Popov declared. "Keep up the good work!"

Andrei greedily gobbled the golden chicken broth with soggy croutons. "Could I have some more?" he asked.

"No. We'll give you more in a couple of hours," Veronica said sternly. "Your system is not ready to receive a lot of food. Meanwhile, Sister Larissa, don't allow Captain Egórov and your mother to tire the patient. I know they will want to visit, but keep it short. Give your husband a warm sponge bath and then re-bandage his wound. I'll come back this afternoon."

"Yes, Sister Veronica," Larissa said obediently. She could see why Dr. Shubin had such great respect for her: she was a perfect nurse. Under her stern façade, Larissa detected a kind nature. Given time, Veronica could become her friend, she thought.

Alone with Andrei, Larissa suddenly felt shy. He was confused and remote watching her every move, with suspicion she thought. Under his stare, she felt awkward, unsure of her actions.

Andrei also felt strange with Larissa. He observed her closely, realizing that she was his wife but seeing only a nurse in strange, nun-like attire. He felt nothing for her. He needed to urinate but was embarrassed to ask her for help. "Do you have any male attendants here?" he asked, finally.

"Yes, we do. Why?"

"Would you call an orderly, please? I need some help."

"I will help you."

"No. I want an orderly."

"I can help you. I am your nurse. I am your wife, I can help you."

"No," he said stubbornly."I want a man to help me."

"Andrúsha …" suddenly she was filled with great tenderness for this suffering young stranger who was her husband. "Andrúsha, my love … Don't be shy with me … You want to pee? I'll help you. Don't feel embarrassed. I have seen you peeing, remember? In Gátchina, on our honeymoon?" She took a urinal bottle from the cupboard under the sink. "You are my one and only love … Let me help you …"

That intimate episode broke down the restraints between them. Awkwardly at first, Larissa attended to all his physical needs, sponged his body with warm soapy water, re-bandaged his injured leg, and exercised his good one. She helped him brush his teeth and exchanged his coarse cotton hospital shirt for a silk one that she had brought from home. She shaved the stubble off his chin and applied fresh smelling eau-decologne. "How handsome you look!" she exclaimed and proffered him a small mirror.

Andrei relaxed under her light and loving touch. He looked at himself in the mirror and saw his eyes welling with tears. "My sweet love … We are together again … Dear Lord, thank You for sparing me!" Larissa knelt at his bed and pressed his hand against her cheek. "Amen," she whispered. "We are together."

Andrei's recuperation was swift. Every day Larissa noticed some tiny improvement in his condition. He and Egórov were soon laughing together as they recalled their adventures to the spellbound Larissa and her mother. Soon even the strict Veronica stayed in Andrei's room longer than necessary, to listen to their stories. She even volunteered some personal information: her brother was an artillerist, fighting in France.

At the end of the first week of Egórov's leave, Andrei insisted on taking a few steps. Egórov and Larissa anxiously watched as he laboriously hopped on his good leg between two crutches. He made it to the bay window and plunged himself in the chair, exhausted. "I guess, I am not ready to walk," he said.

"Certainly, not!" Veronica said sternly as she entered the room. "I am surprised, Sister Larissa, that you allowed your patient to leave his bed!"

Larissa blushed. "I am sorry, Sister Veronica. I thought it wouldn't hurt to see how much he had improved."

"Don't scold my wife, Sister," Andrei said. "I insisted on it. I wanted to see whether I could manage a few steps. And I did! I am just tired now."

"It was my fault. I encouraged him," Egórov said. "Blame me!"

"I don't blame anyone. Just don't do it again. In a couple of days, we will try him sitting in a wheelchair. But not yet!" Veronica said.

"I'll push him!" Egórov exclaimed.

"No. I don't trust you," Veronica said, slightly smiling. "You'll push him too fast."

"No one trusts poor little me," Egórov said, pretending to sigh. "It's the story of my life!"

"I'll trust you to help your friend back into his bed. I don't want him to use the crutches. It puts too much stress on his arms and shoulders. So, you both support him hopping back to bed. Do it now. I want him in bed when I come back." She left the room.

Egórov and Larissa put their arms around Andrei's waist, while he stretched his arms over their shoulders. Very slowly, all three shuffled back to his bed.

"Well, that's that!" Egórov said. "We must obey the higher authority. No walks for you, my boy. However, I would like to talk to you about something very serious. About your future."

"What about it? I'll get well and go back to the squadron. Isn't that what you have done ... and everyone else?"

"Yes, but the situation has changed. The war has changed. It might even be ending, if the situation worsens."

They brought him to his bed and helped him settle in. Larissa cranked the bed to a half-sitting position. "I'll visit with my mother while you two are talking about the war," she said. "She is planning to leave in a few days."

"Give her my love," Andrei said.

"And mine, too. I was hoping that she would stay a bit longer. I wanted to take her to the opera."

"*The opera!* I'll try to persuade her to stay a few more days." Larissa said, removing her coif. Her luxuriant chestnut hair was undone. She shook her head and the hair spilled over her shoulders.

"What a beauty!" Egórov thought. "No wonder Andrei was jealous about her midnight ride with those royal scoundrels!"

Larissa kissed her husband. "I'll be back in a couple of hours!"

"Well, what did you want to tell me about my future?" Andrei said. "Do you see it as any different from your own?"

"Yes. First, because you are much younger and second, because you are married. You must think of Larissa. As I've said, there is a new dimension to this war. Discipline is becoming shaky, especially among the infantry. I have heard that in some units the men refuse to obey their officers. Even more troubling, I've heard that some officers have been murdered by their own men."

"Just frontline gossip," Andrei shrugged his shoulders.

"Perhaps. But people say that in many units there are replacement soldiers who promote the idea of desertion. Even at our own airbase. A new mechanic arrived from Petrograd and urged our mechanics to go on strike! Fortunately, several of them told Kozakov about it. He immediately got rid of that agitator."

"How?"

"He had him arrested and sent to the military tribunal, or wherever they deal with such matters. What I am saying is that we are moving toward total chaos. Killing Rasputin did not solve any of our problems because our problem is the *war itself*. We lost Poland, destroyed hundreds of towns and villages, and we almost lost *you*, Andrúshka! And for what?" As he spoke, Egórov grew more and more agitated. His face turned red and he began to stutter. He grabbed a glass of water from Andrei's night table and gulped a mouthful, only to spit it out. "Hell! Even water doesn't taste like water anymore!" he swore.

Andrei laughed. "Because it is some special 'purified' water they make me drink," he said. "It's full of medical garbage. Anyway, calm down and tell me what plans you have for my future."

"It's not just *my* plans, but Kozakov's. When we thought that you would lose your leg, Kozakov called me to his quarters to talk about you. He did not want to lose you because of it and had thought of a way to keep you flying. He thinks that you are an especially gifted pilot. Of course, I disagreed." He laughed. "*I* am the 'especially gifted pilot'!"

"I agree," Andrei said, nodding.

"I was *joking!*" Egórov was embarrassed. "Anyway, Kozakov wants you to remain in the aviation service as a trainer. They are opening a new School of Advanced Aviation, right here, in Odessa. He wants to transfer you here. Or, rather, keep you here, since you are already in Odessa."

"He wants to get rid of me?"

"Don't be a prick. He wants to *save* you, idiot!"

"Well, I don't want to be *saved*. I am a fighter pilot and I want to stay a fighter pilot. Besides, I kept my leg, so there is no excuse for getting rid of me. I am not a cripple."

"Don't be a fool. Being a cripple is no longer an obstacle for being a pilot. Remember Yuri Gilsher? He is a double amputee, yet he still flies!"

"There you are! I certainly can continue to fly with both of my legs still attached to me!"

"Oh, you are more idiotic than I thought. Of course you can fly! And Kozakov *wants* you to fly, but not at the front, where you would be killed, sooner or later. We all will be killed. He thinks that you are a terrific pilot, and he wants you to teach others how to be terrific pilots."

"That's very flattering," Andrei said sarcastically. "So how are you going to accomplish your plan of making me a trainer against my will?"

"Simple. By command of the Grand Duke Alexander Micháilovich, head of our Air Force. And, to whom, as I remember, *you yourself* wrote when you wanted to become a pilot, against your father's wishes. Am I correct? The Grand Duke remembers you. He wrote you a personal note of congratulations after your adventure on the wing of our Voisin. Am I right?"

"All right, all right!" Andrei was annoyed. "I can still decline the honors, can't I?"

"No. You took an oath to serve your Emperor and the Russian Empire. If the Russian Empire needs you to become a trainer—you will be a trainer." Egórov laughed, enjoying needling his friend. "Your only hope to avoid the reassignment is to plead with Kozakov. But, I must say, it will be useless ... *Kozakov wants you to be saved.* And he will write about his idea to your wife. Once she, and *your* mother, and Larissa's mother know that there is a way to get you out of the hell of combat, they will use all their feminine wiles to keep you safe."

"Then, as my best friend, *you* talk to Kozakov when you get back to the Air Group. Do me a favor, say nothing about it to the women," Andrei said. "There are still a few weeks before I will be discharged, so promise not to tell them anything about our conversation. Promise!"

"I promise. But ..."

"Let's not talk about it," Andrei interrupted. "I am tired."

Egórov's furlough was nearing its end. None of his original plans for having fun in Odessa had been fulfilled; he'd paid no visits to the opera, nor to any of the brothels, and he'd taken very few walks on the seashore. He'd spent most of his time in Andrei's room at Memorial Hospital.

He was falling in love with Larissa.

Everything about her fascinated him. The serene beauty of her young face delighted him. The contrast between her virginal, nun-like mien when in her uniform and her relaxed sensuousness when she removed her apron and coif was startling. It made him rise with desire like an adolescent boy. In his dreams, he visualized her freeing her young, perfect body from that hideous uniform, and he was certain he knew how the texture of her skin would feel under his fingers and his tongue.

When he was awake, Egórov tried not to think of Larissa in carnal terms. In his heart, he felt like an older brother to Andrei, but he was tormented by envy. The strength of Larissa's character, which had made her abandon her comfortable life and follow Andrei to the hospital in Odessa, reminded him of the wives of the Decembrists, the heroic Russian women of privilege who had voluntarily followed their revolutionary husbands into Siberian exile. Yes, Larissa would have done the same had Andrei been among those ill-fated reformers. No one had ever loved *him* that much! Yes, he envied Andrei. An ugly thought ran through Egórov's mind again and again, though he tried to suppress it: Andrei did not deserve his wife.

He felt as if he were a traitor.

On the cusp of his departure, Egórov decided to splurge. He reserved an expensive loge at the Opera House and invited Larissa and Maria Nikoláyevna, who was about to leave Odessa, and Dr. Shubin and his wife to be his guests. The loge was for six; Egórov hoped that Andrei could attend in his wheelchair.

Andrei's recuperation was phenomenal. Only three weeks since waking from his coma, the young lieutenant was already in the convalescent stage. Going to the opera did not seem such an outrageous idea: the worst result could be that the young man would get tired and fall asleep in his wheelchair.

Dr. Shubin gave his permission for Andrei to attend the opera.

Egórov, who had visited with several recuperating patients, spread the news that Andrei was going to the theatre. The prospect galvanized the officers' wing. Officers in the wards begged Egórov to do something for them as well. "For those of us, who are on the mend, there is nothing to do ... we are bored and depressed!" they said.

Egórov was truly sympathetic. "I have been wounded myself and almost died of boredom in a Petrograd hospital. With Dr. Shubin's permission, I shall talk to the Director of the Opera Theatre and get you men a few free seats."

"We can pay," the officers said.

"You have already paid. With your blood!" Egórov countered.

Dr. Shubin thought it was a splendid idea. He wrote an official request asking that the Opera House allocate a few seats at every performance for use by recuperating officers.

Egórov, always an enterprising man, telephoned the *Odessa Times*, informing the paper of the new philanthropic activity at Memorial Hospital. As he'd expected, the newspaper dispatched a reporter to interview Dr. Shubin. The next day, all of Odessa knew about the hospital's brilliant new program to bolster the spirits of recuperating officers. Egórov had no trouble getting an immediate appointment with the Director of the Opera.

Dressed in his pilots' uniform, with his two St. George medals and St. Anne Cross on its crimson ribbon around his neck, Egórov presented himself to the Director. He acted as if the matter of the seats was already settled and suggested that perhaps the best arrangement for accommodating wheelchairs and crutches would be a couple of loges in the *bel étage*. "I am sure that the loges have vacancies these days, due to the war," he said with a charming smile.

The Director agreed. Two loges, providing in total twelve seats at every performance, were reserved for "Wounded Heroes."

Maria Nikoláyevna developed his idea even further. "Since the men must be accompanied by nurses, let's ask the nurses who volunteer for the duty to wear party dresses. Enough of these forbidding uniforms! Let the men enjoy seeing *women* again!"

"You are a treasure, Maria Nikoláyevna!" Egórov kissed her hand. "It's a great idea! The men will do their best to be gentlemen again, and not just suffering soldiers!"

The day before the first scheduled visit to the Opera Theatre, Maria Nikoláyevna took Larissa to the local French *modiste*, Madame Juliette. "We must buy you something suitable for the theatre," she said.

"I can wear my traveling suit," Larissa said.

"No. You must wear a proper evening gown. Andrei must see you as his lovely wife and not as his nurse. Your beauty will encourage him and help him emotionally, to regain his strength."

"What about you?"

"I'll wear my traveling suit, but I suppose I should spruce it up with some frilly blouse. Although ... Dr. Shubin's wife will likely be wearing an evening gown ... and I would look like a governess! No! I must buy a proper evening gown! I am sure Madame Juliette will have something *prêt-a-porter!*"

Madame Juliette knew exactly what they needed. Larissa was easily fitted into a slinky loose-waist gown of pale brown chiffon embroidered in golden bugle beads, with matching silk shoes.

"But, Madame, you cannot wear your underwear with this dress," Madame Juliette said in perfect Russian with a soft Ukrainian accent.

"What do you mean?" Larissa was surprised by her suggestion.

"I mean, this dress is too fragile to wear over your bulky linen pantaloons and corset. The new fashion demands different underwear. Silk. No corsets. Only tiny stocking belts. And a light *bustier*. Try these." She opened a box with pale pink silk undergarments edged with delicate lace.

"They're so light! So filmy!" Lara exclaimed, fingering the garments.

"Try them on," Maria Nikoláyevna said. Larissa went behind the curtain to change.

Maria Nikoláyevna turned to Madame Juliette. "I want to congratulate you on your perfect Russian. Not many French people speak our difficult language. And, so well!"

Juliette laughed. "I am not French! And my name is Julia. I was born here. But my dress shop was going nowhere, until my mother suggested that I call myself Madame Juliette and call the shop 'The Salon.' Since then—I am prospering!"

"You have a clever mother," Maria Nikoláyevna said.

"Thank you! My mother *is* clever. She found seamstresses to make all these clothes. We put my special labels on, and voilà! Madame Juliette creations were ready for sale!"

"You mean … All these lovely gowns and underthings are made by local women?"

"Every one of them. Odessa, being a seaport, has always been a paradise for the smugglers. It still is, war or no war. My father has established some … some connections with certain people, who supply us with the fabrics, and what not."

"What about the designs? How do you know what is in fashion?" Larissa asked from behind the curtain.

"We copy the designs from French journals that the sailors bring us. Our girls are very good: they can copy a gown in just two days," she concluded proudly.

"Fascinating!" Larissa exclaimed, opening the curtain. "Your workmanship is superb. Just look at this charming lingerie, Mama! Isn't it pretty?" She twirled in front of her mother, admiring herself in the tall gilded mirror. "I am so glad that corsets are out of style! Finally!"

"With your figure, you don't need a corset, Mademoiselle," Julia-Juliette said.

"Madame," Larissa corrected her. "I am married. My husband is a pilot. He has been wounded and we are here to care for him. I am his nurse."

"And I am his mother-in-law. However, I am going back to Petrograd soon. My daughter will remain in Odessa with her husband as long as he is in the hospital."

"I hope your husband is doing well," Julia said sincerely.

Maria Nikoláyevna found a suitable dress of dark blue taffeta with an overlay of black lace, still the kind that required a corset, but she was accustomed to having her waist cinched and her breasts pushed up and permanently pocked and bruised by the whalebone stays.

"Do you have any wraps or shawls to go with your gowns? After all, it's winter, and even in Odessa, it gets quite chilly at night," Julia said.

"No, we did not bring any formal clothes with us." Maria Nikoláyevna said. "Would you have anything suitable?"

"I'll think of something ... Perhaps some full-length velvet capes ... Brown for the young Madame and dark blue for you ... They will be elegant, and you won't be cold!"

"We would need them the day after tomorrow," Larissa said. "Can you make them in such a short time?"

"No problem, Madame. You will have them *tomorrow*, I promise!"

"You are a treasure, Madame Juliette!" Maria Nikoláyevna exclaimed."I am so glad that we have found you."

"Well, thank you," Julia said, pinning the hem of the blue taffeta dress. "With this war going on and on, no one orders beautiful clothes anymore. I'll bring the capes and gowns to your hotel tomorrow."

"And don't forget the underthings!" Larissa reminded. "I would like to have at least three sets." She felt embarrassed ordering such flimsy things in front of her mother, but Maria Nikoláyevna nodded in agreement.

Julia Goldberg, aka *Madame Juliette*, was a handsome dark-haired woman in her early thirties. Her strong Semitic features could have been easily mistaken for Southern European, perhaps Greek or Spanish. In profile, she looked as if she were the model for ancient coins. She was stylishly dressed in rustling black silks, with several gold bracelets dangling on her arms and a long, single rope of large iridescent pearls reaching below her uncorseted waist.

Maria Nikoláyevna dismissed the pearls. "Only the Empress would wear *real* pearls like these," she thought. "On the other hand, Julia hinted that her father had some *connections* with smugglers ... What if they robbed some potentate and the pearls are *real*? No. They can't be *real* ... No woman would be foolish enough to wear them so negligently!" she thought.

The gowns and the capes were delivered as promised, with a little fragrant note from Julia and a bill for three hundred rubles, a steep price. On the back of the bill was a short note: "I realize, Madame, that you probably don't carry so much money with you, so at your convenience, you may send this bill to your bank and authorize it to forward payment to my bank in Odessa." There followed the name and address of her bank.

"What a gracious woman!" Maria Nikoláyevna exclaimed. "I wish she were in Petrograd!"

Dr. Shubin conferred with Maria Nikoláyevna about the manner of transporting Andrei to and from the theatre. "Obviously we cannot use a hired carriage ..." the doctor began. "And I am afraid that my automobile is too small to accommodate six people and a wheelchair."

"Why not use the ambulance?" Maria Nikoláyevna asked. "Andrei will be comfortable in his wheelchair, and Larissa and I can accompany him."

"You won't mind riding in the ambulance?"

"Not at all! It's only for a few minutes. And it will certainly be more comfortable for Andrei. He could even lie down if he wished."

"Well ... but ... you'll be dressed in your gowns, and ..."

Maria Nikoláyevna laughed. "You underestimate us, Arkady Petrovich! Larissa and I are much more practical than you think. We'll ride with our Andrúsha. It might even turn out to be a lark!"

"Well, perhaps my wife and I should join you! It might be fun! We all could ride together!"

Andrei was looking forward to going to the Opera. His wounds were healing fast, but he was a bad patient. His wounds were troublesome:

they itched terribly under their bandages and often made him jerk in an uncontrolled spasm of pain. He followed the recuperative procedures with impatience and argued with Sister Veronica about every phase in his treatment. He felt that she was too restrictive of his freedom: he was ready to walk with the crutches, but she kept him in the wheelchair. He complained bitterly to Egórov that even his wife was influenced by *that English bitch,* as he called Veronica behind her back. To his surprise, Egórov was unsympathetic.

"You are a whining brat, my dear fellow. Sister Veronica is a top-notch nurse and if you don't appreciate it, you are a fool. You are recovering so well *because of her.*"

"Larissa is my nurse," Andrei said stubbornly.

"Yes, she is, but she is too young to know what and how to do things for a case as serious as yours. She has to be taught and Veronica is teaching her! Don't be an idiot, and stop carping about Veronica!"

Annoyed by everybody, including his wife, Andrei made up his mind to prove that he was ready to use the crutches.

He waited until he was alone with Larissa. "Dearest, could you manage to bring me a cup of hot chocolate?" he asked.

"Of course, darling! Let me crank up your bed so that you can sit up. Do you want a newspaper?"

"Yes. I'll read while you're out."

Andrei waited until she closed the door and he heard her footsteps in the corridor. Cautiously he lowered his good leg to the floor and then slowly tried to swing his injured leg over the side of the bed, clutching with both hands to the mattress. He cried out in pain but stubbornly continued.

Finally, he saw that his wounded leg had touched the floor, but he could not feel it. "Never mind," he told himself. "Next, get the crutches." They were leaning against a chair beyond his reach. He stretched out as far as he could, but he still could not reach the crutches. He pushed himself to a standing position, but the floor seemed to move under his feet, and his eyes lost their focus. He fell, the chair and the crutches landing on top of him.

Andrei cursed. The pain was unbearable, but the humiliation was even worse. He could not get up.

Larissa returned, a cup of steaming chocolate on a small tray in her hands. "Here is your chocolate!" she exclaimed gaily, her smile turning into a mask of distress as she saw him. "What happened?"

"Nothing. I fell out of bed. Can't you see?" he replied with annoyance. "Help me!"

She placed the tray on the nightstand and bent over him. "Poor darling! How did it happen?"

"What's the difference ... Just help me, stop blabbering," he said. Larissa struggled to lift him back into a sitting position and then to a standing one. Carefully, she guided him back to the bed. She said nothing more as she gently lifted his good leg up to the mattress: Veronica had warned her that Andrei might become impatient and even rude with her. It was all part of the healing process, Veronica had explained when a once-strong man suddenly finds himself as weak as an infant. "Ignore it," Veronica had advised. "It will be his injured male pride talking, not your husband. Later on, he will beg your forgiveness!"

Cautiously, Larissa began to move her husband's injured leg back into the bed. He groaned with pain, hissing at her, "Can't you be more careful?"

She felt anger swelling in her. "I am doing the best I can," she replied, trying to remain calm. "I know that it hurts."

"No one knows how much it hurts!" he said through clenched teeth. "Hurry! And don't blubber to anyone that I have fallen!"

"I won't," she said quietly, as she settled him in, making an effort to keep her temper from exploding at his rudeness.

At half past six in the evening, the opera goers gathered in Andrei's room. Andrei was already in the wheelchair, his knees covered with a light woolen blanket of Scottish tartan, a contribution by Sister Veronica. Larissa, her mother, and Anna Feodorovna, Dr. Shubin's wife, looked elegant in their evening outfits, and the men, Andrei, Egórov and the doctor, dashing. Egórov checked that Andrei's two Crosses of St. George were properly attached to his formal tunic and the pilot wings on his epaulettes were at the exact angle. Egórov also wore his decorations, and even the old doctor had several medals on his chest earned during the Russo-Japanese War.

"What a distinguished company we have here! It feels as if we are about to go to a reception at the Winter Palace!" Maria Nikoláyevna chuckled.

"And your ceremonial carriage is waiting, Madame!" Dr. Shubin bowed to her. "Are we ready?"

The dark-green, bulky ambulance with huge red crosses on its sides and roof was waiting at the front entrance. The driver pushed the wheelchair up a small ramp into the vehicle. Then he stepped aside as Egórov and Doctor Shubin helped the ladies up the ramp.

A surprise awaited the party. Egórov had placed five small armchairs in the ambulance by removing the cots and portable metal seats. He also had a Persian carpet spread on the metal floor, making the vehicle look as if it were a little parlor on wheels.

"How charming!" Madame Shubin exclaimed. "Is this the special ambulance for officers of high rank?" she asked naively.

Dr. Shubin was embarrassed, but Egórov was quick to reply, "Yes, Madame, it is *very special*. The only one suitable for our national hero!"

The driver slammed the metal doors with a bang and took his place at the wheel.

"I have a little surprise to put us in the right mood for the opera," Egórov announced, reaching into a box on the floor. "I think that a glass of Perrier Jouët will do the trick!" He produced a magnum of champagne and six glasses, taking them out slowly, one by one, teasing his audience. "I presume, Dr. Shubin will permit our guest of honor a sip or two?"

"Oh, Egórka, you never change!" Andrei laughed happily for the first time. "That's how we met, drinking champagne on the train, while going to the front!" he explained.

Egórov uncorked the bottle and the cork hit the ceiling with a small bang. "That sounds familiar! Just like at the front, only not as deadly!" Egórov joked. He poured the champagne and lifted his glass. "To our young hero and my best friend, Lieutenant Andrei Rezánov! Let him get well and enjoy life again!"

"To Andrei!" everyone shouted, raising their glasses.

"No more than two sips!" the doctor shook his finger at Andrei.

The champagne unleashed everyone's high spirits. Maria Nikoláyevna was right: their trip was becoming a lark.

The Odessa Theatre of Opera and Ballet looked small in comparison to the gigantic Moscow Bolshoi Theatre or even the Mariinsky Imperial Theatre in Petrograd, but it was a pearl in the architectural diadem of European theatres.

Built in a horseshoe pattern with an exquisite four-story-high entrance in the Italian Baroque style, it was crowned with a sculpture of the triumphant Melpomene, the Muse of Music, in a chariot driven by four fierce panthers tamed by her music. At street level, two more mythological sculptures framed the Grand Entrance: Terpsichore, the Muse of Dance, dancing with a child, and Orpheus playing his lyre for a Centaur.

"What a lovely, lovely building!" Maria Nikoláyevna exclaimed, clapping her hands in delight. "It is so airy, so elegant, so ... so happy!"

"Just wait till you get inside!" Anna Feodorovna said, smiling. "You'll love the acoustics! One can hear a whisper from the stage, no matter where one sits!" As a native of Odessa she could not contain her pride in *'the jewel of Odessa,'* as the opera house was known.

The driver pulled up to the front, and a small crowd of opera goers watched with amusement as three fashionable ladies and a distinguished silver-haired gentleman disembarked from the tacky ambulance. A handsome, dark-haired officer with pilot wings on his epaulettes and two Crosses of St. George on his chest followed him, pushing a wheelchair occupied by a younger, blond pilot with a heavily bandaged right leg.

Egórov and the driver lifted the wheelchair over the marble steps leading to the entrance and proceeded to carry it up the stairs of the Grand Escalier rising in front of them.

The old Head Usher met them at the landing of the *bel étage.* "Welcome, welcome Lieutenant Rezánov!" he cried, bowing and folding his hands in a praying mantis gesture. "We are honored that you have chosen to visit our theatre! We have read about your heroic deeds and we are happy to see you in our fine city!"

"Thank you," Andrei stammered in embarrassment, "Thank you, so much!"

"Would you please show us to our loge," Egórov said coldly, placing the wheelchair down. He could see that Andrei did not appreciate the adulation of the usher and the curiosity of the theatregoers around them.

"Of course, of course, this way please!" He led them to their loge, in the center of the tier, next to the Tsar's loge, which was empty. He helped place the wheelchair in the first row by removing one of the armchairs, looking adoringly at Andrei all the time. "Is there anything you may need, Lieutenant?" he inquired, ignoring the rest of the party.

"Yes. Bring us a bottle of Veuve Clicquot and six glasses," Egórov interrupted. "And find a seat somewhere for our driver. Please," he added as an afterthought, handing the usher ten gold rubles.

"Right away, Captain!" The usher bowed and scurried away to do Egórov's bidding.

The opera house was lavish with burgundy velvet draperies and gilded surfaces. Built in the Louis XVI Rococo style, it was adorned with countless gilded stucco bas-reliefs and carvings. Elaborate gold candelabras and marble busts filled every niche. An enormous crystal chandelier, surrounded by four paintings of scenes from Shakespeare, dominated the ceiling.

Larissa observed her surroundings through opera glasses, thinking that she liked the Mariinsky Opera House much better. "I prefer its elegant pale-blue velvet and tarnished gold ambiance to all this screaming bright gilt. This is a bit vulgar," she thought.

The orchestra in the pit concluded tuning; the conductor, greeted by thin applause, stepped on the podium. The rousing overture of Bizet's *Carmen* filled the hall.

Egórov sat close behind Larissa. Her slender bare neck and the sweet curves of her shoulders and breasts were within his reach. He saw tendrils of her hair that escaped from her coiffure, and he burned with a desire to touch them. He watched as Larissa picked up Andrei's hand and pressed it to her lips. Andrei reciprocated with a similar gesture.

Egórov tried to concentrate on music, but his mind was on Larissa. Her filmy dress cleverly exposed her perfect young body, hidden only by a thin cover of chiffon. It was there, right in front of him, her warm and fragrant body, ready to be loved.

But not by him.

The music of the toreador's triumphant march changed into the tragic theme of Carmen's doom. "Right for my mood," Egórov reflected bitterly. He stood and went to the anteroom, as if for a smoke. The usher was there, struggling with uncorking the champagne. Glad for the diversion, Egórov took over the uncorking. With the usher's help, he filled the glasses and offered them to his guests as the monumental red curtain slowly went up and transported the spectators to the sunny plaza in Seville.

While on the stage sweet-voiced children sang and marched, imitating the changing of the guards, dozens of binoculars were trained on the loge in the bel étage where a young lieutenant with two Orders of St. George on his chest was sitting next to a young and very beautiful woman. The rumor spread quickly among the audience that it was none other than *'the pilot who went out on the wing of the airplane.'*

At intermission a small crowd of admirers gathered in the foyer in front of Andrei's loge.

Dr. Shubin came out to greet the crowd. "Ladies and gentlemen," he began, "I am Dr. Shubin, the director of Odessa Memorial Hospital, and Lieutenant Rezánov is my patient. He is recuperating from very serious injuries and this is his first venture outside the hospital. Please respect his privacy. I know he and his wife would like very much to meet all of you, but not yet. Let him get well first," he concluded with a charming simplicity. The admirers smiled sheepishly and dispersed one by one.

There was no negative physical reaction to Andrei's visit to the theatre. If anything, he was buoyed by his experience. He whistled Toreador's aria and laughed heartily when Egórov sang the same tune with scabrous lyrics.

Egórov had only three days left before he was to rejoin Kozakov's Air Detachment Group that was relocated to Yassy in Romania. There was a direct train connection between Odessa and Yassy, so Egórov planned to stay until the very last minute. He played cards with Andrei, or read aloud to him, postponing by any means the moment when he would have to tell him about the letter that he had received from Kozakov.

That letter weighed like a stone in his heart. It informed Egórov that he was elevated for the post of the second in command, but it failed to gladden him. Kozakov wrote about the heavy losses of the Group. Five pilots were shot down within a month, his friends Platonov and Klembovsky among them. Kozakov also wrote that under the circumstances he had to change his mind about Andrei Rezánov. He no longer could recommend Andrei to some flight school as an instructor; he needed every pilot, his losses being so great.

Egórov said nothing about the letter to Andrei, but he drank himself into a stupor and thrashed his hotel room. On his last evening in Odessa he had dinner in Andrei's room with Larissa and Maria Nikoláyevna, but he hardly talked. They correctly presumed that Egórov's mind was already concentrated on his squadron and his airplane and they did not intrude on his thoughts.

Egórov hugged Andrei and held him in a mute embrace for a long time. Everyone thought that he was praying, but he was bidding a silent farewell to his friend. He had the premonition that it was their final parting: one of them, or even both of them, would not survive the cursed war.

"Be well, Egórka!" Andrei finally said."Give my best regards to all the fellows, and to Kozakov. Tell Platonov and Klembovsky that I am mad at them: not a single letter from any one of them!"

Egórov swallowed hard, tempted to tell Andrei that they were gone, but decided against it. "Let the boy feel good," he thought.

Maria Nikoláyevna blessed him and cried, and Larissa cried and kissed him. They went to the railroad station to see him off, and Larissa kissed him and hugged him again, but she did not run after his train. He might never see her again, Egórov thought.

Egórov locked himself in his compartment. He took a bottle of vodka out of his valise and took several deep gulps, not bothering with a glass. He would arrive in Yassy stinking drunk, he thought, and he did not give a damn. If the security police would arrest him or shoot him, or throw him under the train wheels, he did not give a damn! He was already dead.

A week after Egórov's departure, Maria Nikoláyevna announced that she must leave. She had received an alarming telegram from Andrei's father *'Hooligans broke the glass walls in your Winter Garden. I dispatched Cossacks to guard the house. Come back as soon as possible.'*

Larissa knew, of course, that her mother had to return to Petrograd, but still, it was hard for her to say goodbye. It was the first time in her life that she had really learned to appreciate her mother as a person. She had always loved her, as any child would love a kind mother, but now she knew and loved her mother as a strong, wise woman, full of common sense and reliable opinions.

Andrei also was sad that Maria Nikoláyevna was leaving. He was accustomed to her loving presence and no-nonsense attitude. He actually preferred her company to that of his own mother. His mother, with all her complaints about her nerves or reminiscences about the Dowager Empress, was boring, he thought, while Maria Nikoláyevna was full of information that she fed to recuperating Andrei little by little, like Scheherazade.

Larissa, Dr. Shubin, and his wife accompanied Maria Nikoláyevna to the railroad station, where Larissa said a tearful goodbye to her mother.

"Don't cry, dear child. We'll be together again ... Soon ..."

But Larissa cried.

General Rezánov met Maria Nikoláyevna at the big railroad station on Znamenskaya Square at the far end of the Nevsky Prospect. They embraced as the general's aide-de-camp stood politely a few steps away.

"You have lost some weight in these past few weeks," Maria Nikoláyevna observed the general's newly hollowed cheeks. "Were you ill?"

"No. I am fine ... It's worry about the war and the troubles in the city. This is my new aide-de-camp, Lieutenant Nikolaí Svirsky," the general introduced the young man. Svirsky bowed to Maria Nikoláyevna and clicked his heels.

"I would like him to stay in your house. I also would like you to buy an automobile and sell all your horses," the general continued.

"Wait, wait," she laughed. "Not so fast! You are rearranging my life within the minute of my arrival!"

"I beg your pardon." He offered her his arm. Lieutenant Svirsky walked three steps behind as they walked out into the square and to the General's Packard waiting at the curb.

"You haven't asked me about Andrei," she said, relaxing in the comfortable automobile.

"We'll talk about him later, at dinner. I was in daily touch with Dr. Shubin so I am aware of his progress. Besides, Lara is there, so I know that Andrei is in good hands."

She was surprised at his cavalier attitude, but then that was how he always was: never sentimental. "Not like my Serezha," she thought. "Anyway, tell me about our Winter Garden. Was it badly damaged?"

"Yes. Most of the glass wall on the Nevá side was broken, and all the plants died. I ordered the broken glass removed and the walls sheathed with plywood to prevent further destruction. The little greenhouse, with the seedlings, was also destroyed."

"Who would do such a terrible thing!" she exclaimed. "I hope the vandals were apprehended!"

"Don't count on it," he said. "The police have all the information, but so far, nothing has been done. No one arrested. Now, something else, listen carefully: I want Lieutenant Svirsky and his orderly stay at your house."

"I don't mind, but why?"

"Because it is dangerous to be there alone."

"I won't be alone. I have the servants."

"Mostly women."

"No, I have my butler, and a cook … I have a driver for my carriage and a footman, and my male secretary comes every day. There are plenty of men!"

"Don't argue with me, Maria," he said roughly, pointing with his eyes to his driver and switching into French. "All of your servants are old people and won't be able to protect you if there is trouble. We'll discuss it later, at dinner."

They drove along the Nevsky Prospect toward the bright spire of the Admiralty. Maria Nikoláyevna stared at the familiar landmarks, thinking that perhaps the general's referral to 'trouble' was exaggerated. The city looked the same: people hurried about as usual, schoolchildren walked in pairs, nurses pushed perambulators, and Cossacks rode in small groups, their horses' hooves clattering on the pavement. Although, something was a little different, she thought.

"There are more Cossacks riding around," she said, also in French. "Are there more disturbances in the city? Everything seems peaceful."

"We are on the *Nevsky*," he said with emphasis. "So far it is peaceful, but once you cross the bridges, in any direction, the situation is different. The rabble-rousers are active there. But even here, in the center of the city, two nights ago, someone threw a stone at the Elyseev's Gastronomi-chesky Emporium window and got away with a ham. It happened right here, on the Nevsky Prospect, in the heart of the city!"

"I must ask Ksusha about what is going on in the city," Maria Niko-láyevna thought, watching another Cossack patrol as it trotted on the other side of the street.

"In a couple of weeks I must leave again for Stavka with our latest strategic projections. I don't know why we at the War Ministry are made to sit before our maps with our little colored flags and pins and read all kinds of confidential reports when no one listens to our advice anyway. The Emperor usually smiles that empty smile of his. His Chief-of-Staff is too ill to care, and the rest of them at Stavka are 'yes' men, without any ideas of their own!"

Maria Nikoláyevna was used to Rezánov's complaints. Her husband also had complained about the War Ministry and the other generals. It was all part of the inner politics of the Russian military establishment. She paid no attention to Rezánov's diatribe. "Tell me about Varvara. Is she well?"

"My wife is never well. You should know that. If it is not her nerves, then it is her heart, or lungs, or stomach, or whatnot … But actually, she is strong as a horse!" he said. "She will have a nice cry when you tell her about Andrei. Make it as dramatic as you can! And don't forget to describe the maggots! She doesn't know about them. I kept it from her." His pessimistic mood was broken; he anticipated his wife's reaction to the mention of the maggots. "Would she faint?" he thought with a naughty boy's delight.

They made a left turn to go along the Nevá embankment and continued toward the Orlov's residence. Maria Nikoláyevna saw the high roof of the Winter Garden before she could see the manor house itself. She lifted her gloved hand to her mouth. The domed roof looked as if it were the top of an empty parrot's cage, its giant steel ribs exposed. The feeble winter sun reflected on fragments of glass still attached to the dome.

"Sergei's garden!" she whispered as tears filled her eyes. "How he loved it!"

"I know," the general said with surprising softness. "It broke my heart …"

"So, what happened here while I was away?" Maria Nikoláyevna asked the butler and Ksusha who had appeared in the doorway.

"Oh, báryn'ya, it was terrible!" the old man began.

"Come and sit down. Both of you," she said. "Actually, no. Call all the staff. They will want to know how the young master is doing. Call everybody in!" Ksusha pressed all the buttons on the calling board next to the door and presently, three maids, the cook and his helper, the footman, and even the carriage driver assembled in the hall.

"Come in, come in," she called from the drawing room. Awkwardly, they entered, crowding at the door. None of them had ever been in the drawing room as a guest.

"Sit down. I want to tell you about the young master." She watched as the servants shyly seated themselves on the delicate golden chairs. "Well, my son-in-law was shot down in his airplane, as you know. He was badly wounded by a machine gun." She described Andrei's condition in detail.

Ksusha nodded her head in approval as she heard about Andrei's recovery. Being a privileged person in the Orlov's household, she asked, "And how is my golubushka, my Larochka doing, taking care of her hubby?"

"She is doing very well. Everybody at that big place loves her. I am proud of her."

The carriage driver, an old cavalryman who had served with General Orlov and who, very much like Ksusha, had close relations with the masters, cleared his throat hesitantly. "When the Lieutenant gets well, will he go back to flying his machine?" he asked.

Maria Nikoláyevna realized that his question contained more than his concern about Andrei's future. She hesitated with her answer. "I don't know, Filipich," she finally said. "I suppose like in any military branch, when a soldier is proclaimed well enough, he has to go back and fight again. I imagine the Lieutenant will have to go back and fly his machine again, as you say."

"This cursed war!" the old soldier exploded with venom. "It will end up killing all our young men! And for what reason? What are we fighting for?" Filipich faced the group with his belligerent eyes as if waiting for an answer. There was an awkward silence. Even though they all felt the same about the war, it was dangerous to declare it publicly. It was rumored that agents of the Okhrana, the dreaded secret police, were everywhere, even in private homes. People could not trust one another anymore.

"Well, that's about it," Maria Nikoláyevna said. "You may go now." She motioned to the butler to stay. "I want to talk to you, Semeon Petrovich."

The butler was in tears as he began telling Maria Nikoláyevna about the frightening night when a dozen drunken sailors attacked the Winter Garden with stones.

"I went out, to beg them not to destroy the building, but they knocked me down, tore off my jacket and tie, called me all kinds of names, and kicked me, saying that my time of being a bloodsucker would soon end. They thought that I was the owner of the Winter Garden. When I told them that I was only a butler, they laughed and called me a 'comrade,' then made me gulp their vodka. Then they left, still laughing. I called the police, but by the time they came the sailors were long gone," he sobbed. "I am so sorry that I could not stop them from destroying your husband's garden. I know how much the General loved it!"

"Don't cry, Semeon Petrovich! I know, it was beyond your power to stop a bunch of drunken vandals. What surprises me though, is that the *sailors*, good, disciplined Russian sailors, would do such a thing ..." she said sadly, shaking her head. "It was more than just drunkenness that made them so vicious. It was *hatred!*"

"Oh, Maria Nikoláyevna, I hear from everywhere that this is just the beginning," he sobbed, wiping his eyes with a huge handkerchief and lowering his voice. "People are saying that there will be pogroms, not just against the Jews. This time, the pogroms will be against the monarchy!" He tried to make the sign of the cross but his hand shook so badly that he could not gather his fingers into the pinch needed for the gesture.

Lieutenant Svirsky appeared at Maria Nikoláyevna's house at exactly six o'clock, as the Big Ben-type clock in the hall struck its Westminster chime.

She was ready, schooled from childhood in military punctuality. Attired in a dark blue velvet gown with a double string of pearls around her neck, she looked regal. It was the first time that she had dressed up for dinner since the end of her official mourning period.

Ksusha came out to see her off, as if she were a young woman going out. "Your trip away from Petrograd was good for you. You look beautiful again, Maria Nikoláyevna," Ksusha said. She helped her mistress into her sable coat.

"Oh, you old flatterer," Maria Nikoláyevna laughed, flattered nevertheless. "Make sure that the green bedroom is ready for the Lieutenant."

"Everything will be ready," Ksusha grinned. "Isn't it always?"

Lieutenant Svirsky bowed to Maria Nikoláyevna and offered his arm, escorting her to the waiting Packard.

"Well, tell me about yourself, Lieutenant. Since we will be living under the same roof, so to speak, we must get acquainted. How long have you been with General Rezánov?" Maria Nikoláyevna settled on the soft leather seat of the general's automobile, the young man beside her.

"About six months. There is not much to tell, Madame. I am twenty-three years old. I graduated a year ago from the same Cavalier Guards Academy as your son-in-law; Andrei and I are actually acquainted. My father is a Colonel, attached to General Brusílov's staff. My mother lives in Kiev. I spent three months at the Northwestern front, was wounded in the shoulder by shrapnel, and upon leaving the hospital was assigned to Headquarters in Petrograd. General Rezánov needed another aide-decamp and I applied. My father and General Rezánov know each other, so here I am," Lieutenant Svirsky concluded with a smile.

"It seems that life repeats itself in the second generation. So, Lieutenant, I'll adopt you for a while. I'll write to your mother and introduce myself to your family."

"My mother would like that, Madame."

"Please call me Maria Nikoláyevna. And I'll call you by your first name. Nikolaí, isn't it? Enough of all this formality! I'll call you Kólya."

The Rezánov's manor house on the Fontánka was partially dark, following Government orders to save electricity. "In the old times, it would have been ablaze with light," Maria Nikoláyevna thought. "Now, it looks almost forlorn." There were two automobiles parked near the elegant façade; as usual, the Rezánovs were having guests for dinner. "That habit will probably also change," she reflected. She was glad that her *tête á tête* with Varvara would be postponed due to the presence of guests.

The guests, Rezánov's old friend Cossack General Melekhov with his wife, Suzume, and some other couple new to Maria Nikoláyevna, were gathered in the drawing room. Maria Nikoláyevna exchanged kisses with her hostess, smiled at Suzume, and was introduced to the new couple, Colonel Bolshakov and his wife, Alicia Eduardovna, a famous mezzo-soprano from the Mariinsky Opera.

"How is Andrúsha?" Varvara Mikháilovna managed to ask. Not wishing to risk an outburst of tears, Maria Nikoláyevna smiled widely and made a gesture she had learned from Veronica, making a small circle with her thumb and an index finger, meaning 'everything is fine.' Varvara understood the gesture. She relaxed, returning to her duties as hostess.

General Melekhov resumed the previous conversation. "As I said before, I vigorously protested to our War Minister against another removal of Cossack regiments from the city to the front. General Belyayev assured me that we had enough Cossacks in the city to keep order. But I pointed out that the new replacements are mostly young recruits, unfamiliar with the city, who will be lost among its streets and canals should we have an uprising, God forbid!"

"What did Belyayev say to that?" General Rezánov asked with interest.

"The War Minister just smiled and said, 'Let *me* worry about it!'"

"Do you think we might have an uprising?" Alicia Eduardovna asked.

"Yes, Madame. I do. As long as the city is not able to feed its citizens, the city is vulnerable. I mean, we all are vulnerable. I am sure you have seen the long lines before food stores and bakeries. The stores are unable to supply people with the necessities. There is plenty of food in the provinces, but it can't be delivered to Petrograd because thousands of locomotives are inactive. The motor lorries are also disabled because of lack of petrol. Now, if *you* were a worker at some factory and had a family to feed, and no food available, what would *you* do?" Melekhov stopped for a moment and observed his listeners. "Could you blame that worker if he rose up in anger? And if there were thousands of such men, could you blame them or, would you join them?"

General Melekhov's tirade, unexpected from a Cossack general, created a disconcerting pause among the guests. No one was able to offer a retort or agreement.

The butler announced dinner and the awkward moment passed. Maria Nikoláyevna changed the subject by asking Alicia Eduardovna if she had ever performed at the Odessa Opera Theatre.

"Oh, yes, it is one of my favorite opera houses. The acoustics in that theatre are phenomenal!" the singer exclaimed."Have you been there?"

"Yes. As a matter of fact, I was there just last week with my recuperating son-in-law and my daughter. We heard *Carmen*." She looked at Andrei's mother, sending her a message about Andrei's condition. Varvara Mikháilovna understood, for she gave a deep sigh of relief.

The conversation switched to French. "I read in some dispatches that our severe winter conditions played a role in disabling the delivery of food and fuel to Petrograd," General Rezánov began. "Apparently, the blizzards and heavy snowfalls resulted in the shortage of labor crews to clear the roadbeds. The dispatch said fifty-seven thousand wagons of supplies could not be delivered."

"Fifty-seven thousand!" everyone exclaimed.

"Could it be that the railroad workers refused to clear the snow? Could it be a form of sabotage?" Colonel Bolshakov asked.

"It could. And, maybe, it was ..." General Rezánov said after a pause. "That's what I hate about the whole situation: every new calamity, every new rumor, makes us more suspicious. We begin to believe the rumors ... begin to suspect people of disloyalty. Where is our patriotism? Where is our pride in ourselves as *Russians*? What happened to our Russia?"

"The other day, during the intermission of *Eugene Onégin*, there was a big commotion at the Mariinsky Theatre," Alicia Eduardovna entered the conversation. "Some students in the upper tier released a bunch of pamphlets that floated down to the parterre and the loges. They read: *'Down with the Monarchy!'* By the time the police arrived, the students were gone. However, the show was delayed for an hour because the police and theatre personnel were collecting the pamphlets. It was almost comical! We, the artists, were ordered to remain in our dressing rooms and warned not to pick up any pamphlets. By the time the show was allowed to resume, half of the audience was gone!"

The guests laughed. "Amazing!" General Melekhov exclaimed. "I wonder whether they will write about it in the papers?"

"I doubt it. It is too dangerous, a clarion call for insurrection. The authorities would prefer to keep the general population unaware of it," Rezánov said.

"That's true," Melekhov agreed. "To change the subject, when are you leaving for Stavka?"

"Next week," Rezánov replied. "I certainly don't look forward to it."

The maids served dessert, *Poir á la Melba* in liqueur sauce and the conversation became meaningless chatter. The ladies departed for the drawing room, while the men remained in the dining salon and were served cognac and cigars.

"Would you sing for us?" Maria Nikoláyevna smiled at Alicia Eduardovna. "You have such a magnificent voice! I know, I am rude to ask, but I do so much admire your voice. I heard you in *Samson and Delilah* last year!"

Alicia was visibly pleased. She was not one of those artists who felt offended by such random requests. She loved to sing, and she sang whenever she was asked to, taking the requests as a compliment to her talent.

"I don't mind," she said. "But I don't accompany myself."

"I'll accompany you," Maria Nikoláyevna said. "I am not very good, not like my daughter, but I'll do my best. I always accompany Varvara when she sings."

"Oh? You sing?" Alicia asked her hostess with polite interest.

"Just a little," Varvara blushed.

"She used to sing a lot, when we were young. She has a lovely soprano!" Maria Nikoláyevna said. "At our graduation she and another girl sang a duet from *The Pearl Fishers!*"

"'The Flower Duet'? I know it. Would you like to sing it with me?" Alicia asked.

"Oh, no! I haven't sung it for years. I couldn't!" Varvara Mikháilovna stuttered.

"Yes, you could! I'll get the music!" Maria Nikoláyevna said, lifting the lid of a piano bench and extracting several sheets of music. "Here it is, Bizet's *Les Pêcheurs de Perles!* C'mon, ladies!" She sat at the piano and opened the music.

Alicia took Varvara's hand and led her to the piano, Varvara Mikháilovna still uttering her protest.

Maria Nikoláyevna played the introduction and paused. "I want to dedicate this little impromptu concert to our children, who are in Odessa. They would have appreciated it!" She knew that Varvara would not refuse now.

Alicia subdued her glorious mezzo voice so that it would not dominate Varvara Mikháilovna's pure but untrained soprano, both voices blending easily.

The men in the dining salon stopped their conversation. "That's what we need! Some beauty!" General Melekhov exclaimed, getting up and heading for the drawing room. The others followed. Trying not to disturb the singers, the men seated themselves around the room.

The duet over, the young aides jumped off their chairs and lauded the singers with applause and words of admiration. "More, more," they begged.

"Sing something of Tchaikovsky," General Rezánov said to his wife. "You know, my favorite one, the one about the early spring ...."

"I forgot it," she lied, unwilling to sing solo in front of the famous artist. "Perhaps Alicia Eduardovna will sing it for us?" She turned to the singer. "Will you? Please!"

Alicia smiled and nodded.

Maria Nikoláyevna searched among the sheet music and found two Tchaikovsky songs. "Here it is. 'It Was In Early Spring,'" she said, running her fingers over the keys.

It was a sensitive song of young love during the first days of spring, with text by Pushkin. It was beloved by everyone and included in the repertoire of every Russian singer. Alicia was no exception. She sang it with deep feeling, looking at her husband, who listened to her with misty eyes. It was obvious that the song had a special meaning for both of them.

"That was beautiful!" Rezánov clapped his hands. "Sing 'None but the Lonely Heart'!"

"It requires a masculine voice. Would any of you gentlemen like to try?" With a smile, Alicia looked at the men one after another.

"I would," Lieutenant Svirsky said, his handsome face reddening.

"You?" General Rezánov exclaimed in surprise.

"If you don't mind, sir." Svirsky stood. Like a professional singer, he took his place in the curve of the piano and nodded to Maria Nikoláyevna. She began the introduction.

His baritone was deep and velvety, his articulation precise. When he finished and bowed to his audience, Alicia could not control her admiration. She jumped off her chair and impulsively embraced the young man. "It was *fabulous!*" she cried. "I have never heard it performed with such feeling! You have a *beautiful* voice! Who is your teacher?"

"No one, really." Svirsky was suddenly embarrassed. "I used to eavesdrop at my sister's singing lessons when I was a boy. I tried to imitate her singing. I always *loved* music, especially singing." He was afraid that he sounded childish.

"You are a *natural!*" Alicia cried out. "I must introduce you to the music teachers at the Conservatory! You have a God given talent, Lieutenant, don't waste it! You were *born* to sing!"

"Wait, wait! Don't try to steal my new aide!" General Rezánov interrupted the flurry of her admiration. "Lieutenant Svirsky is not available to change his career. After the war—perhaps, but not yet!" he added humorously.

"Meanwhile," Maria Nikoláyevna glanced at the large bronze clock on the mantel, "I must excuse myself and go home. I am rather tired after my trip." She stood and kissed her hostess, whispering, "Andrúsha is well. I'll see you tomorrow and tell you everything."

"We should be going as well," General Melekhov said.

"And so should we," Colonel Bolshakov joined, but Alicia Eduardovna was not through yet with her plans for Svirsky. "You must promise me, Lieutenant, that you will allow me to introduce you to my music teachers! Where can I reach you?" she insisted.

"The Lieutenant is staying at my house, so you can reach him there," Maria Nikoláyevna said. "And I would like to invite you and your husband to visit with me."

"It would be our pleasure," the colonel replied.

Amid embraces and exclamations of thanks, the guests finally departed.

General Rezánov kissed his wife's cheek. "You sang *beautifully!* You must sing for me again, like you did when we were young." He looked at her for a long moment and kissed her again. Turning to his remaining two aides, who waited politely, he said gruffly, "Well gentlemen, let's go back to work!"

The young men bowed to Varvara Mikháilovna and followed the general.

26

Petrograd seemed to be cruel winter's prime target at the end of 1916. Freezing weather and two-meter-high snowdrifts fettered the city, making even meager deliveries of food impossible.

Wrath against the authorities was boiling over. Mass strikes flared all over the city.

The Tsar had spent Christmas with his family at Tsárskoye Selo. Surrounded by his loving family he enjoyed the simple pleasures of a country squire. He built snowmen with his children, fought snow fights with his aides, went down the hill on sleds, and skated on the palace pond, drinking hot chocolate afterwards. He was warm and cozy, singing English Christmas carols with his family and attendants, not disturbed by his generals' daily briefings or his ministers' bothersome reports about civil unrest in Petrograd.

He ordered his Minister of the Interior, Alexander Protopopov, to see if there was enough flour in the bakeshops for baking Christmas cookies. Protopopov assured him there was *plenty* of flour and everything else, urging the Tsar not to believe vicious rumors. The Tsar was satisfied.

He must have hated leaving Tsárskoye Selo where he and his family were cloistered from hostility. It must have been dreadful returning to Stavka after his holiday. But believing in his divine investiture as *the father of his people,* the Tsar bade goodbye to his wife and children, three of whom were down with measles. He must have felt virtuous and self-sacrificing, abandoning his own sick children for the sake of armies that needed his leadership. He did not realize that in less than three months, his empire would cease to exist.

The first weeks of 1917 remained grim. Russians were losing territory to the Central Powers on all three fronts. Most of Russian Poland was already in the hands of the enemy, as were parts of the Ukraine and Lithuania. There were small victories here and there, but on the whole, everybody felt that Russia was on the brink of losing the war.

The German strategy of attack was methodical and devastating. First, they pinned down adversary forces with a barrage of heavy artillery, pounding the Russian positions day after day, until nothing was left but a scorched land disfigured by craters. Storm troopers would then swiftly move in to clear up whoever might be still alive in the trenches or in the cellars of destroyed buildings. Quickly, they would establish their positions on the abandoned land, readjust the aim of their long-range cannons, and repeat the process. This was known as *Ludendorff's strategy* and it was admired by friend and feared by foe because it *worked.*

Russians could not match the Germans' superior firepower. What they had instead was a pool of millions of undisciplined, poorly trained and poorly armed recruits whom they kept throwing against the Germans.

In February, hundreds of thousands of workers in Petrograd went on strike. They gathered daily in front of their silent and locked factories. They demanded bread, freedom, and the end of the war. With every passing day the crowds grew larger and more aggressive, often vandalizing their plants, and more frequently, the residences of the rich.

February 23 (March 8 in the rest of the world) was International Women's Day. The strike leaders chose it for mass demonstrations against the war. Carrying slogans demanding *"Peace, Bread and Freedom,"* demonstrators encountered Cossacks blocking the entrance to every bridge. To avoid confrontation, the strikers crossed the frozen Nevá over the ice. The Cossacks, as ordered, guarded the bridges and did nothing to stop the people from marching over the ice.

Maria Nikoláyevna watched through her windows as a group of strikers gathered in front of the Imperial Academy of Art across the river from her house. They descended on the ice at a small landing that was framed by two granite Egyptian sphinxes, gifts to Peter the Great from some potentate. She watched scores of people slipping and falling down the slope, while many others slid down on *their* bottoms. Watching them reminded her how she and Ksusha used to take little Lara to that landing with her sled, and how she and Ksusha would slide down the icy hill on their bottoms. "It was such fun, and so many years ago!" she thought, as she watched the crowd.

The strikers made their way through the snowdrifts to the opposite side of the river and climbed up the embankment in front of the equestrian monument of Peter the Great. They passed her house, reuniting with crowds that had crossed the river further up, at the Admiralty and at the Winter Palace, inundating the city. They came from every section of Petrograd: from Vassilievsky Island and Narvskaya Zastava, from Vyborskaya Storona and Lygovka.

Being International Women's Day, there were many women workers among the marchers. It was almost a festive crowd, notwithstanding their somber placards. The women's heads were covered with their best colorful shawls and they smiled and shouted greetings to the Cossacks. The young Cossacks winked and smiled at the women. The Cossacks did not harass them and in return, the marchers parted their ranks to let the equestrians pass through.

Peaceful marchers converged on the huge Znamenski Square in front of the railroad terminal. A small brass band of amateur musicians blasted the air with popular tunes until some anonymous orators began speeches only a few could hear. By dusk, the square began to empty. Everyone thought it was a peaceful rally. The crowds were allowed to use the bridges for their return home.

General Khabalov, head of Petrograd Garrison, ordered the release of some emergency supplies of flour the next day but warned that if the strikers did not return to work, they would be arrested and sent to the front. The threat infuriated the organizers. They issued their reply: they would shut down the city.

They kept their promise. The next day, a Saturday, much larger crowds descended on the center of the city. They tore down Khabalov's proclamations and continued toward Znamenski Square, their mood of peaceful protest turning into angry rebellion.

Everything came to a halt. All stores were shut down, their doors and windows protected by sheets of plywood nailed to the frames. There were no konka wagons on the streets, no automobiles, no horse carriages, no well-dressed schoolchildren, and no nannies with baby carriages. Nothing moved on the broad avenues except the huge flood of people.

Various speakers addressed the crowds from the pedestal of the giant statue of Alexander III in the center of Znamenski Square. This time the speakers used sound-amplifying horns. Bolshevik agitators spoke fearlessly, demanding the end of the war, proclaiming the solidarity of workers and soldiers, and agitating for the end of autocracy. They directed their speeches specifically toward the soldiers, urging them not to shoot at their brothers, the striking workers. Many of the Cossacks nodded in agreement: the workers, indeed, were their brothers, and Russia should get out of the war.

A new company of horsemen arrived, and the crowd split to let them through until everyone realized that the horsemen were the mounted police.

The attitude of the crowd quickly changed. The people cursed the police, spat on them and shook their fists. Someone threw a pavement stone and hit a policeman's horse. The animal reared up in pain.

The policemen lifted their rifles and aimed at the crowd. Suddenly a young Cossack dashed out of the formation and slashed the leader of the police detachment with his saber. The policeman slumped in his saddle, dead. The watching crowd froze in horror.

Then, the crowd cheered. The Cossacks were with the people.

General Rezánov waited at Stavka for the Chief-of-Staff, General Alexeyev. His briefcase bulged with reports and projections from various sections of the Ministry of War, none of them optimistic.

Rezánov hated his role as the messenger of bad news. He hated also that he could not express his opinion. To head off widespread revolt, the Tsar must step down and establish the Duma as Russia's Parliament. To express such an opinion, Rezánov knew, would make him a traitor in the eyes of the Emperor.

Alexeyev entered the room surrounded by his aides. He was balding, and his remaining gray hair was cut very short like a young cadet's. His moustache and small Vandyke beard were showing signs of neglect. He had huge bags under his pale gray eyes. He had recently returned from a sick leave in the Crimea, which apparently had not done him much good. He was suffering from a heart condition and, it was rumored, from cancer. He looked ghastly.

"Ah, Vladímir Petrovich!" he exclaimed, trying to sound hearty. "Good to see you!" He was cordial, but Rezánov could see that he was upset.

"Bring us some good, strong coffee and then leave us alone," Alexeyev said to one of his aides. "Sit down my friend. How is your son, our pilot hero? I've heard that he was seriously wounded."

"Yes, Mikhail Vasilevich. Andrei was shot down. He is at Odessa Memorial now. He is in a wheelchair, but they were able to save his leg. He is getting along fine. His wife is with him."

"Good! Send him my best regards when you write to him."

"I shall."

A young aide returned with two cups of coffee. He put the cups on the table, saluted the generals and left the room.

"Well, my friend," Alexeyev picked up his coffee cup with a trembling hand. "I've heard that things are getting out of control in Petrograd, and elsewhere. I am afraid that we have reached the point of no return. The situation here," he gestured to the room and beyond it, "is no better. The Emperor doesn't want to hear bad news. Right now, he worries about his children, who are sick with measles." Alexeyev lowered his voice. "He is seriously depressed."

"He won't appreciate my reports," Rezánov said. "I have no good news to deliver."

"He may not even receive you. He gave us an order not to disturb him. You might as well leave your papers and go home." Alexeyev's smile was a sad grimace. "I would do the same; go home, if I could. However, since you are here, you might as well stay. Perhaps tomorrow he will see you. He *must* hear what's going on in Petrograd ... All those riots ..." He patted Rezánov on his shoulder as he stood and called his aide.

"General Rezánov will be staying at Stavka," he said. "Please make arrangements."

"Yes, Your Excellency," the captain saluted as the old man left the room. "Would you mind, General, waiting here a few minutes?"

"Go ahead. Send in my aide, Lieutenant Borisov, please."

"Yes, Your Excellency."

Rezánov felt rising anger. General Alexeyev, his old commander and mentor, was obviously suffering from more than physical ailments. The Tsar's neglect must have stung the old warrior's pride. The whole of Stavka was deteriorating, Rezánov thought. The young officers, the aides of various generals, looked bored and arrogant, and the generals and colonels even more irritable than usual. He was infuriated that no one had bothered to inform him *before* he left Petrograd that the Tsar was not interested in reports. The discipline of the High Command was going to the dogs!

Lieutenant Borisov entered and at once knew that his general was furious. He knew better than to ask questions. He saluted and waited for orders.

Over the following two days Stavka was inundated by urgent telegrams. General Alexeyev was finally able to convince the Tsar to listen to Rezánov's report. The Emperor seemed attentive. He thanked Rezánov for his report.

The Tsar left for a long walk in the woods with his aides, and then played a game of dominoes. Only after a nap did he reply to the latest urgent telegram from General Khabalov.

When Alexeyev read a copy of the Tsar's reply, he blanched and made the sign of the cross. "Good Lord!" he whispered. "This is the end!"

The message was very short. The Tsar commanded that order be restored in the city *"as of tomorrow,"* reinforcing his command with a reminder that any disobedience in a time of war was not to be tolerated. The telegram was signed with one word—Nikolaí.

Upon receiving the telegram, General Khabalov called an emergency meeting of his senior staff. He was visibly upset. He read the telegram aloud and then waited until it made its way from person to person and came back to him. "It means, gentlemen, that tomorrow our troops must suppress demonstrations by use of *ultimate means*. I pray to the Lord that the demonstrators march peacefully. But ..." he stopped and looked at their troubled faces. "But, if they carry red banners against the war or against the monarchy, we must open fire. There is no choice, gentlemen; it is by order of His Majesty."

The officers remained silent. The Tsar had thrown down the gauntlet. If troops opened fire on unarmed workers, it would be understood that the Tsar had declared war on his own people. If troops refused to obey, it would mean the end of the Tsar's autocracy.

The President of the Duma, Mikhail Rodzianko, sent one last desperate telegram. He alerted the Tsar that troops of the garrison were openly joining the demonstrators. He urged the Tsar to step down and form a government that would guarantee a constitution. Without a few concessions, the monarchy could topple, he warned.

The Tsar ignored the warning, complaining to his aides that Rodzianko and the others were still bothering him with their gloomy telegrams. He was going to return to Tsárskoye Selo in two days to be with his sick children, he said. Meanwhile, he would like to have a game of dominoes.

27

All through the night, the Petrograd police prepared. They positioned machine gun nests atop building at strategic points of the city. The secret police began to round up all known leaders of the uprising, especially Jews. Some of the leaders had escaped into the Bolshevik underground; they were resurfacing now, ready to lead.

The uprising was finally recognized as an organized rebellion.

The sun rose over Petrograd, and the spell of the pitiless Arctic winter was finally broken. The winds died down and the sky turned brilliantly blue with layers of pink cirrus clouds. The golden spires of the Admiralty shone brightly under the winter sky. It was still cold, but the cycle of brutal winter was broken.

Early in the morning, the soldiers of the garrison, young peasant lads homesick in the big hostile city, gathered in small groups. They were mostly new recruits, hastily trained to replace seasoned troops who were needed at the front. These young recruits felt no allegiance to the Tsar, but felt a deep affinity for the workers, their brothers, who were also of peasant stock.

The soldiers of the Volynsky regiment deputized two of their men to inform the company commander that the regiment would not obey an order to shoot down unarmed demonstrators. The commander listened to them politely. Then, turning to his aides, he ordered the men's arrest.

Instead, the men shot him. After that, there was no choice. The regiment joined the revolution.

Word spread like fire, and by evening, more than sixty thousand troops had switched their allegiance to the revolutionary forces.

Early Monday morning, people began to overflow the broad boulevards of Petrograd. Huge crowds packed the square in front of Kazan Cathedral and spilled to the narrow quays of the Ekateringofsky Canal, near the church built on the spot where in the previous century revolutionaries had assassinated the grandfather of the present Tsar.

The crowds waved red banners and shouted *"Down with the Tsar"* and *"Bread, Freedom and Peace!"* The same scene was repeated at other city squares. Petrograd was pulsating, moving and buzzing, as if it were a colony of aggressive ants. Commands to disperse could not be heard over the uproar of the crowds. Even if demonstrators had heard the commands, they were beyond the point of obeying them.

They became aware of reprisal when the machine guns rattled from the rooftops. The police had opened fire. The marchers began to fall. "Brothers, don't shoot," they shouted to soldiers on the street.

"Fire!" the officers commanded. The soldiers hesitated. Then, as if making a collective decision, they turned their guns on the police. An active battle erupted. The demonstrators tried to hide, but in the huge open square, there was no place to hide.

Finally, machine guns stopped crackling. Commands filled the air. The police units withdrew. The Cossacks trotted away, and the garrison troops marched back to their barracks. Shaken by the slaughter, people were free to leave.

People wounded and dead lay trampled on snow splattered with blood and strewn with discarded placards, torn banners, shoes, and clothes. Bullet holes patterned the walls of surrounding buildings.

The day that the soldiers of Petrograd's garrison refused to obey the Tsar's orders was the beginning of the end.

The rebellious Volynsky regiment, reinforced by other rebel soldiers, had seized the Arsenal. They took possession of thousands of rifles, machine guns, revolvers, and a huge amount of ammunition, which they distributed among the revolutionaries.

The city belonged to them now. The armed crowds grew with the addition of thousands of students and white-collar workers. The people did not march anymore. They roared through the streets and drowned the city under their revolutionary typhoon.

They attacked the Central Police Headquarters, shooting the hated policemen at random. They set the District Court on fire, burned files, tossed documents out of the windows. In their senseless wrath, they prevented firemen from saving the building by slashing the fire hoses. Directed by the Bolsheviks, who had emerged as the leaders, crowds surged throughout Petrograd. Only five large compounds—The Winter Palace, the Admiralty, the Mariinsky Palace, the Peter and Paul Fortress, and the Taurichesky Palace where the Duma was in session—were not yet under the insurgents' control.

The Council of Ministers meeting at Mariinsky Palace listened to General Khabalov's report with growing apprehension. The general was shaken as he described the surrender of his garrison to insurgents. He wiped his face with his sleeve.

"Gentlemen," he declared nervously. "Petrograd is out of our control. Twenty-five thousand more of the garrison troops have joined the rebellion! The Cossacks refuse to leave the barracks if they are ordered to open fire on crowds. Strikers are marching with brass bands now! They are *celebrating!* The bastards opened all the prisons and liberated the prisoners. I beg you, gentleman, do something! Anything!"

The ministers sat in gloomy silence. They knew that they had to untangle the twisted Gordian knot of calamity, but no one knew how.

No one used euphemisms anymore to describe disturbances in the city: Petrograd became the center of a *revolution*. Monday, February 27, was the fifth day of the revolution.

The secret Bolshevik leaders and better-educated soldiers created a new governing body—the *Petrograd Soviet of Workers and Soldiers Deputies.* They had to establish an authority that would guide revolutionary activities. The first meeting of the Petrograd Soviet of Workers and Soldiers Deputies demanded the Tsar's immediate abdication and the initiation of peace talks with the Central Powers.

The Duma was powerless. The Tsar was powerless. Bolshevik agitators knew it was their moment to act. The augury of victory was theirs. Well-disciplined agitators fanned out among Petrograd's workers and soldiers, chanting the revolutionary mantra *"All Power to the Soviet of Workers and Soldiers Deputies."* They urged the masses to keep up the pressure. *"Down with the Tsar! Long live the revolution!"*

Maria Nikoláyevna and her butler stood in the destroyed Winter Garden. The wind blew through the holes in the shattered ceiling. Small heaps of snow piled up along the cracks between the sheets of plywood that covered the smashed glass walls. The marble sculpture of Larissa in the image of Flora was still in its place, but the dwarf orange trees that used to surround it were all dead and the little brook at her feet was frozen.

Maria Nikoláyevna swept a tear off her cheek. "I don't think, Semeon Petrovich, that it would be wise to repair the building. The times are not right," she said dryly, trying not to give in to her sadness. "I think our lives will be quite different, from now on. So, let's move back the barricade. We can start demolishing the garden when the weather turns warm."

"Yes, Maria Nikoláyevna. I'll have the door leading into the house reinforced, just in case," the old man said. "I can't forget my experience with the sailors."

Ksusha met her at the door. "Varvara Mikháilovna is on the telephone. She seems upset."

"She is always upset," Maria Nikoláyevna thought as she went to answer the telephone.

Varvara was in tears. "I don't know what happened to Volódya! He should have been back from Stavka! I can't reach him. Lieutenant Borisov's wife can't reach her husband either! What shall we do?"

"Nothing. Just wait. Look outside: can't you see what's going on along the Nevsky?"

"I am afraid to look!"

"Just sit tight and wait. Make sure all the windows in your house are shut and all the draperies drawn. Stay away from the windows. I'll ask Lieutenant Svirsky to call Garrison Headquarters for some information."

The telephone suddenly went dead. "Allo! Allo!" Maria Nikoláyevna shouted into the horn. Her electric light blinked and then went out. "Well … That's it. The insurgents have taken over the power stations and the telephone exchange. What now?" she thought. She shivered and tightened the shawl over her shoulders.

28

General Rezánov received orders to join the Tsar's entourage, which was en route to Tsárskoye Selo. The Tsar had expressed his wish to talk with him.

"I hope we get there in one piece. Traveling in the Tsar's convoy can be dangerous to one's health," the general joked, as he and Lieutenant Borisov settled into a two-berth compartment on a short but otherwise identical train that always traveled in tandem with the Emperor's train.

The trains stopped at Smolensk to take on fuel and water. While there, at ten o'clock in the morning, General Rezánov was summoned to join the Tsar for breakfast in the small train's lounge car. Rezánov doubted that the Tsar would discuss anything important while drinking coffee and eating his soft-boiled duck's egg.

The lounge car's comfortable furnishings included chairs and sofas upholstered in deep green plush, which were grouped around several small tables. After breakfast, the small tables would sport chessboards and domino sets. For now, they were set with Imperial silver that shone against starched white linen cloths. At one end of the lounge, a group of generals and colonels crowded in front of a long table laden with food.

The Tsar was at a small table with a colonel whose leather jacket had wings on the epaulettes. Both had only coffee in front of them. "Come in, come in, General. Join us!" the Tsar called when he saw Rezánov hesitating at the door.

The general saluted. "Thank you, Your Majesty."

"What would you like to eat?"

"Just coffee, Your Majesty."

"Bring some coffee, please," the Tsar said to an orderly. Then, turning to the general, he introduced the pilot. "This is Colonel Tkachev, the Inspector of Aviation. He knows your son."

"I had the honor of presenting his first Citation of Valor to your son, General Rezánov," Tkachev said with a smile. "I was sorry to hear that he had been badly wounded, but I also know he is getting well. Captain Egórov, who recently returned from a visit with your son, brought us the good news. The Captain is here, on the escort train."

"This is the best news I've heard in a long time!" Rezánov exclaimed, not caring anymore whether the Emperor had any questions for him. He was eager to meet Egórov.

An adjutant stopped at their table and saluted. "Your Majesty, excuse me, but there is an urgent message from Her Majesty with special instructions to bring it to Your Majesty's attention immediately."

The Tsar stood. Everyone present stood also. He smiled shyly at Rezánov. "I must leave. I'll talk to you some other time." He bent his head in a slight bow and left, trailed by his aides and attendants.

When the trains began to move again, word spread that the destination had changed: the trains were going to Pskov, an ancient Russian city. "Why?" everyone wondered. Who would order them to *Pskov?*

The passengers began speculating that the Emperor himself had ordered the change. The idea originated among the telegraphers, who had received a telegram from Grand Duke Mikhail Alexandrovich urging the Tsar to talk to one of his most loyal generals at the northern front, General Nikolaí Vladímirovich Ruzsky. Apparently, news about the revolution had reached the frontlines. Several small infantry units had refused to obey their officers, proclaiming that they would take orders only from the Soviet of Workers and Soldiers Deputies.

"Poor man," Rezánov thought. "If the army is against him, he is finished." His own feelings about the Tsar began to change. His annoyance with the Tsar began to turn into pity for the good but weak man who seemed bound for destruction.

General Rezánov met Egórov in the lounge of the second train. They shook hands, and then Rezánov impulsively embraced Egórov in a bear hug. "I feel that I know you, Captain. Doctor Shubin told me what a great role you played in my son's recovery. Join me in my compartment, and tell me about my boy!"

Lieutenant Borisov rose politely to leave, but the general protested. "No, no, Kólya, you stay. I know that you love Andrei. You have known him for many years. You were one of his Best Men. Stay!"

Egórov began his account of Andrei's life as a pilot. The general listened with great concentration. Finally, when Egórov described the terrifying episode of Andrei's duel with the Albatros, the general covered his face with his hand. "My poor dear boy ..." he whispered. He took off his spectacles and began to polish them vigorously with his handkerchief.

"Andrei is a hero and a talented pilot, Your Excellency. Everybody loves your son, from Commander Kozakov to the soldiers of the support unit. When the order came to transport him to Odessa, everyone who wasn't on duty came to see him off. When I saw him last, he was counting the days until he can return to his unit. Frankly, sir, some of us *don't want* Andrei to return. Our losses are *astronomical!* Kozakov had an idea: there is a new flight school for advanced piloting in Odessa. He wanted Andrei to be assigned as a flight instructor to that school. His impact and contribution to our country might be much greater, and longer lasting, in that role. But Andrei refused, and Kozakov changed his mind. He wants Andrei to come back to the front and fly again. What do you think?"

The general replaced his glasses and said slowly, "The call to fight runs deep in our family's blood. My son has sworn allegiance to the Russian Empire and has already begun paying for that with his life. I am an officer who has done the same, as my father did before me. And my father's father, before him. Andrei will feel deeply that it is a matter of honor to return to his squadron. Kozakov knows, too, that winning the war is more important than one young man's life. I hope you understand this."

"I do understand, sir. Andrei and Kozakov are both honorable men. However," his hands shook. "What if *you* suggested to the Grand Duke Alexander Micháilovich that Andrei be reassigned as an instructor in Odessa?"

"So, you want me to use my friendship with the Grand Duke to keep Andrei out of danger?"

"Well ..."

"I won't do it. My honor as a Russian officer will not allow me to do it. Even though I disapprove of this war, I cannot *'pull strings,'* so to speak, to save my son."

Egórov reddened. "With all due respect, Your Excellency, I am not advocating a dishonorable solution. Andrei would remain in the active service, but in a different capacity. As I said, he is an exceptionally talented pilot and his skills should be used in teaching other young men to be great pilots. His chances of surviving the rest of the war are less than twenty percent, sir! A talented young man's life would be wasted ..."

"What about you, Captain?" the general interrupted. "What about you? You too were wounded, yet you returned to your unit after you recuperated. Why didn't *you* try to get out of active service?" There was a slight tremor under the general's eye.

Egórov thought for a moment, and then said slowly, "I am an older man, General. I am thirty and have no family. My parents died several years ago, and my only brother was killed at the beginning of the war. I have no wife. I have been subpoenaed to appear at my divorce hearings and Captain Kozakov gave me an emergency furlough for two weeks. Thanks to Colonel Tkachev, who invited me to accompany him as his aide, I was able to travel on this pleasant train."

Egórov lit a cigarette and continued, "With Andrei, it is different. He is only twenty-three and married to a lovely girl who adores him. He has both of his parents, who also adore him. His whole life is ahead of him. He shouldn't be wasted. Especially not now, when the country is on the cusp of colossal upheaval."

The general took off his glasses and began to polish them again, saying nothing.

Egórov waited. There was nothing more he could say to the obstinate old warrior.

Minutes of silence passed. The general said finally, "No, I cannot do it. Even as a *father*, I cannot accept it. Andrei must do his duty, as he sees it."

The trains rested at a sidetrack in Pskov, all their windows heavily draped. The Emperor had lunch in his private quarters with Colonel Tkachev and his senior aides. Everyone was in a subdued mood. The Emperor all but said that he was going to accept the proclamation of a Constitutional Monarchy. The men were stunned. There was little more conversation after that, except for discussion about the unusually cold winter. The Tsar seemed to be at peace.

Another short train of only two cars slowly pulled to the parallel track. General Nikolaí Vladímirovich Ruzsky, commander of the northern front, had arrived.

He was well-prepared to meet the Tsar. He carried written agreements from commanders of *all* the fronts, including the Tsar's uncle, Grand Duke Nikolaí Nikolayevich, whom the Tsar had replaced as Supreme Commander. General Alekseyev had been soliciting the commanders' opinions in a circular telegram. They all agreed that the Tsar must step down.

By consensus, the civilian deputies of the Duma reached the same decision. The country had lost faith in their monarch. Two Duma deputies, Guchkov and Shulgin, were already on their way to Pskov to obtain the Tsar's compliance. The revolution had reached a point beyond any negotiation. The promise of a constitution was not enough anymore.

The Tsar had dinner with Generals Ruzsky, Danilov, and Savich. The Tsar listened to the generals with deep attention, a sad half-smile on his face. Ruzsky presented an official form of abdication. As the Emperor read it, he blanched. Then, he stood and said quietly, "I guess this is it. I shall give up the throne." He left for his compartment.

The generals were astounded. The Emperor must not fully understand what he was doing; giving up the throne of the Russian Empire without a word of protest! He was forfeiting three-hundred years of autocratic rule by the Romanov Dynasty as easily as if he were a member of a tennis club passing his racket to another member after a disastrous match! He was signing his name to a document that would affect the lives of *millions* of people, as easily as if he were putting his name on a Christmas card.

In heavy silence, the generals made the sign of the cross over their chests, their numerous medals interfering with their trembling fingers. Suddenly, they felt as if they were children lost in a frightening dream from which there was no escape.

The Tsar returned and handed the signed Manifesto of Abdication to General Ruzsky. He saluted the generals and returned to his compartment without another word. The paper was dated 3:00 PM, March 2, 1917. It was signed *Nikolaí*.

The news flew by wire across the country: The Emperor of all the Russias, Nikolaí II, has abdicated. He has bequeathed the Throne and His Supreme Powers to his younger brother, Grand Duke Mikhail Alexandrovich.

When Duma deputies Guchkov and Shulgin arrived at Pskov, Nikolaí met them with an explanation as to why he had named his brother successor. "My son is a child, and you know that he is not well. I abdicated on behalf of my son as well. It is best for the country that my brother become Tsar and not Regent."

The Grand Duke, sensing the inevitable, rejected the crown, thus ending 300 years of the Romanov dynasty.

Guchkov and Shulgin were touched by Nikolaí's simple dignity. When asked whom they were going to propose as Premier, they said Prince Lvov. Nikolaí nodded without enthusiasm. Finally, he shook hands with them and wished them a safe journey home.

The deputies departed for Petrograd, but the Tsar was forced to return to Mogilev, to Stavka. The road to Tsárskoye Selo was in the hands of insurgents.

29

Being so far away, Odessa had been spared the upheavals of Petrograd, the torments of hunger and cold. Odessa was, however, a revolutionary city. The 1905 mutiny on the *Potemkin* remained in its collective memory. The battleship itself was anchored near Odessa when news of the abdication reached the Black Sea.

The hidden ardor of the 1905 revolution quickly ignited into a raging conflagration among the sailors of the Black Sea fleet. The sailors immediately established the Soviet of Workers, Soldiers and *Sailors* and declared that no orders by officers would be obeyed without the approval of the Soviet. A new battle cry was born: *"Vsyá Vlas't Sovétam! All power to the Soviets!"*

At Memorial Hospital, recuperating soldiers created their own Soviet Committee. Their first demand was integration of the wards. No more separate wards for officers, and certainly no private rooms. The committee ordered Doctor Shubin to immediately move three wounded soldiers into Andrei's room. The doctor tried to invoke his authority, but they were not impressed. They threatened him with a visit from their brother sailors. The old doctor knew what that meant: he would be shot.

He called Larissa into his office. "We have a very delicate situation, my dear," he told her in a low voice. "The revolutionary patients have demanded that we dispense with private rooms and the officers' wards. There are threats of violence. I think that your husband could finish his recuperation more safely in some private location, such as a hotel. Sister Veronica and I can visit him daily, and we will supply you with all the necessary equipment and medications. I am afraid that the situation will only grow worse. Would you be able to take care of your husband in a hotel?"

"Of course, Arcadi Petrovich. We can move to the same hotel where my mother stayed. I'll request a room on the first floor, so that Andrei can use his wheelchair. When do we have to move?"

"As soon as possible. Today. Now. I'll telephone the Otráda."

"Good. I would like to ask a big favor: could you use your official position to telegraph my father-in-law and ask that he and my mother send us some money? Civilians cannot use the telegraph connections anymore, and I have almost nothing left. We have only Andrei's salary, which is not much."

"Of course, my dear. Meanwhile, I can lend you some money."

"Thank you. I think we are all right for about a week. I would like to open an account in the local bank. Both of us have the personal trusts that our parents established at our births. I still have two years to go before I can have my trust, but I know my mother will release some of my funds, given the present situation. Andrei is of legal age already, so he can have his funds now."

Shubin listened to her with admiration. "What a fine young woman!" he thought. "Such poise, such clear thinking, and she is still a mere girl!"

"Yes, my dear. I'll telegraph General Rezánov's office right away," he said. "You go and prepare your husband for the change of venue, so to speak. I'll talk to Sister Veronica about the supplies."

The hospital ambulance moved Andrei to the Hotel Otráda. Larissa had chosen a single room with private bath, thinking of the weeks ahead and the possibility that they would be stuck in Odessa with limited funds.

Andrei was irritable. He felt useless, depending on Larissa's help even to go to the toilet. He hated the world. When he read about the Tsar's abdication, he threw his crutches across the room and cursed like a peasant.

Larissa wasn't shocked: she was sad that life had turned out so ugly that even her sweet, well-brought up young husband began to act like the lowest types. She tried to take the edge off Andrei's bitterness, saying that things would turn out all right, but he refused to be mollified. He yelled that she was nothing but a mama's girl who should sit at her piano and practice her scales.

Larissa continued to unpack their modest belongings, fighting the gathering tears. She recalled Veronica's words that his behavior was typical. He would be ashamed in due time. Meanwhile, Larissa struggled to keep her temper under control.

A second bed was moved into their small room, leaving almost no space to turn around. "Do we have to live in such close quarters?" Andrei complained. "Even at the front I had more space for myself!"

"We have no money for anything better right now," Larissa said evenly. "As soon as we get our trust money, we can move into a suite."

"What if we don't get our money? With what's going on in the country I won't be surprised if the bastards nationalize the banks and steal our money!"

"If that happens, we'll stay where we are and do the best with what we have."

"Yeah, on my pilot's salary! Or, on my *invalid's* pension!"

She decided to try another approach. She smiled and said, "When I was still at school, one of the girls told us a naughty story. It's about *'living on love.'* Want to hear it?"

He still looked angry, but he said, "Alright." She sat on the edge of his bed and took his hand into hers.

"Well, there was a young couple, like us. They were very much in love, like us, but were quite poor."

"Like us," Andrei said gloomily.

"With their money all gone, the young wife was worrying that there was nothing to eat. 'How can we live?' she cried. The husband, trying to cheer her up, said, 'We'll live on love!' So, he went out, looking for work. When he came back, he saw his wife sitting on a stove. 'What are you doing there?' he asked. 'I am warming up your supper,' she replied.'"

Andrei laughed, despite his foul mood. "Come here, my silly darling …" he moved on his bed, clearing a little space for her. Eagerly she came into his outstretched arms. Veronica was right. He came back to her.

That night, when she was giving him a bed bath, there was another pleasant surprise: Andrei had an erection. "Good Lord, I am still alive!" he cried. "I was afraid that my manhood could have been lost forever! Do you think we could try it out?"

"Oh, yes! I had my worries too," she confessed. "But how … "

"The armchair!" said Andrei.

"Yes!" Lara said. But by the time she maneuvered the heavy armchair to the bed, it was too late.

"Never mind," she said cheerfully. "We know now that you are still intact, so we will be better prepared next time. Meanwhile, let's rehearse. You in the chair, and me on your lap."

They took their positions and discovered that it was possible. Soon their rehearsal turned into a performance.

"Good Lord! Thank you!" Andrei breathed. "Do you realize that was the first time since our honeymoon?"

Larissa smiled. "I'd forgotten how marvelous it feels," she murmured as she placed her head on his chest.

After that, Andrei's recovery took an accelerated pace. Although his healing wound was still painful, he was able to tolerate it. The flesh that had formed along the wound was of many colors and sensitive to touch, but he was ready to suffer the discomfort for the sake of making love to Larissa.

Spring was in full bloom toward the end of March. Roses were budding in the Memorial Hospital garden, and lemon and orange trees stood mantled in a profusion of delicate blossoms, the air fragrant with their scent. The velvety nights were warm, and nightingales serenaded their mates with passionate trills.

During the day, the garden was filled with ambulating patients: some limping around on crutches with the help of nurses, others resting on benches, still others confined to wheelchairs, all happy to be in the sunshine, all lucky to be alive.

The young Rezánovs received a note stating that their funds were awaiting them at the local branch of the State Bank of the Russian Empire.

Larissa hired a carriage. After visiting the bank, she wanted to take Andrei on a sightseeing tour of the city and perhaps even to the open air concert in the park.

Andrei needed help into the carriage. The young driver climbed off his perch. "Let me help you, Comrade Lieutenant." He sounded friendly. It was the first time that Andrei and Larissa had heard the new form of address. No more 'Your Excellency' or 'Sir' or even 'Gospodín', mister.

"I know how hard it is to move around when only one leg is working. I was wounded also," the driver said as he helped Andrei navigate the flimsy steps into the carriage.

"Yes. Thank you. When were you wounded?" Andrei asked.

"Last year. At Lutsk. I've got a whole ribbon of machine gun bullets in my left leg. At least, it felt like the whole ribbon!" he said cheerfully. "But the doctors saved my leg. Although I can't bend it anymore."

"I had the same!" Andrei exclaimed, responding to the driver's friendliness. "Machine gun wounds. Only it was in the air, and I was shot down!"

"What do you know! So, you're one of those fellows who fly up in the sky?"

"Yes, I am a pilot."

"Well! Aren't you afraid that your machine will fall down?"

Andrei smiled. "Not really. The machines are good. It's we, the men who fly them, who are not so good."

"Some of you must be good. Last year, when I was still at the hospital, I read in the paper about some young pilot who got out on the wing of his machine and threw bombs at the Germans. Imagine! He was flying his machine and then, sitting on the wing, he threw the bombs!"

"That sounds impossible! Are you sure that he was also flying the plane?"

"Oh, yes, sir! That's what the paper said. He was a *real hero!*" the driver said, climbing to his seat with some difficulty. Andrei and Larissa exchanged amused glances: they both noticed that the driver had called Andrei 'sir,' instead of 'comrade.'

They drove along Deribasovskaya Street, a wide, tree-lined, handsome street with fashionable stores and art galleries on both sides of it.

"There is the bank," the driver said pointing to a large imposing building with four columns framing its massive entrance. "My name is Akim. I will wait for you here."

"Thank you," Andrei said to Akim. Andrei hobbled through the lobby using only a cane. Larissa walked next to him, not supporting him. She wanted him to prove to himself that he was the master of his body again.

The Odessa branch of the State Bank of the Russian Empire looked like its main office in Petrograd. The same large hall with high ceilings and polished marble floors, counters of polished mahogany and fine screens of bronze rods separating the tellers' cages from the visitors. Several individual small rooms, well furnished with handsome leather furniture, were opposite the row of tellers' windows.

A young man in striped trousers and formal morning coat met them. "May I be of help?" he inquired.

"Yes, please. I am Lieutenant Andrei Rezánov, and this is my wife. We received a notice that some of our funds from the central Bank in Petrograd were transferred to Odessa and are available to us."

"Oh, yes. I sent that notice myself. My name is Rostóv, and I am a Junior Executive." They shook hands. "Let me introduce you to our Senior Executive, Mr. Smirnóv. Please, follow me."

He led them into one of the private rooms. "Please, do sit down."

Andrei limped toward the chair and lowered himself gratefully onto the deep seat. "I am not as strong as I thought I was," he chuckled apologetically. "It is my first trip without crutches."

Rostóv smiled uncomfortably, not knowing what to say. Fortunately, Mr. Smirnóv entered the room and Rostóv, with a small bow to Larissa and Andrei, escaped.

Smirnóv was in his late fifties, rotund and almost bald. He was clean-shaven and wore his few remaining gray hairs combed across his scalp. Like the young Rostóv, he was attired in a formal morning coat and striped trousers. He smiled cordially at the Rezánovs. "I am delighted to make your acquaintance," he said, closing the door. "My good old friend Doctor Shubin has told me so much about both of you! My wife and I were hoping to meet you at the Shubins' home for dinner, but the sudden abdication of our Tsar changed everything." He went around the desk and took a seat facing his visitors.

"I shall talk to you as if I were your father, and it may shock you," he began. "But we live in very dangerous times. I can't imagine how the Provisional Government of the Duma *and* the Soviet of Workers and Soldiers Deputies could work in concert. They are natural enemies! In Odessa we are threatened with a repeat of the 1905 mutiny. Now it's even worse. The sailors march down the streets with red flags, demanding 'freedom,' and by *'freedom,'* they mean their right to the property of others!" He stared at Andrei and Larissa with a belligerent expression on his round face.

"I've read that the Provisional Government is contemplating printing new money," Andrei said.

"It may happen. What we'd have then would be three types of money to deal with: gold coins, the Tsarist paper bills, and some new money, which no one would know the value of. Here I come to your particular case: your parents have released portions of your trusts, some sixty thousand rubles between the two of you. That's a *lot* of money. But … if we fall victim to inflation, it may mean that all this money will go up in smoke. It will be worth nothing, not even the paper it was printed on. So, I recommend that you turn part of your money into gold."

"Well …" Andrei began, but Smirnóv lifted his hand, interrupting him.

"I know, you will have a problem: where to keep your gold coins. We can issue you larger denomination coins, but still, you'll have a lot of gold pieces to deal with. Obviously, you don't want to keep it in a shoe box or under a mattress," he chuckled, "or, even in the bank, which might be nationalized." He grew serious. "If the insurgency continues, there will be even more shootings and burglaries and murders and what not, so your money must be well hidden, and yet available to you at short notice!" He paused dramatically.

"So, what must we do?" Larissa asked.

"You must do what Russian peasants have been doing for centuries: You must sew your money *into your clothing* and wear it!"

Larissa and Andrei exchanged looks of incredulity.

"I don't think that I could wear a sixty thousand rubles worth of gold coins!' Andrei said sarcastically.

Smirnóv continued seriously, "Yes, it would be a bit uncomfortable. But, of course, you wouldn't need to hide your *whole* sixty thousand. Half of it could still be in paper, and presumably sitting in the bank and growing interest. As for the rest, your wife would have to sew the gold coins into the hems of her skirts and the sleeves of her coats. And you, Lieutenant, would have to wear a money belt and have a boot maker construct you a pair of boots with faux soles. If we are lucky, and the revolution collapses, you won't need to hide your money. You could redeposit your gold coins. But if we are hit by inflation, you would have saved at least some of your money. Think about it!" he paused.

"Of course, Madame Rezánova, you must buy some inexpensive clothes that would not inspire anyone's envy and an urge to tear them off your back," he continued. "Times have changed. Elegance has become a liability. *À propos ...*" He pointed at Larissa. "I would advise you to ask Doctor Shubin to put you on the payroll. You have been working at the hospital without remuneration, but if we have food rationing, your employment status will affect your ration cards. Without a salary, you probably would get no ration cards at all. The new slogan among a certain group is *"those who don't work, don't eat!'* Don't look so sad," he smiled. "It's just that I believe in being prepared for the worst, especially now."

They left the bank totally confused, carrying their gold coins in a box wrapped as a child's gift in colorful teddy bear paper.

They decided to follow Smirnóv's advice. But until they could conceal the gold in their clothing, they had to protect it somehow, so they locked the box inside Larissa's big *soondook*, a wardrobe trunk that required two men to lift. Still, it was a risk. The solution was obvious: one of them must always be in the room with the soondook.

Larissa needed inexpensive clothes, but how cheap should she go? She wanted to consult someone who was both knowledgeable and discreet. "You rest, Andrúsha, and I will return soon. Watch our soondook with your life!" She laughed. Andrei did not think it was funny. He checked his revolver.

Akim, who had declared that he wanted to be Andrei and Larissa's one and only driver, took Larissa back to Madame Juliette's Salon.

Julia, elegant in her black rustling taffeta silk suit and black patent leather shoes on carved high heels, smiled as Larissa entered. "Madame

Rezánova!" she exclaimed in her rich contralto voice. "What a pleasure! What can I do for you?"

"I need some new clothes, and shoes, but what's more, I need some advice. My mother is back in Petrograd, but my husband is still recuperating. So, we'll be here in your beautiful city for I don't know how long. I brought with me only the bare necessities. I need everything."

"Let's go to my office and talk. Verochka, please bring us some tea and biscuits," Julia said to a young blond girl standing behind the counter.

"Yes, Madame." The girl said with a soft Ukrainian accent. She stared at Larissa. "You are such a beautiful lady!" she declared.

Larissa blushed. In her circles, staring was considered to be bad manners and compliments were given in a more subtle form. "Thank you," she said.

Julia led Larissa to her office. It was tastefully furnished in the fashionable Art Nouveau style with dramatic blacks and whites and only the occasional splash of bright red in silk cushions or fresh roses in severe black vases.

"Do sit down, Larissa Sergéyevna! It's good to see you again. I spotted you and your party at the opera. You and your mother looked very glamorous. And your husband, so handsome! I was curious to see him after I learned that he was none other than *that* famous pilot about whom we'd read so much, so I bought two tickets and took my young son to the opera. He was thrilled to see his hero!"

"That is very kind," Larissa said. "How old is your son?"

"He is eleven. Now, what can I do for you?"

"Well, as I said, I need new clothes ... not fashionable clothes, but plain ones. The type that teachers or secretaries would wear. I realize that you specialize in high fashion, but perhaps you could help me find what I need. I would need a couple of sturdy skirts ..."

"Such as that one?" Julia pointed to a dark woolen skirt on one of the chairs. The skirt looked as if someone was working on it, shortening its length.

"Yes! Just like that!" Larissa exclaimed. "And with the lining also."

Julia laughed. "I know exactly *what* you need and *why* you need it. This is my own skirt, and I bought it for the same reason. Take a look!"

Larissa bent over the skirt. A long string of iridescent pearls snaked out of its half-sewn hem.

"I have always enjoyed wearing my pearls as if they were mere glass beads, but now I must hide them. They could be coveted by someone and confiscated from me in the name of the people!" she laughed. "You and I have the same need to hide our treasures from the voracious appetites of our liberated comrades."

"I did not bring any of my jewelry from Petrograd. But I do have a few gold coins that I must preserve, in case of … well, you know. Actually, it was a banker who advised me to hide the coins in my clothing … in case of inflation."

"Sound advice. I had the same advice from my grandmother even though she doesn't know anything about inflation. But she knows all about robbery. She still keeps some of her jewelry sewn into her clothes!" Julia laughed. "It has become a tradition in our family. When I was very young there was a pogrom in Odessa, and many Jews were robbed, and some even killed." She smiled despite the morbid topic. "I'll help you. We'll go shopping together. We both will need coats and sturdy jackets and at least two skirts. No dresses. No furs. No high heel shoes but flat knee boots with double soles."

"That's what the banker advised!" Larissa exclaimed. "To my husband, that is."

"Actually, you should have some boots also, to hide your pretty legs from our freedom-loving sailors. Our brave sailors are known for their good taste: they *love* to rape women of the higher class," she said with stinging sarcasm. "I am afraid their freedom impinges on ours … I saw some pictures of the new fashions: Paris dictates *very* short skirts, bobbed hair, and shoes with bows or buckles. But this *new* fashion is not for us. We must be clever, subdued and conservative. So, when do you want to go shopping?"

"Anytime. The sooner the better. Tomorrow?"

"Tomorrow. I'll pick you up at ten-thirty, Madame!"

"Please call me Larissa."

"And you must call me Julia."

"I have a friend!" Larissa thought.

"She is the first aristocratic Russian woman whom I like!" reflected Julia.

Verochka brought in tea and cookies, and they sat at the small table in the bay window, pleased with each other.

Julia arrived promptly at ten-thirty, driven by Akim at Larissa's suggestion. Larissa was ready. Both women noted one another's punctuality, another plus in their new friendship.

"We shall go to the Passage," Julia said. "It is the best place to shop. Everything is under one roof."

"Perfect! I am not a good shopper. My mother usually ordered my clothes from her *modiste*. And before that, I wore my school uniform most of the year, except in the summers."

"What did you wear in the summers?"

"Oh, ordinary clothes, blouses and pleated blue skirts, or white dresses with pink sashes. All of them dull. Only when we went to the theatre did I get to wear some pretty dresses of silk or lace. And of course, little white kid gloves and a small pearl necklace! What about you?"

"I come from a different class. No white gloves for me. My father is a shopkeeper. We lived in Moldovanka, the mostly Jewish section of Odessa. We still live there. My parents have a store where they sell just about everything. My father is an *entrepreneurial* type. He has contacts all over the place. He buys and sells things, no matter what or where from. I never ask. He and my mother had practically no education, but they saw to it that my brother and I went to the best Jewish gymnasiums in town. My brother eventually became a rabbi, fulfilling my parents' dream, and I, as you know, became *Madame Juliette!*"

They both laughed.

"You mentioned yesterday that you have a son. What's his name?"

"Yankel. But we call him Yasha. He is a very special boy. He is only eleven, but he is the Odessa Chess Champion! He beats everyone. He has won several matches against adults and there is talk of sending him to compete in America!"

"In America!"

"Yes, my husband is in America. He emigrated there just before the war. We were supposed to join him in a year, but the war started and here we are. Still in Odessa!"

"So, when the war is over, you'll go to America?"

"Yes, that is, if we can save enough money for our journey. Or, unless we change our minds about it."

"Do you miss your husband?" Larissa asked.

"Not really. It's already four years since he left. I know that he has a lady friend and by now, a baby, so I got myself a gentleman friend. Don't be shocked!" she laughed, seeing Larissa's surprised face. "It's just the reality of life."

Akim enjoyed their conversation. He kept smirking and shaking his head. Finally, unable to control his Odessian habit of sticking his nose into someone else's business, he turned to Julia. "That husband of yours doesn't deserve you, *báryn'ya!* Leaving you alone with a little boy, while he has a woman to dilly-dally with in America!"

Julia laughed. "You said it, friend!"

Larissa watched them with amazement. It would have been unthinkable for a carriage driver in Petrograd to speak with such familiarity to a lady. In Odessa, apparently it was quite normal.

The driver stopped his horse in front of the Passage. "Here you are," he said "I'll wait for you across the street, on the shady side."

"We might be a couple of hours," Julia said. "Wouldn't you rather be free to get some other passengers?"

"No, *báryn'ya*. My horse and I will take a nap!" he grinned. "I promised the Lieutenant that I will take care of his wife in our rowdy city," he explained to Julia. "And that's what I am doing," he said. Turning to Larissa, he continued, "Don't you worry, *báryn'ya* . You go and shop. I'll wait for you."

"Thank you, Akim, you are very kind. I am so glad that you are taking care of us!" Larissa said, smiling. "The Odessa people are so unusual!" she thought again.

The *Grand Passage* spanned between two mains streets. Its two entrances were adorned with whimsical marble figures of Fortuna on the ship and Hermes on the steam engine.

"I have noticed that you have a lot of sculptures in Odessa," Larissa said. "Even the façades of private homes display carvings of mythological figures."

"It must be our connection to ancient Greece. The Black Sea and the Crimea are parts of ancient history. All the mythological heroes of the ancient world have been here at one time or another. And of course, their gods and goddesses had to be here also, to help the heroes, or to destroy them. As for the sculptures in the city, it became fashionable long ago to decorate everything with marble statuary, like in Europe. It's your Peter the Great who started the fashion."

"That's true! Come to think of it, Petrograd is the same, full of classical statuary, but the city is so big that often one doesn't see it. It's just *there!*"

They entered the building. Sun streamed through the glass ceiling. The two-tone marble floor between the entrances was dulled by constant foot traffic, but one could still see the original design of Greek keys at the borders.

"Let's go first to the coats section," Julia said.

"You lead the way and I'll follow you like a puppy."

They quickly found what they needed. Each bought a roomy *vátnik*, a traditional coat worn by working people, with vertical rows of cotton wool stuffing for warmth. Next on their list were lighter-weight jackets and skirts. "We should wear only black, brown, and dark blue. Nothing bright. We can have simple white blouses, and even one or two frilly ones for party going," Julia said.

"What about summer? These clothes are too heavy for warm weather," Larissa said.

"For summer ..." Julia hesitated. "I have an idea! Let's go *Ukrainian* in the summer! Let's buy cotton embroidered skirts and blouses and wear boots. With all that heavy embroidery, no bumps will be noticeable! You'll need a sewing machine. It will make your task much easier."

"I can't use the hospital's for this. Do you know where we could find a sewing machine?"

"Right here, in the Passage. My father's cousin owns the Singer Sewing Machine shop. I'll tell him that I need another machine for my Salon, and he will sell it to me for half price. You'll buy it from me."

Larissa was filled with gratitude. "I don't know how to thank you for all of this!"

"Don't worry. I like you and I enjoy your company. Let's go to Uncle Moishe's shop."

With their purchases made, all at reduced prices since Julia had many friends and relatives among the merchants, they were ready to depart.

"I've never had so much fun!" Larissa exclaimed.

"Good. We'll do it again. We still must buy our 'Ukrainian' outfits and purses with double bottoms, and double-soled boots."

"Double-bottom purses? Double-soled boots? Where will we find them?"

"We will order them to be made especially for us. My father ..."

"I know! He has a nephew ... or another cousin!"

"How did you know?" They burst out laughing.

30

Maria Nikoláyevna suffered the nervousness felt by all Petrograd after the Tsar's abdication. No one knew what to expect. The stormy political waters left everyone adrift in the same rudderless boat. Everything was different, and yet, nothing had changed. The workers still demanded bread and freedom. There still was no food in the shops, no fuel for the stoves, and no end to the war. Nothing had changed. Except, there was no longer any order in the city. The police became invisible. Drunken crowds roamed the streets breaking into stores, ransacking wine cellars, and setting random fires.

The Duma appointed the Provisional Government. It was immediately subjugated by the Soviet of Workers and Soldiers Deputies, who selected their own men and appointed them as *'commissars with extraordinary powers.'* The commissars became the *de facto* rulers of the bleeding city.

Two short trains, one carrying the former Tsar, the other traveling as a decoy, arrived in Petrograd. They proceeded to the sidetrack where the Tsar's train was re-routed for the short ride to Tsárskoye Selo, where the erstwhile Emperor would be placed under house arrest.

The generals and officers of Stavka disgorged from the trains, their luggage unceremoniously dumped on the platform.

General Rezánov frowned as he looked at a pile of valises, briefcases, and packages. The platform was crowded with men, but there was not a single porter. A group of armed soldiers lolled at the end of the platform, some of them smoking. Not one of them made a move to assist with luggage. By some sixth sense, none of the disembarked officers had ordered them to do so.

"How quickly times have changed!" General Rezánov thought, picking up his valise.

"Allow me, sir," Egórov said quickly, taking the valise out of his hands. Together, they walked toward the exit, Lieutenant Borisov and Egórov carrying their luggage.

"You stay at my house, Captain Egórov," the general said quietly. "Unless you have some other plans."

"No, sir. I'd be honored."

As they passed the Tsar's private car, they had a glimpse of him at the window. They stopped and saluted their Emperor. He returned the salute. Someone within his compartment drew the shades. It was the last time that any of them would see the Tsar.

The square in front of Nikolayevsky Station looked empty. There were no carriages for hire, no automobiles parked at the curb, not even the electric trams were to be seen.

"We will have to walk home, I am afraid," General Rezánov said. "Lieutenant Borisov, you live too far away. Stay at my house also. You can get in touch with your wife from there."

Borisov put down the suitcases. "Yes, sir," he saluted.

An ironic smile played across the general's face. "Our new overlords surely knew what they were doing when they outlawed saluting: it is impossible when one's arms are loaded with suitcases!" The young men laughed without mirth.

They crossed the square and began the long trek along the Nevsky Prospect toward the Fontánka and General Rezánov's house.

The Provisional Government consisted of representatives of the same antagonistic parties. To reach a compromise was impossible. Every problem, every proposal was discussed and argued to death, each party trying to push its own ideology. It began to look as though only the Bolsheviks with their iron will were able to make decisions. The Bolsheviks agitated against the war among the troops, egged on the workers to take over the factories, and urged peasants to grab the land from landowners, playing on people's desire for peace and exploiting their greed.

The Bolshevik leaders re-appeared in Petrograd. Iosiff Vissarionovich Dzugashvili (Stalin), returned from exile in Siberia, and the main ideologue of the Bolsheviks, Vladímir Ilich Ulianov (Lenin), was smuggled by the Germans from his exile in Switzerland. The Germans secretly supported the Bolsheviks with huge amounts of money through Sweden, hoping that the Bolsheviks would become their final weapon in defeating Russia.

The Provisional Government still advocated the continuation of war. With the help of France and England, who needed Russia to keep the German army divided, the Provisional Government began preparations for a new spring offensive.

The Allies expedited delivery of military equipment and approved huge loans, encouraging Russians to fight. But the Russians did not want to fight anymore. The Russians were exhausted.

The young Rezánovs, still in Odessa, began to re-adjust to the new regime. The Military Medical Committee declared that Andrei was ready to return to active duty.

His spirits perked. He had been terrified that they would make him a trainer, a glorified babysitter for new recruits. He was eager to leave for the front, selfishly displaying before Larissa his happiness at receiving orders. He could hardly wait to be back with his pals, unaware that most of them were already gone. Egórov had never told him that Platonov and Klembovsky were dead, and the young curly-headed Cossack Mironov was demobilized minus both of his legs. Mironov was back at his *stanitza,* on the shores of the Don River, being slowly sucked into the abyss of depression from which he would never emerge, ending his young life by a single shot into his mouth.

Larissa resented Andrei's carelessness toward her feelings. Was being in the company of his friends more important to him than being with his wife? She wished that she could talk to her mother ... but no. Her mother had long ago made peace with men's peculiar need for gambling with their lives. She would understand Larissa's misery, but she would not sympathize with it.

Andrei felt a touch of guilt for not concealing his joy. He saw Larissa blanch as she read the telegram. Her eyes welling with tears, she whispered, "I was hoping that you would stay at the Flight School ... as an instructor ... I thought ..." Andrei did not let her finish. He embraced and caressed her, kissing her eyes, murmuring that it was his duty to go back to his squadron, that he would be close by, in Yassy, that once in a while he would be able to come to Odessa for a furlough, but she kept crying silently, desperately, tears streaming down her smooth face.

He left within three days, Doctor Shubin and Veronica joining Larissa at the railroad station to see him off. This time, Larissa did not run behind his train.

"It's already April!" Maria Nikoláyevna thought as she stood in front of the large bay window in her drawing room, watching the *ledokhód,* the annual breaking of ice on the Nevá. Usually the ice broke during the night and was already on its way to the Baltic by the time people saw the river move.

This time, it happened during the day and she actually *saw* the ice break. At first there was a loud boom as if from a cannon. Then, a series of gnashing and grinding sounds rose from the river as the ice began to crack and split. Huge wedges of ice suddenly jutted vertically, crowding one another, climbing atop each other as if they were pre-historic monsters battling for supremacy. The ice bore several layers of color, the dirty gray of melting snow atop, progressively cleaner shades of white until it burst out in bright turquoise translucency near the water line. Huge chunks floated, colliding with one another and shoving smaller slabs out of the way as they moved toward the Baltic, swift currents churning between them.

The *ledokhód* lasted for several days. Hundreds of people crowded the Nevá bridges to watch its stupendous process, transfixed by nature's mighty display of power. The moist warm air that followed the breaking of the ice always brought the promise of spring and timid buds on trees, though a cold spell would always follow as virginal ice from Lake Ládoga began flowing through the city a few days later.

Maria Nikoláyevna had always loved this time of the year. Ever since she was a child, she felt that something highly dramatic was happening. The Nevá and Lake Ládoga, like two sleeping giants, were breaking their bonds, heaving and gnashing mightily. She liked to imagine that the jutting triangular blue icebergs were sailboats competing in a mysterious regatta, and she was the Snow Maiden. She wished that she could be sailing on one of the ice sailboats.

"Will Russia be cleansed of filth and debris like the river, and blossom again under the spring sun?" she wondered. "The spring and the blossoms, the nightingales and the butterflies, will be back ... but the country will never be the same," she concluded.

31

It was raining hard when Egórov met Andrei at the railroad station in Yassy. He was drenched when he embraced Andrei. "You son-of-a-bitch! Good to see you, boy, still in one piece!" he yelled over the rumble of voices on the platform. Water ran off the visor of his cap and a huge drop hung from the tip of his nose. "How is Larissa?"

"She sends her love. She is fine, working at the Memorial. What's going on here?"

"Nothing much. Let's go to a café and have a drink. They don't have any decent French wines here, but they do have some good English brandy."

They headed toward a café. "No need to hurry, in this weather," Egórov continued as he shook off his wet leather coat and draped it over the back of a chair. A waiter placed two small glasses of brandy and a bowl of green olives in front of them.

"Well, tell me what's going on in Yassy," Andrei said, taking a sip.

Egórov shrugged and rolled his eyes. "We fly reconnaissance patrols, take a lot of pictures, but come home without any fights. The Germans are busy fighting in France, and I think the Austrians have run out of good pilots. The new ones avoid fighting. Everybody is bored. We sleep a lot, but Romanian cots are made for shorter men, so even our *sleep* is not particularly pleasant. I hate it here!"

"Well, there must be *something* pleasant in this city! After all, it is the capital of Moldavia, the exotic city of the Ottoman Empire," Andrei said sarcastically, quoting a travel brochure.

"There *is* something pleasant. The library. It seems that I have plenty of time to read! I have been working my way through Gibbons' *Rise and Fall of the Roman Empire*, but may not have time to complete it. There are rumors that we will be moved north again, to Stanislav, near Lutsk, which is now back in German hands. But of course, the *real* action is in France. Here, in Galicia, no one seems want to fight anymore. The only men still eager to fight are *pilots*, but I believe it is only because we like to fly!" he laughed. "Isn't that the reason *you* are here?"

Andrei nodded. "Yes. And am here because I wanted to be with you and my pals, although I am mad at Platonov and Klembovsky: not even one postcard while I was in the hospital!"

"Well …" Egórov hesitated, looking down at the table.

Andrei sensed that something was amiss. "What happened, Egórka?"

Egórov told him.

"Oh, God! Oh, God!" Andrei struck the table with his fist. The drinks in their glasses sloshed onto the table.

Egórov motioned the waiter to refill their glasses. "To our brothers," he said quietly. They touched their glasses, Andrei fighting tears.

The next morning was dry, but a heavy fog spread low over the airfield. All sorties were cancelled and the pilots lounged in their rooms. Andrei, accompanied by Egórov, reported to Kozakov.

"Welcome back, Lieutenant. I am glad that you are well and ready to join us!" Kozakov said, rising from behind his cluttered desk. He was in shirtsleeves, red suspenders holding up his cavalry britches. Andrei was surprised at the change in Kozakov. He seemed to have lost weight, his cheekbones sharper than ever, and his moustache looked droopy and unkempt. He looked like an old man.

"You'll have your choice of airplanes," Kozakov continued in a tired voice. He did not invite them to sit, so they stood in front of his desk, keeping a semi-formal posture. "We have ten new Spads, six fighters and four two-seaters, and of course, we still have several of our old reliable friends, the Nieuports. You will remain in Egórov's squadron."

"Yes, sir! Thank you, sir!"

"All right. Take him for some instructional flights in the new Spad," he said to Egórov.

"What is the matter with Kozakov?" Andrei asked as they headed toward the parked planes.

"I think he is ill," Egórov replied. "He is terribly depressed. He takes more chances when he flies. He flies brilliantly, of course, but I hate to say it, I think he flies *desperately*. I have seen him breaking into a five-craft formation, shooting down a Fokker Eindecker and then abandoning the fight as if nothing had happened! I wonder if he is courting death. But keep it to yourself, Andrúshka."

"I will,"Andrei said. It disturbed him that his hero was apparently suffering from some kind of emotional or physical illness.

The fog was lifting. They walked toward the airplanes lined along the runway. The mechanics working around the planes recognized Andrei and shouted their greetings. They all liked Andrei and were happy to see him back. A small cluster of replacement pilots, seeing him limp next to Captain Egórov, concluded that he must be the legendary Lieutenant Andrei Rezánov. They were all eager to meet him.

Andrei tried to walk with a swagger to cover up his limp, but Egórov proffered him his own fancy cane with a lion's head at the top.

"Don't be a fool. Who are you trying to impress? Should you stumble and fall before you are fully healed, you would really become a cripple! Use the cane!" he said in a low voice.

Andrei grinned sheepishly and took the cane. The sharp smells of fuel and rancid castor oil invigorated him. He was back where he belonged.

First in the lineup were four Spads, two-seaters, each equipped with three Vickers machine guns mounted on the nacelles. Next to them stood six compact Spad VII fighters. All were painted in the same opaque gray with the 19th Air Corps Detachment insignia on their rudders. White, blue, and red roundels painted on the upper and lower wings and on both sides of the fuselage boldly proclaimed their allegiance to Russian sovereignty. The covers on the wheels were bright red and made the planes look festive.

Andrei suspected that he would not be allowed to fly as an observer. His lame leg would prevent him from standing up during the flights. He did not mind. He preferred the fighters anyway, his attention already focused on the new single-seat Spads.

"Which one is yours?" Andrei asked. "After all, you're an *ace!*"

"That one," Egórov pointed to a third Spad fighter in line with a personal insignia of a rearing black stallion stenciled on the fuselage. "Forever the horseman!" he laughed. Then, he became serious. "Kozakov is not going to let you fly as an observer. You will be my wing man until you get back into the fold. Then, perhaps you'll get your own fight squadron."

"Really?"

"Really! I've come to like the Spads," Egórov continued "They are sturdier than the Nieuports. Want to try one now? I'll go with you and we'll stage a mock fight."

"Can we do that? Can we fly just for fun?"

"Of course we can. Kozakov ordered me to instruct you, didn't he? Now, we'll need a step ladder to help you get into the cockpit."

"I can get in without it!" Andrei protested.

"Don't argue with me. I am your commander, and it is an order!" Egórov said sternly. Turning to the group of mechanics, he said, "The Lieutenant and I are going up for a little practice over the airfield. Have my Spad and another one for the Lieutenant ready. We also need a ladder for the second machine."

"Yes, Captain!" one mechanic saluted. He and three men peeled off from the group and at once began to prepare the Spads for takeoff. A small ladder with a sturdy platform at the top was wheeled next to one, ready for Andrei.

"You be the defender and I'll be the aggressor. Then we'll change roles."

"Fine. I hope I haven't forgotten how to maneuver," Andrei laughed nervously.

"Do not worry. It's in your blood now. We'll meet at 5000 feet and come from the opposite ends of the airfield. Let's give our friends a good show, shall we?"

Andrei climbed into his Spad with the help of the ladder and discovered that it was cumbersome and quite painful getting down into the fuselage. Without the help of the ladder, he probably wouldn't have been able to accomplish it.

Once in the cockpit his anxiety vanished. He felt at ease even though the instruments and wires, levers and knobs, were different from the Nieuports. He felt as if he were in the familiar environment of his study, though some of his things had been replaced. He would need to get used to them, but they presented no real challenge. He ordered the mechanic to twirl the propeller and prepared to fly. Egórov was right: the procedures were in his blood. He did not need to think of what to do.

Within minutes he was taxiing down the runway, ready to rise into the gray sky. Gently, almost tentatively, he eased back the joystick. With growing excitement he felt the vibration that meant the wheels had left the field. He was airborne. He felt the exuberance of his first solo flight and yelled, "I am flying! Look at me! I am flying!"

He climbed steadily and leveled the plane. Where was Egórov? Visibility was poor, and he could barely see the airfield below. The wind blew into his face, bringing back sensations of his frightful experience on the wing of the Voisin.

"Where is Egórka?" He increased his rate of ascent and glanced at the altitude indicator. He was at 4000 feet. "A little more," he thought.

Egórov was there, waiting for him. They wagged their wings in greeting, ready to start their mock battle.

Egórov, as the aggressor, immediately zoomed up and banked his plane to be in position above and behind Andrei, but Andrei anticipated his move. He too was climbing, and when he instinctively felt that Egórov was reaching a point of advantage behind him, Andrei banked sharply and turned in the opposite direction, taking his Spad out of Egórov's machine gun range.

"Good!" Andrei thought, beginning to maneuver his plane for the counter-attack.

They chased one another in the gloomy skies for half an hour, Egórov initiating an attack, Andrei trying to foil it, then staging his own. Finally, Egórov wagged his wings and dived sharply down.

Andrei was not ready to stop flying. He pretended that he did not see the signal and continued making loops and banks, *chandelles*, corkscrew climbs and *piques*, vertical dives with the engine open or shut, testing himself and the new machine, the Spad obeying him instantly.

Finally he made a leisurely circle over the airfield and executed a perfect landing in front of his audience of mechanics and pilots.

They greeted him with applause. Everyone knew by now who he was and that it was his first flight after a long stay at the hospital.

The unanimous opinion of the crowd was that Lieutenant Andrei Rezánov deserved his fame.

Larissa resumed her work at Memorial Hospital. Doctor Shubin authorized the documents necessary for her permanent employment, and she signed a pledge to the new Soviet of Workers and Sailors Deputies stating that she would faithfully perform her duties as a Medical Aide.

Although she was eager to work, she knew that it could not be for long. She was pregnant.

The news did not please her. "I don't want to have a child," she thought. "I am too young! I am not even nineteen! I want to have fun with Andrei, I want to have him just *for myself*. I don't want to share him with a child! I want to be with my Mama!" she cried into her pillow. But her mother was not there to comfort her.

Doctor Shubin confirmed her pregnancy. "Well, my dear, next fall, around November or so, we'll welcome a little Rezánov into this world! Congratulations!" he smiled, his face creasing in dozens of kind wrinkles. "Are you happy?"

"No," she replied without hesitation. "Before it's too late, I would like you to abort it."

"What are you saying! I'll do no such thing! It is against the law and prohibited by our Church. It is the *gravest sin!*" His face, a moment before so kind and shining, was hard now. "Does anyone, besides me, know about it?"

"No. I want to get rid of my pregnancy. I don't want them to know about it."

"Well, *I do!* I want them to know! Why, why don't you want to have a baby? It is such a blessing! Why don't you want it?" he cried passionately. "Why do you refuse God's gift?"

"Because it is a *wrong time* to start a family! Because we are at war! Because I am not ready! Because I am too young! Because I am afraid for Andrei! Because I'll be a terrible mother! There are millions of reasons why!" She burst into tears.

"Nonsense!" he interrupted her. "You'll be a wonderful mother. All your objections are pure nonsense. The war will be over soon, and you are ripe for your first child. I bet your mother was about your age when you were born."

"I had an older brother. She was eighteen when Peter was born," Larissa had to admit, wiping her eyes.

"Well? Don't you see? You are just the right age for starting a family! You'll have a beautiful and healthy baby, you'll make your husband and your family very proud. So, stop talking about an abortion. I won't allow it. And, I know that you are smart enough not to try anything stupid. Am I right?" he looked at her inquisitively. "Write to Andrei and your family. Make them all happy!" he patted her hand.

"I won't do *'anything stupid,'* as you say, and I will have the baby, even if I don't want to, and I will try to be a good mother since I have no choice," she said petulantly. "I'll write Andrei, my mother, and his parents about it. I doubt, though, that Andrei will be too happy becoming a *father* at *his* age. He hasn't been a *husband* long enough! Our entire life as a husband and wife has been a matter of days! Can't you see? He had no time to get used to the idea that he was a husband! And now, I have to shock him with the announcement that he is going to be a *father!*" Tears filled her eyes again.

Doctor Shubin offered her his handkerchief. "Yes, it does take a bit of time to become used to the idea of being a husband *and* a father! I am sometimes not quite comfortable in both of these roles myself, but I wouldn't give them up for anything in the world. I am getting ready for the third role, that is, the one of a grandfather! My eldest daughter is expecting her first child in June," he said.

"Congratulations!" Larissa said, wiping her tears.

"You see? You, who don't want to rejoice at your own good fortune, obviously realize that it is indeed worthy of congratulations! It is God's blessing! I bet Andrei will enjoy having a child."

"I doubt it," Larissa said without conviction.

She procrastinated in writing to anyone about her pregnancy, hoping that she might induce a miscarriage. She had read that women were especially vulnerable to miscarriages in the first weeks of pregnancy and thus should be restrained from physical activities. Even ordinary walking was to be restricted.

Larissa began taking long walks along the wide boulevards and climbing up and down the famous Richelieu stairs, though the only result was that she became stronger and healthier. Finally, she admitted to herself that there would be no miscarriage. She began to think of the gender of the baby. Traditionally, she should hope the first child be a boy, to carry on the family name. But she thought of a girl, a little tender girl, who would be close to her as she was to her mother, and of course, who would never, never go to war.

Whichever it would be, she knew that she could not procrastinate any longer. She had to inform Andrei and the family.

Finally the long-expected order arrived for Andrei's unit to relocate north, to the vicinity of Stanislav, where serious action was flaring up again. The enemy was moving its artillery and troops along the front line, and so were the Russians, both adversaries increasing their air reconnaissance.

On the eve of his departure for Stanislav, Andrei received Larissa's letter.

He was devastated. As usual, he sought the council of Egórov. "I am not ready to be a *father!* What should I do?" he cried out helplessly.

Egórov's laughter was brutally sarcastic. "You have done it already. I know that it is a bad time to start a family, but you have done it, so now you must make sure that Larissa is safe. You should have stayed at Odessa and became a trainer, as I wanted you to be all along! Well, so here you are. A fighter pilot! With your wife all alone and pregnant in Odessa! How far along is she?"

"About three months."

"We must get her back to her family. We can't leave her alone in Odessa," Egórov said, aware that he was taking a lead in making decisions about Larissa's safety. His infatuation with her had not subsided but had taken a new form when he realized that his passion would never be fulfilled. Now, his feelings were that of a protector. "She must go back to Petrograd and be with her mother," he said firmly. "Meanwhile, I'll try to figure out how to get you back to Odessa. I'll talk to Kozakov. After all, it was *his* idea, originally, to remove you from active duty."

Kozakov was unsympathetic to Egórov's plea. "I can't do it. The situation has changed. We are about to stage an offensive and I need *every* pilot in my command," he said, frowning. "That's why I don't like to have married men as my pilots: there is always something wrong with their families, either sick children or pregnant wives! I wish there was a law that only bachelors could be military pilots!"

Egórov readily agreed. "But, is there anything that could be done to help these two young people? Perhaps a short furlough for Andrei so that he can arrange to take his wife back to her family? She is not yet nineteen, a girl really, and she is alone in Odessa, that notorious city. She is a brave young woman. She came all the way from Petrograd to nurse her husband. Without her, our Andrúshka wouldn't have survived. She is a heroic young woman, but in a few weeks she will be helpless!"

Kozakov was surprised by Egórov's compassionate appeal. He twisted his moustache and said slowly, "Well, I suppose I can give Rezánov a short leave …. There will be no action for us while we are moving to Stanislav, so he can hop on the train and go back to Odessa for a week. But there is no train connection between Odessa and Stanislav. How is he going to get back to us?"

"Let him come back to Yassy by train, and then I can fly in and pick him up!"

"So, for a couple of days I'll be minus *two* pilots," Kozakov said slowly. "Ah, what the hell! I'll give him a week off for medical leave … to go back to Memorial Hospital for some … some trouble with his leg. But you must make sure that he will be back in a week!"

"He will be!" Egórov exclaimed. *"Parole d'honneur!"*

Kozakov grinned. "You go through a lot of trouble for that chap, don't you?"

"He is like a younger brother to me. And I do admire his wife."

"Is she pretty?" Kozakov asked, smiling now.

"Is she? She is a real *beauty!*" Egórov exclaimed. He felt that he was blushing. "Blushing!" he thought, "I have not blushed since I was sixteen!"

"All right. I'll prepare the order. I am afraid, though, that Rezánov will have some problems getting his wife on a train to Petrograd. According to a report from Stavka, the train connections are constantly interrupted. The striking railroad workers are becoming bandits. Perhaps Andrei will have to send his wife to Moscow first, and then transfer her to Petrograd. I am sure his father's influence … No. The power of influence has been taken away from generals. It has become rather precarious to be a Russian general!"

"Maybe discipline will be restored," Egórov said.

"Maybe … It is not just the discipline anymore. Those who had been marching demanding *'freedom'* are *free* now. Now it is their time for *vengeance!* They have already turned on the monarchy. Next, they will turn on the nobility. They'll confiscate private property in the name of the people, shoot the men and rape the women. Remember the lessons of the French Revolution. No, don't think of it! It is too depressing," he interrupted himself. "Tell Rezánov to get ready to leave."

"Thank you, Captain!"

"Just make sure that he is back on time so he and I don't have to face the Soviet of Workers and Soldiers Deputies! I'd prefer to avoid an appointment with their firing squad."

There was a regular train connection between Yassy and Odessa, but sabotage along the railroad delayed trains in both directions for a whole day while damage from the explosions was repaired.

Andrei fumed as he paced alongside the immobilized train, using his cane to knock the heads from weeds sprouting between the ties. His excitement at seeing Larissa was overwhelmed by his worry about arranging her journey to Petrograd. He had read a newspaper article reporting that all rail traffic to the capital was going to stop. The paper did not explain why, when, or for how long it would be stopped but advised people to postpone all travel.

"They did not say that traffic *has been* stopped," he thought. "The trains might be still running ... but should I risk placing Larissa *alone* on the train? What choice do I have? If I go with her, I won't be able to get to Stanislav on time," he thought gloomily. "I'd never make it. Kozakov wouldn't be able to save my neck, and he would be court-martialed for letting me go. The Soviet of Workers and Soldiers Deputies would be only too glad to shoot a couple of officers."

He saw no way out of his dilemma. He returned to his compartment. Several hours later the track was fixed just enough so that the train could snail through it and finally arrive in Odessa.

Larissa was working at her new sewing machine, putting the last stitches around the hem of her woolen skirt. Julia taught her how to use the machine, and Larissa found that she enjoyed sewing.

All of Larissa's gold money was now safely stowed away in her clothing. At Julia's suggestion, Larissa had color-coded the denominations of the coins by making tiny embroidery marks under the lining at the points of insertion. "It will be easier for you to reach the amount you may need without taking the whole hem apart," Julia had said. She and Larissa had become real friends, Larissa loving Julia's easy manner and generosity, and Julia enjoying the young Russian aristocrat who seemed to be free of any anti-Semitic prejudices.

Concentrating on her work, Larissa did not hear Andrei's knock on the door. The sewing machine clattered rhythmically, the needle moving quickly up and down, Larissa turning the handle with her right hand, guiding the skirt with her left.

Andrei opened the door and stood, watching her, waiting for her to stop, afraid to startle her. Finally, feeling someone's eyes on her, she turned around.

"Andrúsha!" she screamed and rushed into his arms. "Andrúsha, my angel!"

Their reunion was so intense that at first neither of them could talk. They just clung wordlessly to each other.

Finally, Larissa tore herself away from him and sat down. "I have so much to tell you!" she breathed.

"So do I! I am so happy! We'll have a beautiful baby!"

"Yes! In a few months, we will have *our* baby!" she smiled. Suddenly, both of them felt as if they had always wanted to have a baby.

That night they made love, thirsting for one another in a different, deeper way than their earlier encounters. There was no light-hearted laughter, no jokes, but a desperate expression of need for one another. Andrei found that he could talk to Larissa about his attacks of anxiety, and she understood him and soothed him with her caresses and tender words. Larissa, in turn, confessed her confusion about her sympathies toward the strikers and her anger at the way they were treated by the new authorities.

Without realizing it, they entered a new, adult phase in their marriage.

The next morning, Akim, loyal as ever and overjoyed to have steady, respectful customers, drove them to Memorial Hospital. It was Larissa's day off, and she was not expected at the hospital, but Andrei needed an official document that he required an urgent medical consultation with his doctors. Upon the advice of Egórov, he had telephoned Doctor Shubin and requested an official appointment.

"Come in, come in, Lieutenant! What a pleasant surprise!" Doctor Shubin was all smiles as he welcomed them into his study. "Larochka, you look fabulous! Any complaints? Any morning sickness?"

"No, Arkady Petrovich. I feel really good. Andrúsha and I are very happy about the baby, now," she smiled.

"Splendid!"

"We need your help, Doctor Shubin," Andrei began. "I have to be back at my squadron in less than a week. . With Larissa being pregnant, we think that it would be best if she went back to Petrograd to be with our family."

"A wise decision," the doctor said. "So, how can I help you?"

"Actually I don't know. You have probably read in the papers about the disturbances on the railroads. Obviously Larissa can't go anywhere as long as there are disturbances. But when everything turns back to normal, I won't be around to help her with her trip. That's why I have to burden you with taking care of my pregnant wife."

"Don't you worry, my boy," Doctor Shubin interrupted, taking the liberty of calling him 'my boy.' "I love you both as if you were my own, and my wife and I will take care of Larissa. As soon as the disturbances are over, we'll put her on the train for Petrograd!" He turned to Larissa. "It will be the best solution for you to be with your mother, don't you agree?"

"Yes, Arkady Petrovich. I am grateful that you are willing to help us. But we have another favor to ask."

"It is for me," Andrei said, looking down. He was unaccustomed to asking for favors. "For me and for my commanding officer, Captain Kozakov, who did not ask the Soviet of Worker and Soldiers Deputies for permission to grant me a week of furlough. He may be in trouble on account of it. And, so ..."

"And so, it means the court-martial for both of you, no?" the doctor finished the sentence.

"Yes."

"Let me see your orders."

Andrei handed him his documents. Shubin read them carefully, then smiled. "We have our own Soviet Deputies, only in Odessa in addition to *Soldiers*, we have *Sailors*. To satisfy them, and *to save our necks,*" he added in a low voice," I'll place you back in the hospital for observation for forty-eight hours, after which you *immediately* return to your detachment with the appropriate documents describing your medical condition and treatment. Actually, it *will* be a good idea to check your wounds!"

"Thank you, Arkady Petrovich," Andrei said, "I did not mean to bring you all these problems."

"I know, I know. Meanwhile, Sister Larissa, please take the patient Lieutenant Rezánov to the main ward and start the usual procedure of admittance. Also, please send Sister Veronica to my office." He was suddenly very official, his cordiality gone.

Larissa looked at him quizzically, and he pointed with his eyes to the door. The linen manager, Glafíra Ivánovna, was just arriving at his office.

"Ah, Glafíra Ivánovna!" Doctor Shubin exclaimed heartily, "Look who is back with us for observation! Our hero, Lieutenant Rezánov! Glafíra Ivánovna is the chair of our *Soviet Deputies,*" he explained to Rezánov.

"Well, congratulations! That's a very important position!" Andrei tried to sound cordial. Glafíra Ivánovna smiled and blushed with pleasure, her eyes totally disappearing into her round face.

It was no secret at the hospital that Glafíra Ivánovna had a crush on the famous young aviator. During his previous stay, she had used every excuse to visit his room with a stack of clean towels or an extra plump pillow. She had personally ironed his pajamas, the only patient in Memorial Hospital who had received such a privilege. The rest of the officers wore their pajamas wrinkled, the way they came off the clothesline.

"How long are you going to stay with us, Lieutenant?" she asked almost coquettishly.

"Just forty-eight hours, for observation, Glafíra Ivánovna."

"Ah, too short ... You probably could use some real rest from all that flying."

"The hospital is no place for a 'rest,' Glafíra Ivánovna," Doctor Shubin said sternly.

She did not like his tone. "You don't need to tell *me*," she replied curtly, the ringlets of her hair shaking.

"I am sorry," the doctor quickly apologized.

Andrei and Larissa noticed Shubin's sudden servility. "He is afraid of her!" they both thought.

"I'll bring you your favorite pillow," Glafíra Ivánovna said, looking only at Andrei. "The hospital pillows are all *flat.*" She glanced at Doctor Shubin accusingly.

"Thank you, Glafíra Ivánovna! You are so kind!" Andrei exclaimed with exaggerated enthusiasm.

"You may call me Glásha," she said and sailed out of the study with regal haughtiness.

Doctor Shubin puffed his cheeks out and slowly exhaled. "She is our new boss. No decision can be made now without the approval of the Soviet committee, of which she is the chair. Or, is it *the commissar? Bozhe Moi!* Dear God, what is happening in our poor, foolish country?"

⁂ 32 ⁂

During Rasputin time, everyone was demanding *"Something must be done!"* Now, people were asking themselves *"What is happening in our country?"* Only the Bolsheviks seemed to know the answer: they were taking over. Through their *Soviet of Workers, Soldiers and Sailors Deputies* the Bolsheviks infiltrated every factory, every military regiment, every university and technical school. Their chosen representatives played on people's disaffection with the new Provisional Government, which insisted on continuing the war and dragged its feet in fulfilling its promises of reforms.

Bolshevik commissars exploited this disaffection. They demanded immediate distribution of land among the peasants and confiscation of plants and factories in favor of the workers. Within their own party the Bolsheviks imposed brutal discipline and demanded total obedience, but outside of it they encouraged disobedience. Peasants impatient to grab the land vandalized and burned manor houses. Workers destroyed machinery at plants. Soldiers refused to obey orders.

Russia craved good news, something that would reunite the country, something that would recharge people's patriotism. Russia needed *good* news, but all she had was disorder and despair.

Andrei's parents and Larissa's mother were three people among the gloomy Petrograd citizenry who *did have* good news: they had received letters from Larissa and Andrei announcing her pregnancy.

They gathered at the Rezánov residence for an intimate dinner. The mothers embraced one another, shedding happy tears while the general vigorously polished his spectacles.

"When is she due?" he asked.

"Probably in late October," Maria Nikoláyevna replied. "You know how it is … impossible to pinpoint the exact date. In any case, we must bring her back before that time."

"Yes, of course. But right now it is impossible. We must wait. The Government will not tolerate the disruption of the rail system, even if the Soviets try to prolong it."

"Why do they *do* such things!" Varvara Mikháilovna exclaimed. "Wasn't it enough that they forced our Emperor to abdicate? What more do they want?"

"The Soviets want *power*. They want to rule Russia," the general said. "They believe that they are the voice of the people. But in the process of achieving that power, they are destroying everything. They want to remake the country in their own image and make people grateful for whatever crumbs the Soviets may throw them!"

"Aren't you a bit too cynical?" Maria Nikoláyevna frowned.

"Not at all. I see it coming. Unless there are still some strong, loyal people in our country who can stop this avalanche of lawlessness, soon it will be too late. The Bolsheviks have this clever and charismatic leader. *Lenin* is his *nom de guerre*. I don't know his real name, but he is bent on destruction of the *Imperialist* system, as he calls it … A very dangerous man."

"His real name is Vladímir Ilyich Ulyanov," Maria Nikoláyevna said. "I read something about him in *Pravda*. He is an educated man who has spent most of his adult life in exile, in Europe. But what struck my attention was that his older brother was hanged as a conspirator in the assassination of Tsar Alexander II. So, this Lenin has a good reason to hate the Tsarist regime."

"And the Tsarist regime had a good reason for hanging his brother!" exclaimed Varvara Mikháilovna.

"Ah, enough of these gloomy thoughts!" the general said with false joviality. "Let's drink a toast to our first grandchild. Do you realize, my dears, that soon you two will be *bábushkas*? Would you mind if I call you *Bábushka* from now on?" he teased his wife.

"Don't you dare!" she laughed.

After two days of 'observation', Andrei was armed with certificates signed by Doctor Shubin and Glafíra Ivánovna. Andrei's furlough was over, and he had to return to his squadron.

This time, he was not eager to leave. The fact that his pals were gone lay heavily on his heart. "Who is next?" he thought. "Egórov or me?" The thought of death worried him more now that he was about to become a father. His mind was inundated with questions. Why were Russians suddenly so full of hatred toward each other? An article in *Pravda* demanded the nationalization of all banks and industry and the immediate arrest of their owners and directors. He was glad that he and Larissa had listened to the advice of the old banker and converted some of their money into gold. Paper money was quickly losing its value. Further along in *Pravda*, there was a call for a *class war*. It made him shudder.

Doctor Shubin and Glafíra Ivánovna came to the station to see Andrei off. Larissa and Andrei were driven by Akim in his rickety one-horse carriage, but Doctor Shubin and Glafíra Ivánovna were driven by a chauffeur in the hospital automobile, Glafíra Ivánovna taking full advantage of her new position. Wearing a huge hat decorated with pheasant feathers, she was dressed in a flamboyant yellow suit and sported a red armband proclaiming that she was a Very Important Person. She looked even more round having gained some weight with her new unrestricted freedom in the kitchen larder. She held tightly to a fluffy pillow with a purple stamp of Memorial Hospital on its casing.

Doctor Shubin looked embarrassed sitting next to her.

"I brought you your favorite pillow, Lieutenant," she said smiling. "I am sure they don't have such pillows where you are going!"

"Thank you, Glafíra Ivánovna! I can't accept it. It has the official stamp of the hospital. Your comrades might accuse me of stealing it!" he said smiling. Her sticky admiration annoyed him.

She laughed. "Have no worry. Doctor Shubin will not betray us. Isn't it so, Doctor?"

"Of course, of course! It's perfectly all right!" Shubin laughed nervously.

"Well, in that case, I'll be happy to take your gift," Andrei said, thinking "Good Lord, a distinguished professor has to crawl before this stupid pig!"

"Think of us when you place your head on this little pillow!" she said in a little girl's voice.

"Thank you, Glafíra Ivánovna, I shall!" he said. "I am crawling before her myself," he thought in disgust.

"If you would excuse us for a moment, I would like to say goodbye to my husband in private," Larissa said icily. She'd had enough of this awful flirtation.

"Of course, of course!" Doctor Shubin said quickly. "Goodbye, Lieutenant! Safe journey! Glafíra Ivánovna, let's leave the Lieutenant and his wife to say their goodbyes in privacy, shall we?" He took her arm and placed it on his sleeve, leading her away.

"Goodbye!" she cried over her shoulder, sailing proudly on the arm of the Chief Surgeon of Odessa Memorial Hospital.

The month of May proved to be full of changes. The shuffle of commanding generals continued. The same was going on in the Provisional Government and the Duma. One name, though, that of Alexander Kerensky, seemed to be moving forward and upward with every change. Starting as Minister of Justice, within weeks Kerensky was elevated to the position of Minister of War.

The Provisional Government, afraid to provoke more uprisings among the revolutionary masses, began to eliminate all vestiges of tsarism. All double-headed eagles, the ancient symbol of the monarchy, were removed from public buildings, and the Grand Dukes, who as members of the Tsar's extended family had held many official positions, were fired and placed under house arrests.

At Stavka, the ailing General Alexeyev was left powerless by the deterioration of the Russian armies. He summoned the top commanders of the Army for an emergency consultation. None of them could muster good news. They all reported mass desertions and lack of discipline. All of them reported killings of officers. The battle statistics were dreadful. The losses, from the beginning of the war in August 1914 to May 1917 were over 66,000 officers and *six million* men. These figures did not include the *captured* men, of whom there were over 11,000 officers and nearly three million men.

General Rezánov, who had presented the statistics, observed the group through his gold-rimmed pince-nez. "Gentlemen, there is more. In the past two months we have had at least *85,000* men desert their units. Of course, the numbers may actually be higher. At this point, no one can guarantee the veracity of statistics!"

Alexeyev shook his head slowly. "I received a message from our British allies requesting the scale of our proposed offensive on the Southwestern Front. I informed our allies about the revolutionary activities among our troops. We need a *victory*, gentlemen. We need a *victory* to rekindle patriotism and enthusiasm for the war effort!" He looked from one man to another and said slowly, "Frankly, it doesn't look like we will be ready to begin the offensive by June ..."

The generals had to admit that they were not ready. What's more, they could not guarantee that the troops would follow their command.

"Our new War Minister, Kerensky, expressed his interest in speaking directly to the troops," General Alexeyev opened another topic for discussion. "Should we invite him? He has oratorical skills that might inspire our troops. Perhaps his oratory can challenge the appeal of that Bolshevik orator, Lenin. Shall we try?"

The unanimous decision of the generals was to invite the new War Minister to appear before the troops.

Alexander Fedorovich Kerensky was only thirty-six years old when he became the Minister of War. Of slight build, with a short haircut that bristled like hedgehog quills over his beardless face, his pink ears sticking out like butterfly wings, Kerensky presented a tender image of an adolescent. His youthful appearance was deceptive. Kerensky was a brilliant lawyer and a deputy of the Duma representing the left-of-center liberal party, *Trudoviks*. His eloquence on the Duma floor propelled him into the top ranks of the deputies. His fearlessness in facing the threatening mobs of striking workers and soldiers during the February Revolution had won him a certain amount of trust from all concerned.

As preparations for the big offensive in Galicia continued, Kerensky arrived in Podgaytsy to address the concentration of troops that were to lead the offensive. General Rezánov was entrusted by Alexeyev to attend the historical meeting. He was glad to oblige his old friend. In this particular case, it gave him a chance to see Andrei, who was in Galicia.

Podgaytsy had been a pretty town in the picturesque part of what used to be Poland. Surrounded by verdant hills and green valleys, it was once a prosperous town with a huge Jewish population.

In the beginning of the war, the town was quickly occupied by Austrian troops, and then it was lost to the Russians, who brought epidemics of cholera and typhus with them. By the time of Kerensky's visit, almost nothing was left of the town.

Kerensky arrived in an open car, looking small and insignificant next to the bemedaled generals. He wore a dark uniform without any decorations. There was nothing about him that would suggest his proverbial magnetism.

Dwarfed by the surrounding officers, Kerensky mounted the platform to be met by a roar of welcome.

General Rezánov, standing among the senior officers, was intrigued. "Why are they greeting him with such enthusiasm?" Rezánov wondered, observing the bearded faces of soldiers in front of the podium. "Most of them are illiterate peasants!" he thought. The soldiers, standing in loose formations looked at Kerensky with childlike attention, as if he was their priest.

Slowly, Kerensky lifted the megaphone and began to speak, enunciating clearly. With deliberate simplicity he spoke about *Svobóda*, that great elusive *Freedom* that suddenly had descended upon Russia. From his very first words General Rezánov felt that the man was sincere, that his eloquence was deeply felt and thus hypnotic. His words were often interrupted by shouts of approval and applause. Then he adjured his audience to join *him*, defend their newly won *svobóda*, and expel the enemy from the sainted land of Mother Russia.

The soldiers chanted, *"Svobóda!"* and "Hurrah!" A group of young officers lifted Kerensky on their shoulders and carried him to his car. Some of the soldiers fell on their knees in prayer, some wept, while the officers burst out singing "La Marseillaise" in French. There was no Russian patriotic hymn for them to sing, since "God Save the Tsar" had been eliminated.

Among this hysterical outburst of patriotism, Kerensky saluted the troops as he was slowly driven away.

General Rezánov was shaken. He had never seen anything like that tumultuous reaction of rank and file soldiers. "What is his secret?" Rezánov thought, but he knew the answer. The secret was the magic word *Svobóda! Freedom!*

The general had hoped to see Andrei, but it proved impossible. There was no rail transport, and automotive traffic was limited to troop transport. Even his rank did not provide him the privilege of travel. He had to be satisfied with talking to Andrei by field telephone. They both yelled into the apparatus, exchanging meaningless pleasantries.

Finally, Andrei shouted, "Can you get Larissa back to Petrograd?" but his father could not decipher his words through the noise on the line. At last, they both gave up in disgust.

The general knew that Andrei's unit was scheduled to participate in the forthcoming offensive. He had the premonition that the offensive would fail, knowing the dismal condition of the Russian Army. He wasn't deceived by the enthusiasm of the soldiers who had listened to Kerensky with rapt attention. He knew that Bolshevik agitators were already at work within the ranks of the soldiers.

He hitched a ride back to Stavka on an armored train with a special car attached *in front* of the locomotive. It was loaded with railroad equipment, extra rails and ties, and a crew to repair the rails in case of sabotage.

Alone in Odessa, Larissa was miserable. She did not enjoy her work at the hospital anymore. The wards had been desegregated, and soldiers and sailors mixed with officers. As a result, the nurses' duties had become more complicated. Patients demanded immediate attention, ignoring the protocols of the triage system that gave preference to the most seriously wounded. The sailors were especially rude, treating doctors and nurses with disrespect. They enjoyed shocking the young nurses with coarse language, groping their bodies, and even demanding oral sex. Nurses often fled the wards in tears.

Doctor Shubin tried to bring some order, but Glafíra Ivánovna had no interest in doing so. She enjoyed her popularity among the sailors, hiding her fear of them by ignoring their behavior.

Glafíra Ivánovna became the real power at the hospital. Doctor Shubin tried to avoid her, but every administrative decision had to be approved by the Soviet Deputies, and that meant Glafíra Ivánovna!

Larissa made an effort to be brave and not be upset about the changed atmosphere, but she cried a lot, seemingly at nothing important. If she saw a limping dog, she cried. If she saw a child harshly reprimanded by his mother, she cried again. She looked at her wedding photograph, and she cried some more.

To make matters worse, she discovered a smudge of blood on her underwear. It frightened her. While weeks before she had prayed for a miscarriage, now she was beside herself that she might lose her baby. Near panic, she told Akim to drive her to Madame Juliette's.

Julia was busy at her sewing machine when Larissa knocked on the door.

"Larissa! I was just thinking of you!" she exclaimed, then noticed. Larissa's distraught face. "Is anything wrong?" she asked.

"I don't know ... I think, I may be having a miscarriage. I am bleeding. What should I do?"

Julia led her to a chair. "I did not know that you were pregnant," she said. "How far along are you?"

"Over three months, I think. I am scared. I don't want to lose the baby."

"I understand. I'll take you right now to see my doctor. Is Akim here?"

"Yes."

"Good. Let me close the shop and we'll go to Doctor Gottlieb right away."

Doctor Moishe Gottlieb, Julia's gynecologist, lived and practiced in Moldovanka. His house was shaded by acacia trees in bloom, and the air was filled with their gentle aroma. The house looked prosperous, with large plate glass windows advertising the doctor's services in golden letters in Russian and in Yiddish. Julia pulled the brass ring of the bell and presently a gray-haired woman opened the door.

"Ah, Júlenka!" she greeted Julia. "Come in, come in! And who is this young lady?"

"This is my friend Madame Rezánova, and I beg you, Tóva Moiseyevna, please ask your husband to see her right away. She is three months pregnant and she is bleeding." The conversation was in Yiddish, but Larissa's fluent German allowed her to understand enough of it. She smiled shyly at the doctor's wife, whose calm words and motherly figure reminded her of Ksusha.

"Oh, this is not good," Tóva Moiséyevna said in Russian. "But I am sure my husband will help you, my dear. Please sit down in the parlor. I'll call him right away. He was having a nap."

Julia and Larissa sat on the sofa.

Larissa looked around. It was a large room with a colorful Turkish carpet and three tall windows with lace curtains. The overstuffed furniture was of heavy-looking mahogany, with lacy doilies on every armrest. There were family photographs on the tables and on the mantelpiece of a marble fireplace. But one object in that prosperous middle class drawing room really drew Larissa's attention: a great shiny Bechstein piano.

"Ah, what a piano!" she exclaimed. "A *Bechstein!* Somebody here must really love music!"

There was no time for Julia to respond. Larissa was suddenly dizzy as she felt blood spill out of her. "I think I am having a miscarriage," she whispered, going pale.

"Tóva Moiséyevna!" Julia called in alarm. "We need the doctor! Now!"

"Here I am," Doctor Gottlieb said entering the room. "Hello, Yulenka!" He turned to Larissa, taking her hand and feeling her pulse. "Let's go my examining room," he said.

Julia helped Larissa to her feet and slowly led her to the examining room, Larissa leaning heavily on Julia's shoulder.

"I am sorry, Doctor, I don't know what has happened … I am sorry to bother you …" Larissa tried to apologize.

"Sh-sh ... No apology needed. We'll see in a moment what is wrong."

The examining room was arranged around a strange-looking chair with two stiff protruding contraptions on each side of it. They looked like horse stirrups. Larissa had never been in a gynecologist's examining room, not even when she studied at her Medical Courses in Petrograd. She felt frightened.

"What is your name, dear?" the doctor asked while washing his hands at the sink. "Are you married?"

Larissa answered him, her body trembling.

"And how old are you?" he asked wiping his hands on a small Turkish towel.

"I've just turned nineteen," she said, suddenly realizing that she had forgotten her birthday. She had received no letters, no flowers, not even a telegram. The postal service was totally out of order.

"All right, Yulenka. Help Madame Rezánova to take off her underclothes and then, leave us alone," the doctor said, pointing to the tall screen in the corner of the room. He pulled on rubber gloves.

"Yes, Doctor." Julia helped Larissa out of her skirt and underwear, noticing bright red spots on her old-fashioned knee-length drawers. "She still wears those ugly things!" she reflected automatically. She draped Larissa from the waist down with a sheet and gently led her to the examining chair.

"All right, Yulenka. You go and talk to my wife. We'll call you back shortly," the doctor said.

Julia left the room.

"Now, my dear girl, tell me what happened, and describe the way you felt and what were you doing when you first noticed that you were bleeding. Then, I want you to tell me about your life—your husband, your family, your job, if you have one. It will give you something to focus on while I take a look."

"Now, what bothers me," the doctor said, when he had finished his examination, "is why are you working *night* shifts. In your condition you should be given a less stressful assignment."

"No one at the hospital knows about my condition. That is, no one except Doctor Shubin."

"Well?"

"Doctor Shubin has nothing to do with the scheduling. It is the responsibility of the Soviet Deputies. They run the hospital. Doctor Shubin and the other doctors are in charge only of medical procedures, but even then, all treatments must be approved by the representative of the Soviet."

"My, oh my! I am glad that I am in private practice! Anyway, back to you. First of all, a little spotting is quite common and you are not having a miscarriage. So, stop worrying."

Larissa gave a sigh of relief. "Thank you, God!" she thought.

"But it means that we must be careful," the doctor continued, pointing his index finger at Larissa. "It means that you must stay in bed, at least for a week, until we are sure that there is no more bleeding. Then, no more night shifts for you. As a matter of fact, if you don't need to work, that is, if you can afford *not* to work, I want you to quit working altogether. Can you do that?"

"Yes, Doctor. I was going to quit working anyway, because I'll be leaving Odessa for home as soon as the railroad service is restored."

"Good. Now, where are you living? Is there anyone who can take care of you while you are in bed?"

"I live at the hotel Otráda ... I suppose the maids ..."

"No, no, no!" Gottlieb interrupted her. "You need *real* home care. Have you any friends in Odessa?"

"Only at the hospital. Doctor Shubin and his wife ... Then Sister Veronica, the chief nurse. And then, of course, Julia. But I can't ask any of them to take care of me."

"Nonsense! I'll talk to Julia! You may get dressed." He left the room abruptly.

Larissa lowered herself to the floor and then walked in her stocking feet to the screen. "What now?" she thought putting on her clothes. She still felt dizzy.

Julia and Doctor Gottlieb came back, both smiling. "It is all arranged!" the doctor exclaimed. "You are going to be a *boarder* in Julia's mother's 'boarding house!' You'll have your own room, with a bathroom down the hall! You'll have three meals a day and the company of a fine family! It couldn't be any better!" he said. "You'll be very comfortable with Julia's mother!"

"Yes, Larissa, until Doctor Gottlieb says that you are totally well, you'll stay with us!" Julia smiled. "My mother will take care of you as only Jewish mothers can, that is, she will *love* doing it. And my son, who has had a crush on you ever since he saw you at the Opera, will teach you how to play chess, if you like. And I will enjoy your company!" Julia concluded.

"I don't know what to say—" Larissa began.

"Say nothing. You'll be our guest."

"It is the best solution," the doctor said. "To change the subject, Julia told me that you are a pianist. So am I. Perhaps we could play sometime in 'four hands?'"

"I would love it! Back at home, my mother and I often played in 'four hands.' We have a concert Bechstein also!"

"Splendid! Now go to your hotel and Julia will help you to pack and move to their house. Then you must go to bed and stay there for a whole week, at least. My wife and I will visit you tomorrow. Get going!" he clapped his hands as if for a child, and smiled.

⧉ 33 ⧉

Akim took Larissa and Julia back to the Otráda and waited while they packed. He carried the heavy soondook on his back, and the bulky case filled the whole carriage.

"I'll come back for you, *báryn'ya*," he said to Larissa. "I won't flee with your soondook. Don't you worry."

Larissa smiled. "I trust you, Akim. I am not worried."

Julia glanced at her. She knew that the soondook contained all Larissa's money sewn into her clothes. "I hope she is right," she thought briefly. "Of course, *he* doesn't know what's inside ... But whatever it is, it's still *more* than a poor man has ... To think of it, I am not sure whether the soondook will be safe in *my* house, with my papa poking around!"

Larissa was exhausted by the time she had settled her bills at the hotel. She left a message for Veronica to let her know she was not well and would not be able to work for a few days. She also left a message for Doctor Shubin that she had seen Doctor Gottlieb and asked Shubin to explain to Veronica the reason for her absence.

All that done, she and Julia settled in the Otráda's café to wait for Akim.

Julia's house looked very small from the front facing Degtyárnaya Street. It was narrow, but it extended from the street deep into a shady garden, a long one-story building that had been added onto several times.

The house was painted varying shades of white, each addition a slightly different hue. Set in the overgrown garden was a gazebo made of wooden lattice. Inside the gazebo were several wicker chairs and a wrought iron table set with a chessboard. It looked charming to Larissa.

Julia's mother came out of the house with outstretched arms. "Welcome, welcome to our house, Larissa Sergéyevna!" she exclaimed in a warm, Ukrainian-accented voice. "My name is Mínna Solomónovna," Julia's mother introduced herself and giggled. She was a small woman with a large bust but a slender body. Her dark hair, with a thick white streak starting over her brow, was pulled back into a tight knot at the nape of her head. It was covered with a net made of tiny multi-colored beads. She was a handsome woman, with full lips, dark eyes, and a Semitic profile. "Just like Julia's" Larissa thought.

"I have everything ready for you, my dear, so you get right in bed!" she fluttered. "Yulenka and I will unpack for you, so don't you worry!" She led Larissa through the parlor. An upright Diderichs *pianino* stood against one of its walls, a score of Beethoven's *Moonlight Sonata* on its opened lid.

"Yulenka tells me that you play music! When you feel better, you can play the *pianino* whenever you like! We all love music, and Yulenka, when she was a girl, played the violin. And her son, he plays *her* violin now …" She chattered and giggled.

"That's nice," Larissa said, already annoyed by her hostess's habit of giggling after almost every sentence.

"All right, *Mámole*, let Larissa Sergéyevna rest. You can talk to her later," Julia said firmly.

"Of course, of course!" Minna Solomonovna fussed. "I'll go now." She giggled as she left.

Julia closed the door behind her. "Let me help you," she said, fluffing the pillows. "Doctor Gottlieb told my mother exactly how she should take care of you, so don't argue with anything that she might want to do for you. All right? My mother can be very irritating, but pay no attention to it. She means well. Worst of all is her *giggling*. She developed that nervous habit when I was a girl. I actually remember when it started."

Larissa looked at her quizzically. Julia continued, "It was around the time of the pogroms in Odessa. A band of huge bearded men broke the door of our house and began to ransack it in search of gold. Our house was very small then. We have added to it through the years, a cellar to hide in and a back entrance into the garden, through which we can escape in case of trouble. Anyway, I remember they hit my father hard and knocked him unconscious, and they demanded that my mother give them the gold. She was weeping, swearing that there was no gold. She emptied her purse of all its money, she broke open our toy banks, begging them not to hurt the children. I can never forget the look on her face as she begged them! She looked so pathetic, so *servile*, that I was ashamed of her. I was an adolescent, and I hushed her sharply, as I remember. The men roared with laughter, and she tried to laugh with them. As she turned to me, there was so much pain on her face that I ran out of the room in tears. The men laughed as I ran, and my mother *laughed with them!*"

"How awful!" Larissa said.

"Yes, it was dreadful! Later, she told me that she had been terrified that they would rape me and kill us all. So she tried to ingratiate herself. That terrible laughter of hers turned into a giggle as the years went by. She is not even aware of it ... but I'll never forget how it all started ..."

Larissa nodded solemnly. The thought of facing such a situation with her own child made her shiver. "And your father? I hope he recovered without any dire complications?"

"Yes. Actually, he pretended that he was knocked out, which speaks well for his cleverness but rather badly for his chivalry. But that's my father. He is not known for his sterling character," she laughed. "He is a survivor, in the worst sense of the word. Anyway, rest now. We'll have plenty of time to talk. And don't you try to go to the bathroom. Doctor Gottlieb ordered that you stay in bed and not get out of it, unless there is a fire!" she joked. "Use the chamber pot!"

"Yes, *Comrade!*" Larissa smiled. "That's what we have to call our co-workers at the hospital now!"

Larissa glanced around the room as Julia lingered in the doorway. The room was small, but its window faced the garden. An old apple tree in a profusion of tender pink flowers outside the window perfumed the room with its gentle scent. The room's broad-planked floor was partially hidden by a bright Tatar carpet, and the narrow bed was covered with a knitted white blanket. In the peasant tradition of flaunting the family's wealth, the bed was piled high with a pyramid of fluffy pillows diminishing in size until the last pillow on the top was no bigger than a man's hand. It was called the *doomka*, the dream pillow. Larissa smiled: she had such a tiny pillow when she was a little girl. Ksusha had insisted that she have the doomka under her cheek.

Larissa's soondook was placed in the corner of the room and covered with a large Gypsy shawl embroidered with cabbage-size roses. There was a chest of drawers with a warped mirror and an exquisite Murano glass vase full of apple blossom sprigs. A comfortable armchair in front of the window concluded the furnishings of the room.

"How charming!" Larissa exclaimed. "I love it! Especially the apple tree!"

"Good. Now, rest. We'll have supper together. I'll come to your room to eat, all right?"

"Wonderful! But I would like to meet your son."

"Later. You'll meet him and my father later. They are visiting my brother in Kherson and will be back in a few days. Rest now!" Julia glanced at the soondook and sighed as she left the room.

Larissa stretched out on her bed, her eyes on the apple tree, its fragrant blossoms protruding into her room. For the first time since she had discovered the blood on her underwear, she relaxed. "I'll be fine," she told herself. "I'll do whatever Doctor Gottlieb tells me to do and I'll save my baby. Mother will come to Odessa and Andrúsha will get another furlough and we all will go back home to Petrograd ... and the war will be over!"

She fell into a deep, safe sleep. The little doomka under her cheek was working its magic.

Maria Nikoláyevna also had her little doomka: Ksusha saw to it that her luxuriant bed contained the humble little pillow, which Maria Nikoláyevna did not like but kept, unwilling to offend her old devoted friend. However, its magic did not work on Maria Nikoláyevna.

She slept badly, worrying about Larissa. She wanted desperately to bring Larissa back to Petrograd, or go to Odessa herself, but until the railway traffic was restored, there was no way. Unable to sleep, she watched through her lace curtains as the eastern sky began to turn pink and then orange. "One more month and we'll have our 'white nights,'" she thought. "Revolution or not, Tsar or Bolshevik, no matter what, we'll have our white nights! We'll have our cherry trees blooming, and when they are finished and the white petals cover the ground, we'll have our last cold spell. And after that—the lilacs will bloom! All predictable ...

every year the same, no matter what else is going on in the world. There was definite order in that predictability, and she liked it, especially given the rapid changes around her. Most disturbing was 'Order Number One' issued jointly by the Provisional Government (under duress, she was sure!) and the Soviet of Workers and Soldiers Deputies. *Order Number One* dictated that all orders from military commanders had to be agreed upon and co-signed by the soldiers' Soviet Committees. The order abolished saluting and did away with the use of orderlies. Furthermore, it required that lower ranks must be addressed using the polite form, and finally, it forbade officers from speaking foreign languages. Only the Russian language was to be spoken!

She had no argument about the use of the polite form of address. She had always used that form of address when she spoke to her servants. She sympathized with those who had been offended by being addressed in the same terms one would use with small children or animals, but she thought it was a stupid idea to forbid the use of foreign languages.

"What are they trying to do? Bring *us* down to the level of the uneducated masses?" she thought, admitting sadly that perhaps it was inevitable. "There are more of *them* than of *us!*"

She thought of Andrei's father who was stuck at Stavka. "Even the generals can't travel now!"

It was all too dismal to comprehend. "I must talk to Lieutenant Svirsky. Perhaps he will know something that will be of help," she thought, rearranging the doomka under her head, willing herself to sleep but unable to.

Lieutenant Svirsky enjoyed staying at Maria Nikoláyevna's elegant house. With General Rezánov still at Stavka, he had no duties to perform except providing a masculine presence in the Orlov residence. Maria Nikoláyevna was friendly with the opera singer Alicia Eduardovna, who became a regular visitor at the house. Her husband was back with his troops, and Alicia was lonely. Almost every day she visited the Orlovs' house, often staying for dinner, singing to Maria Nikoláyevna's accompaniment, Ksusha always in attendance.

Ksusha disliked the famous singer. She predicted that Alicia had interests other than singing with Maria Nikoláyevna. "Mark my word, that woman wants Lieutenant Svirsky in her bed!" she announced with a smirk.

"Can you blame her?" Maria Nikoláyevna chortled good-humoredly.

Lieutenant Svirsky was able to obtain a copy of the newspaper *Novoye Vremya* and brought it to Maria Nikoláyevna. Like everything else in Petrograd, the newspapers were not always available. "It is two days old, but basically it is full of news. Mostly unpleasant," he added. "The only good news is the call for a Congress of the Officers Union to be held in Petrograd in a few days. But it's still up in the air on account of the railways situation. How can the men get to Petrograd?"

"Nothing is simple anymore," Maria Nikoláyevna said. "Thanks for the paper." She perched the magnifying spectacles on her nose and opened the paper. "Do me a favor, Lieutenant, try to find out whether I can get in touch with Doctor Shubin at Odessa Memorial Hospital through the military channels. I know it was possible a few months ago, but who knows how it is now. I worry about my daughter. She is expecting."

"Oh, congratulations! I'll get you the information." By habit he saluted, and they both laughed.

Maria Nikoláyevna settled deeper in her chair and began to read the newspaper.

There were dismal articles about the railways crisis, which showed no sign of being settled. There was also an interview with a French military attaché who had visited the Russian front. He reported that in addition to their other problems, the troops were suffering an epidemic of typhus. There were articles about the upcoming Congress of the Officers Union.

She dropped the paper. She could not read any more about the disasters or the proliferation of "congresses." It seemed that every group was holding a congress: the Polish soldiers held one in what used to be Poland, the Don Cossacks gathered in Novocherkassk, the Muslim Tribes of the Caucasian front conferred in Vladikavkas, and the First Officers Union was about to convene in Petrograd. "All they do is argue and argue and appoint committees to argue some more!" she thought in disgust. "Even the clergy is going to hold a congress in Moscow! Nero fiddled while Rome burned. Well, we Russians, we *argue*, while our country goes to hell!"

Annoyed, she called the maid to bring her a cup of tea.

34

Russia was not ready to begin its offensive. After weeks of stormy spring weather when neither friend nor foe could fly, the need for accurate reconnaissance on both sides became crucial. To prevent enemy aircraft from penetrating their front lines, Russian fighter pilots were ordered to invade the skies over enemy territory and fly aggressive missions three or four times a day.

The pilots did not like it. Not only was it physically exhausting and dangerous, but the ambitious young men also knew that their victories, should they have any, could not be confirmed.

The mechanics did not like it either. They refueled and rearmed constantly, and they often had to send planes back into the sky full of barely plugged bullet holes. They felt torn between the Soviets Deputies who agitated disobedience and their loyalties to the pilots and their machines. Before *Order Number One* was proclaimed, there was an air of camaraderie between the pilots and their mechanics: they all loved airplanes. Now—the pilots had become leery of the mechanics, who became sour, bewildered, and even hostile. It created a chasm, which grew deeper and wider with every passing day.

Andrei, who had been acclaimed as a hero among the mechanics, suddenly began to feel coldness from some of them. They did not joke with him anymore and some even turned away from him. He mentioned it to Egórov.

"Pay no attention. They are probably Bolsheviks itching to cut your throat!" Egórov said with unusual venom.

"But why would they want to cut my throat? What did I do to deserve that?"

"You are an *officer* and they are not! You are rich and they are not! And because you are a general's son! We are lucky that our mechanics are Cossacks, the most loyal of Russian troops. So far, they seem to be neutral. We should be more friendly with them. One never knows; we might need their help someday, if things turn really ugly."

"Do you think things can turn even uglier?"

"Yes, I do. I think if our new offensive fizzles, and it *will* fizzle under the present circumstances, the Bolsheviks will stage another *coup d'état* to grab full power. They'll unleash a bloody terror that will make the French Revolution look like a child's game."

They were on their way to the planes, ready to fly behind enemy lines for the third time that day. "How did we lose our country?" Andrei exclaimed, kicking viciously at a dandelion that raised its fluffy round head from the dusty runway.

"It happened when the Petrograd garrison soldiers refused to fire upon the demonstrators. That was *our Rubicon*," Egórov, ever the classicist, replied.

"But the demonstrators were unarmed!" Andrei objected. "They were just marching peacefully ..."

"Oh, Andrúshka, don't be a sentimental fool!" Egórov interrupted. "Do you call *'Down with the Tsar'* peaceful? It was a call for revolution! But that's beside the point. The point is that the troops *disobeyed* orders. Military discipline demands total obedience. You and I know that, and we obey orders even if we don't like them, even if it means we may be killed. That's what *military discipline* means. When it's gone, chaos reigns. That's what we have now, chaos. But today, to create even more chaos, we suddenly have new masters—Bolsheviks. Who are they? Who gave them the right to order us *to obey* their order to *disobey?* Isn't it confusing?"

"So, you won't obey the orders of the Soviet Deputies?"

"I certainly won't!"

"You contradict yourself! Russia is being ruled by two powers now. Whether we like it or not, isn't it our duty to follow military discipline and obey the Soviets, as well?"

"Don't corner me!" Egórov exclaimed angrily. "I don't have the answer!" Finally he said darkly, "I don't know what to do. But mark my words, we are losing this goddamned war!"

"And if we do—what then?"

"Another war. That much, I *do* know. We'll have a Civil War, Russian against Russian," Egórov said, his face grim.

They reached their Spads. The mechanics who were sprawled leisurely on the patch of grass stood and saluted. Egórov smiled crookedly as he returned their salutes. "I thought we don't have to salute anymore," he said.

His mechanic, a middle-aged Don Cossack named Ostap Sukhotin, said seriously, "Captain, we've decided that saluting is the simplest way to let a commander know that you understood an order. We don't like answering all the time *'I serve the Soviet of Workers and Soldiers Deputies.'* So, we'll keep saluting for awhile." He stroked his long drooping moustache and grinned widely.

"Well, in that case, we will respond accordingly. Shall we, Lieutenant?"

"We shall," Andrei said and saluted.

They climbed into their Spads, the bullet holes in the fuselages and the wings patched with long strips of duct tape. It reminded Andrei of a cartoon that he had seen in some newspaper. It depicted a German Fokker airplane crisscrossed with surgical bandages, its wing propped up by a crutch, limping along the runway following an arrow pointing *'to Germany.'* The cartoon was supposed to lift the morale of the troops, but the Russian pilots did not find it funny. They knew that the Fokkers were superior planes and that, more likely, the obsolete Russian planes needed crutches and bandages.

The mechanics helped Andrei climb into the nacelle and hooked his shoulder harness.

Egórov was already in his craft, adjusting his goggles, his irritation with Andrei's logic forgotten. "Ready?" he shouted.

"Ready!" The mechanics spun the propellers and pulled the chocks away. The Spads taxied for takeoff.

"Good hunting!" Ostap Sukhotin waved.

Their flight was over the Austro-Hungarian territory bombed by Russian heavy artillery. Nothing moved down below. It looked like a desert mottled with round craters full of rainwater that sparkled, reflecting the sky. From the high altitude the sparkling craters looked as if they were handfuls of silver coins scattered around the dead landscape.

Andrei was tired and his leg hurt. He did not feel the exuberance of soaring up in the air anymore. Flying had become a routine, a boring chore. By habit he constantly moved his head, scanning the sky for enemy planes, his nerves tight.

Flying ahead of him, Egórov wagged his wings and pointed down: four enemy planes flying in formation at a low altitude apparently were not yet aware of the Russian presence. They were moving west, away from the front lines, most likely returning to their home base. Egórov immediately zoomed upwards, Andrei following. From their advantageous position with the sun behind their backs, they boldly dived into the formation, simultaneously concentrating on the last machine. They hit the Austrian plane with several bursts from their machine guns and quickly banked, climbing again. The surprised pilot did not answer their fire: his forward-firing machine gun must have been jammed.

On his second approach Andrei saw that the pilot they had hit was desperately struggling to unjam the machine gun, but his Fokker D II was hit again by Egórov. A trail of black smoke appeared at its tail. The plane began to spin as it went down. As he watched, the fuselage of his own Spad VII was hit by several trace bullets, so he quickly banked out of reach of his adversaries, soaring upward again.

He briefly saw Egórov coming out of a turn and firing on another plane, but the Austrians were not inclined to engage in battle. They continued on their course, probably out of fuel and anxious to get home.

Egórov decided not to chase them. He gave Andrei the signal to head back for their base.

Dead tired, they landed at their airfield, their Spads carrying new bullet holes. Egórov's win did not bring him any satisfaction: it had been an easy kill and would not be confirmed anyway.

Bad news awaited them: Kozakov was wounded during an air battle over Brzezany. He had managed to land his Nieuport at the home airfield but lost consciousness as he was being removed from the nacelle. He was undergoing surgery, old Doctor Barsky performing it.

Egórov was now in charge. "You go and rest, Andrúshka. I must take a look at Kozakov's orders," he said, wiping his face with his greasy glove. "You go and sleep. You look like shit."

"So do you," Andrei replied. "Can I help?"

"Thanks, but no. I'll let you know if you can help, *bratíshka*." He closed the door to Kozakov's office.

The torrential rains returned that night, pelting the southwestern front. Egórov decided to use the pause in flying to repair the damaged airplanes. Spare parts had finally been delivered.

In an attempt to lower tensions between the mechanics and the officers, Egórov addressed the latter during a daily briefing meeting. He asked for volunteers among the pilots to join the mechanics in the restoration of the damaged aircraft.

Beforehand, Egórov had appealed to Andrei for help. "You see, Andrúshka, if *you* volunteer, some of the men may follow. They all realize how dangerous our old planes have become. They know that we cannot cannibalize the crashed aircraft any further. So, if we can spend a few rainy days fixing our airplanes, it may save some lives and re-establish camaraderie among the men. I think the mechanics will like the idea. It will give them a chance to show off before the officers. It will also show them that pilots don't mind dirtying their hands. What do you say? Are you with me?"

"What a question! Of course I am with you!"

"Good. We'll start right away. I already talked to Kozakov about it and he approves."

"How is he feeling?"

"Much better. He was wounded in his left arm. He may be out of the hospital in a couple of weeks, Doctor Barsky said, but he won't be able to fly."

"Of course. What about the Soviet Committee's reaction to your idea? Will they allow pilots alongside mechanics in the repair shops?"

"I am having a meeting with them in two hours," Egórov said, glancing at his wristwatch. "Want to come? Actually, it might be good if you came. They all know you as the brave hero. It may help if you stir the dying embers of their patriotism, so to speak. After all, we are all *Russians*. None of us wants to die because our planes are falling apart."

"I'll be glad to come and be an *agitator* for a good cause," Andrei said, smiling. "It will be a new challenge!"

The Executive Committee of the Soviet of Workers and Soldiers Deputies gathered in the briefing tent.

"Please do sit down," Egórov said. "I have asked you to this meeting to hear your opinion about an idea for how to use the rainy days, when we can't fly."

"We can play checkers!" someone yelled.

The mechanics burst out in derisive laughter. Egórov joined them.

"Yes, we could do that," he said when the hilarity subsided. "But I think I have a better idea. We, the Russian airmen, know more than anyone that we need *good* airplanes, *good* machine guns, and plenty of spare parts and ammunition. Our enemy has all of that in abundance, while we have to scramble around for every engine, every scrap of canvas to patch our wings, every machine gun that we hope won't jam. We want the war to be over, so we must do everything that we can to make that happen." He could see that some of the Soviet committee members were nodding. He addressed himself to them, telling them of his idea to have pilots and mechanics work together to repair the planes.

"I asked my friend, Lieutenant Andrei Rezánov, to speak to you about it. You all have heard of him. He was that chap who climbed on the wing of the Voisin and unhooked the bomb that got stuck under our wing."

The mechanics met Andrei with applause as he stood.

"*Comrades,*" he began, looking at their tired and grimy faces. "I like this word, '*comrades.*' It describes exactly what we airmen are, for as a pilot I know that without the mechanics, I won't be able to fly. My own teacher at Gátchina Flight School was a master mechanic named Petrovich, who had helped to build the famous *Ilya Murometz* of Sikorsky! Under his guidance, several of us rebuilt a crashed Voisin."

Andrei continued. "Of course, the pilots here don't know as much as you do, but under your guidance, they'll learn, or at least they'll supply another set of strong arms to help! I told Captain Egórov that I would be glad to join you, my *comrades*, in that enterprise. Perhaps, fixing our disabled airplanes, working *together*, will help all of us to get this war over with!"

The chairman of the Soviet committee, Igor Kóshkin, a young man who had only recently arrived from Petrograd, stood. "We must discuss your proposal," he said in a cultured voice. "Please wait outside while we confer with one another."

"Of course," Egórov said politely. He could see that Kóshkin was probably an educated man, perhaps a graduate student from some technical aviation school.

He and Andrei left the tent and waited under the rain cover at the entrance. "Kóshkin sounded different from the others," Andrei said.

"You noticed that also! Perhaps he is one of the new agitators that the Bolsheviks are sending around. We must be careful around him," Egórov said.

It did not take long before they were called back. "The Executive Committee of the Soviet of Workers and Soldiers Deputies has unanimously approved your proposal," Kóshkin said. "Prepare your written proposal and we'll sign it. Meeting is adjourned."

"Thank you!" Egórov shook his hand. "It was a pleasure meeting you!"

"Likewise," Kóshkin replied.

Andrei saluted. "Oh, I'm sorry," he said, lowering his arm.

Kóshkin laughed. "Old habits die hard," he said and extended his hand to Andrei. "I am one of your admirers, Lieutenant!"

Ten pilots volunteered to work alongside the mechanics restoring disabled aircraft. They were all young and from the lower class. None of them were graduates of military academies. The new pilots were closer to the mechanics in their social background than to the officers. A spirit of camaraderie was established almost immediately, but a disturbing thought kept flickering in Egórov's mind: Kóshkin would take advantage of the situation and sway the young pilots to follow him in his Bolshevik ways.

Restoration of the disabled aircraft began at once. Several smashed machines, some of them already cannibalized for parts, were dragged into the tents to be dismantled. Without their wings, the planes had the look of dismembered insects.

Several more pilots joined the group of the volunteers, and by the fifth day of foul weather, there were almost a hundred men working on multiple aircraft.

The men yelled and sang and danced with each other, ignoring their ranks. Since the aircraft were still grounded, Egórov authorized a bottle of vodka for every five men and ordered the kitchens to prepare meat stew for everybody. The feast that followed was without distinction between the officers and men.

Egórov and Andrei personally tested every repaired plane to remove the doubts of pilots who did not quite trust the work of their peers. All planes passed the tests and were ready to join Brusílov's offensive, the name of which the new Minister of War expropriated so that it would become known as the Kerensky Offensive in history books.

The rains finally stopped. The skies turned blue and clear again, but the air was full of the acrid tang of artillery smoke and the septic smell of upturned earth. The offensive began on the first of July with a two-day vicious artillery barrage along the southwestern front. The objective of the offensive was to capture the town of Lemberg (Lvov) and disrupt the connection between the German and Austro-Hungarian armies.

The Russian Seventh Army, the strongest of the three advancing armies, quickly occupied the abandoned Austrian trenches. It was then that the Germans opened up with their devastating artillery barrage. The hollow thuds of heavy shells filled the air as they ripped into the suffering earth. The Seventh Army was quickly pinned down by a fusillade of German fire.

On its flank, the Eighth Army was more successful. It boldly attacked the Austro-Hungarian forces and took several small towns, capturing thousands of prisoners and eighty artillery guns.

A large aviation force was concentrated for the preliminary attack. Kozakov's First Combat Air Group and Ivan Orlov's Seventh Fighter

Detachment were deployed together with several squadrons of French and British pilots, more than 225 planes in all. During the first days of the offensive, the Allied pilots claimed twenty-three confirmed victories.

Egórov's squadron's mission was to keep the vicinity of Tarnopol under constant reconnaissance. It proved to be more complicated than he had thought. His pilots had to watch for and aggressively attack enemy aircraft while risking both heavy artillery shells whose trajectory they were invading and rapid fire from the anti-aircraft batteries. At the height of the offensive, Andrei and Egórov often flew five missions a day. Some days, totally exhausted and unable to make it back to their home base, they landed at airfields used by the French, their crafts barely airworthy.

For a while the offensive favored the Russians, who had at their disposal infantry and cavalry divisions of Siberian and Finnish troops. These forces, it was hoped, were not infected with the germs of Bolshevism. They were supported by more than a thousand artillery guns of various calibers.

However, Kerensky was perplexed that the Germans seemed to refuse to enter the artillery duel. Their infamous Big Bertha guns were silent. The Germans were well aware of the self-destruction of the Russian armies. Shrewdly, they encouraged the fraternization of their troops, even teaching their soldiers what to say in Russian: *don't fight, drop your guns, go home. It's not your war, it's the Tsar's war and the Tsar is gone. Go home!*

Hundreds of Russian soldiers followed the advice.

The Germans and the Austrians did not hurry to retake the little towns and villages. The German strategy was to lengthen Russian supply lines by allowing Russians to penetrate deeper into the no-man's land already destroyed and denuded in recent battles. The Central Powers were taking a cue from Russian strategies proven successful over many centuries, when they defeated invaders by lengthening the distances between the enemy troops and their supplies and communications. The Germans were using the same strategy now. Counting on the total collapse of Russian military and political structures, they spared their own troops and allowed Russia to self-destruct.

When several Russian regiments refused to fight and left the city of Tarnopol open, the Germans easily occupied it, although some regiments fought bravely, defending Tarnopol street by street amidst the staccato cracking of machine guns and the booming explosions of artillery shells.

Kerensky realized that the army was incapable of fighting anymore. A whole cavalry battalion riding in formation with several junior officers at the head deserted the front under a banner, "Going Home." No one bothered, nor dared to stop them.

The war dragged on.

The Germans moved the bulk of their troops to reinforce their armies in the fierce battles with the French and English forces and, soon to arrive, the Americans. They treated with disdain the scorched earth of the sad Russian front. They knew that there would be no more attempted offensives. It was only a matter of time before Russia would collapse. They waited, their troops like some many-bodied mythological beast slowly creeping into the conquered lands, meeting no opposition from the doomed and fatigued people.

35

General Rezánov was finally able to get in touch with his office in Petrograd and speak with Lieutenant Svirsky.

"What's going on at home?" he shouted into the telephone. "Have you been able to get my daughter-in-law to Petrograd?" The line crackled and buzzed, forcing them to shout.

"The Soviet Deputies ... your automobile, sir," Svirsky yelled. "In the name of the Revolution. They issued a ... to your wife, but she refused to sign it."

"What did she refuse to sign?" shouted the general. "Speak louder!"

"The ... paper, sir ... broke her front teeth, but she still did not sign ... with Maria Nikoláyevna."

The line went dead. All that the general could get out of the conversation was that his wife did not sign something and then something about Maria Nikoláyevna and broken teeth. He shrugged and said to his aide, "Let's try to call again tomorrow. I don't understand what's going on there."

He was sorry that someone had broken his wife's teeth. "A tooth, more likely," he thought. "But it won't be easy to find a good dentist now," he thought.

He did not worry about Andrei. So far, he knew Andrei and Egórov were well; the lists of the shot-down pilots were delivered to Stavka daily and their names, so far, were not on the lists.

The Provisional Government had reached an agreement with the railworkers. Several strikes were called off. The Soviets had equipped trains with detachments of armed escorts to protect the passengers from the marauding bands of deserters and criminals, but travel between the big cities was still restricted to official business.

Maria Nikoláyevna was unable to get permission to travel to Odessa. Being the widow of a high-ranking general and mother-in-law of a national hero held no sway anymore. She had to remain in Petrograd waiting for the mail, which was not circulating. Lieutenant Svirsky finally succeeded in sending a telegram through the military channels, addressed to Colonel Shubin and written in an official-sounding language aping the Soviet Deputies. He demanded a report on the state of health of Comrade Larissa Rezánova, Medical Aide. In his reply to the telegram, Colonel A.P. Shubin, Commander, Military Hospital Number One, Odessa, informed Svirsky that Comrade Rezánova was doing well and was under the care of a specialist. Doctor Shubin also understood the new patois of communications.

There was nothing more that Maria Nikoláyevna could do but wait. She concentrated her attention on taking care of her friend Varvára Mikháilovna, who was in a state of mental and physical shock.

Varvara Mikháilovna was ensconced in Larissa's bed, her face disfigured by bruises, her mouth swollen, and her front teeth broken. Knocked out by sleeping pills, she trembled violently now and then and whimpered like a sick puppy.

She had come to the Orlov's residence late at night, disheveled and barely able to talk, her mouth still bleeding. Maria Nikoláyevna had quieted her down with the help of laudanum and learned the gist of her story from the frightened butler who had brought her in. He needed a dose of valerian drops himself before he could relate what had happened.

Apparently, five heavily-armed sailors came to the front door of the Rezánovs' residence and demanded to see the general. Told by the butler that he was at Stavka in Mogilev, they pushed their way into the house. Varvara Mikháilovna, hearing the commotion, came into the hall. One of the sailors announced that "in the name of the Revolution, we have come to take possession of an American automobile named 'Pack Hard.'" She was to surrender the keys to the machine and sign a release that she was doing so voluntarily. Proudly, she refused to sign the paper and ordered them out of her house. The enraged sailor hit her in the face, knocking her down to the marble floor. The sailors grabbed the butler and threatened to kill him if he would not produce the car keys. Fearful for his life, he obeyed. The sailors left, smashing a large mirror in the hall just to "teach the general's bitch a lesson."

"You stay here tonight," Maria Nikoláyevna said to the butler. "Ksusha, please get some money from my purse and pay the driver. Tomorrow we'll get policemen to guard our houses."

Ksusha shook her head mournfully. "That won't help," she said darkly. "The great hatred of one another has settled in our Motherland ... we must prepare ourselves, *báryn'ya*. It will get worse. We can't wait another day. I'll go out tomorrow and buy us some *vátnik* coats."

Maria Nikoláyevna did not listen. She was on her knees before the icons in the corner, praying for her suffering country, for her family separated from each other, and for her dear friend, trembling in her daughter's girlish bed.

Early next morning Ksusha departed for Gostinny Dvor, the arcade on the Nevsky Prospect built like a huge triangle under one roof supported by many arches. There were almost a hundred small shops selling everything from pianos to needles and threads, from shoes to samovars, from sizzling *pirozkí* to ice cream. It was the *'people's'* cluster of shops, where one could get anything for a reasonable price.

Ksusha knew exactly what she wanted: a thick cotton vátnik, dark and bulky, quilted vertically from collar to hem, looking like a winter garment favored by industrial workers and railroad men. It was heavily padded and was much cheaper but just as warm as *touloúps*, the tanned sheepskin peasant coats that smelled forever of sheep.

She examined several vátniks very carefully, paying special attention to the stitching, which was regular and went through the padding. The coats were not lined, their inside seams rough to touch. They suited her purpose perfectly.

Ksusha bought three coats with sturdy metal buttons down the front. She needed one more thing: a strong but pliable fabric for lining the coats. She went to a fabric shop on the Sadovaya side of the Gostinny Dvor and bought several lengths of black sateen. "We still have plenty of goods in the stores," she thought. "It's *food* that we don't have!"

Pleased with her purchases, Ksusha beckoned a carriage-for-hire. "When my Larochka comes home, we'll have a vátnik for her also," she thought. She wiggled her formidable *derrière*, seeking comfort among the flattened cushions of the dilapidated carriage, and relaxed, her bulky packages occupying most of the seat.

Maria Nikoláyevna sent Lieutenant Svirsky and her own butler to check the Rezánov's house.

Their reports worried her. The staff of the Rezánov's household had deserted their employers, scared off by the confrontation with the sailors. Only two old employees, a butler and a housemaid, Agraféna Ósipovna, remained, having locked themselves in their quarters. Tearfully they described the night. The desertion of the servants had upset them more than the invasion by the sailors.

"The servants said that the General's house was 'marked' by the Bolsheviks. We all were frightened for our lives ... the servants said that they didn't want to be paid for the last month because money wasn't worth anything anymore ... instead of money, they said they would take something from the house," the butler began.

"What did they take?" Svirsky demanded.

"Oh, Lieutenant, you won't believe it!" the butler sobbed. "The stablemen took all four horses! They said that the Bolsheviks would confiscate them anyway ... The kitchen staff took a lot of food from the larder and the maids took some stuff from the Madame's room. Probably, her jewels."

"They did not get any of her jewels," the old chambermaid interrupted. "*Báryn'ya* took all her jewels to the bank last week! But, her new maid took her sable coat ..."

"They took most of the pillows and blankets," added the butler. "I called the police and made a report. But the police never arrived. The servants have probably left the city already."

"They wanted me to leave also," the maid said. "But I have no place to go to. I have been with the General and his lady for forty years and their home is my home!"

"Like Ksusha," the lieutenant thought. "I'll call Stavka ... perhaps the General will come home, since it is an emergency. Meanwhile ..." he paused, not knowing what to suggest. "Would you be afraid to stay in the house?" Svirsky asked the maid.

"It's all in God's hands," the old woman said. "I'll stay. What about you?" she turned to the butler.

"I'll stay also," the old man said.

36

General Rezánov requested a furlough to check on his family and home. He was granted three months absence.

Since the direct trip to Petrograd was still impossible, the general and Lieutenant Borisov had to go the roundabout way, through small provincial towns, going to Moscow first and then hitching a ride to Petrograd in a train that had begun to circulate between the two cities. Knowing that their journey would be very uncertain, they reduced their luggage to one small bag each and carried their personal documents and money in special pouches close to their skins. They both had their service revolvers and carried a dagger concealed in the top of their boots. Their sabers, part of the cavalry officers uniform, were more of a nuisance than reliable weapons.

The Stavka cooks supplied them with large packs of French field rations, superior to those provided by Russia. The packs included red wine, which the general rejected. "We are not going on a picnic! We need a couple of thermoses with good, clean water!" The cooks obliged them with water in two American-made thermoses.

From the beginning of the journey General Rezánov was astounded by the amount of rail traffic moving *away* from the front. It was obvious that the Soviets were sympathetic to the deserters on the freight trains. Not only did they provide the deserters with transportation, they treated the exodus as if it was a celebration. The locomotives were decorated with red flags and the slogan *"All power to the Soviet Deputies!"* Most of the freight cars had their sliding doors removed to let even more men jam into them.

These multitudes of angry men were dangerous. Many of them had kept their weapons, prepared to be challenged by loyalist troops along the way. They were dirty and hungry, many of them sick and covered with lice and all of them desperate to survive the war, no matter how or under whose regime. They were peasants eager to get back to their villages and grab the land promised to them by the Bolshevik agitators.

A modest, insignificant-looking passenger train, consisting only of two sleeping cars and several cars with sleeping shelves, was allowed to travel among the *'returning veterans'*, as the deserters became known under the newly created euphemism. The locomotive of the passenger train was also decorated with red flags and five-pointed red stars, but it carried

360

a banner along its side proclaiming it *The Train of Special Designation*. It meant that no one was allowed to enter the cars.

The private compartments in the sleeping cars were filled with high ranking military officers, diplomats, and members of the Provisional Government. They stayed in their compartments for the duration of the journey.

General Rezánov was well aware of the danger. He and Borisov locked themselves in their compartment, checked their weapons, and prepared for a long trip.

The general was sorry now that he had rejected the wine. "It would have been pleasant to have a glass of wine," he thought. He was about to apologize to his aide for denying him the pleasure of a glass of wine, when Lieutenant Borisov unbuttoned his great leather coat and extracted two bottles from its inside pockets.

"I thought that you would enjoy a bit of wine, sir," he said. "I swiped it out of the Stavka kitchen. The orderlies most likely forgot to include it in our food packs!"

The general cleared his throat and said, "Yes. Most likely!"

The French food rations began to look meager by the time they had reached Smolensk. Fortunately, the commissar in charge allowed a dining car to be hitched to the train. The general thought that he had never enjoyed a hot meal as much as in that dining car! His gloomy mood lifted and he began to think that traveling by railroad wasn't as bad as he had always believed. It was quite comfortable and the food was as good as in a restaurant! Perhaps he should try to go to Odessa and bring back his pregnant daughter-in-law, he thought. Why not? It might be possible, even if in a roundabout way.

With several unexpected stops and delays, it took another five days before they reached Petrograd. It was late at night, but the city was in the magical thrall of the last of the white nights and lights were unnecessary—even should they be still functioning.

The small group of passengers from the Special Designation train disembarked and crowded helplessly on the steps of the terminal. There was only one carriage-for-hire at the curb, both the driver and the horse asleep, the horse's muzzle hidden by the feed bag.

Lieutenant Borisov dashed toward it. "Hey, *Dyádyshka*, uncle, wake up!" Borisov slapped his knee. The driver opened his eyes, startled.

"Where to?" he asked by habit.

"First, to Fontánka, then to the Vassilievsky Island, Bolshoi Prospect," Borisov replied holding on possessively to the carriage.

"Yes, Your Excellencies," the driver said with respect, noting the general's uniform. He stowed their bags under his seat and took off the feed bag from his horse's muzzle. "Make yourselves comfortable!"

The city looked peaceful, and the square in front of the Nikolayevsky Railroad Terminal was swept clean, like in the old times. The equestrian statue of Alexander III in the center of the square stood as it always had, though some jokester had placed a red band around the statue's left arm.

The general laughed. "Don't tell me that the Bolsheviks proclaimed Alexander III as their hero!" he exclaimed. "Then, why not? They need decent heroes!"

The general was in a good mood. He anticipated more than anything a good hot bath. He would try to sneak into the house without waking his wife. He was not in the mood for happy tears and conversations. He would tell the butler to fill the tub and shave him while he relaxed in hot, soapy water! What heavenly pleasure, he thought.

The horse trotted evenly toward the Fontánka, the city sleeping as if nothing had ever happened.

They arrived at the Fontánka and stopped under the porte-cochère of the Rezánov's house. Like a young man, the general jumped down on the large granite flagstones of the entrance and ascended three broad steps to the massive door. "You go home, Sereózha," he said to Borisov, using his diminutive name as he pulled on the bronze bell. The house remained silent.

"I'll wait until you are in, Vladímir Petrovich" the young man replied, holding the general's small bag. Following the general's example, he switched to the civilian form of address. They were home, after all.

The general pulled the bell again, then several times more. "What's the matter with them? Are they all deaf in there?" he said without hiding his irritation. There was a commotion within the house and then the high-pitched bark of his wife's little dog.

"At last!" the general exclaimed, his good mood gone.

"Who is there?" they heard the cautious voice of Rezánov's butler through the locked door.

"It's the General," Lieutenant Borisov answered loudly.

"Let me hear his voice, then," the butler replied without unlocking the door.

The general shouted into the keyhole, "It's me, General Rezánov! Open the door!"

"Oh, oh! I am sorry!" There was a sound of several door-bolts being hastily slid open.

The door was flung open. The old butler appeared in its frame. Disheveled and dressed in his long lavender-hued underwear, the yapping dog at his bare feet, he presented a comical figure, but no one laughed. The butler looked frightened.

The general and Borisov both noticed the broken mirror in the hall. "What's happened here?" the general asked, anger rising in the deceptively quiet timbre of his voice. Borisov and the butler both knew that tone of his voice: it foretold the explosion of his temper.

"Oh, sir, we had some terrible things happen here!" the butler began tearfully. "Your automobile ... it was requisitioned by sailors ... and the house staff ... they all left ... only Agrafena Osipovna and I are still here ... Your lady is at Maria Nikoláyevna's house. She is very ill. They took all your horses ..."

"Who took my horses? My wife? Maria Nikoláyevna? Speak some sense, man!" the general thundered.

"The servants, sir, the stablemen when they left ... They took your horses ..."

"Slow down, Grigory Grigorievich," Lieutenant Borisov said gently, taking the situation into his hands. "Tell us, from the beginning, what happened here."

Unnoticed by anyone in the commotion of the revelations, the driver of the carriage stood at the door. "I suppose you won't be going to Vassilievsky Island now?" he said to Borisov.

"No, my good man. Let me pay you."

"I can pick you up here in the morning," the driver said. "It's not easy to get a carriage these days. Most of our horses are requisitioned or killed for food. You can pay me tomorrow. I see that you have a lot of troubles here."

"Oh ... Yes, that will be nice if you can pick me up tomorrow. But we might need you still tonight ... to go to another house. On the Nevá. Can you wait?"

"I can wait," the driver said and went back to his horse.

Wakened by the noise, Agrafena Osipovna came out of her room in the mansards and greeted the general tearfully. "You can't imagine what we went through, Your Excellency," she sobbed, picking up her mistress's little dog.

"Tell me about my wife," the general interrupted. "Was she hurt? How badly?"

"Yes, sir, she was hurt badly …" the servants began almost in one voice.

"You, Grigory Grigorievich, *you* tell me," the general raised his voice, ignoring Agrafena.

"The sailor knocked her front teeth out and she hit her head when she fell on the floor. Madame Orlova is taking care of her now, but Varvara Mikháilovna doesn't talk to anybody … not even to her doctor."

"Let's go inside," Borisov said. He could see that he had to take the lead in the unfolding situation.

The butler bolted the doors. "You'd better get dressed, or at least, put a robe on," Borisov said to the old man. "And then bring us some brandy."

"Yes, Lieutenant," the butler mumbled in embarrassment as he hurried to his room.

As the general listened to the servants' terrifying story, his face darkened. Finally, unable to restrain it, he roared *"Svòlochi!* Scum! Swine! I'll shoot them all myself! I'll hang them over the lampposts!"

The servants and Borisov waited until he had shouted himself out. When he quieted down, Borisov said, "I think, sir, we should drive to Maria Nikoláyevna's house. I know, it's late, but I am sure, she won't mind."

"Yes! Yes! Let's go!" The general rushed to the door. "You lock the house again, Grigory Grigorievich. When I get back I'll ring three times, then I'll pause and ring three times more, so that you'll know who it is."

"Yes, sir … God bless you sir …"

The general and Borisov hurried out. They heard the locks click.

An almost identical procedure was repeated at Maria Nikoláyevna's house. They waited at the massive door, pulling the bell repeatedly until they heard Lieutenant Svirsky say slowly and threateningly, "State your business and identify yourselves."

"Lieutenant, it is your general speaking!" Rezánov bellowed. "Open the door!"

Svirsky recognized his voice. "In a moment, sir!" They heard noises as if something heavy was moved along the marble floor, and then the sound of the opening lock.

"Welcome back, General ... Hello, Lieutenant!" Svirsky was half-dressed in his riding britches and boots, but shirtless, with his revolver stuck into his belt. Behind him cowed the old butler, Stepan Petrovich, wearing a velvet robe and armed with a revolver, still pointed at the door.

"Put your gun down, man," the general ordered.

Embarrassed, the butler stuck the gun into his pocket.

On the top of the landing where the marble stairs split into the two wings stood Maria Nikoláyevna. Her hair in *papillotes,* wearing a Persian shawl over her shoulders, she too, had a gun in her hands, an elegant lady's pistol with an ivory handle. Despite the situation, the general chuckled. "Who are you going to shoot with that toy, Maria?" he asked sarcastically.

"You may be surprised," she replied. "The bullets are real, and they don't care whom they hit."

Svirsky pushed back a heavy cabinet to barricade the front door again "It became a necessity," he explained, "unwelcome visitors have a nasty habit of pushing their way in, once the door is opened. Such a nuisance!"

The general went up the staircase. He embraced Maria Nikoláyevna and they kissed each other's cheeks. "How is she?" he asked in a low voice.

"You'll see. Not good. The doctor thinks that she might have had a serious concussion of the brain."

"Is she lucid?"

"She is, but she refuses to talk. My Ksusha or I are constantly with her, day or night, and there is the nurse also, but she doesn't talk to any of us. Not even to me. I hope she will respond to you."

Maria Nikoláyevna opened the door of Larissa's room. The general was surprised by the incongruity of the scene before him: a pink and blue and white girlish room with mirrors and flowers and a soft-hued Aubusson carpet and a fairy princess bed under a lace baldachin—and on the bed a woman who did not belong there. Her face was smashed into a mass of cuts and blue bruises, her swollen eyes shut.

She did not look like his wife. It was some miserable street creature.

He felt his eyes welling with tears. "My angel," he whispered as he knelt at the bed and lifted her hand. "My darling angel! What have they done to you!"

Varvara Mikháilovna remained unresponsive.

The postal strikes were finally settled by the order of the *Soviet Deputies* and Larissa received a long letter from her mother, sent to the Memorial Hospital. Sister Veronica delivered it to her personally.

Larissa had never seen Veronica dressed in civilian clothes, with her reddish hair in a fashionably puffed pile held together with small tortoiseshell combs.

"You look so different!" Larissa exclaimed. "You look beautiful!"

Veronica did look beautiful with her perfect English complexion and green eyes. Her longish chin and large teeth gave her a slightly masculine but attractive mien.

Veronica smiled. "You have never seen me out of uniform. Sometimes, even I forget that I am a woman with a body, and hair, not just Sister Veronica impersonating a nun!"

"She even *talks* differently," Larissa thought but did not say.

"Everybody at the hospital sends regards and best wishes, including our new boss, Glafíra Ivánovna. I never expected that that *ball of fat* possessed such a nasty disposition. She *rules* the hospital now. Whoever displeases her has to face the *Comrades' Court* where she is Chief Justice. They already gave Doctor Shubin a written warning. He cannot use the automobile without written permission from the Soviet!"

"Dear Lord!"

"Yes, it is kind of awful, but it's also funny. Doctor Shubin is terrified of her."

"What about you? Does she bother you?"

"So far, no. She knows that I am a British citizen and she has no jurisdiction over me. But she is enforcing *Order Number One*, so no more English is to be spoken around the hospital. Even the Latin names of medications have to be translated into Russian. Anyway, how do you feel?"

"I feel pretty well. For a while I was worried that I might have a miscarriage, but Doctor Gottlieb reassured me that *spotting* happens quite often during pregnancies."

"That's true. You probably did not know, but I was also trained in obstetrics. So, if your Doctor needs an assistant, when the time comes,

I am available to help, my little friend. Now, I must go and leave you to read your mother's letter."

"Will you come again? I would like you to meet my friend Julia and her family."

"I'll visit you next week on my day off and I'll stay a little longer. I missed you!" She kissed Larissa on her cheek, a gesture that would have been impossible for *Sister* Veronica. But then, she wasn't a Chief Nurse now. She was her *friend* Veronica!

From the first sentences of her mother's letter, Larissa knew that there was no good news. Maria Nikoláyevna did not try to soften the truth. She wrote unsparingly about every facet of their new life, ending with a *mother's* order that Larissa stay in Odessa and under no circumstances try to reach Petrograd by herself. *"In your delicate condition, I forbid you to take any chances traveling by train. I'll come to Odessa as soon as we make arrangements for Andrei's mother and then, you and I will go to Petrograd together, or we'll stay in Odessa until the baby is born. So 'stay put' my darling, as Ksusha would say. Speaking of Ksusha: she bought us three of the ugliest coats in the world. She is sewing her money into hers and then, she wants to sew all my jewelry into mine and yours. That's Ksusha, for you! So be well my dear little girl and write me about yourself. Let me know what you have heard from Andrúsha. I know only that he is well. His father is being kept informed of his whereabouts through the military channels."*

Larissa read the letter again and cried helplessly for Andrei's poor mother. She realized that her own mother's motives for insisting that she remain in Odessa were valid, but she felt abandoned. She thought, no matter how difficult and dangerous their lives were in Petrograd, they were there *together*, while here she was—all alone!

An old tale that Ksusha used to tell her when she was a little girl came into her mind: "There was an old peasant who was dying. He called his three sons to his bed. 'Bring me the broom,' the old man said to his sons. They shrugged but brought him a sturdy besom made of tree twigs. 'I want you to stay together. Tight as the twigs in this broom,' the old man said. 'No one will be able to break you if you are together. Try and break it,' he told his oldest son. The young man tried to break it and could not. The other two sons tried also, without success. 'Now, pull-out three twigs and try to break them, one after the other.' The young men did so without any trouble. 'So, do you understand what I meant when I said 'stay together'?' The young men nodded. The old man made the sign of the cross and died."

Ksusha always knew the simple truth.

Larissa smiled sadly at the recollection.

Her pregnancy was reaching its half-point. She was feeling strong, her debilitating nausea over, but her mood swings were disturbing. She could change from laughing to tears within a couple of seconds, without any real reason. She attributed it to her need for her family. She read and re-read Andrei's and her mother's letters until she knew them by heart.

Andrei's letters were short and filled with endearments, reminiscences of their short days together, and worry about her health. It amused her when Andrei suggested that they should start thinking of a name for their baby. By tradition, if they had a boy, he should be named after one of the grandfathers. But, which one? Since both grandfathers were equally rich and respected, there was no need to be political for the sake of the inheritance. Andrei suggested writing their names on two pieces of paper and letting Egórov draw one. Egórov, of course, would be the baby's Godfather. He had already agreed. If they had a girl, they would have to be more diplomatic, for both of the grandmothers were formidable ladies—one with her opinions, the other with her reminiscences.

It touched her that Andrei tried to amuse her with his puny attempts at humor. She knew that there was nothing amusing or humorous in his life. In her stead, she too tried to cheer him with her descriptions of Julia's colorful family.

"I have finally met Julia's father, an enterprising charmer who isn't a stranger to the local jail. He's a dealer in many things and his schemes often go wrong. But he is always charming, always finding some plausible excuse for his misfortunes. He has friends everywhere, including the local police, which is strange in the atmosphere of mutual hatred between the Odessa police and the Jews. He performs little favors for both sides, and he knows how to twist some arms too, when he needs to," she wrote.

Larissa liked Julia's father. She had never met anyone as colorful as Isaak Yákovlevich Cohen. He entertained her with amusing stories about Jewish life. Julia had told her that the stories came from the Sholom Aleichem books, but her father insisted that they were from his own life. Larissa enjoyed the stories, not bothering about their origins.

Isaak's wife and daughter did not have much respect for Isaak, but they loved him and forgave him anything as if he were a sweet but mischievous child. "He is nothing but a small time crook who manipulates people," Minna Solomónovna said, dismissing him with a shrug of her plump shoulders.

Larissa refused to believe it. She liked him and the whole family. She especially enjoyed Julia's young son, Yasha. *"He looks like an Italian boy from a Renaissance painting, like a younger brother of Romeo, if Romeo had a younger brother,"* Larissa wrote to Andrei. *"He is a tall, thin boy with a serious face, beautiful dark eyes and curly black hair. He is in love with me. Don't be jealous: he is only twelve years old!*

I often accompany Yasha on the pianino when he plays Kreisler bagatelles on his violin. He is quite good. However I can't raise enough enthusiasm to learn chess from him: he intimidates me with his earnestness. He is the Odessa Chess Champion! At his age! Julia's mother reminds me of it almost every day. She is the proudest grand-mother in the world!"

Indeed, Julia's mother adored her grandson. She constantly patted his head, or kissed him juicily with her thick demanding lips. Minna Solomonovna was a kisser and a hugger as Larissa had discovered to her own embarrassment. But she tolerated the moist kisses and the nervous giggle, knowing the tragic story of its origin.

Julia and Larissa took daily trips with Akim, his open carriage rolling slowly along the leafy boulevards and along cliffs overlooking the sea, as the two women hid from the sun under white parasols. The three of them, so different in their backgrounds, established a peculiar friendship that provided security on their trips through the beautiful city with its undercurrent of constant danger. To reassure the women, Akim showed them a big Nagant gun that he kept under his seat. "Don't you worry ladies, I am a good shot, I have a fast little horse and I swear to God, I will not let anything bad happen to you!"

Julia was forced to close her salon. No one ordered expensive clothes anymore. Besides, it had been seriously vandalized. Two large plate glass vitrines were smashed, the display manikins beheaded, and the elegant clothes they were displaying torn to shreds.

"It must have been some Bolshevik sailors who did it," Akim said as they drove by the locked shop.

Julia agreed. "Yes, it must have been someone who did not know that it was owned by my family. Locals wouldn't have *dared* to vandalize it, knowing my father and his pals would punish them promptly!"

"Are you going to reopen it?" Larissa asked.

"Perhaps, eventually. But not now. We are entering a different epoch in our lives, when elegance in any form, be it speech or fashion or manners, could be dangerous to one's survival. Many of us will have to become *invisible*, I am afraid, at least until we know who is in charge of our country."

"Yes, I begin to think so myself," Larissa said. "Let me tell you what happened to *my* family in Petrograd."

37

By the end of the month, it was clear to everyone that the Kerensky offensive has failed. In Paris, at the meeting of the Allied Governments, a message from the Supreme Allied Commander warned the delegates about the probability that Russia would defect from the Alliance. The Central Powers then would move their mighty armies from the Russian front to reinforce their troops fighting against the Anglo-French forces. It would be disastrous for the Allies.

On the Southwestern front, the Russian retreat continued. The Austro-German forces recaptured the town of Stanislau and established a bridgehead on the Sereth River. The Russian Army was ordered to stop the enemy advance, but the soldiers refused. They requisitioned a train and left the front lines for the hinterlands of Russia.

General Rezánov was ordered to return to Stavka at once, despite his emergency leave of absence. He barely had time to arrange for a platoon of mounted Cossacks to move into his empty stables as special guards, leaving his ailing wife in the care of Maria Nikoláyevna. He and Borisov boarded the military train again, going back to Mogilev, where the stupefying game of musical chairs continued. After Kerensky's dismissal of General Brusílov, General Gutor took over the command but lasted only a week. Kerensky was trying to convince General Kornilov to take the post.

Rezánov was furious. He had nothing to report to his superiors at Stavka. Why was he going back?

Once in the privacy of his compartment he fumed and cursed and bellowed against the Provisional Government and Kerensky, the Soviets and Lenin, the leader of the scum.

Lieutenant Borisov worried that someone might hear and denounce him to the Bolshevik secret police, the *Cheka*, which had taken over from the Tsarist's Okhrana. "Don't shout, Vladímir Petrovich!" Borisov begged. "Someone may hear you!"

"I don't give a damn!" the general bellowed. "Let them all know how I feel! Our country is turning to shit, and all because of those morons at the Duma and Stavka!"

Borisov knew better than to try to pacify his commander, but he hung their coats over the compartment door hoping that it might muffle the sound of the general's angry voice.

At Stavka a dozen generals, twice as many colonels, and at least twenty other officers, gathered for an emergency conference.

The room shone with glossy boots, its aroma a mixture of expensive tobacco, boot polish, and eau de cologne. It was ablaze with gold epaulettes and aiguillettes, Crosses of St. George and St. Anne and St. Vladímir, plus many colorful decorations from the Allied Governments.

Only Kerensky had nothing on his military tunic. His slender body seemed to be lost among the colorful crowd of the chesty military elite. He looked vulnerable and insignificant, like a gray bantam rooster among fancy peacocks.

Kerensky called the conference to order. General Denikin suggested the immediate revocation of the Declaration of Rights of the Soldiers to participate in the decision making, as a means for reestablishing military discipline. He recommended the reintroduction of the death penalty for desertion.

Kerensky objected that it would only invite more anarchy and the massacre of officers.

General Denikin's suggestion was supported by General Alexeyev and all other General Staff officers. Encouraged, Denikin read a message from General Kornilov who demanded the reintroduction of the death penalty as a condition of taking command of the Russian Army.

Kornilov made several other demands.

First: the Provisional Government must have control over military decisions without interference from the Soldiers committees. Second: there must be the cessation of all Bolshevik agitation. Third: the immediate arrest of Vladímir Lenin and his cohorts.

Kerensky agreed to all proposals.

General Lavrenty Kornilov became the Supreme Commander of Russian Armed Forces.

The first news about *raspráva*, the reprisals against the Imperial Family, reached the public through the Bolshevik newspapers: Grand Dukes Mikhail and Paul, the Tsar's younger brothers, were arrested by order of the Petrograd Soviet. Several other members of the Tsar's family left the city for their estates in the Crimea as a precaution.

The fate of the deposed monarch was now in real danger. The Tsar and his family still lived under house arrest at the Alexandrovsky Palace in Tsárskoye Selo, guarded by the Bolshevik Red Guards. The liberal-minded intelligencia leaders of the Provisional Government wished to bring the Tsar to public trial, but with the arrest of his brothers, it became clear that the Bolsheviks had other designs.

Kerensky believed that it was in the interest of Russia's international prestige that the Tsar be brought before the Court and judged *openly* before the world. It would certainly justify the revolution. Of course, the verdict could be predicted: Nikolaí would be found guilty as charged and exiled, but it would be done *democratically!* Nothing could be worse than to allow the Bolsheviks to deal with the Tsar in their own way!

Known to less than six people, under the greatest secrecy, Kerensky arranged that the Tsar and his family, together with a large retinue of retainers, a doctor, the children's tutors, and two pet dogs were to be transported to the remote Siberian town of Tobolsk.

The Tsar's party was to travel in a special train marked as a Japanese Red Cross Mission. By coincidence, their voyage was to take them through the region where Rasputin was born.

General Rezánov returned to Petrograd, this time without any delays along the way.

It was late in the evening and he had to postpone until morning his visit with his wife at Maria Nikoláyevna's house. It gave him enough time to appraise his losses.

In addition to the theft of four fine horses, his expensive American automobile, and of table silver, he had also suffered the loss of his wife's furs and other clothes. He wasn't surprised to see all the blankets and goose down pillows pulled off the beds: peasants valued blankets and pillows.

The small Cossack unit that he had engaged to guard his empty house made a mess of the well-organized stables. The Cossacks ignored the toilet that was attached to the stables and relieved themselves on the straw-covered floors. They did not bother to clean after their horses either, and the clean modern building with electricity and running water had the smell and the look of the proverbial Augean stables.

Grigory Grigorievich, the general's butler, reported that it was impossible to hire anybody to clean the stables. "I tried, Your Excellency …. I tried to hire some peasants at the Gostinny Dvor, but they laughed at me. They shouted, 'let your master clean the … I am afraid they used the most foul language, sir! The people on the streets are very sensitive to their new status, sir. They say that they are *liberated* men and that … that their former masters must serve *them*. They don't even want money anymore. But of course, money isn't worth anything … The Tsar's paper money is nothing but colorful pictures, and nobody believes that the new money is worth the paper it is printed on. They demand gold! But if someone *shows* any gold coins, he is robbed on the spot, or even worse, killed!"

General Rezánov paced the floor of his study.

"Well, don't cry, Grigory Grigorievich," he finally said. "I can shovel the manure into the yard so it can be hauled away. It has to be done. Find me some rubber boots and rough pants. I can't push horse shit in my uniform!"

"Yes, sir! There are rubber boots and overalls that the stablemen left behind when they emptied the stables."

"How considerate of them!" the general said, his face twisted in an angry grimace.

That night the general, with his wife's little dog and his two loyal servants appeared at Maria Nikoláyevna's door.

"We beg refuge at your fine castle, kind Lady!" The general exclaimed with the dramatic gestures of a bad actor. "Cruel scoundrels pillaged our humble domicile and left us destitute. Dear Christian Lady, will you allow us, poor beggars now, to set our tents in your yard for a few days?"

Maria Nikoláyevna laughed. "Come in, come in, you poor, exhausted pilgrims!" she exclaimed. "Stepan Petrovich will take care of your loyal retainers, but you, my *brave knight without reproach* and your shivering little beastie, that looks like a rat, but I am sure is of a noble ancestry, please follow me," she made a low curtsy before him.

Rezánov laughed. "May all the saints in heaven bless you," he lowered on one knee and kissed her hand. He noticed that there were no rings on her fingers; even the gold wedding ring was gone. "A sign of our times," he thought.

"Alright," Maria Nikoláyevna changed her tone. "Enough hilarity. You can take the second guest room on the right. Lieutenant Svirsky is in the first one."

"Let me see my wife. Is she any better?"

"No, my dear. She is the same, unresponsive. Her bruises are healing well, but she still doesn't talk. She cries a lot, quietly, without making any noise. Tears just keep rolling down her face."

"My poor darling," the general said, going up the stairs, Maria Nikoláyevna behind him.

Varvara Mikháilovna was lying on her back, her eyes shut, her arms stretched stiffly next to her body. The room was full of sunshine, and a light breeze moved the lace curtains on the open windows. Ksusha was dozing in the armchair next to the bed.

"Várya!" the general called softly. "How do you feel, my dearest?" There was no reply or any sign that she had heard him.

"She is like that most of the time," Ksusha said, waking up.

The general sighed. "What did the doctor say?" he turned to Maria Nikoláyevna.

"Nothing much. He thinks that Varvara *can* talk, but just doesn't *want* to. We must wait, that's all."

"Well, we'll wait," he said placing the little dog on his wife's chest. The dog sniffed at the blanket and gave a quick lick to his mistress' chin.

"Bijou! My sweet little darling!" Varvara cried, opening her eyes and clamping her hands around the warm, silky body of the little Yorkshire terrier. The dog licked her face as she laughed happily, her mouth stretched in a grotesque smile of broken teeth.

38

Russia's Air Force units were less affected by the disturbances at the fronts than her other armed forces. The officer-pilots and the mechanics still treated each other with respect. Unfortunately, that dedication was not shared by the auxiliary troops attached to the airfields. In no time, the soldiers became indoctrinated by the Bolshevik Commissars who had sprung up like mushrooms after a rain. Scions of the hereditary military elite were no longer eager to join the service, and this forced flight schools to start training non-commissioned men as pilots. The glamour of being a pilot had been tarnished.

Egórov welcomed the new men. Like Kozakov, he took them under his wing for their first few missions, quickly discovering that they were as brave and eager to fly as the officer-pilots. However, they were not good as observers. Their lack of education in mathematics and geography, their poor understanding of topography and navigation, made them unreliable observers.

Egórov thought of establishing a program of remedial education for the new pilots.

"Would you be interested in giving talks on topography and simple map reading, Andrúshka? The poor chaps are like blind puppies when it comes to maps! We must do something about it. They are not dumb; I am sure we can teach them."

Andrei put down a letter from his father. His face was twisted. He could think only of destroying those who had robbed his family, who had almost killed his mother and caused his father to shovel horse shit. "Read this!" He stuck the letter into Egórov's hand, threw himself on his cot, and buried his face in a pillow.

Hatred of the whole lower class consumed him. He, who had never abused anyone, who had always been polite to everyone, suddenly realized that the servants and the soldiers probably had *never* loved him or his family.

Egórov read the letter. He glanced at Andrei still stretched face down on his cot. Egórov recalled his meeting with Andrei's parents, the gruff, authoritarian general and his wife, a fragile, aging beauty. They were so hospitable and sympathetic! They were so gentle with his feelings. But of course, he was *one of them*. He could not imagine either of them giving much thought to the intimate feelings of their *servants*.

"I am not really surprised at the servants' actions," Egórov thought. "They are *not* kind and wise men and women from Tolstoy's novels. You can make one a footman in white gloves, but his fingernails will remain full of dirt. The more wealth is around him, the more envious he becomes. And then, all of a sudden, he is told that he is free to take what he lusts for! Take it! Take it all! It's all yours! What is he to do? Of course he *will take it!*"

Egórov read the letter again. It was bitterly vitriolic and yet pathetic in its impotence. The general realized that for the first time in his life he could do nothing about the change that had taken place in Russia. And he, a liberal-minded person who had welcomed the abdication of the Tsar, had never imagined that *he* would be treated as the enemy of his people.

"What will I do with Andrúshka?" Egórov thought. "He is falling apart."

Andrei *was* falling apart. His separation from Larissa weighed heavily on him. He could imagine how frightened she must be, alone and pregnant ... Andrei's anxiety reached its apogee with his father's letter. "What can I do to be of help to them?" he tormented himself. "I could desert and somehow make my way to Odessa and be with Larissa ... and then, what? I would be shot as a deserter. I can do nothing for anyone that I love," he thought bitterly.

However, one glimmer of hope arose from the blackness. The retreat of Russian troops on the Southwestern Front forced Kozakov's Air Detachment to be moved back. Andrei hoped that their base would be at Yassy again, only a half day trip by train from Odessa. Perhaps Egórov would grant him a short furlough. He even fantasized that he could be wounded lightly and dispatched back to Memorial Hospital. He had such sweet memories of that place, he thought, dismissing the pain, the humiliation of being unable to perform even his most private functions without help.

He thought with sweet nostalgia of Larissa and his parents and of Maria Nikoláyevna, often seeing them in his dreams, only to awaken to the grim reality. His imagination supplied him with visions of revenge against the Bolsheviks who had caused so much pain to him and to his loved ones.

Knowing that Andrei was full of dark thoughts, Egórov postponed elevating him to a position of leadership. "He's too full of hate to be entrusted with command of lower ranks," Egórov thought.

Andrei was grateful not to be given more responsibility. He needed only two more confirmed victories to be acclaimed as an ace, but he did not strive for it anymore. He was suspicious of men of lower ranks, suspecting them of treachery. When two new mechanics deserted the detachment, Andrei had his proof.

Egórov watched him with alarm. "The boy has changed," he thought. Even his appearance had changed. He had let his hair grow long rather than have it trimmed by the soldier barber. "He thinks the barber could be a Bolshevik!" Egórov thought.

Andrei realized that he had changed, but he dismissed Egórov's inquiries with a shrug. "Nothing is wrong with me. I am just annoyed."

Egórov sought the advice of old Doctor Barsky. "Something is wrong with our Andrei," he confessed. "I know you like the boy, and you probably have heard that he is going to be a father in a few months. Perhaps he is just nervous, but I think it is more serious. Talk to him, Doctor Barsky. Maybe he'll open up to you as an older man. His family has suffered greatly at the hands of the revolutionary sailors. And of course, there is his young bride, alone in Odessa, expecting a child in a few weeks! It could make even a *mature* man lose his mind, but our Andrúshka is not a *mature man*. He is only twenty-three years old! He is still a boy!"

Doctor Barsky agreed to see Andrei under the pretext of checking his healing wounds.

"Well, well, how do we feel, Lieutenant?" he greeted Andrei jovially. "Any pain in your leg? Those nasty wounds can hurt for months, or even years!"

"No, Doctor Barsky, the wound has healed well. Although, when I pull on my boots, my leg is too stiff. It's as if my skin is too tight and might split." Andrei replied. "I still limp and I need help getting in and out of the fuselage, but it's getting better," he added.

"Well, it's my duty to follow the recuperation of the most seriously injured men. Besides, I am compiling material for a book, which I want to write. It will be specifically about the war injuries of airmen."

"That sounds interesting," Andrei said, to be polite.

The doctor nodded. "Well, I hope so. I hope it may introduce an understanding of the *mental* state of military pilots. It is my belief that pilots stress themselves beyond any normal endurance. It is my belief also, that not all pilots are born killers, as some people say. Those who are not suffer even more because they *do become* killers!"

"He is talking about *me*," Andrei thought.

The doctor stood and went to the door of his office. "Platonich, be so kind as to bring us couple of glasses of tea and perhaps some honey," he said to his orderly who was in the hall washing medicine bottles in a tub of soapy water.

"Right away, Colonel," the old man replied wiping his hands on his trousers and saluting. The doctor smiled. "You are the only man, who is still saluting!" he exclaimed.

The doctor returned to his office. "Platonich has been my orderly for almost thirty years," he explained to Andrei. "Despite the position being abolished, he continues to assist me greatly. He's a good man."

"Do you *trust* him, Doctor Barsky?"

"With my very life. I trust him explicitly!"

"Then, let me tell you what happened to my parents last month!" Andrei said trying to speak calmly. "They too had long-serving people whom they trusted *explicitly with their lives.*"

Platonich brought in two glasses of dark tea in silver holders and a small crock of honey. "Anything else, Doctor?"

Doctor Barsky looked at Andrei inquiringly. "Anything else, Lieutenant?"

"No, thank you." Andrei felt the urgent need to unburden himself to the doctor. Platonich saluted and left the office.

Andrei began to talk.

"Well, what do you think?" Egórov asked Doctor Barsky two hours later. "Frankly, I am afraid to send him out on a mission in his current state of mind."

"I am not a psychiatrist, so I don't dare to offer a diagnosis, but I do agree with you. He is deeply depressed, but his depression doesn't seem to be the usual, submissive type. Andrei is full of *aggression.* I understand why you are reluctant to send him out. He could be a dangerous man in his present state of mind. He sees Bolsheviks under every bush."

"I thought so, too. He has always had such a sunny disposition, loved the whole world! I have never seen him suddenly so antagonistic and so aggressive in his thinking."

"He told me that he suffers strong headaches and sometimes even deafness right after the flights. It could be signs of a serious brain condition. If I recommend that he be sent for *observation* to ... let's say, back to Odessa Memorial Hospital, would you be willing to grant him a furlough?"

"I certainly would, even though we are getting short of really good pilots."

"Alright. I'll prepare the medical report about his condition and you must make sure that the Soviet Deputies approve it. If they don't—there will be nothing that I can do."

"I think Commissar Kóshkin will approve your recommendations. I have a good relationship with him. He approved my suggestion of remedial training for the new pilots. Actually, he was very enthusiastic about it!"

"Good! Then he owes you a favor."

39

The political situation in Russia was becoming worse with every passing day. The newly appointed General Kornilov became involved in a conspiracy to remove Alexander Kerensky from power. Kornilov ordered Cavalry Corps to move on Petrograd and dissolve the Provisional Government. The march was stopped near Gátchina. Instead of getting rid of Kerensky, it gave him an opportunity to declare himself *the dictator*. The Provisional Government resigned and Kerensky formed the *Third* Coalition Provisional Government with help from the Socialists.

Kerensky dealt swiftly with the conspirators. He issued an order to arrest Generals Kornilov and Denikin. Stavka was left virtually without a High Command, the seats in its musical chairs game suddenly empty. Kerensky re-appointed the ailing General Alexeyev to his old post of the Chief-of-Staff.

While the *new* Provisional Government resumed their ideological quarrels, the Bolsheviks steadily increased their power. They followed the doctrine of Communism, which most of them did not understand but interpreted as the promise of Freedom and *Land*. The Petrograd Soviet of Workers and Soldiers passed a resolution that Russia be immediately declared a Socialist Republic, that all land be given to the peasants and all industry be controlled by the workers. They simplified the idea of Communism as: *"to everyone by his needs, from everyone by his ability."* Even an illiterate peasant could understand that!

When Leon Trotsky was released from prison, the Bolsheviks appointed him the head of the Petrograd Soviet. He immediately armed the Red Guards in Petrograd, Moscow, and other industrial cities, forging them into an exclusive military unit with unlimited powers, answerable *only* to the Bolshevik leadership.

Kerensky tried to curb the powers of the Red Guards, but it was already too late. All attempts to disarm them were ignored. The Red Guards, the loosely knit groups of factory workers, deserting soldiers and the lower class city dwellers, were quickly becoming well-disciplined and ruthless revolutionary soldiers.

The war on all fronts continued. On the Romanian Front, the German Army attacked Munceli, but the Russians repelled the attack with the help of Kozakov's Air Detachment, which staged continuous raids and night bombings of the stalled German Army. In the ensuing halt of military action on the ground, the aircraft were re-deployed to strafe the reinforcements.

It was a brilliant morning with a few scudding clouds, the weather perfect for flying.

Egórov took charge of the first contact patrol. He pushed his Spad a couple of thousand feet above his formation, watching over his pilots from the commanding altitude, Andrei flying as his wingman.

Andrei felt good: Egórov had informed him that after this mission, he would be sent to Odessa Memorial for *observation*.

"Read, *to be with Larissa!*" Egórov told him confidentially. "For a *whole* month!" Andrei felt as if he were suffocating with happiness.

"I wonder how she looks ..." he thought. He could not imagine her pregnant. The only pregnant women he had seen were women of the lower class, who looked repulsive to his jaded eye. In his circles of society, pregnant women concealed their condition as long as possible and then stayed out of sight, re-emerging when the child was born and placed with a wet-nurse for breast feeding. "How does Larissa look?" he wondered, "Has she become ugly?"

Climbing higher over the no-man's land Andrei felt the familiar flow of adrenaline as his actions became instinctive. He and his machine were welded into one being, neither a machine nor a man. It was a strange, unnatural relationship, but he enjoyed it. However, as time went by, he began to discover some of the unpleasant side affects of constant flying, such as the physical fluctuations his body experienced when there were rapid changes of altitude. The sensations during intense maneuvering were disturbing. His arms and legs and his head would suddenly grow heavy, and he would feel as though he were being pressed into his seat, only to be released the next moment to become practically weightless—the price he had to pay for the challenges of aerobatics.

The planes left the no-man's land and crossed the enemy lines. Andrei observed the sky below and above him, on both sides and behind his aircraft, following the imaginary face of a clock with its twelve numbers.

Far on the horizon at one o'clock was a cluster of dark specks. They were German Fokkers, flying southwest in tight formation, away from the Russian lines.

There were six of them. Andrei watched them enviously. The matching new Fokkers were so slick and beautiful in their predatory silhouettes! In comparison, the motley Russian planes were of several different makes, looking drab and decrepit, their wings and fuselages patched with linen.

The Germans suddenly zoomed up, climbing to a higher altitude.

"They want to fight," Andrei thought, his body tightening. He glanced at Egórov who signaled the attack.

The Russians boldly broke into the German formation. They were evenly matched, six against six, and a furious fight erupted. Pilots were engaging and instantly disengaging with quick blasts from their machine guns, firing without using the gunsights. Adversaries zoomed and dived and banked and looped, firing at one another, barely avoiding collisions, demonstrating how fitting it was to describe their actions as a 'dogfight'.

Andrei dipped sharply and concentrated on the last red-nosed machine of the enemy formation. He was above the German, in a perfect position to attack. With the first burst of his machine guns he punctured the Fokker's fuel tank. The German was doomed. Andrei yelled exuberantly, full of self-confidence as if he were still a young cadet. He banked sharply to gain altitude again. In his periphery he saw the pilot of the blazing aircraft bolting overboard into space. Attached to his body was a harness with slender ropes connected to a parachute. It opened up like an umbrella, lowering the man gently toward the ground below. The burning aircraft spiraled down, overtaking the pilot's descent.

Andrei saw him floating down. "Why can't *we* have such useful contraptions?" he thought. But it was not a good time for contemplation: several tracer bullets hit his starboard wing. Andrei quickly banked and began to zigzag in an effort to shake off the enemy who had appeared on his tail.

One of the Russians coming out of a loop gave a short blast of his machine gun toward the parachute and the umbrella collapsed. The gentle floating became a rapid descent.

The Germans seemed eager to discontinue the fight. One by one they pulled out, resuming their previous course, minus one plane and one pilot.

The Russians resumed their contact patrol. There was no time to assess their injuries and the damage to their aircraft. The strafing mission still had to be carried on.

Egórov gave the signal to regroup. In a few more minutes they would to be upon their target, the road choked by troops and equipment.

Troops along the road were forewarned about the approach of aircraft by a sudden barrage from the Archies. Some men rushed into ditches, others plastered themselves on the dusty ground, and a small unit of cavalry stampeded away from the road into the protection of the woods. The success of the Russian mission now depended on the speed of their flight and the terror they brought in their assault.

The operation was one of utter simplicity: they had to pass through a cordon of exploding eighteen-pound shells from the anti-aircraft batteries. They had to swoop down to thirty or forty feet above the ground in a straight line, fire at the troops below, soar up, bank sharply, and repeat the procedure again, becoming the target of the Archies and every machine gun and rifle from the troops below.

Egórov signaled that there would be only two approaches. He dived toward the road, keeping his aircraft in a straight line, both of his machine guns blazing.

Andrei and the others followed. It was almost as if they were practicing takeoffs and landings at Flight School, it was so easy, except that now they carried death. Andrei hated strafing, considering it *barbaric*, but then, the whole idea of war was *barbaric*. "Just do it, and don't torment yourself trying to justify it," Egórov had advised him when he had confessed his doubts. "If you don't do it to *them*, they'll do it to *you!*"

During the second approach Andrei felt a sharp sting in his left shoulder. "I am hit!" he thought. "Oh, God! I am hit! Not again!"

He tightened his grip on the machine gun and opened fire. The earth seemed to be coming up to meet him. Coming out of his swoop and zooming up, Andrei once more became the target of the Archies.

"Dear Lord, don't let me die," he prayed, not knowing yet how serious his wound was. He touched his upper arm. The sleeve of his leather coat was torn and bloody, but there was no big pain, only heaviness and throbbing. "Spare me, dear Lord," he prayed as the peculiar odor of exploding bombs choked him. He pulled his scarf over his mouth and nose, feeling suffocated by the smell of explosions.

Finally, the Russians met at five thousand feet, all machines with badly torn wing coverings and new holes in their fuselages, but still able to fly. The six pilots fell into their positions in the formation and Egórov led them home. He fervently hoped that there would be no challenges along the way. They were sitting ducks: they had used all of their ammunition. He unbuttoned the holster of his gun, knowing that his pilots did the same. Just in case …

Andrei's wound was not life threatening, but it was very painful. It was from a single rifle shot, delivered by some soldier on the ground during Andrei's second approach. He was hit in his upper left arm, almost at the shoulder. Three more pilots were wounded, none of them requiring hospitalization, all receiving the most desired classification of 'ambulatory patient', which excused them from active duty for at least a week.

Egórov escaped being wounded, but his right cheekbone was badly bruised, the purple swelling already spreading around his face. "I hit the edge of the cockpit with my face when an Archie exploded under my plane," he told Doctor Barsky. "I was thinking, 'there goes my handsome nose!'"

The doctor chuckled. "No, my dear fellow, you're in luck. Your noble proboscis is still intact!"

Andrei's wound required awkward bandaging. To keep it from sliding down his arm, it had to encircle his chest and back and shoulder, making his torso immobile on his left side.

"If you are lucky and escape an infection, you should heal very quickly," Doctor Barsky told him. "If you leave tomorrow, you won't need a change of bandage until Odessa. Can you do it?"

"Of course, he can do it!" Egórov exclaimed. "I'll fly him to Yassy myself and put him on the train!"

"Let's hope that the trains are back to normal," the doctor said. "I'll give you some pain-killing medication to take along, but use it sparingly. I wish we could send an orderly with you, to help in case of emergency."

"I'll be alright," Andrei said. "I have some experience with pain and I have developed a certain amount of tolerance to it," he smiled crookedly remembering his suffering some months before. *That* was unbearable.

Andrei slept well without the medicine, but a deep, nagging pain attacked his left arm and shoulder in the morning.

"Alright, my friend, let's get going," Egórov greeted him in the mess tent. "I called Yassy aerodrome and they told me that their train connection with Odessa is almost normal again. So, I booked a sleeping car for you and your companion."

"My companion?" Andrei asked in surprise.

"Yes, my friend. Our Commissar Igor Kóshkin is going to Odessa with you! Well, not exactly *'with you.'* He is going to some Bolshevik conference there, but he has agreed to be of help should you need it."

"Well ... But how is *he* going to get to Yassy?"

"Oh, that's the beauty of it! He had asked for *my* help in getting to Yassy to catch the train. I offered him a plane and a pilot! *Quid pro quo!* So, the four of us will be on our way shortly!"

Egórov left Lieutenant Savchenko in command of the First Air Detachment Group for six hours, enough time for a round trip to Yassy. He was reassured by Commissar Kóshkin's participation in the scheme: there would be no objection from the Soviet about his private use of the aircraft. Egórov ordered one of the new pilots, Ivan Toporkóv, whom he suspected of having Bolshevik tendencies, to be the pilot for Kóshkin. "I don't want to expose any of our pilots to Bolshevik propaganda," he thought. "It will be interesting, though, to see how Kóshkin will try to recruit our Andrúshka for their cause. He'll try, I am sure! Andrúshka would be such *a catch!*"

Andrei and Egórov greeted Igor Kóshkin and Ivan Toporkóv at the officers mess hall.

"Well, Lieutenant, we'll have several hours to spend together," Kóshkin said. "Do you think we should bring along some table games or should conversation be enough?"

"I might be not a good conversationalist right now, considering the painkillers they've given me," Andrei replied. "But if I remember correctly from my last trip on that train, the porter keeps dominos and checkers available. But I think, we should get better acquainted on this trip. The dominos can wait."

"I agree," Kóshkin said with a smile. "Besides, I've heard that dominos are out of favor among the revolutionaries. The former Tsar plays it all the time with his guards!" Kóshkin said, looking at Andrei with a sly smile on his young face. 'So, dominos are considered by some as a *counter-revolutionary* activity!" he finished, laughing. The others for a moment did not know how to react, but they joined Kóshkin in his hilarity.

"I have always been a great admirer of yours, Lieutenant. Ever since your ride on the wing of that airplane," Kóshkin continued seriously. "I am looking forward to knowing you better."

"Thank you," Andrei replied politely.

"Andrúshka will hold his own!" Egórov thought. "Flattery is not going to get him!"

The two Spad two-seaters set their course toward Yassy aerodrome. Andrei's arm hurt him badly: every breath he took sent pain down his whole left side. Egórov watched as Andrei tried to find a more comfortable position for his bandaged arm. "Don't be a hero, take the pill!" he shouted, his own face swollen, the lids of one eye looking as if they were glued together.

Andrei nodded. With his right hand he searched his hip pocket for the little tin box of pills.

⧉ 40 ⧉

The Yassy airdrome looked different from the time that Kozakov's First Air Detachment called it home. It was back in the possession of the Romanian government, whose banner waved from a mast. All signs were now in Romanian or French instead of Russian.

The two Spads landed one after another. Egórov helped Andrei to get out of the confines of the narrow fuselage.

"Are you taking us to the railroad station?" Andrei asked.

"Yes. I want to be sure that nothing goes wrong with the arrangements. Someone from the Memorial will meet you in Odessa .... Don't be surprised if it happens to be Glafíra Ivánovna!" he couldn't resist a tease.

Andrei finally laughed. "Oh, shut up!"

"I will be met by some comrade from the Odessa Soviet," Kóshkin said.

"So much the better. If you don't get along during the journey, you won't need to see one another after that! Now, let's get you boys to the station. As I remember, there used to be a few carriages-for-hire outside the aerodrome. I hope they are still there!" He picked up Andrei's valise. "Let's go, *bratíshka!*"

The train for Odessa was waiting on a sidetrack, still without its locomotive. It was possible that the trip might be cancelled: there were reports of sabotage along the way. However, Egórov's worry lay with his squadrons, which were without an accredited commander. Should anything happen at the aerodrome, he would be held responsible.

He decided not to wait for Andrei's departure. He bid 'safe journey' to Andrei and Kóshkin and, followed by Toporkóv, departed.

Igor Kóshkin's secret assignment in Odessa was to establish a liaison between the pilots of the Navy Aviation in the Black Sea Command and those on the Southwestern front. "Wouldn't it be *great* if I could recruit Rezánov!" he fantasized as they clattered in an old carriage over the stone-paved road toward the station. "A hero, young and good-looking! With his family background, he could become a magnet for some other young officers ... We need well-educated people in our ranks," he thought. He had heard enough gossip about Andrei to know that his family held liberal views. Andrei was not a monarchist, and that meant that he could be made to listen to the Bolsheviks' ideas, Kóshkin thought. "I must be very subtle in my approach ... just be conversational ... His wife is about to have a child ... I suppose, by helping him to get back to her at that time ... Yes! *That* will be the way. I will authorize our Soviet to let him go back when the time comes. It will show our *humanism!*" Kóshkin began to weave a plot to entice Andrei to the Bolshevik cause.

Andrei and Kóshkin settled in their two-berth compartment. An old porter approached Andrei. "I remember you, Lieutenant," he said. "You were going to Odessa last winter, to take your wife to her mother in Petrograd!"

"You have a good memory, my friend!" Andrei smiled. "Well, I did not succeed in taking her to Petrograd. She is *still* in Odessa. Do you know how soon we'll start moving?"

"As soon as they bring the locomotive."

"When will it be?" Kóshkin asked sharply.

"Who knows?" The old man shrugged his shoulders. "I can see you were wounded again, Lieutenant?" he wanted to continue the conversation with Andrei.

"Yes, I was. I forgot your name!" Andrei asked, trying to discontinue the chat in a polite way.

"They call me Osip."

"But what is your patronymic?"

"Ivanich."

"Do us a favor, Osip Ivanich, get us some hot tea! I am frozen stiff after our flight!"

"Right away, Lieutenant, right away," the old man bustled, hurrying into his kitchen corner to check on the puffing samovar.

Kóshkin watched the little scene with interest. It showed him that the lieutenant was obeying *Order Number One*: he addressed the servant using the polite form and not just his first name.

There was an awkward silence, both young men feeling uncomfortable with one another. Kóshkin concentrated his attention on the pile of gravel outside the car's window, while Andrei took time in trying to hang his heavy flight coat, which had a gaping hole from the bullet. The coat kept slipping out of his good hand. In exasperation Andrei cursed, using the juiciest of peasant swear words.

Kóshkin laughed. "Let me help! I did not realize that a gentleman, like you, even *knew* such vile words!" The ice was broken.

"You'd be surprised," Andrei replied, embarrassed. He hated Russian curses. They always involved the word *mother*. He preferred to curse in French.

Kóshkin hanged the coat on a small hook. "I don't like swear words," he said. "But dealing with the uneducated men, who swear *conversationally*, made me immune to the words. However, hearing *you* ..."

"I am sorry that I have shocked you," Andrei said.

"No, no! I wasn't shocked, just ... surprised! And *amused*, I must say!"

"Here you are, gentlemen," the porter said, placing a tray with the tea and little cakes on the foldable table between the berths. "Enjoy!"

"Thank you, Osip Ivanich," Andrei said.

"You shouldn't have called us 'gentlemen,'" Kóshkin said. "We don't use this word anymore. You should have called us 'comrades'!"

The porter looked from one young man to another, Andrei avoiding his eyes. The old man shook his head. "No, sir, I can't call you a *'comrade,'*" he said seriously. "I have never met you before. We cannot be *comrades.*" He made a slight bow with his head and left the compartment with dignity.

Kóshkin and Andrei concentrated on their tea. The tension returned.

There was a shrill whistle announcing the arrival of the locomotive. "Thank God," they both thought.

Andrei kept silent. He thought about Larissa. "Does she have enough food, good food, I mean. I wish she were with the Shubins," he thought, "rather than with some bogus *French modiste.* Who are these new Jewish friends, anyway? She wrote that the father of that family was a crook! How *safe* is it for her to live in their house?" he asked himself.

"Do you know what is Jewish people's basic food?" he asked Kóshkin.

"Jewish people? How would I know? I am not a Jew. Why do you ask?" Kóshkin was surprised.

"My wife is rooming with a Jewish family. She is expecting. I don't know what the Jewish pregnant women are supposed to eat. With the general shortages of food, I don't know whether she has the proper diet!"

"All I know is that the Jews in Petrograd have all become Russian, with Russian names," Kóshkin said sarcastically. "In the leadership of my own party it seems that only Lenin and I are *ethnically* Russian. The rest of them, Trotsky, Kamenev, Zinoviev, Rykov and on and on, are all Jews. But they probably eat the same cabbage soups and oats kasha, as we do. But why is she living with the Jews? Don't you have Russian friends?" he sounded contemptuous.

"It's a long story … You sound as if you *disapprove* of the Jews," Andrei said.

"I *do.* Like all Russians, I dislike and distrust them."

"But why? Did they do something terrible to you or to your family?" he almost said *'as your comrades have done to my family'* but held his tongue.

"No. I just don't *like* them. No reason."

"Well, then you are going to the wrong place, my friend. Odessa is full of Jews!"

Kóshkin did not like the way their conversation was heading. "Anyway, I do know that they eat a lot of matzos, whatever it is, and stuffed fish," he concluded with irritation, "Probably not good for pregnant women, either."

"Probably not ... I think, I'll take a nap," Andrei said. He too, did not like their conversation. "My wound is hurting like hell. I'll take a pill and try to sleep."

The old train rattled and swayed on its worn-out suspensions, the unfinished tea splashing from side to side in their glasses, Andrei's coat swinging on the door back and forth as if it were some enormous pendulum.

The monotonous landscape beyond the window gradually changed, leaving behind the denuded fields and abandoned villages disfigured by artillery fire. As the train clattered further southeast, neat white-washed Romanian villages and lush orchards untouched by war came into view, soon to be replaced by Ukrainian villages with thickly-thatched roofs, white-washed walls and more orchards.

"It looks all the same," Kóshkin thought. "Boring and prosperous, probably not touched by the revolutionary spirit ..." He could not sleep, random thoughts flitting through his mind. He felt that he had said *something* that turned Andrei against him. What was it? Certainly not his admission that he *disliked* Jews? "Everybody in Russia dislikes Jews," he thought. "But why? I have no idea."

He watched Andrei sleep, his injured arm resting on his chest. "It won't be easy to win his trust," he thought. "I would've never believed that *he* was a Jew-lover!"

Larissa was not aware that Andrei was on his way to Odessa. She had not heard from him for more than two weeks and she fretted. She searched the newspapers for some news about the Romanian front, finding instead more political decrees from the Bolsheviks and news indicating that America was getting closer than ever to entering the war.

Apparently, German Foreign Minister Arthur Zimmerman had dispatched a telegram to the German Ambassador in Mexico, suggesting that they involve Mexico, and perhaps Japan, in the war against the Allied Powers. The telegram was quoted in the press. As a reward for Mexican participation in *"making war and peace together"* Mexico would receive generous financial support and reclaim Texas, New Mexico and Arizona.

The Zimmerman telegram created general upheaval and a call to arm American merchant ships with defensive arms. American President

Woodrow Wilson appeared before a joint session of the Sixty-fourth Congress. As if to justify his request a German U-boat sank an Allied merchant ship *Laconia*.

The political situation ment nothing to Larissa. Her interests in life narrowed down to worry about Andrei and to the movements of the child in her womb. She desperately missed her mother, but as a true daughter of Maria Nikoláyevna, she steeled her mind and shut down her emotions, accepting the fact that most likely, she would give birth to her child among strangers, *friendly* strangers, but strangers nevertheless.

Julia watched her affectionately. She admired her fighting spirit, thinking of the ways she could help her, so young and so vulnerable. Knowing that Larissa loved music, Julia began taking her to concerts in the park, bringing along Yasha. Contrary to the tradition of not talking about painful subjects, Julia tried to make Larissa *talk* about her worries instead of locking them up in her heart. It was a new trend arising from the teachings of an Austrian professor, Sigmund Freud. It made sense to Julia. She herself felt better after talking to someone about her problems instead of bottling them.

"How is your mother?" she asked, trying to get Larissa to open up. "When is she coming to Odessa?"

Larissa smiled sadly. "She is still optimistic, but I don't think that she will be able to come. She writes that civilian travel is prohibited. And, she wrote, some terrible things had happened to Andrei's parents. Their own servants *robbed* them and his mother was almost murdered. She is very ill, and is staying at my mother's house. But where is Andrei's *father*? Is he still at Stavka in Mogilev? Is he ill? Or arrested? Or, even … murdered? Mother did not mention anything about him! Maybe she is afraid of the censors who read our mail, or she did not want to upset me, but of course, she *did upset* me!" Larissa began to cry.

"And so did I!" Julia thought. "Perhaps I shouldn't ask her all these questions!" She put her arm around Larissa's shoulders and kissed her cheek . "You poor child … don't cry … it will upset your baby. Let me feel it kick!"

Larissa opened her shawl and Julia placed her hand on Larissa's round abdomen. "She is probably asleep," Larissa said, her eyes still brimming with tears.

"How do you know that it is a '*she*'?"

"I call the baby one time *'she'* and the next time *'he.'* I don't want to play favorites!" She tried to smile.

"You silly goose!" The baby gave a strong kick.

"She probably did not like that you called me *'silly goose'!*" Larissa laughed, at last.

That afternoon, Doctor Gottlieb came to check on Larissa. "I have some good news for you, Larochka! Since you have no telephone here, Professor Shubin telephoned *me* to let you know that your husband is on his way to Odessa, *right now*! Someone at Memorial Hospital received a call from a doctor at the front, to expect your husband at the Memorial …"

Larissa blanched. 'He is wounded! I knew it!" She grabbed at a chair for support.

"No, no, no!" cried Doctor Gottlieb. "He is fine! Well, he is not *totally* fine, but his wound apparently is not serious," he corrected himself, angry that he had talked himself into a hole. "He is being sent to Odessa for *mental observation* … nothing more!"

"Mental observation?" Larissa cried in horror. "Is he … *crazy?*"

"No, no, no! He is not *crazy* … he is … I don't know. You must ask Professor Shubin … " Doctor Gottlieb became totally flustered. He had hoped to cheer up his young patient, but instead he embarrassed himself as a meddling old fool! "I should've left Shubin to deal with it," he thought.

Julia took the situation in her own hands . "So, when are we to expect to have Lieutenant Rezánov among us?" she asked calmly.

"I don't know, Júlenka. Perhaps, tomorrow? Or the next day? Ask Professor Shubin. I really can't tell you anything more." He took Larissa's hand and counted her pulse. It was racing. He felt guilty that he had upset her. He tried to remedy his error. "And how do we feel this wonderful sunny day?" he began with a forced smile. "Did we eat all our fruits and vegetables and Greek-style yogurt? And how is our baby? Kicking a lot?"

Larissa pulled herself together and replied, "Yes, to all your questions." She wanted him to leave so she could go to Memorial Hospital. "I have no complaints. I feel very good."

"Fine, fine! Perhaps you would like to play some Mendelssohn with me?"

"Not tonight, Doctor. I feel very tired."

"You have just said that you were feeling very good! So which is it?" the doctor insisted with a smile.

"Ah, what's the difference!" Larissa exploded, "I don't *care* to play the piano right now! And I don't *know* how I feel! All I want to know is *what's wrong with my husband!*"

Julia glared at the doctor. "I'll take you to the Memorial right now!" she said to Larissa. "Someone there will know something!"

"Thank you, Julia ... I am sorry, Doctor, I was rude."

"Never mind, my dear, I understand. Pregnant women go through sudden changes in their moods, it's to be expected. I am accustomed to it. Would you like me to accompany you?"

"No, thank you, Doctor, Julia will know what to do." Larissa controlled her temper. "Thank you for bringing me the news about my husband."

"You are welcome. I am sorry that I couldn't give you more information but ..."

"It's alright!" Larissa raised her voice. "Please go!"

"Yes, Doctor Gottlieb, please go. Larissa must get ready," Julia said, placing her hand on his arm and steering him to the door.

Doctor Shubin met Larissa with the outstretched arms. "Larochka, my treasure, how well you look!" he exclaimed, kissing her on both cheeks. "How do you feel?"

"I feel fine, Arkady Petrovich, the baby is kicking and I sing to him!"

Julia smiled. "I think the child is probably overwhelmed by this plethora of music! My mother sings Jewish songs, Sister Veronica introduces him to English ditties, and my son plays his violin!"

"Enough, enough," Larissa interrupted. "The baby is fine. What I want to know is how is *Andrei?* I know about him coming to Odessa for observation of his *mental state*. What does it mean?"

"He should be here tomorrow, that is, if the train remains on schedule," Doctor Shubin said. "As to his *mental* state ..." he looked around and lowered his voice, "I think there is nothing wrong with it. He has a wound in his left arm, but not having seen it, I cannot say anything about it. According to the telegraph report of Doctor Barsky, it is a simple flesh wound that ought heal quickly."

"But his *mental* state ..." Larissa insisted.

"I'll tell you about it later, but do not worry. To satisfy the request from the Soviet, we have invited a professor of psychology to evaluate your husband. We'll talk about it later, perhaps at your place. Here," he cautiously glanced around, *"the walls have ears,* as they say. So, go home, sing to your baby and don't you worry. I'll send Stepanich to Julia Isaakovna's house the moment I know anything. Perhaps we can even send an automobile to pick-up the Lieutenant, once we notify Glafíra Ivánovna of his arrival!" He winked. "Don't you worry!"

41

The train crawled along the Odessa platform and stopped. Surrounded by clouds of white steam, its locomotive exhaled a deep sigh of exhaustion. A small crowd of military men disembarked, with a sprinkling of dark-mustachioed and black-eyed Romanian merchants. There were no women or children among the passengers. Railroad travel was too dangerous to be attempted except in case of real need.

Andrei and Kóshkin stepped on the platform. Andrei had not expected to see Larissa, but there she was standing at the door to a passengers' waiting room.

"Larissa!" he shouted and ran toward her, forgetting all caution.

"Andrúsha!" she screamed, making her way through a thin crowd. They embraced awkwardly, his bandaged arm and her swollen abdomen in their way. "My angel, you're wounded!"

Kóshkin observed their reunion with envy: Lieutenant Rezánov was married to a beauty! Dressed in a simple skirt and a jacket as if she were a teacher, her pregnancy obvious, she still looked elegantly aristocratic.

Standing in the wide doors were two older women who were obviously waiting for Andrei along with his wife. One was a handsome, dark-haired woman with the profile of an ancient coin and another, a comical round woman in an ill-fitting military uniform with a red arm band. Both women beamed at Andrei.

"Welcome back, Lieutenant!" Glafíra Ivánovna yelled. "I have an *automobile* waiting for you!"

"She must be the hospital Commissar," Kóshkin thought. "Greetings, Comrade!" he smiled at Glafíra. "My name is Igor Kóshkin and I am the Commissar of Lieutenant Rezánov's Flight Detachment. I ask you to do me a favor, Comrade, since no one is meeting *me*, and I am a stranger in your city. If you have an extra space in your automobile, could you drop me at the Soviet office of the Black Sea Fleet in the harbor?"

Glafíra's face blushed with pleasure. "But of course, Comrade! I'll be delighted!" Turning to Julia, she said dryly, "You'll have to take a carriage."

Julia shrugged. She knew better than to say anything. Besides, Akim was waiting outside, "just in case" as he had said.

"We'll also take the carriage," Larissa said firmly. "Our driver is here."

"As you wish," Glafíra said haughtily. "Let's go, Comrade Commissar!"

"I'll visit you at the hospital in a couple of days, Lieutenant," Kóshkin said, making a small bow before Larissa. "I am so glad to have met you."

"Thank you," Larissa replied, not saying that she, too, was glad to have met him. Glafíra Ivánovna, all smiles, placed her plump hand on his arm and possessively led him to the waiting automobile.

Kóshkin rolled his eyes comically and winked at Andrei, who pretended that he did not see it.

"Good! We got rid of two annoying individuals in one sweep!" Larissa laughed. "I did not like your Commissar. Now, meet my best friend, Julia," she said to Andrei.

They shook hands. "Our faithful driver, Akim, is waiting for you, Lieutenant. He kept watch for every train since we learned that you were coming," Julia said.

"Call me Andrei. I have heard so much about you. I am thankful that you were here for my Larissa, Madame Juliette!"

She smiled. "Call me Julia. I love Larissa as if she were my younger sister. My whole family adores her, even our dog, Zhuchka, who is very particular. Let me have your valise."

"No, no! I can manage."

"Don't argue. You hold your wife's hand and let me carry your valise."

"Do as Julia says," Larissa said, smiling. "Julia and Sister Veronica are two benevolent despots in my life, so I have learned to obey them. They *really* do know better than I what to do!"

Andrei surrendered his valise.

Embarrassed by the changes in her appearance, Larissa felt uncomfortable with Andrei. Larissa held tightly to Andrei's good hand, afraid that he might inadvertently touch her protruding abdomen. Andrei avoided looking at it. He did not know how he should act: Larissa did not look like herself, with her round belly sticking out. She was still beautiful, but somehow, she looked forbidding, he thought. They sat rigidly on the back seat of Akim's carriage, Julia in front with Akim to give them some privacy. Glancing back, Julia noticed that they looked stiff. "They are ashamed of her pregnancy!" Julia thought. "Dear Lord, they are like children! They are not ready to be parents!"

"Where to?" Akim asked.

"Straight to the Memorial," Andrei said. "The aerodrome Soviet needs my official confirmation of arrival to the Memorial. They don't trust officers anymore."

Julia decided to change the subject right away. The young couple needed to *connect*, she thought. "Did your baby kick for his Papa?" she asked Larissa brightly.

"Not yet," Larissa said.

"Oh, but you must introduce them to each other!" Julia said.

Akim laughed. "Yes, Lieutenant! There is nothing like feeling the kick of your baby for the first time! I have felt it three times already with my children, and each child puffed me up with pride!"

Larissa placed Andrei's hand on her abdomen. "This is your Papa, sweetheart," she said gently, and blushed: Andrei would think her silly by talking to her belly. "I think, the baby is asleep..."

The baby kicked, and Larissa felt it turn over.

"I felt it!" Andrei cried. "I felt it *again!*" he beamed at her, overwhelmed.

"I told you!" Akim said grinning, looking at them over his shoulder.

"Does it hurt when the baby kicks?" Andrei asked, still beaming like an idiot.

Larissa smiled "No, you silly boy!" They were at ease with one another again, overflowing with happiness as during the days after their wedding, when nothing mattered except each other. And now—the baby!

"We are having *a baby!*" Andrei jumped to his feet and shouted to the promenading crowds on Deribassovskaya Street. "A baby!"

Julia had convinced Larissa to have Andrei share her room and not move to a hotel. "We have here everything that you need. In case of emergency, God forbid, we are here to help, and Doctor Gottlieb is within a walking distance."

However, Larissa had her reservations about it: her bed was too small. She couldn't imagine how they would be able to sleep in it. But she said nothing. "We can move to the Otráda if it becomes impossible," she thought cheerfully.

Minna Solomonovna had also seen the problem, and while Larissa and Julia were meeting Andrei at the station, she ordered her husband and Yasha to move Larissa's bed out of the room and replace it with her own conjugal double bed.

"How do you expect us to sleep in such a small bed?" her husband complained, looking at the narrow bed. "It's Julia's bed when she was a young girl!"

"It's big enough, and I'll sleep in it. You'll sleep on the couch," Minna Solomonovna declared in a no-nonsense tone of voice, and giggled. He did not dare to object.

Minna Solomonovna took her husband's and her grandson's best suits out of summer storage and the whole house became inundated with the nauseating smell of naphthalene. She opened all the windows to ventilate the house and ironed her husband's best shirt. The Cohen family was ready to welcome the hero into their home.

Akim brought his passengers to Memorial and tied his horse in the shade under a tree. "Good luck, Lieutenant! I hope that this time you won't become a meal for the maggots!"

"Let's hope so," Andrei smiled. "We'll see you shortly."

"I'll be waiting ..." Akim attached a bag of oats under the horse's muzzle and the mare began to chomp contentedly.

Doctor Shubin carefully hugged Andrei and kissed Larissa on both cheeks. He shook hands with Julia and invited them to his office. "I see that our Commissar is not with you ... And I don't see the automobile. What happened?" he said, looking out of the window to the parking circle.

"*Your* Commissar took *my* Commissar to the harbor office of The Sailors' Soviet in *your* automobile!" Andrei said with a suggestion of a sneer.

"Wait, wait! What's *your* Commissar doing in *my* automobile? And why do *you* need to have a *Commissar* in the first place?" Doctor Shubin looked bewildered.

396

Andrei and Larissa laughed. "We all have Commissars now," Andrei said, the sneer on his face growing. "The Commissars watch for our political purity. Kóshkin, who traveled with me to Odessa on some Bolshevik business. He asked *Comrade* Glafíra for a lift to the harbor."

"But where are they now?"

"Who knows? *Comrade* Glafíra is probably showing him around Odessa," Andrei shrugged. "In *your* automobile."

"Alas, the automobile isn't mine anymore. It was requisitioned several months ago!"

"Like my father's," Andrei said.

"Yes, I've heard about the terrible things that happened to your family. I am so sorry." They exchanged meaningful looks.

"Anyway," Shubin said, "to change the subject ... we've written to Kiev, to Professor Ivan Sikorsky, who is the father of one of your own famous fellow-pilots. We asked him if he could recommend someone who is familiar with the *shell-shock* syndrome. He suggested Doctor Gurevich, who is apparently working on research of that particular syndrome."

"Professor Sikorsky's son Igor is not only a pilot," Andrei said. "He is a great inventor and an aviation engineer. My mechanic at Gátchina, Petrovich, was Sikorsky's mechanic at one time. Do you remember him, honey?"

"How could I forget! He brought me a bunch of daisies, which he stole from someone's garden on his way to our wedding!" They all laughed.

"So, Igor Sikorsky is the son of a *psychiatrist.* How interesting!" Andrei said.

"Psychologist," Doctor Shubin corrected. "He is well known in his field. I have been looking forward to meeting Professor Sikorsky, but I guess, it is not possible. So, Doctor Gurevich will interview you. He is arriving from Kiev tomorrow at ten in the morning and will stay at the *Primorskaya* Hotel."

"Am I to go there?"

"No, no. We'll send a car for him, that is, if nothing happened to it and to Glafíra Ivánovna. We shall meet you here, at my office, at one o'clock. It should give enough time for everybody. Meanwhile, Lieutenant, let's go to the Operating Room and examine your new wound. Sister Veronica is waiting!"

Veronica in her immaculately severe uniform was waiting, indeed. "Good to see you Lieutenant!" she exclaimed in English. "As you must have noticed, I did not say 'welcome back,' for I don't enjoy welcoming back my former patients!"

"Well, I am also glad to see you, Sister Veronica, and to know that I'll be in your good hands again!" he replied also in English. "Back at our field hospital, our doctors were in awe of how you saved my leg. Without your care all the wind would have been taken out of my sails and I would be forever … what do you call it in English? A *'gimp'!* That's it! I would've been a *gimp!*"

"You exaggerate my abilities, my friend," Veronica said, pleased nevertheless. "As to the word *'gimp,'* I don't think it is English. I've heard it used …"

"Russian, Russian, Russian! In this hospital we speak only *Russian!"* Glafíra Ivánovna appeared at the door of the operating room, pulling on a doctor's coat over her uniform. She smiled and clapped her hands as if she were addressing a roomful of schoolchildren.

"Sorry," Andrei said. "I was practicing my English. It was all my fault."

Glafíra Ivánovna shook her finger playfully at him. "Don't do it again!"

"Never!" he swore, comically pressing his bandaged hand to his heart. "I swear I'll forget *everything* that I ever knew in *any* language, but *Russian!"*

"Don't overdo it," Sister Veronica said in English, ignoring Glafíra.

42

A few weeks later, during a calm period at the front, Egórov took a furlough and went to Odessa, where Andrei was having another checkup at Memorial Hospital. Upon his arrival at his Odessa hotel, Egórov immediately ordered the attendant to fix him a hot bath, send a barber and a manicurist to his room, and have his uniform cleaned and pressed and his boots shined. "Odessa is still a civilized city," he thought, anticipating the pleasures he would enjoy for the next couple of weeks: a hot bath *every* day! Good whisky and good coffee *every* day! Perhaps a good, clean whore in a good, clean brothel. "Unless the whores too have commissars who regulate their activities," he thought humorously.

He telephoned Doctor Shubin at Memorial Hospital. Shubin informed him that Larissa had given birth to a girl.

"A girl! How wonderful! How is Larissa feeling?"

"She had a hard time, but she's all right."

"And how is the new father?"

Shubin laughed. "Oh, he is a wreck! While she was in labor, he got drunk with Akim and their landlord! He may not even know yet that he is a new father!" They both laughed.

"Thank you, Doctor Shubin!" Egórov said.

"My wife and I will be visiting Larissa this evening. I hope we'll see you there."

"You bet! Don't tell them I am in Odessa. I want to surprise them. I am the baby's godfather!"

"Congratulations!"

Egórov replaced the listening tube. "I must send flowers to Larissa and my new goddaughter," he thought, ringing the concierge.

Julia searched several boxes of unsold merchandise looking for something pretty. She wanted Larissa to look glamorous again, yet it also had to be practical for a nursing mother.

She found something almost at once. It was a gossamer raspberry-colored nightdress of silk chiffon held together with narrow spaghetti straps. Larissa could easily shrug those off her shoulders when she needed to nurse. The garment's transparency was hidden under an elegant peignoir with long, pleated sleeves that resembled butterfly wings, when spread. Julia had ordered the set from Paris in 1915, and her father had smuggled it into Odessa. It was meant for Madam Sylvia, owner of Odessa's most expensive brothel. Unfortunately, Madam Sylvia was unable to collect it; she had been arrested for stealing money from clients' pockets while they were occupied with her ladies.

"Larissa might be embarrassed by the color, but Andrei will love it!" Julia thought. She wrapped the filmy set in perfumed tissue paper and placed it into a large gift box with her logo on the top—*Madame Juliette Salon De Beauté*.

The Shubins arrived with Veronica, all carrying bouquets. Akim was with them, having appointed himself the official and *only* driver for the Rezánovs, Cohens, and Shubins. He and Julia had agreed that in exchange for a monthly retainer, he would be at the disposal of his *friends*, as he referred to the three families.

Akim carried flowers as well, but in accordance with Cossack tradition, his wife had woven them into a beribboned crown. Larissa instantly placed it on her head and entwined her hair with the colorful ribbons.

"You look beautiful, Larissa Sergéyevna. You remind me of a picture of Spring that I saw once. My children gathered the flowers from the field this morning, and my wife made this wreath just for you! Congratulations!" Akim said with emotion.

"Would you like to see the baby?" she asked.

"No, no, no!" he exclaimed quickly. "It's *bad luck* to see the baby before christening!"

"Well, please thank your wife and children for the lovely wreath. I hope to meet them all at the christening and thank them personally!"

"We will be there. We won't miss it!"

Andrei bathed carefully to avoid wetting the bandage that still dominated his arm and chest. His so-called 'light' wound proved to be stubborn in healing. Freshly bathed, he decided to make a quick detour to the Passage and buy Larissa something beautiful and expensive. She had no jewelry in Odessa, except for one small pearl necklace and the gold wristwatch he had bought for her during his previous stay in the city. Worn on the wrist, the bracelet-watches were the latest fashion. Larissa had admired one in the window of a jewelry store. Now, he was looking for something different, something spectacular, something extravagant and even impractical.

Alas, the jewelry store was closed and on its door there was a notice that the store was for rent.

"Well, maybe it is for the best. We must be more careful with our money ..." he thought, disappointed nevertheless.

On his way out of the Passage, Andrei stopped at the florist and bought a large basket of potted white orchids. "My wife just had a baby!" he announced to the florist and at once felt foolish. "What does *she* care?" he thought, looking at the silver-haired woman behind the counter.

The florist smiled warmly and said, "Congratulations, Lieutenant!" Then, looking at his bandages, she added, "You're a pilot ... were you wounded while flying? I am so sorry. My son was also wounded, but he is fine now. Unfortunately, he had to go back to his unit. He is with the artillery."

"I will also go back, as soon as my arm heals. But I'm glad to have been here when my daughter was born!"

"When was she born?"

"Two nights ago!"

"Oh my!" the florist exclaimed. "I am so happy for you! Take these lilies-of-the-valley to welcome your little girl into our world!" She proffered Andrei a small nosegay of fragrant flowers tied with a white silk ribbon. "Tell her they are from Auntie Katya!" she laughed.

"Thank you!" Andrei felt touched by the kindness of the stranger who had joined him in his happiness.

He was finally ready to meet his new daughter.

Three carriages waited outside the doors of the Cohens' house. Among the drivers gathered for a smoke, Andrei saw Akim.

"Hey, Akim Ivánovich!" Andrei called the driver. "Please help me with this basket!"

"Right away, Lieutenant!" Akim dropped his cigarette butt and crushed it with his boot. "More flowers, eh?"

"Yes. I can see that everybody else is here already and probably brought flowers. I wanted to be the first, but because I was celebrating last night, with *you*, this morning I am too late with everything! I am still a little off balance," he said with a chuckle that showed his embarrassment.

"Oh yes. Larissa Sergéyevna was surprised at not seeing you around. Yes, sir, she was even *more surprised* later!" he added with a hint of mystery.

Andrei lifted an eyebrow. *"Another* surprise?"

From Larissa's room came the booming sound of a man's laughter. Andrei instantly recognized it. "Egórka!" he yelled and pushed open the door.

Within a week, Larissa was on her feet, feeling good and strong. She saw no reason to languish in bed, even though Doctor Gottlieb insisted that she stay in bed for two weeks.

Her most important goal now was to reach her mother. More than a year had passed since they had seen one another, and the postal service was not delivering civilian letters. After all the visitors except Egórov had left, she asked "Do you think Doctor Shubin might be permitted to telephone the Botkinsky Hospital in Petrograd and ask someone to visit my mother's house, to check on her and the others? Would they do it, as a favor to Doctor Shubin?"

Egórov responded, "He won't be able to call Petrograd. There are no civilian communications anymore, none, whatsoever! But I have an idea: I know that Kozakov ..." He interrupted himself, "By the way, Kozakov was elevated to the rank of Colonel! Anyway, Stavka has ordered Colonel Kozakov go to Petrograd and join the Council of the Knights of St. George. We can ask him to visit your mother and give her your letters."

"Oh, Vasya!" Larissa cried and kissed him impulsively on his cheek. "What a great idea!"

Egórov continued, "I am puzzled though, why the Council of the Knights of St. George would hold a meeting *now*, when just *the sight* of an orange and black ribbon raises the hair on Bolsheviks' backs."

"I think it is too complicated," Andrei said. "However, I am sure, Kozakov would agree to visit Maria Nikoláyevna, but how will we get letters to Kozakov? We could try to reach him through Memorial Hospital, but to do that we must get permission from Glafíra."

"Is she still *in love* with you?" Egórov winked.

"I don't think so. I think she switched her affections to Kóshkin."

"Why not try Commissar Kóshkin?" Larissa said. "He was very sympathetic when I told him of my worries about my mother. He told me that the Bolsheviks were not *heartless,*" Larissa continued. "He even authorized adding several weeks to Andrei's furlough, so that I wouldn't have my baby without any family around."

Egórov looked at her for a few moments without saying anything then said, "I think, Andrúshka, our Larissa has a good point. Remember when I warned you that Kóshkin would try to recruit you to their cause? He may think that helping your wife will create a good connection between the two of you ..."

"You see? He'll help you!" Larissa added.

"To call Kóshkin, we still need Glafíra's authorization!" Andrei was not yet convinced.

"So what? We'll go to Glafíra's office, you'll charm her again, and she'll have a chance to become involved *personally* with the *two* most handsome young men in Russian aviation! She won't refuse such an opportunity!" Egórov laughed. "Let's go, *bratishka!* And you, my lovely, start writing to your mother!"

Glafíra Ivánovna dissolved in smiles when Lieutenant Rezánov invited her to see his new baby and relayed a message from his wife that Glafíra was welcome to visit them at *any time*. She was smitten. Handsome Captain Egórov *kissed* her hand!

"We would like to ask you a personal favor," Egórov said, looking intently into her eyes.

"What kind of a favor?" she asked coquettishly.

"We would like to get in touch with our Commanding Officer Colonel Kozakov, who is about to leave for Petrograd on a mission," Egórov began. "As you know our mail service to and from Petrograd is shut down right now ..." he paused dramatically, "... and so, we thought that perhaps Colonel Kozakov might visit Maria Nikoláyevna while in Petrograd and let her know about her first granddaughter. Frankly, it is our *only* hope of getting in touch with her. You are the *only* person who, as Commissar, can grant Lieutenant Rezánov permission to use the military telephone connection. Will you do it for our Lieutenant? Please?"

"They are not asking too much," Glafíra thought. "When is your Colonel leaving?" she asked to appear efficient, even though she had already made up her mind to participate in their little scheme.

"Frankly, I don't know."

"I'll call Commissar Kóshkin right away about your request. I cannot talk directly to your Colonel. It must be done through our Soviet *political* channels, Commissar to Commissar. Comrade Kóshkin will follow it up through the channels."

Egórov exclaimed, "Wonderful! Thank you so much for your help, Glafíra Ivánovna! You are an *angel!* Let's call him now!"

Kóshkin answered the telephone. At once, he saw his chance for ingratiating himself to Andrei. He listened impatiently to Glafíra.

"Fine. Let me talk to Lieutenant Rezánov!" he said.

Andrei picked up the receiver. "Igor, I need your help," he began, deciding to be truthful in his request. "I have told you what happened to our families. For months, neither my wife nor I have had any contact with them. I thought of asking Kozakov for help in reaching them, to give them our letters and bring back news of our family. By the way, Larissa had a little girl! Her mother will be so happy to hear it!"

Kóshkin laughed into the telephone. "Congratulations! A new papa, eh? Of course, I'll help you! I'll send someone to Kozakov's quarters and ask him to come to the radio-telephone in my office. I'll call you back shortly."

Andrei and Egórov settled on the oilcloth-upholstered sofa in Glafíra's office. "Now, we have a new problem: getting the letters to Kozakov," Egórov said. "Ah, for the convenience of dropping a letter into a mailbox …"

"I think I can ask the old porter on the train to take the letters as far as Yassy. But that's where I am stymied. How can the letters be forwarded from Yassy to Kozakov?"

"Ask Igor Kóshkin about it," Glafíra suggested. "By now there is probably a branch of the *Soviet Soldiers Deputies* in Yassy."

"Good thinking, Glafíra Ivánovna!" Egórov exclaimed. "Of course! Since Kóshkin agreed to help, I think he will see it to the end!"

Colonel Kozakov readily agreed to deliver the letters to Maria Nikoláyevna. He was to leave in four days, so there was enough time to organize the complicated arrangement.

Kóshkin promised to transfer the letters from Yassy to the Russian aerodrome. "I was planning to visit our new Soviet office in Yassy anyway, so tell your porter to leave the letters with the station master in Yassy, and I will personally pick them up. No problem. Glad to be of service to the new parents!"

"Well, Glafíra Ivánovna, you have our deepest gratitude," Egórov said. "And to show it, I would like to invite you to lunch with us at my hotel tomorrow, after the Lieutenant and I take the letters to the station."

Akim took Andrei and Egórov to the railroad station the next morning. The train to Yassy would depart Odessa in the afternoon. If the old porter was aboard, half of their hopes would be fulfilled.

They were lucky. The old man was shuffling around the platform carrying a handful of kindling for his samovar.

"Osip Ivanich!" Andrei called. "I was looking for you!"

"Oh, Lieutenant! Going back already?" the old man stopped.

"No, no, Osip Ivanich, not yet! My wife just had a baby, a little girl!"

"What do you know! I didn't even know that you were *married!*"

"Well, I am! And I am a father now! Meet my best friend, and the godfather of my baby, Captain Egórov. Take good care of him when he goes back to Yassy in a couple of weeks."

"I shall!" The old man nodded to Egórov and smiled, displaying an almost toothless mouth.

"We hope you will do us a favor, Osip Ivanich," Andrei said. He explained their request. "Will you do it?"

"Give me your letters. I'll be glad to let your folks know about your baby!" the old man mumbled, smiling.

Andrei handed him three unsealed letters, one from him to his parents, and two to Maria Nikoláyevna; one from Larissa and one from Egórov. Egórov had suggested leaving the letters unsealed, an indication that they contained no secret information.

"Here is something for your trouble," Andrei said, placing a ten ruble gold coin in the old man's wrinkled hand.

"No trouble, Lieutenant, but thank you! I haven't seen a gold coin since our Tsar Bátushka, God bless him ..."

"Lower your voice," Egórov interrupted.

The old man waved his hand in resignation and resumed his walk.

Glafíra was waiting for them in her automobile at the Primorskaya Hotel entrance.

"Did the porter agree?" she asked.

"He did," Egórov said, offering her his arm. "Now, we'll celebrate the arrival of my goddaughter! Do you like champagne, Glafíra Ivánovna?"

"Oh ... It depends." She had never tasted champagne, though she would never admit it.

"Of course," he agreed politely.

They were a curious trio: two handsome, highly-decorated pilots, one of them carrying his arm in a sling, and a short, fat woman in military garb wearing a red band over her arm. Under the stares of dozens of well-dressed patrons, mostly foreign, male executives and beautiful young women, they were escorted to a table in the bay window. The other diners were a reflection of the so-called 'silver age' of the Russian Renaissance, the waning light of which Odessa was still enjoying. It was an era of exploration and freedom, not only in the arts but also in open sexual entanglements and the use of cocaine and opium, which sailors of the international fleets smuggled to Odessa.

Andrei let Egórov choose the wine and make selections for their meal, although he would be paying; he was still the richer of the two.

Glafíra quickly became inebriated. She swallowed champagne as if it were *kvass*, a peasant beverage made of fermented bread. "To your baby!" she clinked her glass against Andrei's with such force that wine spilled over the rim. She laughed loudly, proclaiming, "I am having such a good time!"

After lunch, Andrei and Egórov, supporting the staggering Glafíra, deposited her in the waiting automobile. "I'll take you back home Andrú-sha," she declared. Come with me in my auto-mo-bile!"

"Thank you, Glafíra Ivánovna, but I have some business I must attend to with Captain Egórov!"

"I'll wait."

"No, no! Don't wait! I don't know how long it might take!"

"I can wait," she insisted.

Egórov stuck his head into the chauffeur's window and said quietly, "Go!" The man grinned and started the machine.

"Ooph!" Andrei exhaled with relief.

Egórov laughed. "I am surprised you refused a ride in her *auto-mo-bile!* So, what is your plan for the rest of the day?"

"To go home, admire the baby and take a nap. And you?"

"The same, except for admiring the baby. I'll postpone that pleasure until tomorrow. I must let you rest without my constant presence."

"Oh, don't be a prick!"

"All right! I must let *me* rest without *your* constant presence!" They both laughed.

"See you tomorrow!" Andrei jumped into Akim's waiting carriage.

Egórov opened the door to his balcony, pleased to find the air was still warm. He moved a wicker chair closer to the railing, put his legs on the ledge, and lit a pipe. Pipes were his latest habit; he had started a collection and already owned six of them.

Staring at the darkening sea through his smoke, he thought about the convoluted contrivances of sending letters to Maria Nikoláyevna. A feeling of shame for playing up to Glafíra and Kóshkin overwhelmed him. "What has happened to us?" he asked himself. "How did we allow the Glafíras and Koshkins to set the rules? How did we lose our country to them? Once in power, they will never give up. We will have to fight them. But who will be *our* leaders? Certainly not Kerensky. He is no match for Lenin. And of course, no members of the Imperial Family. Then, who?" The names of famous generals and members of the Duma flashed through his mind. None of them seemed to match the mysterious Lenin in his ability to rouse the masses. "What is his secret?" Egórov thought. "He is an insignificant-looking little man with a speech defect. He is a cosmopolitan, a Marxist, who has nothing in common with the *common* Russian man, yet they follow him. Why? Because he flaunts a glorious picture of triumph for the common man through the 'dictatorship of the proletariat'? Yet, he himself is not a proletarian."

These thoughts made him feel depressed. He thought that perhaps being on a furlough gave him too much time for fruitless thinking. It was better to be constantly on duty; to think of nothing but his airplane, his mission, and his buddies.

He stood up, straightened his jacket and went downstairs to the lobby bar.

Near a bay window at a small round table sat a woman dressed in black and wearing a large black hat with red roses, a short veil shadowing the upper part of her face. A small glass of absinthe was in front of her. She looked like Anna Akhmatova, the famous poetess, very dramatic and poised, but as Egórov came closer, he recognized the familiar profile.

"Julia Isaakovna!" he exclaimed in surprise.

"Oh, Vassily Sergeyevich … Are you meeting someone? If not, would you like to join me? I am in a need of a friend."

"With pleasure!" He took the seat opposite her. "Whisky," he told the waiter who appeared at his elbow. "I'll ask you the obvious question. What are you doing here?" It was unusual for 'decent' women to be alone in public drinking places.

"Oh, I was saying *adieu* to someone," she said, "and I feel a little sad. It's always sad when a love affair ends badly. Perhaps you understand."

"I do. But most of the time, it's for the best."

'Yes, but it still hurts! In this case, I should have ended it years ago."

Egórov was surprised that Julia was talking so freely about her love affair. Perhaps this was Odessa's Renaissance culture.

"Will it help to talk about it?" he asked.

"Perhaps," she shrugged. She finished her drink and ordered another. "As you probably know, my husband is in America. Yasha and I were to follow him there, but the war interfered. Now, my husband has a new family there. It's fine with me. If I ever get to America, I'll divorce him and allow him to make his new children legitimate. We'll remain friendly."

Egórov listened, and it occurred to him that the only happy couple he knew was Andrei and Larissa.

"And so, I took a lover," she continued. "My *'bon ami'* was a newspaperman working for the Kherson paper. I suppose he was talented, and at first it was fun. He told me the plots of his satiric stories. We laughed a lot and made love a lot. He was poor, and I helped him financially. I knew that he had no money for the luxuries that I enjoy, so instead of denying those pleasures to myself, I paid for both of us … I did not mind."

She stopped and took a sip of absinthe. Egórov knew what was coming: the man began to deceive her. "A familiar story," he thought, as the image of Tatiana, his erstwhile wife, appeared in his mind's eye.

But Julia's story was different.

"Soon he started 'borrowing' money from me. We both knew that he had no intention of paying it back. I thought nothing of it, knowing that he really could *not* pay back the loans. He had nothing. Then, I discovered that he was helping himself by *stealing* money out of my purse or out of the cash box whenever he came to my salon. I caught him one day. He wept, begging forgiveness, saying that he needed money for his sick mother, forgetting apparently that he had told me his mother had died when he was a boy."

"So, what did you do?"

"I showed him the door, of course. We had a stormy argument, he pledged his undying love and so forth, but I remained unmoved. He made his exit by threatening to get even with me. I told him to go to hell!"

"Good for you!"

"It wasn't *'good'* for me. My salon was burglarized last year, before I closed it down. Rumor was that the burglars were drunken sailors, but, through my father's connections, we learned that my *bon ami* was the instigator. My father's pals beat him to a pulp, and I must say I had no pity for him. I did not lift a finger to save him from punishment."

"What a story! I wonder if he is going to write about it someday!"

She laughed bitterly but ignored his comment. "But the strangest thing happened *today*. That's why I am here," she said. "I received a message that he must see me on a matter of life or death. He said that it was too dangerous for him to be seen with me, so we met in the garden. He told me that my son would be *kidnapped* by Mishka Japónchik's gang!"

"Who is Mishka Japónchik?" Egórov asked.

"He is the leader of Odessa's most powerful gang and a friend of my father. Mishka and his pals *adore* my Yasha! They would *never* harm him. They are proud of him. They bet their money on him at the chess matches. They protect our home, making sure that nothing bad happens to any of us. And now that includes Larissa, Andrei, and the baby."

Egórov said nothing, but he did not like that his friends were under the protection of a criminal gang. "So, what happened today?"

"He tried to scare me, saying he knows that there is an order from Mishka to kidnap my son. I asked him how he knew this, but he refused to say anything more. I insisted of course, and he finally blurted out that if I give him ten thousand rubles in gold, he would be able to bribe Mishka."

"What did you do?"

"I laughed in his face. I told him that Mishka Japónchik is my father's friend. I also told him that if he ever tries to see me again, I'll ask Mishka to pay *him* a visit. I know I've scared him, but it left an awful taste in my mouth. I acted like a true daughter of a gangster. I threatened the man with violence."

She began to cry.

"Don't cry, Julia. You did the right thing. You did not let the scoundrel blackmail you. Don't cry. Let me take you home," Egórov said.

"I don't want to go home. Take me to your room."

Their unexpected union was mute and spontaneously passionate. They both were starved for sexual closeness. When it was over, still breathing hard, they looked at one another and laughed. "Well, what do you know!" he exclaimed. "Surprise, surprise!"

"Yes! Did you ever think …" Julia began and laughed. "I never thought that I …" she stopped and placed her head on his moist, bare chest. "It was wonderful," she murmured, kissing his chest. "Thank you!"

"Yes, it was wonderful …" he said and moved a strand of her black hair from her face. "Oh, Julia, it was so wonderful!"

They slept in each other's embrace. Egórov viscerally enjoyed the nearness of the woman's warm body. His encounters with women since his breakup with Tatiana had never involved *sleeping* together.

They made love again, tenderly this time, then had a huge breakfast on the balcony, both cuddled in a blanket and sharing their toast with the cooing pigeons.

"It's a shame that you must be leaving soon," Julia said. 'Let's use every available moment to enjoy each other without any obligations or explanations. Let's take our unexpected liaison as it comes. Let's not strangle it with conditions."

"Agreed."

"If Andrei or Larissa ask us what's going on, for they will notice the difference in our relationship, would you mind if we tell them the truth?"

"Not at all. There is nothing to be ashamed of. I know they will welcome it, especially, Andrei! He keeps urging me to fall in love!"

"Let's not talk about *love!* Let's be voluptuaries and enjoy what we have discovered. Perhaps Larissa will be a little shocked, but it's time for her to grow up and see life as it is. She is a good person who loves us both. I think she will be glad that we have found a few sweet moments of pleasure with each other in this cruel world."

She was right: Larissa and Andrei, though surprised, welcomed their liaison.

43

Alexander Kozakov landed his Nieuport 17 at the Gátchina Flight School aerodrome. He was exhausted. Instead of going from Yassy to Petrograd by train, Kozakov had chosen to fly, not trusting the erratic railroad service. He hopped from airbase to airbase, stopping at each long enough to have his Nieuport serviced and fueled, have a quick meal, and make use of the toilet facilities.

Not yet recovered from his wounds, Kozakov had overestimated his strength. At the end of the first day of flying, he had spent the night as a guest at some small aerodrome, sleeping on the cot of a pilot who had been shot down. He awoke engulfed in pain. The second day was even harder. He was feverish. He perspired in his heavy flight suit only to shake with chills the next moment. His vision played tricks on him. The insignia of his 19th Detachment kept appearing before his eyes, even though he knew that he could not see its skull and bones. He realized that he was hallucinating.

"I *must* get to Petrograd … Sick or not, I must get to Petrograd," he thought, shivering, urging himself not to succumb to the threat of illness. "What if it is typhus?" The thought quivered in his mind like a captured little bird.

Stubbornly, Kozakov continued on his northeast course. He knew that he was flying erratically. He went up and down, gaining and losing altitude, desperately willing himself to stabilize his craft. To a superb pilot, as he was, the uncertainties in his technique were inexcusable. "Concentrate!" he ordered himself sharply.

The possibility of being seriously ill took possession of his mind. "I hope it isn't *typhus* ..." The threat of having contacted the dreaded disease overwhelmed him. "I shouldn't have visited those *typhósny* pilots at the hospital in Yassy!" he thought. "I've probably exposed myself to the infection ..."

The intermittent fever shook him again. He had a sudden urge to dive down and crash his plane. He could see himself going down in a corkscrew pattern. "Concentrate!" he yelled and slapped his face, shaken by the dangerous symptom. With a last surge of failing strength, he landed at the Gátchina aerodrome. He could not make the remaining forty versts to Petrograd.

Kozakov shut off the engine as his body drooped forward helplessly, still restricted by the security harness. He had no energy to unhook the belt and throw his legs over the edge of the cockpit.

The doctors were amazed at the number of old scars on his wiry body. There were also several recent shrapnel wounds that looked disturbed by the constant rubbing of his clothing; they were oozing and needed re-dressing. He was feverish and delirious.

"He must stay with us for a few days," Doctor Nikanòrov of the Gátchina medical unit declared to his staff. "He is utterly exhausted."

Kozakov's skull-like face twisted into a weak grimace. "I think, I may be *sick* with something ..." he mumbled. His voice sounded to him as if it was coming from the bottom of a deep barrel. "I visited the typhus ward last week ..."

"Don't fret about it, Colonel ... We'll watch over you, and if it turns out to be typhus, we are here to catch it early enough. Meanwhile, we'll take care of your infected shrapnel wounds."

Kozakov closed his eyes and surrendered himself to the ministrations of the Gátchina doctors.

After a week in the comfort of the little hospital on the premises of Gátchina Palace where the Grand Duke Mikhail was being kept under house arrest, Kozakov felt better. Apparently he was not infected with typhus, but his reopened wounds were bothersome and slow to heal.

Kozakov's mandate was to attend the meetings of the Knights of St. George, but he still could not comprehend what such meetings could accomplish. By the order of the new Military Revolutionary Committee, the decorations of the Cross of St. George had been *abolished*.

"Who is in charge?" Kozakov thought. "We have the Provisional Government to run the country, but it is not in charge of anything. Its members lock themselves in the Winter Palace and argue among themselves. We have the High Command at Stavka to run the war, but all these Soviets of Soldiers and Sailors and Workers run the war in their own way. Who is *truly* in charge of our country?"

He shared his concerns with Colonel Gorshkov, the Commanding officer of Gátchina Flight School, when the Colonel came to visit him at the hospital.

Gorshkov, an old friend, was pessimistic. "It looks like you've made your long trip for nothing, my friend. Your meetings have been cancelled by the Military Revolutionary Committee," he said. "More proof of the anarchy in the country."

"Well, I still have a couple of meetings to attend, although they are of personal nature. I promised one of my pilots that I would deliver some letters to his family since there is *still* no civilian connection between Petrograd and the rest of the country. Perhaps you remember the fellow. He was one of your cadets."

"What's his name?"

"Andrei Rezánov."

"Of course I remember him! He became one of our heroes, with his famous ride on the wing of the Voisin! His photograph is hanging in our mess hall!

I always liked him. And do you know, he was married right here in Gátchina!" Gorshkov laughed. "He married a beautiful girl, the daughter of the late General Orlov."

"Yes, he is a fine young chap and an *excellent* pilot. Right now he is on medical furlough, and his wife just gave birth to their first child. I promised to visit his family in Petrograd and deliver the news to them."

"That should be a pleasant duty," Gorshkov said. "But take my advice: don't *fly* to Petrograd. Leave your Nieuport here. It will be safe with us.

"Why shouldn't I fly into the city?"

"Because the Military Revolutionary Committee could requisition your Nieuport."

"Can they do that?"

"Yes, they can. Not only *can* they do it, but most likely they *will* do it. They requisition people's homes, their businesses, and anything else they want. I shall send you to Petrograd in one of our motorcycles with our school's license plate. What's more, I'll send one of our mechanics, a member of the Soldiers Soviet as your driver. Our local Soviet is still friendly to the officers. You are a hero among our men, so your escort will be proud to take care of you in the city. We'll give you all necessary passes and permits that will allow you to move in the city without being arrested."

"Is it *that bad?*"

"It is," Gorshkov replied. "And it is going to get even worse. Stay at the Astoria Hotel. It is safe, so far, because all the foreign diplomats stay there, so the Bolsheviks don't bother the guests. But I recommend that you share your room with your driver. Just in case. If you don't mind."

Kozakov smiled. "I am enough of an egalitarian not to mind."

Kozakov and his driver, a twenty-year-old mechanic named Morósov wearing a red band on the sleeve of his left arm, bundled themselves up in their warm flight suits. Kozakov lowered himself with a grunt into a narrow sidecar, his old wounds aching with his every move and his new ones itching maddeningly as they slowly developed new skin.

Morósov observed his passenger with curiosity; the famous Russian ace did not look too impressive. His skull-like face looked even bonier after his illness, and his body seemed to be lost in the huge, fur-lined flight suit.

Kozakov proffered his hand to the mechanic, and Morósov shook it.

Their first stop was to be at the home of General Rezánov. It was beginning to snow. When they reached the bridge across the Fontánka, the croups of its famous equestrian sculptures were blanketed with white covers.

Morósov drove under the porte-cochère of the general's mansion and turned off the engine. The elegant house looked deserted. Tall, heavily-carved front doors encased with bronze adornments were crossed diagonally by two boards nailed to the doorframe. A small, official-looking proclamation nailed over the boards quivered in the wind, threatening to be blown away.

Morósov jumped off his seat and walked over to the door. Glancing furtively around, he tore the proclamation off and quickly returned to the motorcycle.

"The house is requisitioned," he announced dryly as he handed the proclamation to Kozakov. "Hide it. You can read it later." He started the motorcycle and raced away from the house, turning into the first narrow street along the Fontánka and then back to the Nevsky Prospect through the labyrinth of backyards of the stately homes.

"You obviously know your way," Kozakov shouted over the noise of the motorcycle.

"I grew up in the city," Morósov shouted back.

Kozakov was anxious to read the proclamation. It burned his chest pocket. "I wonder where the General is? Perhaps, still at Stavka. He probably doesn't even know that the Soviets have taken his house. But where are his wife and servants? Have they all been arrested?" he thought.

They drove along the Nevsky Prospect toward the Nevá. At the junction of Nevsky and Morskaya, a Soviet patrol stopped them to check their documents. Three sailors carrying rifles with attached bayonets barred their way. They passed Kozakov's papers from one man to another, reading them slowly with their lips moving, obviously unaccustomed to the art of reading. Kozakov observed them coldly. "These are the new rulers," he thought with derision.

"Why aren't you wearing your uniform?" one of the sailors demanded rudely. "It says here that you are a Colonel. Are you trying to *hide* your rank?"

"This *is* my uniform. I am a pilot." Kozakov replied icily.

"It's true, comrades! This pilot here, he is the best Russian ace ... he is Alexander Kozakov! This is his uniform, honestly!" Morósov chatted with servility. "That's all he ever wears! He is the best pilot in Russia, ask anyone!"

"Let 'em, go, Philip. The man looks sick ..." another sailor interrupted.

"Yes, Comrades, this pilot was in our hospital for more than a week with many wounds! Ask anyone!" Morósov informed the sailors.

"Oh, keep going!" the sailor returned the papers to Kozakov. "Who gives a damn about his uniform. He is an officer, and we beat the officers!" He roared with laughter, the other sailors joining him.

Kozakov stared stonily ahead and only a tiny muscle twitched under his left eye.

They reached the river and followed the embankment, searching for Maria Nikoláyevna's house. Kozakov saw the ruined remains of the Winter Garden and knew that they were in front of the late general's house. "Andrei wrote good directions," he thought.

The ornate gates at the front of the Winter Garden were locked with a large padlock. Morósov drove slowly along the wrought iron fence to the second set of matching gates, which were also locked, but there was light in the two lanterns on both sides of the porte-cochère behind the fence.

The huge house looked deserted. Every window was shaded with draperies and the steps leading to the front doors were covered with snow bearing no footprints.

Morósov dismounted and pressed the button of the electric bell at the gate. Presently, the draperies moved in one of the windows facing the gates, and a bearded old man appeared in its frame. Morósov explained with gestures that he wanted to be allowed inside. The draperies closed, then reopened again, as another face appeared in the window, that of a woman. She observed the visitors through small opera glasses. Finally, the massive doors of the house opened, and an old servant hurried to the gate with a set of keys.

"Welcome, welcome," he muttered as he opened the creaking gate. "The lady of the house recognized the Gátchina emblem on your motorcycle," he smiled awkwardly.

Morósov drove to the front door. "Is it safe to leave my machine?" he asked.

"You had better let him park in the garage, Stepan Petrovich," Maria Nikoláyevna called from the opened door of the house, "the motorcycle might be too tempting for someone. And lock the gates."

"Yes, Maria Nikoláyevna. Please follow me," the old man said to Morósov, locking the gates with a padlock again.

Kozakov ascended the wide steps. "I am Colonel Kozakov, the commanding officer of your son-in-law," he introduced himself with a bow." Seeing that she blanched, he quickly added, "I have letters for you from your daughter and from Andrei."

"Oh, *Mon Dieu!*" She gasped and pressed her hands to her chest. "Letters! From my little girl! Oh, dear Lord! Letters! God bless you, Colonel, come in, come in!" she bustled, suddenly out of control. She felt that she was on a verge of hysteria, her stoic character finally collapsing under the weight of *happy* news.

Kozakov entered the large hall embraced by a graceful double-winged white marble staircase.

"Ksusha, Ksusha!" Maria Nikoláyevna called loudly into the open space over the staircase. "We have letters from Larissa and Andrei! Oh, Colonel! Take off your ... your ... It is some kind of a special suit for flying, isn't it?" she bubbled.

He smiled slightly. He could well sympathize with her excitement as he too had received no news from his mother and sister in Sevastópol for more than a year. "Yes, it's our new winter flight suit," he said, shedding his cumbersome attire.

"Let's go to the kitchen. It is the only warm place in the house," Maria Nikoláyevna said, taking control of her emotions. She led Kozakov to a large kitchen, which was indeed very warm.

Stepan Petrovich was already there with Morósov. "I thought you would want the driver to come in," the old butler said.

"But of course! I am Maria Nikoláyevna," she introduced herself to Morósov.

"Morósov!" he bowed. "I am a mechanic at Gátchina's Flight School."

"Welcome," she said. "If you'll excuse me, Colonel," she turned to Kozakov, "I'll leave you here while I read the letters. Ksusha will make you a cup of tea. She is my friend and companion."

Kozakov saw an old peasant woman wrapped in several shawls wobble into the kitchen.

"We are living in the kitchen now," Ksusha explained, pointing to four blue velvet armchairs crowded around the large kitchen table of plain wood. "We use our bedrooms only to sleep. The rest of the house is closed up. Sit down, sit down, sir! We'll have some hot tea now. Stepan Petrovich, help me to lift that samovar!"

"I'll help you," Morósov said quickly, seeing that the old man was frail and his hands were trembling. "Where do you want it?"

"Right here, on the table. What's your name, young man?"

"Morósov, Mátushka."

"No, give me your Christian name!"

"Nikolaí."

"All right, Nikólenka, be a good fellow and start the samovar," she said kindly as if Morósov was her own son. "We are old folks here and we are barely able to lift it. We boil water for our tea in a cooking pot!

But we have guests now," she smiled at Kozakov and Morósov, "and we want to celebrate with them in the traditional way, with a good, hot tea from the *samovar!*"

"Yes, Mátushka, I can do it! Where is your kindling?"

"Right there, at the stove" Stepan Petrovich said.

"What about water? Do you have running water?"

"Yes, so far we are lucky. We still have running water!" Ksusha said.

Morósov filled the samovar from the faucet in the kitchen. Then, he stuffed the dry kindling vertically into the samovar chimney and lit it from below. The flame quickly enveloped the kindling and in no time, the water was boiling and the samovar was puffing.

Ksusha filled a china teapot with boiling water from the samovar, sprinkled two teaspoonfuls of dry Indian tea into it, and crowned the samovar with the teapot, to steep.

Kozakov observed the tea-making ceremony with nostalgia. He used to help his nurse with the samovar. It was a pleasant family ritual. He became painfully aware that he missed his own family.

"Unfortunately, we have nothing to offer you with your tea," Ksusha said. "We have already used our daily rations. At the end of the month, we should get our coupons for flour ... But today is only the 24th ..."

"Don't worry, Mátushka, we brought along some food," Morósov said brightly. "I raided our kitchen at School, just in case ..."

"Good thinking!" Kozakov exclaimed.

"Glad to be of service, Your Excellency," Morósov replied crisply and then blushed. He had forgotten that he was a member of the Soldiers Soviet!

He removed a sizable packet wrapped in brown paper from inside his flight suit. "Here is some ham and white bread with butter. And two hard-boiled eggs. Also a small tin of cookies from England."

"We'll have a feast!" Ksusha clapped her arthritic hands encased in woolen gloves without fingertips. She was about to call to Maria Nikoláyevna with the good news of the food, but Maria Nikoláyevna had good news of her own.

"Larissa had a *baby!*" Maria Nikoláyevna shouted from the door, her face wet with tears, her trembling hands clutching the letters. "They had a little *daughter!* Oh, *Bozhe moi!* What happiness! Oh, my God!"

Kozakov offered her his arm and helped her down into a blue armchair. She was trembling, unable to collect herself, and kept repeating, "*Bozhe Moi, Bozhe Moi!* What happiness!"

Finally, she took a hold of herself. "Tell me how they both look. Do they also suffer from lack of food as we do in Petrograd?"

"I have not seen them, Maria Nikoláyevna," Kozakov said. He described the convoluted arrangements that Andrei and Egórov had made in order to send their letters to Petrograd. "As you can see, so far I have only half-succeeded in delivering the letters. We were not able to reach General Rezánov. His house was requisitioned." He took the proclamation out of his pocket and placed it on the table.

Maria Nikoláyevna did not look at it. She covered her face with her hands and began to sob pitifully.

Ksusha stopped portioning Morósov's food and joined Maria Nikoláyevna in her sobbing.

Kozakov and young Morósov were stunned by the sudden flood of tears. They looked at the old butler. "What happened?" Kozakov demanded sharply.

"The general and his lady are both gone ... About three months ago ... of typhus ... right in this house ..." Stepan Petrovich was able to say as sobs, sounding like hiccups, began to overpower him as well.

Maria Nikoláyevna collected herself. She wiped her face with a handkerchief and swallowed some tea.

"It was so terrible," she began. "Our house became a virtual charnel house. Not only General Rezánov and his wife died here, but also three of my servants. We had no medical help. Even our doctor succumbed to the disease. Ksusha and Stepan Petrovich and I were the only survivors ... General Rezánov's aide, Lieutenant Svirsky, had resigned his commission just in time, and the general's Chief-of-Staff, Lieutenant Borisov, had been killed at the front."

"We had to make two guest rooms upstairs into hospital wards," Ksusha joined in.

"The general suffered terribly, fighting the disease, but it was of no use," Maria Nikoláyevna continued. "His wife, my best friend since childhood, did not even know what was happening. She was badly injured by some sailors. She was already dying when typhus hit her ..." Maria Nikoláyevna began to sob again. "My poor Váren'ka ... forgive me ... I'm being so morbid, but we have lived here surrounded by such horrors."

Morósov looked down, not knowing how to react. He felt ashamed, as if he were somehow responsible for the tragedies of the Rezánov family.

Ksusha patted his arm gently. Then turning to Maria Nikoláyevna she said sternly, "Stop crying, *báryn'ya*. Think of our Larochka and Andrúsha, and their new baby! We should be celebrating now. Our friends and relatives are gone and buried, but we have a new baby in our family! Rejoice!" She made the sign of the cross, bowed before the icons in the corner and tried to smile, her own old eyes full of tears.

Kozakov was at a loss for what to say. Not yet feeling well himself, his head throbbing with pain, he longed for a rest. In the back of his mind, too, was a suspicion about Morósov that hastened his desire to leave. How was the young Bolshevik reacting to this? Was he sympathetic, or would he report the conversation to his superiors for further recriminations?

"I am so sorry, Maria Nikoláyevna, to hear such sad news. I'll leave Andrei's letters to his family with you. I don't know if Andrei had any cousins or other relatives."

"No. The general's only brother was killed during the Japanese war. He was a bachelor."

"I'll stop by in the morning to pick up *your* letters to your daughter and Andrei, and I promise, upon my honor, to have them delivered."

Maria Nikoláyevna smiled gently. "I can't describe how very grateful I am to you for bringing me the news about my little family!" she said. "I feel badly that I can't offer you to stay at my house, but you see how we live. So, go with God's blessings! May our Lord keep you safe!" she made the sign of the cross over his chest as she embraced him. "You too, Kólya Morósov, may our Good Lord keep you safe!"

"Thank you, *Báryn'ya*," he replied quietly. He thought of his own mother. She used to say the same words to him.

"Thank you for sharing your food with us," Ksusha said. "I had forgotten the taste of white bread and butter!" Stepan Petrovich nodded in agreement.

"And so did I," Maria Nikoláyevna tried to smile. "We all thank you."

44

"Well, Nikolaí, what is your impression of our visit to Maria Nikoláyevna's house?"Kozakov asked as they settled down in their large room at the Astoria Hotel.

"Sad," Morósov said. "Very sad … The house is like a palace! But the *báryn'ya* and her servants are so *sad!* I think her servants really love her … She must have been kind … I think she never *exploited* them."

Kozakov suppressed a smile. The young man must have been indoctrinated into believing that all upper class people were *exploiters*.

Morósov continued. "It felt good when I saw how *happy* they were when you gave them their letters. I thought of my own mother. She hasn't heard from me for more than a year. But I can't write to her: she can't read or write."

"I thought you were from Petrograd!"

"I am, but my mother left for her village in Rostov when the war began."

"And your father?

"He was killed near Lutsk. He was an airplane mechanic."

"Was his first name *Eroféy* by any chance?" Kozakov asked with sudden interest.

"Yes, sir. Eroféy Eroféyevich Morósov."

"Then, I knew your father! He was one of my best mechanics at the 19th Air Detachment! At the beginning of the war he was sent to France, to learn about the Nieuports. He came back and taught *our* mechanics about the new French airplanes."

"He taught me, also," the young man said with pride.

"Eroféy Morósov was your father …" Kozakov repeated slowly, shaking his head. "I was devastated when I learned that he was killed. We suffered great losses at Lutsk …" He stopped and shivered. He wasn't feeling well again.

"Are you all right, Colonel?" Morósov was full of concern. Kozakov had suddenly become to him not just a famous pilot but a friend, someone who had admired his father. "Let me fix you a hot bath. My parents always sent me to the banya when I wasn't feeling well."

Kozakov nodded weakly. "A bath and sleep in a good warm bed is probably all that I need."

Morósov disappeared into the bathroom. Kozakov heard the vigorous surge of water into a deep tub.

"While I am soaking in the tub and taking a nap, you might as well take a walk through the city. See what's going on," Kozakov said through the open door.

"You won't mind?"

"Not at all. You go, but be careful."

Morósov walked along Morskaya Street toward the graceful Arch that led to the Palace Square. The huge square resembled a labyrinth or some intricate fortress as it was chock full of thousands of cords of stacked wood. Dozens of troops wearing red arm bands unloaded platform trucks with still more cut wood, stacking the cords around the Alexandrovsky Column and along the faded russet-red Palace walls. During the long Russian winters, the Palace Square sometimes served as a storage area for the firewood needed to heat the monolithic fifteen-hundred-room Palace and the adjacent private theatre of Catherine the Great. Now the vast square had been utilized for a more crucial purpose. Behind the cords of wood nestled machine guns aimed at the Palace. The Bolsheviks were getting ready to storm the Winter Palace, which had become the seat of Kerensky's Provisional Government.

Morósov was surprised that no one demanded to see his papers. Was it because of his youth and red arm band that he was not suspected of being an officer? He walked undisturbed, fascinated with the preparations for something so ominous. He thought of his father and what would have been his reaction to the changes in the country, if he had lived long enough. "He wouldn't liked it ..." Morósov thought.

He walked along the curve of the General Staff building and then along the Nevá embankment. There too the soldiers were stacking wood, but there were also several ambulances unloading stretchers with the wounded.

He watched as the patients were brought into the Palace, which had become a huge hospital. At the outbreak of the war, the Tsarina had established in the Winter Palace a special hospital for the convalescing officers. But as soon as the Imperial Family had moved to Tsárskoye Selo, the hospital began to accept wounded patients of all ranks.

Morósov pondered how was it possible to provide proper medical care to hundreds of patients stuck among the rich ambiance of gilded furniture, sparkling mirrors, priceless paintings and statuary, not to mention thousands of other beautiful but useless objects. He had a glance of the Imperial ambiance at a more modest and smaller palace in Gátchina when he was snuck into it by his friend who had worked there as a footman. "That was before the Grand Duke Mikhail was arrested ..." Morósov thought, and wondered how was the Grand Duke managing under the house arrest. Morósov had seen him several times walking slowly through the park, with two guards behind.

Morósov continued his walk. He took a shortcut through a small park at the Admiralty toward the St. Isaak Cathedral Square and the Astoria Hotel, still surprised by the quietness of the city. Almost at his destination, his attention was caught by a large open automobile. In the back seat was the familiar figure of a slender man with protruding ears. Kerensky. The car was speeding, racing through the empty streets without slowing down or blowing its horn at the intersections.

"He must be in a hurry," Morósov thought, not knowing that indeed Kerensky had to hurry to escape arrest by the Military Revolutionary Committee, which was poised to move against the Provisional Government. He was heading out of the city toward Pulkovo and then on to Pskov and beyond, to Stavka in Mogilev, hoping to rally the loyal troops, (if there were any of them left), for the defense of Petrograd.

45

"What if we order *another* breakfast, will they serve it to us?" Morósov said the next morning as they ate their breakfast of tea, omelets, and rolls with sweet butter and jam.

"They will," Kozakov replied. "This is a hotel for rich foreigners. Are you still hungry?"

"No, sir, but I thought we could take it to the old folks when we pick up their letters."

"What a good idea! Of course! Let me call room service," Kosakov turned the handle of the telephone several times and asked if there were any meat dishes.

"Yes, Colonel," someone on the other side of the line replied, "we have some English kidney pies left."

"Fine. And make *three* extra omelets. Everything for three more persons. Bread and butter and some jam. I expect some important guests."

"Yes, Colonel. Right away!"

He replaced the receiver and grinned at Morósov. "You are a genius, Nikolaí Eroféyevich Morósov! It was a great idea to bring some *real* food to our friends!"

Morósov's face reddened. "Being praised by Kozakov! This is a high honor," he thought.

They arrived at Maria Nikoláyevna's house while the food was still warm, the plates, minus silver domes, packed carefully into Kozakov's valise.

Maria Nikoláyevna, wrapped in several shawls like a peasant woman, even behaved like a peasant woman. She and Ksusha embraced and kissed both men, Maria Nikoláyevna discarding her court manners with apparent ease. Only Stepan Petrovich maintained the dignity of his profession.

"What a feast!" Maria Nikoláyevna was choked with emotion. "Sit down, sit down, let's eat!" Ksusha was already dividing the omelets and the kidney pies into five small portions.

"No, no!" Kozakov stopped her. "We have eaten. It is all for you. Besides, we must hurry back and check out of the hotel before they notice their fine plates are missing! So, if you don't mind, Maria Nikoláyevna, let me have your letters and we will be on our way."

While Maria Nikoláyevna was retrieving the letters, Kozakov cautioned Ksusha and the butler. "It would be wise to remain inside for the time being. Morósov told me yesterday that there was something important going on in the city. He saw machine guns being set up on the Palace Square and today, on our way here, we saw a battalion of Cossacks riding with the *Red Flag!* Imagine that? The Cossacks! And I read in *Pravda* that Lenin was calling for the *proletarian* insurrection."

"I read it also," Maria Nikoláyevna said as she proffered him a thick sealed envelope. "I believe in being well-informed about the Bolshevik actions, so I read *Pravda* whenever I can get hold of that horrible paper. Anyway, take these letters and go, my friends! Go before it's too late and they barricade the roads. Tell my children how happy I am ..."

"How happy *we all are,*" Ksusha interrupted, "What a blessing to have a new baby in our family! I used to be Larochka's nurse," she told Kozakov, holding his hand tightly. "I wish I could be the nurse for our *new* little girl!"

"Go with God's blessing! Take good care of Colonel Kozakov, Nikolásha, even though you are apparently ..." Maria Nikoláyevna hesitated.

"I am *not* a Bolshevik, Maria Nikoláyevna," he said. "I was elected to represent the mechanics in our School's Soviet. That's all. I don't believe in killing officers ... I don't want to kill anyone ... I want the war to end!"

Ksusha grabbed him in a tight embrace and kissed him loudly on both cheeks. "We all do! God bless you, my boy! I knew that you were a good boy! God keep you both safe! But now—GO!

Kozakov climbed into the sidecar as Morósov started the motorcycle. They heard the front door being bolted behind them and saw Ksusha drawing the draperies over the windows. Passing through the tall gates, they waved to Stepan Petrovich who struggled with his keys trying to lock the gates. He lifted his arm in a last salute.

46

"All my things are at the hospital. You'd better take me there," Kozakov shouted over the noise of the machine, unwilling to admit he was feeling ill again. His body felt on fire, and his sweat had the unpleasant odor of wet hay. He had a sharp, persistent throb in his head and weakness in his extremities. "What the hell is wrong with me? I am falling apart!" He turned to Morósov. "Thank you for driving me and being a good companion. If you ever get tired of fixing the airplanes *crashed* by the cadets, I'd be glad to have you at my detachment."

"Thank you, Colonel! I would be honored to be in your command. As a *pilot!*" He shouted in reply, and a broad grin spread over his boyish face. "I have been accepted in the next group of trainees."

"Good luck! You ought to make a fine pilot, with your knowledge of machines. But don't hurry to graduate. Wait until the war is over. I say it as an older person, not as a Commander."

"As a Commander, you *need* new pilots. I understand!" Morósov laughed with the spirit of youth. He felt good, fearing nothing and expecting a good life ahead, no matter who ended up in charge of Russia. *He* would be in charge of an airplane, not only on the ground, but up in the sky! His future looked good!

Despite his pain, Kozakov smiled. The enthusiasm of the young mechanic was infectious. Years ago, before his body was crippled and torn, before his loyalties were challenged and spat upon, before his spirit was all but broken, he had felt the same way. "How long ago was it?" he thought. "Only a few years ... But it feels that it was long, long ago ..." He shivered.

"Are you feeling unwell?" Morósov glanced sideways at Kozakov.

"Yes. I am having shivers and shakes again. Whatever I had yesterday and the day before yesterday and two weeks ago, and it seems forever, is back. It comes on and off, all over the body. Very debilitating."

"We are almost there," Morósov turned to a side street for a shortcut and in a few minutes stopped the motorcycle in front of the hospital. "Here we are, Colonel. Let me help you," he said, noticing that Kozakov was having difficulty getting out of the sidecar.

Kozakov was immediately placed in a private room and covered with warmed blankets.

Doctor Nikanorov gave him a small dose of a sedative dissolved in a cup of hot tea with honey. He suspected that Kozakov had fallen victim to a debilitating disease called Mediterranean Fever. It was an infectious Zoonotic disease passed on from animals to people, often through contaminated milk or infected meat. It was a difficult illness, often requiring months of treatment, tormenting its victims with severe headaches and muscular and joint pain that came and went, like the ebb and flow of undulating tidal waves. In the extreme cases it led to death.

"Where could have I picked up such a malady?" Kozakov complained to the doctor. "I haven't been close to any animals for months! Not to horses or dogs! Not even to cats!"

"But you have drunk raw milk, haven't you?"

"Yes, it was one of the small luxuries that I enjoyed in Yassy. The Romanian peasants supplied us with goat's milk and fresh eggs."

"There is your answer: unpasteurized goat milk is the most common carrier!"

Kozakov had nothing to say.

Early the next morning Doctor Nikanorov entered Kozakov's room in great agitation. He did not greet him nor ask the usual question, *'How do we feel today?'*

"They took the Palace!" he announced, his face pale.

"Who?" Kozakov asked.

"The Bolsheviks! Last night! They took the Palace! The members of the Provisional Government are under arrest. We received a telegram from the Central Medical Headquarters with the orders *not to discharge* any recuperating officers from the hospitals until final orders."

"Does that mean that I can't leave, even if I feel better?"

"That's correct. Although, in your case, we would not discharge you anyway. You are *not* better. Your temperature is still much too high and you will feel sick again in a short while. For weeks and months it will be like that."

"Gracious Lord! The hell with my fever!" Kozakov cried angrily. "Tell me about the revolution!"

"I know nothing more than that. As I understand, Colonel Gorshkov is dispatching someone to Petrograd to report *unofficially* on what's going on there, probably that young mechanic who took you to the city yesterday. It's very unprofessional, but the times are changing."

"Morósov is an intelligent young man. He is not *totally* indoctrinated by the Bolsheviks. He'll bring back a true picture of what's going on in the city. Meanwhile, I want to get out of bed and see Colonel Gorshkov."

"No, sir. I want you to stay in bed at least for a couple of days. I'll tell the Colonel that you wish to talk to him. He can come and visit you here."

Kozakov nodded. "Frankly ... I don't feel too well ... I am dizzy and I hurt all over." He had finally accepted the fact that he was seriously ill.

Gorshkov came to Kozakov's room, his arrival heralded by the squeak of his brightly polished cavalry boots.

"So, my friend, it took a cup of goat's milk to knock you off your feet, eh?" he twisted his moustache.

Kozakov smiled weakly and twisted his own moustache. He had noticed that twisting one's moustache was like yawning: if one person yawned, soon the others in the room would begin to yawn also.

"The doctor tells me that you are sending young Morósov back to Petrograd. Good choice. He is a bright chap. But let me report to you the tragic story of Andrei Rezánov's family."

Gorshkov moved a chair closer to the bed. "I am anxious to hear it."

Morósov filled the sidecar of his motorcycle with a bag of food, enough for two days, and two large cans of extra fuel for the machine. The cans were out of sight, in the nose of the sidecar in the tight space for passengers' feet, camouflaged with a tarpaulin and a pile of books and magazines. "No one would be tempted to search a machine full of books," he thought. He attached small red flags to each side of his handlebars to make sure that anyone would recognize the machine as belonging to a *revolutionary*. He checked and oiled his father's old Nagant handgun, loaded it, and stuck it into his pocket. He had no holster for it. He was not a very good shot, but just in case, he thought, he should be ready for anything. *Just in case* had become the mantra of all Russians.

It was an unpleasant ride. The snow was falling heavily and the biting wind from the Baltic blew it into his face. Fortunately, the goggles protected his eyes. He drove, bending over the handlebars and burrowing his chin in the folds of a silk scarf. He looked like a *pilot*, he thought, wearing a leather helmet and his father's old leather jacket. He *liked* the way he looked!

The first sign of trouble met him on the border of Petrograd. The great Putilov factory, the main producer of heavy weapons, was on fire.

Morósov decided not to stop. It was obvious that the Bolsheviks were the ones who had carried out the deed. There had been enough propaganda against the Putilov Works during the previous months to inflame the revolutionary hatred," Morósov thought. He kept going on, toward the center of the city.

A huge crowd was gathered on the Palace Square. Morósov drove his motorcycle at the lowest speed, maneuvering it among the labyrinths of wood and clusters of people, balancing it with one foot on the ground.

Finally he stopped at a group of young men that looked like students. "What's going on, fellows?" he asked with a friendly smile. "We at Gátchina Flight School know nothing about what's going on in Petrograd!"

"Are you a pilot?" one of the young men asked.

"Yeah," Morósov replied in bored tone, as if he was tired of such obvious questions. "Tell me what's going on in the city."

"The Revolution!"

"The Red Guards took the Palace!"

"The *Aurora* shelled the Palace last night!"

They all shouted, interrupting one another, frenzied by the deadly situation, excited by the danger, not knowing yet how to react to it.

"Naval vessels were involved?" Morósov asked. "Are there lots of sailors ashore?"

"Lots and lots!" A young woman joined the group. "I've just seen a bunch of them disembarking at the Nevá entrance to the Palace!"

"Did anyone try to stop the sailors?" Morósov asked.

"You must be joking! No one would *dare* to stop the sailors! They are the fiercest of the Bolsheviks!" someone shouted. "They shoot without provocation!"

Morósov noted that there were no officers anywhere in the crowd. Regardless of rank, they could be shot on the spot and apparently they preferred not to test their luck by appearing in public.

"Well, thank you," Morósov said. He kicked the starter of his motorcycle and drove slowly, toward the river entrance of the Palace, circumventing groups of people. He wanted to see for himself whether the bridges on the Nevá were raised to let naval vessels through. It was going to be even more dangerous in the city if thousands of sailors were there, Morósov thought.

He came out to the Palace Embankment and stopped. The familiar panorama of the broader part of the Nevá opened up before him in all its magnificence. On his right, across the still unfrozen river, was the old Fortress of Peter and Paul with the golden cross topping the spire.

Morósov was on this very spot only the day before and had noted its peacefulness, but it looked different now. The embankment was filled with hundreds of soldiers, sailors, and men in civilian attire carrying weapons of all kinds, their chests criss-crossed with machine gun belts of bullets.

Morósov decided not to risk leaving his motorcycle unattended. In such a big crowd of angry men no one and nothing would be safe. He would wait until he could catch someone's eye and begin a conversation.

He did not need to wait long. A middle-aged worker, encircled with a belt of machine gun bullets, stopped at his side. "Can you spare a smoke, comrade?" the man asked.

"No, comrade, I don't smoke. But I can share a piece of chocolate!"

The older man laughed. "Where could you get *chocolate*? I haven't even *seen* chocolate for more than three years!"

Morósov opened his flight bag and took out a chocolate bar. "It's from England. We at the Gátchina Flight School receive little gifts from our fellow-pilots in England and France. This muffler is a gift from some pilot in France," he pointed to the white silk scarf around his neck that he had bought at a street market.

"Have a piece!" he broke off some chocolate.

"Thanks!" the man said.

"Say, what's going on here? Looks like everyone is going into the Palace and no one checks their documents. Why is the *Aurora* here? Is she going to shoot at the palace?" he pointed to the cruiser anchored across from the Palace, its guns aiming at it.

"She already did! Last night. See that hole at the cornice of the second story? They say it was Alexander III's room! I was there. I even picked out a souvenir! See that picture?" He took out of his pocket a small photograph in a fancy filigreed frame. "It must be his daughter," he said. "But I feel guilty ... I am not a looter!"

Morósov shrugged his shoulders. "Nowadays it could mean the opposite. You just took back what belongs to *you*. That's what our Commissar says."

"That's what I thought too, but I heard that Lenin ordered people to stop looting or be shot on the spot."

"Anything else?"

"I've heard that Lenin is going to speak to us, but where or when, I don't know. It would be great to hear *Ilych* speak!" The man had used the patronymic of Lenin's name as if he were one of his intimate friends. "In any case, we have *won!* I used to be a welder at the Putilov works. Now, I am a Red guard. Or, I try to be ..." he laughed. "I am a peaceful man!"

"On my way here I saw a big fire at the Putilov's works. It looked that there were no firemen around."

"That's all part of the revolutionary design. Destroy everything! Then start from scratch!" the man said. Morósov could not say whether he meant it as a joke. He preferred to say nothing.

47

A proclamation by Lenin announced that the Provisional Government had been overthrown and the power was now in the hands of the Military Revolutionary Committee of Petrograd.

"Hail the Revolution of the Workers, Soldiers, Sailors and Peasants!" screamed the headlines in the Bolshevik newspapers, and public notices appeared on the walls of Petrograd buildings announcing the victory of the proletariat.

Lenin shrewdly issued several immediate orders that crippled any possible opposition. He shut down all the newspapers except the Bolshevik's, and arrested their editors adding them to the deposed members of the Provisional Government incarcerated at the Peter and Paul Fortress. An order went by wire to all the main cities of Russia that the power was now in the hands of the Military Revolutionary Committees, and that all previous political and military leaders must be placed under arrest at once. The old order had collapsed. The new Bolshevik order was about to take its place.

The first heavy snow blanketed the ground of Petrograd during the night. In the morning, sleighs appeared on the streets, the horses feeling playful, enjoying the first *real* snow. In the following days Lenin authorized a slight increase in food rations, and the local railways began to function again. The armed patrols became more friendly, and the peasants began to bring milk and vegetables to the street markets.

The peasants did not want money. The Tsarist money became dangerous to own, the currency printed by the Provisional Government was worthless, and carrying gold was risky. The peasants preferred *things*. The street markets became strictly *barter* markets where one could sell and buy anything, a head of cabbage or a bag of potatoes in exchange for a chair or a gold ring. Even the prostitutes refused to accept money. Fresh lemons became their preferred method of exchange.

The news about the Bolshevik victory reached Odessa in two days. The reaction of Odessa's citizens was sharply demonstrated by the ethnic divide. The Russians were bewildered, but the Jews were triumphant. Most of the leaders of the Bolsheviks were Jewish, and some younger Jews talked of a just revenge; the pogroms and long history of discrimination against Jews in Russia were not easily forgotten in Odessa. But what united both groups was their fear of the sailors.

In Moldovanka at the Cohens' house, Julia and her parents had an important discussion in Yasha's room. They talked in whispers, so as not to disturb Larissa with the new problems: what to do if the sailors of the Black Sea Fleet were let loose in the city and came searching for officers? Their house would certainly be an object of the sailors' interest because of the presence of Andrei. Everyone in the neighborhood knew of Andrei.

"Andrei should hide his uniform," suggested Julia's mother.

"He should hide *himself*," Julia's father snorted.

"Where?" Julia wanted to know. "Under Larissa's bed? We can't hide him in the house. They will surely find him, kill him, and burn down the house!"

"What about the catacombs?" Yasha suggested. "Grandpa knows some good hiding places there."

"That's a good idea!" Julia exclaimed and kissed her son. "What a smart boy you are!"

Yasha blushed. Encouraged, he continued, "I also think that we should place little red flags on our house and on the garden gate. Let the sailors think that we are Bolsheviks."

This time his grandmother grabbed him and covered his face with juicy kisses. "You are the smartest boy in Odessa!" she declared. "Let's go to my room and make a couple of little flags. I am sure I can find some scraps of red cloth."

They left the room followed by Julia, who went to prepare Larissa for the *"possible complications."*

Larissa reclined in a wicker rocking chair, gently swaying her sleeping baby. Her lap was covered with a Scottish tartan throw, a gift from Veronica. She crooned softly an old Cossack lullaby that Ksusha used to sing to her when she was a child.

"What a lovely *tableau*," Julia thought as she paused at the door. "I'll never get used to her beauty."

Larissa's bountiful hair was loosely braided in a single plait, some strands falling freely on her shoulders covered with a white down shawl. It barely hid her full breasts. Her face expressed such tenderness and happiness that Julia caught her breath. "Raphael's 'Madonna and Child'..." she thought.

"Look at her," Larissa whispered, looking at the child. "Isn't she beautiful?"

"Yes, she is," Julia smiled. "I have something to tell you. Where is Andrei?"

"He is with Egórov at the Memorial, having his bandages changed. Something very strange happened. Glafíra Ivánovna paid me a visit!"

"Again? For the third or fourth time?"

"Yes, but listen! She offered her help in hiding Andrei and Egórov in case the sailors go searching for officers! So our men are now at the hospital, hiding! Andrei as a patient in bed, and Egórov in the uniform of an orderly carrying the bed pans!" she chuckled. "Glafíra came in the car and took them both with her! How do you like that?"

"Do you trust her?"

"I do. I think she is not a bad person, just a silly one, but I really think she is kind. She is putting herself in danger to help our boys. Anyway, what did you want to tell me?"

"That the men must be hidden from the sailors when they come searching. But Glafíra apparently solved our problem! However, we must make *you* look less desirable. You know that one of their favorite activities is raping upper class women. In your case, they surely would be tempted!"

"Let her lie in bed as if she were sick," Julia's mother said, coming in. "We can say that she is *typhósnaya*, and perhaps they will leave the house as fast as their feet will carry them!"

"We can paint Larissa's face with Mama's rouge," Yasha suggested from behind his grandmother's broad back. "It will look as if she has high fever!"

"I told you that he was a genius!" the grandmother exclaimed proudly and giggled.

The October Revolution was celebrated in Odessa with the desire to smash anything that was not to the liking of the solid mass of marching men and women carrying red flags on the broad boulevards. The sound of their voices penetrated the whole city, making the citizens tremble behind their bolted doors.

In the Cohens' house, Julia and her mother donned dirty kitchen aprons and stuck their hair under dark kerchiefs, while Yasha hid his treasured possessions, the violin and the ivory chess set, under a pile of dirty towels in the laundry basement. The women moved the basket with the sleeping baby into Yasha's room, the safest in the house since it faced the garden, and tucked Larissa in bed, her face and hands rouged. They tucked her hair under a dark kerchief as well and hid Andrei's and Egórov's tunics and military decorations under Larissa's mattress.

Julia's father decided to pretend that he too was infected by typhus. He stretched himself on the bed, covered his own face and hands with rouge and dampened his hair to create an impression that he was sweating. "It's the best possible way to protect my money! It should be safe in the double mattress and under my own body," he thought.

"Now—we wait. Just don't show them that we are scared," his wife admonished everyone. "We shall behave as if we have nothing to hide, so we aren't scared. Seeing two people sick with *typhus* will *scare them!*"

"I hope so," murmured Julia's father from his bed.

"What if the baby cries?" Larissa worried.

"I'll take care of her," Julia said. "You stay in bed! Our safety depends on you and Papa playing your parts!" she ordered. "Understand?"

"Yes," Larissa whispered.

"Do you understand, Papa?" she insisted.

"Yes, yes, I understand!" he replied with irritation. "I stay quiet!"

They could hear the sailors invading Moldovanka. The roar of the mob was truly frightening, for among the shouts of "All power to the Soviets!" there were individual calls for *Bei Zhidóv! Kill the Jews!"

Larissa, her eyes shut tightly, her body trembling, prayed that their house would be spared.

Her prayers went unanswered. She heard the loud banging on the front door, the frightened voice of Julia's mother crying, "I'm coming, I'm coming," the door opening with a crush, and she could see in her mind's eye a crowd of armed sailors bursting through it.

There were ten of them. "Where is the Tsarist officer?" a man with a booming voice demanded. "Where are you hiding him?"

"We don't hide anyone," Julia stepped forward. "The officer returned to the front weeks ago. There are only two people, my father and my cousin, both sick with *typhus*. Come and look for yourself."

Larissa heard the shuffling of many feet and the clanging of weapons as the men crowded through the narrow doors from one room to another. They burst into her room and stopped at the door.

"What's the matter with her?" the leader demanded.

"She has typhus ... And so does my father."

Larissa's tensed body made an involuntary shudder, and the sailors scrambled into the hall. The leader made no effort to stop them or to continue his search. "Let us know if there are any officers in the neighborhood," he said brusquely.

"We shall, *sir comrade!*" Julia's mother cried with servility, bowing before him. "We shall!"

The sailors, pushing one another, left. Julia and her mother bolted the door.

"Stay in bed!" Julia ordered. "More of them may still come!"

All through the night the citizens of Odessa trembled at the gunshots and piercing sounds of broken glass, women's screams, and the hysterical barking of dogs as the sailors went on a rampage in the dark and terrified city. They were not interested anymore in the 'Tsarist officers.' They were after the wine shops and restaurants. They emptied the private wine cellars of the rich and the beer taverns of the poor. The drunken crowds of sailors spread along the boulevards and the beaches in staggering masses, shouting and swearing, singing and fighting, and finally falling down somewhere having totally lost control of themselves. The city had never seen such disgraceful demonstration of disorder.

The Commissars of the abandoned ships requested the help of the Red Guards to round up the unruly sailors. A few Bolshevik naval officers who had replaced the murdered ones gathered for an emergency

meeting with the Commissars to figure out how to deal with the malevo-
lent sailors. There was not enough space in the brigs to lock them all up,
so they decided to do nothing. As for the city, well, the Commissars suggested that the city ignore the citizens' complaints and the murder of the
officers. No great loss. Blood must be shed. It's the Revolution, after all!

48

The next morning Julia sent Yasha to take a look at the destruction in
Moldovanka and check the homes of their friends. He returned with the
information that the beautiful plate glass vitrines with the gold-etched
name of Doctor Gottlieb were smashed, and the doctor had a black eye.
The Bechstein piano in his parlor had its keyboard smashed, and the
equipment in his examining room was destroyed. On the wall of his dining room was written "Bey Jidov! *Kill the Jews!*"

Larissa broke down in tears. "Poor Doctor Gottlieb," she sobbed,
"Why would they be so cruel to *him?* He wouldn't hurt a fly!"

"Because all Russians hate Jews," Julia's father spat vehemently.

"It's not true!" Larissa objected. "I am a Russian and I don't hate you.
My best friend is your daughter! And I don't hate your wife! And I *adore*
Yasha! And I love Doctor Gottlieb and his family! And I love you! How
can you say that *all Russians hate Jews!*"

"Well ... all right! Not *all* Russians ..." the old man finally agreed.
"Some Russians."

They sat around a small table in the gazebo, the weather being unsea-
sonably warm. An old samovar puffed peacefully, and Yasha munched
on his third piece of his grandmother's *mandelbrot.* The baby slept in her
laundry basket while Larissa worked on attaching lace to a tiny bonnet
she was preparing for the Christening. It was a peaceful tea-time and it
was hard to imagine that only a few days before the air was filled with
curses and gunshots and terrified people hiding from other people bent
on murder.

A klaxon sounded on the street. Yasha recognized the sound. "Andrei and Captain Egórov are back!" he shouted and rushed to open the
door.

Glafíra Ivánovna accompanied the pilots as they entered the garden.
The men were wearing gray wool sweaters of British aviators. It was
safe attire, without any insignia. They looked good, resembling young

athletes ready for cricket or rugby or whatever games British young men played. Provided by the British Red Cross via Sister Veronica, the sweaters looked cozy, as if some loving grandmother had knitted them for her grandsons.

"Andrúsha!" Larissa rushed into his arms.

Egórov bowed to Julia's parents and kissed Julia's hand. "Well, how did it go here last night? The sailors did not bother us too much at the Memorial. Glafíra Ivánovna was *a peach!* Without her I don't know how we could have managed to escape the sailors!"

She blushed with pleasure. "I kept chattering and flirting with them and I think they had no time to think of anything but how to get rid of *me!* But we saw a lot of damage in the city as we drove through it right now. Anyway, I must go! Good to see that you are safe!"

Julia led her to the door. "Thank you, Glafíra Ivánovna! You are truly our savior!"

Glafíra smiled and her slit eyes disappeared. "Never mind!" she said. "When is the Christening?"

"We don't know yet. We still cannot get a date from the church."

Glafíra Ivánovna looked thoughtful. "We have a small chapel at the Memorial and a priest on retainer. I can authorize the use of the chapel for the Christening. But you must do it fast. Before religion is officially prohibited."

"How about tomorrow?" Egórov said.

She laughed. "Well, tomorrow may be a bit *too* soon. Lieutenant Rezánov must get in touch with the priest and so forth, but the day *after* tomorrow, I think it might be possible."

"Good. It will also give me time to arrange for my trip back to Yassy. We don't even know if the trains are still running!" Egórov said.

"I'll stop by tomorrow to arrange the details," Glafíra said. "Good bye, now!" She took a peek at the baby and left.

"I told you that she was a kind woman!" Larissa said to Julia. Then, she turned to Andrei.

"Anyway, have you heard *anything* from Kozakov? Has he delivered our letters? I had hoped that *by now* Doctor Shubin would certainly have some news from Kozakov."

"No. Nothing. There is still no mail or telephone connection with Petrograd. Nothing."

Larissa made the sign of the cross. "In that case I may *never* see my mother!"

"I hate to be so pessimistic, but it is quite possible," Egórov agreed. "In any case, I must return to the squadrons immediately, since Kozakov might be unable to get back."

Andrei hated the idea of Egórov leaving. His own leave was to expire in two more weeks. After that—back to flying and shooting and being shot at. Where was his love of flying? He did not want to think of it. He had noticed that his attitude toward life had changed. Nothing seemed to be pleasing anymore. Why wasn't he as happy with the baby as Larissa was? Foreboding thoughts about the future crowded his mind, excluding any semblance of joy.

"Why would you want to go through all this trouble to get back to that stupid war that is almost over?" Isaak asked. "The Bolsheviks are talking about peace with the Central Powers."

"Because, my friend, I swore to protect my country against her enemies, and the Central Powers are her enemies," Egórov said. "Because, I am an officer of the Russian Military Air Service and it's my duty to be with my men. It's my duty. It is as simple as that."

There was a moment of silence, everyone moved by his sincerity, but not necessarily agreeing with its premise.

"I'll help you pack," Julia said quietly, standing up.

"That would be wonderful," Egórov smiled.

In the morning, Julia finally helped him pack. "Well, a few more hours, and you'll be gone. Then—what?" she said, watching him shave. She was on the verge of tears.

"Who knows, what ..." Egórov said. "What are *your* plans?"

"I don't have any. Although for Yasha's sake, I should go to America."

"Then do it quickly, while it is still possible to leave Russia. Do you speak English?"

"No. But Yasha does. He is taking English instead of French at school."

"Good! But start learning English. Larissa can teach you."

"I'll think about it," she said. She made an effort not to weep; "I am in love with him," she thought, feeling sad.

Egórov was subdued. He enjoyed Julia's company, her wit and her passion. He thought that he could actually come to love Julia. "She would be *loyal*," he thought. It was sad that they were to part within hours, perhaps forever.

Egórov ordered breakfast. "Do you want me to come with you? To the station, I mean?" Julia quickly clarified her question.

"Better not ... Maybe we should say our farewells now. Privately. Besides, if there are no trains going anywhere, I'll have to figure out some other way to travel. I don't want to drag you around while I am making enquiries."

"I can't let you go!" she exclaimed suddenly, surprising herself. "I love you, Vassily!" She threw her arms around his neck, kissing his face, sobbing with desperation, allowing her feelings to explode. Egórov was stunned. Like most men, he did not know how to deal with women's tears. He stroked her shiny black hair, at a loss for what to do. He probably should have said that he loved her too, but he could not.

Julia sensed that he could not say it, and dropped her arms. She searched her pockets for a handkerchief but could not find any. Grabbing a napkin from the breakfast tray, she wiped her face.

"I had better go. Now," she said, her voice unsteady.

"I'll take you home."

"No. You hurry to the station. Good luck. Be safe!" Julia tried to smile, but tears welled in her eyes again. She grabbed her coat and purse and hurried out of the suite, forgetting her hat and gloves.

Egórov stood where she had left him, his face moist from her tears. "I am a scoundrel!" he thought. "Why had I nothing to say to her?"

The large central hall of the station was empty. There was a notice on the wall next to the closed ticket windows proclaiming that there would be no train departures or arrivals until further notice. No reasons were given.

Egórov fumed. He hated the Bolsheviks who were the cause of the chaos in the country. But at that moment he hated himself for acting so cold toward Julia. He should have told her that he too was sorry to part from her. ... He should have ... A glass of cognac! He prohibited himself from thinking of Julia. He headed toward the bar.

Several Romanian artillery officers crowded around a small table covered with a flashy Tatar tapestry. The officers seemed to be in high spirits with glasses of cognac, laughing at some joke, one of them a bemedaled general. Egórov clicked his heels and saluted crisply. He took off his leather coat and his three St. George crosses glistened on his tunic. The Romanians noted his rank and the fact that he was undoubtedly an ace.

"Would you like to join us, Captain?" the silver-headed general asked in French.

"It would be my pleasure." They introduced themselves to each other. General Ionescu beckoned a waiter who brought another glass and a fresh bottle of cognac.

"I see that you are in the same predicament as we are. You need to leave Odessa and there is no way of doing so," the general said pleasantly.

"Yes, Your Excellency. I was on leave, visiting with a wounded friend, and now I must return to my Air group, which is partially in your country."

"By any chance, in Yassy?" the general asked with a smile.

"No, Your Excellency. We *were* stationed in Yassy for a while, but then the front stabilized and my squadrons were moved north."

"Oh, yes. Our offensive at Marashesti had fizzled. Were you a part of the Russian group that bombed the Germans so successfully?"

"Yes. I led the eleven craft group. Originally, we caused them heavy losses, but, unfortunately, the offensive *fizzled*, as you've said."

"Yes. The Germans counter-attacked and advanced about eight miles into our territory after we removed you Russians from our front! Our Command decided to withdraw all Russian units from the sector as *untrustworthy*. I am sorry to say, but your troops refuse to fight!"

Egórov looked straight into his face. "I agree with you, General. Russians have became *untrustworthy* allies, and I am afraid that it is going to become even worse."

"That's what I have been wondering myself!" General Ionescu said. "Anyway," he perked up, "*we* are on our way back to Yassy and are waiting for a special train that has been dispatched to pick us up. Perhaps we can help you, Captain Egórov. If you wish, we'll take you along."

"Dear sir! You are God sent!" Egórov exclaimed. "I don't know how to thank you!"

General Ionescu smiled. "You don't have to. We are all military men. We all were raised since boyhood to stand up for each other and be of help to our brothers-in-arms."

Egórov bowed to the general. "I am truly grateful," he said.

"*Bon!* Tell us now, what's going on in *your* country? We arrived in Odessa for a special meeting but the meeting was cancelled. No one seemed to know what had happened, why there was no transportation or any working telephone or telegraph. We remained isolated in our hotel until I received a hand delivered message from our Consulate that we will have a special train to take us back to Yassy. So, what's going on?"

"You haven't heard, Your Excellency? The Bolsheviks staged another revolution in Petrograd!" Egórov said. "They are now poised to take charge of the whole country!"

49

A scant train of one car and a locomotive bearing the colors of Romania on its chimney arrived at the Odessa main terminal. The locomotive was unhooked and maneuvered onto the sidetracks to be turned around and attached to the car again at its other end for the return journey. The stationmaster reported to General Ionescu that the train was ready for departure.

"Shall we go, gentlemen?" General Ionescu said, rising. "Let's take along a couple of bottles of cognac for the road. Please pay what we owe, Lieutenant, and get a receipt," he said to one of his aides.

"Please, allow *me*," Egórov said. "As a small token of my appreciation for your kindness."

"It is not necessary," the general said, "but if you insist ..."

Egórov paid the bill and felt good about it. It was still substantially less than his fare would have been for the tickets across the frontier.

They boarded the car and the general announced that he would like to take a nap. The conductor brought out a fluffy pillow and a large Tartan blanket and helped the general take off his tight jacket and boots. With a sigh, the old man stretched out on the couch. "Wake me up in two hours," he said to his aides.

"What a charming old chap!" Egórov thought as he settled into a chair by the window and sat staring at the passing landscape of orchards and straw-roofed whitewashed huts. His thoughts turned to his last moments with Julia. "Why didn't I comfort her?" he thought. "She took me by surprise. I could not lie to her..."

He felt rotten. Julia's tormented face stayed in his mind's eye.

Julia came home mentally flogging herself. She threw herself on the bed, pummelling the pillows with her fists. She sobbed, not caring whether anyone heard her.

Larissa came into the room. "What happened?" she asked.

"I am so ashamed!" Julia sobbed. "I behaved like some lovelorn Tatiana confessing her love to Onégin! I told him that I loved him! I am so ashamed of myself!"

"What did he say?"

"Nothing! He offered to take me home."

"There must be more to it," Larissa thought. A flash of memory brought to her an episode from her own life. She embraced Julia and said quietly, almost into her ear, "Something like that happened to me. Andrei and I were engaged and he was about to leave for the front. I went to his room and gave myself to him *before* we were married. His parents were furious, but my mother understood how I felt, and she defended Andrei before his parents and did not shame me. It is one of my sweetest memories ... letting him know how much I loved him. Don't feel ashamed."

Julia wiped her tears. "You are truly *a special* person, Larissa," she finally said. "Fine. I won't feel ashamed of myself anymore. I'll concentrate on the fact that Vassily did not *lie* to me. He was a gentleman. He did not love me and he did not lie to me that he did. As for my outburst ... well, I am an impulsive woman and Vassily was leaving for the front ..." she tried to smile. "It is a good excuse for my behavior."

"That's better!" Larissa said. "I know that he was fond of you. I think he was *infatuated* with you. As for love, Andrei had told me that he was desperately in love with some married woman who apparently did not share his passion," Larissa said.

"I feel better now. I behaved stupidly, yes, but I really cannot blame Egórov for anything. What could he have done differently?"

"I agree. And, don't worry, I won't tell Andrei. There are certain things that are strictly between women."

"Agreed!" Julia said. "You are so young. How did you come to possess so much wisdom?"

Larissa laughed. "It's not *'wisdom.'* It's simply common sense!"

The train arrived in Yassy in total darkness. All lights at the terminal were extinguished as a precaution against air attacks. The train had been stopped twice along its route by saboteurs who blocked the tracks with chopped down trees. Egórov helped General Ionescu's aides remove the tree trunks off the rails, grateful that there were no hidden explosives buried in the roadbed or snipers hiding in the tall weeds.

General Ionescu extended his benevolence toward Egórov even further. "You stay tonight at our headquarters, Captain. In the morning one

440

of my aides will take you to our aerodrome with my written request to assist you in returning to your detachment base."

"Thank you for your kindness and understanding, General. Without your help I would've certainly risked being court-martialed if I failed to return to the base on time!"

"Don't mention it! It was your good luck and my opportunity to help that brought us together," he smiled. "So, let's shake hands and wish each other some more good luck. *Bon chance, mon Captain!*"

The next morning, Egórov and a Romanian pilot climbed into a two-seater Spad A.2 and set course northeast to the Russian positions.

"Back to the old routine," Egórov thought as he faced his desk. He was annoyed as he could see that in his absence someone had riffled through his desk and his papers. That 'someone' most likely was the Commissar, he thought.

Igor Kóshkin lifted the flap of Egórov's tent and knocked on the inside pole.

"May I come in?" he asked, grinning. "Welcome home!"

"You are already 'in,'" Egórov replied, not too friendly. "Have you heard from Kozakov?"

"As a matter of fact, yes. He has been stuck in Gátchina Flight School, very ill with some kind of fever, but he is coming back as soon as they can arrange for transportation."

"Is it typhus?"

"No, something different. Something that I've never heard of before. Something that stays with a patient for several months, gets better, and then gets worse again. I forgot the name. Anyway, how are our friends in Odessa? By now Larissa Sergéyevna must have had her baby."

"Yes. She had a girl. By the way, the *enchanting* Glafíra sends her love!" he said with deliberate touch of nastiness. "You were sort of ... close, weren't you?"

"You must be joking!" Kóshkin laughed without rancor, either being a good actor or not catching the insult. "What is the baby's name? You are her Godfather, no?"

"By proxy. I could not stay for the Christening. We had to ask Akim to stand up for me."

"Akim? The *isvóschik*, the cabdriver? I can't believe it! My, oh my, how the mighty have fallen!" he broke out in laughter, slapping his knees and jumping like an adolescent. "To have an *isvóschik* for a Godfather! Hail to the Proletarian Revolution! Only a year ago the godfather would have been some Grand Duke!"

Egórov felt livid. He controlled himself. "The child's name is Nina," he said dryly. "Now, please go. I have things to do." He turned his back to the Commissar, pretending to arrange his disturbed papers.

Kóshkin quieted down. "Before I go, I must tell you about some new directives that were issued while you were away. First, all officers' ranks are *abolished*. No more generals and captains and so forth. Soon we'll be informed about the new ranks and the correct forms of address. Second, all foreign languages are *abolished*. Only Russian is to be spoken. That order was issued once before, but most of you gentlemen-officers paid no attention to it." He scowled. "You continued speaking French among yourselves, and the rest of us could not understand what you were saying. From now on, you must speak only *Russian*. Those who disobey will be severely punished!"

"By a firing squad?" Egórov asked coldly. "Anything more?"

"No. For the time being that's all. But there will be more directives, I am sure." Kóshkin smiled and left the tent with a jaunty gait.

Along with abolishing ranks, Lenin did not waste a moment in granting more and more power to the Soviets. He dissolved the legal system and abolished the legal profession. All political crimes from then on would be handled by the Revolutionary Tribunals. He demanded liquidation of the *enemies of the people*, a new term that was invented to identify the so-called *former class*. Lenin fanned the flames of hatred toward the *former class* into a conflagration, urging his disciples to become instant judges and executioners.

To undermine whatever remained of the discipline of the troops at the fronts, the Bolsheviks issued the *Declaration of Soldiers Rights* that granted troops the right of selection of their commanders and discussion of their orders. It allowed the soldiers to refuse obedience to any order. It also gave them the right to condemn their commanders and to execute them.

The commanders were helpless. Only one of them took his own draconian measures against the deserters and the agitators: General Kornilov, the son of a Siberian Cossack. He ordered the hangings of deserters at every crossroad in his section of the front, treating them as harshly as the Bolsheviks treated the officers.

Kerensky, having escaped to Stavka, still held the title of Supreme Commander and still hoped to inspire the remaining loyal troops to continue their fight against the Central Powers. He began by reshuffling his Commanders, removing some of them, accusing others of incompetence and even treason. He started by arresting General Kornilov. Four other generals followed. All five demanded a public trial to prove their innocence and were incarcerated in an old monastery in the ancient town of Bykhov.

Meanwhile, Lenin's supporters seized Moscow and several other cities. The tentacles of the Proletarian Revolution reached farther and deeper into the land. By mid-November the imprisoned generals realized that there was no one left to stop it, unless *they* led the counter-revolution. They escaped, making their way south to Cossack lands on the Don and the Kuban rivers where a nucleus of the Volunteer Army was forming. Hundreds of officers whose troops had deserted made their way singly or in small groups to Novocherkassk to volunteer. They pledged their lives to liberate Russia from the Bolshevik insurrection.

The Civil War had begun.

50

On every level the country was exhausted by war, and the Bolsheviks promised *to put an end to the war*. Lenin pursued his bid for peace by sending a delegation led by a gentlemanly Jewish intellectual, Adolf Joffe, to Brest-Litovsk, an ancient Polish town at the confluence of the rivers Bug and Mukhovets.

On December 3, 1917, a large Russian delegation faced a smaller group representing the Central Powers. The Russians were specific in their selection of the members of their delegation. They wanted to symbolize the *new* Russia of the Soviets and flaunt their new equality by having a *woman* delegate and a *Jew* heading the delegation. In addition, the Bolsheviks brought to the conference four symbolic men—a worker, a soldier, a sailor, and a peasant, who were to represent the new egalitarian Russia.

The representatives of the Central Powers had great fun ridiculing the Russians' manners, noting with amusement their reluctance to use dinner napkins, wiping their fingers instead on their trousers. The *'symbolic'* representatives preferred to use the same spoons for everything, and the better-educated members of the Russian delegation, who had proper dinner manners, burned with embarrassment. To spare themselves more humiliation and ridicule by the press, the Russians requested to be excused from attending formal dinners.

While Joffe tried to negotiate an armistice, Lenin continued reshaping the lives of millions of Russian citizens. With a stroke of a pen, Lenin nationalized factories and workshops, schools and universities. Everything was to be the 'property of the people.' The requisition of private property was increased. The banks were nationalized, private accounts frozen, and any kinds of private loans annulled.

Andrei and Larissa were hit hard by the nationalization of the banks. Their monetary assets in Petrograd and Odessa were now frozen, soon to become confiscated. Still having no news from their families, they presumed that the same situation enveloped their parents as well. The only money that Andrei and Larissa still had was his salary as a pilot and the gold coins sewn into their clothing.

Andrei was due to return to his detachment. His arm wound had finally healed, but the problem of how to get back to his detachment was as difficult as ever. He was perturbed about leaving Larissa and his infant daughter in the revolutionary Odessa. Even though he knew that Julia and her family would take good care of them, they were not *family*. Besides, being Jewish, they had their own troubles to deal with.

They read in the Bolshevik newspaper that the manager of the Odessa bank had been executed by the sailors. Prior to his arrest he apparently destroyed all the documents dealing with conversion of paper money into gold, which he had advised *his cronies* to do, the newspaper said.

"He probably saved our necks," Andrei said. "I am sure we were among his so-called *cronies!*"

"I am scared, Andrúsha," Larissa confessed. "We are like little children now. We must obey every order or be punished on the spot! No one says a word of protest!"

"I am scared also. Scared that there is no one there to oppose this Lenin and his bunch. I am sure there are hundreds of thousands of men like me, who feel the same way."

"The opposition must unite and develop a plan. Stage a counter-revolution!"

He faced her angrily. "You sound like a typical stupid woman! It's easy to say! *'Stage the counter-revolution!'* How can we *do it* when we have no way of getting together even to *plot* it? When I *must go* to my detachment? When we can't even get news about our parents! Are they still *alive?* We don't know. And they don't know whether *we* are still alive! And you say *'Counter-revolution!'* How? By walking to Petrograd? The Bolsheviks are all over the country now! They control everything! Everything!" He was shouting now, choking in his fury.

The child began to cry, awakened by his shouting.

"Stop it!" Larissa ordered in her mother's imperious voice. "You've upset Nínochka!"

"I'm sorry," Andrei muttered.

"Oh, Andrúsha, let's not argue or insult one another. If we start fighting, we'll lose each other …"

"I'm sorry. I shouldn't have called you stupid … Forgive me!" Andrei face was red. "I just feel helpless …"

"I know," she said softly. "I did not take it personally." She picked up the baby and unbuttoned her blouse. The child greedily attacked her nipple.

Andrei watched her, his heart overflowing with tenderness while his mind kept telling him that there was no exit from the labyrinth that his life has become.

Ironically, Andrei's problems were partially solved by Lenin himself. With only three more days before he was due to report at his aerobase, Glafíra Ivánovna arrived at the Cohens' house with a handful of mimeographed orders from the *Sovnarcom*, the Soviet of Peoples Commissars.

She smothered Larissa in her plump arms. "Good news! The trains are running again! Your husband can leave soon and not miss his date of return! Comrade Lenin ordered the rail traffic to be restored! And the telegraph service with Petrograd is back, at least for the official use."

"At last!" Larissa said with a deep sigh. "Maybe we can go home now!"

"It may not be possible. Not yet. Petrograd is in danger from the *counter-revolutionaries,* the papers say. It's much safer here. Perhaps your mother can come back to Odessa and take care of the baby, while you work. Because you *must* work!" Glafíra Ivánovna said severely and shook her finger at Larissa. "We have a new slogan: *Those who don't work, don't eat!'* I'll recommend our Soviet at the Memorial to take you back after your *'maternity leave.'*"

"What's that?" Larissa asked.

"It soon will be one of our new laws, *the maternity leave!* Women with newborn babies will be given a few weeks off, *with pay.*"

Larissa was speechless. She had never considered the plight of the working woman: go back to work almost immediately after giving birth. "It is a *good* law," she said finally. "And the Bolsheviks had suggested it?"

"Yes," Glafira smiled. "It *is* a good law. They also promise to make education free for everybody, from kindergarten to university!"

"That I would like to see!" Andrei snorted with sarcasm. Larissa threw him a warning glance, but Commissar Glafira only smiled.

"You *shall* see it, but you must be careful with *what* you say and *to whom,*" she said. "If you talk like that among some people, you may start counting your days. No, your *hours!* I am telling it to you as a friend," she said.

"We appreciate it," Larissa replied as the icy fingers of fear touched her spine.

Andrei departed the next morning on the first train going to Yassy. Akim drove him and Larissa to the station. The big waiting room was crowded with the relatives and friends of soldiers returning to their regiments. All officers, including Andrei, were without their epaulettes or any symbols of rank or decorations. They looked embarrassed as if they were undressed. They secretly hoped that once they were back among the loyal troops at the front, *maybe* things would change. They yearned to be respected again, many of them thinking of the nascent Volunteer Army that was forming in the Cossack lands.

Larissa clung to Andrei, trying not to give in to her desperation. Julia had told her that any emotional upset might dry up her milk, but the tears kept gathering in her eyes, spilling over her face.

A sharp whistle announced the departure of the train and the crowd poured out onto the platform. The women and children sobbed, not hiding their distress anymore, knowing perhaps that they were seeing their husbands and fathers for the last time.

Larissa waved her handkerchief and saw Andrei waving back to her. The train began to move, then gather speed and then, it was gone.

Upon arriving in Yassy, Andrei took a carriage to the aerodrome. He needed to send a message to the 19th Corps Detachment that he was ready to be picked up. That done, he ordered the driver to take him to the Grand Hotel Traian, a huge building designed by Gustave Eiffel. Andrei barely glanced at the famous building. He was consumed by nervous energy, worried suddenly about his father. Deep in his heart he feared that his father was gone. "Has he been arrested? With his hot temper he certainly could have been ..."

Andrei was anxious to talk to Kozakov. "He should be back from Petrograd. He would know what is going on!" His thoughts became incoherent as he threw himself on the bed, lost in an uneasy sleep.

Kozakov was still in Gátchina, prevented from leaving by the illness that kept him in its grip. He witnessed helplessly as his beloved Nieuport 17 was confiscated during a brief fight between the striking Bolshevik ground personnel and the officer-pilots. A new Commissariat of Aviation and Aeronautics was created to disband the aviation units made of officers that were suspected of being counter-revolutionary.

The purges of the aviation ranks began at Gátchina Flight School. It was renamed First Socialist Flight School, and Colonel Gorshkov was arrested and replaced by a non-commissioned military pilot.

Kozakov observed the changes with silent fury. He still suffered from sudden fevers and shook uncontrollably, or burned with sudden heat and sweat. On other days, though, he felt almost normal.

"I must send Maria Nikoláyevna's letters to Odessa," he thought. "The postal service is supposed to be back to normal." The letters burned his pockets, those pathetic letters that she must have written with her blood and tears. Kozakov wished that her letters could bring some happiness to her daughter and son-in-law, but he knew that they would only increase their despair.

But it had to be done. The surest way to send the letters was by military dispatch. Andrei Rezánov should be back at the base after his stay at the hospital ... Egórov must be watching him, not sending him yet on patrols, saving his young friend from being shot down in the last days of the war. "The last days of the war! What a joke!" he corrected himself. "The war will continue, only now we will be killing our own brothers who are *already killing us!*"

Kozakov shivered; another bout of cursed fever was to lay him flat again. He called in the orderly. "Please, call mechanic Morózov from the repair shops. Right away!" he said, trying to prevent his teeth from chattering.

Shortly Morózov arrived wearing his grease-splattered overalls and pilot's goggles.

"Good to see you, Colonel!" he greeted Kozakov. "What can I do for you?"

"I want you to do me a *great* favor. I must mail Maria Nikoláyevna's letters to Lieutenant Rezánov. He is at the Stanislav Air base. I can't do it … I am still sick as a dog! Will you do it for me, Nikolaí?"

"What a question! Of course, Colonel! I think, though, the letters could get 'lost' at the censors. The Lieutenant's mother-in-law might have written something that our Bolshevik censors may not want to pass through. I will place the letters into a large *official* envelope and mail it as personal and confidential mail to your second-in-command, with your request to deliver the papers to Lieutenant Rezánov. I can seal both envelopes with the official seal of the Soldiers Soviet."

Kozakov could barely speak, his teeth chattering. "What a brilliant idea! My second-in-command is Captain Vassily Egórov, the best friend of the Lieutenant!"

"Then the problem is solved! We'll do everything *officially*. You just write a note to Captain Egórov. Do you know your Commissar's name?"

"Yes, I do. He is Igor Kóshkin. Thank you my friend," Kozakov said. "Now, let me rest for a couple of hours … I am exhausted …"

The plan succeeded without a hitch, Kóshkin correctly suspecting that the packet contained some vital information about the Rezánov family. He felt smug. It was he, after all, who had arranged the complicated scheme of sending Andrei's letters to Petrograd! Kóshkin, the inveterate Bolshevik, was delighted. He held hidden admiration for certain members of the military nobility. He envied their easy manner with each other that seemed to suggest respect and assurance of belonging to a chosen group. Despite the Bolshevik propaganda, Kóshkin wished that he were one of them. He admired Rezánov, Egórov, and Kozakov. His envy was not of a sick, vicious variety that resulted in hatred. Rather, it was an abstract, adolescent envy that a young man might feel toward some famous winner of a steeple-chase or a piano competition, whatever his personal interests were. And of course, he envied them their women. The image of Larissa, even pregnant, was often in his mind.

Egórov received a message from the telephone shack that Lieutenant Rezánov was in Yassy, ready to be picked up. "Aha! He made it! Good old Andrúshka!" he thought. He picked up the receiver of his field telephone and requested to be connected with Commissar Kóshkin. "Rezánov is back," he said. "I am on my way to Yassy."

"Could you deliver a bunch of *Pravda* to their airfield for me?"

"Why not? Bring it to my Spad," he said, then thought, "What the hell, I'll deliver the Bolshevik papers.... It's too late to stand on the principles of noble opposition!"

Three days later, Egórov tossed a packet on Andrei's bed. "Look what Kóshkin has brought me! Something for *you* from your *First Socialist Flight School formally known as Gátchina Flight school*. Open it!"

"Here is a note from Kozakov addressed to you." Andrei passed it to Egórov. With his Swiss Army knife, Andrei tore open the thick envelope. "The letters are only from Maria Nikoláyevna. Nothing from my parents ..." he said, his heart sinking.

"Read the letters." Egórov suspected bad news. "I am sure there is some logical explanation. I'll be back in a while ..." he said, leaving with Kozakov's note.

Andrei felt his hands shake as he unfolded the letters and began to read.

🙧 51 🙧

Maria Nikoláyevna still hoped that a new Constituent Government would be elected and repudiate the Bolsheviks reforms. However, with every new decree, her self-induced optimism crumbled like a dry biscuit. The nationalization of the banks was the final blow. She knew what would come next: the requisition of her house.

Ksusha and Stepan Petrovich knew it also. "We must save some of the important things before it's too late," Ksusha said. "Let's go around the house and see what might be easily hidden and bartered. Then, we'll go to *my* house in the islands and prepare it for moving in. I don't think that the Bolsheviks would want *my house* without running water or indoor toilet."

"Yes," Maria Nikoláyevna said. "Let's decide what we need to survive. Obviously anything that I am accustomed to is useless now. We must think only of practical things. First, we'll need to secure whatever money we still have. I suggest that we pool our money. We are old people and our expenses should be low."

"All my money was deposited in the bank, except for a few rubles in my wallet. I have nothing," Stepan Petrovich said. "I had hoped to get back to Ekaterineburg where I was born and my sister still lives, but now I don't have enough money for a train ticket!"

"I have everything sewn in my clothing, but it is the Tsarist paper money, so it is worthless," Ksusha said.

"The same with me. All my money, paper and gold, is in the bank. But I still have some jewelry. Let's hide the jewels before they confiscate them. We'll barter and sell the jewels for things as we need. The first thing we need is a train ticket to Ekaterineburg!"

"God bless you, Maria Nikoláyevna!" the old butler exclaimed, tears gathering in his old reddened eyes.

"Yes, yes! Much good a blessing will do!" she said with irritation.

"Don't be blasphemous! God will punish you!" Ksusha raised her voice.

"He is already punishing *me*. And He is punishing *you*! And rewarding the Bolsheviks! Where is His *justice?*" The old servants had no answer.

They selected the most important items for a basic life, concentrating their search in the servants' quarters. They needed pillows and woolen blankets, sheets and pillow cases, Turkish towels and knitted throws for extra warmth. No more silky quilts and embroidered sheets and pillow-cases from the masters' beds! A medium-size copper samovar instead of a huge silver one, cheap mugs and plates and imitation silver for eating utensils, although Ksusha suggested packing a set of real silver utensils for bartering a piece at a time.

Next came Maria Nikoláyevna's sables.

"Let's save the coats," Ksusha suggested. "Of course, you couldn't wear them in public, but if things get worse, we can easily trade them with the Bolshevik women. Meanwhile, we shall sleep under your coats and capes if it gets too cold." She stuffed Maria Nikoláyevna's and Larissa's precious furs into the horses' feeding bags from the empty stable. "What else?"

"Cooking utensils," the butler said. "You will need a frying pan or two, a big pot for soup and a couple of smaller ones. Then two or three glass containers with tight covers to store your flour and grains." He had already excluded himself from their planning. "I am going to be out of here, in the Urals, away from the cursed Petrograd!" he thought.

"What about shoes and clothes?" Maria Nikoláyevna said, "I have no sturdy shoes or felt válenki."

"I will get you something at the Gostinny Dvor," Ksusha said. "I have some friends among the merchants, as you know. We can barter a ring for shoes and válenki. But the rest of your jewelry we must hide in our clothing tonight! Who knows what will happen tomorrow."

Maria Nikoláyevna smiled without mirth and patted Stepan Petrovich on his stooped shoulder. "I shall miss you, my friend ... How many years have we been together?"

"Thirty-five, *báryn'ya*. And I was with the General for five more years, before you were married to him," he said, his eyes misting again. "I was his orderly when he was a young cavalry officer ..."

"Yes, I remember." she said. "And look at us now ... Anyway, let's not get too sentimental! In the morning we shall load Larissa's sled and the two of you make your way to Ksusha's house in the islands. I will stay here, in case the *'requisionners'* come."

Ksusha and Stepan Petrovich repeated their trips several times during the following week, becoming utterly exhausted by the journeys. The elderly travelers trekked over the ice of the frozen Nevá, dragging the heavily laden sled behind them, preparing the small hut for habitation as if they were squirrels. But they did not complain.

Through Ksusha's connections, Maria Nikoláyevna was able to sell one of her rings for two hundred rubles in small bills. She gave the money to Stepan Petrovich for his journey, and Ksusha contributed another twenty rubles, hoping that it would take him to the Urals if the trains continued to run. Maria Nikoláyevna added three silver spoons for an emergency. Ksusha baked some black bread, sliced it thin, and dried it in the oven to feed him on his long journey.

Maria Nikoláyevna and Ksusha went to the Nikoláyevsky Station to see him off to Moscow where he was to change trains for the Urals. They wept as they kissed him goodbye, knowing that it was forever.

Back at the frozen, forlorn mansion, they bolted the doors and moved heavy furniture against them. Returning to the warm kitchen, they sat down in the elaborate drawing room chairs around the kitchen table and dissolved into tears. Ksusha cried with loud laments in the peasant style while Maria Nikoláyevna sobbed silently and desperately, both women's spirits finally broken.

Another week passed. Maria Nikoláyevna began to hope that perhaps her fears of having her house requisitioned were unfounded. No one bothered them. Maybe the Bolsheviks would allow her to continue to live in her house, in the servants quarters. Maybe she should *offer* her home as a house for some famous artist or scientist? Or even a diplomat? It would make a marvelous embassy! "We could rebuild the Winter Garden and hold diplomatic receptions there," she thought, her imagination replacing reality.

But the reality won out.

One afternoon, three Red Guardsmen and several sailors arrived in two armored cars and stopped in front of the locked gate. They rang the bell and when the gate wasn't opened at once, yelled that they would shoot the padlock off.

Ksusha ran out of the house in her carpet slippers. "Don't shoot *golúbchiki*, I am coming!" She called, using the term for 'little doves', sounding as if she were a kind grandmother and not a scared old woman. Several of them smiled, perhaps thinking of their own grandmothers, but the others looked foreboding. They were there to perform a serious duty.

With their guns cocked, the men entered the house. "Who lives here now?" the middle aged man demanded. He was dressed in a handsome double-breasted black leather coat with the traces of the removed epaulettes, obviously an aviation officer's coat belonging to someone who wasn't around anymore. His chest was criss-crossed with machine gun belts of bullets. "Who lives here?" he repeated.

"We do," Maria Nikoláyevna said, entering the hall and facing the group, showing no fear. "I am Maria Nikoláyevna Orlova and this is my friend and companion, Ksenia Potápovna Tarásova."

"Any men living here?" the leader glanced at his papers. "It says that a general lives here."

"Not anymore. My husband passed away almost three years ago and my son was killed at the front. My daughter is in Odessa."

"We must search your house," the leader said not looking at her.

"Go ahead," she said and made a sweeping gesture toward the marble staircase.

She and Ksusha remained in the kitchen. There was no need to accompany the men. If they fancied anything, they would take it, without regard for the owner's presence.

Maria Nikoláyevna heard their loud footsteps throughout the house, cringing but willing herself not to show fear. Ksusha, on the other hand, cried softly, afraid to attract their attention but unable to stop.

In half an hour the men returned carrying rolled military maps from General Orlov's study. "We are confiscating the maps as evidence of sabotage," the leader announced, avoiding meeting her eyes. "Here is the receipt." He placed on the kitchen table a piece of paper with dimly stamped official seal. "And here is the order for the requisition of the house in the name of the Sovnarcom. You have twenty-four hours to leave the premises and you may take with you whatever you can carry."

Ksusha raised her voice in loud lament, increasing the volume until it became a wail.

Maria Nikoláyevna cringed but said nothing.

"Do you understand?" the leader demanded loudly, staring at her now. "Shut up!" he ordered Ksusha.

Maria Nikoláyevna met his stare. "Yes, I understand very well!"

The men departed, somewhat intimidated by her bearing and courage. The leader spat at his feet, saying under his breath, *"Whore!"* as he entered his armored car.

Maria Nikoláyevna locked the gate and returned to the kitchen. "Let's have some tea and decide what we must do next," she said, churning with hatred but speaking calmly.

"What do *you* want to do?"

"I want to break everything to pieces and leave, cursing them all to hell!"

"Then *do* it! Smash everything! Leave nothing for the cursed scum!"

Maria Nikoláyevna stared at Ksusha for a moment. "Yes! That's what I shall do! I shall destroy *everything* that we loved and cherished!" She grabbed a heavy silver candle holder from the table and ran to the entrance hall. She swung the candelabra at a marble bust of Athena at the foot of the stairs and knocked off the goddess' nose.

She went methodically through the house, smashing every mirror, every glassed cabinet holding some precious bric-a-brac, tossing the small items against the walls and crushing them with her feet.

She paused at the music room and stared at the concert piano. The great instrument smiled at her with its eighty-eight teeth, inviting her to make music. "I shall never touch it again," she thought. She hit the keys with the candlestick again and again, the piano responding with pathetic cries of pain.

Ksusha stood at the music room entrance, overcome by Maria Niko-láyevna's orgy of destruction. She felt a sudden urge to join in. She returned to the kitchen and attacked the blue damask chairs with kitchen scissors, tearing the silk upholstery to shreds. The feeling of revenge was new to her, and it was exhilarating. She slashed the seats of every chair and sofa in the drawing room. The lacerated furniture gaped at her, stuffing protruding through vicious wounds.

The women demolished everything. In the China Room they smashed every plate and cup of the exquisite Meissen and Sèvres dinner sets. In the Linen Room they tore apart fine sheets and embroidered pillowcases. In the bedrooms they mutilated the mattresses. The liberated coils sprang at them as if they were some mysterious vibrating creatures from the bottom of the sea.

Maria Nikoláyevna spared nothing, and Ksusha, infected by her mean spirit, followed her from room to room. Finally, in the general's study they paused in front of a large equestrian portrait of Nicholas II. The Tsar was depicted astride a white stallion, his chest emblazoned by shining stars and crosses of many decorations, his face kind.

"It is because of *him* that Russia is suffering!" Maria Nikoláyevna whispered fiercely. "It was because *he* was unable to govern! Because *he* *was weak!* I have never thought that I would come to hate the Tsar, but I *do* hate him now, I *hate* him with all my heart!"

Ksusha attacked the portrait with her scissors, making a gash in the Tsar's neck. "I was afraid to hit the horse," she said apologetically.

Maria Nikoláyevna suddenly broke into laughter. She bent over, laughing hard, tears rolling down her gaunt, unhappy face.

Ksusha stared at her. "Let's go to the kitchen and have that cup of tea," she said.

"It would have been *terrible*, to hit *the horse!*" Maria Nikoláyevna was finally able to say through her paroxysm of laughter. "Yes, let's have that cup of tea, and then go to your house on the island!"

"We may need to skip the tea. Do you know what time it is?"

"No. We have broken all the clocks." Maria Nikoláyevna laughed again. "But you are right. We must go now, before it gets light."

Ksusha knew well that imperative tone. It precluded any discussion. She shuffled to the kitchen closet. Silently they pulled on felt boots and quilted coats, heavy with sewn-in gold coins and jewelry. Covering their heads with heavy woolen scarves, they sat for a moment on the ruined chairs as the tradition required, praying silently.

Maria Nikoláyevna kissed the house keys and placed them on the table, while Ksusha spat over her left shoulder and repeated three times, *"I curse you all to hell and damnation."* Then, they left the house and crossed the street to the granite embankment and the snow-covered steps of the boat landing. Ksusha glanced at the house through gently falling snow, but Maria Nikoláyevna did not look back.

The child's sled bumped behind them on the slippery steps with its last load: an album with family photographs, three small icons, and a box with General Orlov's medals.

52

The letters devastated Andrei. Maria Nikoláyevna's description of his mother's humiliation and her slow descent into silence and death, or his father's desperate fight against typhus, made Andrei numb with grief, but that grief quickly turned into a murderous rage.

The requisition of the Rezánov's house on the Fontánka was the last drop in a bitter cup. It hit him with such force that he could not breathe.

Egórov entered the tent, a bottle of cognac in his hand. One glance at Andrei told him the story. "Here, take a sip!" He poured a little into a glass. He watched as Andrei grabbed the glass with a trembling hand and gulped it.

"Read this!" Andrei said, giving Egórov the letters. "There is more, but I haven't read it yet. I can't take it!" Andrei's face was blotchy, his eyes full of tears and his hair disheveled.

"Don't say that!" Egórov said sternly. "We are men. We must face the horror of our times and then decide on action. Are we going to let the Bolsheviks take over, or shall we fight? I choose to fight!"

"So do I!"

"Pull yourself together. Read the rest of the letters and then let's go out for a walk." He swept the tent with his eyes, mutely suggesting that *'the walls have ears.'*

Ten minutes and another glass of cognac later, they walked away from the tent, toward the dark forest on the edge of the airfield.

It had stopped snowing. It was quiet in the forest, without the constant buzz of aircraft engines. For two days, there had been no activity in their sector, as if both adversaries had given up their hostilities. The aircraft parked in two flight lines looked more than ever like a flock of nesting birds with their wings burdened by snow. The tarpaulins over the fuselages suggested horse blankets, creating the impression that the airplanes were some stout mythological half-birds, creatures never meant to fly squatting on broad snow runners that looked like long flippers.

"There are thousands of men like us," Egórov said quietly. "Men who will fight the Bolsheviks. We can't let the scum rape our *Matush-ka Rossiya!* But we must be smart about our next move. We should ask Kóshkin for back issues of *Pravda.*"

"Don't joke!"

"I am not joking. We must be well informed. We must know what's going on in the country. And Kóshkin will be pleased to see us reading them. He'll never suspect our next move."

"Which is?"

"You know as well as I about the Volunteer Army organizing in No-vocherkassk. We should *go* to Novocherkassk with a couple of aircraft!"

"You mean, become deserters? Steal planes?" Andrei was conflicted, caught between grief over his parents and rage toward his tormentors.

Egórov stopped walking and grabbed him by the shoulders. "Yes," he hissed. "Unless you're willing to swear allegiance to the Bolsheviks!"

"*Now* you are joking!" Andrei said icily.

The Commissar was predictably delighted. "I *was hoping* that you would become interested in our ideology," Kóshkin said. "With your background and some Communist education you could become valuable members of our revolutionary forces! Perhaps even achieve command-ing positions in the Soviet Air Force!"

"Not so fast, Comrade, not so fast!" Egórov laughed good-naturedly. "As you know 'Rome wasn't built in a day!'"

Kóshkin smirked. "What about you, Comrade Rezánov? I know, the news about your family must have been devastating, but now that you are as poor as I am you might as well join *us.* Together we build a new *socialist* society where everyone will be equal!" He noticed that Andrei's face reddened. It pleased Kóshkin to see Andrei humiliated. "That son-of-a-bitch!" he suddenly thought. "He doesn't deserve Larissa!"

"Anyway," he continued, "I am glad that you are interested in reading *Pravda.* It's a good title—*Pravda,* the *Truth! We tell the truth!*"

With their arms full of back issues of *Pravda,* Andrei and Egórov returned to their tent.

"All right," Egórov said, "let's start reading and planning. God *knows* what else Lenin has in store for us!"

"God *doesn't* know anymore. God was also cleared out," Andrei said, opening one of the papers. He willed himself not to think about his lost family. Egórov was right: it was time to think of *revenge*.

Andrei's despair morphed into a burning hatred that demanded action. *Pravda's* articles and slogans inflamed him, showing him whom he needed to fight. It was not the Germans anymore. His acute and single-minded need for revenge pushed out of his mind Larissa, the baby, and anything else sweet and comforting that used to give him so much pleasure.

He found a short article mentioning that counter-revolutionary forces of Tsarist Cossacks were organizing an army in the Crimea. They were calling it the *White* Army. Local Bolsheviks challenged them, but the Cossacks, aided by money from Imperialist countries, had won their first battle. Flaunting their victory over the Bolsheviks, the Cossacks sent Petrograd two freight cars stocked with Bolshevik corpses. The article had been written to inflame readers with wrath, but Andrei applauded it. "That's the way!" he cried, slapping his knee.

Egórov looked at him in astonishment. "If it's true, Andrúshka, I find it distasteful! We are becoming as brutal as our enemies!"

"It's the only way to deal with them! 'An eye for an eye!' No pity!"

Egórov cleared his throat. "You and I must leave for the Crimea right away, before they start to administer the oath of allegiance to the Sovnarcom. If we refuse to swear the oath, we'll be *put against the wall*, as they say now. We should take two Spads and load them with ammunition and guns, and if possible, with spare parts."

"It's a great idea, but how can we? The airfield is under constant observation and most of the service personnel are Bolshevik."

Egórov was undaunted. "We'll think of something," he said. "Perhaps we'll have to steal a couple of horses instead and gallop away, like the good cavalrymen we used to be!"

"Perhaps we'll have to *walk* away," Andrei said cynically.

"Perhaps! But one way or another, we must leave for the Crimea!"

53

The Cease-Fire agreement was reached in Brest-Litovsk on December 16th 1917. A great jubilation prevailed among the troops, while the

Officer Corps remained confused. The High Command at Stavka still pursued the war, so many units remained at the front in perpetual limbo. Meanwhile, the killings of officers by revolutionaries increased, leaving many with no hope but to make their way to the Don River and join the White Army.

The volunteer troops under Ataman Kaledin, a Cossack general, captured Rostov, a city recently taken by the Bolsheviks. It was a great victory for the fledgling White Army. Intoxicated by their victory, Kaledin's men executed the Bolshevik prisoners and Rostov Soviet. It was a feeble attempt at revenge, which showed the sobering reality: There would be no mercy in Russia for anyone. Within a short time the Reds dispatched an armored train and retook Rostov. They executed all wounded Whites in retaliation.

A new year, 1918, was about to arrive. It promised to be a hungry and severely cold winter, especially in Petrograd. As activities at the front abated, troops continued streaming home in a murderous flood of hungry men infested with lice, many sick or dying of typhus and infected wounds.

The pilots of the 19th Detachment were idle for more than two weeks. First it was the inclement weather that prohibited flying, then came the order from the Soviet of Soldiers Deputies to cease all action. Commissar Kóshkin had a secret order from the Military Revolutionary Committee to guard the airplanes from being hijacked by officers. Many were deserting and joining the resistance forces. Kóshkin had become the *de facto* commander of the detachment. Kozakov was still in Petrograd, ill and under investigation by the Cheka for refusing to join the new Red Air Force. Egórov and Andrei were voted *untrustworthy* by the Soviet of Soldiers Deputies after Vassily Yanchenko, another famous officer ace, went to the Whites in Novocherkassk, flying away in one of the detachment's airplanes.

The desertion of Yanchenko honed Kóshkin's Bolshevik watchfulness; he could not afford to have another escape with an aircraft in his dossier. He appointed trusted pilots and mechanics to guard the planes day and night, with special attention to men like Andrei and Egórov. He was not fooled by their interest in the Bolshevik newspapers.

Egórov and Andrei quickly discovered that they were being watched. It became clear that to follow Yanchenko's example would be impossible. Even if they managed it somehow, what about refueling? They could not carry enough cans of benzene and castor oil to take them over such a long distance. They had to abandon their romantic notions and concoct some more realistic action.

"I think we should go back to Odessa," Andrei said. "We have friends there and we will already be halfway to Novocherkassk!"

"In Odessa we'll be in the midst of the most fanatic Bolsheviks!" Egórov said. "I know you want to be near Larissa and the baby, and I don't blame you, but practically speaking ..."

"Practically speaking, we'll be *already in the Crimea!* It's still in our hands, despite the sailors! We may not even go to Novocherkassk! In Sevastópol and Evpatoria there are Flight Schools that operate under the old command! We can become instructors! And Odessa has an aircraft factory! We can become test pilots! There is an advanced flight school in Landsdorf, remember? You tried to send me there, remember?"

"I remember," Egórov growled.

"There must be a lot of pilots like us! Men with kindred spirit! We can organize our own anti-Bolshevik squadrons! And we *know* how to get to Odessa!"

Andrei's eyes sparkled with boyish excitement. "We will fly to Yassy with Kóshkin. He mentioned that he had to go to Yassy for some propaganda business, and he actually asked if I would fly him there. The Bolsheviks are becoming really impudent about watching us, but in Yassy we can get rid of Kóshkin somehow and bribe someone on the train to Odessa to sneak us in. If our old friend Osip Ivanich is still there, we'll have no problem. I know it sounds childishly simple, but it may work!"

Egórov looked at him seriously. "Stop, stop, stop! It sounds plausible," he finally said. "All right. Let's assume that you'll fly to Yassy with Kóshkin. Where do you fit *me* in your plan?"

"Simple!" Andrei exclaimed enthusiastically. "Since Kóshkin is going with some other chap, *you* can fly *him!* We'll take two two-seaters. I bet Kóshkin would agree, since he likes keeping his eye on both of us! Taking both of us along, we will be right there under his nose!"

Egórov's smile was wide.

As Andrei predicted, Kóshkin was delighted to have both pilots under his observation. He and his assistant loaded two planes with stacks of *Pravda* and propaganda slogans in Romanian to be presented to the pilots and mechanics to help them stage their *own* revolution. Lenin saw to it that the Russian Bolsheviks were generous in offering their help to any country that might be inspired by the Russian example!

Andrei and Egórov, like two schoolboys bent on an adventure, anticipated with alacrity their return to Yassy, even though there might be serious complications with their identification papers. Each of them had two sets of identification. One set, issued by the Kerensky Provisional Government, was supposed to have been destroyed when they received the new Military Soviet papers, but they hid the documents along with the certificates of their St. George decorations in thin kid leather envelopes plastered under their shirts.

The envelopes were Andrei's invention, and he was very proud of them. He had made them out of Larissa's opera gloves on Minna Solomonovna's sewing machine in Odessa. The thin, pliable leather never bulged under their clothing and was never itchy.

"Well, what else?" Egórov asked as they counted their money. Together, they had a little over five hundred rubles in gold, a small fortune, but scarcely enough for a long journey to Novocherkassk.

"Let's use the money prudently and resist our tendency to spend on champagne and cognac," Egórov said, meaning himself. "I need the restraint that my *'parole d'honneur'* would impose on me!" he joked.

"Avec plaisir, mon Capitaine!" Andrei laughed. They swore to one another that not a kopek would be spent on frivolities.

To reduce Kóshkin's suspicions, they left behind some clues indicating that they intended to return.

"We leave some clothing, of course, and our extra boots ..." Egórov said. "It's too bad, though ... I have just primed a new pair!"

"We need to leave something very personal. I know! I'll leave the first photograph of my baby!" Andrei exclaimed.

"Are you willing to part with it?"

"Yes! I made copies of it to give to friends after the Christening! As a matter of fact, I brought one of them for Kóshkin!" he laughed.

"Marvelous! And I'll leave the picture of my erstwhile wife!"

"Good riddance!"

Upon arriving in Yassy, Egórov stayed close to Kóshkin while Andrei investigated the possibilities of getting on a train, explaining his absence from the airfield as his need to buy some *'baby things'* for Larissa.

Andrei hired a one-horse carriage decorated with faded naïve paintings of flowers and birds in the style of peasant wedding carriages. Pulled by an emaciated horse in blinders and driven by a melancholic Romanian peasant with a long drooping moustache, the carriage barely moved along the streets paved with round stones. Using a French-Romanian pocket dictionary, Andrei told the driver to take him to the fashionable part of the city.

"Wait for me at the fountain. I won't be long," he said, pointing to the center of the square. In case Kóshkin had someone to spy on him, Andrei now had an alibi.

He went through the shops looking for a store with baby things. The series of upscale shops reminded him of Petrograd's Nevsky Prospect and The Passage in Odessa. It was fun just to walk through it, even without making any purchases.

Within minutes he found what he was looking for: the *Prêt- á- Porter pour les Petites Enfantes.* He was overwhelmed by the plethora of cute things in pink and blue. The matronly lady with a splash of silver among her raven black coiffure greeted him, all smiles. The young Russian pilot was obviously a new father. He was awkward, gingerly fingering the tiny things as if they were fragile. Noticing that he was basically looking at the pink things, she showed him tiny girls shoes, soft as the belly of a kitten, and little frilly white dresses, cuddly blankets, and soft flannel sheets for swaddling.

"What's the name of your little daughter?" the sales lady asked.

"Nina," he said.

"What a lovely name! Would you like to have a little silver cup and a spoon with her name engraved?"

He would, but he could not afford frivolities. "No thank you. I'll take the dress and the shoes, and one blanket, though."

"As you wish!" While she wrapped his purchases in tissue paper, then arranged them in a large box with the name of the store on it, Andrei quickly glanced out the window to see whether there was anyone suspicious. It looked peaceful enough, but then how would he know if anyone was watching him? He had read many spy stories when he was a boy, and he remembered that the hero had always checked whether anyone was watching him and *never* used the same hired carriage twice.

"Here you are!" the woman said, passing him the parcel. "Isn't it wonderful that the war may be over, at last?"

"Yes, it is!" he said, paying her, and thinking, "but not for us! Our war is only beginning!" He thanked the woman and returned to the waiting carriage.

Andrei dismissed the driver and, on foot now, went around the square pretending to be interested in the window displays of the local flower shops and the bakeries and tobacconists. He hired another carriage a few streets away. "Take me to the train station," he told the new driver.

It felt like spring, although it was still late December. Yassy looked bright in the winter sunshine, and some of the flowering bushes, which kept their foliage green all year around, were full of fat spring buds. Andrei observed the beautiful old city from his carriage and thought how much more prosperous Yassy looked in comparison to the Russian provincial cities. People were well dressed, the streets were clean, and children played in the well-kept parks.

The peaceful scene was not enough to distract him from his immediate task.

He realized that should they succeed in getting away, Kóshkin would logically presume that Odessa was their destination. "He would immediately telegraph the Odessa Soviets. We would be met in Odessa by a unit from the Cheka ... Maybe we should go straight to Novocherkassk ... But how can we get there from *Romania*? No, we have to take a chance and go to Odessa."

He ordered the driver not to wait for him while he went into the station looking for Osip Ivanich. Not seeing the old porter anywhere, Andrei asked for the Stationmaster who turned out to be a middle-aged mustachioed man with military bearing, a former Cossack who recognized Andrei.

"I remember you! You want to go to Odessa," he said in a booming voice. "How soon?"

"Today, if possible. With my friend. He is also a pilot."

The man observed Andrei closely. He could see that the pilot looked ill at ease. He had no distinguishing symbols of his rank, and he did not wear a red star on his cap or a red band on his sleeve. He wasn't a Bolshevik.

"Odessa is now partially in the Bolsheviks' hands," the Stationmaster said cautiously.

"My wife and an infant child are there," Andrei said. He thought that it was a good explanation for a mature man, who did not seem to be a Bolshevik sympathizer.

"Then, to lessen the risk, I suggest that you go to a different city, one not far from Odessa. I suggest Tiraspol," the Stationmaster continued, "It is on our suburban link of the railroad line, very close to Odessa, actually, less than one hundred kilometers, and right now it is still *safe*. My cousin is the Stationmaster there. He will help you. You can stay there *incognito*, perhaps growing beards and big moustaches," he smiled, "and then, if the situation changes, go to Odessa, or make arrangements to get your wife and child out. Do you think this may fit your plans?"

Andrei decided to be totally honest with the Stationmaster. "Sir, you can't imagine how much this fits our plans! Our lives are in danger at the present time. We are officers. So far we were lucky: we made it to Yassy, but we must get away from here *today!* We cannot return to our airfield."

The Stationmaster nodded. "Please sit down." He pointed to a chair opposite his own at the desk. "Does your Commissar know about your family in Odessa?"

"Yes."

"In that case, you and I must be even more careful. Your Commissar and his Bolshevik friends will come to see me if you leave. No doubt about it. They will demand to see our records and the receipts from the sale of tickets. He will threaten me with arrest if I refuse. But I'll let them see my records and receipts willingly!" He looked at Andrei with a sly smile. "You'll go to Tiraspol *without tickets*. My cousin will take care of you there. You'll pay *something* to my cousin, but I don't want your money. I am happy to be of help to an officer, just as the Cossacks were always of help to the Tsar."

His eyes were proud, and he stroked the end of his moustache. Then, he outlined the plan for Andrei and Egórov's escape from Yassy.

54

Kóshkin was exultant after his meeting with the Romanian pilots. He could not stop talking about it. He felt that with a little more persuasion, he would be able to convert many of them to the Bolshevik cause. He had joined Andrei and Egórov in a small parlor of their guest house, and the three of them relaxed in the comfortable chairs, puffing on fat Romanian cigars and sipping French cognac.

"What I need is a few men who will become my *'cadre'* in Romania," Kóshkin kept repeating, as if trying to convince himself how close he was to his goal.

Andrei and Egórov played the role of sympathetic listeners. Andrei demonstrated his goodwill toward Kóshkin by showing him the purchases for the baby; they both turned sentimental as they fingered the fragile-looking tiny items.

"Well, I had better go to bed," Kóshkin finally said. "Tomorrow I must conduct another important meeting, this time with the mechanics," he continued, stretching himself and yawning. "What about you? Want to come with me tomorrow?"

"Oh, no!" Egórov cried in pretended horror raising his arms above his head. "No meetings for me! Especially, the ones where the interpreter repeats every word at least twice!"

"I feel the same!" Andrei said. "I think I'll go sight-seeing tomorrow. Yassy is a picturesque old city with a five-hundred-year-old monastery. I had no time to examine it when we were stationed here."

"No monasteries for me! I would rather visit the *House Of Ill Repute!*" Egórov said with a lewd smile. They all laughed.

"Watch that you don't pick up some French disease there!" Kóshkin said, puffing on his cigar.

"In the *Romanian* whore house? It would be unpatriotic!" Egórov exclaimed with exaggerated pomposity. Kóshkin doubled up with laughter."

'Well, then I'll see you in the morning," he finally said.

"Not too early, please! Allow us a chance to sleep late! But, let me say this: you were *very good* at the meeting today! Lenin ought to promote you to the Red Air Marshal one of these days!" Egórov said.

Kóshkin blushed, a feeling of camaraderie toward the pilots overwhelming him. "Ah, go on!" he waved his arm as he went to his room.

Andrei's and Egórov's rooms were separated from Kóshkin's by a short corridor that led to the toilets and the showers.

"If Kóshkin hears us passing by his door, we can pretend that we were going to the toilet," Egórov said in a low voice.

"With our flight bags?" Andrei said sarcastically.

Egórov sighed comically. "Oh, Andrúshka, you have no imagination! If Kóshkin comes out of his room our goose is cooked, whatever we carry! We must *rush* him, tie him up, gag him. If worst comes to worst, we may have to cut his throat! Our lives are at stake now!"

"I hope we won't need to do that, but if it becomes necessary ..." Andrei did not finish. Neither of them welcomed the idea. They were pilots, not murderers!

They did not disturb anyone during their escape. They heard Kóshkin snoring contentedly in his room as they passed it. There were no guards around the guest quarters. There were no guards at the airfield either. It looked as if the whole city had suddenly abandoned its wartime need for security. The Romanians had signed the documents of the cease-fire. There was no need anymore for military patrols and other precautions.

That was lucky for Egórov and Andrei. Despite their careful planning for escape, neither of them thought of the *distance* between the airfield and the railroad station. Being so careful about the abstract details, they failed to secure a carriage to take them to the railroad station.

Egórov said, "Check your gun, although what good would it do if we are caught? Just pray!" He made the sign of the cross. It was the first time Andrei had seen him do it.

And so they began their long trek along the country road leading toward the city.

The country road was enveloped in darkness, the moon providing only dim light to make their progress a little easier. Doggedly they marched, their senses attuned to their silent environment.

The booming of heavy artillery came from a long distance away, and bright flares burst here and there along the horizon. "The Germans are on the move again," Andrei whispered. "I thought we had a *cease-fire!*"

"Apparently the cease-fire did not work," Egórov responded. "The Huns are shooting again!" Suddenly he stopped. "Do you see that blinking red light? There, on the right, in that side street ... Do you know what it is?"

'No, of course I don't know!"

"It may be a whore house!"

"What a time to think of whores! "Andrei exclaimed. "Your mind is forever on fucking!"

Egórov ignored him. "They may have a *carriage* that could take us to the station! Whore houses usually retain the drivers for the clients!"

They turned into the narrow street, walking toward the red light. Within a few minutes they reached a dark, three-story house with a fancy red lantern over its heavy front door. It *was* a whore house. Most important, in front of the house there *was* a carriage! The horse was covered with a blanket, a feedbag tied under its chin, and the driver, stooping low on his perch, was sound asleep.

"Hey, grandpa," Egórov said quietly, touching the man's knee. "We need a ride!"

The old driver woke up at once. "Where to?" he asked in Polish, but his accent was Ukrainian.

"To the train station," Egórov said, glad to hear his soft accent. The Ukrainian and the Russian languages were somewhat similar. It would have been more complicated to talk to the driver if he were a Romanian.

"Are you Russians? I don't take Russian money."

"We'll give you ten rubles in gold. But you keep your mouth shut about it, understand?" Egórov said in a threatening tone.

"I ain't no fool," the old man said with a chuckle. "Get in."

The horse trotted evenly on the thin cover of snow.

"Do you have any patrols?" Egórov asked.

"Only in the center of the city. Everybody there is hiding something, money or food or officers … The patrols make *a lot* of money there! They don't arrest the rich people if they pay them."

"What about you? Do they bother you?"

"No. They allow me to work for the whore house. I've been doing it for years! It's a good, steady job and the customers are all from the center of the city, so they always pay well."

"And the girls? Are you ever take a tumble with one or two?" Egórov asked.

The old man guffawed. "When I was younger, sure. But now, my pecker don't stand up no more, and the girls tease me."

Andrei smiled in the darkness. "That Egórka!" he thought. "True to himself, even now!"

They arrived at the station and in the light of a single bulb could finally see their driver, a small, dried up old man. He was dressed in a short sheepskin Cossack coat and wore a gray curly lamb *papákha* that was perched on his head at a rakish angle. His long gray moustache reached well below his chin, and it looked that he might even have the Cossack's *choob*, a single long lock of hair from the top of the head, partially hidden under his *papákha*. He looked like Taras Bulba, the hero of Gogol's famous story.

They paid the driver, picked up their flight bags, and walked through the unlocked doors of the main station building and then out through the side door, to the wooden platform for the local trains. There was a sound of a puffing locomotive, but otherwise everything was eerily quiet. Once in a while a cow mooed in the distance. At the end of the platform loomed the dark form of a shack and a blue light.

They walked in, bolted the door and turned the blue light off, as the Stationmaster had instructed.

Groping along the walls in total darkness they came upon a long bench.

"Now we'll wait," Andrei said, placing his small bag on the bench and sitting down.

"So far, so good. We are becoming adventurers, Andrúshka! Next stop: the great city of Tiraspol."

Andrei was about to reply, but there was a gentle tap on the door. They waited, and in a moment it was repeated and the subdued sound of someone clearing his throat. "Open the door," a low voice said.

"I have been waiting for you since eleven o'clock. What kept you?" the Stationmaster asked when Andrei let him in.

"We couldn't get away from our Commissar," Andrei said. "And then we had to pick up a ride here."

"Good. I brought you some clothes that you must wear *now*. You can't go around wearing officers' coats and caps. You must mix with the crowds until you reach the Volunteer Army. I presume that it is your destination." He handed them a couple of *touloúps*, raw-sheepskin coats, and two *papákhi*, Cossack hats. "I also brought you peasants' shirts," he continued. "The officers' white shirts could cost you your lives, but in these clothes you ought to get to Tiraspol without any problem. Once there, my cousin will take good care of you."

"How will we recognize your cousin?" Egórov asked.

"His name is Ivan Kusmích Prokassov. He is totally bald and he is fat. He has a habit of whistling. He whistles very well, all kind of songs, Russian and Ukrainian, and most of the time he doesn't even realize that he is whistling. It can be very annoying. But he is a good, Christian man who will help you. What else?" he asked himself. "Oh yes, start growing beards and moustaches, and try *not* to talk too much. Your cultured speech will give you away, just as your clean fingernails will."

"Thank you, sir," Andrei said "But we don't know your name."

"I am also Prokassov, Sergei Petrovich. Anyway, hurry up and change your clothes. I'll take you to the train that departs in thirty minutes. Have you eaten anything? Have you any food for the journey?"

"No, to both of your questions, Sergei Petrovich," Egórov said, pulling the rough homespun red shirt over his head.

"Oh ... Never mind, I'll make you a small package of food for the road. Anyway, it's not a long trip!" Prokassov said cheerfully.

"Thank you sir, not only for your help, but also for your good advice," Egórov said without his usual touch of sarcasm. "We are sorry that we cannot thank you in some more tangible way."

"Not to worry. My old man had a simple theory about gratitude. It went like this: if *I* help *you* in your time of need, in return *you* help *someone else* in his time of need, and *he*, in his turn, helps *someone else*, it will continue forever. Simple, isn't it ? We all get rewarded by the knowledge that we helped someone in need! It's a *good* feeling! As I told you before, I don't want your money. I'll take your leather coats, though, and keep them for a while. If things don't change, I'll sell them. If we return to our previous way of life, you can write to me and I'll send them back to you! Agreed?"

"Agreed!" They handed their coats and caps to Prokassov and donned the *touloúps* and *papákhi*.

They stepped out of the shack and Prokassov locked it with a key. It was still very dark. "Oh, oh! I almost forgot! You carry the officers' bags!" he exclaimed, stopping short. "It will never do! We must get you burlap sacks! There will be some empty sacks in the service car, so you stick your things into them ... Let's hurry. I want you out of town before dawn!"

He jumped off the platform, and the pilots followed. At a trot they crossed the rails to another rail bed where they could see the outlines of a short train with the puffing locomotive and several cattle cars and a service car hooked-up at the end. The pungent smell of cattle enveloped them.

"Good luck!" Prokassov said in a low voice. "Sorry that I have no better accommodations for you, but the cattle train under the circumstances is the safest way to travel. Climb on the upper sleeping shelves and *stay* there! Don't leave the car until you reach Tiraspol and my cousin will come after you. I'll bring you a little food for the trip in a moment."

468

In a few minutes he was back with two parcels wrapped in gaudy head scarves. Peasant women during harvests gave such food parcels to their men.

"Happy journey!" Prokassov said. "My cousin will take good care of you, as if you were our own kin. He might arrange your trip to Odessa by boat, which is safer than by train. He will know. I'll lock you up from the outside, but there is a small door in the *'crapper'* through which you can escape in case of trouble. Good luck!" He slid the heavy door. They could hear him locking the padlock.

55

Larissa was fast becoming a typical military wife like her mother, the difference being that instead of taking care of charities or rolling bandages while being served tea and French pastries, Larissa nursed her baby and washed diapers. The infant Nina became the *raison d'être* of her life. The weeks after Andrei's departure from Odessa swept by like fallen leaves on the Primorsky Boulevard. Larissa still had no news about her mother or of the rest of the family, and she wept helplessly worrying about them.

Then, suddenly, the postal and telegraph services with Petrograd were reinstated. The Soviets of Postal and Telegraph Workers had reached political agreements with the Sovnarcom, and letters and telegrams began to circulate in the country again.

Maria Nikoláyevna took advantage of the new situation: she wrote to Doctor Shubin at Memorial Hospital asking him to pass a letter to her daughter.

With shaking hands Larissa opened the long, heart-breaking letter. Maria Nikoláyevna wrote almost in code, in an attempt to escape the censor's blackouts. She hoped that Larissa would be able to decipher it; Maria Nikoláyevna described what had happened to their family. She did not avoid anything. She wanted her daughter to face the truth. Larissa needed to be aware that she was no longer a young, beautiful aristocrat, pampered and adored. She needed to become practical and unsentimental, thinking of the welfare of her child and of her own survival as a *protector* of that child. Even her love for Andrei should become secondary to her own welfare. Yes, Larissa had to learn to be selfish! As for herself,

Maria Nikoláyevna wrote, she would do everything possible to reunite with Larissa. But apparently, not yet …

Blinded with tears, Larissa could not continue reading. The image of her mother rampaging through the house gave rise to Larissa's own wrath. She felt a physical need to strike at something, *anything*, in her own impotent rage. If she were in her own house, she would have probably broken a few things to release her building up tension, but she was not in her house. She made an effort to calm down.

She picked up her two-months-old baby, and the baby smiled. "Julia, Julia," she called, excitedly, "Nínochka smiled at me!"

Julia and, behind her, Minna Solomonovna and Yasha, rushed into her room. They all peered at the swaddled little creature on Larissa's lap, and the infant rewarded them with the sight of pink toothless gums and what looked like a smile.

Larissa's rage was quickly displaced by deep sadness. "My poor baby … What kind of a life will she have?" she thought.

That night she read the rest of her mother's letter. She debated with herself if she should notify Andrei about the loss of his family and both of their homes, and decided to wait. She should not introduce more pain into his life, she thought. Andrei was in constant danger as it was; he did not need to be told about the tragedy. Not yet …

She felt suddenly hopeless. "We have lost everything, our parents, our homes, our money … We are *really poor* now! What future do we have?" She could see no future. She felt that her head would explode if she did not talk to someone.

"Julia!" she called desperately. "Julia, Julia, please, help me!"

Andrei and Egórov arrived in Tiraspol in the morning. The train stopped before it reached the platform. They waited, listening to the sliding doors of the cattle cars being opened and the noisy procedure of unloading the cattle. Among the commotion of shouting men and lowing animals, they suddenly heard someone whistling *"La Donna é mobile."*

They exchanged smiles. Indeed, it was Prokassov. He fumbled with the padlock and pushed the sliding door open. The pilots stood in its frame, burlap sacks over their shoulders, looking like gentlemen masquerading as peasants. Prokassov thought that they looked comical. The noble bearing instilled in them from their childhood could not be hidden.

"Welcome to Tiraspol!" the Stationmaster said with a wide smile. He was exactly as his cousin had described him: jolly looking, middle-aged, fat, and with a drooping Ukrainian moustache. "Who is who?"

"I am Vassily Egórov."

"And I am Andrei Rezánov."

"And I am Ivan Prokassov. Do you know anything about building garden fences?"

Andrei and Egórov looked at each other and shrugged their shoulders.

"That's what you will be doing around my house while I make arrangements for your travel. Nothing better than hiding in plain sight! Let's go!"

By now the whole train was surrounded by peasants unloading cattle and trying to hoard them into manageable clusters. It wasn't easy without the proper chutes and enclosures. The men ran after the cows, shouting and swearing, the dogs nipping at the cows' hocks. The terrified animals mooed, trying to break through the thin cordon of young peasant boys blocking their escape.

The pilots jumped down to the ground. In the pandemonium at the cattle cars no one paid attention to them. Prokassov led them to a small stucco house under a red tile roof, part of a small group of buildings some distance away from the station. The house had a picturesque Mediterranean look. It was surrounded by a perimeter of posts that protruded from the muddy ground like dragon teeth, obviously the supports of the fence that they were to build.

The Stationmaster said, "Let's go in and have something to eat while getting acquainted." They followed him around the house to the so-called *'black'* entrance, a back door for servants and traders that led directly to the kitchen. "I must treat you as if you were deserters whom I hired to finish my fence. I'll seldom speak to you in public, do you understand?"

Egórov and Andrei nodded.

"I suggest that you don't speak much to each other, either. Limit your conversations and don't meet people's eyes. Take off your hats when you speak to me or to my wife. Try to look *inferior*. I know it will be difficult for pilots!" he joked and laughed.

Egórov and Andrei joined him in his laughter. There was something pleasant about him. He began to whistle an old Siberian Cossacks' song, "Ermak."

"What should we call you?" Egórov asked.

"Call me *khozyáin*. It's respectful enough. The boss! And call my wife *khozyáika*. Or Anna Platonovna. It's a little sweeter and she is a very *sweet* woman. You'll sleep in the shed behind the house. It will be cold there, but my wife will give you plenty of blankets."

"Don't worry, *khozyáin*," Egórov said, trying the new form of address. "We are used to being cold. When we fly up there, it is so cold that our balls freeze!"

"I can imagine!"Prokassov laughed.

"Who is in charge in Tiraspol?" Egórov continued.

"I don't really know. For a while we had Bolsheviks running all over the place, confiscating everything in the name of the Revolution. Then the Ukrainians began to take back what was confiscated, there were some fights, of course, people were killed on both sides, until some new group arrived. They fought everybody and called themselves *'the 'Blacks.'* But now they are gone also, and we have no one. But I've heard that next will be the Germans or Austrians. They are on the move! The cattle that have just arrived is what the people in the west are trying to save from the Germans! What a crazy world. Is it true that the government ordered our troops not to fight?"

"What Government? " Egórov asked with a frown. "Our Government doesn't exist. The Bolsheviks are running it in Petrograd, but who is running the country elsewhere? But to answer your question, yes, the order was issued to stop fighting."

"God help us!" Prokassov crossed himself and made a tiny bow toward the church belfry that rose not far away. "We should know in a few days what's going on in Odessa. Perhaps it's better if you go directly to Novocherkassk. We know for sure that it is where the Whites are."

"I have my wife and an infant daughter in Odessa," Andrei said. "Before I go anywhere, I want to see them and make arrangements for their safety."

"We thought that perhaps we could join the aviation units in the Crimea. It seems that the Crimean aviation is still outside of the Bolshevik domination," Egórov added.

There was a sound of the front door being opened. "Must be my wife," Prokassov said. "We are in the kitchen, honey!" he called.

An imposing, stately woman entered the kitchen. The pilots stood up.

Prokassov laughed. "This will never do!" he declared. "Peasants would never *stand up* at the appearance of a woman!"

Anna Platonovna smiled. "But it was nice," she said with a charming accent. "Please, sit down." She wore a fine Romanian *poloushúbok*, a lambskin coat embroidered with colorful silks in intricate designs. Her wheat-colored hair was covered with a Gypsy shawl printed all over with huge red and yellow roses. She looked beautiful with her pink cheeks and large blue eyes as if she stepped out of a cover of a Palekh lacquer box, the image of the ideal Russian peasant beauty.

Prokassov looked at her with pride. "He is in love with his wife!" Egórov thought, watching Prokassov and feeling envious. "What a lucky man!"

Anna Platonovna took off her *poloushúbok* and shawl. She was dressed as a traditional Cossack married woman with her thick hair sleek on her head and gathered in a knot at the nape of her neck contained in place by a knitted hairnet. She wore a frilly white blouse that outlined her ample bosom. Several white petticoats peeked from under a blue woolen skirt with many folds that exaggerated her hips. She was magnificent in her mature ripe beauty, despite muddy boots that did not fit with her perfect image.

"I think, I'll bake a cabbage pirog in honor of our guests." She smiled, dimpling her round rosy cheeks. "Will you help me to chop some cabbage, Ivan Kusmích?" she turned to her husband.

"With pleasure," Prokassov said, contrary to the tradition that men despised doing women's work.

"We all will," Egórov chimed in, surprising himself.

"Give us some knives, Anna Platonovna, and show us how to do it!" Andrei said, trying to sound jolly, but he made no effort to continue the conversation. He chopped the cabbage silently, his thoughts on Larissa and the baby, making him appear listless. Egórov understood his concerns and tactfully stayed away from uttering the empty words that *"everything will be all right."* He too, worried deeply about Larissa.

56

A strange friendship developed between Larissa and Glafíra Ivánovna. To Larissa's surprise, Glafíra turned out to be well-read and quite familiar with foreign literature through translation. She was dismissed by most people as a clownish woman, not worthy of serious consideration because of her roundness and fussy curls, the high girlish voice and slit eyes. Through the years Glafíra acted as if she were, indeed, an empty-headed woman, man-crazy and often obnoxious. She learned to live with this caricature of herself and did nothing to dispel it. She suffered silently and deeply, finding solace in reading. No one was interested in her political ideas, but Glafíra was a Bolshevik who had offered her services to the clandestine cell of Odessa revolutionaries at the beginning of the war.

When she was appointed by the Workers Soviet to be the hospital Commissar, she found her *raison d'être*. She blossomed like some insignificant plant that blooms once in a generation.

The first tangible proof of her sudden power was the hospital automobile. She took pride in allocating its use to some and denying it to others, especially Doctor Shubin, who had never shown any respect for her as the hospital's linen keeper. It amused her to see how the famous physician tried to ingratiate himself to her so that she would allow the chauffeur once in a while to drive him home.

Glafíra became beguiled by Larissa from the moment of Larissa's and her mother's arrival in Odessa. She was not jealous of Larissa's beauty, but she envied her the naturalness of her manners and her easy social relationships. Glafíra wished to be friends with her, but they had nothing in common, she thought. As she had become Commissar, it became virtually *impossible* for her to befriend Larissa, her dreaded *class enemy*. Yet, she continued to admire the young woman and yearn for her friendship. It bothered her that Larissa lived in the Jewish neighborhood and was friends with Julia. People like Julia were *the bourgeoisie, the bloodsuckers of the working class!* The very people that the Bolsheviks had sworn to eradicate!

The chance to become friends with Larissa had come unexpectedly when Glafíra hid Andrei and Egórov in the hospital during the sailors' rampage, and helped send Larissa's letters to Petrograd. She risked her life by helping Larissa.

To Glafíra's surprise, the whole Cohen family had warmly accepted her in their midst.

Having no friends otherwise, Glafíra began to visit Moldovanka, bringing little morsels of scarce sweets from England or France that Memorial Hospital received through the Red Cross. As rumors began to circulate that America was joining the war, gift packages addressed to Larissa Rezánova began to arrive from the American Red Cross.

Larissa had no idea how her name had appeared on the list of the recipients of the American Aid Program, but she suspected that Glafíra Ivánovna had something to do with it.

One of the magnets that drew Glafíra to the Moldovanka was the baby. Glafíra loved the infant. She enjoyed watching Larissa nurse the baby or bathe her in the kitchen sink and cherished the times when Larissa allowed her to hold Nina.

Glafíra's admiration of Larissa and her baby was annoying at times. "She is so *cloying*," Julia complained, "every time I turn around, there she is!"

"I like her! She brings me candy!" Yasha said.

The women laughed. "Oh, we are so easily *seduced* by candy!" Julia said, mussing his curly hair. "But we should not discourage her friendship. She could be useful to us again. She has *power* over our lives!"

Larissa said, "It's sad that we base our friendship on her usefulness."

"That's life," Julia said pessimistically.

"I like Aunt Glafíra! She's funny!" Yasha insisted. "I told her that she looks like a girl's doll. Her eyes hide in her cheeks, like in the dolls that open and close their eyes."

"What did she say?" Julia asked.

"Nothing. She just smiled and her eyes disappeared!"

Glafíra arrived at the Moldovanka house in great excitement. "I have received a telegram from Commissar Kóshkin with some news," she announced. "Your husband and Vassily Egórov have deserted their squadron, and no one knows where they are. The Bolshevik headquarters in Odessa has been notified and our comrades are watching *you*. You could be arrested. I cannot help you. You can help *me* by not telling anyone that I warned you."

"We won't tell," Larissa whispered, her lips trembling. "Do you know where they are?"

"I have no idea. They might be on their way to Odessa, but I hope not. I must go. Be strong. And don't talk about your husband to anyone!"

"I understand," Larissa whispered. "Thank you!" Glafíra took a quick look at the baby sleeping in the laundry basket and was gone.

Larissa lowered herself into a rocking chair that Julia's father had presented to her at the child's birth. She was terrified. Like a small child, she yearned for her mother. She wanted to be with her, to hide in her arms. She felt despondent that their reunion had become impossible:

a new *prikaz* forbade travel to Petrograd or Moscow without a special permit. To get such a permit required lengthy applications and hearings of the housing commissions. The result was almost always the same: the application was denied.

Andrei and Egórov were constantly on alert those first days while working on the fence around Prokassov's house, but no one bothered them. They seemed to have melted in the changing pools of deserters and peasants in transit.

Prokassov insisted that they should not hurry to leave. "The Bolsheviks are on the lookout for you. They *know* that Odessa is your destination. I am sure there is already the order to shoot you on sight. Stay here for a while."

"And what if the Reds take over Tiraspol?" Andrei asked.

"Well, in that case you must leave and hide somewhere, even in the woods ... As for me and my wife, the safest thing for us would be to stay put and accommodate them. To assure them that we are sympathetic without joining them. It is a dangerous game, but I can see no other way to survive. Think of it: where can people go to escape from them? With you, the military men, it is different. You have a choice. You either fight them or become one of them. One way or another, you end up *dead*. Sorry to be so blunt, but that's how I see our world now." Prokassov's face reddened.

"Sh-sh," his wife said, "Don't shout, Ivan Kusmích ... Someone may hear you!"

"You see? We are already living life in fear of someone hearing us!'

"You put it just right," Egórov said. "But Andrei and I think that not everything is lost, even though our government had to escape to Samara! If we only stop arguing among ourselves and allow our elected officials to *govern!* Our allies will help us. They'll come to our aid!"

Andrei listened to Egórov with an air of boredom. His own belief in the opposition to the Bolsheviks was badly shaken. "No one will aid us," he thought. "The Bolsheviks will destroy us and everything about us ... We allowed it to happen. Perhaps we deserve it!"

57

Andrei and Egórov hid in Tiraspol through the end of 1917. At the end of their first week at the Prokassov's house, Andrei transferred twenty gold rubles from his money belt to Prokassov's. It was a fair exchange. Their host was more than generous with his hospitality, but he apparently was unable to make arrangements for their further journey. There was no way to leave Tiraspol except by foot. The Dniester River was already partly ice-bound, making escape by boat impossible. The territory around Tiraspol was still under Romanian rule, but Odessa was in the no-man's land with Bolshevik sailors concentrating their forces for another attempt to grab the whole city. They already dominated the harbor and the railroad connections, not allowing any traffic in or out of Odessa without their authorization.

To be useful to their host, Egórov and Andrei started building a gazebo with the lumber left over from the fence.

"I was thinking," Egórov said, lowering his hammer. "There are only two ways for us to keep moving. First, we can get horses. We'll move faster, but we'll become more visible. In our precarious situation, we must remain as invisible as possible. It leaves us only one choice: walking. So if we have to walk, let's start walking! We can't stay in Tiraspol and wait for the Bolsheviks!"

"I am ready." Andrei hit the nail with such force that the board split. He glanced at Egórov with a sheepish smile. He had ruined several boards already.

"Take it easy!" Egórov laughed. "These are wooden boards, not the Bolsheviks!" Turning serious, he continued, "I think, we should move along the shore of the Dniester, from farm to farm, avoiding the villages and people, until we reach the delta. That delta is huge. Maybe we can move through the limans in a rowboat."

"What about the Reds? Wouldn't they be hiding in the estuary as well?

"It will be risky, but we have no choice. We must move on! I think the way we look now, dirty and with overgrown whiskers, we can easily pass for deserters returning to their homes."

"All right. Let's assume that we'll survive and reach Odessa. What then?"

"I don't know. Perhaps we can let Shubin know where we are, or Glafíra … Or, Akim! We'll stay away from the harbor and the railroad, but somehow we'd have to get in touch with our own people."

"It sounds simple enough, but what is the reality of succeeding?" Andrei insisted.

"We shall deal with the reality as we go. So far it has worked for us. Hasn't it?"

Andrei nodded in agreement. He hit another nail and the board split. "I'll never learn to be a carpenter!" he exclaimed, throwing down his hammer in disgust.

Prokassov came out of the house with two mugs of hot milk. "My wife thought that you must be frozen here," he said, handing them the mugs.

"Thank you," Egórov said, taking one. "And we have something to ask you about." He described their plan. "Do you think it's plausible?"

"Yes. Dangerous, but possible. Otherwise you might be stuck here all winter. The Ukrainian farmers around Tiraspol are anti-Bolshevik. They fight for their land, which the Bolsheviks want to confiscate. They will help you. What's more, they are all interrelated by marriages, so they'll pass you from one family to another."

"I think we must be armed again," Andrei said.

"If you want to be armed, let me get you a couple of bolt action rifles like the deserters carry. Handguns are for officers."

"Good thinking!" Egórov nodded. "Personally, I think it is safer for us to carry no weapons. If the Reds ambush us, guns will be of no help. Without the weapons, we might talk them out of shooting us. However, we should have a couple of good knives."

"I agree," Prokassov said, "but the rifles will be alright," he said. "Deserters always carry them. I'll get you a couple!"

Prokassov arranged with his wife's cousin who had a horse breeding farm to take them in for a few days and then send them to another cousin whose vineyard and orchards were on the edge of the deltas of several rivers further south. The limans that they created never froze, so Andrei and Egórov could travel to Odessa by rowboat. "Before the Bolsheviks became active, this particular cousin regularly traveled by boat to Moldovanka with the fruits from his orchards," Prokassov said. "Now it has become dangerous. The Bolsheviks arrest the merchants as enemies of the people. But I know that somehow Cousin Feodor still manages to sneak into the city with his apples and grapes! In any case, I think Feodor is the best man to get you to Odessa without the official permits," Prokassov agreed. "All these cousins of my wife are well-to-do farmers who have no love for the Bolsheviks. They will be sympathetic to your plight."

They finished building the gazebo in two days and prepared to leave. Anna Platonovna was to accompany them to the farm and introduce them to her cousin.

"Good luck, my friends, safe journey!" Prokassov hugged each of them. "Perhaps we meet again, when things settle down. Thank you for building the gazebo. We'll think of you as we drink tea there in the summer."

"We'll think of you more often than just when we drink tea in the summer," Anna Platonovna laughed. "You became like sons to me!" She kissed her husband. "I'll be back tomorrow, my *golúbchick*, my little dove, my little piglet!"

The men followed Anna Platonovna, their rifles and burlap sacks with their few possessions over their shoulders. Shuffling behind her, with their beards and long, uncombed hair, they looked like bona fide deserters.

"Good Lord, you do look ugly, my friend!" Egórov laughed, observing Andrei from head to foot.

"You are not too pretty, either," Andrei retorted.

"Never mind," Anna Platonovna said, turning serious. "I shall go ahead, and you follow me in a few minutes." She unlocked the garden gate at the back of the house. "At the end of the street there is the "Horse and Carriage Rental Stables" building. My cousin owns it."

"Another cousin?" Egórov lifted an eyebrow.

"I have a lot of them!" she laughed, her laughter sounding young and cheerful. "I am going now. Wait about ten minutes, and then go, straight to the end of the street. I'll be there, waiting for you."

Without their watches, they had to guess when it was time. When it felt that it was about right, they began to walk. In the falling dusk they soon saw a long squat building with several huge sliding doors all locked with the padlocks. It was the stables. A kibítka, a four-wheeled permanently enclosed vehicle sat in front of the stables with two bays hitched to it. On the high driver's seat was Anna Platonovna holding the reins. "Get in," she ordered in a low voice.

The pilots obeyed. She switched the reins over the horses' backs and they took off.

The horses' hooves clattered unhurriedly over the street paved with river stones lightly powdered by new snow, the pilots invisible in the cocoon of the kibítka.

Anna Platonovna, a vision of a Russian beauty in her colorful shawl and embroidered coat, held the horses at a slow gait through town, but once outside its limits, she urged them into a fast canter. "I want to get to the farm before night!" she shouted over her shoulder.

She drove the horses with a sure hand. She looked back at them and laughed, exposing brilliantly white teeth, enjoying the ride and flaunting her command of the horses before the cavalrymen. "Good, eh?"

"She's a remarkable woman!" Egórov said to Andrei. "Imagine how beautiful she must have been when she was young! How old do you think she is?"

"I don't know. Forty? Forty-five?"

"I bet she's over fifty!"

"She looks good. I actually was afraid that you might try to seduce her!"

"Oh, Andrúshka, is that what you think of me?" They both laughed.

"To tell the truth, yes! If I were a woman, I would have fallen madly in love with you the moment we met! This mysterious married woman with whom you are so hopelessly in love is a fool for not surrendering to you!"

"If you only knew!" Egórov thought and chased the image of Larissa out of his mind.

The horses slowed their gait to a steady trot once they entered the forest. The rhythmic sound of the hooves was soothing to the men trained to be around horses since boyhood. They felt drowsy.

"I think, I'll take a nap …" Egórov pulled up the collar of his smelly touloúp.

"I'll do the same," Andrei said. "If I am lucky, I'll see Larissa in my dreams!"

Egórov said nothing.

The persistent barking of dogs woke the men. The dogs surrounded the *kibitka*, running parallel with the horses, barking excitedly, but whether in welcome or in threat, the groggy pilots could not tell. In the light of the moon that seemed to be brighter than usual because of the whiteness of snow, they saw the outlines of several white-washed squat huts, wattle fences and thatched roofs, all under plump pillows of snow. "Well, here we are," Anna Platonovna shouted. *"Khoútor Svyáto-Petrovsky,* Cousin Peter's farm!"

She stopped the horses at the gate of the main hut.

A light flickered in one of the small windows, and presently a stoop-shouldered, barefoot old man in a long homespun shirt and wide pants appeared in the doorframe. The dogs wagged their tails, running toward him. Obviously he was the *khozyáin.*

"He looks like Lev Nikolayevich," Egórov said, thinking of the famous photograph of Tolstoy.

"He does!"

Anna Platonovna jumped off her high seat. The pilots followed. "It's me, Annúshka!" she ran to the old man. "I brought you some guests, Sávvushka!" she embraced him.

"Get in Annúshka, may God bless you! Welcome!" The old man opened the door wider and the dogs rushed in, their tails wagging, their pink tongues hanging down, and their sharp teeth gleaming. He tried to shoo them out, but they paid no attention. They knew that they were loved in that house.

"This is my cousin Sávva Ilych," Anna Platonovna presented the old man. Andrei and Egórov shook hands with him, introducing themselves by their military ranks. Prokassov had informed them that the old man had been a Cossack commander during the last Turkish war. He was proud of his military past, including his Cross of St. George. "You'll find a true kindred soul in Sávva Ilyich!" Prokassov had told them.

It was warm in the house. The huge *petch*, a huge brick stove, the heart of any peasant hut, still glimmered behind its gate-size iron dumper after a day of baking. The air was filled with the friendly aroma of baked bread.

Neither Andrei nor Egórov had ever seen a peasant petch. Seeing the petch for the first time, Andrei was instantly intrigued by its construction and utility. It was built of homemade bricks and clay, and it occupied at least a quarter of the hut. Intricate, winding vents were constructed to regulate and retain its heat. All cooking and baking was done at different layers of shelves within the petch. On the top of it, about three feet below the ceiling, a large brick platform was always kept warm. It was the *'lezhánka,'* and it was meant for sleeping.

Andrei saw three small blond heads over the ledge of the *lezhánka*, the children looking with curiosity at the new arrivals. He stuck his index fingers at each side of his head, acting as if he was going to charge them like a bull. The children giggled.

Anna Platonovna smiled. "You'll be a good father to your daughter when you are reunited, Lieutenant," she said.

"Thank you," he replied.

Sávva Ilych ordered his adolescent grandson Timóshka to take their guests to the empty banya, the family bath house, for the night. The banya was still warm from being used some hours before, but its wooden benches and shelves were already dry. With several quilts and straw bags for the mattresses, the pilots ought to be comfortable, the old Cossack thought.

Anna Platonovna was given the bed of one of his daughters, Prásha, a husky young woman with a badly pock-marked face. Exposing the muscular calves of her bare legs under her night shirt, Prásha climbed nimbly up to the *lezhánka* and joined the children already there.

Egórov whispered in French, "Have you ever seen such powerful legs?"

Andrei only smiled.

The next morning, they bade farewell to Anna Platonovna. She kissed them both and cried a little, blessing them several times. "Goodbye, my friends ... We probably will never see each other again, but I'll pray for your safety every night."

Anna Platonovna climbed on the drivers' seat of her *kibitka*. She swished the horses' backs lightly with the reins, and in a few moments she was gone.

"Annushka told me that you both were cavalrymen before you began to fly," the old Cossack said, leading them back into his hut. "Why did you give up the horses?"

"Oh, Sávva Ilyich, it's hard to explain ... There is something magical in flying free as a bird ..." Egórov said.

"There is something magical in galloping on a horse, free as the wind!" the old man retorted.

"We have had both," Andrei said. "The birds and the wind!"

"Would you like to see my horses? Or, what's left of them? I used to raise horses for His Majesty's special regiments. The horses were chosen by matching colors. My specialty was dappled gray, the most difficult color to match. I raised fifty dappled greys just for the big parades in 1913, for the three hundred year Jubilee!" he said proudly. "But now, I have only five of them left ... The Bolsheviks raided and stole my horses, right out of the barns ..." His old eyes filled with tears. The pilots pretended not to notice.

"We would be honored to see your horses, Sávva Ilych!" Andrei said.

The old man and his grandson, Timóshka, led them to a long build-ing way behind the huts. "These stables used to house forty horses. Now they are empty. I have a smaller stable where I used to keep my pregnant mares. But they are gone too. The scum did not want to bother with the pregnant mares, so they shot them. The only reason that I still have five horses is that they were in the far pasture with Timóshka, and the Bol-sheviks did not know about them."

"How did the Bolsheviks know about your horses to start with?" Egórov asked.

Sávva Ilyich took a deep breath and replied, "We had a stableman who used to beat horses. I fired him. He joined the Reds and paid me back."

"Was he ever brought to justice?"

"Oh, yes! My son, Timóshka's father, found him in Tiraspol and shot him. But the Romanians arrested my son for murder, and he is sitting there in jail. He will be freed if the Bolsheviks take the city. They always liberate the prisoners. So, we are praying now for *them!* There is your justice!" he said with a bitter laugh. "We pray for the Bolsheviks, who kill us!"

58

Sávva Ilyich was a widower. His farm contained several well-con-structed huts where his six sons lived with their families. When Andrei and Egórov arrived at the farm, only one of his sons was in residence, a severely maimed soldier who had been caught in a poison gas attack. Aside from Timóshka's jailed father, his four other sons were still at the front, still faithful to their oath to serve the Fatherland.

While the men were at the front, their wives and the adolescent chil-dren carried on the heavy load of raising horses. The well-established routine of work was never interrupted under the falcon eye of the old Cossack.

The pilots volunteered to work in the stables with the adolescent grandsons of their host while they waited to make their next move. The boys at first smirked watching the strangers currycomb the horses, brush and plait their manes and tails, feed them and water them. The youngsters became impressed that the men knew exactly how to do these mundane tasks. Although Andrei and Egórov had never needed to do it, having soldiers to take care of such chores, they still remembered the routine.

Sávva Ilyich was also impressed. "Would you like to take a ride with me around the exercise grounds?" he asked.

"Yes, Sávva Ilyich. We would be honored."

"All right boys, saddle up three horses …" Sávva Ilyich ordered brusquely. "No, saddle all five. Timóshka and Petyushka will ride with us." The chosen boys puffed up with pride and rushed to obey their grandfather's order.

Andrei and Egórov jumped into the saddles with panache. Quickly they took control of their prancing horses, aware that the old Cossack and the boys watched their every move, ready to mark mistakes. But nothing had been forgotten! They were still superb horsemen.

They trotted on each side of the grand old man who rose majestically on his Don River silver steed. It was easy to picture him in command of a hundred Cossacks riding into a battle. The two boys rode behind, emulating their grandfather, already showing that someday they would be fine Cossacks themselves.

The horsemen left the compound and followed the road to an exercise field where Sávva Ilyich used to train his prize horses. He spurred his horse into a fast canter. The other horses picked up the speed without being urged.

The horsemen circled the field twice at different speeds, when suddenly Sávva Ilyich yelled *"Sháshki dolói! Roúb-it!"* a cavalry battle cry to attack with sabers.

They carried no sabers, but the old man made a gesture with his right arm as if he withdrew his saber from its scabbard while holding the reins in his left hand. The men and the boys copied his gestures. The horses pinned their ears and with nostrils flaring burst into a gallop. They too apparently pretended that they were on the battlefield.

The riders galloped through the open field in their imaginary attack, yelling wildly. Waving their arms over their heads and pretending to chop through the air as if they were lopping off Bolshevik heads, they chased the invisible enemies around the field.

Finally the old Cossack slowed. "We cut down all of them!" he declared, looking at his grandsons and replacing his imaginary saber in its imaginary scabbard. "I am proud of you, men! We haven't lost a single man or a horse!"

The next morning the courtyard was teeming with Sávva Ilyich's grandchildren who were on a recess from the school that was part of the compound.

"Our host must be quite a progressive man," Egórov said. "He has a private school for his grandchildren!"

"He certainly has enough of them to fill the school! How many do you think he has?"

"Thirty? Forty?" Andrei laughed. "I like him! I must confess, despite what we are going through, I am really enjoying myself. Since we left our squadron, I've learned more about Russian people than I had ever known! They are *likable!*"

"Well, we were lucky so far to meet only likable people. Don't forget those who caused your mother's death and confiscated your property and money. They are also Russian people!"

Andrei's enthusiasm was quickly extinguished. "Egórka is right. I mustn't grow soft," he thought. "Sávva Ilyich probably did not bat an eye when his son murdered someone. Most likely, he ordered it done!"

After three nights of sleeping in the bath house, Sávva Ilyich told them that he would move them into the school building. "You can't sleep at the banya anymore. We always start our bath-taking procedures on Tuesdays, one family a day, so the banya must be heated and full of hot water every day. At first, I thought of placing you with my son's families, but all my *babi* have been without their men for many months, and you are young studs. Women are like bitches, they go crazy without fucking, and everybody knows that! To avoid temptation, you shall stay at our school, and I shall give the children a holiday!"

Andrei and Egórov glanced at each other with amusement.

"The children will be pleased," Andrei said awkwardly.

"Oh, yes, especially the older ones. The little ones like going to school. They learn to read and write and do sums, but when they turn ten or twelve they have had enough of learning. They want to be Cossacks!"

"What about the girls?"

"The girls are no problem. They start early to learn the women's work. They have to be ready for marriage.'"

"At ten or twelve?" It sounded incredible to Andrei.

"No, a bit older, as soon as they get their monthlies. But their mothers start training them when they are about seven, so by the time they are ready for marriage, they can run the house. At least, my granddaughters can!" he said proudly. "I shall go to Cousin Feodor's tomorrow. We shall figure out how to get you to Odessa. Meanwhile, you stay at the school-house."

Porfíri Timoféich, the teacher of *Svyáto-Petrovsky Khoútor*, was an old drunkard who ended up at Sávva Ilyich's farm after being fired from several village schools. The old Cossack had pitied the teacher and hired him upon his promise to stop drinking. The indigent teacher, having no family and no possessions of any kind except the clothes on his back and a few books, realized that his employment at the *khoútor* was the final stop in his life. He made an enormous effort to keep his promise and, to his own surprise, succeeded.

Porfíri Timoféich refused remuneration. He had no need of money. If he needed new boots or anything at all, he would mention it to Sávva Ilyich and a pair of new boots would appear at the door of his room in the school building. Food was delivered to him every day, the obligation evenly spread among all the families. Often he was invited to participate in the family meals, treated as if he were a favorite uncle. His students adored him and he reciprocated in kind. He taught the multitudes of children rudimentary Russian and arithmetic, a little bit of geography and history.

Porfíri Timoféich discovered that he was happy. His craving for vod-ka to drown his loneliness had disappeared altogether. He kept his prom-ise. He stopped drinking.

Sávva Ilyich and Timóshka returned from Feodor's orchards late in the evening. Sávva Ilyich was too tired to talk to the pilots, but he sent Timóshka to the schoolhouse with a week-old issue of *Pravda* that his cousin had brought back from Odessa.

"Grandpa will see you tomorrow," the boy told them. "Uncle Feodor said that the paper has much news."

"Thank you, Timóshka," Andrei said.

The pilots and the schoolteacher crowded around a small table to scan *Pravda* for news. Porfíri Timoféich opened a lined notebook to take notes, a pince-nez perched on his long nose.

"Well, let's see what our comrades in Petrograd want us to do now," Egórov said, unfolding the skinny newspaper. "My God! It's mostly about America sending her troops to Europe!"

"Do you mean ground troops, that is, infantry and cavalry and artillery? Not just volunteer pilots?" Andrei asked.

"Yes!" Egórov spread the paper on the table. "There is some other, more 'local' news: Finland proclaimed her independence from Russia. And so did Estonia ... Oh, here is something about Odessa! 'The Bolsheviks formed its first Aviation Otryad (AO) in Odessa, under the command of military pilot Barbaco.' Have you heard of him?"

"Never," Andrei said. "What else?"

"Romania signed an armistice ... Trotsky and the others in Brest-Litovsk continue the provisional peace talks with the Central Powers ... And finally, an order for workers, soldiers, and peasants to stop fighting and *stand shoulder to shoulder against the forthcoming American capitalist invasion.'* That's all."

"In other words, Russia is out of the war and America is in!" Porfíri Timoféich said. "The war goes on. We shall accept the defeat and its consequences. Our country is ruined, and millions of our people are dead or maimed. So in the end, what were we fighting for?" he asked rhetorically.

59

"Well, my friends, let me tell you what Cousin Feodor has suggested for getting you to Odessa!" Sávva Ilyich said, twisting his long moustache. He and the pilots were having breakfast. They sat at a planked table covered with white cloth embroidered by one of his daughters-in-law with roosters and flowers. In front of each of them were steaming crocks of hot milk under the golden crust of thick cream, just taken out of the petch. In the centre of the table rested a round dome of black bread, its aroma spreading around the room. While the men waited for the bread and milk to cool, a young woman served them fried eggs and potatoes.

"Cousin Feodor says that the Bolsheviks are having a hard time in Odessa. The citizens don't embrace them as they had hoped, but around the harbor the Bolsheviks are strong. The sailors are tough. They harass everybody. But in the city people live more or less like they have always lived, except that instead of money they barter. Cousin Feodor deals mostly with the Jews in Moldovanka, and says that there is no problem there. He went to a brass band concert in the park, and people came with their children to listen to the music!"

"That's good news!" Andrei said. "My wife lives in a Jewish home in Moldovanka."

"Apparently, Moldovanka is the safest place so far. They have some local person there who deals with the Bolsheviks, and they leave the Jews alone. So far, that is. Feodor says that man is a hero in Moldovanka, admired for his ability to manage between the Bolsheviks and the current authorities. They call him Mishka Japónchik, because he has slit eyes, like the Japanese."

The pilots exchanged glances. "We have heard about him," Egórov said. "Has your cousin met him?"

"No. But he heard that it was this Mishka Japónchik who had organized the concert in the park, requesting that the sailors not be permitted to attend. People are afraid of the sailors."

"How well we know it! Anyway, what is your cousin's plan for *us?*" Egórov asked.

Sávva Ilyich broke the golden skin on the milk with his wooden spoon and took a swallow. "Good!" he smacked his lips. "Nothing in the world is better than hot milk, baked in the oven!" He cut three thick slices of bread. "Cousin Feodor will hide you while he gets you the needed documents. He says that the Bolsheviks have established a new way with the documents that is almost foolproof. They attach people's photographs to the identification papers!"

Andrei frowned. "But how can we have our photographs taken under the circumstances?"

"Cousin Feodor says that he'll get the standard blank documents before you get to Odessa. They will have spaces left open for the names and photographs. When you arrive, someone will take pictures of you and paste them inside the papers. Someone will also stamp the pictures as proof that they are authentic. But it will cost a lot of money. In gold. Only in gold. And here is where Mishka Japónchik comes into our plan!"

"I thought so!" Egórov exclaimed. "The moment you mentioned his name, I knew that somehow he would be involved."

"Are there any guarantees that we won't be betrayed?" Andrei asked.

"No. Up to the time that you get to Odessa, I guarantee that no one will betray you, but once in Odessa … God only knows. You'll be on your own. Now, I realize that one hundred rubles in gold is a lot of money, and you probably don't have it. I will lend it to you. When we succeed in getting rid of the Bolsheviks, you'll pay me back. With small interest. But if the Bolsheviks win and take over the country, it will make no difference if you owe me anything. People like you and me will be shot dead anyway."

"Thank you, Sávva Ilyich," Andrei said, touched by the old Cossack's generosity, "but we have one hundred gold rubles. You'll need your money to save your own family if the times come to it. But thank you for the offer!"

Egórov had a sardonic expression on his face. He said nothing but thought that it was stupid of Andrei to dip into their small stash when they were offered such a good deal. "But that's the difference between me and Andrúshka!"

"Back to Mishka Japónchik ..." Egórov said.

Sávva Ilyich spoke through a mouthful of buttered bread. "He is the one who can supply the false papers. He will need to bribe some people, so I think he won't keep all the money for himself."

"We don't care how he is going to spend the money. All we care about is having the proper papers to allow us to stay in Odessa." Andrei said.

"What about your cousin Feodor? How much is he asking for helping us?" Egórov asked.

"Nothing. He is happy to help someone like you. We know that you are trying to reach the Volunteer Army. We both are too old to fight, but we wish to help those who still can. We know that you are willing to gamble with your lives for our mutual survival. So, don't worry, gentlemen, we are honored to be of help!"

For several days there was no news about their further travel. The pilots began to worry. "What if Feodor was arrested by the Bolsheviks?" they wondered. Sávva Ilyich sensed their concern.

"Remember, my cousin goes to Odessa only once a week or even less often if the weather is bad. Give him a few more days ... I am sure he would prefer that you stay here rather than freeze in some duck blinds on the limans!" The pilots had to agree.

A young man with fuzz struggling over his upper lip and chin arrived to the farm, and Sávva Ilyich introduced him as his nephew Vládik, one of Feodor's sons. The pilots had lost count of all the cousins and nephews, so they greeted Vládik as if he were their own cousin. "Why did it take you forever to ride to your Uncle Sávva's house?" they asked jokingly, not expecting an answer.

Shyly Vládik apologized. "I had a bellyache and the trots ... I had to stop ... Twice!"

Egórov laughed. "That's a good enough reason! How do you feel now?"

"Better. But I must run again!" He hurried out of the door, to the outhouse.

"Poor fellow," Andrei said.

"Not to worry! My Paláshka will cure him in no time!" Sávva Ilyich said. "My old woman, God rest her soul, taught our daughter all kinds of cures. She'll give him something to drink and he'll be as good as new!"

Vládik was indeed as good as new the next morning, and Sávva Ilyich announced that the pilots could leave on horseback, riding to meet Cousin Feodor. Timóshka would bring back the horses.

"Won't your grandson be afraid to ride back alone?" Andrei wondered.

"Perhaps. It will be a good challenge for him. He is an excellent rider, and the horses like him, so he'll do very well, I'm sure.

"But what if he runs into the Bolsheviks?" Andrei insisted.

"It's all in God's hands. So far as I know there are no Bolsheviks after we pushed them to the other side of the river. Our scouts tell us that their unit is very small, about ten men and badly equipped. Not even a machine gun. They have only one horse, for their Commissar."

"What about the dozens of horses that they stole from you?"

"It was a different unit, strong and well-armed. But let's not talk about it ..." he said. "I feel my blood boiling when I think of it!"

Sávva Ilyich took his grandson to the stables for a private talk. Palasha prepared four parcels of food. She filled four flasks with hot milk, adding to it some vodka for the men and honey for the boys. In Vládik's pack she placed a small bag of dried blueberries, just in case his 'trots' were not over.

Sávva shook hands with the pilots and wished them well. Their teacher friend Porfíri Timoféich arrived as well to see them off. "I brought you a map of the region, including the Odessa limans," he said, handing them a folded parchment.

"Marvelous! It will help us immensely! Thank you!" the pilots shook hands with the teacher and mounted their horses.

Palasha came forward solemnly and walked next to Timóshka's horse, holding onto the stirrup in the Cossack tradition of women saying farewell to their men going into battle. Andrei thought it was very touching.

He glanced furtively at Egórov and saw that he too, was touched by the scene.

Timóshka made an effort to appear nonchalant, but it was the first time that he was treated as a man. He tried not to become emotional. He mumbled, "Don't fuss, I'll be back," as if indeed he were going to the front.

Vládik and Timóshka rode in front of the pilots along a firebreak that created a natural corridor between two rows of trees with thick pillows of snow on their branches. It was very quiet, the steady trot of the horses muted by soft snow. Once in a while they would see a rabbit scurry out of the way or hear a branch snap and fall. They rode in silence for several hours, respecting their environment that demanded silence, until they reached a fast, still unfrozen stream that rushed between the stony shores.

Timóshka pulled on the reins, slowing down his horse. The others followed his signal.

"We usually stop here to rest the horses and let them drink," Timóshka said, playing his role as the leader of the group. "But the horses are not tired and not overheated, so if you want, we can keep going."

"Let's keep going. I would like to be at your uncle's place before dark," Egórov said.

"How far is it?" Andrei asked.

"About the same distance. Wait!" Timóshka raised his arm, "look there!" he pointed to a space between the trees that looked like a narrow but definite path. The snow was marked with fresh imprints of horse hooves.

"I don't like it …" Egórov said quietly. "It might be a Bolshevik scout. Let's load the rifles, just in case," he turned to Vládik and Timóshka. "You, boys, obey my command if there is trouble. Your duty is taking care of the horses. Don't let them scatter. Do you understand?"

"Yes, sir," they saluted like real Cossacks. Andrei and Egórov loaded their guns, and the four riders crossed the stream.

The light wind increased, and it began to snow. At first it was a thin, lacy veil of gently falling flakes, but soon it became a white curtain that the stinging wind blew into their faces, reminding the pilots of high altitude flying.

The horses ran in tandem at a steady gait, Egórov leading, Andrei in the back, protecting the rear. They had passed several miles without any interference when a shot suddenly pierced the silence. Vládik jerked in the saddle, ready to fall. Andrei grabbed the reins of Vládik's horse, stopping both horses. Egórov and Timóshka turned their horses around.

"What happened?" Egórov shouted.

"Vládik is shot!" Andrei shouted back. Another shot whizzed by them, and they saw a horseman emerge from the treeline and gallop away.

"Stay with the boy!" Egórov yelled as he spurred his horse and bolted after the shooter.

Andrei and Timóshka lowered the wounded boy. He was in pain, bleeding profusely from his left leg. Andrei knew that he had to stop his bleeding, but how? They had no first aid equipment. Without hesitation Andrei reached into his sack and pulled out the white baby blanket from the Yassy shop. He tore it roughly into strips. "Dump all the things out of my bag," he ordered Timóshka while bandaging the boy's leg. "Fill the bag with snow and put it over his leg." Timóshka did his bidding.

Andrei tried to remember how he had dealt with the wound when he was hit in the thigh. He could not remember. Vládik seemed to be unconscious. "At least he doesn't feel pain ... A tourniquet! Yes! I must stop the bleeding," he thought. "Get me a small branch," he ordered Timóshka. He tightened a strip of the baby blanket across Vládik's leg with the help of the small branch.

In the distance they heard a shot and then immediately another one. A flock of crows rose up with harsh croaking, then everything was quiet again. Andrei froze. "Egórka ... not my friend ... Please God, not Egórka!" he prayed in panic.

They waited for a full minute. The snow under Vládik turned red, and still they waited.

The horses heard something before the people did. Their ears twitched, and they turned their heads in the direction from which soon appeared a mounted figure leading a second horse. It was Egórov, his head bare, galloping with another horse on the lead behind him.

"What happened?" Andrei shouted, weak with joy.

"I killed the bastard!" Egórov yelled, dismounting his horse. "The scum ambushed me ... I killed him. He must have been a lone Bolshevik scout ... I killed him." Egórov was breathing hard, his words clipped. He barely glanced at the wounded boy, repeating again and again, "He tried to escape! I killed him!"

Andrei realized that his friend was in a shock. "Drink this," he said, proffering his flask with milk and vodka. "Have you lost your hat?" Egórov gulped the drink voraciously and stared at Andrei uncomprehendingly. "I killed him!" he said again.

"Yes, I know. Good riddance. But we must go. We must bring Vládik home. He is badly wounded. Put the boy on my horse in front of me." He jumped into the saddle. "We must keep going, Egórka! The boy is bleeding to death."

Egórov pulled himself together. He lifted the wounded boy and placed him in front of Andrei. Then he arranged the bag with snow against Vládik's leg and tied the two riderless horses behind his and Timóshka's saddles and looked at Andrei for further instructions.

"Let's keep moving," Andrei said. They nudged the horses and followed Timóshka along the snow covered road.

"Egórka must have had a nervous shock," Andrei thought as he trotted, holding Vládik with one hand. "He had never killed at close range, face to face … It must have been terrible killing at such close range, or perhaps even shooting a man in the back …" snatches of thoughts filled Andrei's mind. He tried to think of something else, something pleasant, like his baby, but his mind refused to change his thoughts. The baby was an abstraction. He tried to think of Larissa, but his mind stubbornly returned to Egórov.

It was almost dark when they arrived at a large orchard with naked fruit trees planted in precise rows, their trunks half-painted white. Against the whiteness of snow it made the trees appear stunted.

"Is this the place?" Egórov asked.

"Yes," Timóshka answered. The travelers rode between the rows of trees. The tired horses picked up the pace, sensing the nearness of a warm stable and food.

Andrei's arms were numb from trying to protect Vládik from sliding off the horse. The boy's eyes were open, but Andrei thought that Vládik was not aware of what was going on. "We are home," Andrei said in case Vládik could hear him.

There were spots of light blinking between the trees and momentarily the house with a piqued tin roof and a detached barn came into view. The house looked different from the Ukrainian peasant dwellings. It had the look of a provincial city house of a prosperous official.

The riders dismounted, Andrei carrying the wounded boy. Egórov went ahead and knocked on the door while Timóshka held the horses.

The door was opened by a small tow-headed boy in an oversized shirt and no pants.

"Where is your Pa?" Egórov asked.

"Sleeping," the child said.

"Wake him up!"

The boy ran inside the house, his tiny buttocks exposed. "Pa!" he yelled, "Some men want you!"

The pilots stepped over the threshold and Andrei placed the wounded boy on a broad bench at the wall. Vládik was unconscious, his improvised bandage brown from the congealed blood.

Andrei looked around. It was obviously a wealthy household. There were several beautiful icons in expensive silver *rizas*. Embroidered white towels edged with lace were draped around the icons. Red crystal lampadas flickered under the icons, spreading waves of soothing aromatic incense about the room. On the long table in the center of the room stood a large silver samovar. A Tatar carpet on the wooden floor gave the room its cozy and rich appearance. And of course, there was the petch taking a large part of the room.

"You must be the pilots," they heard a deep voice. "Welcome!" Their host, Feodor Nikítich, a tall bearded man, entered the room with outstretched arms. Then he saw the body on the bench. "My boy!" he cried.

"Yes, sir. We were ambushed in the forest … Your son was wounded in the leg … He has lost a lot of blood …" Andrei said.

"Who was it?" Feodor Nikítich thundered. "Who wounded my boy?"

"We don't know, sir. I killed him," Egórov replied, in full control of his nerves again.

Feodor Nikítich touched Vládik's cold face. "We don't have a doctor anymore. …" he sounded lost, certainly not the figure of a fearless person who made regular clandestine trips into hostile territory.

"We shall help, Feodor Nikítich," Andrei tried to sound optimistic. "I had a similar wound, and I was treated in Odessa Memorial Hospital. I remember something from my treatment there. Let's not lose our heads. First of all we must clean his wound. We need plenty of towels and boiled water. And good soap, if you have any. Do you have any medicine?"

"Our doctor used to live minutes away, so he had all the medicines ... But he died several weeks ago. We have only iodine. The doctor told us to use it on the children's scratches."

"Good! Have it ready. Now, show us where we can wash up with warm water ... we shall need a lot of it to—"

A young girl entered the room and froze in shock. "What happened to Vládik?" she cried and began to lament shrilly. She moved her thin body back and forth in a half-bent position.

Egórov grimaced with irritation. He grabbed her by the shoulder. "Stop that! Instead of yelling, help your brother! Boil a lot of fresh water and bring clean towels or sheets for bandaging. Shoo!" He clapped his hands and she fled like a bird, terrified by the rough-looking strangers.

"We always keep a bucket of boiled water in the petch," Feoder Nikítich said. "We can also heat some in the samovar."

"Good, do it while we wash."

"I've put the horses in the stables and gave them some hay," said Timóshka, wiping his feet at the door. "How is Vládik? Can I help?" He was calm and prepared. His father was right, Andrei thought. He would be become a great Cossack.

Andrei and Egórov washed and scrubbed their hands and arms with hot water and soap. They took off their dirty shirts and dropped them on the floor. "Is there a chance that someone will wash our clothes while we are here?" Egórov asked. "We shall pay, of course!"

"Of course. Take off your things and my daughters will wash them," Feodor Nikítich replied, not looking at them. He was holding his son's lifeless hand, praying silently.

"We have no change of clothes," Andrei said.

Feodor Nikítich glanced at them for a moment, his prayer interrupted. He called loudly, "Sonya, bring two of my night shirts!" Turning to the pilots, he said, "Gather all your dirty things and the girls will wash them." His prayers must be postponed, he realized.

Andrei and Egórov looked ridiculous in their host's night shirts coming down to their hairy calves. At a different time, they would've laughed about it, but under the circumstances they remained grim.

Andrei took charge of the procedures. He recalled Sister Veronica using some spirits to sterilize her hands. "Do you have any spirits in the house?" he asked Feodor Nikítich.

"Only the home-brewed vodka."

"It will do! Pour some over my hands!" The old man took a bottle of home-made vodka out of a cupboard and emptied it slowly over Andrei's hands.

"Good. Now, cover the table with a folded sheet and place Vládik on the table," he ordered. Timoshka removed the samovar that was already beginning to puff and spread a clean sheet over the table.

Feodor Nikitish lowered his son on the table. The boy was still unconscious. Andrei felt his brow. It was burning.

Andrei tried to remember Sister Veronica's basic instructions to her young aides about cleansing the wounds. "Be gentle. Do not hurry. Remove any debris and dirt from the surface surrounding the wound. Don't get inside the wound, let the medicine work inside it," she used to say. Medicine! What medicine? Andrei had nothing to offer. "Fill three or four small pillow cases with snow and we'll put them around his body, to cool him," he ordered Timóshka.

Andrei willed himself to stay calm. Sister Veronica's instructions seemed to be simple enough to follow. "Remove his bandaging gently," he ordered. When the bloody wrappings were removed, the wound began to pulsate blood, slowly gathering and spilling out over the edges. He tried to work fast, wiping and cleaning the skin around the wound with warm soapy water. "Make me a thick square of the towel," he said. "We must stop the bleeding."

Egórov folded a towel several times and handed it to Andrei. "Is this what you want?"

"Perfect!" He smeared the skin around the wound with iodine and covered the wound with the folded towel. "Now, I shall hold it in place and apply pressure, and you tear the sheets into bandages."

Egórov and the boy's father did what they were told, and within minutes they had wound Vládik's leg in a plausible wrap.

Vládik opened his eyes. "My leg hurts," he whispered hoarsely.

"I know, son, I know," Feodor Nikítich held his hand.

"Pa! I can't move my leg. It's burning ..."

"I know, my boy ... You'll feel better soon," he murmured, wrought in anguish.

"Give him some milk and honey from his flask," Egórov suggested. They lifted the boy into a half-sitting position and placed the flask to his lips. He drank thirstily and smiled weakly. "It was good!"

"We must put him to bed," Andrei said. "Perhaps he will sleep now."

With Vládik safely in bed, the household began to return to its routine.

Sonya emptied the bloodied water from the wash bowls. She wiped the table with a damp rag and spread a tablecloth over it. The room again took the appearance of a wealthy peasant's household.

Natalia, the eldest daughter of Feodor Nikítich, a tall and hefty girl accustomed to farm work, came to collect the pilots' clothes. She wasn't as pretty as her younger sister, but she had a fleeting smile that lit her features and made her look attractive. "Your banya is ready," she announced in a pleasant contralto.

The pilots instantly became aware of their ridiculous appearance. They tried to look nonchalant. "She is just a farm girl," each of them thought. But she was a woman, and no young man wished to look ridiculous in the eyes of a woman.

Natalia grinned, noticing their embarrassment. "You will feel better after the banya," said in her deep chesty voice.

60

For two days Vládik burned with fever, slipping in and out of consciousness, thrashing when he was lucid but limp and delirious most of the time. On the third day, Andrei noticed that the edges of the wound were turning a greenish color, and the wound was collecting something creamy inside it.

"The wound is infected. It is full of puss ..." he told Egórov quietly. "It is probably going to turn into gangrene ... What shall we do?"

They were at the stables taking care of Feodor's fine horses. "We should take the boy to a hospital ..." Egórov sighed.

"Of course we should!" Andrei spat. "But where to? There are no hospitals within a hundred versts! Unless we take him back to Tiraspol!"

"No. We must take him to Odessa." Egórov said evenly.

"To Odessa? Are you serious?"

"Yes. Our own plans are not simple anymore. Feodor Nikítich won't be able to attend to our problems under the circumstances. We have to figure out how we can combine his dilemma with ours. It's apparent though that both of our problems lead to Odessa. I propose that we get in touch with Glafíra. We'll beg her to accept Vládik at the Memorial. I have a feeling that she'll help. She has risked her head for us before ..."

"How do you suppose we can get in touch with her? No telephones, nothing ..."

"I don't know. Perhaps Feodor Nikítich will have some ideas. After all, he has good connections in Odessa. The great Mishka Japónchik!"

Feodor Nikítich was in his room, changing a compress on his son's forehead. The boy looked as if he had shrunk, lost among the traditional pyramid of pillows on the bed.

"We must talk to you, Feodor Nikítich," Egórov began. "We must take Vládik to a hospital. In Odessa!"

"Yes, Feodor Nikítich, Vládik's wound is showing signs of being infected," Andrei joined. "He is burning with fever. If we don't get him proper medical help, we shall lose him."

Egórov took over, improvising his plan as he talked. "We think that we can arrange to have Vládik admitted to the Odessa Memorial Hospital, but we need to get in touch with someone in Odessa to arrange it. We are willing to risk getting there without the documents."

"To place Vládik in the hospital," Andrei added.

"Yes. The question is: How can the four of us get to Odessa? Can Mishka Japónchik get us to the city without the documents?" Egórov continued. "Can he help us to get in touch with our friends and admit Vládik to the hospital? Can he hide us, until we have our papers?"

Feodor Nikítich looked bewildered. "It will be dangerous for all of us to enter the city without permission. For you it may mean a firing squad, for me—arrest and confiscation of my boat and the cargo ..." he did not finish.

Egórov put his arm around his shoulder. "Let's figure this out logically, step by step," Egórov said patiently. "By what means shall we travel? That is, how do you go there on your regular trips?

"I go to the river in a wagon with crates of produce. I load the crates into a boat and sail or row it all the way to the delta. It takes a lot of time. Two or three days. Then, a friend who has a shack in the liman helps me reload the cargo into his cart. Two or three brokers, Mishka Japónchik's men, are always at our meeting place and we barter our produce for anything that we ordered on our previous visit. Shoes, clothes, tools, weapons ... We don't go into the city itself because we have no permits. Before the war, I used to have agreements with several food shops in

Moldovanka, but now … now the Bolsheviks arrest the traders and confiscate their wares."

"But are you willing to take us at least to the outskirts of the city?"

"Yes. It will be risky, but we have no choice, do we? It might work
… you and the Lieutenant will go as my helpers! In case of Bolshevik
patrols, I shall say that you are my cousins, deserters, who are helping to
take my wounded son to the hospital. I'll say that we are sorry to travel
without permission, but it's an emergency. When they see Vládik, they
will believe us, I am sure … After all, the Bolsheviks also have children."

Feodor Nikítich squeezed his son's hand and prayed one last time.

Two powerful black draft horses pulled a large sleigh loaded with
crates of apples and cabbages, Natalia driving. She was bundled up in a
men's touloúp and knee-high felt boots, a red woolen shawl covering her
head. Between the crates there was a bag of straw to serve as a mattress
for the wounded boy. Feodor Nikítich sat behind his daughter, holding
Vládik's head on his lap.

Andrei and Egórov rode behind the sleigh astride two Don River
riding horses. They nodded to one another in approval of the superior
breed of the horses. The noble animals matched perfectly, including their
'Roman profiles', the slightly convex muzzles. Feodor Nikítich was obviously a wealthy man to own such expensive horses. It was likely enough
to place him on the official list of *enemies of the people*.

The Percherons moved at a slow, even pace to the Dniester River, the
edge of their host's lands. The early morning air was bitingly cold, the
wind penetrating their heavy clothing. Vládik, his forehead hot and dry
under a fur cap, thrashed and moaned in pain, calling, "Bat'ya, Bat'ya," a
childhood name for father.

Feodor's mind churned with thoughts of how to shorten the long
trek. "The best way to save time would be to forget the cargo," he thought.
"To hell with it! Whoever is in charge at the delta, the Bolsheviks or the
Ukrainian partisans, will have pity for my boy," he thought. He touched
his daughter's shoulder. "Stop for a minute. I want to talk to the men."

Both pilots thought it was an excellent idea to forgo the cargo. They
also realized the risk: if the patrols were unsympathetic to their plight,
they could be shot on the spot. Like all pilots, though, they maintained
a philosophical view about their lives: by becoming pilots, they symboli-
cally made the pledge to risk their lives day by day. This was just a varia-
tion of that pledge.

The Dniester was wide at the point where the boat was hidden. A high cliff with an old forest confined the western shore of the river, while its eastern bank was in the flat, steppe-like land, a subject of annual floods during spring. The river was free of ice, but strong winds from the northeast disturbed the river, topping the waves with white caps.

Feodor Nikítich ordered Natalia to leave for home with the unloaded crates and the riding horses. He kissed her on her forehead and made the sign of the cross over her. Natalia kissed her father's hand as an obedient daughter should. The pilots thanked her once more for washing their clothes, and within a few minutes she was on her way back to the farm with the saddled horses tied to the sleigh. It was not the first time that Natalia was left in charge of the farm. Her father knew that she was capable of managing her responsibility.

The pilots shouldered their rifles and helped Feodor Nikítich hoist Vládik on his back in a blanket tied like a backpack.

A huge pile of debris on the river shore came into their view. "Where is your boat?" Egórov asked looking down the cliff.

"On the beach. Inside that pile."

"Good job! It is perfectly hidden!" Egórov exclaimed. The boat was invisible from above.

It was a steep walk down the cliff descending along a barely visible zigzagging path leading to the beach and a large pile of small trees, broken limbs and branches looking as if it was the debris left by the floods.

Feodor Nikítich placed his son on the ground.

"Let's open the entrance ... it's about ... here," Feodor pointed to a spot not any different from the rest of the barricade. The pilots dragged off several small trees with branches full of dead leaves. The seemingly random brush was hiding a narrow passage to the mooring where rested a small sail boat looking as if it was part of the debris as well. On the deck, with its planks beginning to hump, there was a dilapidated wheelhouse with a broken window.

A single mast in the center of the deck appeared to be sturdy with its square sail furled tightly. Hanging on the wall of the wheelhouse was an old life-saving ring made of cork that was crumbling.

Feodor Nikítich disappeared into the wheelhouse to make a bed for Vládik. "Good!" he called from the wheelhouse, "Now, hide the entrance from the inside." Quickly the young men restored the camouflage.

Feodor Nikítich and the men used oars to push the boat away from shore. It bobbed and rocked from side to side, looking as fragile as an old weather-beaten toy forgotten on the beach by some careless child. Feodor Nikítich took his place at the tiller and the pilots unfurled the sail.

They were on their way. The mined waters of the liman were only a few versts ahead.

Feodor Nikítich knew the river well. He steered the boat close to the shore, knowing that it was the safest way to remain undetected. It was easy sailing in the open river, but as they reached the delta and the Dniester began to split, it became complicated. Feodor Nikítich had to be on constant alert for the proper channels into which to steer his boat.

Toward evening, the wind finally died and a dense fog descended over the delta. Their surroundings became all but invisible and further progress impossible.

They had to stop. They rowed the boat into the bulrushes and prepared for the night.

It became frosty during the night. They protected the injured boy from freezing by holding him across their knees, huddling close together on the bottom of the boat, their shoulders touching. The warmth of their bodies should keep the boy a little warmer, they hoped, as they covered Vládik with the remaining blankets.

"It will be a tough night," Feodor Nikítich predicted. He reached for a basket of food that his daughter had prepared. There were apples and bread, several hard-boiled eggs and milk with honey in a vodka bottle. "I'd hoped she had also packed the real vodka!" he said in disappointment, probing in the basket. "The milk is for Vládik. Oh! I think there is another bottle! I hope it's vodka!"

It was vodka. Their spirits rose as each took a swig, aware that vodka had to last them for the whole night.

Vládik stirred and cried, "I am thirsty, Bat'ya!" They lifted the boy to a half-sitting position and he yelped with pain. "I am thirsty!" he repeated.

"I know, I know, my boy ... Here is some milk. Drink!" His father pressed the bottle to his lips. Vládik drank greedily. "I can't see anything," he said. "Where are we?"

"We are on the boat. We are taking you to a doctor." The men stretched him on their laps again, tucking the blankets about his thin body.

It was totally dark now. "I curse myself for not bringing a lantern ..." the old man said.

"There is nothing we can do but wait for the morning," Egórov fumbled by touch in the basket and came up with an egg, then two more for his companions. "Now we have everything! Bread! Eggs! Vodka! Relax, my friends! Tomorrow we shall be in Odessa and drink champagne!" he exclaimed, pretending to be cheerful.

It was one of the most difficult nights any of them had ever experienced. Aside from being physically uncomfortable, frozen and stiff by sitting with their legs stretched out to accommodate the boy, they suffered Vládik's every toss and cry of pain. They slept by fits and starts, feeling deeply for the boy. His bandage should have been changed and the wound should have been cleaned, but nothing could be done under the circumstances. The wound began to smell.

They prayed silently, Andrei thinking how could it be that his life had been so irrevocably changed in such a short time? His heart was full of bitterness and hatred for the Bolsheviks. He tried to think of something pleasant, like his baby. He thought of Larissa. Was she working at Memorial Hospital again to be eligible for better food coupons? Who was taking care of the baby?

Egórov also thought of Larissa. His love for her went through a drastic change, from a carnal passion to a familial devotion as he made peace with the fact that he would never possess her. He thought of Julia, also. His cold treatment of her weighed heavily on his conscience, even though he felt that he had behaved honorably. He could not tell her that he loved her. He did not love her. He loved Larissa.

61

The morning was cold and bright. Vládik was in a coma, spared suffering his terrible pain. The men stretched, trying to restore the feeling in their legs and bodies.

The sun was rising steadily, bringing no warmth but restoring the beauty to the river and lifting their sagging spirits. Soon the whole sky was ablaze with color. The old fir trees on the shore stood stripped of snow by the wind of the previous day, their branches sparkling with the new morning frost reflecting the rosy colors of sunrise.

The men finished the vodka and chewed the remnants of the bread sprinkled with salt. The eggs and the apples were all gone.

"All right, friends, let's get going!" Feodor Nikítich declared. "We must use only the oars because the sail would be seen over the reeds. I shall guide the boat, but we must go slowly. The smaller streams often change their channels … It makes going through the wetlands more difficult," he explained.

"We have a map of the delta," Andrei said. "Your cousin's schoolteacher gave it to us."

"It will do me no good. I can't read maps."

"Not to worry. Feodor Nikítich knows his river," Egórov said encouragingly.

Andrei glanced at Vládik. He felt pain in his own old triple wound. The boy's delirious cries and murmurs were as familiar to Andrei as if they were his own.

The old boat creaked and moaned as it plied ahead, looking as if at any moment it would give up. The water was frothing at its sides, its oars suffering under the stress, but the boat kept going, slicing through the water as if understanding the importance of its mission. Stubbornly they rowed, the old man steering the boat through the labyrinth of the bulrushes that had no end.

The estuary of the Dniester was a complicated conglomeration of several large rivers starting in the Carpathian Mountains, all breaking their way to the Black Sea, each splitting into the tributaries that in turn split into smaller rivers and even tiny creeks. Having been trained to observe the terrain from a birds-eye-view, the pilots had no trouble visualizing the web-like topography of the delta.

It was huge. Hundreds of channels connected with one another, uniting here and there, then separating, forming shallow lakes from which the new streams evolved to become small ponds choked by reeds that grew taller than a man. Water was everywhere, lying dark and quiet in the deeper parts or sparkling at shallow points when their boat scraped the ground and they worried that its bottom would split.

The pilots were fascinated by the enormity of the delta. They consulted their map, pinpointing to Feodor Nikítich their approximate location, making him wonder how could they be so clever. They in turn, wondered how he, who was barely able to read and write, could be so perfect in his navigation!

It could have been a pleasant experience were it not for the reason they were there. The boy was dying. One glance at Vládik was enough to make them keep going with all their strength. They could not imagine that under the best of circumstances they could get the poor boy to Odessa in time to save him.

Unnoticeable at first, the reeds thinned out slowly and there was more open water ahead. "We are almost at the liman," Feodor Nikítich said. "We should stay hidden in the reeds for a little while, watching. If all is quiet and the wind blows in the right direction, we shall raise the sail and go faster. But we must watch out for the mines. Mishka Japónchik's 'trading center' is on a narrow spit of land connected to the mainland. His men are there every day. Remember, Mishka and his men are bandits, and they are serving only themselves. Mishka is their king. You must pretend that you respect them, but keep in mind that they are as ruthless as the Bolshevik sailors!"

"I think one look at Vládik would convince anyone about our emergency," Andrei said.

"They will have no problem with Feodor Nikítich's need to be there, but the two of us? Why are we there? How can we explain it, if asked?" Egórov raised the question.

Feodor Nikítich replied. "I'll say that I needed you to sail the boat while I took care of my son. I think they won't be suspicious. But don't volunteer any information on your own. Keep silent."

"I believe in our basic Russian goodness," Andrei said. "We will be fine. They'll believe us!"

"Oh, yeah?" Egórov laughed with brutal sarcasm. "It's all around us, that Bolshevik basic Russian goodness!"

Andrei preferred to say nothing more.

Feodor Nikítich docked the boat as the sun began to set over the liman. He lifted his lifeless son. The boy was surrounded by the terrible, unmistakable odor of gangrene and the smells of urine and feces that had accumulated in his blankets. The pilots, dirty, hungry, and exhausted, tied up the boat and climbed on the dock.

A small shack stood close to the dock, the dim light of a kerosene lamp seen through the window. There was a neat naval cater tied to the landing, suggesting that sailors might be inside the house. It did not look good to the pilots.

Feodor Nikítich thought the same, but there was no other way except forward. Egórov pounded on the door.

There were three men in the shack drinking tea, a samovar puffing peacefully on the table in front of them. One was the owner of the shack, Kubánetz, the other two were Jewish men of Mishka's gang, unknown to Feodor.

"Well, what have we got here?" Kubánetz said with a grimace of disgust. "Smells like shit!"

"It's my son … He is wounded and we must take him to the hospital!"

The Jewish men stared at the comatose boy while the pilots stared at them in utter surprise: one of them was Julia's father, Isaak Yákovlevich Cohen!

"Isaak!" Andrei muttered in disbelief, "I am Andrei Rezánov!"

"And I am Vassily Egórov!"

Isaak stared at one, then another, not recognizing them.

"How is my … my wi-wife?" Andrei stuttered in his excitement. "My b-b-baby?"

"They are fine," Issak replied automatically, not believing that the dirty-looking peasants could be Andrei Rezánov and Vassily Egórov.

"They are fine!" Andrei cried exuberantly. "Did you hear it, Egórka? They are fine!"

"I heard it. Isaak Yákovlevich, we need your help," Egórov said, raising his voice over Andrei's jubilation. "We need to get in touch with Glafíra Ivánovna and beg her to help our friend here. We must take his wounded boy to the hospital. Can you do it, can you get in touch with her at the Memorial?"

Julia's father blinked, suddenly recognizing his friends. "Yes. We can try. Who do we have in the military medical administration?" he turned to his companion. They talked in Yiddish briefly. Switching back to Russian, Isaak said, "Yes. We'll call Yakov Feitelson … He is the commissar at a medical facility in Big Fontaine. He will call Glafíra."

Julia's father lifted the lamp and concentrated its light on the corner of the room where there was a field telephone on a small table. His friend, Joseph, was already cranking the handle of the phone.

"We will tell Glafíra that you are here but have no papers," Isaak told the pilots in a soft voice. "She will understand the situation."

Joseph replaced the hearing tube. "Yakov will call us back as soon as he talks with Glafíra."

"Good," Isaak replied. "You must be hungry," he said to the pilots. "Sit down. Have a glass of tea and some food." The pilots and Feodor Nikítich gratefully crowded around the table.

In about an hour the telephone rang. Joseph answered it. The conversation lasted no more than ten seconds, but it felt like eternity to the men who had brought Vládik all this way. Finally, disconnecting the telephone, Joseph said, "Your Glafíra is sending an ambulance to pick up the boy. She is going to have the chief surgeon standing by."

"God bless you, comrade bárins!" Feodor Nikítich burst into tears, using the Bolshevik and the old Tsarist's forms of address.

It took another hour at least, before the ambulance arrived, an old rickety box on wheels, dark green, with huge red crosses on its roof and the sides. Andrei and Egórov smiled in recognition: it was the same ambulance that Egórov had chartered to take them to the Opera House some years ago!

The driver and his helper, placed Vládik on a stretcher and carried him into the ambulance. Isaak, Feodor Nikítich, and the pilots followed, leaving Joseph in the shack with Kubánetz in case Mishka Japónchik had any other 'business' to conduct. There was always someone who needed Mishka Japónchik's shady but successful interference.

They rode through the sleeping city, stopped only once near the harbor where a Bolshevik patrol wanted to check the ambulance documents. It could have been a dangerous moment, but one look at the suffering boy was enough for the patrol to wave them through.

Andrei was eager to ask Isaak about Larissa, but Isaak was laconic in his replies. Obviously he did not want to talk. Egórov wanted to ask about Julia but thought better of it. Feodor Nikítich seemed to be in a coma himself. He sat motionless, his eyes closed. Only his hand gently caressed the dry, hot hand of his son.

The nearness of death demanded respectful silence from them.

The ambulance stopped at the receiving entrance. The orderlies wheeled a gurney to its wide doors and quickly transferred Vládik's body to the receiving station. The smell of his wound and his body was overwhelming: the boy was rotting alive. The orderlies covered their faces with masks as they began to strip him of his filthy rags.

"You had better wait in the reception room," a male nurse told them. "It is—"

"We know where it is," Egórov interrupted. He led his companions to the wide staircase and on to the second floor.

Glafíra Ivánovna and Doctor Shubin were waiting for them. Among warm greetings and exclamations of surprise at their changed appearance, Doctor Shubin and Glafíra felt ill at ease. They were risking their lives if any of the Bolsheviks were to know the identity of these dirty young men, equally dirty old peasant, and his dying son, all of them lacking any permits for being in Odessa.

Glafíra announced sternly that the pilots must go immediately to the hospital banya, shave, and be ready for the hospital barber in the morning. She had prepared shaving kits for them, along with underwear and hospital robes from the Scottish Red Cross. They would be registered as recuperating patients who had been exposed to typhus and thus quarantined in a special ward under observation, she declared. They would remain isolated for a few days in a two-bed ward, with the same nurses taking care of them to eliminate the danger of infection. Glafíra glanced at her notes. "The nurses' names are Larissa and Julia," she said coldly, not looking at the pilots, pretending to read the names. She looked at them at last, and a slight smile lit her face. "By the way, Julia works here now."

62

It was getting late. Isaak decided not to go home, but rather rush to Mishka Japónchik's headquarters in an old warehouse in the heart of Moldovanka. He needed documents for the pilots. Immediately! They both would be listed under false names as aviation mechanics of lower rank. In addition to their new identification papers, they would be given three months provisional permission to live in Odessa, with the right of renewal. All they needed now was to have their photographs taken and embossed with a special stamp through the bottom of the photo.

Isaak had to deal with Mishka's second in command, Bennie Levinson. "Never mind," he thought, "when Mishka comes back I'll remind him that he was paid already and more than he had bargained for, thanks to my information!"

Bennie Levinson was a talented forger. He had stacks of blank documents stolen from various official organizations that required only the names of the new recipients to be typed in and the photographs pasted.

He used to work as a forger for the Tsarist Secret Service, but during the revolution he had joined forces with the Bolsheviks, doing the same work for them. When Mishka, his childhood friend, proclaimed himself the King of Moldovanka, Bennie joined him without abandoning his position with the Bolsheviks. Money was plentiful with Mishka, and his survival was protected by his association with the Bolsheviks.

"How soon can my friends have their papers?" Isaak asked him.

"As soon as we have their pictures. I'll send the photographer to the Memorial today. It will take him a day to print the pictures. Then, I'll sign the papers and age them overnight so they look old and used. Are your friends ready with their payment?"

"Oh, I am sure they are! If for some reason they are not, the wife of one of them is renting a room at my house. I know that she has some good money stashed away, so don't you worry! You'll be well remunerated!"

As he said it, he felt a tiny prick of conscience. "Now, why did I brag about it?" he thought. "I have already told Mishka about it! Oh, well ..." But an uneasy feeling about his digression remained.

In the nurses' changing room, the baby finished nursing and was falling asleep. Larissa placed Nina over her left shoulder and patted her back lightly. Julia had taught her that little trick to help the baby burp any air swallowed during nursing. She changed Nina's diaper, swaddled her in clean flannel sheets, and placed her back in the laundry basket. The baby granted her a smile. "Ah, what a darling!" Larissa said, wishing that she did not have to go back to work. She kissed the child on her tiny pink head. Julia's mother was already on her way to watch over the baby.

Akim was in front of the house, Yasha sitting next to him in the driver's seat, his violin in its casket-like case between his knees. Akim now drove Yasha to school. Lately, the streets of Odessa had become dangerous for children, especially Jewish children. Gangs of homeless children, a new class of junior 'Mishkas', attacked and beat the Jewish children, robbing them of their musical instruments, shoes, and clothing.

Akim picked Yasha up after school as well, along with a couple of other young musicians and delivered them to their homes. Then he would drive to the hospital and wait for Larissa and Julia.

This arrangement suited everybody. Akim was well remunerated. The parents of the young musicians, who were still allowed to conduct their businesses of shoemakers, tailors, and grocers, were generous with their payments in groceries and feed for the horse or wood for his stove. Some paid with repairs of his family's shoes and clothes, all exchanges more valuable than the worthless paper money.

Every day Akim drove Minna Solomonovna with the baby to the hospital for Larissa to nurse. He particularly enjoyed this chore, cooing over the infant as if he were a woman. "Nínochka *smiled* at me today!" he would announce to Larissa, or "Nínochka is fussy today!" Larissa and Julia would laugh and agree among themselves that Akim was a sweet man. He took his position as a proxy godfather very seriously.

Sister Veronica looked them over. "You don't need to wear your head coverings for the next few days," she said. "You are assigned to a non-sterile special ward that is restricted to visitors. Only you, Doctor Shubin, the Commissar, and myself are permitted to visit the patients."

"When was this decision made? Are the patients already there?" Julia asked, flustered by the break in routine. Veronica pretended not to hear. She turned her back and closed the door.

Larissa was perturbed, but she and Julia dutifully went up the main staircase to the second floor, stopping at the door with a sign that the ward was proclaimed 'contagious.'

"There must be a mistake," Larissa said. "We have a baby at the house, and the room is contagious!"

"She would not send us to a contaminated room. She knows about the baby!" Julia said, but they stood at the door, hesitating to enter.

The pilots luxuriated after bathing, enjoying clean beds and clean clothes for the first time in weeks. They shaved without hurry in the attached bathroom, saving their long moustaches and overgrown hair for the barber's scissors.

Their breakfast waited for them: Soft-boiled eggs! Pink slices of ham! Brioche! A whole pot of coffee with thick cream! Sweet rolls! Strawberry jam! They looked at one another and laughed like young boys. They were going to live it up!

With a burst of laughter Egórov shouted, "I shall eat all of it and leave nothing for you, my friend!"

"What a pig!" Andrei laughed happily.

Larissa heard the laugh. "Andrei," she whispered, her eyes sparkling as she turned the doorknob. "It's Andrei!" she screamed, "and Egórka!"

The men jumped to their feet, upsetting the coffee that spilt over the saucers and onto the tablecloth. Andrei opened his arms and Larissa clung to him. Egórov paused for a split second, then opened his arms wide. Julia rushed into his embrace.

All four started talking at once, not listening, starting a sentence and not finishing it, laughing, Larissa crying, smudging her tears over Andrei's face, he kissing her hands, her hair, whatever was within the reach of his lips.

Julia and Egórov were more subdued, her face buried on his chest.

Finally, the outburst of their happiness subsided and they settled down around the table, Julia and Egórov apart now and looking a little embarrassed, and Andrei and Larissa unable to look at anybody except each other.

"How is my baby?" Andrei finally asked.

"You'll see her in a couple of hours!" she replied, her adoring eyes on his face. "Oh, Andrúsha, I am so happy! But you both are so thin!" She realized that she had all but ignored Egórov. "Forgive me … I got carried away! Oh, Egórka!" she embraced him. "God, I am so happy to see you both! And not even wounded! And even more handsome!"

Julia was the first to regain equanimity. "We interrupted your breakfast," she said. "Let me get you some fresh coffee!" She wanted a few moments alone to fully compose herself. She picked up the coffee pot and left the room. Egórov instinctively stood to follow her, but then remembered that he and Andrei were to remain incommunicado in that room.

About fifteen minutes to twelve, Akim brought Minna Solomonovna to Memorial Hospital. As always when she went to the hospital, she looked very formal, wearing a hat and gloves, her best patent leather high-button shoes, and a special coat with a red fox collar. "I am not a nursemaid. I am almost a grandmother of the baby!" she announced to everybody.

Holding the infant swaddled in a pink woolen blanket that she had knitted herself, she awaited Akim to help her down from the carriage and accompany her to the main entrance. With a flourish Akim opened the door for her and she sailed in as a proud grandmother, proceeding to the receptionist on duty. "Please inform Sister Larissa that Madame Cohen has brought the baby." Then, as was her unfortunate habit, she giggled nervously and destroyed her impressive arrival. Meekly she proceeded to the nurses changing room to await Larissa. That routine had never changed, even if at first the orderlies and the nurses made fun of her. Her pride in the infant and her devotion to the young Sister Larissa were touching. Soon they began to respect and even envy her. She was lucky to be friends with such famous people! Many remembered the imposing Maria Nikoláyevna, and no one could forget Lieutenant Andrei Rezánov.

"Your baby is here, Sister Larissa," the orderly said, raising his voice at the closed door of the ward.

"I'll be right there!" Larissa called back. "I'll try to bring in the baby when she is finished feeding," she said to Andrei, lowering her voice in case the orderly was listening at the door.

"Can't you nurse her here?"

"No! It would be against the regulations," she laughed. "I'll be back in half an hour and maybe I can sneak the baby in. Julia, be a dear and talk to Glafíra. Perhaps she can figure out how to show our Nínochka to her father and godfather."

Julia was only too glad to have another excuse to leave the room. She was torn. Her impulsive reunion with Egórov was so sweet! But now she felt embarrassed. "What will he think of me throwing myself at him like that after he rejected me?" she thought. "Where was my pride?" She had no answers. She was happy to see him again.

Larissa unbuttoned her dress, eased out her left breast that was beginning to ache from its need to be emptied, and wiped her nipple with a mild Boric solution. Settling herself in an armchair that Sister Veronica swiped from the reception room, Larissa was ready for her most pleasant duty—nursing her baby.

"Andrúsha and Captain Egórov are here," she said in a low voice to Minna Solomonovna. "I don't know how long they are going to hide in the hospital, and what are their plans, but do you think we could hide them if necessary in that wood cellar of yours?"

"Isaak told me. He also said that the wounded boy probably won't survive. Feodor Nikítich, his father, is staying in that cellar now," she giggled most inappropriately.

"Yes, yes," Larissa said, "but is there enough space for two more people should we need to hide our men again?"

"What I am saying is that the old man wants to go back to the limán, but Isaak is making arrangements for him to have a permit to stay in the city so that he can visit his son. He won't need to hide in the cellar when he gets his permit. He will be safe. And Andrei and Captain Egórov can also stay with us, openly, once they have their new documents, Isaak says. Then, they too will be safe. Well … maybe not safe, but a little safer!" She smiled, not offended by Larissa's rudeness. "No one will need to stay in the cellar!"

Larissa felt relieved. "As soon as I am through nursing, let's take Nínochka to meet her Papa!"

Glafíra sat enthroned behind a massive desk taken out of Doctor Shubin's office. It took most of the space in her tiny office, leaving no place for more than two chairs. Julia confided her dilemma of showing Andrei his little daughter, and Glafíra came upon a clever idea: she would call for a mandatory emergency meeting of hospital personnel in the conference room located in the basement. She would read some new orders from the Party, and for half an hour or so, even if the baby cried in the 'contagious' ward, no one would be near enough to hear it.

She quickly composed a short announcement requesting the immediate presence of all personnel during their lunch break. Only those on special assignment would be excused. Her secretary mimeographed the order to be delivered to the employees.

"What about those who are not your supporters?" Julia insisted. "Won't they be curious why you called a meeting in the middle of their lunch break?"

"I don't think so. Nowadays it is safer to be not curious, and people know it. What is that saying about curiosity and a cat that was killed by it? Well, people have discovered that it must have been true. To avoid the fate of the cat, they refrain from expressing too much curiosity!" She laughed, pleased with her wit.

About thirty employees joined Commissar Glafíra at the basement archives.

"Be seated," she said dryly, all business. "First of all, I want you to know some statistics about our hospital." She began to read the dull reports about admissions and discharges that no one cared about. Glafíra could see that her audience was not interested. The orderlies yawned, and a couple of nurses closed their eyes. Glafíra continued to recite the statistics.

It was easy for her to speak extemporaneously: all political expressions were already created by someone to become convenient stencils for the speakers, even Lenin himself. It was simple to use the stencils at the proper places. The leaders were always 'glorious', the country was always 'great.' All other countries were called 'imperialist' or 'capitalist' with a dash of sneer.

"We, the architects of a new Soviet nation must know what is going on in the capitalist world that hates our great country and its glorious leaders. We all know about America, that most imperialistic capitalist country in the world," she said. "There is a possibility that America will openly join the Allies in their war against Germany and Austro-Hungary. The American President has come up with a plan for how to divide the world after the Allied Victory. He calls his plan The Fourteen Points."

She opened an issue of *Pravda* and began to read Woodrow Wilson's thesis. She too was bored, but as she reached Point 6, her own interest perked-up. It dealt with Russia.

"Now, listen to this," she raised her voice authoritatively. "We all know that our glorious comrade Trotsky and his colleagues are trying to reach a permanent armistice with the Central Powers to get us out of the war. Here is something that the capitalist American President suggests." Slowly, she read Woodrow Wilson's recommendation to the new Bolshevik government; that they demand the evacuation of all Central Powers forces from the Russian territories. "Do you understand what that means?" she asked.

No one dared to say 'yes' or 'no.'

"All right. Let's send a telegram to that Vudro Vilson that we approve point six of his plan! Who's for it?"

They all raised their hands.

"Who's against?" No one raised a hand. "Good, the recommendation to send a telegram to the American President Vudro Vilson is approved unanimously."

She glanced at her watch. Almost an hour had passed since the meeting began. "All right. The meeting is adjourned. I'll compose the telegram and offer it for discussion by the Executive Committee."

The people began to disperse. "Why should we send a telegram to the American President? He wouldn't give a damn about an approval of his proposal!" she thought. "But what the hell! To send a telegram to the American President! Under my signature! It is impressive! They might even mention it in *Pravda*!"

½ 63 ½

The documents were delivered as promised, the photographs taken, affixed, and signed by the forger. For an additional fee of ten gold rubles, the photographer took several pictures of the baby with Larissa and Andrei and even of Julia, Egórov, and Minna Solomonovna with the baby. Larissa was beside herself with happiness. She could send the pictures to her mother, whom she hadn't seen for almost two years!

Postal service between the cities worked more or less normally. Larissa and her mother exchanged letters, both desperate to be reunited, both realizing that it was impossible.

Having paid Isaak handsomely for their false documents, the pilots did not need to hide in the 'contagious' ward anymore. They were free. However, they had scratched the bottom of their secret stash of funds. Egórov had only twenty gold rubles left in his money belt. Andrei had more, but not enough to finance their voyage to Novocherkassk. Fortunately, there were still several thousand gold rubles sewn into Larissa's clothing stored in the soondook.

"Please take a thousand rubles out of our stash, darling," Andrei asked Larissa.

Her heart sunk. "He is leaving again …" she thought. "He's not staying …" She knelt at the soondook with the key to the padlock, her eyes clouding with tears.

As she was about to insert the key, she saw that the padlock was already opened.

"Andrúsha!" she cried in alarm. "The lock is broken!" Andrei dropped the newspaper he was reading and tore up the lid. The soondook was empty, all of Larissa's clothes with their hidden treasure gone. They looked at one another in a shock.

"When did it happen?" Andrei asked, stupefied.

"How would I know?" she replied defensively. They sat on the floor like two children in front of an empty toy box, not knowing what to do.

"I think I know who did it," Andrei said slowly in a very low voice.

"Who?"

"Julia's father."

"No! He's our friend! He arranged everything, your documents, everything! He is our friend!"

"Yes, but we do know *who* he is. Julia herself told us that he's a *thief.*"

"I can't believe that! Not Isaak Yákovlevich! He loves us! He risked his life by hiding you and Egórka! He wouldn't do this to us ..."

Julia and Egórov knocked on the door. "What are you doing on the floor? Checking your toy box?" Egórov joked. Julia took one look at the empty soondook and blanched. She glared at them and without a word ran out of the room in search of her father.

She found him sitting in the kitchen with Minna Solomonovna drinking tea.

"Why did you do that!" she yelled, snatching a newspaper out of his hands and knocking the spectacles off his nose. "Larissa is like a sister to me! You *gonif*, how could you do it to her!"

"What? What has he done?" her mother cried. "Julia, darling, get hold of yourself!"

"How can I get hold of myself when this thief, this husband of yours, this ... this father of mine, has robbed my dearest friend!"

"What? Is it true? Did you do that, Isaak? Tell me the truth!" Minna Solomonovna knew that it must be true. Her husband was a thief. She had become used to it through the years, pretending not to know about it, accepting his pleas of innocence and attributing his incarcerations to Tsarist anti-Semitism.

Isaak pressed himself deeper into his chair. "It was Mishka Japón-chik," he mumbled. "He ordered the robbery. I did not do it! I wasn't even home when it happened!" He looked at the floor, avoiding her accusing eyes.

"But how did Mishka know that Larissa had money?" Julia demanded harshly, not deceived by his humble mien. "Did you tell him?"

"Not exactly ... " he stalled. "Not to Mishka anyway, but ... to some fellows ... We were chatting ... about the best way to hide money from the sailors when they come with their search warrants. I said the best way was to sew the money into some heavy garments."

"And that was all?" Minna Solomonovna was ready to exculpate him of the crime. "Everybody knows that people sew money into their clothing."

"But he told them that Larissa had it in her soondook!" Julia cried.

"No, I did not! I did not tell them where it was ... I just mentioned that our tenant had done so ... Julinka, you should know that I would never steal money from Larissa! Never! Never!" He was sobbing now, sincerely believing in what he was saying. "I love Larissa and the baby as if they were my own! They are like family to me!"

Minna Solomonovna pressed his balding head to her ample bosom, glaring at Julia. "See what you have done? You made your father cry!"

"You are both imbeciles," Julia shouted and rushed out of the kitchen.

Andrei, Egórov, and Larissa with the baby in her arms sat gloomily around the table in Larissa's room. "What shall we do?" Andrei asked, not expecting an answer.

"Not much," Egórov said. "The money is gone. Perhaps we can make some deal with that Mishka to watch over Larissa and the baby so they can survive without you, or even reunite her with Maria Nikoláyevna, but I doubt if that would be possible. I don't think that he could be of much help to us from now on. We have nothing to barter for his help."

"Don't worry about us," Larissa said. "I have all the proper permits to live in Odessa, and a good job. Glafíra is watching over us. What about you? How will you manage with all our money gone?"

"Somehow we'll manage. We always do. When we get to the Volunteer Army, we'll be pilots again, or cavalry officers if there are no airplanes. If we don't get to there, we'll get jobs as mechanics," Egórov said with a bravado that did not fool anyone, including himself.

Andrei was silent, distraught. He imagined Larissa with her infant, alone in the city … And he, a factory worker. If that's what was in the cards for them, he would rather … No, he would not even think of it! The solution was in the destruction of the Bolsheviks.

"I guess we'll have to call for Mishka Japónchik's help again," Egórov said. "He is probably the only one who can arrange anything. We'll have to beseech him through our honest broker and friendly thief, Isaak. Let bygones be bygones, we must tell him. Mishka has been paid more than enough for taking care of us. He owes it to us! Perhaps he can arrange a sea voyage to Novocherkassk?"

They tried to take an optimistic attitude toward the theft. "It was just money," Egórov offered the usual bromide. "What would we do without our ever-available clichés?" he thought.

"How can you say that!" Larissa exclaimed angrily. "Of course it was *just money!* Something we can't live without, something that has been stolen from us first by the Soviets and now by the Odessa bandits, with the help of our *friend!* What else can they take? They even took my winter clothes!"

"So what do you want me to do? Call the police? Go and shoot down every man with a red star on his hat? Shoot Isaak? What can I do, tell me?" Andrei shouted back at her. She broke into helpless tears, but he wasn't going to comfort her. He left the room, slamming the door. The baby began to cry.

The klaxon sounded in front of the house, and Larissa knew it must be Glafíra.

"Must be something important," Larissa thought. "The boy!" She placed the baby back into her basket and went to the kitchen to investigate.

She and Glafíra exchanged kisses on their cheeks. "How is Nínochka?" Glafíra asked in a low voice.

"She is fine, thank you. She's sleeping. What happened? It's Vládik, yes?"

"Yes. He died a couple of hours ago ... We could not save him. I came to fetch his father. He was with him all night, and the resident ordered him to go and rest. The boy died shortly after he had left. He never regained consciousness."

"He was already in a coma when we brought him to the hospital," Egórov said quietly. "Poor boy ..."

"How old was he?" Minna Solomonovna asked, sniffling.

"About fifteen," Andrei said.

Feodor Nikítich came into the kitchen. Everyone looked at him. He did not need to be told that Vládik has passed away; their somber faces told the story. "When did it happen?" he asked.

"A couple of hours ago," Glafíra replied. "I came to take you back. You must decide about the funeral."

"There is nothing to decide. I am going back to the liman, get into my boat, and then take him home. We'll bury him at the farm, in the orchard under the tree that I planted when he was born. Could you get me a coffin?"

"Of course. We'll take you to the liman in our ambulance." Glafíra said, her slit eyes welling with tears.

"Glafíra is really a kind woman," Larissa thought.

"Thank you. May our Lord keep you safe in these cruel times," the old man said simply. "And I thank you and your husband, Minna Solomonovna, and you, my friends. You risked your lives to help my son ... I'll pray for you for the rest of my days."

"We are coming with you to the liman, Feodor Nikítich," Andrei said. He did not consult Egórov: he knew his friend would be in agreement.

The pilots and Feodor Nikítich joined Glafíra in the automobile and returned to the hospital. The old man collected the necessary papers, including the death certificate still printed on the Tsarist's standard form with a double-headed eagle. Glafíra requested a coffin to be brought from special storage in the basement, and the body of Vládik swaddled in a white sheet was placed inside.

Doctor Shubin shook hands with Feodor Nikítich. "I am so sorry that we couldn't save your boy," he said quietly. "He was too far gone ..."

"I understand. We are all in God's hands." The orderlies placed the coffin into the ambulance, and the pilots and the grieving father took their places around it. "Good bye," Feodor Nikítich waved to Doctor Shubin. "God bless you for everything!" The ambulance moved on.

64

Larissa worried that her milk might dry up. Minna Solomonovna had warned her against any emotional upheaval, but losing their money was a major disaster. By unspoken agreement, neither the Rezánovs nor the Cohens spoke of it anymore. The money was gone, and to blame Isaak was pointless. Andrei and Larissa from childhood were trained in the British stiff upper lip tradition, which discouraged self-pity. As for the Cohens, they were accustomed to finding suitable excuses for Isaak's actions. It was a shame that the money was gone, but nothing could be done about it.

But Julia continued to suffer deeply for her friends' misfortune. She did blame her father for the burglary. He was not a stupid old man given to bragging. Oh, no! Her father was a shrewd gangster, a thief all his life and he was not above stealing money even from his own daughter when she had her salon. She had caught him red-handed twice, each time forgiving him after his tears and promises to never, ever do it again! She believed that he sincerely loved the young Rezánovs and adored their baby and was willing to hide Andrei and Egórov, but ... when it came to money, money outweighed his loyalty. He simply had to have it.

"Don't worry about your breasts going dry," she advised Larissa. "You are a healthy young woman, you'll have plenty of milk for your little Nínochka! Don't listen to my mother. She is an old woman, and full of crap!"

Despite Julia's encouraging talk, Larissa could not stop worrying. Andrei and Egórov were planning to leave for Novocherkassk, which was even farther from Odessa than Yassy. It presented a serious problem in terms of how to get there without running into a Bolshevik firing squad.

The Don River Cossack lands were at the hub of the huge horse breeding estates that supplied the empire with its horses. The Cossacks were fiercely independent peasants, never enslaved by serfdom. They were allowed to have their own forms of government under the rule of democratically elected military leaders. Every male member of the Cossack community from eighteen to thirty-eight years of age had an obligation to serve in the Russian Imperial armed forces, providing his own horse and equipment. In return, the empire granted him land in the most fertile regions, like the Don River valley. As the result of generations of military service, the Cossacks became the wealthiest peasants in Russia, deeply religious, highly disciplined, and devoted to the Tsars, with their own regiments under the command of their own officers.

They were a handsome bunch, the Cossacks. Properly fed from childhood, they were healthy, seldom suffering from the common diseases of the Russian peasantry. They lived in well-built houses and were superb horsemen. They bragged that even before they could walk, they knew how to sit on a horse. Excellent swordsmen as well, the Cossack boys from the time they were eight years old were trained to split a cabbage head or a watermelon while riding bareback at full gallop.

The Cossack women were known for their beauty. Usually tall and stately, they were famous for their singing. Every evening the multi-voiced groups of women and girls would gather to sing their melancholy songs about their men fighting and dying somewhere in foreign lands. The mysterious 'foreign lands' were always places of no return in their sad songs. The women sang in natural polyphonic harmony and the melodies were so heart-rending that they found their way into the Russian operas of Tchaikovsky, Rimsky-Korsakov, Mussorgsky, and others.

The Cossack settlements, some of them as big as small towns, usually consisted of two or three streets, a well-appointed church, a school that provided education through the fourth grade level, several stores, and a doctor's office.

Every house in the settlement was white-washed and topped with a thatched straw roof, surrounded by an orchard and a large vegetable plot along with roomy stables for their beloved horses, as well as separate quarters for farm animals such as ox and cows and pigs. Chickens ran freely through the yards and the orchards. The young animals, calves or lambs, were taken into people's quarters and kept close to the warm petch. Needless to say, the air in the huts in such cases was unpleasant, but otherwise the Cossack houses were usually immaculate, contrary to most peasant dwellings.

"I think that even if we manage to arrange our trip with some fisherman, it will take forever," Egórov said. "Remember our trip along the Dniester? Well, this would be even worse. We would have to sail over *two* seas. God only knows how long will it take in a small boat! And of course, the winter storms—"

"So, what do you suggest?" Andrei interrupted.

"We must fly!"

"How? On a witch's broom?"

Egórov laughed. "No, seriously, we must get an airplane and fly to Novocherkassk! We will be welcomed, especially if we bring an airplane!"

"Where would we get an airplane? On Deribasovskaya Street? Or, perhaps in the Passage?"

"I am serious," Egórov said. "We'll steal it from the Anatra factory. Let me finish!" he lifted his hand. "We'll go to Anatra and apply for a job as test pilots, or even as mechanics. We don't need to hide our true identities from them. Most likely, they will be thrilled to have us, two experienced aces. We'll fly for them for two or three days to make them trust us, and then we'll take off for Novocherkassk! It should be easy!"

"I just love you, Egórka!" Andrei exclaimed. "You are always so full of crazy ideas! The way we look, though, they won't believe that we are pilots ..."

"They are no fools. They know what precarious times we live in. Besides, we'll show them both sets of our documents, and they can check our identities through the official papers of the 'former' Imperial Russian Air Service."

Andrei liked the plan. "Sounds good to me! Let's go tomorrow! But I must prepare Larissa."

"By all means. As a true daughter of our former military establishment, she will accept your duty call without protest," Egórov said optimistically, but a vision of Larissa running after the train was vivid in his memory. She had protested his leaving ... in her own way!

That night Andrei and Larissa made love for the first time since the birth of the baby. Doctor Gottlieb had forbidden her to engage in intercourse for several weeks after Nina's birth since it was 'dangerous for her genital health,' as he had put it. Doctor Shubin agreed, but for a more pragmatic reason. "You are at the most fertile age, when even a kiss could make you pregnant. I am joking of course about the kiss, but seriously, if you don't want to risk pregnancy at these particularly bad times, restrain yourselves from intercourse."

At first it was simple to refrain from sex. Andrei had to go back to war while Larissa was still torn after giving birth. Then they were separated almost immediately.

After his dramatic return from Yassy, Andrei deliberately withheld himself from Larissa. He slept on the floor. He felt that he was still dirty and smelly and was afraid to touch her. Behind his rationalization, was his real reason: Andrei convinced himself that he was becoming impotent. He based his suspicions on the fact that he had stopped having sexual dreams that used to relieve his urges.

He was reluctant to confess his fears to Egórov. "Egórka would make fun of it," he thought, and he was really afraid to confront Larissa with his shame, for it would be shameful to be impotent at his age, he thought. He suffered silently, unable to face his self-imposed problem.

Larissa could not understand his reluctance to make love to her. He seemed to love her no less, but unwilling to make love to her. What was the matter with him? Why did he prefer to sleep on the floor on a bag of straw rather than share her bed? Surely, the bed, even crowded, was more comfortable. The baby was quite happy in her laundry basket, so he wasn't endangering her by his presence in Larissa's bed.

"Why doesn't he want me anymore? I want *him! Why does he deny himself?*

She decided to force him to make love her.

That night she joined him on his straw bag on the floor. Without a word of explanation, she attacked him with kisses and caresses, to which he quickly responded with an erection. Her caresses reached the lower part of his body and soon she engaged, for the first time in her life, in an active performance of fellatio.

Andrei squirmed in embarrassment, as he was unable to stop the flow of his semen. She laughed. "Next time we'll do it for each other … I think this is the ultimate declaration of carnal desire …. Now, let's make love in the usual way!"

"I don't know if I can now…"

"Nonsense. You can. And you shall!" she said and laughed. "I sound like my mother when she used to make me do something that I was not accustomed to doing!" She caressed his body again, enjoying touching and loving every part of it, his smooth skin, his hard musculature, his penis coming back to life.

"You see?" she whispered against his neck. "You are ready…"

65

Akim drove the pilots to the gates of the Anatra Aircraft Factory located on the outskirts of Odessa, not yet infiltrated by the Bolsheviks. It was a compact enterprise consisting of two squat industrial buildings under half-domed roofs supported by heavy metal frames and walled with tall never-washed windows. The huge sliding doors of both buildings yawned open, exposing four airplanes in various stages of assembly. The planes were surrounded by a cluster of men in greasy work clothes. Only one of the machines, a Nieuport, had its dragonfly wings. The other three, still wingless, looked like mutilated bugs.

Short spiral staircases led from the building floors to a half-dozen offices and two metal overhead bridges connecting the opposite sides. The gallery provided easy positions for observation of the work below.

"Good luck, friends! You look so prosperous, as if you are *buying* this factory and not asking for a job!" Akim joked.

"Oh, yes! That's exactly what we are, very prosperous! So prosperous that we are wearing someone else's funeral clothes!" Egórov pointed to their somber suits with long black coats favored by Jewish rabbis.

"Be glad that these are not your own funeral suits!" Akim laughed. "I'll be waiting for you," he said.

Andrei and Egórov paused before the great doors. No one seemed to pay any attention to them. "Well, here we go!" Egórov said, stepping onto the work floor. "Let's look for the office of the boss!"

The 'boss' of the aircraft factory was Artur Antonovich Anatra, the manufacturer of several types of French-designed reconnaissance aircraft. The factory produced mainly Farmans, Nieuports, and Voisins. The models were quite familiar to Andrei and Egórov.

Mr. Anatra sat in his rather modest office behind a large desk piled up with papers, rolled charts, and maps. Well over fifty, his dark hair was still plentiful, neatly divided on the left side of his head, slick and shiny with brilliantine. Although of Italian origin, Anatra looked very British in his Savile Row brown suit with narrow beige stripes, brown silk bow-tie, two-tone brown shoes, and beige spats with shiny buttons. He was clean shaven except for a small moustache that was well waxed, its ends pointing up—not as high as Kaiser Wilhelm's, but high enough to look comical.

"What can I do for you gentlemen?" he inquired, raising his eyes from an official looking document, correctly assessing them as being gentlemen.

They looked at each other and, in unison, stretched out in salute.

"Squadron leader Captain Vassily Egórov and my deputy, Lieutenant Andrei Rezánov, Your Excellency! Our detachment has ceased to exist, and we found ourselves stranded in Odessa," Egórov reported smartly, breaking their cover and throwing themselves at the mercy of the factory boss. They saluted again, clicking their heels in the best tradition of the Imperial Guards officers.

Anatra smiled slightly, and his moustache ends moved upwards. "What detachment was it?"

"The Nineteenth, sir, at the Romanian Front. Colonel Kozakov's Detachment."

"Oh yes, I know your commanding officer. I hope he is well. If I remember correctly he became seriously ill while in Petrograd attending some meetings."

"Yes, sir," Andrei said. "We knew that he was called to Petrograd! As a matter of fact, the Colonel was kind enough to carry some letters to our families."

"We haven't heard about his illness," Egórov added. "Of course, the Colonel had been wounded so many times, perhaps it was something connected with his not being completely healed."

"As I understand, it was something different. But as you know, any second-hand information gets stale with time and one never knows what to believe. So, what can I do for you?" He had already guessed what they wanted: jobs! They were not the first ones; there were already several pilots who were in need of employment after their units were disbanded at the shrinking Russian fronts. They inevitably found their way here, trying to stay ahead of the Bolsheviks and their malevolence toward officers.

"We hoped that perhaps you could use us as test pilots, Your Excellency," Egórov said. "We thought that perhaps—"

"Unfortunately, I cannot offer you anything in Odessa," Anatra interrupted him. "However, we've a new facility in Simferopol. But first, let me see your papers: your authentic documents and then your fake ones. I know that you must have them, the fake ones, I mean. All prudent men have learned to fake something or other these days," he said, looking at their suits. They all laughed.

"Yes, sir!" They proffered him both sets of their documents.

"Rezánov ... Rezánov ..." Anatra repeated slowly. "For some reason your name sounds familiar to me ..."

"It's familiar to a lot of people, sir!" Egórov said, smiling. "Lieutenant Rezánov was that famous pilot who took a ride on the wing of a Voisin a couple of years back!"

"And dislodged a bomb! Yes! I remember! So, it was you!" Anatra exclaimed.

"Yes, sir. Captain Egórov was the pilot." Andrei was always ready to share his fame with Egórov.

"Well! Two famous pilots! Two Knights of St. George! You certainly will be welcome at our enterprise," Anatra said, returning their papers. "As long as the Bolsheviks don't get their hands on our factories, you have a home with us. If you are willing to relocate, I shall telegraph to Simferopol to expect two new test pilots. How soon will you be ready to leave?"

"Any time, sir, although the Lieutenant must make arrangements for his wife and child. Is there any chance of accommodating them in Simferopol? Odessa is like a powder keg ready to blow up!"

"The whole country is. There is no safe place anywhere. But you would have to find out about that in Simferopol, although I don't see why not. Anyway, come back tomorrow and meet with my business manager who will arrange and explain all the details of your employment and so forth. Our remuneration is very modest for we are never sure anymore of the legitimacy of our currency. However, we accommodate our employees in some other ways, such as their quarters and food. In a way, it's similar to what you were used to receive in your Military Aviation Service. Not very much!"

He stood up, indicating that the interview was over. "See you tomorrow, at nine!"

The pilots saluted again, but Anatra shook his finger at them as if they were naughty boys. "No, no, no! Remember, saluting is against the law! We have not been requisitioned yet, but we don't flaunt the fact!"

Instead, they shook hands.

Larissa's eyes were red from crying as she waited impatiently for Andrei's return. She had received a long letter from her mother, describing her new life.

"I live now in Ksusha's house on the islands, a stone throw from the Malaya Nevka where your friend Yousoupov murdered Rasputin," she wrote. *"I don't think that you've ever been in Ksusha's house. It is a sturdy, one room peasant hut with a tin roof that makes terrible noise during the rains. The house has no running water, and the toilet is outside. Ksusha, God bless her, takes good care of me, teaching me how to live in a 'proletarian style.' She made a lot of connections with the local merchants that are still allowed to function, but it begins to change. I can see several little shops that are suddenly sealed, their owners gone. Ksusha says that they were arrested as the bourgeois enemies of the working class. But I don't understand it: they were peasants, working people, proletarians who just happen to live in the city and sell a few things in their tiny shops! Obviously, 'bourgeois' is a misnomer. Oh, well ... I don't understand a lot of things lately!"*

Maria Nikoláyevna expressed her delight at receiving the photographs of Nina and Larissa.

"Ksusha and I placed the pictures under the icons and every night, before going to sleep, we look at them through a magnifying glass. You may wonder where we got a magnifying glass; Ksusha exchanged her gypsy shawl for it and a box of writing paper and envelopes in a stationery shop (that is now closed!) More enemies of the people!

"I read in Pravda that the Bolsheviks are signing an armistice pact with the Central Powers. If they succeed in ending this stupid, devastating war, I'll bow low to them in gratitude. God willing, we will be reunited! Of course, all of us are dirt poor now. Your and Andrúsha's inheritances were in the bank and all my formal court jewels ... they became the property of the people!" Can imagine some vulgar Bolshevik baba wearing my diamond tiara? My

heart fills with hatred. How are we going to live? I do not know. I still have a few little pieces for barter, but how long will they last?"

Larissa cried as she remembered her mother's rampage through the house. "My piano!" she thought recalling her beloved piano, her father's gift on her fifteenth birthday. "She must have trashed it too ... She wouldn't have left it for the Bolsheviks to bang on!" The image of the noble instrument with its keyboard smashed and the wood bearing the deep scars of her mother's rage was on her mind as Andrei entered the room.

"What happened?" he asked in alarm noticing her tear-streaked face. "Is anything wrong with the baby?"

"No, she is fine. It's my mother's letter. She wrote about some sad details of her new life with Ksusha."

"Cheer up, dearest girl! We got jobs! In Simferopol! As test pilots! We all shall go to the Crimea, where it is always warm and there is plenty of fruit!"

She smiled in spite of her sadness. "He is still such a boy!" she thought.

That evening as usual she sent Andrei and Egórov to smoke in the garden; because of the baby no one was allowed to smoke in the house. They sat in the gazebo talking in low voices about their plans, sipping cheap Bessarabian wine from Isaak's personal stash. They both had new pocket watches from a large collection that Isaak kept in a locked box under his bed. "Choose any watch you like! Even the gold ones," he offered. "I am glad to be of service!" he declared with generosity born out of guilt. And take this little lady's watch for Larissa!" Isaak said. "Give it to her on her birthday!" He picked up a small watch from the pile.

Andrei recognized the gold watch. He had given it to Larissa for her birthday! "She'll be glad to have it back," he said dryly. Isaak pretended not to hear.

Isaak hoped that he had been forgiven. The most unforgiving soul in the Moldovanka house was Julia. She barely spoke to him and would leave the room as soon as he entered. She blamed herself for not following her intuition. She should have done something ... But what? Where could Larissa have hidden her little fortune? Bury it in the ground?

Julia was also torn by the nearness of Egórov. She was tormented by her desire for him. For the sake of her pride she had suppressed her feelings, but she watched him surreptitiously, blushing like a young girl when she thought that he had noticed it.

Life in the little house was charged with the unhappiness of hidden passions, but the most all-consuming passion was Andrei's and Egórov's hatred of the Bolsheviks. The proud golden boys of Russian aviation, the admired heroes were brought down to their knees by virtual poverty. Wearing someone's clothes, sleeping on straw, and hiding from the authorities like criminals, they longed for revenge.

"What do you think we should do now?" Andrei asked, trusting his friend's judgment.

"Obviously, since we have no intention of working in Simferopol or anywhere else," Egórov began, "we must go to Simferopol and begin looking for a way to escape again. It may take a while, but there will be a chance."

"What about Larissa and the baby? Should we move them to Simferopol? Perhaps it is safer?"

"No! We don't know how long the Crimea will remain safe. Here in Odessa at least she has a good job and friends. In addition to Julia and her family, Larissa has the Shubins and Veronica and even Akim."

"Don't forget Glafira!"

"Of course! Glafira and her automobile! Let Larissa stay where she is. She's safer here than anywhere else, believe me."

"I believe you ..."

"Well, my friends, let me introduce you to Mr. Mamontov, or Comrade Mamontov, as he prefers. I think he aims to become the first Commissar when the Bolsheviks come for us! He is practicing being called 'comrade,' just in case," Anatra joked. "He'll make all the arrangements for you. Come with me."

They followed Mr. Anatra to the opposite side of the gallery and a similar looking small office. The door was open, and the pilots could see the shiny top of someone's bald head. The rest of it was hidden behind the spread of *Pravda.*"

"Ivan Petrovich, allow me to introduce our new test pilots, Captain Egórov and Lieutenant Rezánov. They are ready to start immediately, so go ahead and process their documents. Make our new pilots *'legitimate'!* I'll leave you in the capable hands of Comrade Mamontov. See you before you leave for Simferopol." He turned around and began to descend the spiral staircase to the work floor.

"Thank you, sir," the pilots said to his back, not saluting. They eyed Ivan Petrovich carefully. He knew their real identities. Now their lives were in his hands.

Ivan Petrovich Mamontov was an older man with a long, cartilaginous nose on the tip of which was perched a gold pince-nez on a black silk cord. Attired in an old-fashioned black frock suit with striped trousers, he looked like a pre-war senior bank clerk.

"He doesn't look ambitious enough to be a Commissar!" Andrei thought.

"He certainly doesn't look like a 'comrade'!" Egórov thought.

"Have you read *Pravda* today?" Mamontov asked without acknowledging them in any other way.

"No, sir. We don't have access to that paper," Egórov replied.

Mamontov stared at them over the pince-nez with his pale blue eyes. "Never mind. Apparently General Kaledin's Volunteers captured a town and killed all members of the Workers Soviet. All of them! Such barbarism! But of course, they are the Cossacks!" he said with disdain.

"They must have followed the example of the Bolsh—" Andrei began testily.

Egórov cut him off. "What else is new in the paper? What about the armistice negotiations?"

"Stalled," Mamontov replied without elaborating. "How soon can you leave for Simferopol?"

"As soon as you want."

"Tomorrow?"

"If you wish." Egórov adapted his laconic manner of speech.

"Fine. Tomorrow, then. You'll fly on the Voisin VI two-seater directly to Simferopol, using your flight for test purposes along the way as well. I understand you both are familiar with the Voisins."

"Yes, sir," the pilots replied.

"Well, this particular machine you'll fly is Voisin VI, and you will test certain small modifications. Now, let me have your papers." The pilots placed both sets of their documents on his desk. Mamontov glanced through them quickly and then stared at the men with his rheumy eyes.

"Why do you wear these clothes? Are they required by your religious affiliation? You look *Jewish,*" he said with disgust.

"No, sir. We are Christians. We were traveling incognito from Yassy to Tiraspol and then to Odessa through the territory under the threat of the Bolsheviks, trying to be lost in the crowds of deserters ..." Egórov explained, trying to keep his hatred of the Bolsheviks out of his voice. "Our Jewish landlord supplied us with these clothes."

"Never mind. While I go through the necessary formalities to legitimize your documents, you might as well go and get your proper flight suits, boots, and whatever else you need. Last door on the left from my office. Come back when you are through with the outfitters."

Andrei and Egórov looked at one another, grinning. For the first time in almost two months they were again wearing the pilots' black leather coats, officers' trousers, and military leather caps.

"I had forgotten how handsome we are!" Egórov joked.

Mamontov entered the room and handed each of them a folder of papers. "Here are your new legitimate documents. I advise keeping your fake ones handy, in case you come against some hostile elements. Believe it or not, I am not the one you need to fear," he said dryly but without the caustic air of his previous comments.

"Thank you Comrade Mamontov," Egórov said sincerely. "Would it be possible to see the modified aircraft that we'll be flying? And the list of the modifications?"

"I am sure it would be possible, but it's out of my jurisdiction. You must consult Artur Antonovich. I'll let him know that you are asking to see him."

The landing field was at the former grounds of the hippodrome, behind the main buildings of the Anatra works. The mechanics rolled the Voisin VI out of its tent hangar, and Andrei felt his throat tighten. He loved that airplane! He suddenly realized how much he had missed flying. With all their convoluted peregrinations of escaping, it had been a long time since Andrei was at the controls of an airplane!

Egórov, too, was smiling at the Voisin. "I never thought that I would be so glad to see the good old crate!"

They settled in their familiar positions: Andrei in the front of the fuselage on the observer's seat and Egórov at the controls behind him. Both were given mimeographed pages of modifications.

At first glance there was not much that could be called 'modifications.' The plane was a little more streamlined, and steel tube spars were added to the wings. The fuel tank was slightly redesigned to prevent leakage of fuel in case of a puncture. According to the written report, there was also an aluminum firewall between the engine and the fuel tank.

"Let's just have a quick touch-and-go flight over the airfield a couple of times," Andrei said. "We can check the modifications tomorrow on our way to Simferopol."

"Or, to Novocherkassk."

Andrei looked at him quizzically. "Do you mean …"

"Yes. Why not? We are stealing the aircraft one way or another. And we have no intentions of being test pilots. We want to get to Novocherkassk as soon as possible. So, why not go straight there, if we can?"

Andrei dreaded telling Larissa about their plans. He rehearsed his speech in his mind, trying to find the most compelling words, which would explain his decision and convince her of its urgency.

Egórov watched him closely. "Stop fretting! Larissa is the daughter of Maria Nikoláyevna. She knows how much you hate the Bolsheviks, and she feels that way herself. Look what they did to her mother! Larissa has already sent you into battle. Several times! She will understand."

"Yes, but how can she manage with the baby, with all our money stolen, and of course, with her job?"

"She will meet her responsibilities!" Egórov said impatiently. "Just make sure that you don't impregnate her until the Bolsheviks are gone!"

"You're always joking!" Andrei objected, annoyed with his friend. He stared at the broad back of Akim, who was driving them home. "You and I can fight for our beliefs and for our lives, if it comes to it, but what can she do if she is arrested? What will happen to our child? Who will protect her?"

Egórov had no answer. He knew that any usual words of comfort would have been banal and empty.

"Don't worry, Lieutenant," Akim turned on his seat to face them. "Larissa Sergéyevna is in the safest place, right now, right here, in Moldovanka! The Cohens and the other Jews have a great organization among themselves, taking care of one another. They even have a secret commander, a man by the name of Mishka Japónchik. He is a real bandit, but he takes good care of his people. As long as Larissa Sergéyevna is staying with the Cohens, she is safe, believe me!" He turned his attention back to his driving. "So don't worry, Lieutenant, go and fight the Bolsheviks. I may join the Volunteer Army myself if they will take a cripple like me!" Akim said over his shoulder. "I have my own score to settle with them!"

66

The shores of the Crimean Peninsula on the Black Sea were peppered with the great palaces of the members of the Imperial family and sumptuous estates of the ruling nobility. After the Bolsheviks took Petrograd, the Crimea provided a comfortable gathering point for members of the Imperial family and some aristocratic survivors of the revolution. The picturesque Crimea beckoned the newly dispossessed.

"When exactly must you report to Simferopol? And when do you plan to escape to join … you know," said Larissa, not wanting to say it out loud. She had known for a while that a test pilot job was only the first step on the road to Novocherkassk.

"Tomorrow."

"Tomorrow! So soon!"

"I know, but we have no choice" he lied, noticing that no tears had clouded her eyes. "How she has toughened with motherhood!" he thought, not sure that he welcomed the change: Larissa, emotional and passionate, was more to his taste. Andrei had prepared himself for a torrent of tears, but nothing melodramatic followed. Larissa only lowered her head. "Alright," she said quietly.

"Alright," he echoed. "I'd better pack." There was not much to pack: a few toilet items and a set of new underwear and socks, gifts from the Red Cross through Sister Veronica.

Egórov had similar items to pack in a soft canvas bag with a Red Cross emblem. He wanted to give Andrei and Larissa a few hours alone so he stayed in Yasha's room, making calculations for their flight while the boy was sleeping over at his friend's house.

It looked to Egórov that they should remain in Simferopol for a few days after all. The Voisin could not make it to Novocherkassk in one flight. They would have to refuel along the way. But where? There were no airports along their route. They would have to carry additional fuel, perhaps as much as twenty gallons, but how and where could they find so much extra fuel? They would have to find some clandestine connections in Simferopol, which of course meant Mishka Japónchik. Never a procrastinator, Egórov knocked on Isaak's door.

"Isaak Yákovlevich, we need your help," he began at once. "We'll need five cans of aviation fuel in Simferopol. Can you get it for us? As you know, Andrei and I don't have any money, so we can't pay for it. Can you somehow manage through your friends to get it for us?"

Isaak turned to his wife, "Go to the kitchen and fix us some tea and something sweet," he said. "I must talk to the Captain in private." Minna Solomonovna giggled and left the room. She was accustomed to the 'private conversations' of her husband.

Isaak was quick with an answer. "I can arrange it. Actually, it will be very simple, and it won't cost you anything. Mishka needs to send a package to Sevastópol. Since you are going to Simferopol, his agent can pick it up there. Can you handle a valise of this size on your airplane?" He bent down and pulled a valise from under his bed.

"Easily," Egórov said. "Is it something illegal?"

"Yes. Twenty Browning handguns and twenty boxes of ammunition," Isaak said without hesitation. "If you agree to take them, someone will pick them up from you and you'll get your five cans of fuel within a day or two. Upon my honor!"

Egórov smiled ironically. "What honor?" he thought. "Why are you telling me what is in the valise? Aren't you afraid that I might betray you?"

"No, Captain. To whom would you betray me? To the Bolsheviks? Besides, I know that you and Andrei were raised with the different code of ethics. Betrayal has no part of it."

"Ethics change, my friend. Someday you and I, if we survive, ought to have a discussion of 'ethics.'"

Isaak ignored his comment. "Somebody is going to meet you in Simferopol. We'll make sure that he is an employee of Anatra. When he asks, go with him. He will be one of Mishka's agents."

"How can you arrange it so fast? We are leaving tomorrow!"

"Have you heard of such a thing as the telephone?" Isaak asked with a sly grin. "Let's go to the kitchen and have some tea and something sweet!" Isaak said. They went to the kitchen and had tea with Minna Solomonovna and talked about the weather.

"Well, I'd better go to bed," Egórov finally said.

"And I must make a telephone call," Isaak said.

'Egórov raised an eyebrow. "Where do you find a telephone at this hour?"

"In my bedroom. We all have military field telephones now."

"I should've known!" Egórov laughed.

Julia came into Yasha's room and turned the key, locking the door. "I wanted to say goodbye to you," she said to Egórov. "Most likely, we'll never see one another again. I know where you are going. I also know that very few of us will survive when the Bolsheviks take over our city," she said. "I love you, Vassily, and this time I am not ashamed of declaring it. Don't say anything."

Egórov remained silent. He just opened his arms.

Andrei and Larissa also made love, but there was no uncontrolled passion. Andrei was cautious, afraid to impregnate Larissa. Later, he rocked the baby to sleep. He held the child in his arms, examining her sleeping face, imprinting it in his mind.

The baby looked like a baby now, and not like some wrinkled creature that failed to awaken any paternal feelings in him. Now, at almost three months of age, she was a child, his child. He stared at her tiny nose and a few blond wisps of hair, her perfect tiny hands with their miniscule fingernails, and he was filled with sadness. "This is my daughter," he thought. "I shall never see her grow up ..." Caught in the tragic web of life, Andrei made an effort not to dwell upon his melancholy thoughts.

Akim was ready to take Larissa and Julia to the hospital and then continue his drive to Anatra Aircraft Factory with the pilots. Doctor Shubin came out of his office to wish them good luck, and Glafíra stuck her head out of the door. "I'll watch over them," she shouted. They both knew that the pilots were heading to join the Volunteer Army. They had to avoid saying anything compromising. Glafíra especially had to watch her tongue. What she had done to help her friends would be considered high treason if the Bolsheviks were to find out about it.

Sister Veronica came out to see the pilots off and take Larissa and Julia inside. As the women left with final glances at their men, Veronica waved to the pilots. "Godspeed and good luck, *wherever* you're going!" she shouted fearlessly, protected by her invincible British passport.

The Voisin VI was waiting for them, fueled and clean with little tags attached to indicate the new experimental touches. Egórov jammed the valise into the observers' part of the fuselage, which had more floor space than the pilot's compartment.

"What have you got there? A bunch of stones for ballast?" Andrei murmured with irritation. He was in a bad mood. Larissa had begged him not to go to Novocherkassk, but rather stay in Simferopol and become a test pilot. They had quarreled. He had even yelled at her that it was his sacred duty to fight the Bolsheviks who had destroyed their family. He had called her selfish, and she had finally broken down in tears and the baby cried also, making it impossible for him to sleep. He had spent the rest of the night on the straw mattress on the floor.

Egórov glanced at him and decided to say nothing about the valise or the deal with Isaak. "He is too upset now," he thought.

Before starting on their journey the pilots again took a close look at the visual improvements of the craft. There were other visually un-observable modifications that they would test only by flying and going through certain aerobatics, but those they could discover later. They knew that the weight of the machine was somewhat increased, and it worried Egórov: the extra weight of Mishka's contraband was going to increase it even more.

Artur Antonovich Anatra came out of his office to wish them safe flying. "Have a good trip. Be very thorough. But be honest in your evalu-ation. Don't hesitate to mention the negative features. A lot depends on your report. We have potential orders for more than a hundred machines. I've made reservations for you at the hotel Europa until you find some permanent housing for yourselves and your families. So, Godspeed, and His blessings for your safety!"

The familiar commands of 'All clear!' and 'Contact!' were given, the wooden chocks under the wheels removed, and the Voisin VI taxied to the takeoff line.

It was a clear, crisp day made for flying. "It is going to be a pleasure flight, not threatened by the Albatroses or Fokkers," Egórov thought. Of course, they had to test the aircraft, to submit it to stress and various maneuvers that could actually lead to a crash. But it was all part of the game, part of the challenge of being a pilot, part of the daring life that they had chosen.

Andrei waited for the familiar exaltation of being in the air to take over him, but it never came. Instead, the tear-smudged face of Larissa was in his mind's eye, mutely accusing him of being cruel. "I was cruel," he thought. "I dumped on her my inability to protect her and the baby … I failed to acknowledge that she worried about me … Instead, I gave her a lecture … I am a real cad…"

He made an effort to remove the picture of Larissa from his mind and concentrate the plane's modifications. He noted that the newly-de-signed protective harness was meant to be locked around the observer-gunman's body. Since the gunman had to shoot the machine-gun while standing, it was permanently attached with sturdy belts to the walls of the airplane. It virtually excluded the possibility of the gunman falling out of the aircraft during active maneuvering aerobatics.

They reached the sea and flew over it until the mountainous outline of the Crimean Peninsula came into view.

The Voisin performed well in the hands of the experienced pilot, but Andrei doubted whether a less seasoned pilot would find it easy to manage. The craft seemed to have some problems with lateral controls and stability, probably due to the shift in weight. Its Salmson radial engine functioned well, and despite its increased weight the Voisin VI was 20 km/h faster than previous models of the plane.

Egórov circled over the city of Simferopol. It was easy to find the factory and its landing field: a flight line of three Nieuports rested on its northern edge. Egórov lowered his machine and wiggled his wings to greet the small crowd below that had come out to greet them.

"Well, here we are in the beautiful Crimea," he shouted to Andrei over the decreasing noise of the engine. "Our new adventure is about to start!"

He landed perfectly. The Voisin VI was immediately surrounded by mechanics and several very young men in matching leather jackets without epaulettes, obviously cadets of an aviation school.

"How was it?" they wanted to know.

"It worked fine," Egórov replied. "We'll tell you about it in detail later, after we report to your head designer, Gospodin Khioni," Egórov said, smiling. He could sympathize with the cadets' eagerness. They probably had only recently passed their solo flights. They were newly in love with aviation.

"I'll take you to Comrade Khioni," a middle-aged man stepped out of the crowd, emphasizing the word comrade. "Afterwards, you will meet with Commissar Krávchenko. "As I understand, you shall be staying at the Hotel Europa, so if you have some luggage, I can send it there while you are busy with your reports," he said.

"It won't be necessary ..." Andrei began, but Egórov interrupted him.

"That would be very nice. There is a valise in the observer's part of the fuselage and a couple of small canvas bags with our shaving gear. That's all we have."

"Good. I'll send one of my men with your luggage to the hotel," the man said. "Meanwhile, follow me."

"Must be the Commissar," Egórov thought.

Several hours later, after they concluded their reports to the management of the Anatra Factory, they hired a one-horse drozhki to take them to their hotel. "So what have we brought to Simferopol in that mysterious valise?" Andrei asked.

"Weapons. Handguns and ammunition, to be exact."

"What? We smuggled guns? For whom?"

"For Mishka. In exchange for five cans of fuel to take us from here to Novocherkassk. Isaak arranged it."

"Well!" Andrei was stunned. "So, when are we going to receive the fuel? And where are we going to store it?"

"The second part of your question bothers me also. Maybe someone in our hotel could be bribed to store it ... or perhaps there is some friendly soul around who can take care of it for a few days. We must investigate. As to when we should receive the fuel, I think probably tomorrow."

"We also must find another suitable aircraft. And manage to transfer our fuel to the plane. How shall we do it?"

"I don't know ... we probably should wait a few days before we find answers to all our questions. So, let's relax. Let's try to enjoy Simferopol. As I remember, Simferopol was once the center of the Scythian Empire and there are some ancient burial mounds. Could be interesting, don't you think?"

"Yes," Andrei said without much enthusiasm. "Could be interesting."

The next day, blessed with a cerulean sky and sunshine, the pilots enjoyed breakfast on the balcony, waiting for their fuel. But nothing came. No telephone calls, no messages, and no fuel. Egórov had a gut-wrenching premonition that they had been hoodwinked once again: the clothes that he had packed over the guns had been neatly spread on one of the beds when they came to the hotel, and the valise and its contents gone. But there was no message about the fuel.

He mentioned nothing about his premonition to Andrei, but Andrei had a premonition of his own, similar to Egórov's, that they had been "had" by Mishka Japónchik.

67

The next morning, and the morning after, there was still no fuel. Egórov asked the Commissar of the Anatra factory twice daily if there were any messages for them, but the reply was always negative: no messages.

"Looks like we'll be stuck here for a while," Andrei said. "Actually, I think the Crimea may become one of the action locations in the Civil War. Have you noticed the formations of armed workers training in the parks? They wear red bands quite openly. It reminds me of Petrograd in the early days!"

They discovered that they had plenty of free time on their hands. The Anatra factory production of aircraft was constantly interrupted by strikes of revolutionary workers throughout the city, who would shut down the water or electricity, stop the city transportation system, or simply barricade some streets, stopping traffic and shutting down deliveries of food and fuel.

The pilots worried that their presence at the Anatra could become superfluous and they would be fired. There were two other test pilots at the factory who had seniority over them.

"I talked to Commissar Krávchenko about our precarious position at the Anatra, and he agreed that our employment could not be guaranteed," Egórov said on their fifth day of idleness. "He suggested that we offer ourselves to a flight school as instructors. There are new schools in Evpatoria and, apparently, there are vacancies. He even offered to telephone to Evpatoria and inquire on our behalf."

"That was kind of him. Can we really trust him?"

"I don't know, but he knows who we are and still offered to help us. He could be useful to us, as Kóshkin or Glafíra—"

There was a knock on the door. "Fuel!" they both thought.

"Who's there?" Egórov called.

"Commissar Krávchenko."

Andrei and Egórov looked at each other. "What does he want?" each thought. Andrei felt his pulse elevate. Despite his offer to help, Andrei was suspicious. Still, they had no choice. Egórov opened the door.

Krávchenko walked in with a broad smile. "Hello, gentlemen. I know that you have little to do right now, so I thought I would offer to take you sight-seeing. I'd be your guide, if you don't mind. If you are interested in the city at all, I ought to go with you for your protection."

"For our *protection?*"

"Yes. Right now the city is no place for former Imperial officers. Even if you don't wear your epaulettes, you *are* officers. I'll go with you, and my red band will protect you," he touched the band over his left arm. "I hope you don't mind. Besides, I know quite a lot about Simferopol. I was born here."

"This is very considerate of you. We don't mind, of course," Egórov said cordially. "Actually, it will give us a chance to get better acquainted." He winked at Andrei.

Krávchenko looked like a typical Bolshevik factory worker. Dressed in an old cracked leather coat with the red band on his arm and a cloth cap, he must have been in his late forties but looked older.

"Do you have your Anatra factory documents with you?" he inquired. "Just in case. We have sailors patrolling the city, and they can be quite unforgiving."

"What would they do?" Andrei asked.

"Anything they want to. Arrest you. Or beat you up. They might even shoot you. They have a license to shoot counter-revolutionaries."

"Let's go," Egórov interrupted. He did not like the direction that their conversation was taking. He suspected the Commissar was not exactly what he was supposed to be. Like Kóshkin, his turns of speech were not compatible with the appearance of a factory worker. His vocabulary suggested that he was an educated man.

They hired a drozhki driven by an old Tatar in baggy black pants, a soiled shirt collar protruding at his neck. He was wearing an exquisitely embroidered skullcap that somehow did not go with the rest of his dirty appearance. His round yellow face with the slit eyes reminded the pilots of Glafíra: as he smiled bargaining for his fare with the Commissar, his eyes disappeared into his cheeks.

"Ah!" Andrei thought. "She is a Tatar!"

They drove through the city, giving the right-of-way to the Tatars' cumbersome carts pulled by little donkeys. The carts were overloaded with anything, from a pile of cabbages to old furniture, from chopped wood to bunches of small dirty children. It was incredible that the little donkeys could pull so much weight.

The drivers, ensconced on the top of their loads, all wore similar looking leather slippers and embroidered *tubeteiki*, skullcaps.

Krávchenko directed the driver toward the Old City, where the streets were unpaved, narrow, and crooked, covered with manure. Two carts going in opposite directions had only a hand's width for passing one another, which led to the shouting of both drivers and the braying of donkeys suffering beatings by their masters as they tried to pass one another. A drozhki could not enter certain streets at all.

The houses of the Old City were dilapidated, squat one-story hovels without doors or windows, the entrances covered with colored carpets. The air of poverty would have predominated were it not for the carpets. The carpets, big or small, were everywhere, dazzling in their colors and designs. They were spread on the ground in front of the houses and around the fire pits where the people prepared their meals.

It was obvious that the denizens of the Old City lived on the streets around their fires, not changing much from their ancient ways.

"This is the stink hole of Simferopol," Krávchenko said. "I really don't know how they keep themselves clean! They probably don't. The Russians despise the Tatars and don't allow them to use our public baths. The Tatars hate the Russians also. Few people, except for tourists, ever dare to visit this place, especially at night. Tatars are known for their savagery. I think even the sailors avoid the Old City. They know that all slashed throats in the city are committed by the Tatars. I also hate them, even though I shouldn't. The Bolshevik goal must be the unification of the Proletariat! And that must include the Tatars. They are the proletarians also, aren't they?" Krávchenko concluded his little bit of Bolshevik propaganda with a sardonic smile.

Prudently the pilots restrained from commenting.

Krávchenko sighed. "Let me show you something more pleasing to the eye, something that I have always enjoyed, ever since I was a boy. It is a tree. Actually, *several* trees."

"Alright. Show us your tree," Egórov said with comic resignation." But I think *one tree* should be enough."

The Commissar said something to the driver. The old man nodded.

"Do you speak the Tatar dialect?" Andrei asked in surprise.

"Just a few words. We all do. We speak a few words in their tongue and they speak a few words in Russian, and somehow we manage to understand one another."

They rode for almost half an hour through quiet streets until they finally saw the tree that Krávchenko so wanted to show them. Andrei had to admit that it was truly an unusual tree. It consisted of *five trunks* that eventually divided into hundreds of big branches.

"It's an ancient chestnut tree. During the summer when it's in full bloom, it's an enchanted garden all by itself. The chestnut flowers are like little forest nymphs dressed in cone-shaped white dresses, all lined up as if on parade," Krávchenko said with a dreamy expression on his worn face.

"Why, my dear Comrade Commissar, you are a poet!" Egórov was smiling. "I know what you mean. I had a similar impression when I saw some chestnut trees in bloom in Paris .... Only instead of nymphs or angels I saw the little ballerinas of the Corps de Ballet of the Paris Operá!"

"You would too, wouldn't you!" Andrei laughed.

The commissar laughed, too. He ordered the driver to take them back to the hotel. Halfway back, he said quietly. "I called Evpatoria. They have some trouble there. A decant of sailors landed in their harbor unexpectedly. Perhaps it is better if you wait a little ... if you know what I mean."

They knew very well what he meant. The Tatar brought them back to their hotel.

68

There was no fuel. They realized that they had been swindled.

To make matters worse, Krávchenko telephoned, asking them to come to his office at once. It sounded ominous.

"I have some terrible news from Evpatoria," he announced. "Sit down!"

They obeyed.

Krávchenko began his recitation.

Evpatoria had been shelled by a cruiser, fortunately causing little damage as the gunners apparently were not well trained. The sudden appearance of the revolutionary sailors in Evpatoria was a real surprise for the peaceful town known mostly for its healthy mud treatments. Those who dwelt along the shore in elegant villas watched fearfully as naval cutters brought wave after wave of armed sailors to their pristine beaches.

A resistance group was hastily organized under the command of the retired Colonel Vygren, but lacking machine guns they were unable to hold back the fanatical revolutionary sailors. Colonel Vygren formally surrendered to the sailors by presenting his ceremonial sword to the victors. In reply, the sailors seized the elderly Colonel and threw him *alive* into the roaring furnace aboard the cruiser.

Commissar Krávchenko was visibly shaken. "It's lucky that *you* were not there. Stay in Simferopol. I'll see that you get more assignments. You have less competition now: one of our test pilots deserted to the Whites."

"What?"

"Not only has he deserted, but he took along the plane he was testing!" Krávchenko looked grave. "And I helped that son-of-a-bitch to get his job! If I ever see him again, I will kill him."

Andrei and Egórov resisted the urge to exchange glances, both glad that a telephone ring distracted Krávchenko's attention. He waved them out of his office.

"We must be very careful now," Egórov whispered. "They are watching us!"

More trouble was brewing. Even though military action against the Central Powers had stopped, a new domestic rebellion erupted within Russian borders: the Ukraine proclaimed her independence from Russia. Petrograd promptly declared war against the Ukraine.

Various military decrees followed to centralize and strengthen the Red Army, starting with a new name—Workers and Peasants Red Army, or RKKA, for short. This decree was followed by another one declaring the creation of the Workers and Peasants Red Military Airfleet with a similar jumble of capital letters, under the command of People's Commissariat of Army and Navy.

Only one more large military branch remained to be re-shaped into a Red organization—the Navy. The Baltic Fleet was renamed Workers and Peasants Red Fleet, and its Command Quarters moved from Helsingfors in Finland, which had declared *her* independence from Russia, to Kronstadt Island in the Baltic sea, within sight of Petrograd.

Andrei and Egórov watched the constantly changing situation in the country by reading the issues of *Pravda* in Krávchenko's office. They refrained from discussing the news with the Commissar, and he did not press them, both parties deliberately avoiding the obvious conflict of opinion. The pilots wondered why the Commissar had made no attempts to recruit them or turn them in, and they decided that perhaps he himself was not totally devoted to the Bolshevik's mission.

Krávchenko knew very well *who* they were, and he suspected that they were planning desertion. He arranged that they be sent to test only one-seat fighters and never at the same time. One of them was always to be kept at the plant while the other was up in the air. The Commissar was sure that they would not try to desert separately.

The pilots in their turn had already decided that they would wait until they had a two-seater to test to attempt the escape. Meanwhile they looked for a kindred soul among the mechanics, whom they could involve in their plans: they still needed that extra fuel.

The solution to their problem came surprisingly with the actions of the Central Powers. Annoyed by the Bolsheviks who kept stalling signing the armistice agreement while Lenin waited for a proletarian revolution in Germany, the Central Powers declared resumption of the war with Russia and ordered their armies to move again.

They met no resistance at the exhausted Russian front. Their re-activated troops quickly moved along the railways in two directions: north toward Petrograd and southeast toward the Crimea. They made quick progress in both directions and within days, Germans were expected to be on the doorstep of Simferopol. Commissar Krávchenko gave orders to the factory employees to save the aircraft by flying them to Sevastópol, which was now in the Red's hands. As the pilots took to the air with the completed machines, the others on the ground set fire to the factory and its unfinished aircraft.

In the commotion, Krávchenko abandoned his watch over Andrei and Egórov. They took advantage of the situation by loading a two-seater Voisin VI with four large cans of benzene and two small cans of lubricant oil and took off not south, toward Sevastópol, but north, toward Novocherkassk.

On March 3rd, the Soviets signed the Treaty of Brest-Litovsk, surrendering the territories of Poland, Finland, Latvia, Estonia, Lithuania, Belorussia, and the Ukraine, depriving Russia of about 30% of its pre-war population.

The Bolsheviks established the *Supreme Military Command* headed by Trotsky, who began to reorganize the Red Army. Serving in the army became compulsory.

On March 9th, Lenin offered the country another big surprise: the capital would be moved to Moscow, away from the shores of the Baltic Sea that Russia shared with several European countries.

The Soviet government secured itself in Moscow, behind the thick walls and the huge locked gates of the ancient fortress of the Kremlin. The Kremlin became a fortress once again, a territory forbidden to enter to anyone without a special permit.

One of the first announcements from the Kremlin was the ratification of the Brest-Litovsk Treaty. That done, the *Soviet Forces of Special Purpose,* better known as the Cheka, were ordered to Mogilev to abolish the former Stavka, arrest the remaining officers of the Supreme Command, and have them shot. That was done without delay.

69

In mid-March the Reds occupied Odessa and began a campaign to recruit former Tsarist officers into their service. They badly needed *educated* officers. To assure that those who had joined their forces would not betray them, the Cheka watched the *families* of the new recruits, thinking of them as hostages not yet incarcerated. But Lenin realized that to frighten the converts into submission wasn't enough. The recruited officers were allocated extra food rations and other privileges, a system that continued with success for many years to come.

The Reds occupied Odessa but did not stay long. The Austro-Hungarian forces were right on their heels, giving the Reds barely enough time to send their battleships to Sevastópol for safe-keeping. While still in Odessa the Reds confiscated as much as they could from its citizens, including the supplies and medications from Memorial Hospital.

Doctor Shubin and the nurses watched helplessly as the Reds swept off the shelves their irreplaceable medications and the supplies of bandages and rubber gloves. Shubin protested when they took the trays of surgical instruments. They rudely pushed him away. "Go away, old man! Our wounded comrades need all this stuff!"

Commissar Glafíra Ivánovna remained silent as the soldiers stripped the beds and loaded the gurneys with the sheets and towels from the linen room, taking the loot to the ambulance, which they also confiscated.

"Comrades, it's the only ambulance that we have! We *really* need it!" Glafíra finally pleaded.

"We need it more," was the reply. She knew better than to protest any further.

Glafíra was heart-broken that the ambulance was confiscated, but at least the precious automobile was safe, she thought. She and the driver had secreted it in the old dilapidated barn where before the revolution the hospital had kept its two horses and medical carts. The horses were long gone, but the carts were still there under tarpaulins. Glafíra and the driver piled up empty cartons and other debris and hid the car under the tarpaulins between the carts. The Reds were not interested in the old carts, and the automobile had survived confiscation.

Larissa and Julia worried about Andrei and Egórov. There had been no news about them for almost a month. Julia received a letter from her husband in America through the American Consulate informing her that he had gathered the necessary documents for her and Yasha's emigration and deposited the needed funds with the consulate.

"What should I do?" she cried to Larissa. "Should we go?"

"I am not the one to advise you ... But of course, you were planning to go to America even before the revolution. Perhaps you should do it, while you have a chance. I don't know ..."

"But, would you leave if you had a chance?" Julia insisted.

"My situation is different. My mother is in Petrograd and my husband is somewhere nearby ... It is different for me. Talk to your parents. But most of all, think of Yasha. What kind of future would *he* have in Russia?"

If she were in Julia's place, Larissa thought, she would leave. However, she wasn't in Julia's place; she painfully missed her mother. In her heart of hearts she thought that she missed her even *more* than she missed Andrei. She wondered if she would *ever* be reunited with her mother after the new directives of the rights of general population were announced.

Every urban person was to be assigned to some particular place that could not be changed. People were forbidden to travel without an official permit given only to a few important people. Even within the same city people were not allowed to change domiciles without permission. Every change of location had to be approved by a special committee. It took *months* for one's application to be considered and most likely denied. It looked as though unless the Reds were defeated and all their draconian laws repealed, it would be impossible for Larissa and her mother ever to be reunited.

Larissa received an official *propíska*, a permit to occupy one room in the Cohens' house. The house itself was confiscated and became the property of the State. The Cohens were allowed to occupy it, but they would be permitted to keep only two rooms for their family; the parlor and the dining room would be assigned to someone *"qualified"* under the new housing laws. The kitchen and toilet would be for communal use by all occupants.

70

In Petrograd the pitiful lives of Maria Nikoláyevna and Ksusha were ever harsher. To cope with the new regulations they developed a work-sharing routine: while Ksusha did the bartering for provisions and dealt with the authorities that required negotiations, Maria Nikoláyevna took care of the domestic chores. Ksusha taught her how to prepare and knead the dough and bake bread, how to cook gruel, and how to bake potatoes over red-hot coals without burning them. Together they washed their clothes in a large metal tub that leaked. Ksusha plugged it regularly with wax from a spent candle. They pumped water every morning from a public pump and cleaned their outhouse. At first Ksusha tried to prevent Maria Nikoláyevna from cleaning the outhouse. "I can't let you!" she insisted. "You are a lady, you are my *mistress!*"

"Yes, and as your *mistress* I order you to shut up and remember that I am not a lady anymore. I must learn a lot of new things. And, don't call it a shithouse! Let's at least avoid using street language!"

Maria Nikoláyevna learned how to look like a gray-haired peasant baba, attracting no attention from the militia patrols. Dressed in cheap dark clothes with her jewelry hidden in every seam, she blended with the multitudes of women.

But she had to learn how to *speak*. No more was she to use such expressions as *may I*, or *please*, or even *thank you*. Her politeness stamped her immediately as a *'former person,'* a new classification that found its way into the Russian language. Maria Nikoláyevna and Ksusha decided that only Ksusha should speak in public. She had the necessary intonation and diction and a superb talent to cajole, beg, and even shed tears at the right moment. With that talent, Ksusha was able to wrangle miniscule pensions for herself and Maria Nikoláyevna as two war widows as well as the permit to live in the little hut. It had become nationalized and they were made to pay rent to the housing authority. They also received an allocation of cut firewood for their petch.

It was a miserable life without any future. Maria Nikoláyevna, who had hoped that by selling some of her hidden treasure she would be able to scrape enough money for a ticket to Odessa, had another disappointment. With the proclamation of the new travel restrictions and housing laws, she had no hope of being reunited with Larissa.

For weeks at a time she heard nothing from Larissa. The postal service was in chaos once again. The letters were often left undelivered and discarded, or would arrive weeks later, all bunched up. Try as she could, she was unable to free herself from the ever-tightening coils of depression.

Ksusha was more optimistic. "Just wait for our men to get organized and go to battle against the Reds!" she kept saying. "Our friends in the other countries will come to our rescue, you just wait and see!"

"What friends? All our *friends*' are terrified that Communism will spread to their own countries!"

"That's why they'll come to our help! They don't want to suffer our fate!" Ksusha insisted.

Maria Nikoláyevna shrugged her shoulders. She had no hope herself. Having heard rumors about three Commanders in the south trying to organize an Anti-Bolshevik army and knowing the propinquity of political arguments, she had no hopes that the commanders would achieve much. "They will fight one another for supremacy," she thought. "They will argue like our ministers and deputies did before the revolution. Instead of creating a democratic government when they had a chance, they allowed the *Red Terror*' takeover!"

The *Triumvirate of Generals*, as they were called, consisted of three famous military leaders, each of whom had a great reputation and his own crowds of followers. The eldest of the three was General Mikhail Vladímirovich Alexeyev, whom Maria Nikoláyevna knew very well. He was the commanding officer of her husband even before he had become Chief-of-Staff to the Tsar. Like so many Russian military leaders, he had welcomed the February revolution, hoping for the democratic election of the Constituent Assembly. With the Bolshevik revolution in October, Alexeyev's hopes were shattered. He had found himself in need of organizing the opposition to the new regime. Being in ill health, Alexeyev nevertheless took command of a few hundred kindred souls and issued the call for volunteers to fight the Bolsheviks.

The other two generals were Anton Ivánovich Denikin and Lavrenty Georgievich Kornilov. Maria Nikoláyevna knew less about them but was convinced that Alexeyev was an unsuitable man for ultimate leadership. Aside from being in poor health, he was known by his staff as being too gentle. She recalled General Rezánov's complains about Alexeyev not being *tough* enough. "That's not what is needed now!" she thought angrily. "We don't need a nice, polite man to lead the army. We need a *brute* to fight the *brutes!*"

That *'brute'* seemed to be General Kornilov, who had personally arrested the Tsarina in Tsárskoye Selo. He was adored by his soldiers. Kornilov had adopted the Bolsheviks' own slogan of *"No Prisoners."* His soldiers were only too glad to oblige. For each act of brutality by the Reds, the Kornilov soldiers answered with a *double* measure. Alexeyev and General Denikin, were shocked by Kornilov's tolerance of brutality, but they did nothing about it. Kornilov was the hero to his troops and a champion recruiter for the anti-Bolshevik cause.

The Triumvirate shared their Headquarters in Novocherkassk in a former palace of a Cossack ataman. Unfortunately they acutely disliked one another and rarely spoke. They preferred to exchange messages from one office to another.

Similar situations reigned around the country. There were many counter-revolutionary groups throughout Russia, from its European borders to Siberia, each headed by a former military leader or an adventurer, each followed by a group of demobilized soldiers, loyal only to him, if to anyone. Should all these diverse groups unite, they could have represented a real threat to the Communists, but as it was, each pursued its own agenda and ambition. At best these small armies of fighters could be called partisans, at worst—plain bandits.

Such were the thoughts of Maria Nikoláyevna gleaned from the information she obtained from the pages of *Pravda* pasted on the walls of the buildings in Petrograd. She was astute enough to read between the lines of communist propaganda and make correct conclusions. She was convinced now that the Whites would be unable to overcome the Reds and began to prepare herself for the new reality.

Ksusha held different views. She believed that God would punish the Bolsheviks. She prayed on her knees every night for the Bolshevik's defeat, for Andrei's life, and for her *sweet little Lárochka and her baby Nínochka,* all alone, somewhere in Odessa.

Maria Nikoláyevna could not pray. She had lost her faith.

71

Novocherkassk, the capital city of the Don Cossacks, was a young city by Russian standards. It was built at the junction of the Aksai and the Turlov Rivers, both tributaries of the mighty Don, and it became the cultural and administrative center of the Don Cossacks nation.

Egórov and Andrei circled low over the city looking for an aerodrome, noting two triumphal arches at opposing ends of a broad boulevard, a couple of monuments, a park surrounding a large building that looked like a palace, and a Byzantine Cathedral. The streets were built as a compact grid, evidence that it was indeed, a modern, well-planned city.

They found a small aerodrome, really a large field on the outskirts, with three big tents, each housing an airplane. A long shack, obviously a workshop, was next to the tents. A smaller shack with a windsock pole, probably an office, was across the landing strip, and a motorcycle with an attached gondola was parked at the entrance.

Egórov checked the windsock and gently landed into the wind.

The buzz of their Voisin attracted the attention of several men who came out of the workshop to watch them. Egórov taxied to the building and turned off the engine.

"Greetings!" he called. "I am Captain Vassily Egórov, Squadron leader of the 19th Detachment of Colonel Kozakov. This is Lieutenant Andrei Rezánov. We came from Simferopol to offer our services to the Volunteer Army. May we dismount?" He grinned. He used the cavalry term, noting that all men wore cavalry boots with spurs: like him, they were originally cavalry officers.

One of them, a man in his late twenties, stepped out of the group. "I am Captain Vladímir Markov, Commander of Novocherkassk Aviation Detachment. Welcome!" Egórov and Andrei climbed out of the Voisin and, for the first time in months, saluted without fear of recrimination.

Captain Markov drove them in his motorcycle into the city and took them to the Hotel Europe where he and the other pilots were billeted. He was not surprised that Andrei and Egórov had arrived without any luggage, lacking even toothbrushes. That was how most of the volunteering officers arrived. With their lives at stake, they had to travel light.

"Do not worry," Markov said, taking them to his room and offering them French cognac. "We have a Ladies Help Society here. I have already left the standard request for some things that you will need until you make your own requests. The ladies will supply you with everything. They are mostly the wives and daughters of our senior officers, and they are well organized. Once in a while they give charity balls and concerts, and there are some lovely young ladies to dance and to flirt with," he added, looking with a smile at Andrei.

"The Lieutenant is a new father," Egórov said, "But I might enjoy a bit of flirting with some lovely young ladies!"

"Oh, you would, wouldn't you?" Andrei grinned.

"So, what's going on in the Crimea?" Markov asked, turning serious.

"When we left Simferopol, the city was neutral. But yesterday, the Anatra Commissar ordered his men to fly all workable aircraft to Sevastópol, which is in the Reds' hands. We preferred to use the opportunity to fly here, instead."

"The Commissar expected the Austrians to take the city," Andrei explained.

"Well, he was correct: the Austrians are entering Simferopol as we speak," Markov said. "You made it just in time! The Austrians have taken the whole of the Ukraine already! But let me tell you about our squadron here. We have only four workable fighters. Now, with your two-seater, we have the capacity of six. It's good news for us. The French are promising to send us four new Nieuports, but *when* is an open question. Since we are out of the war, they are not particularly sympathetic to our plight. Anyway, our activities here are just being organized. We have four pilots and three Cossack mechanics, who are good but know nothing about the aircraft. The French sent us one old man, who is an excellent mechanic, but he doesn't speak Russian and Cossacks don't speak French. So far we are managing, but to have you two, who are experienced military pilots, is a blessing to us. Of course, you speak French, don't you?"

"We do." Andrei said.

"Wonderful! Now we *really* can start moving!" Markov exclaimed. "We have received a small shipment of spare parts for Nieuport 17s and perhaps you and Monsieur Gilot could teach our Cossack mechanics how to use the new spare parts to fix the old machines."

"Tell us about the Civil War," Egórov said. "What is the situation? What will we be doing?"

"Our duty has been reconnaissance and light bombing of the Red reserves. So far, we have not been challenged, which probably means that the Reds have no aviation. As we begin to advance on Rostov, I am sure we'll see a lot of action, but I am also sure that there won't be any air battles. We will harass their land forces, scatter their cavalry and so forth. Meanwhile, we will continue trying to recruit more *ordinary soldiers.*"

"Any luck?"

"Not so far. We get only officers, of which there is a dwindling supply in Russia. So officers are fighting now as infantry privates," Markov said. "I've read in our news bulletin that the French are lending Alexeyev's army several million francs. Perhaps we will receive some kind of salaries from that loan. Right now, the Volunteer Army can afford to pay only for our lodging, food and medical care. And that's all. I hope you have some private funds to tide you over."

"We don't," Egórov said. "We have about one hundred and fifty rubles between us. But Rezánov needs to send money to his wife and baby in Odessa: he and his wife were robbed there."

"Sorry to hear that. I'll try to wangle a reward of some kind for you for bringing us the Voisin. It certainly deserves a reward. First, though, I would like to take you to meet General Alexeyev."

Andrei and Egórov cleaned themselves up a bit with their host's toiletries, rinsed their mouths with Boric solution, combed their hair, and dug the dirt from under their fingernails. They were ready to meet the old general.

It was already quite dark and the streets of Novocherkassk were illuminated by tall and elaborate streetlamps as impressive as those in Petrograd.

Markov straddled his motorcycle and Egórov and Andrei took the passenger seats—one behind the rider, another in the gondola.

"This is a nice city," Markov shouted over the noise of the motorcycle.

It *was* a 'nice city,' indeed. The streets were clean and on both sides of the wide central boulevard behind elaborate iron fences were handsome villas surrounded by trees.

Markov pointed. "See that Triumphal Arch? It was built in commemoration of our victory over Napoleon. There is an identical arch on the other end of the boulevard. The city fathers did not know from which end of the city to expect the entrance of the victorious army, so they built *two* arches!"

"And whose statue is that?" Egórov pointed to an equestrian statue in the middle of a spacious square.

"It is Ataman Platov, the Cossack leader who was the founder of the city. And the big building behind that fancy fence is Platov's palace, where our High Command of *three generals* are presiding over the creation of the Volunteer Army." Both pilots thought that they caught a hint of sarcasm in Markov's reference to the three generals.

Markov turned inside the opened gates of Platov's Palace Garden and stopped his machine. He showed his documents to a very young Cossack guard.

"These officers are to see General Alexeyev," Markov said with emphasis.

"Proceed," the guard saluted. He turned toward the striped black and white barrier erected beyond the formal gates and, turning the handle of some primitive mechanism vigorously, lifted the barrier. Markov drove his machine under the porte-cochère entrance at the side of the palace, and the pilots dismounted.

"We have a meeting with General Alexeyev," Markov announced to the officer on duty. The pilots and the duty officer saluted one another.

"Proceed to the second floor. The duty officer there will escort you to the General's office," he replied.

The office of General Alexeyev was rather small with two windows facing the wintry garden. The general's desk stood between the windows. On the wall behind it was a large colorful map of European Russia. Parts of it were still peppered with little flags.

The general sat behind the desk wearing his old uniform with its epaulettes and military decorations of St. George. He had the pasty appearance of a sick man in need of fresh air. His thin hair lay flat on his head and even his full moustache that was always twisted up with bravura, seemed to have lost its optimistic élan.

The three pilots stretched to attention, their right arms raised at the correct angle in salute.

"Captain Vladímir Markov and the pilots from the 19th Detachment of Colonel Kozakov," the duty officer announced crisply. Alexeyev lifted his eyes from reading the newspaper. It was *Pravda*.

"Welcome," he said, putting the paper aside. "Please come in and sit down." The pilots seated themselves around a small round table covered with a decorative tapestry. "Please order us some tea and biscuits if we have any. If not, just tea."

"Yes, Your Excellency, right away!" the duty officer saluted, made a sharp turn, and left.

"Well, what good news have you for us, Captain?" Alexeyev asked, turning to Markov.

"We have two pilots who arrived with a Voisin VI from Simferopol, Captain Egórov and Lieutenant Rezánov," Markov said. The pilots stood up, bowed stiffly with their heads, and clicked their heels.

"Sit down, sit down," Alexeyev waved them back to their chairs. "Rezánov … Rezánov …" he repeated slowly. "Are you by any chance related to General Vladímir Petrovich Rezánov?"

"Yes, sir. He was my father." Andrei said. "He died of typhus last year."

"So I have heard. What a shame! He was a good man and a great tactician. So, you are the young man whom I was asked to persuade *not* to become a pilot!"

"Yes, sir. I remember when my father brought me to your office in Petrograd."

"We can see how effective that was!" Alexeyev laughed, his pale eyes becoming surrounded by a web of fine lace of wrinkles. "And you, Captain? Did you have any objections from your family to your choice of career?" he turned to Egórov.

"No, sir. My parents were already gone, and I had served in the cavalry for two years before becoming seduced by aviation."

"I like your choice of words! *Seduced!* That was exactly right in those early years. The young men were *seduced* by aviation! Well, anyway, tell me how you came to be here with us."

An elderly orderly, looking more like a family retainer and not a soldier, brought in tea and a plate of stale biscuits.

Egórov and Andrei described their epic journey in detail. They felt at ease with the old general. He was friendly, endearing himself as he asked Andrei to help him to take his medicine. "Mix these powders with water, Andrúsha," he said. "I hate to call the duty officer each time I need to take my medicine. I should be able to prepare it myself, but my hands shake and I spill the powders." He reached into his chest pocket and extracted a small square packet of some powdered medicine.

Andrei took the packet and emptied it into a heavy cut glass. He filled it with water from a large decanter and, with a spoon that lay next to it, swirled the powder until it dissolved. "Here you are, sir," he handed it to the general.

"Thank you, my boy. And how is Varvara Mikháilovna?"

"My mother has also died. They both were staying with Maria Nikoláyevna Orlova after their house was confiscated and my mother was beaten by the Bolsheviks. She never regained her health and I think her mind either, and she died shortly after my father."

"Oh, how sad. You have more reason than most to hate the Bolsheviks. And now you are joining our Volunteer Army," he said with gravity. "As Captain Markov must have told you already, we are in a rather pitiful circumstances. No money to pay our soldiers, no money for heavy weapons or ammunition, only the determination to defeat the powers that brought us this tragic situation. We *must* destroy this Bolshevik power! It will be up to us, a few devoted sons of Russia to restore order in our country. I was reading their *Pravda* … what a misnomer it is! It says that now the Reds are trying to recruit *our officers!* Have you ever heard of such impudence?"

"Yes, sir, their Commissars made some veiled approaches to us," Egórov said.

Alexeyev laughed. "I can see that they haven't succeeded in *'seducing'* you, as you called it!"

"No, sir. Just the opposite. They convinced us instead to join you in the fight for the liberation of our lands." Egórov knew that he sounded as if he were quoting from a political leaflet, but he did not care. That was how he really felt.

"So when we win, I don't say *if* we win, for there are no *ifs* for us, who do you think should be at the helm of our country?"

"A freely elected Parliament under a constitution," Egórov replied with sincere conviction. "I don't want any compromises. No, sir! I wish for a simple and democratic Parliament with a simple and democratic constitution that will respect the rights of all citizens and classes. Sort of like in the American system of government."

"Bravo! Bravo!" Alexeyev laughed a clapped his hands. "I'll nominate you, Captain Egórov, to be one of our first deputies!"

"I second it!" Andrei joined. "Captain Egórov expressed my own exact sentiments!"

"Mine also," Markov said, all by forgotten under the weight of Egórov's and Andrei's personalities. "I was wondering, Your Excellency, would it be possible to award a prize to Captain Egórov and Lieutenant Rezánov for bringing a new aircraft to our squadron?"

"I can propose it at the next meeting with the Triumvirate. It's a good idea. It may encourage the other pilots who will be volunteering to join us to come with their aircraft. Meanwhile, it is getting late, so I will let you go. I'll be in touch with you shortly. There will be a lot of flying for you when we move on to Rostov! So, good night!" he stood up. The officers rose to their feet, saluted, and remained standing until the old general left the room.

72

The pilots and the French mechanic Gilot immediately established mutual respect: they all *loved* airplanes! Gilot checked the Voisin and the modified construction of the machine gun as Andrei demonstrated its capacity against a target pinned to a forgotten haystack rotting in the field outside the aerodrome. The haystack was torn to shreds by Andrei's precise bursts of fire. The old mechanic was impressed, but Andrei only laughed. "It was nothing!"

Egórov smiled paternally. "The Lieutenant was our best sniper at the 19th Detachment," he said to Gilot.

The Frenchman was delighted by the new pilots. They amazed him with their impeccable French and surprised him with their knowledge of the workings of an airplane, a non-existent combination among the new crop of pilots. As for Andrei and Egórov, they were only too happy to be able to speak their elegant second language.

In preparation for the attack on Rostov, the Triumvirate needed new reconnaissance of the enemy troops. Captain Markov designated Egórov and Andrei to do it. They were the most experienced pilots in his motley crew of airmen; both were aces and Cavaliers of the Order of St. George, a distinction that he himself lacked.

Attired in new fur-lined winter flight suits and wearing special leg warmers provided by the English Red Cross, the pilots climbed into the Voisin, watched by the entire squadron. It was to be their first flight under the banner of the Volunteer Army, and their explicit orders were to avoid engagement with the enemy and produce strategic photographs of its forces on the approaches to Rostov—a very important city along the railroad line that led to Taganróg, the city on the Sea of Azov that opened the way to the Black Sea and the Crimea. This triangle of rich Cossack cities was valuable to both adversaries. It provided huge supplies of grain, cattle, coal, industrial ore and *horses*, much needed thousands of horses for the cavalry.

Egórov opened the throttle, and as the tail of the Voisin lifted and the wheels began to skim the bumps on the runway, he pulled into the wind and began to climb. The plane obeyed him like a good horse obeys a skillful rider.

Egórov followed the railroad tracks from the start. There were several trains at the city terminal, none moving, some lacking a locomotive. He signaled to Andrei to start photographing.

Andrei peered down and around. Dark green patches of woods came into his sight and then a little later the confluence of two rivers—the Aksai and the Turlov, still partially under ice. There was a large settlement with the gold cupola of a church shining brightly in the winter sun. "Must be some Cossack *stanitsa*," he thought. They continued on their course without seeing any movement on the railway, until Egórov pointed down. "There they are," he yelled.

Andrei saw what looked like dark caterpillars of military transport crawling along the silver threads of rails. But instead of the caterpillars moving *away* from Rostov, it looked to Andrei that they were moving *toward* Rostov.

Andrei shouted to Egórov, "Look at the direction of the troops! That must be the reinforcements!"

Egórov banked the plane and descended to take a closer look.

Almost at once the air around the plane exploded, and familiar puffs of gray smoke appeared around it: the Voisin had entered the anti-aircraft zone, and the Reds had them in their sights. Andrei concentrated on his work, trying to ignore the barrage, photographing the railroad and troops through the sudden screen of exploding shells.

Egórov began to climb again, out of reach of the anti-aircraft batteries. Their order was to produce a series of photographs, and they had done that! It was time to go home rather than risk being shot down.

Twice more in the next few days they were sent on the same mission. It was clear that the Reds were not ready to give up Rostov. They were getting ready for battle.

Then, the *impossible* happened: the Volunteer Army had to give up its city. The Reds entered Novocherkassk almost without a battle while the Whites retreated. The puny squadron of Captain Markov followed the Army in retreat, tossing a few small caliber bombs on the Red troops but causing no significant damage. As the Reds seemed to grow ever stronger subduing town after town, the Whites suffered several disasters, one of them being the death in battle of the legendary General Kornilov.

While the Reds and the Whites continued their death struggle, competing in cruelty and mutual destruction, the Germans and the Austro-Hungarians swept through the Ukraine and the former Russian territories, confiscating anything movable: aircraft and small ships, live cattle and food supplies that they badly needed in their own devastated territories.

The Austrians occupied Kiev and then entered Odessa, quickly subjugating the Anatra factory. But they were also generous to the citizens of Odessa who had suffered losses during the Red occupation. They restocked Memorial Hospital with medication and replenished the confiscated medical instruments. To Glafira's delight, they even presented the hospital with a new, modern ambulance.

"Why did we hate Germans so much?" Glafira thought. "They are kinder than our own people!" Of course, she kept her thoughts to herself.

Larissa and Julia found themselves in great demand as interpreters. Larissa spoke German, and Julia, using Yiddish that was based on German, was able to translate simple requests and give some uncomplicated explanations or directions.

The Cohens were assigned two Austrian non-commissioned officers to lodge with them. Minna Solomonovna gave them Yasha's room, moving the boy in with Julia. Yasha immediately surprised the lodgers with his chess prowess. The Austrians proclaimed him a *genius*. It made Minna Solomonovna the proudest grandmother in Moldovanka.

Isaak quickly became a good friend of the former enemy and organized a profitable little business in Tatar carpets that the Austrians seemed to covet. He bartered the rugs confiscated from the Tatars by the Reds and then, stolen from the Reds by Mishka Japónchik's gang.

When he discovered that the Austrians treasured the carpets, Mishka suggested a barter. The lodgers didn't have much, but they offered him a connection to someone who had plenty of French champagne stolen from wine warehouses in captured territories. The collection was initially claimed by the military and it traveled in the baggage cars of the senior officers of the Hungarian forces. As the war with Russia had ended, the collection had disappeared, finding its way to Odessa and ending up in Isaak's cellar. What Isaak's plans were for his stash, no one knew, but he wasn't going to waste such a valuable commodity on the proletarians. He would wait for a better class of customers.

Isaak buried the wine bottles under the floorboards in his cellar. Over the hole he piled up several broken chairs and old suitcases, some mice-chewed mattresses and an old Singer sewing machine in need of repair.

⅗ 73 ⅗

Spring was always beautiful in Odessa. The devastating winter storms when the sea was black with anger were over. The water turned green and then blue again, the dolphins leaping joyously over the waves.

The stately trees along the boulevards and in the public gardens of Odessa blossomed in myriads of flowers, perfuming the salty air with an intoxicating aroma. The little garden behind the Cohens' house was in full glory as well. The apple tree in front of Larissa's window offered its shaggy paws full of blossoms, extending the exquisite flowers into her room as she opened the window.

Larissa kept her baby in the old carriage in the shade of the gazebo during the day, believing in Veronica's Scottish tradition that growing up in plenty of fresh air was essential for the baby's health. Minna Solomonovna disagreed with that notion. She believed that too much fresh air was dangerous for little babies. She wheeled the carriage into the kitchen or wherever she was in the house, making sure that by the time Larissa returned from the hospital, the baby was back in the gazebo.

The child was growing fast, surprising and delighting them all. One morning she stood up in her carriage! The protective sides of the carriage were not high enough to prevent her from falling out. She needed now to be on the floor but restricted in her freedom to crawl away, for she was already trying to do so.

It was Akim who came up with a solution. He constructed something like a square cage, a tall wooden frame with fine chicken wire walls and a floor covered with a blanket. It was an unsightly contraption, but it was perfect for keeping a fast-growing baby safe. They moved the cage from one place in the house to another as needed, which was not easy, the cage being quite heavy, until Yasha suggested placing it on wheels. Then, little Nínochka was pushed from place to place like a circus tiger, keenly observing life around her. She had toys now: a yellow rubber duck for her bath and a cat-faced rattle, and she was slowly being introduced to solid food. There were a couple of bright pink buds in her mouth that soon turned white, announcing the appearance of her first teeth. Nínochka had become the main point of interest among a few satellite friends in the orbit of her short life.

Among many new laws that governed the country now, there were a few unspoken rules created by the people themselves. No one spoke about the Bolsheviks anymore or about those who had been shot by them. It wasn't safe. No one *dared* inquire about the disappearance of relatives and friends or even what had happened to the deposed Tsar and his family. They were gone without a trace, it seemed.

After the October Revolution shook Petrograd, it became dangerous to inquire about the fate of *any* of the Romanovs. There were rumors that the Cheka executed Grand Duke Mikhail. Several close relatives of the Tsar were hunted down and executed. Some of the Romanovs managed to escape to their properties in the Crimea and the Caucasus, while the others fled Russia altogether.

The monarchists hoped that the Tsar's family would be given refuge in England, but it did not happen. The British Government refused to offer refuge to the Russian Tsar, afraid of starting a revolution in their own country with their own disaffected proletariat.

Meanwhile, the Volunteer Army began to concentrate under General Denikin's leadership following Kornilov's death. General Alexeyev was too ill to be an active commander of the troops.

The Cossacks retook Novocherkassk after a short occupation by the Reds and had hanged all the Commissars they were able to capture. Andrei and Egórov returned to Novocherkassk with Captain Markov's squadron that had grown twice as large with the addition of new Cossack pilots and aircraft, but without two of their mechanics who had deserted to the Reds. The pilots now had to make small repairs to their machines themselves under the tutelage of Monsieur Gilot, but the spirit of all pilots was high: the Volunteer Army was growing and now had several important victories in the field.

However, both adversaries suffered the lack of aircraft and were in constant need of fuel, trying to conserve it by using their planes sparingly, mainly for deep reconnaissance. Instead, both parties relied heavily on cavalry, that staple of Russian warfare. Most of the White officer-pilots who were originally cavalry officers found themselves in the saddle again. The vicious cavalry skirmishes became the legends of the Russian Civil War, in time becoming part of the folklore and the subject of songs.

Andrei and Egórov volunteered to join cavalry reconnaissance patrols whenever the weather prohibited flying. The suave Egórov and the boyish Andrei, everybody's younger brother, were immediately adopted by the Cossacks, who respected their skill with horses.

The pilots took part in a night patrol of five men riding along the railroad tracks. Their target was a small stanitsa that Andrei had photographed on their first flights some months before. Their order was to investigate whether there were any Reds as a vanguard of the new attack on Novocherkassk that was expected to come.

It was a foggy night. Their faces were damp from the moisture in the air, but it was an easy ride as they followed the rails. The horses' hooves clattered rhythmically on the old shale at the side of the railroad embankment. It felt peaceful.

They reached the sleeping stanitsa, with only a few dim candles still blinking in some of the houses. With the horses at a walking pace they entered cautiously, following the main street, accompanied by a chorus of barking dogs behind latched fences. At the church they dismounted and tied the horses to a railing, leaving one man to watch them. Captain Popónov, the leader of the patrol, knocked on the door of a small structure leaning against the church with a light in one of its windows. It was undoubtedly the priest's house.

A very old man with long overgrown white whiskers opened the door. He looked like an ancient prophet from some primitive painting, barefoot and dressed in a long homespun shirt. "Ah, Cossackí! Come in, come in!" he greeted them kindly. "What can I do for you?"

"Thank you holy *Bátushka*. We won't bother you," said Captain Popónov. "We are from Novocherkassk and are searching for the Reds who might be hiding in your stanitsa."

"*Niet*, we don't have any Reds here ... Not anymore. But we did have two who lived among us. We thought that they were teachers and we liked them and sent our children to them. They were nice, quiet, did not drink or chase our *babi*. Then, everything changed when the Reds took Novocherkassk. The teachers put on red bands and went from house to house with the Red Guards taking away peoples' stuff and livestock, *arresting* those who refused to give them what they demanded. One of them even tried to take the icons from our church! Our *babi* threw him out of the church. So, he *pissed* on the church door!" He looked at the men with his rheumy eyes. "We have no more Reds," he continued. "If you go to the main square, you'll see the gallows with two bodies."

"What happened to the men they had arrested?" Egórov asked.

"The Reds shot them before they left," the old man said. "All of them, the fifteen-year-old *khloptsy*, and the old *frontoviki*, the grandfathers. All of them ... May our Lord bless the souls of the new martyrs!" He made a wide sign of the cross over his concave chest. The Cossacks and the pilots did the same.

"We won't bother your people with a search," Captain Popónov said. "But if you discover any Reds around here, send someone with the news to us in the city, and we'll come and get rid of them. Don't try to deal with them by yourselves, promise?"

"I promise," the priest said. "Go with the Lord," He watched as they mounted their horses and waved as they rode away.

They did not go to see the bodies.

The year 1918 was nearing its end. Russia was out of the world conflict, but poor Russia continued to bleed. The Reds were winning more territory with the promises of a better life for the working class and dangled land distributions for the peasants. By promises of a better life or a threat of immediate execution, the Reds imposed harsh discipline on the population.

The Whites desperately tried to turn back the clock. The more educated among them still dreamed of a democratically elected Parliament, but instead of democracy and justice, they faced chaos in all structures of industry and agriculture, more confiscations, more spilled blood, and the threat of a great famine looming above it all.

In October General Alexeyev died of a heart attack. The old soldier was spared witnessing the total collapse of his beloved country that was to come.

When the news trickled in that armistice discussions were going on between Russia's former allies and the Central Powers, few people paid attention to it. *Pravda* was laconic about the news. For Russia, the war was already over with total humiliation, defeat, and ruination.

On November 11th 1918, the Armistice was proclaimed. There was jubilation around the world. In Russia, a new hope was ignited among the Whites that the former allies would intervene now and help Russians to defeat the Bolsheviks.

Then a world-shattering event took place among the defeated enemy. *The revolution* that Lenin so fervently promoted exploded in Berlin! *Pravda* was ecstatic in its descriptions: Kaiser Wilhelm II was forced to abdicate and flee into exile. Several other abdications followed: the King of Bavaria, the King of Würtemberg, the King of Brunswick, and Carol I of Hungary all stepped down from their thrones.

The Reds celebrated, but to Lenin's disappointment, the populace of the respective countries did not support the revolutions. After a few weeks of disturbances, order was restored and the affected countries switched from monarchies to republics.

In Odessa, still occupied by the Austrians, the churches celebrated the end of the war with the traditional ringing of all the bells. It was a tremendous display of the intricate mastery of the church bell ringers. There were two large Cathedrals and several smaller churches in Odessa, and when they all rang the bells at the same time, all conversations were stopped. One could hear nothing but the bells.

Larissa always loved it. She wondered whether bells were also ringing in the churches in Petrograd and in Moscow. "Probably not. The Bolsheviks would not allow it," she thought.

It was the last time that she heard the church bells.

74

The new year 1919 began with optimism for people around the world. The devastating war was over. But not so in Russia. Two years after the revolution that was staged in the name of workers and peasants, people continued to die. Russian workers and peasants were slaughtering *each other* now, suffering mass requisitions of grain and livestock.

In the cities, the forced requisitions were often conducted by the criminal element under the auspices of the dreaded Cheka. In Odessa the *'criminal element'* was organized under Mishka Japónchik.

Mishka thought of himself as a sort of Jewish Robin Hood and his band of small crooks as the merry men of Odessa. They robbed the rich and not so rich, and they helped the poor, that is, themselves. They had established a system of extorting money from citizens and businesses in exchange for "protection." Those who refused were beaten or suffered unexpected calamities. Their women and children were harassed, the girls raped, and their dogs and cats hung in front of their doors.

But Mishka did not allow any murder. Like Robin Hood, he was a benevolent man.

The Bolsheviks, trying to create a better image of themselves among the citizens, arrested Mishka. Within an hour a huge crowd of heavily armed men surrounded the jail. They demanded Mishka's immediate release, threatening to blow up the jail. The guards quickly complied.

Sensing his importance, the Bolsheviks decided to recruit him, appointing Mishka a Commander of the Odessa Soviet Unit and the 54th Soviet Revolutionary Regiment. In addition to his own men, the regiment consisted of the anarchist militia and the mobilized Revolutionary Students of the Novorosissk University.

The new regiment had no uniform, but no matter. They marched through Odessa in parade, wearing whatever hats they had, from the straw boaters of summer tourists to the shiny stovepipes of the city fathers, from the Tsarist *foorázhki* to the sailors' flat hats with the names of the ships on the ribbons stamped with golden anchors.

Mishka marched ahead of his troops attired in black leather with mirror-shiny black boots and a naked saber in his black-gloved hand, his face set in a stony expression of Bolshevik determination.

Behind the marchers followed several machine gun carts, each pulled by two horses. The horses were requisitioned by Mishka's men from the city's carriage drivers, Akim among them. He watched from the sidewalk as his two old horses pulled a cart with a machine gun aimed at the crowds and a scowling young student in his University uniform kneeling behind it. Akim was not upset about the horses: Isaak promised that the horses would be returned to him after the parade.

It was a comical parade, but the spectators did not laugh. They stared at the marching crooks, wondering who would be the next to squeeze them even tighter.

In the weeks after the parade, Mishka's men terrorized the city without regard for anything but Mishka's directives. Meanwhile, Mishka ignored the directives of the Bolshevik leadership. It didn't take long for them to realize that Mishka was impossible to handle. He was a liability, turning the people of Odessa against the Reds. He had to be eliminated.

It was done without delay. Mishka was ambushed near the town of Voznesensk and shot dead in July 1919. His killer was awarded the Order of the Red Banner, while Mishka Japónchik entered the folklore of Odessa. Books and songs were written about him in the following decades, making him indeed the Jewish Robin Hood of Odessa.

In the vacuum of leadership, adversaries emerged, fighting viciously with one another. Several large partisan groups, calling themselves Blacks or Greens, often changed their allegiance between the Whites and the Reds. They fought and killed holding no real allegiance to any ideology. Their method of attack was simple: sweep down on a village or a train, shoot the men, rape the women, grab anything, and disappear as fast as they had appeared. Their cavalry was accompanied by machine guns and snipers who fired indiscriminately. They were not interested in occupying villages or establishing their own regime. They were pirates, masters of the lightning attack and lightning disappearance. All people, including the Reds, feared them.

The Communist High Command in Moscow became alarmed with the growing association of their military forces with the extreme actions of the 'criminal element.' The Cheka were ordered to start a purge in every city, and it opened the gates for the flood of denouncements to settle old scores and quarrels.

With Mishka gone, so was Isaak's status and the protection of his home. Someone denounced Isaak Cohen as a contraband dealer in French champagne.

One night a dark-panelled car stopped in front of the Cohens' house.

Several men in dark clothes spilled out of the car and knocked on the door. Minna Solomonovna peeked through the curtains. Seeing the "Black Raven" vehicle in front of her house, she knew that she had to obey.

Trembling with fear she opened the door. The men armed with hand guns pushed her out of the way as they burst into the house.

"Where is your husband?" the leader demanded.

"He is sleeping," she mumbled and giggled. "Come back in the morning."

"Wake him up!"

"Yes, sir comrade, in a moment, sir comrade! Would you like a glass of tea and a few Mandelbrot cookies? I baked them last morning!"

The leader pushed her aside. With his heavy boot, he kicked the bedroom door. He pulled Isaak up roughly and tied his hands behind his back. Minna Solomonovna began to giggle again and one of the men pointed his gun at her. "Stop laughing or I'll shoot you between your old eyes!" he hissed. Terrified, she made an effort to stop her nervous habit, continuing to tremble violently.

Isaak, despite the desperate situation, seemed to be unshakable. "I don't know why you are here, Comrades," he said, smiling. "It must be some mistake."

The leader of the Cheka group said, "Where is it, the French champagne?"

"I don't know what are you talking about?" Isaak tried to wiggle out of the accusation, "I have no French champagne, not even our own Crimean champagne. I prefer good *proletarian* beer!" he made an attempt to joke. The leader nodded to one man, who aimed his fist at Isaak's face and hit him with full force, breaking Isaak's nose. Bleeding profusely, Isaak fell backwards, hitting his head on the piano.

"Tell them, tell them!" Minna Solomonovna screamed. "Tell them or they'll kill you!"

"That's right," the leader said calmly. "You had better tell us where it is."

"I know where it is," Yasha said. "It's in our cellar." He stood at the door in his night shirt, trembling. "Please, don't hit Grandpa anymore!"

"We won't, if you are telling the truth," the leader said, almost kindly. "Where is the cellar?"

"I'll show you," Yasha said.

Julia in a bathrobe, with her hair undone, knelt next to her father, wiping his bloody face with a towel. She glanced at her son but said nothing. "The boy thinks that he is saving his grandfather," she thought. Yasha led the men to the cold cellar. "It's down there, buried in the ground," he said. "Under the junk."

"All right. Go back to bed. You are a good boy," the leader said. Yasha scurried up the stairs.

The men cleared the junk and removed the floorboards. They dug for a few moments and saw the stash of bottles with French labels. "Good job!" the leader said. "Take the *evidence* to the machine." He returned to the parlor.

Isaak sat on the floor, leaning against the piano. Minna Solomonovna was spread on the sofa in a semi-conscious condition, crying and giggling. Julia and Yasha were holding a compress against Isaak's broken nose.

"Get up, Cohen, you are under arrest," the leader said brusquely, his mild manner changed as his men kept moving back and forth between the cellar and the car carrying the bottles.

Minna Solomonovna screamed. The leader grimaced. It was always the most unpleasant part of his duty: to witness the family's anguish while taking a person away.

Isaak struggled to his feet. Minna Solomonovna threw herself on the floor, grasping at Isaak's legs. "No! No! I won't let you take him away!" she cried clinging to his feet.

The leader grimaced again. "Take your mother away," he said to Julia. "We are only doing our duty."

Julia and Yasha struggled to help Minna Solomonovna to her feet but she fought with them. She clung to the feet of the leader now, kissing his boots. Yasha tried to unhook her fingers one by one off the leaders boots, ashamed of his grandmother's behavior. The leader finally shook her off distastefully.

"I shall leave the order for the arrest on the table," he said. "You will be legally notified in a couple of days of further decisions." Then he and the men carrying the last bottles left the house, gently closing the front door.

⁑ 75 ⁑

Larissa was petrified hearing the commotion and screams at the main house. She prayed fervently that the baby would keep quiet and the 'searchers' would not come to her room. All her documents obtained through Isaak were excellent forgeries, but they were *fakes* and she never felt safe when she had to produce them.

She heard the men digging in the cellar and knew that whatever Isaak was hiding there was discovered. For a moment she was glad that God had punished Isaak for the harm he had done to her and Andrei, but almost immediately she felt ashamed. It was wrong to have joy at someone's misfortune.

The baby continued to sleep peacefully. Larissa heard the men leave the house and then the sound of the automobile driving away. Still, she was afraid to leave her room. What if some of the searchers were still in the house? She dressed and stayed awake, worrying, until the rose fingers of sunrise painted her room pink. Everything was quiet in the house. She decided to investigate.

Yasha was sitting alone in the parlor, bent over his chessboard. "Are you playing against some ghost?" Larissa joked. "I hope you are winning!" He lifted his face toward her. He was crying.

"They took my Grandpa," he said.

"Oh, no! Where is your Mama?"

"She is with Bábushka … Bábushka is sick … She was screaming …"

"I know … I heard her … Did they say *where* they were taking your Grandpa?"

"No, but Mama told me that they took him to jail. Mama told Bábushka not to worry, she said that it would not be the first time that Grandpa went to jail. But Bábushka yelled that this time it was different and they were going to kill him this time!"

Larissa made the sign of the cross as Julia came out of her mother's room. "Yes, this time it was different," she said. She was still undressed and disheveled and her striking face looked sharp and ugly. Larissa had never seen a person change in appearance so drastically in such a short time: Julia suddenly looked like an old woman. "I can't go to work and leave Mother alone," Julia continued, "She is not herself, she babbles, she has lost her mind … What shall we do?" she asked Larissa, who usually asked *her* the same question.

And the girl who had always done what she was told, said calmly, "You stay home, take care of your mother and Yasha. I'll take the baby with me and keep her in Glafíra's office. Let's be optimistic and hope that they'll release your father," Larissa said. "Meanwhile let's decide what to tell people while you and your father are absent. We'll say that you both are sick. With a cold? No, that's too trivial. It must be something more serious."

"With *pneumonia*," Yasha said.

"All right, let's pretend that it is *pneumonia*," Larissa said. "But you, Yasha, also must *pretend*. If you tell anybody about what happened here last night, your Mama and Bábushka may be also taken away. So, let's all pretend that your mother and Grandpa have pneumonia. We trust you as a *grown man*, do you understand?" Larissa said earnestly, holding his cold hands in hers and looking deep into his eyes. "Don't *ever* let anyone know if you are scared. Act natural, joke with your friends, play your violin, beat everyone at chess!" she said. "You must pretend that everything is all right, even if it hurts!"

Yasha looked scared. Larissa smiled. "I did not mean to scare you. But I wanted you to know the truth. Be on the alert. You are the only man around here. Do you understand what I mean?"

"I do," Yasha said without hesitation. "It is up to *me* to keep you safe. I am over thirteen. I had my Bar Mitzvah. Yes, it makes me the only *man here!* I'll keep you safe!"

"You said it, boy!" Larissa exclaimed seriously and shook his hand.

Glafíra held drooling Nina, who was teething, waiting for an orderly to tie two padded armchairs facing each other seat to seat, creating a soft bed for the baby.

"Good!" Glafíra said. "Nínochka will be safe and comfortable in her daybed and have fun watching everybody visiting the room! You may go, Antonich, thank you!" The orderly made an awkward bow and left.

"So tell me again, what happened last night at your house," Glafíra said to Larissa.

Larissa began to recite the sad story again.

Glafíra sighed sadly. "So, your idea is to pretend that Julia is ill to provide an alibi for her absence from work. All right, we can do it for a few days. But if Minna Solomonovna is in such bad shape, it will make her feel even worse when she finds out that her husband was shot. We must think of—"

"How do you know that Isaak was *shot?*" Larissa interrupted, turning cold.

"You said that it was the Cheka that came. Well, there is a new directive ordering cooperation with the Cheka in its efforts to eradicate the activities of all counter-revolutionary gangs. Mishka was liquidated already, so I can bet my last gold ruble that Isaak will be liquidated also. The Cheka does not procrastinate!"

"So what shall we do?" Larissa was close to tears now. Isaak, that lovable, sweet grandfather, that thief and robber and hapless scoundrel, was probably shot ... It was too monstrous to imagine.

"You do nothing," Glafíra said sternly. "Do your work, take care of your child and sit tight. You have enough baggage of your own to carry. Have you heard from Andrei?"

"No, not lately. But I have a short letter from my mother. She writes that Ksusha is not well ... and Ksusha is old! She must be close to eighty now."

"She won't survive," Glafíra said coldly. "She is too old."

"Don't say that!"

"Your mother wouldn't be writing to you about 'just a cold!'" Glafíra said with finality. "She is preparing you for Ksusha's death."

Akim came to take Larissa home at the usual time. "So, Julia Isaakovna is sick, eh?" he said. He had noticed when he picked up Larissa in the morning that Julia was absent, the boisterous Minna Solomonovna was nowhere to be seen, and Larissa was bringing the baby to the hospital with her. It all suggested that something drastic had happened in the Cohen household. But out of prudence and politeness, he had not pried.

"Yes, Akimushka, we had some big troubles last night." Larissa explained the situation. Akim was a loyal friend and she saw no reason to keep the truth away from him. "Glafíra Ivánovna is going to keep her eye on the baby for a few days while I work."

"And what shall you do after a few days? If Isaak is shot, his family will be kicked out of their house, most likely."

"I don't know. We must wait and see," Larissa said, "Let's hope it doesn't happen."

"I read in a leaflet that was dropped by the Whites that Denikin's troops are heading for the Crimea. It may mean that your husband and Captain Egórov might rejoin us in the very near future. I also heard some rumors that the French are moving through the Ukraine toward Odessa!"

"That would be wonderful! I knew that our allies would not abandon us!"

"There was also interesting information about Colonel Kozakov. Wasn't he your husband's Commanding officer?"

"Oh, yes! Andrei and Captain Egórov *loved* Kozakov! I hope the news is not that he had been killed."

"No, no. Just the opposite. The news was mentioning that in the Murmansk-Arkhangelsk section the British have landed an expeditionary force and several famous Russian pilots had joined it, including your friend, Colonel Alexander Kozakov. I thought you would find it interesting."

"Oh, yes, Akim Ivánovich! I am so glad that we are getting some support from our former allies. I only hope that there will be more of it!"

"Don't we all! But what are you going to do if the Cheka throws you out of the house? Do you have a place to go to?"

Larissa shook her head.

"I thought so. Well, you come and stay with my wife and me. We don't have a fancy place, but we'll have a bed for you and a cradle for Nínochka. My wife and the children will help you, so don't you worry. You stay with us!"

"Oh, Akimushka, you are such a dear friend! Thank you! Let's hope that Isaak returns home, Julia's mother survives the tragedy, and we stay where we are, but it's good to know that in case of the worst to come, I'll have a place to go to."

Yasha found a sealed envelope under the front door. He brought it to his mother. She tore the envelope with trembling hands and read the short typewritten message: *"Upon the order # 345 / 21 of The Revolutionary Commissariat of Odessa District, Citizen Isaak Yákovlevich Cohen, member of the notorious criminal gang under the leadership of the bandit known as Mishka Japónchik, was condemned to be shot for his criminal activities. The sentence was carried through."* It was signed by the Commissar of the Cheka of the Odessa district and witnessed by two Comrades who added their scribbled names. The official seal of the Cheka Commissariat concluded the document.

76

General Deníkin renamed the Volunteer Army the *Armed Forces of South Russia* (AFSR) to be distinct from the army of Nikolaí Yudénich in the Baltic region that was named *Northwestern Army* and the forces of Admiral Kolchák in Siberia, who had proclaimed himself *'Supreme Ruler of Russia."* There were several other 'armies' under various generals who often disagreed with the strategies of the AFSR command and fought their own battles while the Reds doggedly concentrated their efforts on the unification of their forces and upholding discipline through the Cheka.

The peasant population suffered no matter who was in charge. The Reds and the Whites supplied and fed their armies through expropriations from the peasants. At first the Whites insisted on paying for the requisitions, but as the requisitions intensified, they followed the example of the Reds—any disobedience to the expropriations became punishable by a firing squad or hanging, which was cheaper since it did not require bullets.

Andrei and Egórov were the most valuable reconnaissance team in Denikin's AFSR. The radius of their work was huge. It included the Don and the Kuban Cossack lands where great cavalry battles took place, with the cities and the stanitsas going from one side of the conflict to the other, both Armies bleeding the once rich lands.

Each time the AFSR moved its positions closer to the Black Sea, and to Odessa, Andrei applied for a few days of leave. He has not seen his daughter since her birth, and now she was already learning to *walk!* Each time his hopes were shattered. His fine reconnaissance maps and photographs were needed more than ever by the constantly moving White Armies. This new war was not a trench war, when the opposing armies often sat for weeks buried in deep holes as if they were prairie dogs. This war was one of constant movement, a war of unending advance and retreat, when yesterday's reconnaissance was already obsolete. This was the war that depended on pilots like Andrei and Egórov. They could not be spared.

One of their latest reconnaissance missions brought information that a large contingent of Red cavalry reserves was approaching the Kuban stanitsa Berezínskaya. There were no forces nearby that could stop the Reds. The Whites decided to strafe and scatter the moving reserves, the aircraft mowing down soldiers in the open fields with machine gun fire. To Andrei and Egórov, it was a most distasteful operation, but Captain Markov designated his best pilot, Vassily Egórov, to lead the attack. Markov and Andrei would fly in tight formation as the wingmen, all using three new Sopwith Camel fighters from a recent shipment of aircraft from England.

The planes lifted into the air one after another and quickly fell into a small Delta formation. Their course was north along the railroad tracks, always the easiest landmark to follow, and before long they reached the coordinates where the previous day they had discovered the moving column of Red cavalry. The Reds had moved closer to their destination, but the planes were right on their tail.

Egórov raised his arm and jerked it sharply, pointing down as he banked to reach a lower altitude. The cavalry regiment was in clear view now, their red flags unfurled, moving four abreast along the road. Behind the regiment moved several carts and armed field machine guns.

Not yet aware of the airplanes above, the clatter of hooves of hundreds of horses muted the drone of the approaching aircraft.

Egórov raised his arm once more to signal his descent. He peeled off from the formation and plunged at the moving column as if he were a falcon sighting his prey. Andrei and then Markov followed closely, swooping down on the horsemen.

With his fingers holding down the triggers of his two synchronized Vickers machine guns, Egórov zipped low over the column, spreading death below. The column was in a panic, scattering like ants. Egórov climbed up in a wide arc to leave space for his wingmen to fall into their places behind him.

Andrei repeated his friend's maneuver, his head empty of any thoughts, his actions automatic as he aligned his gun sight with the remnants of the column and opened fire.

Down on the ground a bloody mass of injured people and horses was in total disarray. With no place to hide, no woods, no buildings, nothing but the empty space of the dusty steppe and a two-way railroad bed, the wounded men and horses fell into bleeding heaps like mowed grass. The maddened horses swerved and galloped into the steppe, many without their riders, the carts obliterated and their machine guns useless.

Before order could be restored there was a cry, *"Here they come again!"* Every man stared at the sky in mute terror: the screeching menace was coming down, the deafening sound of the engines reaching deep under the skin of every man and animal. The spooked horses reared, stomping over the fallen bodies.

The planes went over again, but the pilots did not shoot the machine guns this time. Instead, they dropped twenty-pound bombs in the midst of the bloody carnage, each explosion blowing apart more men and horses, raising fountains of dirt and sand, sections of rails and wooden ties. The planes zoomed up again, regrouped, and for a final time dove at the remains of the doomed column.

The few terrified survivors and limping horses scattered around the killing grounds, trying to escape the murderous machines that were coming at them *again*. There was no resistance. There were no anti-aircraft batteries to fight the murderous planes. A few horsemen managed to fire one or two rifle shots at the aircraft, but it was useless. After the explosions of the bombs, there were no attempts to stop the assault.

Egórov allocated five minutes for the free-wheeling carnage on the ground. Pursuing the wounded men that hobbled in terror with their arms raised in surrender ... it was too much for him. Shooting the wounded horses that dashed in panic one way, then another, probably blinded and in great pain ... no, he could not participate in it! He gave the signal to leave. Andrei followed him immediately, but Markov failed to see the signal in the heat of a chase. He continued to pursue and shoot at anything that moved, rejoicing at the carnage. Finally noticing that his friends were climbing up again, Markov banked his plane gently and zoomed up in pursuit of his friends.

77

The spring offensive of the White forces seemed to be successful. Admiral Kolchák's armies moved their forces in Siberia, followed by General Deníkin taking Khárkov and Baron Vrangel wresting Tsáritsyn after fierce battles on the Volga. But the White Army's luck began to change.

In September, the British who held the positions north of Petrograd began to evacuate their forces from Murmansk, and soon the devastating news reached Andrei and Egórov: their beloved Commander Kozakov had been killed while serving with the Slavo-British aviation group. The news reached them some weeks later, transferred across the nation by field telephones from one air group to another by grieving airmen.

There was not much military action in that sector. The peasants accused the British pilots of trying to grab the Russian land. To pacify the peasants and to fight the boredom of the garrisons, the Commander of the Slavo-British Group asked Kozakov to demonstrate some aerobatics for the entertainment of the locals.

With a crowd of spectators watching, Kozakov lifted his Sopwith Snipe into a cloudless sky going straight up as if to execute a loop and then ... something happened. Either his engine had stalled or he had a stroke or he had *deliberately* crashed—nobody knew. To the horror of all who had witnessed it, the plane plunged to the ground.

Kozakov was dead. With all military honors that were deservedly his, the most famous Russian ace was buried in the small village of Beneshnikí. He was almost thirty-one years old.

Andrei and Egórov were devastated. Both felt that it was the end of an era. Both had the same thought: "I'll be the next." For months they tried to hide from each other that they were depressed, but Kozakov's death unlocked their hearts. While Egórov with his customary devil-may-care attitude still talked bravely about victory with the help of the Allies, Andrei had no such hopes.

"It comes down to simple arithmetic, Egórka. There are more of *them* than of *us*," he predicted gloomily.

The Reds were taking back one town after another. Their superiority lay in the unlimited supply of human reserves and the *'red terror'* that subjugated populations to their will. By the end of 1919 the Reds regained Omsk, Khárkov, Kiev, and Ekaterinodar. In January 1920 they took Tsáritsyn and Taganróg on the shores of the Azov Sea. Shortly after, Novocherkassk also fell. The Whites were losing the war.

In February, vicious winds swept through Odessa, uprooting trees on the boulevards, breaking levees on the limans, and embracing the city in an unprecedented cold spell. In the midst of this, the Reds entered the city once more, unopposed.

Glafíra called Larissa into her office, where Nínochka slept peacefully in her makeshift bed of two armchairs. Glafíra locked the door.

"I want to tell you something in great confidence," she began in a low voice. "You must be as careful as possible now. There will be a purge of the personnel at the Memorial. We have a directive to fire all *bourgeois* employees. It means Doctor Shubin, Doctor Popov, you, and Julia. I don't have to worry about Sister Veronica. She is leaving us, going back to her country."

Larissa nodded. "Yes, she told me. It is a great loss for the Memorial, but I don't blame her."

Glafíra continued as if she did not hear Larissa. "I might manage to save the doctors, we need them badly, and you, but not Julia. Because of her father and her former ownership of that salon, she is a marked person. So, here is what I want *you* to do … Do you realize that I am risking my own head?" She stared at Larissa through the slits of her eyes.

"I understand," Larissa whispered, feeling a tremor in her body.

"First, I want you to convince Julia to leave for America," Glafira continued. "Leave, now. Tomorrow."

"What about her mother? She is sick. Julia won't leave her mother."

"She will have to. If she wants to save her son, she will do it. But you must help."

"But what about Minna Solomonovna?" Larissa insisted, thinking of her own mother. Would *she* abandon her?

"I've made arrangements with a Jewish group who have a home for the elderly in Kherson. They'll take her in and as long as she keeps from mentioning Isaak, she will be safe. So, it's up to you to convince Julia to leave, while she still can."

"I understand," Larissa said. "But what must *I* do to avoid the purge?"

"Nothing, as yet. Just keep working as usual. If anyone approaches you about becoming a Bolshevik, show interest. Frankly, pretend that you *might* be converted. But most of all, *don't talk about Andrei*. If asked about him, say that you don't know where he is and ..."

"I don't need to pretend. I don't know where he is," Larissa said.

"There is more to it. Pretend that *you really don't care* where he is. Can you do it? Can you pretend that you don't care for *Andrei?*"

"No ..."

"Think of her," Glafira pointed to the sleeping child. "For her sake you must pretend that your past is just passed, and you are ready to start a new Soviet life!"

To Larissa's surprise she had no trouble in convincing Julia to leave. Julia was relieved that her mother would be taken care of and did not ask for any details. She realized that the less she knew, the easier it would be to leave. She had a talk with Yasha and told him frankly that they must leave at once with a minimum of luggage and without his grandmother. Yasha, being a smart boy and becoming even smarter after he assumed his role of a *man*, had no qualms about leaving his grandmother. He understood the situation. His mother and he had to save themselves.

Next morning, carrying only two small valises with a change of clothes and some toiletries, the ivory chess set divided and packed among their clothes, and the violin in its coffin-like case, Julia and Yasha asked Akim to drive them to the American consulate.

Akim, usually so curious, did not ask any questions. He waited until they were admitted into the front door by an American Marine guard and whispered, "Good luck, Julia Isaakovna ... Yasha ... God be with you! Have a safe journey!"

The door closed. Akim heard the sound of a heavy bolt placed across the door—the sound of irreversible finality.

Glafira sent an ambulance to pick up Minna Solomonovna and deliver her to the railroad station where a representative from the *Hadassah Facility for the Elderly* met her and accompanied her to Kherson. Minna Solomonovna was stretched out on a gurney, her eyes wide open but unaware of anything around her. The orderly wheeled her into the second class car where a middle-aged nurse was waiting for her. The nurse signed the documents of the transfer, and the orderly departed. That was all.

The train moved slowly along the platform, but there was no one to wave a handkerchief and wish her a safe journey. Minna Solomonovna seized to exist.

One of the first things that the Reds did in Odessa region was to restore the rail traffic. With their usual draconian methods of governing, they made the system work. The trains were running again, bringing in supplies and reserves for the Red Guards, and the mail that for months accumulated at various small towns along the rail connections to Odessa.

With the first delivery of mail Larissa received three letters from Andrei, one from Egórov, and several severely censored letters from her mother in Petrograd.

Hungrily she tore off the envelopes of Andrei's letters. As a good military wife she knew that there would be no information of his whereabouts. He wrote only about his love and his longing for her, of his yet unfulfilled feelings as a father. He wrote about General Alexeyev and their reminiscences of Andrei's father. And the most recent letter contained the sad news about Kozakov.

Egórov's letter also mentioned Kozakov, and it ended with a humorous hint that they might soon be nearby, *lolling on the beach and teaching Nínochka how to swim*. This last sentence cheered her up, only to remind that the Reds were in the possession of the city and under no circumstances would Andrei and Egórka be in Odessa! But wouldn't it be wonderful if they could?

Her mother's letters, being from Petrograd, contained pages of thick black lines across most of the text, except the first line of greeting and the mention of Ksusha's death.

"I had her buried next to your father," she wrote. There followed another long line of the censor's black ink. "It's such *important* information, not to be disclosed," Larissa thought with hostile sarcasm.

The Cohens' empty house looked sad to Larissa. She went from room to room putting away various items that were left in disarray, Nínochka following her around like a puppy. Nínochka was almost three years old, a sweet blond child who loved to sing and dance. She knew many songs taught to her by Larissa or by Yasha, who often played his violin for her while she danced, daintily holding the hem of her skirt as Larissa had shown her.

Nínochka wasn't shy. If asked to sing, she willingly obliged and sang her favorite song about snowflakes, dancing and pretending to be a snow-flake. Her little voice was pure, capable of following the melody, which was quite unusual in a child so young. She was a happy child surrounded by adoring people. She used to call Isaak 'Grandpa' following Yasha's ex-ample, but now they were gone. Everybody was gone, her friend Yasha, her Grandpa Isaak, her Grandma Minna, and her Aunt Julia, and she was alone with her Mama in the empty house.

Growing up without a father, she knew about him only from the little stories that Larissa had told her. She often kissed his photograph, seeing her mother doing it, and whenever she heard the drone of an airplane, she pointed to the sky, saying "Papa!"

She was searching the house now, looking for Yasha. "Where is he hiding?" she kept asking, looking under the beds and into the armoire in the big bedroom. "Where *is* he? Where is *everybody?*" she wailed.

"They are gone to see Yasha's Papa," Larissa told her, hoping that it would quell her anxiety.

"When are they coming back?"

"I don't know. Probably soon."

"Oh, all right!" Nínochka was quickly satisfied. But not for long. "When are *we* going to see *my* Papa?"

For a moment Larissa was stunned by the question. "When it will be warm," she finally said, not looking at her daughter.

78

Glafíra worried. Larissa, alone in a house, in the most dangerous sec-tion of Odessa ... it was only a matter of time before the lovely young nurse and her angelic child became victims. Larissa could be raped, the baby kidnapped ... Glafíra worried.

While Isaak was alive, they were safe. Isaak had his own notoriety, even without Mishka Japónchik. And even earlier, during Andrei's long recuperation, Larissa was safe as the young wife of the famous pilot who rode on the wing of the airplane. The thieves and the bandits always idolized brave people and the presence of Andrei and Egórov in Moldovanka gave the whole neighborhood a certain romantic air. But that was long ago.

Glafíra decided to do something drastic: to keep Larissa and the little girl safe, *she* would move into the Cohens' house herself! It had been requisitioned before the Cohen family fell apart, so it already belonged to the Odessa Housing Authority to be resettled with some needy people. Glafíra's scheme was clever in its simplicity: she requested the house to be used as a dormitory for the junior medical personnel of Memorial Hospital. Instead of having the newly-recruited young nurses and orderlies live all over the city, why not have them concentrated in one place with Glafíra in charge of it all?

She appeared before the Housing Committee in her full regalia of a Commissar. Her proposition was so unusual and enticing that the Committee voted unanimously to accept it.

"One room has been occupied for years by one of our nurses and her child, so we'll leave her where she is. I'll take the smallest room as my office, but there are three more rooms. We can make two dormitories, one for each gender, and keep the dining room, next to the kitchen, as a communal room," she told the Committee.

"This house has been well run and there is a lot of furniture that we can use. We won't need to buy anything," she continued. "We'll have eight or ten young people whom we can accommodate there and we can use the extra beds from the hospital storerooms," she added, assured now that they were impressed by her plan. Their district with its bad Moldovanka reputation soon would become famous for creating a truly communal living space for young professionals!

"I visualize our Medical Support Dormitory as a self-running administration," she improvised. "We shall establish a schedule of duties. All our male members will be responsible for the security and physical upkeep of our residence. All the females will take care of cooking, housekeeping, and shopping," she continued. "We will demand that everyone will be responsible for everyone else, in the true spirit of communist society! *'All for one—! One for all!'* she declared the famous slogan of The Three Musketeers.

The Committee members applauded. All her suggestions were approved for immediate action.

Glafíra moved immediately into Yasha's room. She did not want the news to spread that a lone young woman with a baby lived in that house. She sent a carpenter from the hospital to reinforce all the windows and doors with bolts and double locks and had a telephone installation crew place a telephone line into the hall with extensions to two rooms—Yasha's, that is her office, and Larissa's.

That night Glafíra and Larissa sat at the kitchen table drinking tea from Minna Solomónovna's copper samovar and chewing stale cookies. Nínochka, having outgrown her baby carriage, slept peacefully in her mother's bed that they now shared.

. Glafíra's fast actions had bewildered Larissa. Not knowing Glafíra's motives, Larissa attributed it to greed.

Glafíra felt intuitively that Larissa had a wrong impression about her moving into the Cohens' house. It was time to talk *po dushám,* heart to heart.

"You know, of course, that I am a Tatar," Glafíra began. "My father was wealthy, and we lived in the best house in a Tatar village west of Odessa. My father was a thief. I had a lot in common with Julia!" She laughed without mirth. "He was a horse thief. There wasn't a thoroughbred horse in the whole of the Crimean Peninsula that was safe from my father." She sounded proud. "The horses he dealt with were Arabian riding horses and trained dressage horses, and he stole them on commission. His clients were the wealthiest men in Russia, the Grand Dukes and the princes. My father was paid very well for the horses and his important clients protected him from the police. Of course, he also had a lot of enemies. The other Tatars hated him. I remember only that he was always nervous and had armed men living with us. But I adored him. He had two wives and *five* daughters. No sons. I was the daughter of his eldest wife, a woman from whom my twin sister and I inherited our shape. His younger wife was a beautiful Persian girl, and the three daughters that she produced were all beautiful. My father often joked that someday his little girls would be worth the price of good horses. But not I or my twin. He said that in our case, *he* would have to pay a good price to someone to marry *us!*"

"It was cruel! Yet, you said that you had adored him?" Larissa asked, lured by Glafíra's uncharacteristic openness.

"Oh, yes, he was cruel. But the Tatars are cruel people, didn't you know that? As a child I thought he was teasing us. I did not know that I was ugly," she continued weakly, becoming emotional. "It was 1905, the year of the first revolution, when Odessa was inundated with sailors and striking workers. There were shots on the streets and people were killed. I was thirteen years old and had my first monthly that year. I remember the night when a gang of drunk sailors with red bands on their sleeves and red stars on their caps burst into our house. They shot our guards, dragged my father out of the house, and hung him from the tree in front of our house. Then they ransacked the house, raped my mother and the young wife and all of us, the five young girls--" She stopped, overcome with the memory.

Larissa put her arms around Glafíra. "Don't ... Don't talk about it ..." she whispered, tears gathering in her eyes.

"No, it's good to have it off my chest. It's the first time after all these years that I am able to *talk* about it! I *must* tell you everything ... I remember the screams of my young sisters as the brutes forced themselves into their little bodies. And I have never forgotten my own pain as one man and then another and another tore me apart ..." She was sobbing now, tears rolling down her round cheeks.

Larissa tightened her embrace. "Don't talk," she whispered again. "I can't take it ..." She felt Glafíra tremble.

"No, listen," Glafíra continued through her sobs. "I *must* tell you everything." She swallowed a little tea, and it seemed to stop her trembling. "I don't remember how I got out of the house. Someone found me in the morning, on the grass, and took me to the hospital. The sailors apparently tried to set the house on fire, but it did not burn completely, so the dead bodies were found: two women and three little girls, all of them under ten years of age, the youngest the age of Nínochka. My twin sister was never found."

"Did the authorities punish the sailors?"

Glafíra's face wrinkled in a grimace of a bitter smile. She was not sobbing anymore. "Not that I know of. I was too young then to know, but as I grew older and heard stories about it, I was too ashamed to mention it to anyone. In my late adolescence I researched the newspapers in the public library and found a reference to the hanging of my father and the burning of the house. But there was nothing about the rape of the little girls and their mothers. It simply said that my father was a notorious horse thief and was killed in the traditional way of punishing horse thieves: by hanging." Glafíra spoke coldly now, with a steely sound to her voice. "Ever since then I hated the Communists ... Come to think of it, I hated *all men!* I thought of ways of avenging myself, but how could I, an unattractive, undereducated girl, raised in a charity institution? So I thought of *joining* the Reds and doing whatever I could against them, doing it from *within*. The rest you know."

"Weren't you afraid?"

"Not really. Actually, I enjoy this double existence. It is exciting and profitable. I am never hungry, I have all the privileges, and I can help certain people, as you know. And frankly, I feel quite comfortable in my role. I think my Tatar bloodthirstiness is satisfied in having power over people. But on the other hand—I might be ... *crazy*, as I was certified when I was still a girl." She was smiling now. "So, now you know ... Please understand that you and Nínochka are the bright lights of my life. I'll do anything to keep you safe."

Glafíra's commune proved to be a great success. The young nurses and orderlies, none of them older than twenty, all of them from the working class, were accustomed to living in crowded rooms. For them the Cohens' house represented luxury. They eagerly followed the schedules and the rules established by Glafíra: two people were always to be on duty at the house, a man and a woman rotated daily. She taught everyone how to use the telephone, made them memorize the emergency numbers of the hospital and the militia station, and demanded that every night all locks on the doors and the windows be checked and secured.

The young people willingly obeyed. They were afraid of Glafíra. Their very lives were in her hands—literally. She knew it, and liked it. She did not encourage familiarity and insisted on being called *"Commissar."* Only Larissa was allowed to call her by her name, and Nínochka, who called her Auntie Glásha.

Nínochka became the center of the universe in the commune. Everyone adored her and she loved them all in return. She called them her aunties and uncles, creating a feeling of family among the inhabitants.

Larissa began to relax. She felt safer now. If only she had some news about Andrei! If only her mother were with her! If only the devastating Civil War were over! If only! Sometimes she did not even care which side would win. She just wished it were over.

Maria Nikoláyevna in snowbound Petrograd harbored the same thoughts. Clear-headed as always, she saw no chance for the Whites to win. She began to read communist literature in the public library. To her surprise, she discovered that she was in agreement with many of Lenin's ideas for the future: free schooling and healthcare, elected representatives, respect for women, and cooperation among people of all classes.

All these new ideas made sense to her. "Now, if only they would be implemented," she thought darkly.

Since Ksusha's death, life became much tougher for Maria Nikoláyevna. She lacked Ksusha's ability to barter or cajole and did not have Ksusha's connections. Maria Nikoláyevna knew only the name of an old jeweler to whom Ksusha sold a couple of things taken out of her padded coat. But how could she find this man whose shop was undoubtedly requisitioned?

She decided to go to the *tolkúchka*, an illegal market in an alley near Ksusha's house, and try to find someone who knew Ksusha. She realized that it was a crazy idea, but what else could she do? She had to establish her own chain of supply. The minimal food rations for unemployed persons were barely enough to keep her alive. And she *must* stay alive for the sake of Larissa and the baby whom she had never seen, she thought.

She removed one of the less valuable rings from her vátnik. It was a small round ruby surrounded by tiny diamonds, which she put on her little finger. She remembered the ring: it was Larissa's first ring given to her by her father when she turned ten years old!

"I hadn't realized that I lost so much weight," she thought, twisting the child's ring around. She covered it with a heavy-knitted glove.

In her clumsy vátnik with her white hair under a knitted shawl, Maria Nikoláyevna looked like any peasant grandmother. She carried an empty basket, hoping that she would fill it with provisions. Despite her usual confidence, she felt timid. She was going into unfamiliar territory, where even her speech could betray her.

Tolkúchka, meant literally "push around" and it was well named. People milled around, pushing one another, the stronger ones shouldering the weaker ones aside, all selling or buying something. There were no booths except for vegetables and meat, but even those booths were collapsible, made out of empty boxes. It was one of many of such illegal markets, which could be dismantled at the first signal of a raid. It was a noisy place where the sellers advertised their wares by shouting. Those who had something to barter timidly displayed their items. They were mostly women, shabbily dressed but obviously from the educated class, displaying something from their former lives—a Meissen tea cup or sable boa. They looked scared, intimidated by the robust peasant women who shouldered them out of the way.

Maria Nikoláyevna was not going to be one of them. She watched as a young pale woman dressed almost in rags tried to barter two volumes of Tolstoy's *War and Peace*. "It is autographed by the author, and it has pictures," she was saying politely. "I'll exchange it for a couple of eggs and a cup of cottage cheese." Nobody was interested in her books.

"She is from a good family," Maria Nikoláyevna thought. The young woman reminded her of Larissa.

She made an effort not to think of Larissa now and attend to the business of bartering, something that she had never done before.

She stopped near a clumsy booth presided over by a formidable woman in a sheepskin coat. A little pyramid of duck eggs and a small bag of coarse flour were displayed before her, with a larger bag at her feet. The woman observed Maria Nikoláyevna, noticing that her basket was empty. It was obvious to her that Maria Nikoláyevna was new at the market and had something better to offer than books or a pretty teacup. She had something *hidden*, and that always meant gold coins or jewelry.

She smiled at Maria Nikoláyevna. "And what have you got to sell, Bábushka?" she asked pleasantly. "Maybe I can help. What do you need?" She sounded very friendly.

"Do you know a woman by the name Ksusha?" Maria Nikoláyevna asked. "She used to shop here."

"Ksusha!" the woman exclaimed. "Of course I know Ksusha! But I haven't seen her for a while."

"She has died."

The woman made the sign of the cross. "Rest in peace. So, she was your friend or a relative?"

"A friend."

"She was a good customer. She had only good stuff for barter, if you know what I mean." She looked shrewdly at Maria Nikoláyevna. "Do you have anything like what Ksusha used to have?"

"I might," Maria Nikoláyevna said evasively. "I need some flour and eggs and potatoes. And a roasted chicken and honey. Enough for a week. You have only eggs and flour."

The woman laughed. "I have the chicken, but no potatoes or honey. But don't you worry, I'll get you potatoes and honey also. So what have you got that is worth so much?"

"This." Maria Nikoláyevna removed her glove. "It's ruby and diamonds."

"Is it gold?" the woman asked.

"Of course! It was my daughter's."

"It's too small for my finger," the woman said. "I'll give you five pounds of flour and ten eggs for it. Or, instead of eggs, you can have a chicken." She reached under her flimsy counter and produced a rosy roasted chicken. "I brought it for myself. It is stuffed with apples and kasha."

"No deal." Maria Nikoláyevna said. "It is a good piece of real jewelry and you can always have it enlarged." She replaced her glove, hiding the ring. "Nice talking to you!"

"Wait!" the woman cried. "Just because you were Ksusha's friend, I'll give you what you want. The chicken, the eggs, and the flour."

"And potatoes and honey."

"Oh, you are a tough costumer, Bábushka!" the woman laughed. "Alright! Let me have the ring!"

"Fill my basket first."

"You don't trust me?"

"I don't know you. And the times are bad. Sorry, but fill the basket first."

"But why should I trust *you*? What if you run away with your basket full?"

"At my age? I wouldn't get far," Maria Nikoláyevna said sternly.

"Oh, alright. Hey, Katúshka" the woman yelled over her shoulder. "Let me borrow ten potatoes and a crock of honey! I have a customer!"

"Right away! I'll send Vanúshka!"

While they were waiting for Vanúshka, Maria Nikoláyevna studied the handsome, stocky woman of about thirty. "What's your name?" she asked.

"Daria. And yours?"

"Maria Nikoláyevna."

"Do you live nearby?" the woman asked. "Don't answer. You don't know me!" she said ironically. "But I already know that you are a lady. You don't talk like we do."

Maria Nikoláyevna smiled. "You are a smart woman, Daria! What else do you know?"

"I know that you shouldn't wear your vátnik to the tolkúchka. Or anywhere. The thieves know that when a *báryn'ya* is wearing a vátnik, it is probably full of jewelry. They'll knock you dead for it!"

"She is clever," Maria Nikoláyevna thought. Aloud she said, "Don't you think that some people might wear them because they are warm garments?"

Daria laughed. "But not you. I know who you are. You are Ksusha's mistress and you trusted her to do all the purchases. Now she is dead and you must do the bartering yourself. Am I right?"

"Yes," Maria Nikoláyevna decided to admit. "Which I don't quite know how."

"You did very well with me," Daria said, smiling cunningly.

"I don't think so. A piece of fine jewelry for a little food that will be gone in a few days?"

"That food may help you to survive the famine," Daria said seriously. "If the famine spreads to the villages, I might barter this ring for food also! Oh, there is Vanúshka with potatoes and honey!"

A freckled boy of about ten with snot on his upper lip dumped a small bag of potatoes and a clay pot of honey on her flimsy counter. The boy grinned at Daria and ran back. Daria placed the potatoes, flour, and the chicken wrapped in the newspaper on the bottom of Maria Nikoláyevna's basket. Then she made a conical bag out of the rest of the newspaper and carefully filled it with the eggs. There was no more space for the honey.

"Can you carry the crock under your vátnik? Maybe between your tits?" Daria suggested.

"I can try ... Maria Nikoláyevna opened her vátnik and stuck the crock between her formidable breasts. She noticed that Daria tried to see the insides of her vátnik, but it was impossible to detect the bulges of the hidden jewelry. Ksusha and she were good with a needle. "It will work! Thank you, Dásha," she said. It was no use to pretend that she was a peasant. Daria was too shrewd.

"Will you come back next week?" Daria asked. "Tell me what you need and I'll have it ready for you. As for me, I would like to have a pair of earrings. Just dreaming!" she laughed.

"And I am dreaming of butter and eggs, perhaps some pork and of course, flour and potatoes and honey! Such pleasant dreams! I dream of cabbage and carrots and beets, also!"

"Maybe our dreams will come true."

Maria Nikoláyevna shuffled away, holding her heavy basket with one hand and supporting the crock of honey between her breasts with another.

79

"It's fortunate that the tolkúchka is so near," Maria Nikoláyevna thought as she puffed her way toward Ksusha's house. The basket was heavy, and her stretched arm soon began to hurt. She stopped several times to rest. Soon the arm supporting the crock between her breasts began to hurt as well, but she was less than a block from the house. With a final effort she shuffled the remaining few steps to the front door.

Stuck into the door was an official-looking envelope. She placed the basket at her feet and with great care extracted the crock of honey. She fished the keys from her pocket and unlocked the door. The letter fell, but she felt dizzy, afraid to bend down to pick it up. "It can wait," she said. Lately she was talking aloud to herself, she had noticed.

The room was cold. She sat on the bed, catching her breath. For a moment a dark thought reverberated in her mind, "I hope it isn't my heart!" But after a while she felt better. She took off her vátnik and stocked the petch with the remnants of her supply of wood. Tomorrow she must barter something else to get some wood, she thought.

Then she remembered the letter. "I wonder what is prohibited now," she mumbled as she picked it up.

It was from the Petrograd Housing Authority. It informed her that she must appear at their offices to be reassigned new living quarters. No explanation was given.

The next morning she started out early on her way to the Housing Authority. It was located on the Fontánka near the Anichkov Bridge with its famous four equestrian sculptures, close to the Rezánov's old residence. She had enough coins for a one way trip, or if she split the money, for one part of each way. The tram consisted of two cars with long parallel benches on each side. The ticket conductor in each car collected the fees at the beginning of each new section. The conductors and the tram drivers were usually women, tough and unforgiving, summoning a militiaman by whistle to arrest nonpaying or unruly passengers.

"It probably will be better if I split the money," Maria Nikoláyevna thought. "I'll walk to the Nevá and catch a tram before the bridge. Then I'll ride along the Nevsky Prospect to the Fontánka. On the way back I'll reverse my trip. If I am lucky there will be a seat."

The trams were always crowded. During peak hours, men and women hung like bunches of grapes over the steps of the cars, clinging to the hand bars and to one another.

A new law was passed requiring that the four seats directly behind the driver be allocated for passengers with small children or pregnant women. Occasionally the conductors demanded that some young lout give up his seat to an elderly person, however the cars were always so jammed that conductors rarely were aware of who was sitting where.

Maria Nikoláyevna liked the law about the pregnant women and the passengers with small children. "The Bolsheviks are showing signs of compassion," she thought.

She arrived at the Housing Authority office located in the former mansion of Count Gureisky. She knew the house well. She had been a guest at Gureisky's parties many times. The Count was a hospitable man, and his parties were famous for their exquisite suppers. She wondered for a moment what might have happened to the Count. Was he shot by a firing squad? Was he dying somewhere in Siberia? Or had he escaped abroad as so many aristocrats had been able to do?

She climbed the wide steps leading to the front door of the mansion and stopped to catch her breath.

The vestibule was full of people standing in lines that moved rather briskly. She joined one line. Within a few minutes she was directed to a large room that she remembered as the Music Room. Its walls were still decorated with the bás-reliefs of muses and garlands of flowers, but the intricately inlaid parquet floor of different woods was dirty, scratched, and covered with spit.

The room was filled with dozens of desks, each with a chair for a visitor. A huge letter of the alphabet was suspended over every desk, and small queues formed in front of them. Serious-looking women in red kerchiefs presided over each desk.

Maria Nikoláyevna went to the desk under the letter 'O'.

Three people stood in a queue under it and one more sat in front of the desk talking with the young woman behind it. Maria Nikoláyevna took her place in the queue. She wished she could sit, but there were no extra chairs.

She observed the crowd. All people were holding summons similar to hers, and the queues moved fast, people apparently raising no objections to anything.

"I had never seen our Russians behaving so well," she thought. "Are they afraid to ask questions or are they *really* satisfied with their allocations?"

Something about the young woman in the red kerchief at the 'O' table looked familiar. "I know her," she thought. "Where have I seen her?" Then suddenly, she knew! "It's Natalia!" She saw in her mind's eye a slender young Natasha, her daughter's favorite maid, who had left to study nursing. It *was* Natasha, the same pretty girl who was now a woman. A *communist* woman, she corrected herself.

For a moment she felt trapped. "Natasha will recognize me," she thought. "There is no more anonymity." She thought of leaving the office and coming back another day. "No, it won't work. I am already registered as a *'former person.'* I've never assumed a new name ... I must take a chance ..."

Her turn came and she took the chair, grateful to be off her feet.

"What is your given name and patronymic?" Natalia asked automatically, looking at the summons instead of the person in front of her desk.

"Maria Nikoláyevna."

The young woman raised her eyes in surprise. "Maria Nikoláyevna? Orlova? Maria Nikoláyevna! I am Natasha! I used to work for your daughter. Don't you recognize me?"

"I do recognize you! How are you, Natasha?" Maria Nikoláyevna felt the heavy burden of apprehension drop off her shoulders. Natasha was happy to see her.

"I am fine, fine! How about you? Where is Larissa Sergéyevna? Where is her husband? I have a million questions to ask! Let's do this: I'll see the man behind you, and then I'll take my dinner break and we'll go to the employee mess hall and have a bowl of soup! You'll be my guest! You remain seated. This young man won't mind standing!"

They went by the back stairs to the basement with several plain tables and benches that in the old times had been the servants' dining room.

It was empty except for an old woman in a white apron presiding over a large pot steaming on a kerosene stove.

"Ah, Natáshenka! I was about to leave. I thought you were not coming today!" she exclaimed.

"No, Auntie Frósya! I would never miss your soup! Can you spare a plate for my old friend, Maria Nikoláyevna?" she asked pleadingly.

The old woman observed Maria Nikoláyevna. "Do you have your dining coupons?" she asked sternly.

"No. I am unemployed," she replied.

"I'll give you my coupons," Natasha said quickly.

Frósya frowned. "No. You need your coupons for yourself. Sit down. We'll manage. Just don't tell anybody or they'll start bringing in their parents and children, do you understand?" She looked at Natasha with pretended severity.

"I understand," Natasha said like a little girl.

They sat at the table and Frósya ladled cabbage and beet borsch onto two plates. "Do you have any bread?" Frósya asked.

Natasha shook her head.

"Oh, Natáshka!" Frósya sighed with reproach. "You never learn! You should *always* carry a little bread with you! Just in case! All right. I'll give you two slices from the emergency supply. Just keep your mouth shut."

Maria Nikoláyevna thanked the cook for her soup and bread. "I haven't tasted anything so good for months!" she said. Frósya looked pleased.

"Tell me about Larissa Sergéyevna, and the rest of the family," Natasha reminded.

"There is not much to tell," Maria Nikoláyevna lied. She could not tell the long, sad story. Natasha didn't have time for that kind of tale. "Larissa is fine. She is in Odessa with a small child who is perfectly healthy. Her husband was a test pilot nearby, but I am not sure where he is now. Everything is fine," she said with false joviality. "Anyway, what about you? Have you finished your nursing training?"

"No." Natasha said with embarrassment. "They dismissed me from the courses. I could not tolerate touching the wounds, so the doctors said I wasn't fit to be a nurse. I was glad to be released. So, I enrolled at the workers training school. I learned how to type and do office work. They assigned me to the Housing Authority. I like it so much better!"

"Are you married?"

"No, but I have a man. He is a Commissar. I want to get married, but Dimka has a wife somewhere and a couple of boys, so he keeps stalling."

"If you ask me, he is a piece of *shit*, your Dimka!" Frósya said. "If he is married and has children, but sleeps with you and strings you along, he is deceiving all of you. Leave him and get yourself some decent fellow!"

Natasha was embarrassed by Frósya's crudeness. "I am sorry," she said to Maria Nikoláyevna.

"I agree with Frósya," Maria Nikoláyevna said. "You are much too good for such a man."

Natasha felt uncomfortable. "I've thought about it, but ... I love him!"

Frósya snorted scornfully. "Love!"

"Anyway, thank you, Auntie Frósya, for the soup and bread and for allowing me to bring my old friend," Natasha said, rising. "I must go back."

"Any time, *sólnichko*, my sunshine," Frósya replied, full of smiles again. She turned to Maria Nikoláyevna. "Since you are Natashka's friend, you may come back sometime, after hours. I always have a little soup and bread stashed away for my friends!"

"Thank you, Frósya, I am glad to have met you. I will come, when I am really hungry. I am not proud. I am grateful to you!" Impulsively she kissed Frósya on her cheek.

Natasha and Maria Nikoláyevna returned to the big room. Most of the people were gone, and the women in red kerchiefs were clearing their desks.

"I will try to get you the best room in my files," Natasha said, unlocking the desk. "I think you should live closer to the center of the city, near the tramlines, in a proper flat with running water and electricity. And I have such a room available. It is on Vassilievsky Island, on the Bolshoi Prospect, in one of the old apartment buildings that used to have elevators." She looked at her files. "The room has two windows, which means that it is probably bigger than your allocated nine square meters. You will have to pay extra for more meters. It used to be a private residence belonging to ..." she looked at the papers again. "To some doctor, so it is a *good* flat. There is a bathroom and two other rooms. They are occupied by ..." she consulted the document, "by a single man, a school teacher. Second room is taken by a mother and daughter, a secretary at the militia! You'll have educated people as your neighbors and militia worker for security! It says here that there is no furniture, but perhaps Ksusha had some that we can take along! I am so happy!" She was radiant.

"Dear Lord, it was such good luck that I ran into you, Natasha! Thank you, thank you dear girl, with all my heart!" Maria Nikoláyevna whispered, her voice trembling. Her stoicism had broken, and she dissolved in a torrent of liberating tears.

Natasha embraced her. She did not need to be told of Maria Nikoláyevna's ordeal. She could guess.

80

On Natasha's day off two days later, she took Maria Nikoláyevna to see her new room and meet her new neighbors. They rode a tram to Vassilievsky Island, the largest in the archipelago of islands on which Peter the Great had built his Imperial Capital. It was separated from the rest of the city by the Nevá River spanned by its many long and graceful bridges that were raised up every night for the passage of ships to and from the city. The island was built in a strict geometrical pattern along three main boulevards running parallel and bordered by leafy trees. Peter's plan was to flood the island, creating his own Venice with a grid of interlocking canals, but he had died before his plan could be realized.

Maria Nikoláyevna had second thoughts about the room. Since it was larger than her allocated space, she would have to pay more. "Where is the money to pay for it? Of course, if Larissa manages to come to Petrograd, she and Nínochka will move in with me. Besides, *I* want to live in a decent room, with running water and electricity! I could get a job, like Frósya. And I still have some of my jewelry ..." she thought, not listening to Natasha's reminiscing about Larissa's wedding.

"They were such a beautiful couple! Lieutenant Rezánov was so handsome, we all fell in love with him! Well, not *really*," she hurried to clarify her outburst.

Maria Nikoláyevna smiled, relieved that she had made her decision. "I too could have fallen in love with him! Let me show you a picture of them with the baby!" She searched in her reticule for the photograph. She found the envelope with the picture. "Here it is. Nínochka is almost three years old now," she said. "Larissa writes that she is very pretty, she sings and dances and is altogether a lovely child. The tragedy is that her father hasn't seen her since this picture was taken!"

"Is he still ... flying airplanes?" Natasha asked delicately.

"Yes. He was seriously wounded and that's why Larissa is in Odessa. She and I went there to take care of him. When he got better, I returned to Petrograd, but Larissa stayed in Odessa. Then, Andrei had to return to his detachment. But the railroads stopped functioning and it became impossible for Larissa to return to Petrograd. Now, one must have a special permit to travel."

"I know. I tried to go to Vólogda when I heard that my parents had died but was unable to get the permit, even though I am a Communist Party member!" Natasha said. Seeing nervousness in Maria Nikoláyevna's eyes, she said quickly, "You don't have to worry about me or Dimka. I know that you are a good person, and he is not inquisitive. Even though he is a Commissar, I doubt that he would bother you with questions."

They came to a handsome nineteenth-century four-story apartment building of gray stone with two caryatides supporting the frame of a large front door decorated with bronze accoutrements. Several full-grown linden trees shaded the front of the house, each tree trunk surrounded by intricate iron grates at its roots. "Like in Paris!" Maria Nikoláyevna reflected. "I like it!"

They entered the vestibule with the non-working lift and began to climb to the third floor. It was easy. On every landing there was an elaborate iron bench. Resting on each for a few moments, Maria Nikoláyevna thought again that it reminded her of Paris. She had no trouble reaching the third floor.

There were two apartments facing one another, with the names of the occupants and the number of rings of the bell required to be admitted. "That's clever," Natasha said. "That way the occupants know by the number of rings if it is for them." She read the names. "Here we are, the *'authorized representative' Comrade Pushkin*. How do you like it! Pushkin *himself* is going to be your neighbor!" they laughed as Natasha touched the button of the electric bell for a single ring.

Shortly the door was opened by a balding man in his sixties wearing a soiled undershirt and a pair of pants with hanging suspenders. His feet were shod in moth-eaten velvet slippers.

"Comrade Pushkin? I am a representative of the Housing Authority, Natalia Makarova," Natasha introduced herself. "I brought your new neighbor, Maria Nikoláyevna Orlova, who has been assigned a room in your communal flat. Do you mind showing us the room? Here are her documents." Natasha proffered him the papers.

Pushkin searched in his pockets for his spectacles. Placing them on his long nose, he examined the papers. "Everything seems to be in good order," he finally said. "Follow me, if you please. You must excuse my appearance. I hadn't expected any visitors."

"Don't worry!" Natasha smiled. "Besides, this is not a social visit!"

"Nevertheless, I shouldn't be receiving you *déshabillé.*"

"I like him," Maria Nikoláyevna thought. "He must have been a gentleman in his previous life. And he speaks French!"

"The flat has three rooms, and yours is the last one in the corridor," Pushkin continued. "Let me show your room first." He opened one of the three doors in the entrance hall and turned on the light in the long corridor. "Your room has its own Holland stove, so you won't need to share your heat with another room. Your room has two windows and a glimpse of the river and the St. Isaak Cathedral." He took a bunch of keys from his pocket and searched for the right one. "As a long-time tenant of the flat, I was chosen by the other tenants to be their representative in all disputes within the flat and before the authorities. Also it is my responsibility to watch for the security of the tenants and the general upkeep of the apartment, so if something is broken or needs to be repaired, I must be notified. At the end of each year the tenants hold the election of a new representative, so we might even elect you, Maria Nikoláyevna! I have been doing this job since the Revolution, when the house was first nationalized! So I have served my time in the name of democracy!" he concluded with a sly grin.

It was a pleasant, bright room with crown molding at the ceiling. The parquet floor that had not been waxed since the Revolution was still good, its squares and triangles looking like an intricate puzzle. In the corner of the room rose a tall stove covered by shiny squares of sky-blue ceramic tiles. The walls had pale blue wallpaper of small bouquets of forget-me-not flowers. The wallpaper was still good, except under the windows where it was hanging loose.

Two double-framed windows with old lace curtains that had survived the post-revolutionary tenants, faced the linden trees in front of the house; in the space between the trees she could glimpse the gray waters of the Nevá and beyond it, the shiny cupola of the gigantic St. Isaak Cathedral. But the most striking sight for Maria Nikoláyevna was the view of *her own* former residence with its naked ribs of the dome of the destroyed Winter Garden.

Both women recognized it immediately. Mutely, they looked at one another and Natasha squeezed Maria Nikoláyevna's hand.

Natasha took over Maria Nikoláyevna's resettlement. She washed the floor and the inside of the windows. She made sure that the allocated firewood was delivered, and Dimka stacked it next to the Holland stove. Dimka checked the stove to make sure that it worked and glued back the loose wallpaper.

With his help, Natasha took apart Ksusha's metal bed with its decorative curlicues at the headboard. There was not much more to transfer except a set of wrought iron garden furniture that Maria Nikoláyevna had given to Ksusha when the Winter Garden was destroyed. Ksusha used it as her dining set, the table always covered with a clean tablecloth and chairs made comfortable by colorful cushions. Now it was back in Maria Nikoláyevna's possession, continuing its service as a dining set.

They piled Ksusha's belongings into a small truck that Dimka expropriated for a day from his office at the Red Triangle Rubber factory. They stripped bare Ksusha's little house, taking everything, including a box of used nails. "You might need them," Dimka said. "You can't buy nails."

Dimka was right. One could not buy nails.

In two days Maria Nikoláyevna was settled. The room looked almost pretty. Together they examined the old curtains and Maria Nikoláyevna decided that she could repair them; she was good with a needle.

"We must ask permission of Comrade Pushkin. The curtains are government property," Natasha said.

"But they are no good! The government will have no use for them!" Maria Nikoláyevna objected.

"No matter. They are mentioned in the description of the room. You must have an affidavit from the tenant representative that they are useless. I think, Comrade Pushkin will sign it without trouble. I'll prepare the papers for his signature."

"You are so good to me, Natasha! I don't know how I can ever reciprocate!"

"You don't need to. You and Larissa Sergéyevna were always kind to me, and I loved Ksusha. She was like a mother to me. When I lost my own mother ..." There were tears gathering in her eyes as she said softly, "truly, Ksusha was better to me than my own mother ..."

"If you allow me, I shall be your new *'Ksusha,'*" Maria Nikoláyevna said, opening her arms. Natasha clung to her without hesitation.

81

During the fall of 1919, encouraged by several substantial victories, the Whites began to dream of an offensive against Petrograd via General Yudénich's Northern forces. At the same time, General Deníkin contemplated marching against Moscow.

Warned by spies of the possible offensive, the Red Commissar for War, Lev Trotsky, hurried to Petrograd.

Within days Trotsky turned the city into a fortress. Barricades were built across strategic intersections and machine gun nests hidden in the surrounding buildings. Rows of sharp stakes and sawed-off pieces of steel railroad rails were erected to serve as the first rebuff against armed vehicles. Miles of barbed wire were strung across the city streets, and gigantic anti-aircraft balloons hung in the sky over the main bridges.

All the roads leading to Petrograd were fortified against cavalry with tons of ball-bearings collected from factories and repair shops and spread on the roads to make the horses stumble and slip. Factory workers were armed and placed on a twenty-four hour alert. Trotsky ordered that every citizen fight for every street and every house, for every flat and every room, with no retreat and no surrender.

But the Red forces stopped Yudénich at Gátchina, only thirty miles from the city. The White offensive was poorly organized, its front too extended. The Whites lacked supplies and reinforcements, and there was no harmony among the Command.

Deníkin's progress was stopped at Orël, about a hundred miles southwest of Moscow, for the same reasons. The Whites had to retreat, losing dearly won territories once again.

Deníkin was disgusted by the in-fighting among his staff and by the absence of discipline among his troops and deeply discouraged by the heavy losses and dwindling reserves. He had to admit to himself that the Whites' cause was lost. *Pravda* gloated that the Red Army had reached over *five million* men, not counting various partisan groups that harassed the Whites on their flanks and in the rear.

His spirits crushed, General Deníkin resigned his Command. The White Army would never again seriously threaten the Reds.

Andrei and Egórov followed the retreating Army to the Crimea and their new headquarters at the Sevastópol aerodrome. Being so close to

Odessa, Andrei again requested a week's leave to see his family. "I haven't seen my child since her birth and she is now almost three years old!"

Egórov took Captain Márkov aside. "I know it will incapacitate the Squadron, but *please* grant Andrúshka his request. He is desperate. He'll do something foolish, like flying to Odessa without permission. Then we'll lose him, and not just for a week, but forever!"

"What about *you?* Do you also want a week off?" Márkov asked.

"I do. But I'll stay. I have no family and no one waits for me. I'll stay."

Márkov did not need to be persuaded. He had become accustomed to relying on Egórov's judgment. The fact that the great Alexander Kozakov had entrusted Egórov with running the detachment in his absence was always on Márkov's mind. Actually he was surprised that Egórov had made no move to replace *him!*

He signed the papers granting Andrei a week's leave after one more photographic reconnaissance flight over the Turkish Wall of Pericóp.

The morning of the reconnaissance mission was crisp and bright. Flying two Spads at high altitude, Andrei and Egórov were able to see clearly their targets. The fortifications of the narrow isthmus separating the Crimea from the mainland were reinforced by General Vrángel and closely packed with troops.

The famous Turkish Wall built by the Ottomans centuries ago looked like a piece of old dirty thread. "It's hard to believe that once it was considered to be *'impenetrable,'*" Andrei thought, aiming his camera at the wall. "Of course, for cavalry in the old days it must have been true. The ditch alone would have made it impossible to cross for the horses. But today, with a couple of well-aimed bombs, the whole wall could be demolished in no time!"

The Whites' new concrete fortifications down below looked formidable bursting with Vrángel's troops. Built in depth like a huge labyrinth with several thick lines of concrete, the trenches and the bunkers connected with each other by short corridors for easy communications. Large caliber artillery, mostly guns captured from the Germans during the war, were concentrated throughout the wall and along the Sivash Lake shore.

The Reds would be hard pressed to break through, but they were gearing up for the attempt. Beyond the White fortifications, Andrei and Egórov could see the columns of Red soldiers and artillery.

Egórov wagged his wings and dived sharply for a better look. Andrei followed. There were only the two of them up there in the blue skies and instantly they became an easy target for the enemy's gunners as they entered the barrage zone of the anti-aircraft batteries.

Ignoring the fire, the pilots continued to photograph the fortifications and the terrain. Andrei could clearly see the activity of the massive Red forces concentrating for the assault on the isthmus. Several cavalry regiments moved in tight formation toward the target. Closer to the isthmus, long ribbons of infantry and artillery stretched in the same direction.

"They are going to throw their horse armies against us," Andrei thought, trying not to get distracted by the flack of the murderous explosions around him.

Egórov signaled that it was time to go home. He zoomed up, and Andrei followed him. "In just a minute we will be out of reach of the Archies," Andrei thought. He noticed Egórov's Spad flying erratically. It dipped, then surged up and forward and, to his horror, Andrei saw a small red tongue of fire appear near the fuel tanks. Egórov had been hit.

"Egórka!" Andrei screamed. Egórov's body leaned precariously to one side of the fuselage. It looked as if he was trying to level the aircraft. Andrei moved his own plane as close as was safe for a better look.

Egórov grinned at him, but Andrei could tell that he was badly injured. Fire was now licking the whole aircraft. The plane went into a screw dive toward the ground, trailing thick black smoke behind.

"Egórka! I am with you!" Andrei yelled, but of course Egórov could not hear him.

The Spad plunged into the ground with its tale pointing up to the sky, its wings broken and Egórov's body still in the protective harness hanging helplessly over the edge of the cockpit.

Andrei landed carelessly nearby. Once it must have been a small meadow leading into the woods, but now it was a pock-marked wasteland from exploding artillery shells. His own Spad had a broken wheel, but he didn't care. His eyes were on the burning plane as he ran toward it.

"Andrúshka, help me!" Egórov screamed.

Egórov's Spad was burning furiously. Immobilized by horror Andrei saw rampant tongues of flame reaching his friend's distorted face. Egórov's leather coat was crinkling on his back, gathering in small bubbles. "Shoot me!" Egórov yelled hysterically. Andrei had never heard such a desperate voice. "Shoot me!" Andrei ran helplessly around the burning plane, unable to do anything.

"Shoot me for Christ's sake, shoot me, don't let my fry!" Egórov screamed.

With his hands shaking, Andrei reached for his gun. He shut his eyes and emptied the gun into the burning body of his beloved friend. When the bullets ran out, he lobbed the gun into the flames.

Without a glance at his own crippled aircraft, without a thought of the explosion behind him, without a thought of anything, Andrei ran toward the woods and threw himself on the ground, wishing to die.

82

The men who found Andrei the next morning were neither Red nor White. They picked up the detritus of both sides and called themselves 'partisans', but in reality they were bandits without any affiliations or ideology. They mainly robbed the wounded and the dead after a battle. They had little pity for the wounded and no respect for the dead.

Andrei's leather coat immediately attracted their attention.

"Hey, look at that coat! What a coat!" cried their leader, a husky old man with a long unkempt white beard. "It's *mine!*" He placed his hand on the gun in his belt, daring anyone to oppose his claim. The men jumped off their horses and surrounded Andrei.

"Who are you?" demanded the leader, remaining in the saddle. "Are you Red or White? Are you wounded?"

"No." Andrei replied. "My name is Andrei Rezánov." The men roughly pulled his coat off his shoulders and threw it to the leader. Andrei's medals shone brightly on his tunic.

"So! You are a White flier and a *hero,*" the old leader exclaimed sarcastically, glancing at the wing emblems on Andrei's epaulettes. "You have been awarded the Order of St. George! You *must* have done something really brave! And what is that other one, on the red ribbon?"

Andrei did not want to answer but replied, "St. Anne," his instinct of self-preservation taking over.

"Take off his shirt," the leader ordered his men.

"They are going to shoot me," Andrei thought. He unbuttoned his tunic, and the men pulled it off. Watching with indifference as they unhooked his medals and gave them to the leader, he felt no rage, no sorrow, only emptiness in his heart.

"What were you doing here anyway?" The leader demanded as he examined the medals. "That one is beautiful," he said admiring the Order of St. Anne. "All this red and gold … Do you think it's real gold?"

Andrei shrugged. He did not care anymore for these little pieces of bright enamel and imitation gold, once the objects of his pride. In his mind's eye he saw the burning Spad and Egórov hanging over the nacelle. "His medals must have melted …" a thought flashed through his mind.

"So, who are you?" the leader turned his attention back to Andrei. "Speak up!"

"I am Andrei Rezánov, a military pilot, formally of the 19th Detachment. You have my papers and the orders. They are in the inside pocket of the coat."

"Hey, Nikítka, read me the papers! I'm not too good at reading," the leader said, taking the papers out of the inside pocket of the leather coat. A young man with fuzz on his pimpled face took the papers. "It says here that he is Lieutenant Andrei Rezánov and is *'on leave'* for a week. The other paper says—"

"Enough! He must be what he says he is," the old man interrupted. "So, what were you doing here, all alone, instead of enjoying your *leave?* Speak up!"

"There were two of us. We were photographing the advance of the Reds. My best friend was shot down and burned … and I killed him … I shot him …" Saying it made Andrei feel that he was suffocating. He gasped for air.

"It takes a lot of guts to shoot your best friend!" the old man said. "You must be tough! And who is this woman? Your wife?" he held up a photograph that was among his papers.

"Yes," Andrei said hoarsely, "And my baby. They are in Odessa."

"And you want to go to Odessa."

"Yes … My airplane is wrecked …" as he said it, he realized that there was no way to get to Odessa or anywhere from that devastated clearing in the no-man's land.

The old man observed him critically. "Can you ride a horse?"

"Yes."

"Nikítka, bring the spare bay. We'll take you to the railroad. It's working again, and at its end is Odessa. We are partisans, free men, going wherever we want to, doing what we want to, so we'll put you on the train to Odessa! Why not? It will give you a few days with your wife before you must go back …"

"I won't be going back," Andrei said quietly, surprising himself. "I am through with this war."

"You mean, you'll *desert?*"

"I am through," Andrei repeated. There was a sudden new steely quality to his voice. "I won't go back. I won't kill anymore."

"That's fine. We all feel that way sometimes. But it is necessary, to kill. Will you fight and kill if *necessary* to get to Odessa?"

"Yes," Andrei said.

"Good!" Noting that Andrei was shivering in his thin undershirt, the leader turned to young Nikítka again. "Find some kind of a shirt and a good coat. The Lieutenant is freezing!" The young man ran to a four wheeled open-sided wagon pulled by horses. It was loaded with piles of loot among which protruded a barrel of a Maxim machine gun.

"Here!" Nikítka handed a rough shirt and sheepskin coat to Andrei.

"Thank you," Andrei mumbled.

"Don't thank me. Thank my Grandpa," the young man snarled.

"Listen up, everybody," the old man called out, "We are going to stop a train!" He turned to Andrei. "As we force the train to stop and have everybody out, you sneak in and hide until we are done. We'll leave, and it will be up to you to keep on hiding or threaten everyone with your gun."

"I have no gun," Andrei said. "I threw mine into the fire."

"We'll give you another one. No man can live without a gun. So, get up on the horse and let's go to the railroad. If you are lucky, tomorrow you may be fucking your wife!" the men laughed and some slapped Andrei on his back.

"Mount your horses, brothers and nephews and cousins! Let's have some fun with the train!" The men eagerly mounted, laughing and joking as if indeed they were going to some place of entertainment.

"You probably have never seen a *family* fighting together," the old man said, riding next to Andrei. "We are all members of the same family. We lost our homes and our women during the war. The Reds and the Whites, the Ukrainians and the Romanians. Our village was wiped out by the artillery of all of them. In grief, all of us, fathers, brothers and sons, cousins, uncles and nephews, banded together and declared our own war on *everyone!* We rob and we kill, and it makes us feel better. We die also, but we die for good reasons: we avenge ourselves!"

"I know exactly how you feel," Andrei said. "I too, have lost everything, my parents, my home, everything. And now, I lost my best friend. All I have left is my wife and the baby ..."

"Consider yourself lucky," the old man said. "Here. You will need these." He proffered Andrei his documents. He did not offer to return Andrei's coat or medals, but Andrei didn't care.

"What's your name?" Andrei asked.

"They call me Kusmích," the man replied. "No other name."

The band consisted of fifteen men. They were well organized with two supply wagons in addition to a cart with its machine gun. Behind each wagon trotted spare horses on short leads.

"I like to stop the train in the middle of nowhere," Kusmích explained to Andrei. "The surprise of the attack scares everyone shitless. There is no place for them to hide. The convoy usually surrenders without a fight. All very simple. It usually takes less than an hour."

Despite his grief, Andrei was captivated by the old leader. "Doesn't the convoy defend the train?"

"Not really. As a rule, passenger trains have one armed man for each car, usually some man who is no good as a soldier anyway. At the sight of us, he shits in his pants! We don't touch the trains with the real military convoys that transport troops. And now, since the Reds restarted the railroad traffic, we have one passenger train going between Taganróg and Odessa every day!

They trotted out of the forest that was not a forest anymore, but a large space of broken trees without branches or canopies. It was a desolate landscape, like an illustration in a fantasy story about the final destruction of the earth. Nothing moved. There was not a rabbit scared by the horses, nor a squirrel scurrying across their path, not even a flock of crows disturbed by their approach. The forest was dead. It must have been a birch forest at one time, and its naked white trunks stuck out of the snow like the broken teeth of some prehistoric animal.

"Sad, eh?" Kusmích said.

"Yes," Andrei agreed.

The steppe spread before them as they left the dead forest. Covered with snow, it looked as flat as a tabletop under a white cloth, but in reality it was full of hidden craters from artillery barrages. Nothing relieved its blandness now except a frozen river and a trestle railroad bridge. Constructed of logs with catwalks on both sides, it looked puny and fragile.

"We shall wait for the train under the bridge embankment. As they stop, we'll attack," Kusmích said.

"How do you know that they will stop at the bridge?"

"Because we'll *make* them stop. We'll have a tree over the rails before the bridge."

Two horsemen galloped back to the dead forest. Shortly they were back, dragging a tree trunk by an attached chain. They placed it across the rails and piled snow at both ends to make it difficult to remove. It was done quickly, all men taking part in creating snowdrifts on both sides of the rail bed.

"The engineer will be able to see our barricade and slow down the train," Kusmích explained, reaching into the chest pocket under his coat and retrieving a handsome gold watch. "The train usually crosses the valley about noon, so we won't need to wait too long," he said. He showed Andrei the expensive watch. "I picked it up from some minister of something or other. It says something in French, I think. Can you read French?"

"Yes." Andrei looked at the back cover of the watch. It was engraved *'À bon copain'* and signed *Vladímir.* "It says *'To a good buddy, from Vladímir.'"* Did you kill the man?"

"Probably. I don't remember." Andrei did not ask any more questions.

They heard the distant whistle of a train. "Alright brothers, let's take our positions. We'll wait until the train stops and they get out to remove the barricade. We'll swoop on them from both sides. So, watch for my signal. Godspeed, my friends!" the men took off their hats and made the sign of the cross.

Asking for God's grace struck Andrei as incongruous. "They are thieves and killers, about to commit a crime, yet they ask for God's blessing! How truly *Russian* they are! *Egórka, brother of my soul, you were right!"* Andrei thought bitterly.

He followed Kusmích down to the river bank and the understructure of the bridge. "Egórov was never sentimental about the *'goodness'* of Russians," he thought. "He believed that we were still the wild *'Scythians with slanting and covetous eyes',* as Alexander Blok wrote. "Yes, we are, and I am one of them," Andrei thought.

It was a short train consisting of one passenger car and two *teplúshki,* cattle cars. It chugged peacefully toward the bridge, its teplúshki full of horses that comprised the security detachment of the new Cheka unit assigned to Odessa. Its sliding doors were tightly locked.

"There is no easy way to check the teplúshki before we attack," said Kusmích.

The train was going at a full speed, the engineer not yet seeing the barricade across the rails.

"There must be someone important on that train," Andrei said. "The passenger car is two-tone brown. It means first class. The ordinary passenger cars are usually green."

"Our new rulers are changing their colors!" Kusmích snorted. "Soon they'll create their own ruling class!"

It was a pretty picture of a little train puffing white smoke, scampering through the white spaciousness of the steppe, reminding Andrei of his boyhood picture books. "We met on the train," he thought of Egórov again, deep pain swelling in him.

The train was approaching the bridge. Andrei was rigid with tension. He fingered the gun in his pocket. Memories of the times when he and Egórov were hiding together on the way to Tiraspol flooded his mind. "We were always together ..." he thought. "Sometimes we even *enjoyed* the danger."

The train slowed to a crawl and stopped. They watched as three men with large coal shovels jumped out from the locomotive and, looking cautiously at the mute steppe around, trotted toward the barricade.

Kusmích raised his arm and yelled "NOW!"

His horsemen charged out of the ambush, shooting into the air. The trainmen dropped their shovels and rolled down the embankment in search of cover. The horsemen split into two groups, racing toward the train, shooting at it from both sides. Andrei galloped next to Kusmích, looking for a spot where he could get into the train.

All three cars looked tightly locked. The passenger car windows had the shades drawn and the only people he could see were the trainmen down the embankment and an engineer who ducked behind his window at the first sounds of gunfire. The train looked dead.

But not for long.

The huge doors of one of the cattle cars suddenly slid open and three men spilled out, opening a barrage of rapid, concentrated handgun fire at the horsemen. Andrei saw Kumisch slump in the saddle, and before Andrei had time to react, he felt bullets tearing into him as well.

Andrei fell face down into the snow, his mortally wounded horse pinning him down. Kusmích tried to catch up with his retreating men, but his horse, also wounded, was unable to carry him. It collapsed under him, with one of the old man's feet caught in the stirrup. Two other gang members lay dead in the snow bank.

The shooting stopped. The Red soldiers, all specially trained hand-gun snipers, carefully examined the fallen men and removed the barricade that the trainmen had abandoned.

"All clear!" the commander shouted. Two men and a woman came out of the passenger's car. Dressed in black leather and knee-high boots, they clutched cocked guns in their hands.

"Two dead, two wounded, two horses dead. Probably ten or twelve have escaped. It seems that they are gone, Comrade Commissar," the commander reported.

"Who were they?" the woman demanded "White guardsmen?"

"No, Comrade Commissar. Some kind of partisans. I think, we have their leader. An old man. The other man may be a pilot. Most likely, he was a prisoner. What is your order?"

"A pilot, you say? How funny! Take us there," she said briskly.

The woman was the notorious Cheká Commissar, the executioner known as *Zemliáchka*, roughly translated as 'a close neighbor.' In her forties, she was a fanatical disciple of Lenin and famous for her cruelty. She seemed to derive pleasure from torture and executions. *"Rasstreliát!* Shoot them!" was her standard order. She spoke often of the need for ruthless and relentless pursuit of the Whites who were *"hiding from the sword of proletarian justice."*

Zemliáchka and her aides walked around the locomotive to the other side of the train. There, lying on the snow, were two horses, their huge dead bodies slowly trickling dark blood. Next to the horses were two men, one partially under the horse, his face in the snow, and the other with a white beard and leather flight coat, his leg still in the stirrup, probably dead.

Zemliáchka kicked the younger man with the tip of her boot, and he moaned. "Remove the horses," she ordered.

"Yes, Comrade Commissar," the commander said. The soldiers dragged aside the dead animals.

"Lift the young one up," she ordered, snapping her fingers. "He is still alive." Two men lifted Andrei and propped him in a sitting position against the car. His eyes were open but unseeing.

"Are you a pilot? What is your name?" she demanded.

Andrei was silent. The snow around him was red with his blood.

"What's your name?" she repeated. Andrei remained silent. "Search him!" she ordered. Her aides reached inside Andrei's coat and extracted his documents.

"Let me see!" she grabbed the papers. "It says here that he is Lieutenant Andrei Rezánov ... Cavalier of the Order of St. George ... *and* the recipient of St. Anne!" She looked at another document. "Why, he was *on leave!* We could have had some *fun* interrogating him! Here is the picture of his family. Look!" she showed the photograph of Larissa to her companions.

"Very beautiful woman," one of them said.

"Yeah!" Zemlyáchka laughed harshly. "I wonder how *beautiful* she would be after you boys were through with her!" The men around her laughed.

"So, what were you doing here, Lieutenant Rezánov, the Cavalier of St. George and St. Anne? The husband of a *beautiful* woman? Why are you dressed in a stinky shirt and not in your fancy pilot's coat? What were you doing with these low-class bandits? Why weren't you enjoying your leave in Odessa? It's a *beautiful* city!" She scoffed.

Andrei remained silent, his head hanging over his chest, his eyes unable to focus on the dancing shadows of people around him. He did not hear what they were saying. He was aware of nothing around him.

"He is dying, Comrade Commissar," said the commander, trying not to show any compassion.

"Good riddance! One son-of-a-bitch less! *Rasstreliát!*" Seeing the commander hesitate to follow her order, she unhooked her Nagant and calmly pressed the trigger.

Andrei's body jerked as he fell sideways in the red-stained snow.

Zemliáchka said over her shoulder, "Add him to our roster. Let's go, comrades. You can drool over his *beautiful woman's* photo on the train. Or even better, you can fuck her when we have her in our cellars!" she laughed.

83

Winter arrived. The Crimean mountains were powdered with light snow while the rest of the peninsula and Odessa were shrouded in fog and rain. The sea became black again as the high waves vaulted over the sea walls, licking the golden beaches with their curly white tongues. On the boulevards, the winds stripped off every leaf of the linden trees.

The Volunteer Army was girding itself for the defense of the Crimea. Yet, General Vrángel prudently stockpiled coal and oil and food in case he might have to retreat across the sea. He made clandestine arrangements for emergency evacuation with the French, whose squadron of ten ships was in Sevastópol. He made an agreement with the Turks to provide the vessels to evacuate thousands of troops and their families and give them temporary refuge should the need arise.

If he could hold the Crimea over the winter, Vrángel hoped the Allies would come to his aid with weapons and equipment. Come spring, he would be able to lead his re-organized army in a grand offensive, unifying the smaller groups that still continued to resist the Reds throughout the country.

However, Vrangel was prudent enough to prepare for defeat as well. The odds were against him. He had only about one hundred thousand fighting men at his disposal, while the Reds had concentrated three times as many against him.

November 7, 1920, was the third anniversary of the Bolshevik Revolution. The Reds were especially motivated to celebrate it with a *great* victory, and a strange phenomenon of nature had come to their aid. Only once or twice in anyone's lifetime had hurricane winds blown from the northwest toward the Crimea with such force that they dried the shallow foul-smelling waters of the Sivash Lake salt flats that lay on the approaches to Perekóp, but it happened on the night of November 7th in 1920. Temperatures fell so low that the muddy bottom of the shallow flats froze, making it possible for the Red infantry to cross it. It was an epic march through four miles of knee-high mud. It was an eerie sensation suggesting to many the crossing of the Red Sea described in the Bible.

The Reds suddenly appeared at Vrángel's rearguard positions, and the Whites were snared in a trap. They had no hope of winning the battle. On November 9th, General Vrángel gave an order to retreat. He told the entire army to evacuate the Crimea. He issued an order that all wounded, the officials of his government, and the remains of the Russian Army High Command must be evacuated before the Reds took possession of the Crimean Peninsula. They would be allowed to take along their families and those who *'might be in danger if they fell into the hands of the enemy.'*

On November 11th, he ordered all designated ships to proceed across the sea to Constantinople.

To guarantee the safe passage of the ships, French Admiral Dumenil telegraphed the Red Commander of the Southern Front a request '*not to pursue or bother*' the refugees in any form. He warned that should even one of the ships in the convoy be attacked, he would consider it an attack on the French Republic. He would reply by immediately bombing Russian ports on the Black Sea.

The Reds agreed. They were exhausted. They actually felt *relieved* to be excused from the tiresome duties of finishing off the defeated enemy.

General Vrángel left the Crimea aboard the cruiser *General Kornílov*, as the last of the exiles.

Amidst prayers and curses, but most of all copious tears, tens of thousands of refugees bade farewell to their beloved country forever.

84

The Reds and their followers were jubilant and celebrated the end of the civil war. The clarion call went over the country proclaiming that *"The Proletarian broom will sweep the rubbish of the rotten bourgeoisie!"* The headlines howled *"He who is not with us is against us!"* That was the new popular slogan that began to appear above lists of the few surviving members of the upper class, writers and artists, scholars and engineers.

The threatened citizens began to destroy all the vestiges of their past, photographs of family members in Tsarist uniforms, school records, medals, birth certificates, and other evidence of connection with the past regime.

The fear to be classified as the *enemy of the people* enveloped the whole country as a new all-encompassing terror descended on the suffering Russia.

It was *Gólod*, the famine.

Gólod showed its first signs during the last months of the World War, when Russian people began to suffer the lack of food. The traditional 'bread baskets' of the Ukraine, Poland, and Belorussia became the killing fields of the warring armies instead of fields of golden wheat or rows of potatoes or lush meadows for cattle. But gólod only got worse after the ultimate Red victory.

The freaky phenomenon of nature that froze the Sivash Lake had turned against *all* Russians by denying snows during the winter and rains in the summer. *Pravda* reported that the temperatures in Central Russia rose up to those of Egypt, and the resulting drought affected more than 25 million people.

The country was exhausted and nearly destroyed by six years of unstoppable battles and then by the multitudes of demobilized soldiers as they returned to their villages and towns. All of them needed work, all of them had to be housed and fed by the country that was in the throes of typhus epidemics and drought. The requisitions of grain had forced the peasants of Central Russia to deplete their supplies of seed for next year's planting. The region, always a dependable supplier of grain and produce for the country, became an impoverished conglomeration of towns and villages where people perished from the lack of food.

As in any large scale famine, the starved people often succumbed to the ultimate deterioration of character—cannibalism. At first it was considered to be vicious rumors spread by the surviving 'enemies of the people,' but eventually the authorities had to face the situation and ban the sale of ground meat once it was proven to contain human flesh.

The alleged cannibals were hung en masse and left dangling as a lesson. Crows pecked at the corpses, arguing, enjoying the sudden plethora of easy food while the emaciated people observed the display with dull indifference.

Odessa, being an international port city, suffered less than the rest of the country. The sailors were always good sources of contraband, including food. Moldovanka became a little island of stolen goods and illegal food markets.

Despite the loss of Mishka Japónchik and his generals, the clandestine group of thieves continued to operate in Moldovanka. They were more secretive now and stopped flaunting their power, but they were still active and some of them even prosperous.

Glafíra has established a profitable, if extremely dangerous, contact with a couple of members of the gang whom she knew only as Gríshka and Yúrka. In her capacity as Commissar, she was free to go wherever she wanted in the hospital, including the pharmacy stockroom. She made it her official duty to visit it for 'inspection.' Every week in exchange for medications that she filched, Gríshka delivered to the house in Moldovanka flour and butter or sugar, sometimes even ham or lamb. Yúrka supplied Glafíra with potatoes, cabbage, and onions, enough for a large cauldron of soup.

Glafíra had no pricks of conscience for stealing the medications. It did not bother her that somebody may have suffered because of the lack of particular medication. She hated all Reds, but she especially hated the ones who had fought at Perekóp. They now occupied beds in the Memorial Military Hospital.

The hospital still had large quantities of medications and supplies obtained through Sister Veronica, but with the unending stream of wounded Red soldiers and Glafíra's pilfering, the supplies were fast diminishing.

"Everybody is *gone*," Glafíra reflected. "Doctor Shubin and his family, gone with Vrángel ... And so is young Doctor Popov, *gone* ... The whole Cohen family is dead or gone. Veronica, *gone*. And no word from Egórov or Andrei. Are they also gone?"

She watched Larissa with concern. Her adoration of Larissa and the child had grown into an obsession. She surrounded them with an invisible net of protection and jealously excluded anyone who seemed to break that net.

Larissa's thoughts about Andrei were even darker. It was more than a month since she had received a note about his impending furlough. Since then—nothing. Could he have been shot down? And Egórov, also? There was that mass evacuation from the Crimea. What if Andrei went away with Vrángel? No, it was not possible! Andrei would never desert her and his child! But, what if ..." She willed herself not to think of it, but the cruel thought continued to gnaw at her heart.

There was no way to find out what might have had happened to Andrei and Egórov. With the departure of Vrángel's forces, the illicit White newspapers perished. Glafíra warned Larissa to remain calm and not make any requests for information. Being the daughter of a Tsarist general and the wife of an officer, Larissa was in real danger now.

Another month passed with no news. In a letter to her mother, Larissa confessed her fears that Andrei had deserted her. Maria Nikoláyevna wrote back angrily that Andrei would have *never* done such a thing. Larissa had to admit to herself that she could deal with him being shot down: she was a military wife, a military daughter. She had lived with that fact all her life. But the suspicion that Andrei may have *deserted* her was painful beyond endurance.

Glafíra bravely tried to comfort Larissa. She was grateful that the young people in the communal house distracted little Nínochka from noticing Larissa's frequent weeping.

But Nínochka was also waiting for Andrei, in her own way. She pestered Larissa with questions about Papa, how soon he would come home and whether he would stay with them *always*.

Her questions tore at Larissa's heart, and she was unable to suppress her tears. The child then would climb on her lap, wipe her tears with her skirt, saying, 'Don't cry, Mámochka, Papa will come when the weather will be warm!" repeating Larissa's own saying to her.

Glafíra watched them, feeling close to tears herself.

Another month passed. The inhabitants of the commune watched Larissa trying to present a happy picture for the sake of her daughter. Akim regularly brought Nínochka a bottle of milk from his wife's goat and a few eggs from her hens, never accepting any money.

"Don't insult me with offering me money," he told Larissa. "Nínochka is my goddaughter, even if by proxy!" He was almost sure that by now he had become a *real* Godfather.

It was early in April when Glafíra received a confidential list of names distributed only to the Commissars. It was a long list of liquidated 'enemies of the people' in alphabetical order, describing former careers and affiliations. All of them were officers, highly decorated for bravery. Egórov's name was not among them.

Glafíra turned the page and Andrei Rezánov's name leapt at her. He was described as "a whelp of the Tsarist general, a reckless pilot, who had crushed several valuable airplanes, a spy on his way to Odessa under the pretext of a furlough. He was caught trying to blow up a bridge, riding with a bandit gang, dressed in peasant clothes, but the sharp-eyed Red Commissars were not fooled by his masquerade. They shot him on the spot before he could do any harm to the peaceful Soviet Citizens of Odessa."

Glafíra pondered whether she should show the lists to Larissa. "She is already at the bottom of her endurance!" she thought. "On the other hand, it's better that she face the reality … She'll survive the shock. She has her Nínochka to think about. She is strong, like her mother."

Glafíra decided to tell Larissa. She would do it at the hospital, where Larissa's reaction could not be heard and seen by the child.

She called Larissa into her office and shut the door. Larissa knew at once that Glafíra had bad news. "It is about Andrei!" she exclaimed, blanching.

"Yes." There was no use trying to prepare Larissa. She already sensed it. Glafíra handed her the report. "Read it."

Larissa lowered herself into a chair while Glafíra turned to the window, staring at the greening garden below and not seeing it.

Larissa read the report twice, her eyes dry and her face set as if it were carved of stone. Her tears were all shed during the months of uncertainty. Now she felt a wave of rising blind wrath, when she wanted to smash everything around her, like her mother had.

Glafíra came to her chair and embraced her. "Think of Nínochka ... think only of Nínochka!" she whispered. "Don't do anything stupid ..."

Larissa looked at her as if not recognizing her. "Yes ... Nínochka ... She will never know her Papa ... I will tell her about him ... I'll always talk to her about him ..." she began to shiver.

"Sh-sh," Glafíra said, stroking her head as if she were a young girl. "Tell Nínochka about him later, when she is older. But not now ... Not yet ... Don't talk about him to *anyone*. Tell the curious that he is *'missing in action.'* It is safe enough."

"Yes ... Missing in action, wasn't he? My Andrúshka ... Missing ... In action. I shall tell Nina that he won't be coming to us when the weather turns warm ..." She finally burst into tears.

Despite her best intentions to behave as if nothing had happened, Larissa succumbed to deep depression. She could not sleep or eat. She wept constantly. Finally, she could not lift herself up in the morning and go to work. Glafíra and the young people tried to take care of Nínochka, but she felt intuitively that something was very wrong with her mother. The unfamiliar feeling of *fear* bothered her young mind. No more did she sing and dance. She became fearful of loud noises, was petulant, disobedient, and cried seemingly without a reason. She began to wet her bed.

Akim noticed the change in Nínochka. "Let me take her to my house for a few days until you are feeling better," he said to Larissa. "She will play with my children. It will be good for her! What do you think, Larissa Sergéyevna?"

"If you wish," Larissa replied apathetically. Glafíra and Akim exchanged glances of mutual concern: Larissa's depression was beyond their ability to help. She needed medicine. She needed a doctor.

"Does her mother know that her son-in-law was killed?" Akim asked Glafíra in the kitchen as they waited for Nínochka to wake up from her nap.

"I don't think so. I don't think that Larissa has written to her."

"Well then, I think *you* must write to her mother. Maria Nikoláyevna is a wise woman. She won't be able to come to Odessa, but at least she will write to her daughter and give her support."

"Yes, let's write to her. But I must disclose the whole truth. And what about the censors?" Glafíra's round face crinkled as she thought of the possibility that her letter may never reach the addressee. In a few moments she smiled. "I know what I'll do! I'll write on my official stationary with our official seal and address it to *Comrade* Orlova and request an official signature that the document has been delivered!"

"It might work!" Akim said.

"It will! I'll write in the official political jargon, not mentioning the Lieutenant's name. She'll understand! She is *wise*, as you say!"

Nínochka woke up and came into the kitchen, dragging her blanket behind her. "Uncle Akim!" she cried happily as she ran to Akim. He picked her up and whirled her around. She squealed in delight.

"How would you like to go for a ride with me in the carriage and then come to my house for a few days and play with my girls? Would you like it?"

"Yes!" she cried.

"Alright! Tell your Mama that you are going with me to my house."

"Mama is sleeping. She is sick."

"I'll tell her when she wakes up," Glafíra said. "Let's go and get dressed."

"Will you let me hold the reins, Uncle Akim?" the girl asked.

"Of course! You can sit on my lap and help me drive!"

Followed by Glafíra, Nínochka skipped happily into her room to get dressed.

85

Maria Nikoláyevna opened Glafíra's *'document'* with concern. She immediately understood Glafíra's ruse: the letter had reached Petrograd without a censor's interference and in only four days, as if it was still in the good old days. Glafíra requested information about the *maggot treatment*, and then mentioned that a pilot who had been given such a treatment was recently executed as an enemy of the people, adding that his wife and child were still in the same place, waiting for the child's grandmother.

She read the letter several times, with ever deepening desperation. Her poor, poor girl, and the baby, her pride and joy. They needed her help! And Andrei! That golden boy, whom she had known since birth and loved as if he were her own son ... *executed*, not shot down. There was a great difference between the two.

"*My darling Larissa,*" she wrote.

> *My heart breaks that I can't be with you and share your sorrow. But I won't go into the descriptions of how I feel. You know how I feel. You know how it is when a part of your heart is torn out of you.*

> *What I want to tell you is just what we both must do, right away! We must be together to support one another and to raise our little girl in an atmosphere as happy as we can create. You must join me in Petrograd. I have a beautiful big room now, big enough for all three of us, in an old handsome building on the Bolshoi Prospect. It's near the streetcar lines and a short walk to the Soloviévsky Garden where our little one can play at the children's playground.*

> *What we must do now is to save enough money for your train tickets. The trains to Petrograd are back to running now, more or less regularly. You must obtain an official permit to travel. I think your friend Glafíra could get it for you. I'll get a permit for you and the child to join me for a visit. I think I could get it through Natasha. You know who she is. She works at the Housing Authority, but her common law husband is a Commissar. I think he likes me. I can ask him to pull some strings and get permits for you to come to Petrograd.*

> *So, start saving money for the tickets! I'll do the same. If we are lucky, we'll be together in a few months, my darling girl!*

> *I can't write anymore ... I am too devastated. Kiss Nínochka for me.*

> *Your mother*

She included a short note of thanks to Glafíra and mailed the letter in the provided return envelope plastered with postal stamps bearing the new Soviet emblem of hammer and sickle. It was addressed to Comrade Commissar Glafíra Ivánovna Khádji and was stamped *'confidential.'*

There was no specific medication against depression *anywhere* in the whole country, Glafíra thought. She did not want to talk about Larissa to the new personnel of the hospital. All new doctors were Communists, and few would be sympathetic to Larissa because of her political background. In fact, they might report her to the Cheka.

Suddenly she remembered the old Doctor Gottlieb. "I wonder if he is still alive," she thought as she trudged along the street looking for the doctor's house.

She found the house, its large windows still without glass after the latest pogrom, sheets of plywood nailed to their frames. A plaque with the doctor's name, once shiny, was now green with mold and hung crookedly on one nail.

She rang the bell and shortly the door was opened by a gray-haired woman dressed neatly in an old-fashioned dark frock with a white lace collar. She looked very formal and stern, like a schoolmistress.

"Citizen Gottlieb?" Glafíra asked. The woman, seeing someone attired in black leather and with a gun at her belt, began to tremble. Her formality instantly melted into servility.

"Yes," she mumbled apologetically, "I just needed a few potatoes to make some *latkes* for my husband ..." she said nervously. " He is sick ... he asked me to make him some latkes ... He loves my latkes..."

"What are you talking about?" Glafíra interrupted rudely.

"On the black market ... I bartered my wedding ring to make the latkes ... I know it is against the law but I needed—"

"I have no interest in your ring or your latkes. I want to talk to your husband about Julia's friend, Larissa, who needs medication. Her husband was recently killed, and she is sick with grief. She doesn't eat, doesn't get out of bed, and doesn't take care of her little girl. I need something to get her well ... She is my friend." Glafíra saw that the old woman visibly relaxed. "So, may I see the doctor?"

"Yes, yes! Please sit down ..." the woman pointed to an overstuffed chair upholstered in a balding dark red velvet. "I'll call him." She hurried out of the room.

Glafíra looked around. The parlor was furnished with heavy wood furniture and overstuffed chairs and a sofa. It had an overall sad air of abandonment and quiet despair.

A grand Bechstein piano dominated the room. Over the fireplace was a dusty mirror speckled by flies. Cold ashes spilled out of the fireplace.

Doctor Gottlieb, dressed in an ancient threadbare velvet robe with a matching cap with a tassel, looked comical as he entered the room.

Glafíra now remembered him. He used to be a sprightly gentleman, always dressed in expensive suits, with a well-tended little beard and moustache. Now before her stood an ancient man with his hands trembling, his eyes tearing behind his pince-nez attached to a black velvet ribbon patched in several places.

"What can I do for you, Madame?" he asked politely.

"I came for some medicine. Not for me," she added quickly. "It is for Larissa Rezánova, who used to be your patient. She is sick with grief. I thought that perhaps you have some medicine that could help her."

"Unfortunately, Madame, our pharmacology is way behind in research of mental disorders. But we have something. Tóva, my love, bring me a bottle of laudanum. The big bottle." His wife, who stood at the door during the conversation, left and quickly returned with a quart-size bottle of laudanum.

"Take the whole bottle … I have no more patients. Give her no more than a spoonful each time, mixed with water. Two, three times a day."

Glafíra nodded. "How much money do I owe you?"

"Food is more valuable than money these days," he replied. "Three potatoes would be fine!"

"I-don't-carry-potatoes-with-me!" she said with open irritation.

"It's alright. I understand. You can bring them tomorrow. I trust you, Madame."

Courteously he escorted her to the door, dragging his feet along the dusty floor. Clutching her bottle of laudanum, Glafíra hurried out of the house.

86

The laudanum slowly brought Larissa out of her paralyzing depression, but it was the absence of Nínochka that struck her back to reality.

"Where is my daughter?" she demanded. She felt weak and out of balance when she pushed herself out of bed. Then she remembered: Nínochka was with Akim's family. Nínochka was safe.

Larissa looked at herself in the mirror, and a strange woman stared back at her. Her hair was matted, her cheekbones protruded sharply, and her eyes were rimmed in red. Larissa touched her hair, and the woman in the mirror did the same. "*Bózhe Mói,* dear God," she thought, "I am an old woman!" She felt faint.

It was quiet in the house. All the young people were at work, and the only man on duty at the house was in the garden planting tulips. He saw her through the window and grinned, glad to see her up.

Larissa tried to gather her thoughts. None of them were clear, except one that throbbed in her head—*Andrei was executed.* That frightening phrase floated in her mind as if it were a rudderless boat rising up on a wave and disappearing into the deep, rising up, and disappearing—*Andrei was executed* ...

Andrei was gone from her life. Gone forever ... *executed* ... Gone ... She would never see him again. Her child would grow up without ever knowing her father, without *ever* sitting on his lap ...

The thought of her daughter shook her up. "Nina must be with me. Nina must *always* be with me! There is no one to protect Nina but me ... We must leave Odessa. We must go back to Petrograd, to Mama. She will know what to do ... But my Andrei ... *executed*, probably by a shot to his head, his hands tied behind his back, his blood everywhere ..." Squeezing her temples with both hands, Larissa screamed.

The young orderly heard her. He dropped his tulip bulbs and ran into the house. "What happened?" he cried.

"Where is my daughter?" Larissa shouted.

"She is fine. She is with Akim and his wife! Don't you remember?"

"No, I *don't* remember. Yes, I remember ... I am all confused. ... Where is Glafíra? Where is everyone? Who are you?" she continued to shout.

"I am Victor, an orderly. I played *balaláika* for your daughter when she danced. Remember?"

Larissa squeezed her eyes and a slow smile spread over her emaciated face as the fog in her head began to lift. "Yes, now I remember. You are Victor and you played balalaika! So, you say Nínochka is with Akim? That's good. He is her Godfather, did you know? And he loves her."

"We all *love* her," Victor said. "When I have children of my own, I want them to be like Nínochka!"

She smiled appreciatively, her pulse slowing. "Thank you, Victor. You are very kind," she said in her modulated upper class voice.

"I'll call the Commissar," Victor said. He helped her to the chair.

"Tell her to bring back Nínochka. I am alright now," she said, but as she said it, that cursed word *executed* flashed through her mind like lightning.

Larissa tried to brush her long hair without success. It was hopelessly snarled, impossible to untangle. She retrieved the scissors from her sewing basket and without hesitation chopped her hair to a crooked uneven length just above her shoulders.

A short piece of red ribbon with gold edges at the bottom of her sewing basket caught her attention. It was a spare replacement ribbon for Andrei's Order of St. Anne. Andrei's Order ... She quickly put back the scissors and closed the basket. She could not look at it.

Facing herself in the mirror, she thought that she looked like some thin adolescent boy out of a Shakespeare play. She made her way to the kitchen and tried to light the stove to warm some water for washing her remaining hair, but her hands shook violently. She had to call Victor for help.

"What have you done!" he exclaimed, coming into the kitchen "You chopped off your hair!"

"It was just a nuisance."

"I bet your husband won't like it when he sees it. Men *like* long hair!"

"He'll never see it. My husband is ... is dead," she said, avoiding the dreaded word.

"Oh my God! I did not know ... I'm so sorry!" He made the sign of the cross, he a godless Communist! Awkwardly moving around her as if she were made of some breakable substance, he lit the kerosene stove and placed a large pot of water on it. "I talked to the Commissar. She will bring Nínochka in her automobile."

"Nínochka will love it!" A shadow of a smile crossed Larissa's face.

"Are you hungry?" Victor asked. "What a stupid question! We are *hungry* all the time!" He was at a loss as to how to speak to someone who had lost her husband. "The Commissar left two eggs to feed you when you are ready. I can make you a fried egg and save another one for tomorrow."

"Wonderful! But let me first wash up. As I've noticed, we still don't have running water. If you don't mind, bring a laundry basin into my room, and a bucket of hot water. I'll wash in three parts to save water. First hair, then body, then feet."

"That's how the *soldiers* in the trenches used to do it!" Victor said.

"Now *we* are in the trenches," she replied.

Glafíra carried sleeping Nínochka into the room just as Larissa finished combing her short hair.

"What have you done to yourself!" she exclaimed, placing the sleeping child on her lap. "Why did you cut your hair?"

"Because I wanted to look like a modern Soviet woman! Short hair and red kerchief. And a dangling cigarette. And a few swear words. Boots would help, and spitting on the floor, also." Larissa joked, but it did not sound funny to neither of them.

"Don't you *ever* say anything like that," Glafíra said, alarmed.

"Sorry. My hair was impossible to comb, all matted like a horsehair blanket. The only solution was to cut it short."

Nínochka stirred on her lap and opened her eyes. She looked at her mother, not recognizing her. She stretched her arms toward Glafíra.

"Aren't you glad to see me?" Larissa asked, stung by her reaction. "I am your Mama!"

"No you are not." Nínochka looked at Glafíra. "Auntie Glásha, pick me up!"

"She *is* your Mama! Look closer!" Glafíra said.

"She is a nice Auntie but she is not *my* Mama!" Nínochka said stubbornly. She tried to wiggle out of Larissa's arms. "Let me go, Auntie!"

Larissa broke out in desperate tears. She released her daughter, but the child remained sitting on her lap, staring at her. Suddenly Nínochka exclaimed, "Mama! You *are* my Mama! Don't cry Mámochka, don't cry! I love you, don't cry!" She began to wipe Larissa's tears with her little hands, smudging her face with dirt. "Don't cry. I know you're my Mama, I *know* it!"

It wasn't easy to save money for the train tickets to Petrograd. Larissa's salary was small and allowed her to save only kopeks and not rubles.

To help, Glafíra tried to appoint her to the vacated position of Chief Nurse. She suggested it at the meeting of the Executive Committee of the hospital. "Nurse Rezánova is well qualified for that position. She was trained by our former Chief Nurse Veronica. The entire staff likes her. I collected petitions from the young aides and nurses who know her even better by living in the same house. They also recommended her for that position."

The Executive Committee was unmoved. "Nurse Rezánova may be an excellent nurse but she is from the *former class* and she can't be placed in the position of authority. We don't trust those people. We'll allow her remain where she is as a regular staff nurse, but should we have a *proletarian* nurse apply for a position, Rezánova will be fired." That was that.

Maria Nikoláyevna was only slightly more successful in raising money for the trip. She sold several pieces of jewelry through Frósya, but the money became practically worthless because of debilitating inflation. People were dealing now in denominations of *millions* instead of twenties or hundreds. It was hard to comprehend that a pair of felt *válenki* now cost over a *million* rubles. But by summer Maria Nikoláyevna had scraped up enough money for an adult and a child ticket for third class travel to Petrograd. With the help of Commissar Dimka, who had telegraphed the money to Commissar Glafíra, she was assured that the money would reach her daughter.

But an even more difficult problem still remained unsolved—obtaining the permits for Larissa and the child to leave Odessa, and another permit to enter Petrograd for a visit. The permit to stay permanently in Petrograd would be taken care of when Larissa arrived. Dimka promised that he would take care of it.

Larissa applied to the Cheka for permission to visit her elderly mother in Petrograd. She sweated over the lengthy questionnaire and with help from Glafíra answered the most dangerous questions about her and her parents' occupations.

There was no trouble with her own occupation: she was a nurse. With the advice from Glafíra, she wrote that her father was a soldier. "He was a general, wasn't he? Well, generals are soldiers." Glafíra said to classify her mother as a 'housewife,' but the most difficult question about social origin stumped even Glafíra. The accepted social origins were *Peasants, Workers,* or *Meschánins,* the city proletarians. None of these categories applied to Larissa or her parents.

Finally, Glafíra thought that she had found the solution. "There is a space that says *'other.'* Of course it would be a death sentence to write *nobility,* but why not write *Educated Citizen*? It will be the truth. It will suggest to them that you are a smart person, just the kind that the Communists encourage to join them. They already know that you are a *working nurse*. I think, it will be acceptable.

"But what if it is *not* acceptable?"

"Then we'll think of something else," Glafíra said optimistically, not sure herself that the Cheka would accept that new category of social origin.

For weeks Larissa waited for a reply from the Cheka, and when she finally received an official letter, she was disappointed. It informed her that her request was under consideration and that she would be notified about the decision in due time.

"Don't despair," Glafíra advised. "At least there was no order for you to visit their offices to *explain* your answers!"

Several more weeks passed. Autumn was in its first colorful glory. Larissa watched Nínochka run happily in the garden each day, gathering heaps of falling leaves then throwing them up into the air, laughing if any of them fell on her head.

There was no word from the authorities. Glafíra tried to explain it by saying that the new bureaucracy hadn't yet learned how to be efficient. "They are too busy hunting spies and saboteurs," she said. "Granting permission to travel must be the last on their lists of what to do!" It seemed to be a poor excuse, but there was nothing that anyone could do about it. So Larissa waited, worrying now about arriving in Petrograd during winter. She had no clothing for Nínochka or for herself that was suitable for Petrograd's biting winters.

Christmas arrived and Akim invited Larissa and Glafíra to spend it at his little house, not yet confiscated. He was going to have a forbidden Christmas celebration and have little gifts for the children. Akim had five children by now. The older boy, seven-year-old Kólya, was the only one who had ever seen a Christmas tree.

Akim cut down a small fir tree outside the city, breaking two laws simultaneously—cutting a tree on public property and having a religious celebration. If caught, he would have faced a stiff prison sentence if not a firing squad.

Akim had been planning his Christmas celebration for months. Since it was impossible to buy Christmas decorations anymore, he made his own. He collected the silver linings of the boxed cigarettes used by the sailors of the foreign merchant ships visiting Odessa. By December he had a sizable batch of neat shiny golden squares that he sliced into four strips each, to make links for a long chain to be hung on his tree.

He whittled out of chunks of wood the figures of the Snow Maiden and Grandfather Frost, and various animals: dogs, cats, horses, and birds. His wife decorated them with colors from an artist's paint box pilfered from an art supply store and forgotten by a thief in Akim's carriage.

He was especially proud of the large five-pointed star for the top of his tree. Risking his very life he broke it off the pole of a communist flag at the railroad station. He repainted the star gold and put it on the top of the Christmas tree.

Glafíra also took a great risk when she rearranged the silk red ribbon around the portrait of Lenin in the hospital. The ribbon was just right for a bow for Nínochka! Glafíra shortened it by enough length to make one great bow for Nínochka and two smaller ones for Comrade Lenin. No one knew the difference. She was also able to get a bit of flour, sugar, and butter to make the Christmas *kréndel*, a large sweet bread in the form of a giant pretzel decorated with raisins and almonds.

On Christmas Eve, Akim picked up Larissa and Nínochka and then Glafíra at the corner of Deribasovskaya Street. He almost missed her. He had never seen Glafíra wearing women's clothing.

Nínochka could barely contain herself with excitement. She was going to a party! She was wearing a new dress! Her mother had made it out of her old batiste nightgown edged with lace and narrow ribbons. She had new shoes! Uncle Akim had made them from his leather driving gloves, and the best of all, Auntie Glásha tied a new big red bow on her head!

Akim's three little girls gathered around Nínochka. She felt very beautiful turning this way and that to allow everybody to admire her finery.

"Already vain!" Larissa smiled, watching her daughter. "Was I that way also when I was four?" She could not recall. She remembered only that her father had given her a pony for Christmas, but her friend, eight-year-old Andrúsha Rezánov, mounted the pony at once and would not let her ride it. "You are too *young* to ride," he had told her. *That* she remembered!

Her Andrúsha … She felt tears welling up in her eyes.

Glafíra and Akim both noticed. They knew what she was thinking. Glafíra quickly turned to Nínochka. "Sing a song for us! You look so pretty! Like a fairy princess!"

"All right," Nínochka nodded regally. "I'll sing and dance for you about the snowflakes. Mama, sing with me!" Larissa smiled through her gathering tears but began the simple melody: *"We are snowflakes and we came down to you from that dark cloud above ..."* Nínochka picked up the melody and began to swirl around, pointing above her head to the imaginary cloud. "Dance with me!" she invited Akim's little girls to join her. "Do what I do! Pretend that you are flying!"

The adults, forgetting for a moment the bitter reality, watched the four malnourished, tow-headed little girls as they danced around the tree. "They are like little angels," Akim's wife whispered and brushed away a tear.

The feast that followed was joined by the local old priest who had baptized all the children. He brought a small bunch of church tapers for the tree, which made it even more festive. More guests and their children came bringing a couple of bottles of vodka and some gifts—pickled cucumbers and a loaf of bread.

It was the first time that Larissa participated in the Cossacks' celebration. One of Akim's buddies brought a large accordion, and the party grew even livelier. Nínochka and her friends performed their dance again and again to the applause of the guests, until the men took over the floor and danced the *komárinskaya*, a tricky peasant dance in a squatting position, throwing one's legs in front of oneself. Finally, Akim's wife joined the male dancers, sailing demurely among them with a white kerchief in her upturned arm, her feet moving in tiny steps, making it look as if she were floating among the whirling dervishes.

Despite her sadness, Larissa was enchanted with her daughter's participation in the festivities. The child showed no shyness. She danced and sang and counted up to twenty-five demonstrating how smart she was. She begged Akim to make her a crown from the gold cigarette papers, and she wore it proudly in addition to her red bow as she finally dozed on her mother's lap, clutching the wooden Snow Maiden from the tree, Akim's Christmas gift.

87

The first two weeks of the New Year of 1922 were even more difficult for Larissa. She became aware that her job at the hospital was in jeopardy. No one had mentioned it, but she felt that a certain chasm had suddenly appeared between her and the other employees. Apparently, Andrei's execution had become known to everyone. People discussed it behind Larissa's back, and as the widow of an *executed* officer, she became a marked woman.

The old employees of Memorial Hospital liked Larissa. They remembered how she and Maria Nikoláyevna came to Odessa to take care of the dying lieutenant. They were of the upper class, of course, but they were respectful. They were always polite.

To the new *communist* personnel of the hospital, Larissa was the enemy, not to be trusted, and she felt the hostility. She mentioned it to Glafíra, who agreed. Glafíra felt that the new personnel also disliked *her*. The men resented her powerful position, while the women ridiculed her fat body and Asiatic eyes. The new nurses laughed behind her back calling her a 'pumpkin in uniform,' speculating about her love life since no one had ever seen her with a man. But soon it wasn't enough. Soon her *friendship* with Larissa became the subject of their suspicions. A rumor began to spread that Larissa and Glafíra were lesbians.

The young nurses and orderlies living in the same communal house were constantly questioned about the two women, but the young people refused to spread the lie. The punishment for homosexuality was severe—several years of incarceration—and so they defended them against the rumors. But the others at the hospital refused to accept the truth. The idea was much too juicy to abandon.

Larissa still had no permission to travel to Petrograd. She felt that the sword of Damocles was hanging over her head. The hostility of some employees was so strong that she knew it would end with her being fired.

In March a local one-day extraordinary Congress of the Black Sea Commissars was scheduled to take place in Odessa. Glafíra looked forward to it, although deep in her heart she was scared. She did not know what was going to be discussed at the congress—the political success of the Communists, or the famine that still tormented the country, or even the peasant uprisings here and there. Glafíra hoped that there would be no investigations of the administrations of local institutions. She had to protect herself from such an investigation. She had raided the hospital's pharmacy and storage rooms for months to exchange for food. What if the Congress chose to investigate the hospital?

Days before the Congress, Glafíra stayed late at her office going over the lists of medical supplies used during Doctor Shubin's and nurse Veronica's tenure. The storage shelves were now almost empty. To cover her pilfering, she burned the lists. She inserted a postdated note in her files that most of old the pre-revolutionary medications were confiscated or destroyed during the invasions of Odessa by hostile troops. They were never replaced, although there had been requests on several occasions. She included copies of three requests to the Commissariat of Health.

That was all she could do to protect herself, she thought. She hoped it would work.

The Congress was to take place at the Opera Theatre. The building was cleaned from top to bottom by an army of 'volunteers' who were ordered to give up their Saturday and work without pay. The Opera Theatre was decorated with red flags inside and out, and a huge portrait of Lenin at the top of the grand staircase replaced the one of the Tsar that had hung there for decades.

The Commissars began to gather at the Grand Foyer for registration. It looked as if they were clones of one another, all attired in leather jackets, riding breeches and knee-high boots, all carrying guns on their hips. There were a few women, but they too, wore men's leather clothing and guns.

Glafíra was dressed like everyone else, but she felt uncomfortable in this crowd. She wished she could disappear in the leather-clad mass, but her peculiar round figure attracted curiosity instead.

"Hey, Gláshka!" she suddenly heard. She turned around. A tall man with a small beard cut in a fashionable goatee, like Lenin's, grinned at her. "Don't you recognize me? I am Igor Kóshkin, formerly the Commissar of Alexander Kozakov's Detachment! I was the Commissar of Lieutenant Rezánov and Captain Egórov who, I think, were your friends. Do you remember me now?"

"Yes! Now I *do* remember you! Are you still the big boss over the pilots?"

"I am in Sevastópol now. I am the Commissar of the Black Sea Naval Aviation Group."

"Very impressive," she said.

"And you?"

"Still at the same hospital."

"You probably know that Rezánov was shot down."

"He was *executed*," she corrected. "His name was included in the official lists. His wife is a nurse at my hospital."

"Larissa? I don't remember her patronymic." An image of Larissa appeared before his mind's eye. "I used to be smitten by her," he thought. "She was a beauty!" he said instead.

"She still is. And her little girl …"

"So, she is a widow with a small child? Where is *her* mother? Still in Odessa?" I remember she was a formidable woman."

"She is in Petrograd, and Larissa is trying to get back to her. So far without success."

"It will be a long time before people like her will be allowed to travel. Can't you, a Commissar, help her to get the proper documents?"

"I am not important enough."

He laughed. "I have some connections in Petrograd. As a matter of fact, I might even move there myself. *Maybe* I can help. Let's get together after the meeting. You can take me to her, if you know where she lives. I would like to see her."

"We live in the same house. We are friends."

"Great! I'll bring some wine …"

"Better bring some *bread*."

"Is it *that* bad in Odessa?"

"Yes."

"I'll bring some food," he said. "Meet you right here, after the meeting."

The meeting was long and tedious. Igor Kóshkin must have become a very important man, for he was sitting on the stage at a long conference table covered with red cloth. Twelve people were seated at the table, including a woman, who was presiding.

"Who is she?" Glafíra asked a man sitting next to her.

"*Zemlyáchka*. She is a big shot," he replied. "I don't know her real name, but she is very powerful."

Zemlyáchka stood and ordered people in the audience to take their seats.

One by one the men around the table introduced themselves and their organizations, proclaiming their loyalty to the Communist Party and Comrade Lenin. Their speeches were almost as identical as their attire. Only Igor Kóshkin's was different. He simply said: "I am Commissar

Igor Kóshkin and I bring you the greetings from the pilots of the Black Sea Naval Aviation Group," and sat down.

"Is that *all?*" Zemlyáchka asked him sarcastically.

"For a while—yes," he replied evenly. The audience laughed, but Zemlyáchka scowled at him.

The meeting continued. Zemlyáchka took the floor - literally. She marched in front of the table and began a long harangue against the *former people.*

"The loathsome Tsarist vipers are still active. It is your duty as Communists to get rid of them once and for all. They are everywhere, hiding from the proletarian justice. Some of them are pretending to be workers or peasants. Why, just recently, my colleagues and I came upon such a nest. We were on our way to Odessa, when a bunch of Whites dressed as peasants attacked us. They stopped the train with a barricade and peppered us with machine gun fire while we had only our side arms. I myself shot one of the leaders with this gun!" She slapped her hand on her holstered gun. "Yes, comrades, I shot him, point blank! We *knew* who they were! Despite the fact that they were dressed like peasants, they failed to fool us!" She laughed harshly. "I shot that son-of-a-bitch, disguised as a peasant, and we discovered that he was a *fighter pilot!* He was heading for Odessa on a *furlough.* What kind of *furlough* would a peasant need?" She spat on the floor.

Glafíra trembled. She realized that Zemlyáchka was talking about Andrei.

Zemlyáchka's call for proletarian vigilance was met with long applause. One by one the deputies rose to their feet to denounce the *former people.* Finally, Zemlyáchka called for a vote on a resolution to get rid of all *former people* immediately, suggesting their liquidation as a class.

The resolution was adopted unanimously without any abstentions.

Glafíra met Kóshkin in the foyer. "Do you want to go now? I have my car," she said.

"Oho! A car! Fine! But let's stop first at my hotel. I have some tins of condensed milk and sausages, some chocolates and good coffee. And white bread with raisins."

"Dear me! White bread with raisins! I forgot that such luxury had ever existed! Where did you get that stuff?"

"In Sevastópol. We receive food packages from America. The Americans seem to be sympathetic to us, welcoming our revolution, calling it democratic. They are debating in their Congress special shipments of food for Russian children."

"Good. It might save millions of lives!" She changed the subject. "Nínochka will be so happy with a piece of chocolate! I don't believe that she has ever tasted it."

"Who's *Nínochka?*"

"Larissa's daughter. She is almost five, and she has never seen her father. The Lieutenant was away all these years. He saw the baby only when she was born. And not since."

"It's tough!" Kóshkin said. "How did Larissa take Andrei's death?"

"Very badly. She was seriously ill. Nínochka finally pulled her out of her depression. But what will happen to her now? We'll have to fire her on account that she is a *former person.*"

"She must return to Petrograd.'

"It's easy to say! But how? I've tried to get her a permit to leave Odessa, but no luck. Larissa is a fine person, a good nurse, even though she is not a proletarian. I love her as if she were my sister."

Kóshkin twisted his moustache, thinking. "I will help her," he said finally,with a slight smile. "Meanwhile, try to keep her employed for as long as possible so that she can continue to receive her ration coupons. But I'll get her to Petrograd!"

She grabbed his hand and looked into his eyes. "Thank you, Comrade Kóshkin!"

"Call me Igor."

Larissa was on duty at the hospital, and Nínochka was being watched by Liza, a nursing aid. Liza was peeling potatoes while Nínochka labored over a drawing, her tongue sticking out in concentration.

Kóshkin stared at the child through the window of the house. She looked cherubic, except that she had no baby plumpness. She was malnourished, thin and pale, her blond hair almost silvery. Observing her, he felt a sudden surge of tenderness.

"Auntie Glásha! Look what I have drawn!" the little girl exclaimed as Glafíra opened the door. "It is a house!" Noticing Kóshkin, she placed her drawing behind her back, looking embarrassed.

"This man is your Mama's old friend."

Nínochka curtsied, holding her skirt with two fingers.

"What's your name?" Kóshkin asked with a wide grin.

"Nina Rezánova" she said formally. "What's yours?"

"Igor Kóshkin," he replied, placing his box on the table and making a bow as if he were a gentleman from some French comedy. "At your service!"

Nina giggled. "You can't be *Kóshkin*! *Kóshki*, cats, have *kittens*, not real *boys*!"

"Well, my Mama must have been a special *magic kóshka* and she had me, instead!" he said with a smile. "Will you show me your picture?"

She proffered him her drawing. "It's a house. For me and my Mama." she said.

"A beautiful house!" he exclaimed, looking at a lopsided house with screws of smoke coming out of the crooked chimney.

An impish look appeared on her thin little face. "I can draw you and your mama, if you want to live in that house!" she said, taking back the drawing.

"All right!"

"Here!" she exclaimed in a little while. "This *kóshka* is your Mama, and you are her kitten!" She handed the drawing to him. "Your Mama is the bigger one."

"She looks exactly right," he said seriously. "Mamas and Papas are always bigger than their children."

"I don't have a Papa. He is in heaven flying in his airplane and watching that nothing bad happens to me and Mama."

Kóshkin felt a spasm in his throat.

Glafíra carried the boxes of food to her office to lock them in her safe. She felt sorry for her hungry housemates, but she was not going to share with them the bounty from America. It was for Nínochka and Larissa and perhaps a little for herself: a bit of coffee with condensed milk and a slice of raisin bread, and the same for Kóshkin.

"I want to save as much as possible for Nínochka. She worries me. There is so little for her to eat, just potatoes and a little bread. Fortunately, Akim is her proxy Godfather. He brings one egg and a small bottle of goat milk each day, but it's not enough for a growing child," she said.

"Who's Akim?"

"An invalid Cossack. Our horse cab driver. He and his wife share their limited food with Nínochka even though they have five young children themselves. They are truly kind people!"

"So, Larissa is quite *democratic*, eh? Having a cab driver as a Godfather for her high-born child!" Igor said sarcastically. "How *low* the mighty have fallen!"

Glafíra's eyes narrowed. "Don't be an idiot! Neither Andrei nor Larissa were ever *mighty*. Neither was Egórov. They were fine young people—liberals who welcomed the abdication of the Tsar!"

"Don't talk about those two. I trusted them, but they almost caused me to be court-martialed!"

"Well, I don't know anything about their escaping, but Andrei and Egórov were decent men, more honorable than any of our men who execute people without even asking for their name! Like that whore Zemlyáchka!"

"Lower your voice! As for me—I used to be their admirer also. I *envied* them their education, their good looks ... Even the way they sat a horse!" he said. *"And I envied Andrei his Larissa!"* he thought to himself.

There was a sound of a key turning at the front door. Glafíra led Kóshkin into the dining room. Through the open double door, Kóshkin could see Larissa entering the house accompanied by a limping man in a Cossack hat. Nínochka ran into the hall and hid behind the coats.

"Where is my little snowflake?" the Cossack shouted from the door. He pretended to look around the coat rack where Nínochka was hiding. "I am going to find you!"

"No you won't!" she laughed, jumping out from behind the coats. "Grrr," she growled. "I am a bear! I'll eat you up!"

"Help!" Akim cried, limping into the kitchen, Nínochka in hot pursuit, growling behind him.

Glafíra smiled. "Larissa, we have a visitor. Someone you know. Igor Kóshkin."

"Kóshkin? Andrei's Commissar?"

"One and the same!" he said. "Glad to see you again, Comrade Rezánova!" He could see that she did not like being called *'comrade.'* "May I call you Larissa?"

"Please do", she replied dryly.

He swallowed hard, absorbing her disdain. "I was told that you are having some difficulty in getting permits for going back to Petrograd. I can help you, if you wish," he said smiling, trying to disarm her obvious hostility. "Just let me know when you want to leave!"

Her lovely face softened. "I am ready now!"

"I understand," he smiled. "But realistically?"

"As soon as possible. In two weeks? I have to buy some winter clothes for my daughter and myself."

"I can help you with that as well. Just tell me what you need and you'll have it within a few days! And it will cost you nothing! The American Red Cross will be happy to oblige you!"

She looked doubtful.

"He is serious," Glafíra said, reading her thoughts. "He is a big shot now."

"How can you perform such magic?" Larissa asked.

"Because his mama is a *magic cat!*" Nínochka shouted from Akim's shoulders as he burst into the dining room. "He told me so!"

"That I did! My mother was the famous Russian Grey." They all laughed.

Back at his hotel Kóshkin thought of Larissa. It broke his heart to see her so sad, with her hair chopped short, her luscious body gaunt, those beautiful dark eyes seeming even larger on her thin face. He could see that she was worn out. He wondered how long she would last under the present circumstances, with the ever-present fear that all people of her class must be suffering. The Cheká was vigilant in pursuing its mandate.

He was glad that there were such people as Glafíra and Akim who cared for Larissa, but they were not completely safe themselves. He was sure that Glafíra would soon be replaced by some ambitious Commissar. Her looks alone were not a good representation of an iron-willed communist ideologue. As for Akim—well, as a former Cossack he was already a potential candidate for liquidation.

No, they were not secure enough themselves to save Larissa and her child.

Going to the starvation-chocked Petrograd was not a good solution, either, he thought, but he realized that being with her mother was the best possible option for Larissa and her daughter ... and for him. "I'll get her to Petrograd," he thought, "And then, I'll marry her!"

88

Koshkin's infatuation with Larissa had flared up anew, but with a deeper feeling of tenderness and pity. "She must be no more than twenty-four," he thought. "And she looks so … so wasted! As if her life was over!"

It was a happy coincidence that on his last trip to Petrograd he was offered the position of Commissar at First Socialist Flight School, formerly the Gátchina Flight School. It would certainly be an advancement in his career, but he wasn't sure whether he would like to move from the sunny Crimea to frozen Petrograd. Now—he knew what his answer would be: he would be happy to accept the offer and relocate to Petrograd with his wife and a small child.

With his decision to marry Larissa firm in his mind, he needed help from Glafíra and Akim. They should convince Larissa to trust him. In order to provide her with the permits to travel to Petrograd and to remain there, it was necessary to create a new biography for her. She had to pretend that they were married and Nínochka was his child.

As for the *real* marriage—it was too early to raise the subject with Larissa.

He telephoned Glafíra and asked to meet with her and Akim.

Kóshkin described his plan. Glafíra was ready to help, but Akim was more cautious.

"You and Larissa are political enemies. Don't forget that. Your people destroyed her life. Wasn't it *you* from whom Andrei and Egórov were escaping? You would have had them shot if they were caught, isn't it true?"

Kóshkin hesitated with the answer. "True," he finally said. "But it was in the middle of the war and …"

"Of course … blame the war. But *your* people executed Andrei when the war was *over*. Larissa would never forgive you, a Red Commissar!"

"Then, how can I help her if she *hates* me?" Kóshkin exclaimed.

Glafíra sighed. "Use Nínochka. For her sake, Larissa will accept any deal," said Glafíra. She felt as though she were betraying Larissa, and the memory of Andrei, in some way. But without Kóshkin's help, Larissa's future was bleak. "With our help, she will accept your plan. She is no fool. She is Maria Nikoláyevna's daughter!"

"That she is," Akim nodded. "But be *honest* with her from the start. Lay your cards on the table and tell her the truth of her desperate situation. Pretending to be married to you would involve acting like a wife, including sleeping in the same bed … And of course Nínochka *must* call you Papa".

"This probably will sting her more than anything," Glafíra said thoughtfully. "But it must be done! Akim is right: tell her the *truth*. She is a strong woman, even though she seems so fragile. She will make the right decision. Of course, you too, will have to pretend to be her husband and treat her accordingly." Glafíra eyed him seriously.

"It won't be hard!" he laughed. He almost told them that he had been infatuated with Larissa from the moment he had seen her photograph years ago. He remembered vividly how he had envied Andrei for possessing such a beauty. Yes, he would have ordered to shoot the White pilots, the bastards who believed that it was their born privilege to be well-educated, have no lack of money, and have such beautiful women. He remembered how bitterly he had *envied* Andrei! Actually, how he *hated* him!

He controlled himself. "The tables are turned now! I will have Larissa!" he thought.

That evening Kóshkin arrived at the Moldovanka house. Glafíra was alone with Nínochka, working on official reports in her room. Nínochka played on the floor at her feet, building a tower with domino tiles.

Glafíra let Kóshkin in.

"Uncle Kóshkin!" Nínochka cried in delight, jumping up and upsetting her construction. "See what you have made me do? You are a *bad puss!*" she shook her finger at him.

"*Meow!* I am so sorry!" he apologized. "I'll never do it again!"

"See that you don't! Or you'll have to stand in the corner!"

"Oh, no!" he cried in pretended horror.

Nínochka laughed. "I was just joking!"

"I brought you something, if you are a good girl," he said.

"I *am* a good girl, ask Auntie Glásha! What is it?"

He pulled a small package from his pocket. "Help me unwrap it and you'll see."

Glafíra passed him the scissors. He snipped the strings tying the package and invited Nínochka to tear off the heavy wrapping paper. She tried, but the butcher paper was too tough for her little hands.

"I can't do it. I am just a little girl," she said with a sigh.

He was enchanted. "Let's do it together! I'll tear it open and you pick up the paper. Alright?"

She nodded. "Alright."

He tore off the wrapping paper, and she dutifully pushed it off the table. A securely sealed carton box was before them. "What should I do now? How can we open it?" he asked.

"You must use scissors," she said.

"Yes! Of course! Oh, you are so *smart!*" Quickly he cut through the sealing tape, Nínochka watching him closely. "What do you think is inside? And what would you *want* to be inside?"

"Toys!" she said without hesitation.

"Oh, *hell!* I should've thought of it!" he thought. "No, not this time, but if you are a good girl and promise to wait patiently, maybe the next time …"

"I promise," she interrupted. "I'll wait!"

"And now I'll show you what I have *just for you!* Close your eyes!" She closed her eyes as he took out a small flat box and extracted a bar of Hershey's chocolates. "Open your eyes, it's for you!"

She had never seen chocolate before and was not impressed. "What is it?

"Take off the paper, smell the bar, and then, bite it," Glafíra said. "It's candy!"

Nínochka did as she was told, and a happy smile spread over her thin face. "I like it! I like it very much! Thank you, Uncle …"

"Call him Papa! You can pretend that he is your Papa and you are his little girl, just like you pretend to be a snowflake for your Uncle Akim!" Glafíra said.

"Or, how I pretend to be a butterfly for the people in our house!" Nínochka added.

"You won't need to pretend to be anything for me! You are *my every-thing!*" Larissa said, entering the room.

"Mámochka! Look what Papa brought me! It's candy! Try a little piece, you'll like it!"

Larissa tried not to flinch. It was painful to hear, but it was necessary. It was one of the conditions. She was loath to think of another one, which was yet to come: sharing a bed with Kóshkin. Both Glafíra and Akim agreed that he was the *only* person who could arrange her return to Petrograd. What was more, it had to be done quickly.

Glafíra had shown her the new secret mandate to all Commissars in Odessa to eradicate the *former people.* "It isn't safe for you to remain in Odessa. Any day now the Cheka will begin the purge. Igor Kóshkin is willing to save you and Nínochka. You shouldn't object to the conditions of your rescue. It is your *only* chance to save yourself and Nínochka!" Glafíra declared.

Larissa had to agree.

Three days later Kóshkin returned to the Moldovanka house. It was still early in the morning, and he waited in the back garden until only Glafíra remained in the house. He knocked on the kitchen window, gesturing to open the back door.

"Good morning!" he said, opening his leather portfolio. "I brought all the documents necessary for Larissa and Nina. Both of them now bear my name. I used Larissa's maiden name in her new papers for obvious reasons, but kept Petrograd as her place of birth. It will qualify her to get permission to remain there, in case anything happens to me. Nowadays no one is completely safe."

"How true! What else will she need now, aside from money?"

"She will need some documents about her employment. Can you get me some blank official forms for employment used by the hospital? My forger can fill them in. We can change her name in your files as well, or even better: we can *destroy* your files pertaining to Larissa."

"That is better. If *all* the files are destroyed, not only Larissa's—it would be much safer. Less suspicious."

"Fine!" Kóshkin said. "Then my men will pretend to be some ordinary city bandits. They will *confiscate* your typewriter and vandalize your offices, remove all your personnel records, and burn them. That's a good plan, easy to stage!"

She agreed, thinking that such a burglary may even cover her pilfering of the hospital supplies.

"I'll be back tomorrow with some clothes. My men are coming from Sevastópol with clothes from the *American* Red Cross."

"Those capitalists are very generous with their gifts! I wonder how long will they continue to be so friendly," Glafíra said with a sarcastic smile.

"I know what you mean. As soon as they hear our new slogan, *"Catch up and overtake America!"* they'll sing a different song! We'll challenge their oppression of the working class. Their workers will rise and join us in our fight for the World Revolution! Then *we'll* be sending *them* food packages!"

89

In a few more days everything was ready for their departure. The documents were authenticated by the authorities, including a fake marriage certificate from the no longer functioning church. There were also new certificates for Nínochka's birth and christening.

"It feels as though my whole life has been wiped out," Larissa thought. "Who am I? Who was my father? I am suddenly Larissa Koshkina ..." The plebeian name stung her pride. "How long will I have to live under that stupid name? Will my child be able to use her real name?" She pestered Glafíra with questions to which Glafíra kept saying not to worry, just think of reaching Petrograd.

"I suppose she is right," Larissa thought. "But I would like to have my original documents," she told Glafíra. "How can I get them?"

Glafíra shook her head. "I don't know. I suppose you can ask Igor about it. Be honest with him. Tell him that you would like to keep yours and Nínochka's surnames once the emergency situation ceases to exist. I think he'll understand."

Larissa was doubtful. She felt that Kóshkin was motivated by something more than the Quixotic tradition of helping a maiden in distress. She could feel his suppressed desire just as she had felt it with Egórov. She had always known that *she* was that married woman, the object of Egórov's secret passion.

Kóshkin's reaction to her request was swift and brutal.

"I broke my ass trying to help you! I am risking my *life!*" he yelled, his face turning red. "You want your surname back? All right, I'll give back your damn old documents, and I'll bail out of your life! See how *far* you will go! If your name means so much to you, go ahead, be my guest!" he reached inside his portfolio and fished out a stack of papers. "Here!" he threw them into her face. The papers spread over her chest and slid on the floor. "Just think of what will happen to you and your daughter!"

Larissa was frightened. She hadn't expected such an immediate hostile change. She suddenly wondered if she had been wrong to go along with Igor's scheme. "I'm sorry," she protested timidly. "I just thought ..."

"No need to explain. I *know* what you thought. And I tell you what *I* thought: I thought only of *fucking* you. But I also wanted to *marry* you and be a *real* father to your child. That's what *I* thought! So, you decide, what will it be: If you are ashamed of me and my proletarian origins, so be it. I'll leave you alone. I'll leave you this minute!"

Larissa was sobbing. "No! I'm not ashamed of you," she began between the sobs, "I just don't know how I can—"

"Save your Nínka by yourself in this meat-grinding century? You can't. I am here to help," he said softly now, his anger gone at the sight of her tears but a steely edge still in his voice. "I promise, I won't talk to you about marriage. I know, it's too soon for you. But I'll *sleep* with you, Larka, of that you can be sure!"

She noticed that he had called her and Nina in the peasants' way of adding '*ka*' to the stem of their names. It could be used as an expression of familiarity among good friends, but also could mean disdain. It was used by military men as a sign of camaraderie, as between Egórov and Andrei, but never among polite society. Now—she and her daughter became Larka and Nínka, as if they were peasants. She felt tears gather in her eyes again, but she said quietly, "No, you stay, Igor. I *do* need you. Please, forgive my outburst."

"Don't mention it!" he exclaimed, cheerful again. "I happen to hate *your* social origins as much as you hate *mine*, it's true, but I am willing to ignore them. It's not our faults that your father was a general and mine a poor priest. You and I can be friends and save our Nínka and each other. Smile!" he said, picking up the documents and stuffing them back into his portfolio.

Larissa was still afraid, deeply afraid, but she tried to smile a little. "You must be a *good* man, Igor Kóshkin!"

"Oho! You'll be pleasantly surprised!" He winked lewdly.

Once more Larissa felt revulsion but made an effort not to show it. "I'll have to tolerate him only for a few days, until we reach Petrograd," she thought. "Once he meets my regal mother, he will run from us as fast as his legs can carry him!" But deep in her heart, she knew that her *regal* mother's attitude toward life would be different. Most likely, she had tried to become invisible among the multitude of proletarians who surrounded her now.

They left Odessa on a sunny spring day in March. Riding in Akim's open carriage along broad boulevards surrounded by the innocent glory of spring—when the sticky young buds covering the trees strained to burst open—it was hard to believe that the country was in the grip of devastating famine, its citizens subdued by hunger and fear of arrests and executions.

Larissa thought how much she would miss the Odessa climate. A letter from her mother had reminded her of Petrograd's terrible weather. A series of spring blizzards tormented the city and disrupted transportation. Peasants could not bring food to the city to barter for gold coins or rings with those who still had something left for barter.

Maria Nikoláyevna watched with alarm how her hoard of jewelry was diminishing. She still had Ksusha's vátnik with its own small stash of gold coins sewn into the lining, but it could not be substantial. Ksusha's coins were probably not equal to one of Maria Nikoláyevna's bracelets.

But she felt happy! Larissa and the baby were coming, and everything would be alright. They would be together, at last! She bartered a set of gold earrings for a bag of flour and a small crock of fresh butter with her new friend Daria from the tolkúchka and arranged with Frósya to make cabbage *pirozhki*. She was confused by Larissa's mention of someone named Igor Kóshkin who apparently had arranged her travel permits and was to accompany her. It was good that she was not traveling alone in these dangerous times, but what price had she paid to that *Kóshkin*? Maria Nikoláyevna suspected that Larissa had to pay for her return to Petrograd with her body.

But there was no other way. *"If one lives among the wolves, one must howl like a wolf,"* she thought, quoting the old proverb. "So be it!"

Larissa and Glafíra, sitting side by side in Akim's carriage, held hands. They both regretted the forthcoming parting, realizing that it was most likely forever.

Kóshkin, across from them, mentally recounted the steps to be taken before they reach Petrograd. He would need to warn Larissa about the possibility of delays along the way. And there was always a chance that they might be ambushed by anti-Soviet partisans. Igor was well prepared to defend his family, as he now thought of Larissa and the child. He had two guns fully loaded, and his pockets were bulging with ammunition. In addition, he carried a powerful shotgun in his luggage. He was going to take it out as soon as they left Odessa.

He debated if he should warn Akim of the forthcoming danger to his little enterprise of driving for hire. He had read in a bulletin that a new wave of confiscations was about to begin.

He slapped Akim on his shoulder. "Listen to me, Akimka. Listen carefully." Akim placed Nínochka on his other knee and half-turned toward Kóshkin.

"I am listening."

Kóshkin told him the bad news. "You need to sell your horse and the tack and the carriage immediately. Then, apply to some factory for a job. Take anything that would pay you a salary, even a night watchman. You need to establish yourself as a *working man* to get the proper ration cards for your family. Do it right away. After the fifteenth it will be too late."

"Thank you for the warning," Akim said. "It will be very hard to sell everything in such short time ..."

"Perhaps I might help," Glafíra said. "The hospital needs another vehicle. With the difficulty of obtaining fuel, the Executive Committee has opted to buy a horse and a carriage as an auxiliary ambulance. I shall recommend Akim's horse and whatever goes with it, including the driver!"

"Brilliant idea!" Kóshkin exclaimed. "Do you think the hospital bosses will approve it?"

"I am still the Commissar! They will approve." Glafíra replied archly.

The train waited at the platform, the locomotive breathing like some huge beast surrounded by clouds of white steam, but no people crowded the platform, no porters burdened by baggage scurried around, and no conductors checked the passengers' tickets. Instead, the Cheka agents closely watched everybody.

Larissa felt a squeeze of pain at the pit of her stomach as she watched Igor present their documents to the agent, but the agent just nodded to Kóshkin. "You and your family may board, Comrade Commissar," he said politely.

Larissa and Glafíra, both in tears, kissed, while Akim handed Nínochka to Kóshkin.

"Take good care of them, Comrade Commissar" he said quietly. "Larissa Sergéyevna is a fine person!"

Nínochka watched the little commotion on the platform. "Why everybody is crying? Aren't you coming with us for a ride?" she asked.

"Not this time, my little snowflake," Akim said, wiping his eyes with a tight fist, "Enjoy your ride!"

Glafíra made the sign of the cross over Nínochka. The Cheka agent was startled to see *a Commissar* doing it. Igor smiled at him and said with disdain, "For babas it's hard to forget the old habits!" The agent nodded.

"Well, farewell now. Be well and write to us!" Kóshkin said.

Larissa was speechless. She clung to Akim, then to Glafíra, tears rolling freely over her hollow cheeks. "Goodbye, my dear friends!" she kept repeating. "Goodbye …"

"Why are you crying, Mama? Are we going away? Aren't we coming back?"

"No, my dear, we are going to your Bábushka!" Kóshkin said. "And I have a surprise for you, as soon as the train starts moving!"

"Oh, alright! Let's go then!" She said as Kóshkin helped Larissa enter the car.

The last whistle announced the departure. Kóshkin unlocked the window in the compartment and, holding Nínochka with one arm, placed his other arm possessively over Larissa shoulders. She stiffened but did not withdraw.

They stood at the window, waving to Glafíra and Akim, who walked along the slowly moving train until the end of the platform. Then they stopped and waved white handkerchiefs until the train was out of view.

"Can I have my surprise now? I am a good girl!" Nínochka said.

"Indeed you can!" He lowered her on the floor and shut the window. "Help me with this package," he said, wishing to distract her from noticing that Larissa was weeping again.

With the Swiss Army knife that he had swiped years ago from Egórov's abandoned luggage in Yassy, he cut the strings around the pack of American canned foods. On the top of the cans there was a small brown gutta-percha doll.

"A doll!" Nínochka exclaimed. "For me?"

"Well, it *must* be for you! I don't play with dolls. I am a *boy!*"

She giggled and dashed to him, embracing his leg and laughing happily. "Look, look, Mámochka! Look at my doll! She looks just like that brown lady we saw in the kino. She was dancing … Remember?"

Larissa smiled through her tears. "What do you say?"

"Thank you, Papa!"

"I'll call her Zee-Zee!" Nínochka announced.

"What a strange name! Where did you get it?" Igor asked.

"I don't know. I just like it!"

"I used to have a kitten when I was her age. His name was Zee-Zee," Larissa said, wiping her eyes. "I've told her about it."

"Zee-Zee she will be!" he proclaimed.

"Thank you," Larissa mouthed to Igor.

The train was gathering speed and rocking gently. "I'll go and check the other passengers," Igor said. "You lock the door and keep it locked. I'll knock three times slowly, and three times fast, like that," he demonstrated. "Then you can open the door. Can you shoot a gun?"

"Yes. Andrei taught me. I used to be quite good at target shooting."

"Good. I'll leave one of my guns under the pillow in the upper bunk. I think a *certain party* won't be able to find it there."

"I'll watch that *certain party.*"

"In case of trouble, hide under the lower bunk bed, wrap Ninka in the blanket, and hide there yourself. Keep the door locked! Do you understand?"

"Of course. But you frightened me! What kind of trouble?"

"One never knows."

Kóshkin stepped into the corridor running the length of the car with six compartments on one side of it, each for four people, all of them men.

At one end of the car there was a tiny cubicle for the porter who was already preparing a samovar for the travelers' tea. At the other end was a single toilet with a sink and a cold water faucet for washing up.

Igor walked through his car, peering into the open doors of the compartments, trying to guess who the occupants were. They all looked like demobilized military men of lower ranks, covered with whiskers, all surly.

Kóshkin noted that he was the only Commissar among them. He crossed to another sleeping car. It was also full of men. The stink of unwashed bodies and cheap tobacco was nauseating even to him, who was used to large conglomerations of soldiers.

"Hey, Pops" he addressed the elderly Chief conductor who was coming down the corridor from the opposite direction. "Who are all those soldiers?"

"The remnants of the prisoners of war from Galicia. Most of them are from the Kiev region ..."

"I didn't see them boarding the train in Odessa," Igor said.

"They were already on the train. They were not allowed to leave their compartments. At one of our stops along the way, they abducted a young Cossack woman, right off the platform. Keep your wife locked up when you are not around. And stay at the door when she is in the toilet."

"Where is the Cossack woman?"

"We left her in Odessa. She was almost dead, God bless her." He made the sign of the cross.

The rest of the train consisted of three baggage cars converted into third class, with shelves for sleeping but no blankets or pillows and open holes in place of the toilets through which one could see the railroad ties below. The cars were chock-full of men sleeping as Igor peered in through a small window in the first door. The car was locked. He did not need to go inside. He knew that the conditions there would be intolerable. He had seen such cars full of sick men before. By the time they arrived in Petrograd, most would be dead.

He made his way back to his Second Class sleeping car. Stopping at each compartment, he ordered the men to gather in the corridor in ten minutes. He knew that seeing the insignias of a political Commissar, the men would obey him.

"How was it?" Larissa asked.

"Awful! Dirty, stinky, ugly. The men look as if they are on the verge of murdering anyone for any reason. The men in the locked cars are sick, but nothing can be done. No doctors, no medicine. Whatever illness they have could spread. That's why they keep those men in sealed cars." He did not mention the Cossack woman. He did not want to frighten her.

"How terrible! Perhaps I could help and take care of the sick. After all, I am a nurse!"

"Don't even think of it! Are you crazy? Before you take someone's temperature, they will gang rape you! The conductor suggested that I keep you locked up, and that's exactly what I'll do! So, you'd better do nothing heroic and stay with Ninka. Do you understand? *Stay with Ninka!*" There was a steeliness in his voice suggesting that he expected total obedience.

"I understand," she said softly.

The men gathered in the corridor as they were ordered. Igor was glad to see that none of them looked ill, even though all of them were skeleton-thin and dirty. They constantly scratched themselves; they were infested with lice.

"Comrades," he began, standing on a crate in the middle of the corridor so that everybody could see and hear him. "My name is Kóshkin and I am on my way to take a new command as the Commissar at First

Socialist Fight School, near Petrograd. Are there any pilots among you?" the men looked from one to another, no one volunteering an answer.

"Apparently not," Kóshkin smiled. "Never mind. I am the senior ranking member on this train, so it is my duty to address you. As you probably know, we are traveling through territory that is infested by different *bandit* gangs. Until we reach Kiev, we could be surprised any time by any of them. Now, I know that you are armed. In case our train is ambushed by bandits, I expect you to rise up in mutual defense!" Some of the men nodded, the others stood silently, their grim faces stony. It seemed that they did not care one way or another.

"We can't expect any help from the men in the three locked cars. All of them are very sick and dying."

"You don't need to tell this to us," said one of the men. "We have been traveling with them since Galicia!"

Kóshkin nodded. "So comrades, let's check our weapons, and let's not be caught by surprise! I'll go now to the other car and tell them to join us." He picked up the crate and headed for another car. The men began to disperse to their compartments, looking glum.

The first stop on the 2,000 km trip was at the small town of Vosne-sénsk. It was snowing lightly, and Larissa and Nina, bundled up in the warm American Red Cross finery, enjoyed their walk along the snow-dusted platform. Kóshkin followed them closely, keeping his eye on a group of men from the Second Class cars. It was certainly not a sight that was suitable for observation by Larissa and Nina, he thought: the men were relieving themselves at the edge of the platform.

"Let's go back. It's getting cold," he said, taking Larissa by her elbow.

"No, Pápochka, not yet! I like the snow!' Nina begged, but Larissa turned her around. She too saw the urinating men.

The train left Vosnesénks within an hour but was stopped again in the open field just outside town. Kóshkin locked Larissa and the child in the compartment and went to ask why the train was stopped. Before he found anyone who would have known the reason, he saw it through the window in the corridor: the doors of the Third Class cars were opened, and groups of disheveled men spilled out and under the embankment of the railroad. It was the compulsory stop for the natural needs of those who could still walk, and it was repeated twice daily along the trip. It was a revolting scene. Kóshkin warned Larissa to keep Nínochka from looking out the window at such times.

During the stops, the porters cleaned the cars, filled the water cisterns with fresh water, and placed daily food rations of bread and salted pork fat or a hard boiled egg on each man's sleeping shelf. Toward the evening, large kettles of cabbage soup were brought into each car, and the men filled their metal bowls. Using the spoons that they carried in the wrappings of their leggings or inside the tops of their boots, they wolfed the watery soup without complaint. They considered themselves lucky: the Soviet troops had liberated them, and they were going home. To complain *now*, to be ungrateful to the liberators, could have meant arrest. No one was willing to risk it.

Even Kóshkin avoided leaving their compartment when the Third Class cars were open. The scene was just too gruesome. He tried instead to think of something pleasant, such as his forthcoming first night of making love to Larissa.

Larissa was also thinking of making love, not with pleasure but with dread. She felt that she was betraying the memory of her beloved Andrúsha, prostituting herself for a few cans of condensed milk and some fake documents. She tried to think of what her mother's reaction would be if she knew about her deal with Kóshkin. What would her mother advise her to do? She thought she knew: her mother would justify it as a necessity for their survival.

Unfortunately there was no hot water at the train toilets. Larissa prepared herself for the night by thoroughly washing herself with soap and cold water to remove any unpleasant odors. She even went as far as to apply a few drops of perfume around her neck. "My last gift from Andrei that he brought from Yassy. A small flacon of *French* perfume … Now I am acting as if I am a cheap whore about to serve a rich costumer!" she thought harshly. Despite her pragmatic approach to the situation, she felt miserable. The idea of having intercourse with an *enemy* of her husband, so soon after his death, filled her with self-loathing. But it was the price she had to pay for saving her child and herself. It was also the price for reuniting her with her mother. In the end, it would be worth it.

90

Larissa kissed Nínochka. "Good night, my angel. Sleep well …" She tucked her in one of the lower beds. The little girl smiled and, clutching the new rubber doll, fell asleep at once, lulled by the rhythmic sound of the wheels.

Larissa sat down on the opposite bed, thinking of what she should do next. Kóshkin was in the corridor, smoking with the men.

"I suppose, I should get in bed. I don't want to undress in front of him," she thought. Undressing was easy to do since she had stopped wearing corsets in her third month of pregnancy. Removing her shoes was also easy ... no more button hooks on elegant half-calf footgear. She wore ugly but warm válenki. As for changing into night clothes, that small luxury was all but forgotten. Larissa's one and only nightgown that had survived the revolution had provided enough fabric to make two dresses for Nínochka. On hot Odessa nights, Larissa usually slept in the nude. Otherwise, she slept in the same knee-length drawers and cotton vest supporting her breasts that she wore during the day. It was ugly-looking underwear, but it was the only type that was available in stores.

"I am sure that Kóshkin has never seen beautiful underwear," she thought. "After all, who is he? Some peasant boy, probably with no more than six years of village school education!" The centuries-old schism between the upper and the lower classes opened before her again. She was to give herself to a *mouzhik*! *C'est honteux!* she thought in French. *French* ... She hadn't spoken French for years! It will be fun to speak it again, if only with her mother! To read *'Illusions perdues'* again ... Balzac ... she used to *love* Balzac!

There was a coded knock on the door, then the key was inserted into the lock and the door opened. Kóshkin filled its frame with his muscular body surrounded by clouds of smoke from the American cigarettes that came out of the Red Cross gift package that he had generously shared with the men. Larissa had a sudden spasm of sexual stirring, the kind she had felt at the sight of Andrei's naked body, a sharp sign of arousal concentrated in her genital area. She used to be able to recreate this feeling by deliberately thinking of it, but she had never done it again after she had learned of his death. But there it was, back again, just from *looking* at a man whom she barely knew!

While that feeling was physically pleasant, she was disgusted with herself. How *could* she respond in that intimate way to some stranger, a *mouzhik*, a communist!

"Oh, you are already in bed!" Igor exclaimed. "Is Nínka asleep?"

"Yes."

Igor quickly shed his military uniform and boots. He took his gun out of its holster and placed it under the pillow. He stood in front of her in his baggy long underwear with dragging ties at his ankles, looking unattractive and comical, a far cry from her Andrei, who always wore English officers' trim white underwear of shorts and a sleeveless undershirt that displayed his fine physique.

She shut her eyes and moved closer to the wall to give Igor more space on the bed. He plunged himself next to her and embraced her around the hips, his hand on her buttocks.

"At last!" he whispered, trembling with excitement. Larissa turned off the light over the bed.

Kóshkin was gentle as he explored her body with his greedy hands, not devouring her as she feared he would. His kisses were hot but not disgusting for he did not force them on her. His was the caress of a lover, not the attack of a rapist. She began to relax as he kissed her breasts.

"Touch me!" he whispered. She obeyed and discovered that he was big with a full erection. "I love you, Larka," he whispered into her ear.

Despite herself, her body demanded him with its own primordial need as she guided him into her body. She tried to pretend that she was with Andrei, but her mind refused to obey. Andrei was not there. But neither was Kóshkin. It was no one in particular, but a vigorous young male whose demand for her plunged her into a sensual abyss, reawakening her long forgotten physical responses.

Their coupling was furious, and it left them spent. They lay next to one another, sharing a flat pillow, breathing heavily, exhausted. They did not talk, and Larissa was grateful for that.

Early in the morning, Kóshkin dressed quickly to be one of the first in line for the toilet. "If you hurry up, I'll hold a place for you," he said matter-of-factly. There was a new *à propos* tone in his voice, as if they were a long-married couple accustomed to one another's habits.

"I'll hurry," she replied in a similar tone.

The train moved peacefully through a bare, flat landscape under the cover of the slow-melting snow of early spring, approaching the woods where the thick stand of trees split, opening a tunnel for the train. Larissa stood in front of the window, looking at the woods, waiting for her daughter to announce that she had finished making her *pee-pee* in a small bucket.

Suddenly, the woods came alive as dozens of mounted men appeared between the trees, firing guns at the train.

"Bandits!" Larissa grabbed Nínochka and shoved her under the bed. She pulled the blankets from both beds and all the pillows she could grab and joined her daughter under the bed as Kóshkin had instructed.

"You hurt me, Mama," the little girl protested.

"Sh-sh! Don't talk. Stay quiet!" Larissa whispered as if the bandits could hear her. Barely able to move under the low bed, she wrapped the child in both blankets and surrounded her with pillows. "Don't make a sound!" she told her.

"I want my Papa!" the girl demanded. "I am scared!"

"He is busy. Keep quiet, or I'll spank you!" Larissa hissed. She could hear the bullets hitting the sides of the car. There was a sound of broken glass as a bullet hit their window. "Oh, my God! Just a minute ago I stood in front of that window!"

Nínochka must have been frightened by the strange commotion outside for she quieted down.

Larissa prudently remained under the bed with Nínochka, but the train was slowing down, she could feel it. "I must get the gun," she thought. Making snake-like movements with her body over the dirty floor, she slithered to the end of the protection of the bed. Quickly rising up two rungs on the little ladder, she reached under the pillow on the upper berth. The gun was still there. She grabbed it and dived under the bed again.

Kóshkin and the men fired their hand guns from the windows without inflicting any visible losses. The bandits were too fast, their guns blasting, racing maniacally along each side of the train, peppering it with bullets.

The train was forced to stop. The mounted men surrounded the train and aimed their rifles at the men in the windows, but they did not shoot. Their horses were steaming and lathered with sweat. A man under the Black Flag of Anarchy raced his horse along the stopped train, showing off. He ignored the locked cars, apparently knowing that those men were unable to offer any resistance and were of no importance to him.

"Stop your fire, comrades! We don't need anything from you. All we need is your locomotive. If you continue your fire, we will kill the engineer and his crew, and still take your locomotive. But if you stop now, no harm will come to anyone. Do you understand? We'll just take your locomotive."

Kóshkin stepped into the opening between cars. "I am Commissar Kóshkin," he shouted. "I protest your seizure of our train, which is full of *liberated prisoners of war*. We have no valuables on this train. Why don't you let us pass and let these men who have suffered so much, go back to their families. Let us pass, Comrade!"

The man under the Black flag laughed. "You are very persuasive, Comrade Kóshkin," he sneered. "Unfortunately we *really do need* a locomotive. But we'll help you and your prisoners of war who have suffered so much, as you say. After we leave with your locomotive, I personally will call Kiev and request that they send another locomotive to pick you up. I promise!" he shouted and, spurring his horse, dashed toward the locomotive where the crew was already unhooking the train. The bandits on horseback watched the cars closely from their high saddles but made to attempt to harass the passengers. Apparently, it was a highly disciplined band: there was no pilferage and no random shootings, and all that they took indeed was the locomotive.

It was unhitched and, sounding a farewell of three parting whistles, it was gone. The mounted men melted among the trees, disappearing as suddenly as they had appeared. A strange silence surrounded the five railroad cars left forlorn in the middle of nowhere.

"Why would they want a *locomotive?*" Igor thought as he jumped to the ground and went along the train to examine the damages. All cars were struck by the neat patterns of bullet holes reminding him of the airplanes coming home after dog fights. Dozens of compartments had broken windows, including his own.

"Larka!" he thought as he jumped back onto the train and ran to his door. With his hands shaking, he inserted the key into the lock, forgetting to knock. As he threw the door open, he faced Larissa, aiming her gun at him. "No!" he yelled.

The shot hit the door frame over his head. "My God ... I almost killed you!" Larissa rushed to him. "Oh, my God!"

Nínochka began to wail, crouching on the floor among the pillows.

Kóshkin put an arm across Larissa's trembling shoulders. "It's all right, Larka. No harm done ... I should have knocked. It was all my fault. You did everything right!" He sat down on the bed, and Nínochka clung to his leg. "Tell Mama not to shoot us!"

"She won't, baby! It was a mistake, an accident. It was a mistake!" he kept saying, patting her little head. "Everything is all right!"

The child quieted down and climbed on his lap. "I love you, Papa,"

"I love you too, my sweet *kóshechka*, my little kitten! My little snow-flake!"

Larissa was torn apart by contrasting emotions of relief, of self-hatred, of gratitude to Igor, and of acute jealousy in seeing her daughter's obvious affection.

Igor put the girl on the floor. "Go to your Mama, and tell her that we love her!" he said to her. "Go!" He gave her a little push.

"We love you, Mama!" she said, but Larissa continued to cry.

It took three days for the promised locomotive to arrive. During that time, conditions on the train did not improve. Food and clean water were running low, and the sickness in the locked Third Class cars claimed more lives. For each grim death, Kóshkin had the men dig holes in the forest, and Kóshkin himself performed a funeral service that he remembered from his father. He avoided any mention of God or making of the sign of the cross, but the men surrounding the grave treated the funeral as if it was still a traditional Christian ceremony.

The Chief conductor gave Kóshkin a folder with the documents of the departed and requested his signature, so that he could inform the authorities of their deaths. To mark the grave, the Chief conductor knocked together a wooden cross. He read aloud a few verses from a Bible that was still kept in the crew's quarters and concluded the sad ceremony.

Larissa asked if the men in the locked cars could be let out for fresh air and exercise. She wanted to tend to the sicker ones to see if she could stave off death until they could reach doctors, but Kóshkin forbade it. "Are you crazy? We don't know what kind of diseases those men carry. You may catch something and pass it on to your child! Have you thought of that? Those doors must remain *locked*."

"This train is truly a charnel train," Larissa said bitterly.

"I don't know what you mean," Kóshkin retorted.

"In the medieval times, there used to be special charnel buildings or vaults for storing human bodies or bones. In our case, we have a whole *charnel train!*"

"Where did you get this awful ghoulish thing!" he exclaimed, his face turning red. He hated being caught ignorant about something, no matter what.

"It's just an historical fact," she said, surprised at his reaction.

"No need to rub my nose in my lack of education!"

"I had no intention to ..."

"Let's stop this conversation!" he interrupted and turned away from her, ashamed.

Larissa did not realize that with her innocent remark, she had touched on his most sensitive point—his lack of education. It used to be one of his main reasons for hating and yet admiring Andrei Rezánov and Vassily Egórov: they were well-educated young men, unburdened by the absence of knowledge.

On the fourth morning, a new locomotive finally appeared behind the stranded train. Since there was no way to maneuver it to the head of the cars, the locomotive had to push the train from behind, all the way to Kiev, where the Third Class cars were unlocked, and the occupants spilled out, headed toward their own small villages. The Koshkins were to proceed to Petrograd on a regularly scheduled train, disembarking from Kiev on the following night.

Kiev! Larissa had never been to Kiev and wished they could stay there a little longer to get acquainted with that great capital of ancient Russia, the cradle of Christianity! The city that changed hands *nineteen* times during the Civil War, where two ancient cultures, the Russian and the Ukrainian, mingled harmoniously. Kiev, the city of famous architectural monuments, of universities and concert halls, of medieval churches with gold and blue cupolas that could be seen from far away! The city of great beauty, green with parks and gardens, shady streets lined with flowering trees, the mighty river Dnieper and the polyglot population!

This paean was on Larissa's mind as their train was pushed into the side track of the main railroad terminal. Kiev was not spared by the famine, but in Kiev's best hotel they still could count on good hot meals. But the best that Kiev had to offer was a *hot bath*, the first *really* good bath in years, when one did not need to heat miniscule amounts of water and save the soap. The hotel still had its fragrant soap in the bathrooms and even little stacks of cut toilet paper.

"I had forgotten that such luxury ever existed," Larissa exclaimed as she gave Nínochka the first real bath of her life. Larissa allowed her to splash in the huge marble bathtub on lion's paws, and Nínochka played in the water with her Zee-Zee doll, proclaiming that she wanted to live in that hotel forever and take a bath twice a day!

When the child was finally asleep in the bedroom alcove, Larissa took a bath herself. She washed her hair in the sink and wrapped it in a towel, then she stepped into the tub, relaxing finally in the soothing warm water.

She hoped that Kóshkin would wait for his turn in the tub, but no such luck. He came into the bathroom in a robe and greedily observed her naked body.

He shed his robe and stepped into the tub, splashing water on the floor. He sat in the water facing her. A picture of Andrei in the same position during their honeymoon in Gátchina flashed through her mind. How happy she had been! How playful they both were and how daring she sounded even to herself when she demanded to see him standing up with his arousal!

Now it was the other way around. It was Igor who wanted to see and touch, Igor who wanted to love every inch of her body, to possess it forever, to engulf it with his own body.

"I must have you … Now!" He reached for a terrycloth bath sheet and lifted her up, enclosing her in the sheet. Dripping wet himself, he carried her into the sitting room part of the suite and lowered her on the divan. He was aggressively aroused. The sweet memory of Andrei was gone, leaving this reality to take its place. She opened herself to Igor's overwhelming desire and responded to it with her own. "I might as well enjoy it," she thought cynically.

﷽ 91 ﷽

The bell rang three times, the code of rings for Maria Nikoláyevna to open the door for her visitors. Hearing the rings, she shuffled along the dark corridor, holding on to the wall, muttering to herself. "It has been *weeks* since the last electric bulb burned out, and it has still not been replaced!" How many times had she complained about it, but all without any results! "One of these days I'll break my neck!"

The bell continued to ring in three short bursts. "I'm coming, I'm coming," she raised her voice. Whoever it is must have some urgent business with her. "What business? I have no business with anybody!"

She unlocked the door, and Natasha rushed at her, almost knocking her off her feet. Dimka, Natasha's lover, followed close behind.

"They will be here *this week!*" Natasha cried. "They are already in Kiev!"

"Who?" Maria Nikoláyevna asked irritably.

"Your daughter and Nínochka!"

"I have a telegram from Commissar Kóshkin that your daughter and granddaughter are on the last leg of their journey to Petrograd," said Dimka. "They are traveling with the Commissar, under the name of *Kóshkin.*"

"What? They are coming *here?* It's a miracle!" she could not believe her ears. Then, the full weight of what Natasha had said struck her. "But ... my Larissa is now ... *Kóshkina?*"

Natasha patted her arm. "Don't worry, Maria Nikoláyevna! It was probably necessary for her to get all the permits to come to Petrograd."

"So, she's married to this ... this *Kóshkin?*" Maria Nikoláyevna spat out the plebeian name.

"Not necessarily," Dimka said. "We have new laws now that permit people to live together and have children without getting married. What is marriage, after all? Just a piece of paper! Women don't have to change their names anymore if they don't want to! At last marriage is free of bureaucracy. At last marriage is democratic!"

Maria Nikoláyevna suddenly realized that they were still standing in the hall. "Come on in, come on in," she fussed. "Be careful in the corridor, we don't have any light there." She led the way back to her room at the end of the corridor. "I am so glad that they are on their way. It's a dream come true! But who is this Commissar *Kóshkin?* Do you know him?" she asked Dimka. The name *'Kóshkin'* affronted her to such a degree that she momentarily felt no happiness that at last her daughter and granddaughter would be reunited with her.

"No. But it won't be too hard to find out. I'll request information about Commissar Kóshkin."

"He must be a very important man since he was able to get all the permits for your daughter and grandchild," Natasha said.

They stopped on the threshold of the sunlit room. "You'll need another bed," Natasha said. "And perhaps a crib for Nínochka ... How old is she?"

"Five. She must have already outgrown cribs."

650

"Not to worry. The Housing Authority has a warehouse full of furniture! I'll get you a double bed and Larissa can share it with Nínochka, that is if Commissar Kóshkin isn't planning to ..."

"No! I won't allow a *strange man* living in *my* room!" Maria Nikoláyevna objected hotly. "I won't tolerate it!"

Dimka and Natasha exchanged amused glances. "She must have forgotten that she is not at her great mansion on the Nevá but in the *communalka* flat!" Dimka thought.

Natasha said, "Anyway, we'll get you a comfortable bed with a clean mattress. A good blanket and a couple of pillows. I think I can get some sheets and pillowcases through Auntie Frósya. Her niece works at a textile factory. For a little bribe one can get anything!"

Maria Nikoláyevna wasn't listening. She stood in front of the window staring at the skeletal ribs of a cupola of the Winter Garden across the Nevá, tears rolling over her wrinkled cheeks. Her darling Larissa was finally coming home ... *Home* ... Where was their *home?*

While Igor took Nínochka to the park, Larissa luxuriated in the warm bath, a cup of coffee sweetened with condensed milk on the floor within easy reach. She had to decide how to solve the problem of Igor's insistence on marrying her. She realized the advantages of marriage under the circumstances. She even sort of *liked* making love to him and appreciated his affection for Nínochka, but she could not accept that Igor used to be Andrei's enemy. She could not accept Igor's communist beliefs. She could not discard his lack of education and his rough manners.

She did not want to share her life with him. She could not love him as she had loved her darling Andrei. She still considered Igor to be her adversary.

Igor and Nínochka returned from the park in good spirits. The child's cheeks were rosy again for the first time in a long while and looked a little plumper, as the cheeks of a child her age should be. The American oatmeal and condensed milk must have been beneficial. Larissa kissed her cold face. "Did you have fun in the park?"

"I did! Papa and I made a snowman!"

"Was there enough snow for that?"

"Yes. The workers pushed it off the paths and there were many children playing in the snow," Igor said.

"One bad boy threw a snowball at me and knocked my hat off!" Nínochka laughed.

"What did *you* do?"

"I threw a snowball at him! Only I missed," she said. "But Pápochka didn't miss! He threw a snowball right at his nose! The boy cried. His nose was bleeding."

"He was a nasty brat!" Igor said. "It will teach him not to throw snowballs at little girls!"

Larissa's mouth set at the thought of Igor's demonstration of adult superiority against a child. Andrei would never have done something like that. She could see that Igor was embarrassed.

"Anyway," he continued, "Tomorrow we'll be on our way to Petrograd! It will be a pleasant experience. We'll travel in the *international* car, in a compartment with its own toilet. *You* should feel at home there! You must've traveled like that before!" he added with a bit of sarcasm, looking at Larissa.

"Why does he keep reminding me that I am one of the *former people?* Does he think that I should be ashamed of it?" she thought. Aloud she said, "It will be such a pleasure to travel in a *civilized* way for a change!"

The express train was luxurious. Even Nínochka noticed the difference.

"This train is pretty," the girl said, "There are mirrors in the doors and pretty lamps. They look like lily of the valley flowers. But the uncles and the aunties speak differently. I don't understand them."

"I don't understand them either," Igor told her. "But your Mama would know. These people are *very* different from you and me." He glanced at Larissa in a rather unfriendly way. "They are from another country. They are foreigners. They speak their own *American* language." Kóshkin sounded disapproving.

"They are from the country that Yasha and his Mama went to, remember?" Larissa said evenly.

"Yasha? Yes, I remember! He went to … *America!*"

"Right! These people are *Americans* and they don't speak Russian."

"Oh … Do they know Yasha? And why don't they speak Russian? I am little, but *I* speak Russian! I am smart! Will Yasha speak American language also?"

Larissa laughed. "Yes, my darling! He will speak it. He is also very smart. And *you* are *very* smart! Someday you, too, will learn some other languages and will talk with people from other countries!"

"It'll be fun! I'll learn all the languages in the whole world! And I'll read all the books in the world also!"

"That's my girl!" Larissa laughed.

The Americans traveling to Petrograd were members of several American relief organizations, including the Red Cross. Petrograd was their final destination. They watched with interest the small Russian family of a good looking, broad-shouldered young man with a pistol at his side, obviously an important official, his young and slender wife, and an adorable little blond girl who boldly came to their group and introduced herself: "I am Nina and I am five years old."

"What did she say?" the Americans asked their interpreter.

He smiled. "She said that her name is Nina and that she is five years old!"

"How charming!" exclaimed one of the American women. "Glad to meet you, Nina!"

"What do you say?" Larissa prompted.

"*Spasíbo!*" Nínochka said and made a curtsy as she was taught by her mother.

"It means *'thank you,'*" Larissa translated.

"Oh, you speak English?" the woman exclaimed smiling at Larissa.

Caught by surprise, Larissa said, "Yes, I do." She realized that it was a mistake. Igor took her by the elbow and led her into their compartment. Nínochka smiled at the Americans and waved to them before Igor closed the door.

"Why did you brag that you speak English?" he demanded roughly.

"I did not *brag*. It was just an answer to a question. I've never realized that speaking a foreign language was something to be ashamed of, something to hide."

"I don't want you to become friendly with them," he said coldly. "They could be capitalist spies, and we would be accused of establishing contact with them. My reputation is at stake, if not my head, so *remember* that."

Larissa stayed in the compartment for the rest of the trip, for there was *really* no reason to leave it. They had a toilet inside and the porter supplied them with a teapot of hot water for their tea and brought their food from the dining car, usually cabbage soup and several slices of coarse bread.

But not Nínochka. With every opportunity she snuck out of the compartment and soon they could hear her singing the snowflake song for the Americans. Igor would go out and retrieve his 'daughter,' not too politely. The Americans soon understood that the Commissar did not want his family to fraternize with them.

In the morning of the third day the train arrived in Petrograd.

Maria Nikoláyevna, Natasha, and Dimka were getting ready to go to the grand train station, renamed *Oktyábrski Voksál* in honor of the revolution. Dimka had arranged to have a car with a driver for Maria Nikoláyevna, but he rode his motorcycle with a side car.

"I suggest that Commissar Kóshkin ride with us in the motorcycle," Natasha said. "Let Larissa and her mother have some privacy, get re-acquainted and have a good cry together. It will take a few days before Maria Nikoláyevna welcomes Kóshkin."

"She never will," Dimka said. "Not Her Imperial Majesty!"

Natasha frowned. "I know that she can be imperious sometimes, but she is a kind old lady, smart and well educated. She has been dealt some bad cards in her life. She was always very kind to me."

"To each his own," he said dryly. "To me, she's the typical *former person* still living by the *former* standards. She needs to accept the new reality."

Maria Nikoláyevna waited nervously for the train. Also waiting for the arrival of the train was a small group of Americans. By their conversation, she had learned that they were from the American Embassy and were waiting for some delegation. There were two Russians among them, easily recognizable as commissars by their leather coats, holding welcoming bouquets of roses.

The train pulled slowly along the platform. Maria Nikoláyevna was waiting for car number three and so apparently were the Americans. The number three slowly passed by, and the Americans and Maria Nikoláyevna's group hurried in pursuit.

Kóshkin waited in the compartment until all Americans descended from the car and were surrounded by their greeters. He watched a group of three people waiting on the platform, two women in shapeless vátnik coats and fur-lined hats with ear flaps accompanied by a man in a leather coat with a Colt at his hip. "Commissar Dimka," he thought. He felt as if he knew Dimka from their long distance correspondence about Larissa's fake papers. He wondered what price Dimka would demand for making it possible to bring Larissa to Petrograd. So far—he had asked for nothing.

"There she is!" Larissa exclaimed. "Look Nínochka, there is your Bábushka! Mama, Mámochka!" she burst into tears as she jumped off the steps of the car and ran toward Maria Nikoláyevna.

"Larissa, my baby!" They fell into each other's arms, tears blinding them as they kissed and hugged and cried and laughed all at once. Nínochka boldly approached them and tugged at her grandmother's coat. "Look at me, Bàbushka! I am Nina!"

"Of course, of course! Oh, my little angel, my darling ... Look at you! How big you are!" Maria Nikoláyevna bent down to the child.

"I am five!" Nina announced. "But I can't see your face!"

"Here! Here is my face!" the old woman cried. She untied the earflaps of her hat, tearing it off her head and dropping it to the ground. Her white hair was disheveled, her face beaming under the tears. "Here is your Bábushka, my sweet little angel!"

"I like your hat!" Nínochka said. "It looks like goats' ears," she picked up the hat and touched the flaps. "It must be warm!"

"It's yours!"

"Hurray! I'm a goat! Beh-eh-eh," she bleated.

Larissa and her mother laughed, locking again in an embrace. The stiff vátnik, enclosing Maria Nikoláyevna like a medieval chain-link battle dress, made their embrace awkward.

Kóshkin, Natasha, and Dimka were touched by the reunion. They knew the troubles these two women had gone through, and Kóshkin, though he despised the *former* class, felt good about reuniting them.

The American delegation on their way to the exit smiled at Nínochka and her grandmother. "It must be the reunification of a grandmother with her granddaughter," one American said.

"It certainly is! It is the first time that we met!" Maria Nikoláyevna replied in English.

One of the women from the delegation took two roses out of her welcome bouquet and proffered them to Maria Nikoláyevna and Nina. "Congratulations upon your reunion!"

"Thank you!" Maria Nikoláyevna replied and, turning to Nínochka, said in Russian, "Repeat after me: *"thank you!"* she said slowly.

Nínochka dutifully repeated the foreign phrase and made a polite curtsy.

"You are welcome, dear!" The American said and was herded from the platform by their greeters.

"*Thank you!*" Nínochka repeated the newly learned words. "Does it mean '*Spasíbo?*'"

"Yes, it does," Maria Nikoláyevna smiled.

Larissa embraced Natasha and the two had their own small reunion on the platform.

Maria Nikoláyevna finally turned her attention to Kóshkin, who was pretending to be in deep conversation with Dimka and Natasha. "I must thank you, *sir*, for helping my daughter to be reunited with me. What is your Christian name and patronymic?" She hated his last name so much that she did not want even to say it.

"Igor Nikítich," he replied, offended by her icy tone and using the forbidden form of address '*sir.*'

"Well, Igor Nikítich, thank you for returning my daughter and granddaughter to me." Maria Nikoláyevna said it matter of factly.

"It was my pleasure," He responded evenly. He placed his arm possessively across Larissa shoulders. "Give the flower to your Mama!" he ordered Nina.

"Why?" she challenged. "The auntie gave it to me!"

"Do as your Papa tells you!" he said sharply. Nínochka pouted but obeyed.

"There!" he thought, looking at the old woman victoriously.

She understood his maneuver, as did the others. Kóshkin had established his authority.

"Well, let's go!" Maria Nikoláyevna said. "I have a little lunch waiting for us in celebration! And I have a surprise for my *smart* granddaughter!" she smiled. "Perhaps you would like to join us?" she asked Kóshkin politely, letting him know that he was a stranger and needed an invitation to join them.

"No, Maria Nikoláyevna. Larissa and I have our own little surprise waiting at our hotel. We want to celebrate the occasion with champagne, as you would do in the olden times! So you are welcome to come with *us* to the Astoria!"

Larissa realized that a game was being played, and she was the prize. It was time to act! She turned calmly to Kóshkin.

"I am sorry, Igor, but this is the first time that I've heard about our staying at the hotel with you. Our agreement was to end with my return to Petrograd. We both fulfilled our agreement. So let's celebrate it at my mother's flat as she has planned," she said firmly in the no nonsense tone of her mother.

Maria Nikoláyevna and Larissa riding in the car held tight to each other's hands, their eyes damp with happy tears. Nínochka sat on her grandmother's lap and played with the flaps of the *uoshánka*, imagining that they were indeed a goat's floppy ears. As the car sped along the Nevsky Prospect toward the Palace Bridge that would bring them to Vassilievsky Island, Larissa observed the familiar landmarks, switching her eyes back to the beloved face of her mother. "How she has aged!" she thought. "She looks as if she were seventy! How thin she is … her beauty is gone … poor Mama. Oh, there are the Fontánka Bridge equestrian sculptures …" she thought. "They did not change. And there is the Rezánov's house … Mother and I came there when Peter was killed and Father died … The Rezánovs shared our grief. How happy we used to be in that house!" she smiled through her tears.

"Old memories?" Maria Nikoláyevna asked, understanding her emotions.

She nodded, "Yes … sweet old memories … Also, the bitter ones … Do you realize, Mama, that only the two of us who have survived?"

"But we have our Nínochka and it is up to us that she also survives!"

"Nínochka will help *us* to survive!" Larissa added, noticing that the girl was listening. "Won't you help us, baby?"

"I will help," Nínochka said eagerly. "What does it mean to *survive?*" she asked.

"It means to live happily ever after," Larissa replied. "Like in a fairy tale."

"Oh, that's easy! I always live happily! I know how to do it. I will help you to *survive.*"

Kóshkin, seated behind Dimka on the uncomfortable seat of the motorcycle, did not look at the marvels of classical architecture or the beauty of the cathedrals and monuments. His mind was occupied with Larissa.

"I won't let her slip out of my life," he thought. "I'll make her love me, maybe not the way she loved her Andrei, but in her new, passionate way. I *know* she likes fucking me, I know it, she cannot fake it … She *wants* me. And little Ninka *needs* a father … I'll make the old bitch accept me.

She is supposed to be a liberal … Well, I'll play on her *liberalism*, I'll listen to her, I'll flatter her … I'll ask her opinion … and of course, I'll keep them all alive with food. If she is as wise as she is supposed to be, she will soon realize that they *need* me. I'll win her over!" He began to feel better. "I'll lay low for a few days. I have to report to Gátchina anyway, so it will give them enough time to realize that they need *me!*"

They reached the Admiralty at the beginning of the Nevsky Prospect, turning right toward the Alexándrovsky Column in the center of the Palace Square.

"What a tall tower!" Nínochka exclaimed. "There is an angel on the top!"

"I will take you there sometime! It's called a *column*," Grandmother said.

"*Co-lumn,*" the girl repeated slowly, glad to learn another new word. "You'll take me to the top? To see the Angel?"

Maria Nikoláyevna laughed. "No, it's impossible to go to the top, but we'll go around it and look at it. I'll tell you a story about it."

They crossed the Palace Bridge and followed the University Embankment until the turn that led them to the Bolshoi Prospect and the apartment house where Maria Nikoláyevna now lived. As they followed the embankment, Larissa stared across the river, at the exposed half-moon ribs of the ruined Winter Garden and the imposing house with the colonnaded entrance attached to it, her childhood home. Maria Nikoláyevna noticed the tears filling Larissa's eyes. She did not say anything. She guessed her daughter's thoughts, and she did not want to give the ever-curious Nínochka any access to that Pandora's box. "The child shouldn't know," she thought.

They stopped in front of the new residence of Maria Nikoláyevna, and Dimka chained his motorcycle to the iron grate under the tree. He helped Kóshkin to unload his English duffel bags and Larissa's pitiful luggage from the trunk, then he dismissed the driver.

Maria Nikoláyevna led the party along the broad staircase to the third floor, stopping at every landing along the way to catch her breath. Larissa watched her, alarmed.

"Are you out of breath, Mama?"

"No, no … Its only when I'm going up the stairs … it hurts a little."

"We'll get you to a good doctor," Igor said, seeing another opportunity to make himself indispensable.

Larissa and Natasha supported her as they slowly made their way to her apartment door. Maria Nikoláyevna searched in her pocket for an old iron key and handed it to Natasha. "Please, Natáshenka, unlock the door with this monstrosity."

"Let me do it!" Dimka said. "You must request at your office that they install a *modern* lock and keys," he said to Natasha.

"I'll do it tomorrow!" she said. "This one looks as if it came from the castle of The Beauty and the Beast!"

"I know that story! Let me see the key!" Nínochka exclaimed. "Oh, it's *big!* Bigger than my two hands!"

Maria Nikoláyevna led them to her room along the dark corridor. "I told the apartment *leader* that my family was coming and we needed a light in the corridor and he promised to get it, but we still don't have it!" she complained.

Kóshkin quickly said, "I'll get it for you! Right *now!*" He had noticed that in the entrance hall over a mirror there was an intricate arrangement of electric bulbs under the glass *abajours* in the form of lily of the valley flowers, so popular at the beginning of the century. It was quite elegant, obviously left over from the pre-revolutionary times, with only one bulb lighted, for economy sake. He quickly returned to the hall, hoping that the other bulbs might still be functional. He checked them at random. He was right.

In a moment there was light in the dark corridor. Everybody clapped, " Bravo, Igor Nikítich," Maria Nikoláyevna said. "You performed a miracle! For more than a *month* I kept begging for a light, and you produced it in a moment! Thank you!"

"*Thank you,* Pápochka," Nina said in English. "That is in American language, and it means *spasíbo!*"

They all laughed, Larissa and Igor exchanging proud glances.

"You are welcome!" Igor said. "Let's celebrate a stupendous occasion, *the reunification of a family!* How many years has it been?" he asked Larissa.

"Six years ... no, even longer! Nínochka is almost six! Mama left Odessa long before Nínochka was born!"

"Well, the occasion deserves a celebration, so I'll ask our youngest member to help me to unpack this bundle. Who do you think is the youngest among us?"

"I am the youngest!" Nina jumped up and down. "I am the youngest!"

"That's right. So help me to unpack. You know what to do."

Kóshkin cut the strings around a large parcel of canned foods: condensed milk, powdered eggs, and meats. There were even three cans of sliced peaches and a bag of whole wheat flour. And of course, a bunch of Hershey chocolate bars!

Maria Nikoláyevna's eyes filled with tears. "God bless you, Igor Nikítich." She grabbed his hands, feeling guilty for misjudging him. "He must be a kind man!" she thought.

Kóshkin, not a sentimental man, was nevertheless moved. "You are welcome. It is from America. Being a Commissar has its little advantages," he winked at Dimka.

"You said it, Comrade!" Dimka replied and reached inside his roomy leather coat, taking out a bottle of French cognac.

Maria Nikoláyevna had only four cups and saucers and four plates. She had two forks and three spoons, three knives, and one large bread knife.

Igor looked at the pathetic collection. "Can your office do something about this?" he asked Natasha. "She needs dishes and cutlery, pots and pans. I can write a request for the necessary equipment."

"Happily," Natasha said.

"Alright everybody!" Maria Nikoláyevna clapped her hands. "Let's get organized. It will be a little awkward to serve our *banquet*," she joked, "but we are all friends, aren't we? Let's move the table between the beds, and we'll sit on the beds. There are only six of us, so it won't be too crowded!"

Nínochka declared, "I shall sit next to my Bábushka!"

"No, my little angel, you'll sit on your bábushka's lap!" Maria Nikoláyevna said. "I have been waiting for this moment all these years! And you and I will sit in my one big chair as if we were the *Tsarítsa* and the *Tsarévna!*" As she said it, she realized that she had committed a really great faux pas. "I mean, like in a *fairy tale!*" she added quickly, but everyone was unperturbed by the reference.

They ate pirozhkí, small half-moon pies stuffed with cabbage and chopped eggs, a traditional dish beloved by all Russians. They opened the cans that Igor had brought and had a small feast. Dimka started the samovar, and Maria Nikoláyevna brewed enough tea for everyone.

"Bábushka, please give me my surprise," Nina asked politely. "I don't think that it was pirozhki. They are for *everybody*, not just for me!"

"You are right, my precious girl! I do have a surprise, just for *you!* She opened a drawer in Ksusha's old chest and took out a package wrapped in bright red paper. "I hoped that you would be here for Christmas and it would have been your gift ..."

"It doesn't matter," Nínochka said. "I'll be here next Christmas and you can give me another surprise then!" Nina patted her grandmother's hand as if she needed some encouragement.

Everybody laughed.

"Well, open it!"

Nina tore the red paper off and two colorful books of fairy tales revealed themselves. "Fairy tales!" she cried in delight. "How did you *know* that I like fairy tales?" she asked, pressing the books to her chest.

"A little bird told me! See that big tree in front of the window? Well, there lives a little sparrow and she tells me a lot of secret things. I'll introduce you to her when she comes back from her winter home."

"Where is her home in the winter?"

"In Odessa," the grandmother said with a sly smile.

Nina's eyes grew wide. "In Odessa! That's where we came from," she squealed.

It was getting dark. Nínochka, exhausted by the celebration, was sound asleep on Maria Nikoláyevna's bed, still holding her new books.

"Well, comrades, it's time to part and let Maria Nikoláyevna rest," Kóshkin said. "I must report to Gátchina tomorrow, so I won't see you until the day after. We can make our plans when I return."

Feeling more benevolent toward Maria Nikoláyevna after a bit of cognac, Kóshkin decided that he would use a new tactic: he would make a proposition that *included* Maria Nikoláyevna. Let the old Grandma join his family! Let *all of them* be his family! He would call her Mama or Bábushka and Larka and Ninka would be his wife and his daughter. Tomorrow he would apply for a flat in Gátchina and they, as the Commissar's family, would join him there and receive special ration cards. In his mind he saw an ideal family. He was almost sure that he would convince them to accept his plan. "We shall hire some country woman to cook and to wash, so that Grandma could take care of Ninka, while Larka will get a job at some hospital, and I, being a Commissar, will be assigned an automobile!" he thought.

A happy, ideal family was on Kóshkin's mind when he kissed the sleeping Nina, embraced Larissa and then Maria Nikoláyevna, kissing her juicily on both cheeks. Surprised, she returned his kiss and pecked him on his cheek. She, too, felt a little more friendly toward him. "For a *communist* he is not too bad," she thought.

ꑥ 92 ꑥ

Kóshkin was greatly surprised when he arrived in Gátchina to find that the flight school was no longer there. It seemed that no one had bothered to inform him. In the Administration Building, two men in civilian clothes were doing some remaining office work, but the sky was empty of airplanes. The parking tents were also empty, gaping like open mouths with missing teeth. There were no cadets or mechanics around the silent repair shops stripped of their equipment. The school was *gone*.

"You must be Commissar Kóshkin," said the older man, getting up from his desk. "We were informed of your coming. I am Tatárov, in charge of the final stages of moving the school archives."

"And I am Pávlov," the younger man said. "We expected you last week."

"There were some troubles in our travel from Odessa. I arrived to Petrograd only yesterday evening. What happened to the flight school?"

"I have an urgent order for you," Tatárov said. "It explains everything." He proffered Kóshkin a sealed pack of papers. "You may use that desk," he pointed to a desk with two chairs and a wastepaper basket piled on top of it, a sad witness to the process of abandonment.

Kóshkin took down the chairs and the basket and settled at the desk. As a military Commissar, he did not expect any *explanation* of the order, but he was stunned by this particular order. He was to proceed *immediately* to Zaráisk, near Moscow, and then on to Sevastópol—*back* to the Crimea! Gátchina flight school and Zaráisk flight school were merging with the Sevastópol flight school in one large Aviation Flight Training Center.

The written order was accompanied by train tickets and special food ration coupons for the next two weeks.

He was furious but held his temper. He was a Party member and his primary duty was to *obey* the Party orders, otherwise … he did not want to think of what may happen otherwise.

"I would recommend that you take the night train to Moscow. You have already lost almost two weeks in getting to Petrograd from Odessa, so the High Command may not be sympathetic," Tatárov said.

"I understand. I'll leave tonight," Kóshkin said weakly.

"I need your signature that you have received your orders," Tatárov said.

"Yes, of course!" Kóshkin signed the form. "I must leave. Goodbye now."

"We'll see each other in Sevastópol! I'll be glad to escape from this cold and foggy city for the warmth of the Crimea. Won't you?"

"Yes," Kóshkin said darkly. "But I must hurry now!" He stuffed his orders into the British dispatch case that he wore over his shoulder.

"Wait, wait!" cried Tatárov. "How are you going to get back to Petrograd? There will be no trains before three in the afternoon!"

Kóshkin swore. "Perhaps I can hire someone with a motorcycle, or a car ..."

"Comrade Pávlov, will you take the Commissar back to Petrograd? How much will it cost?"

The younger man, busy scribbling in a large journal, placed his pen down. "It depends ... If the Commissar is willing to part with three special purchase coupons and pay for fuel, I'll be willing to take him."

"I am willing! Let's go!" Kóshkin said quickly. He had to make sure that Larissa wouldn't slip out of his life completely. He felt it in his gut that she would refuse to follow him to Sevastópol.

"It looks that our new administration is as corrupt as the old one," he thought grimly as he perched on the uncomfortable seat behind Pávlov, his luggage stowed in the motorcycle gondola. "Where is our proletarian idealism and honesty?"

Pávlov did not talk as he drove. This was fine with Kóshkin. He was not in a chatty mood.

"Where to?" Pávlov asked over his shoulder when they reached Petrograd.

"Vassilievsky Island." They sped along the Nevsky Prospect. Kóshkin noticed many *private* shops had sprung up under a temporary decree from Lenin. It was called the New Economic Policy, the NEP, and it reinstated some minor private enterprises.

But did the NEP work? Apparently it did. The plate glass windows of the shops displayed beautiful foods and baked goods, colorful fabrics and shoes, and there were small clusters of people gathered in front of the windows, admiring the merchandise. But who had the *money* to spend on fresh oranges, or silk stockings, or whatever there was to buy? Only a few, called derisively *speculators*, could afford the shops. The *people*, in whose name the Revolution was staged, were still dying of hunger.

"What's happening? Are we succumbing to the old bourgeois ideas of *private property?*" Kóshkin felt utterly confused.

"Stop at that house," he shouted. Pávlov stopped the machine.

"Let me pay you," Kóshkin said. He took out his new ration coupons. "Which three do you want?"

"Doesn't matter. They are all of the same value. And give me ten rubles for the fuel."

It was too much, but Kóshkin did not argue. He opened his wallet and extracted a crisp, newly-printed bill.

Kóshkin pressed the electric bell three times. Larissa opened the door.

"Igor! We thought you were in Gátchina!"

He grabbed her and kissed her hungrily. She stiffened in his embrace and kissed him on his cheek.

"We were about to have some tea," she said. "Will you join us?"

"Of course! I have a lot to tell you," he said. "Something *very* important."

She felt her legs suddenly becoming weak. "Some bad news?"

"Yes and no," he said, entering the corridor.

"Papa!" Nínochka squealed as she rushed into his arms.

He lifted her up and kissed her smooth cheek. "How is my little snowflake?" he was overcome with love for that little girl who greeted him with such happiness.

"Hello, Igor Nikítich," Maria Nikoláyevna said. "Is anything wrong? You look disturbed."

Kóshkin took off his leather coat and relocated the gun to his field shirt belt. "Yes, I am *very* disturbed. I am ordered to depart immediately for Sevastópol."

"But you just came from there!" Larissa exclaimed.

"Let's sit down and have a cup of tea while Igor Nikítich tells us what happened. Nínochka, help me to set the table!"

"Yes, Bábushka," she was eager to help.

"Call me Igor," Kóshkin said to Maria Nikoláyevna.

Briefly Igor described the new situation. "I have no idea if I shall retain my present position. Most likely not. The school is going to be three times as large as Gátchina ever was. Most likely some big shot from the Sovnarcom will be appointed as the Senior Commissar, and if I am lucky, I shall be the Commissar of one of its sections. It's all speculation on my part. I might be appointed Commissar of Timbuktu, for all I know!"

"I like this word! Tim-buk-tu, Tim-buk-tu," Nínochka began to sing.

"Anyway," he continued, smiling at her, "I have a plan that concerns all of *us*." He took a deep breath. "You know of my wish to marry Larka and adopt Ninka. But I want to take it even further. I want *you*, Maria Nikoláyevna, to live with us, all of us becoming a family. To be frank, as a *former person* you may be exposed to some political ..." he paused for the right word, "*persecution*. But by becoming a member of *my* family, you would be safe, and you and Larissa will become members of the *new* ruling class! Think of it! I must leave for Moscow tonight and then for Sevastópol, but we can finish some of the formalities before I go. What's important right now is to secure your safety and the future of the little one. Think of it!" he repeated, staring into Maria Nikoláyevna's eyes.

She did not know how to react. Kóshkin talked as if there was no doubt anymore about the stability of the new Soviet system. Yet, there were constant uprisings against it, some supported by international powers.

"What if the League of Nations should decide to declare a war against the Communists? It is still possible, isn't it?" Maria Nikoláyevna thought. "What would happen to people like Kóshkin? Would they be *liquidated* by the *anti*-communists? I bet, they would!"

Kóshkin pressed her. "I say the four of us go to the vital statistics bureau *right now*, and I marry Larka and apply for the papers to declare Ninka as my daughter!"

"I wish you'd stop calling her 'Ninka'. It's *street* language, used by uneducated people. We are civilized people and should use civilized language," Maria Nikoláyevna said with irritation.

Kóshkin was stung, not knowing what to say. He ignored her. "I'll deal with *that* later," he thought. "My *only* concern right now is to save Larissa and her child," he continued coldly. "As the wife of the Red Commissar, she would be safe."

"But what if your Soviet power *doesn't survive?* What if the international forces get together and overthrow your *Dictatorship of the Proletariat?* What will happen to Larissa 'as the wife of the *executed* Red Commissar?'"

"That is insidious talk, María Nikoláyevna, and I refuse to participate in it!" Igor raised his voice.

"Sh-sh-sh!" Larissa placed a finger to her lips. *"The walls have ears."*

Nínochka giggled. She imagined big meaty ears attached to the walls.

María Nikoláyevna smiled, but Kóshkin was too angry to smile. He could already see that Larissa shared her mother's point of view. He felt her slipping away. He felt desperate.

Larissa said quietly, "Mama, maybe Igor and I should talk in private."

"Yes. Nínochka and I will go to the park while you two settle your differences," María Nikoláyevna said. "We all *know* what we want. Get your coat and hat, my angel!"

Larissa and Igor faced one another across the round table, Larissa feeling strong, her self-determination reinforced by the brutal honesty of nocturnal conversation with her mother. She had told her mother about the vicious *red terror* of the Cheká in Odessa. She told her about Glafíra's information that the Cheká had begun a new campaign against the *former people,* and her name was on the list. She mentioned Igor's report about Andrei's execution by Commissar Zemliáchka. She did not hide from her mother the price she had agreed to pay. She told her *everything*.

Her mother realized that Larissa had no other way out. Being listed as a marked person, she would have been denied employment. It would have forced her to sell herself, not just to Kóshkin but probably to many others. It had become a shameful fact of life among the surviving members of the *former class* that the young women saved themselves by becoming mistresses of the new rulers. Had Lara refused Kóshkin's protection, she could have been shot. María Nikoláyevna did not judge Larissa. "For centuries women used their bodies as payment for much lesser prizes than survival," she said.

Both of them, however, agreed that Larissa should not marry Kóshkin. "You are *class enemies* as they call it, far apart in your backgrounds. Have you ever told him that you *loved* him?" María Nikoláyevna asked.

"No. Never. He knew that I loved my Andrúsha and I was grieving for him. He kept telling me that soon I would forget Andrei, that Nínochka needed a father, and that she already *loved* him. It was all true. Except, for forgetting my Andrei!"

"That also will be true, someday," her mother thought but did not say.

"I don't *dislike* Igor. He is mostly kind and honest with me. And he really loves Nina. But he is also so uncouth, so vulgar that sometimes I can't even look at him. The way he eats and talks with his mouth wide open. The way he burps, the way he uses unprintable words talking with Nínochka about the bodily functions ... I suppose, they are just *ordinary words* among peasants, but ..."

"Ksusha used to do that too, refer to the bodily functions in a peasant's *patois*. I was worried that you and Peter might use that language yourselves, but you never did."

"Oh yes, we did! Peter and I used that lingo among ourselves, being naughty! Anyway, it all makes me very uncomfortable. It makes me afraid that Nínochka would pick up his behavior. Nothing escapes her. But Igor is not a *bad* man." She paused. "Do you realize, Mama, that Andrei and I spent less than *six months* together as a married couple? I looked at my journal and counted the days. During most of our marriage we were separated. All these years I have been faithful to him, even though my body was hungry ... When Kóshkin came into my life and offered his help and stated his conditions, I agreed. I thought I would think of Andrei and pretend that it was him, but I couldn't do it. No one could be *my Andrei!* But still, I didn't dislike it. Have I shocked you, Mama?"

"No, my darling girl," she replied, recalling her own sudden *explosion of desire* when her husband was away at the Turkish war. She'd had a brief affair with a young lieutenant, a junior aide of her husband. So long ago! She understood the physical longings of her daughter ... But for Lara it wasn't an explosion of desire; it was a *payment of debt*, she thought.

"So, tell me about your reassignment," Larissa began. Briefly Igor described the situation. "What's most important to me, is what *we* are going to do now," he concluded.

Larissa was ready for it. She folded her hands calmly in front of her. "I am going to stay with my mother and get a job at some hospital. I'll start by registering with the Employment Bureau, and then, I'll go to the Botkin's Hospital where I was trained and perhaps they will give me a job. If I can't get a job at the hospital, I can become an interpreter. Surely, the new authorities need interpreters when so many educated Russians are not around anymore. And finally, I can give music lessons. Let my years of playing the scales pay for themselves!" she joked.

"Then, according to your plans, there is no place for me?" he said, outwardly restrained but sizzling with anger. "Apparently you don't realize that all these wonderful choices of employment will *not* be available to *you*, with *your* past!"

She felt the rising of her own hot anger. "You sound as if I deserve to be punished for *not* being born in a proletarian family! As if I am some kind of a criminal!"

"Yes!" he shouted. "Yes! But I am willing to forget it and give you a chance to start a new life! Do you think you can survive without my protection? No, my dear lady! At the next purge, you and your dear mama will be flushed out and end up in a labor camp up north, and Ninka will be raised in some stinking orphanage!" he practically spit the words.

"I don't believe you. Your Lenin is an educated man himself and he knows that the country *needs* educated people. Look, he has created the NEP and soon the famine should be over. Things are starting to settle down. Lenin won't allow the terror and famine continue without a limit!"

"This is a *stupid* conversation," Igor exclaimed vehemently. "You know nothing about Lenin! Who do you think ordered the liquidations of your *former class? Lenin!* Your *'educated people'* are our class enemies, and they must be swept out of the way. We'll create our own *educated class!* In any case, back to our *private* problem. You refuse to marry me?"

"Yes," she replied, looking him in the eyes. "I cannot marry you. I am grateful to you for your help. I respect you and I'll be your friend forever, but I don't love you, Igor. There is *nothing* in common between us!"

"How about fucking?" he threw the vulgar word into her face. "You *loved* it, didn't you?" he shouted. "You wanted more, didn't you? I want to fuck you *forever.* I want to have children with you!"

She restrained herself from reacting to his outburst.

"You enjoyed it, admit it!"

"Yes," she finally said. "But that is not a solid base for a marriage. Don't harangue me with accusations, Igor … I will not marry you because I do not love you. I am grieving for my husband …"

"Some grieving! Banging me as if there was no tomorrow!"

"I know, you want to hurt me … and you *do* hurt me. But it won't change my mind."

"What about Ninka? Who'll protect her? What about her?" He was aware that he was losing his argument. "Ninka *loves* me!" he shouted in desperation.

"I know. But she is very young and with time …"

"She will forget me, I know." He felt that his cause was lost. "But I am not giving you up! I'll go to Sevastópol because I must. Maybe by that time you'll realize that you need me. I don't mind if you marry me out of need. I love you. And let me tell you, you shall *need* me and *need* me badly. And there is a short step from needing someone to loving someone."

Larissa had nothing more to say. "You had better go now, before Nínochka comes back. It will be easier for you."

His shoulders sagged, defeated. He sat silently for a moment, staring at the floor. Then, he slowly stood. "Goodbye, Larka ... But remember, I am not giving you up!" His eyes were now full of tears. Looking at him, Larissa felt her own eyes welling.

"Goodbye, Igor ... One last thing: I would like to have back all my original documents and Nina's birth certificate."

His first reaction was anger. He wanted to say that he had destroyed the documents and that she must use her new identity that had made her into his *faux* wife. But he could not lie to her. Instead, he opened his portfolio and handed her a sealed packet with her documents. "They are all there," he said.

She embraced him and kissed him on his wet eyes. "Thank you!"

"Oh, Larka ..." He squeezed her in a bear hug and kissed her hard on the mouth. Then he released her and almost ran out of the room. She did not follow him.

93

It took Larissa several weeks to get used to her new life in Petrograd. The first week was heady with the excitement of rediscovering her beloved city, of digging into her scant reserves of money to take Nínochka on long rides on the streetcars. The rides bored the child. She was still too young to appreciate the beauty of the city or be interested in its history, and the April weather was still brutally cold and the snow too deep to spend much time in the parks.

There were a few moments of excitement when some furniture, dishes, bed linens, and kitchen utensils arrived. None of it was new, but it was given to them free of charge. It all had been confiscated from someone's destroyed life and kept at government warehouses.

Maria Nikoláyevna and Larissa did not discuss their new bounty, both feeling humiliated by using someone else's private possessions yet realizing that they were lucky to be the recipients of so many needed items. Maria Nikoláyevna briefly wondered who was using *her* possessions, but she chased the unpleasant thoughts out of her mind.

As advised by Dimka, Larissa signed the receipts for the deliveries as "Requested by Commissar I. N. Kóshkin." Natasha assured her that there would be no inquiries of any kind. "Everything was requested according to law, so you don't need to worry. The Commissar has a solid reputation and the fact that he doesn't live at this address right now means nothing. These days most men are still not living with their families. Look at Dimka! The men are needed by the Soviets somewhere else." Larissa thought that Natasha was being sarcastic, but no, she was sincere.

Natasha arranged for Larissa to have a permanent registration that gave her the legal rights for nine square meters of living space in her mother's room. It meant that Lara had become again a legal citizen of Petrograd, and it meant that her mother no longer had to pay the special tax on her room.

In the second week, Larissa began her new life by making a trip to register with the Employment Bureau. "You must be prepared to make several visits there before you get an assignment. Of course, you'll have a better chance if you use Igor's name as his wife," Dimka had counseled her.

"No!" she exclaimed. "I shall use my own name. I think that my working credentials and the letter of recommendation from the Commissar of the Odessa Soviet Memorial Hospital should be enough to open the doors for me."

"Don't be too optimistic. We are suffering from severe unemployment. Hundreds of desperate people will be competing with you for the same job. Any job."

Discouraged but still determined, Larissa walked toward the Geological Institute on the Nevá embankment where a local branch of the Employment Bureau was located. At the front of the Geological Institute along the broad steps leading to its entrance there were two massive marble sculptures of the *Rape of the Sabine Women*, a realistic representation of brutal force and hopeless resistance. She remembered how as a girl she had gazed at the sculptures and wondered why those men were so cruel. She pitied an infant on the ground who must have been torn out of his mother's arms. She had forgotten who the Sabine women were and who the attackers were. "I must start re-reading classical history," she reflected. "I have forgotten so much!"

But that day something else dominated her attention. It was a long line of poorly clad men and women forming a queue that snaked out from the massive doors of the Institute, down the steps, all the way to the sidewalk—unemployed citizens who had come to register for a job.

She took her place at the end of the line and in a few minutes ten or more people joined the line behind her.

Surprisingly, the queue moved briskly. As Lara discovered, it was a line where people only registered their names and addresses. There were no interviews. People gave their names and addresses, the women clerks in semi-military attire typed them in triplicate and gave one copy to the applicant.

From listening to the conversations along the queue, Larissa soon learned that the real problems were going to start with the interviews: the applicants, even for a janitorial job, would be *interrogated* by a team of women who had no sympathy for anyone's situation, according to the experienced applicants.

That did not bode well for her, Larissa thought.

The grand vestibule of the Institute was crowded with desks over which floated balloons with crudely written letters of the alphabet.

Larissa searched for the letter 'R'. The air was filled with the rhythmic clatter of typewriters and the sounds of coughing. It seemed that every person was sick and should have stayed in bed. People coughed without covering their mouths, some spitting their phlegm on the floor. "It will be a miracle if I leave without picking up some disease," Larissa thought, pulling the end of her scarf across her mouth and nose.

She found the desk under the letter 'R'. In front of it there was an old man leaning on a cane desperately trying to explain something to a grim-looking woman at the typewriter. He spoke with a strong French accent, mispronouncing Russian words and making the woman in a red kerchief increasingly annoyed the more he tried to explain himself.

Larissa felt sorry for the old man. He probably was a surviving member of some rich household, a butler perhaps, who got stuck in Russia after the revolution. She listened as he pathetically tried to explain to the clerk that he was a sous chef.

Finally, ignoring the decree that speaking a foreign language was forbidden, she offered her help to the old man. She explained to the clerk that he used to be a cook's assistant and was looking for any job anywhere. She dictated to the clerk his name and address.

The clerk pouted but followed the procedure and gave the old man his registration.

"Merci, merci, Madame!" He almost doubled over in a low bow and then choked in a paroxysm of coughing. Still coughing, the old man limped away.

"So what are *you* doing here?" the clerk addressed Larissa, sounding a little friendlier. "This is a registration office for the lowest unskilled jobs. You are obviously educated, so this is the wrong place for you."

"I am a nurse," Larissa replied, "and I badly need a job. I'll take anything that's available."

"Take my advice: go directly to a hospital and apply for a job on the spot! Most likely the very first hospital will hire you! Go! Don't waste your time here. It's not for you!"

"Thank you," Larissa said, but the woman waved her off and called, "Next!"

Larissa waited for a streetcar for the Pertrográdskaya Storoná, where her old hospital was located, and took a seat near the conductor, who smiled at her, a rare thing in those days. People had forgotten how to smile.

For a short time Larissa was the only passenger since she boarded the streetcar at the end of its loop.

"Could you tell me where I have to get off for the Botkin's Hospital?" she asked the conductor.

"Sure, honey, it's a long way, on the other side of the city."

"Yes, I remember that it was quite far."

"Are you a nurse?"

"Yes. I used to work in a hospital in Odessa," she said. "Why am I telling her about myself?" she thought. But it was too late. The conductor was full of questions.

"Is it true that in Odessa there are many criminal gangs?"

"Well, I don't know ... Odessa has a bad reputation because of the bad behavior of the sailors, but I don't think that it's worse than in any other large city. How about Petrograd? I have been living in Odessa since the war, so I don't know what's going on here."

"Oh, it is horrible here! We have gangs made up of children!"

"Children?"

"Yes. Twelve, thirteen year-old boys organize themselves into gangs and terrorize the city under the command of seventeen, eighteen years olds."

"But who are they, the boys?"

"They are homeless boys whose fathers were killed in the war or shot after the war, whose mothers have died or abandoned them. There are hundreds of them in the city. Maybe even thousands. People say the boys kill as easily as they spit. They have no one to take care of them, so they take care of themselves. They work as a team and rob anybody. I have been robbed right here on this tram four times already, and a friend of mine, who works on the Lígovka line, has been robbed seven times!"

"And the homeless girls?"

"They don't rob. They become whores."

The car began to fill up. Two elderly women climbed the steps to the back platform and bought tickets for three sections of the trip. A young woman with a baby took a seat close to the exit, followed by an old man covered with a thick white beard, like Father Frost. As the streetcar began to move, a sick-looking boy, dirty and in tatters, jumped on the back platform and plopped himself on the bench without paying.

"Where are you going, boy? You must buy a ticket," the conductor said mildly. The boy ignored her.

She looked at Larissa and pointed at him with her eyes. Then she pointed with her eyes to Lara's purse. Larissa understood: the boy was a scout, and they could expect a visit from the rest of the gang at any moment. The other passengers apparently did not need to be warned: at the first sight of the boy, they began casually probing inside their pockets, trying to relocate their money, while the boy watched silently.

Larissa did not have much money, but she certainly did not want to lose whatever she did have. She reached into her purse as if to get her handkerchief, feeling her way around a few things on the bottom, and scooped the coins into the handkerchief. She wiped her nose and then pushed the handkerchief with the coins through the top of her válenki.

At the next stop there were no regular passengers waiting, just a tight knot of ragged adolescents. As the streetcar stopped, they split into two groups and calmly entered both cars.

"Give us your money, or I blow your fucking heads off!" a boy about fifteen yelled at the passengers, pointing a Nagant gun wildly, while the rest of the boys quickly felt in the passengers' pockets and purses. The boy with the gun pointed it at the conductor, and she quickly pressed the valves of the contraption hanging on her chest, releasing the coins that were stored there. The coins dropped almost soundlessly into the boy's dirty cap. It was all done very efficiently.

The boys, including the scout, left the streetcar at the next stop and disappeared down a side street.

"Oophs!" the conductor sighed. "We are lucky that they did not take our coats and boots!"

"Don't the militia patrol the city?" Larissa asked.

"They do, but there are too many bandits. They arrest the men and send them to the labor camps. They lock the younger ones in some special children's homes, where they get a bit of schooling. But it usually doesn't work. The boys run away and rejoin the gangs. It's all very sad. A whole generation of our children is gone, destroyed, wiped out!"

"She is better educated than her job requires," Lara thought. "What sort of work did you do before you became a streetcar conductor?" she asked.

The woman smiled wryly. "An arithmetic teacher in a girls' school."

The old hospital looked less formidable than Larissa remembered. It was dilapidated, its paint peeling, the waste bins that used to be out of sight now were in full view next to the main entrance.

Larissa entered the lobby and looked for a doorman or a receptionist who could guide her to a proper office. As she remembered, that particular part of the hospital had never looked like a hospital. It looked like a nineteenth century middle-class parlor, including a piano under a bouquet of wax roses in a crystal vase. She smiled, remembering the garish bouquet. There used to be a large painting of the Tsar over the fireplace, and there still was a large painting, but it was of Lenin.

Larissa heard the sound of a typewriter from behind one of the doors. She knocked, but whoever was there did not hear it. She opened the door.

A middle-aged man was typing laboriously with two fingers on a tall Underwood machine.

He looked annoyed. "What do you want?" he asked rudely.

"I am sorry to disturb you, Comrade, but there was no one I could ask about directions ..."

"So, what do you want?" he repeated impatiently.

"I wanted to inquire whether there was an opportunity for a position on the nursing staff. I was trained at this hospital during the war, and I—"

"There are no positions open," he interrupted. "Besides, you must apply to the Commissariat of Public Health. *They* do all the hiring." He turned back to his typing.

"Perhaps you can help me. Where is the Commissariat of—"

"I am not the Bureau of Inquiries."

"I am sorry that I disturbed you," she said politely but churning with anger.

"So, you are sorry. Good! Now, leave. Or I'll call an orderly to escort you off the premises!"

Once outside the room Larissa sat on a stuffed chair to calm herself. She was furious. "Who was that terrible man?" she thought. "Why was he so hostile?"

A young dark-haired woman carrying a stack of papers entered the parlor. "May I help you?" she asked in a low, business-like voice.

"No, thank you, I was just leaving ... Who is the man in that room?"

"Our Commissar, Comrade Toumánov."

"A Commissar? He doesn't look it. He is not a military man, is he?"

"Oh, no. He is a civilian. The times are changing, Comrade! Did you want to see him?"

"No, thank you. He just threw me out of his office when I inquired about the possibility of working here. I am a nurse."

"Yes, the Commissar can be very rough," the young woman agreed. 'Did he tell you to inquire at the Commissariat of Public Health?"

"Yes. Where is it?"

"At the old Smólny Institute."

"Smólny Institute! My own alma mater!" Larissa thought.

"I would not advise you going the Commissariat right now, unless you don't mind working in a field hospital somewhere in the provinces. They would mobilize you on the spot and send you somewhere."

"I cannot go away from Petrograd again. I have just come back from Odessa to take care of my aging mother. I also have a very young daughter. I can't leave them."

"And you have no husband?"

"No. I am a widow. My husband was a pilot."

"Oh ... Then he was an *officer*, wasn't he?"

Larissa hesitated. Inadvertently she had said more than was wise. But it was too late to correct her mistake. "Yes" she said.

"Well, right now it will be *impossible* for you, to get a job at the city hospitals. But try the Women's Hospital on Vassilievsky Island. They are a little different. Women continue to give births, even during the class wars," she joked. "Ask for Doctor Kline. Perhaps she could help you. Tell her that Sonya suggested it. Good luck!"

"Thank you, Sonya! You made me forget your rude Commissar!"

Sonya smiled and disappeared behind the Commissar's door.

The Women's Hospital was built by Catherine the Great as a part of her plan to bring Russia into the cultural and scientific climate of her European neighbors. *The Birthing House,* as it was called, was Catherine's gift to the Russian women and babies who were prone to childbirth deaths.

At first people ignored the hospital. They mistrusted the idea of organized medical help, preferring the old canon of *'All in God's hands.'* To convince her subjects of the importance of their new hospital and its services, Catherine made an example of *herself* by getting vaccinated against smallpox. She knew that merely ordering her subjects to get vaccinated was not enough. The Russians had to be reassured. Slowly they began to accept the idea of concentrated medical services.

The upper class women, who had always given birth at home, reacted to the hospital with utter disdain. They considered all hospitals to be strictly *charitable* institutions and ridiculed the idea of pre-natal care. They laughed at attempts to save the lives of the endangered infants. "The indigent masses breed like mice! Why spend money on *saving* their babies? Let the nature take its course."

However, as the eighteenth century progressed, the hospital became a welcome institution. During the various pandemics that regularly decimated Russia, hospitals became bastions against the dreaded diseases. During the First World War, the Women's Hospital was used as a military facility, but in the early 1920s, the Soviets returned the building to its original designation as a maternity hospital.

A large building of gray stone built close to the Academy of Sciences among a park-like setting, had one of the most magnificent views in Petrograd. It looked out on the Nevá and the Admiralty embankment with its classical architecture and statuary.

Larissa entered a reception hall handsomely sheathed in dark wood. The leather furniture and the carved wood tables, the bookcases along the walls and tall bronze lamps, reminded her of her father's study. "This elegance certainly doesn't belong in a hospital! It looks like a Noblemen's Club!" she thought.

She stopped in front of a desk presided over by a young woman with a red kerchief on her head.

"May I help you, Comrade?" the young woman inquired.

"Yes," Lara replied. "I would like to see Doctor Kline, if I may."

"Do you have an appointment?"

"No."

"Are you her patient? If yes, I'll have to get your records." She sounded friendly.

"No, Comrade. I have never met doctor Kline. I am a military nurse, but I worked at Odessa Memorial all these years. Is there a chance of getting a job here?" She decided to not waste her time seeing Doctor Kline if there was no chance.

The receptionist met her eyes. "Doctor Kline might be surprised why you, an experienced military nurse, should seek employment at a *birthing* hospital! Wounds and amputations are your expertise, not screaming women and yelling babies!"

"True," Larissa said. "I went to the Botkin's, but they told me to forget about a job in any of the hospitals. A kind young woman, Sonya, suggested that I see Doctor Kline. So, here I am!"

"Did they explain why they thought that you shouldn't even try?"

Larissa decided to be totally honest. "Yes. Basically, because I am a widow of a pilot and ..."

"A *former person*," the receptionist finished the sentence.

"Yes."

"Well, whoever it was who told you that, was right. But our hospital is a little different. We don't discard people who are willing to work hard, no matter their class background. We *need* people who are well educated, who speak foreign languages. Do you speak French?"

"I do."

"You see? You are exactly the type of a person that we *need!* Go to the second floor. Doctor Kline's office is third on the left. Her name is on the door."

Larissa knocked on the dark-paneled door with Doctor Kline's name neatly printed by some calligrapher on a cream-colored card and inserted into the central panel.

"Come in!"

Larissa entered and stood at the door.

"Do sit down," the doctor pointed to a chair in front of her desk.

"Thank you. I have been recommended to see you, Doctor Kline, by a kind stranger, a young woman, called Sonya," Larissa began.

"Yes?" Dr. Kline lifted her eyebrows. She looked very small and thin, like an adolescent child were it not for her graying hair gathered tightly into a knot at the back of her head and scores of tiny wrinkles on her Semitic face. Dressed in a severe old-fashioned black dress with a white lacy collar and seated behind a huge mahogany desk, she looked like a strict schoolmistress.

"So, what is the reason for your visit? Are you in need of medical help?"

"Oh, no, Doctor. I am in need of *work*. I am a widow, with a small child, trained at the Botkin's during the war. I have arrived from Odessa couple of weeks ago to rejoin my aging mother."

"Why were you in Odessa if you were trained here?" Doctor Kline asked.

"Because my husband was severely wounded and was in Odessa Memorial Hospital. I went to Odessa to take care of him."

"Did he die?"

"Not at that time. He survived and returned to his detachment. He was a pilot. He died a few months ago …"

Doctor Kline looked at her, reading correctly her identity as a *former person*.

"Do you speak any foreign languages?" Doctor Kline asked.

"Yes. I speak French, English, and German."

Doctor Kline imagined Larissa in a white silk ball gown, with white kid gloves above her elbows. Yes, she knew who that young beauty was, she thought.

"Why don't you apply for a job as an interpreter or some office position requiring your type of education?"

"Because I was trained as a nurse and was good at it. Also, because of my political situation, I may not fit the present regulations."

Doctor Kline nodded understandingly. "So, how did you meet Sonya?"

"She came to my rescue when I was denied even a short conversation with an official at the Botkin's hospital. She suggested that I come here, and talk to you."

"How old are you, Larissa …?"

"Sergéyevna," Larissa introduced her patronymic.

"Larissa Sergéyevna. How old are you?"

"I am twenty-four. I have a daughter, almost six years old."

"Do you live in Petrograd?"

"Yes. My mother and my child and I live in a communal flat nearby."

"And what about your father?"

"He died before the Revolution. Heart failure."

"I see ... Was he in the military service?"

"Yes. At the time of his death he was in the Tactical Advisory of the General Staff."

"In what rank?"

The doctor's point blank questions put Larissa on guard. This information was enough to get her arrested. She hesitated for a moment, then decided to be truthful.

"When I was born he was already a general."

"In other words, your family was the hereditary nobility?"

"Yes," Larissa said, meeting her eyes.

Doctor Kline observed Larissa with open curiosity. "The young woman is obviously smart. She is aware of the consequences of trying to hide her origins. Or is she *stupid*, talking so openly to a stranger?" she thought, staring at Larissa.

"Doctor Kline doesn't like me ..." Larissa thought. "She won't help me ..." but she remained seated in front of the desk, her folded hands slightly trembling on her lap.

"I'll tell you what I'll do," Doctor Kline finally said. "I'll employ you on a *temporary* basis as a nurses' aide. Since you don't know anything about pre-natal care, you'll have to learn about it while doing the most disagreeable tasks. Your salary will be small, but you will receive food stamps, which in times of famine are more valuable than money. At the end of a month, my nursing staff will evaluate your work. I think, they will be fair in their evaluation even though they will quickly realize that you are from the *former class*. It is written all over you, but they are kind people. If these conditions suit you, I'll take a chance on you."

Larissa felt her eyes filling up. "Thank you, Doctor Kline. I am not afraid of any work, however unpleasant it may be. Thank you!"

"Leave your documents with me. Come back tomorrow morning, and I'll return them. Meanwhile, I'll discuss your application with the management and our political Commissar. Don't worry, we are less rigid than the Botkin's!"

"I'll be forever thankful to that Sonya!" Larissa exclaimed. "I wish I could write to her, but I don't even know her last name!"

"It is Kline. Sonya is my niece."

⠿ 94 ⠿

The Commissar of the Women's Hospital was a middle-aged woman named Vera Petróvna Gavrílko, a Ukrainian communist from Vínnitsa, a city on the Southern Bug River. In her big office full of spring sunshine, the walls were covered by bookshelves. Two huge portraits dominated the space between the windows. One was of Lenin, another of Michaíl Frúnze, the Red General who had forced Vrángel's army out of the Crimea. One bookshelf contained biographies, from Marco Polo and Christopher Columbus to Isaak Newton and Charles Darwin. Another shelf was filled with the works of Russian explorers, Krusenstern and Lysiánsky, Béring and Bárents. The other bookshelf was full of political writings, predominantly Lenin's.

Larissa was surprised by the choice of books. Either the Commissar was extremely erudite or she had inherited the books from the pre-revolutionary administrations. "The latter, most likely," she thought cynically as she observed the Commissar—a tall, angular woman with copper-colored hair cut very short. The deep furrows on the Commissar's forehead made her look permanently disapproving of something, or someone, in this case—Larissa, who intuitively felt that the Commissar did not like her.

The Chief Nurse was just the opposite. Also of middle age, Raísa Grigórievna Stern was all warm smiles as she welcomed Larissa to their 'family.'

"I understand you have a little girl. After you get acquainted with our operations, perhaps you should take a look at our Children's Center. We started this new program for very young children while their mothers are ill and unable to take care of them. Most of them have no fathers. We keep the children during the day, and we feed them and allow them to be *children* as they run in the garden, all under the supervision of young women who are in training to be kindergarten teachers."

"What a great idea!" Larissa exclaimed.

"The cut-off age for our program is six," the Commissar said, guessing the Chief Nurse's idea.

"Larissa's daughter could still qualify until she turns six," the Chief Nurse objected. She turned to Larissa. "The ARA, the American Relief Administration, has our Children's Center on their lists. We are guaranteed regular distribution of food, while the general population of needy children might never be included in those lists."

"It's a very good idea," Doctor Kline joined the conversation. "Let's see if Comrade Rezánova's daughter could be added to our program. Bring your little girl with you tomorrow," Doctor Kline said decisively. "Meanwhile, let's show Comrade Rezánova our facility."

It was huge. In addition to the doctors' offices, library, and large dining room, there was a lecture hall in a horseshoe-tiered pattern. Larissa was shown three large birthing wards and three dormitory-style wards where the beds stood side by side separated from one another only by small night tables.

Behind the wards were the toilets for the patients who could walk. The toilets looked like medieval chambers of horror. Raised about a foot over the marble floor was a platform with several pairs of giant footprints made of stone. Between each two sets of prints were gaping holes. The user of the toilet had to place her feet on the footprints and squat low over the holes without anything to hold on to. A rough lever nearby was used for flushing, spilling water over the footprints. Obviously antiquated versions of the toilets were still in use.

Larissa assumed that cleaning of the toilets would be one of her duties. She could see that the Commissar was waiting for her to recoil in disgust, but she would not give her that satisfaction.

"I presume that the hospital has some more modern toilets as well?" she asked the Chief Nurse.

"Oh, yes!" the woman laughed. "These toilets are historical exhibits of sorts."

"The Government is allocating a lot of money for restoring historical facilities!" Commissar Gavrílko said.

"There are many *more* important expenses than restoring ancient toilets," said Doctor Kline. "I would rather have new surgical instruments! I would demolish this *exhibit!*"

"Oh no, we can't! These toilets are historical!" the Commissar objected seriously. "We may relocate them to the Museum of Ethnography as an example of the Imperial attitude toward its slaves! We'll *never* get rid of them! They belong to the people!"

Doctor Kline raised her eyebrows skeptically. "Now you are carrying your zest into the realm of fantasy, Comrade Commissar! They are nothing but eighteenth century *crappers!*" she said contemptuously. "Anyway, enough of that! Let's show our new comrade some of the more inspiring aspects of our organization!"

When Larissa returned home there was a letter and a package from Kóshkin. She was pleased. It was the first time that he had written to her since they had parted. Not hearing from him, she presumed that he had turned his back on her.

"All his proclamations of love are easily forgotten," she thought with a certain amount of disappointment that she did not want to acknowledge. But now, holding his letter in her hands, she felt ... well, she felt *happy!* But this feeling, she did not want to acknowledge either.

"*My Dearest Lárochka,*" Igor wrote, calling her for the first time in the affectionate, upper class form of address.

"*There is not a day or a night when I don't think of you and cry into my pillow. Don't laugh, I truly cry,*" he wrote.

His letter was short and full of both spelling and grammatical errors, but Larissa knew that it was from the heart. The most interesting news was that Igor had enrolled in accelerated courses for "*total immersion in everything,*" as he wrote.

"*The Soviet Government has realized the lack of educated people,*" he wrote." *It has decreed the creation of a new educated class. Thousands of teachers are being mobilized right now to teach tens of thousands of young communists! I am one of these students!*"

The food package accompanying the letter included a variety of dry fruits, flour, sugar, a tin of lard, and several packets of powdered yeast. Kóshkin addressed it to Maria Nikoláyevna with a short note that there was a recipe in English in the sugar tin. "*You won't have any trouble following it since you speak the language!*" he added in his schoolboy's handwriting.

There was also a coloring book and a set of coloring pencils for Nínochka. "*Let her draw me a picture!*" he requested.

"*Please write to me, Larissa. Let me know what you are doing, where you are working, and if you need anything. I might be able to come to Petrograd in July or August. I love you, Lara, and I swear! I'll win your love when I am really educated!*"

The last sentence of his letter made her sad. "Poor Igor! He believes that we are divided only by his lack of education!" she thought.

She let her mother read the letter. Maria Nikoláyevna contemplated it seriously and then said, "He really *wants* you! But he could be dangerous since he considers you as already *belonging* to him. You must be careful and never encourage this belief. Be friendly, be supportive of his ambitions, but be *very* careful in dealing with his feelings. Rejected lovers are the most *dangerous* men!"

Larissa took her mother's advice to heart. She wrote Igor about her adventures, describing searching for a job humorously and making fun of the *'historical treasure'* of the toilets.

"I am glad that Nínochka passed the scrutiny of Commissar Gavrílko. Actually, she brought a smile on the Commissar's face. Nina asked permission to touch her flaming red hair. The Commissar was confounded, but Nínochka insisted, saying that it was very beautiful and looked so-o-o soft. Before the Commissar could refuse, Nínochka was already on her lap, petting her hair, saying that she just loved it! She declared that she would have the same hair when she grows up!"

She wrote, *"We are so proud of you, Igor. You have taken on an enormous responsibility. But knowing you, as I do, I am sure that you won't give up! When you get into the groove of your studies and have a little time for 'reading for pleasure,' start with the short stories of Tourgeniev's "Notes of the Hunter." His themes of Russian village life will be familiar to you. You'll be at home around his characters and the woods and the fields, and his hunting dogs. When you become used to reading for pleasure, then branch out to Chekhov and Tolstoy's War and Peace. It's a long book, but it will give you a new perspective of our country's history. From the highest nobility to the poorest peasants, you'll discover that all Russians loved Russia!"*

She let her mother read her letter, and Maria Nikoláyevna declared it "Just right! Except the sentence about *'all Russians loving Russia'.* I would take it out."

Larissa re-read the sentence and agreed.

Several weeks passed. Larissa worked hard, doing the most menial jobs. She did everything with good cheer, keeping out of Commissar Gavrílko's way. Doctor Kline tried several times to elevate Larissa to the position of an Operating Room nurse, but the Executive Committee, which consisted mainly of Gavrilko's appointees, always voted it down.

"We cannot trust somebody like her in the operating room. She is a *former person*, who probably hates us. There is no guarantee that she won't commit some kind of sabotage in revenge," they argued.

Doctor Kline was indignant. "We are wasting a talented nurse because we don't like her pre-revolutionary background when she was a young girl who skipped rope and played the piano! It is *stupid* and very short-sighted!"

"Let the *aristocratka* clean the crappers of the working class for a change! It will teach her a lesson!" Gavrilko declared.

But there was also a small victory for Larissa: Nínochka was accepted into the hospital's kindergarten.

The short Petrograd summer arrived, and people felt the surge of new energy. The white nights came in June when there was but a couple of hours of crepuscular light separating the day from the night in that most *magical* time. People exhausted by famine and sickness, broken down by deaths, suspicious of one another, suddenly found themselves strolling during the night on the embankments of the Nevá or enjoying the new greenery in the leafy private parks that the Soviets had opened for all citizens. The young people were falling in love again, the old reminisced about their youths. It was that magical time in a jewel of a city.

Larissa became close friends with Natasha, her former maid. They were the same age, only now their positions on the ladder of social standing were reversed. Larissa was at the bottom, while Natasha was ascending.

On a soft night when it seemed that no one could sleep and the sky was pink and orange, they took a street car to Yelágevsky Island and its famous Strélka, a small spit of land that intruded into the Gulf of Finland like a tip of an arrow.

It was a part of the park surrounding a classical small palace. Through the centuries its royal owners landscaped the park with exquisite marble statuary and surrounded it with flowers in elegant marble urns.

It used to be a private park, but it was now open to the general public, and it became the perfect spot for watching a sunset. A long, broad alley with allegorical marble statuary among the trees led through the park to the Strélka where two large marble lions guarded it at both ends of the broad terrace. The lilacs in full bloom, planted in small groves here and there, filled the air with its intoxicating fragrance, mixing it with the salty sea air.

Suddenly Natasha stopped and pointed to a white marble statue in the lilac grove. It was of a young woman holding flowers, hesitating at the edge of a small water pool, carefully testing it with her foot .The real water at the pool barely touched the toes of the sculpture.

"Do you recognize it?" Natasha said in a whisper as if someone might hear. "It's *you!*"

They came closer. Sure enough, it was the sculpture of Larissa for which she had posed when she was sixteen.

"Yes, I remember! Ksusha was always there to watch over me and not allow that Italian artist to have any liberties with me." They both laughed. "Ksusha would adjust the *chitón* over my naked breast by pulling it up, while the Italian artist tried to pull it down, as a far as possible! It was hilarious to watch them try to communicate with one another. One time, when the Italian tried to expose my breast a bit more, Ksusha struck his hand and cursed him. She cursed him using the most terrible swear words!"

Larissa looked at the image of herself and felt twinges of nostalgia and sadness.

"It's good to know that the sculpture wasn't destroyed, but placed instead in the park, for everybody to enjoy!" Natasha said.

They sat on the bench and stared at the sky reflected in the peaceful shimmering ripples around the shallow sea at the Strélka. They did not talk anymore but stared at the water, feeling at peace.

Suddenly, two young sailors plopped themselves on the bench next to them, ogling them, ready to flirt. The magic of the white night was broken. It was time to move away.

Nínochka blossomed in her kindergarten. The extra nutrition restored her health, and the children admired her. Before long the children followed her in singing and dancing her snowflake song, as well as another song where she wore a paper flower hat and sang a solo welcoming the arrival of spring.

Everyone adored her, and she returned the affection in equal form. She especially loved Commissar Gavrílko and her copper hair. Whenever the Commissar visited the Children's Center, Nina climbed on her lap and touched the flaming bristles on her head. "It's so beautiful!" she would sigh. Soon the other children began to compete for the privilege of sitting on her lap and touching her hair. The adults found it cute, but Commissar Gavrílko did not share their opinion: she found the other children repulsive with their runny noses and dirty hands.

At the end of summer, Larissa received a letter from Igor that his official visit was cancelled. Larissa was disappointed. She had looked forward to seeing him and frankly, hopping in bed with him! This she did not admit to her mother.

Maria Nikoláyevna did not ask any questions. She had noticed that Larissa's feelings toward Igor were changing. She also noticed a change in Nínochka, who began to talk about having *two papas*—one in heaven, flying in the pretty airplanes with the angels, and another with whom she had traveled on the choo-choo train. She missed *that papa* a lot, she kept saying. Larissa did nothing to stop Nínochka from fantasizing that her *airplane papa* could bring her *Kóshkin papa* to Petrograd on his angel airplane.

It was all very sweet and cute, but Maria Nikoláyevna did not like it. In the softening of Larissa's attitude toward Igor was a microcosm picture of the whole country, she thought, where the opposition to the Soviet rule was visibly changing in favor of the Communists. She still hoped that the Allies would come to their senses and dislodge the Bolsheviks from Russia's borders. But the Allies were comfortably ensconced in Switzerland, drinking hot chocolate and arguing politely in their new League of Nations about *World Peace and Democracy.* "It's probably too late to save Russia," she thought.

Nínochka broke down in tears when she learned that Kóshkin wasn't coming. All day at school she was subdued.

The Commissar noticed. "What is the matter with my Nínochka? Why are you so sad?" she asked.

"Because my Papa isn't coming. Mama doesn't know when he will come. I miss my Papa so much!"

"The child is delirious!" Gavrílko thought, probing Nina's forehead if she were feverish. "Her father is *dead!*"

Seeing the Commissar's puzzlement, the child explained patiently. "You see, I have *two Papas.* The *invisible* Papa Andrúsha flies with the angels, and the other Papa, Kóshkin, who came with us to my Bábushka, is not *invisible. But he doesn't live with us.* My Mama doesn't know when he will come to be with us, and my Bábushka says that he is *not* my *real* Papa, and I shouldn't wait for him. I don't know what to believe!"

Gavrílko put Nina down. There was something strange in the child's story. Maybe it was nothing—the confusion of a small child—but that little tidbit of information deserved investigation. With those treacherous *former people*, one could never be too sure about anything.

95

Doctor Kline called Larissa into her office. "I have some unpleasant news for you, Larissa Sergéyevna," she began in a low voice. "It is strictly confidential. But I want to give you some advance warning so that you won't be caught by surprise. The Commissar has found something in your dossier that she finds suspicious, so she has called a meeting of the Comrades' Court. Do you know what that is?"

"No, but I presume I will be accused of something," Larissa said, a cold wave of fear binding her instantly, like the numbing fear that she had known in Odessa during the searches of her room by the revolutionary sailors. She possessed nothing illegal or subversive. She had no photographs of men in Tsarist uniforms, nothing that could be used to tie her to the enemies of the Revolution. Yet, the searchers always managed to confiscate something, like an extra pair of scissors, saying that one pair was enough for the family use, while the extra pair could be classified as a weapon.

"I don't know what they might accuse you of, but they know everything about you, so you must answer all questions truthfully. Look into the eyes of whoever is questioning you. You might ask friends who know you well if they would be willing to appear on your behalf, but don't be surprised if the answer is negative. People are afraid to get involved, even with the so-called Comrades' Courts. They are not very *comradely!*"

Doctor Kline lit a cigarette. "The main thing, *don't look scared*," she continued. "The popular belief is that only guilty people have reason to fear judicial procedures! The court will meet tomorrow. It doesn't leave you much time to prepare. You may leave early today, if you wish."

Larissa took a streetcar to the Housing Authority office. Natasha was about to leave when she spotted Larissa at the door.

"What happened?" she exclaimed in alarm. "Has anything happened to Nínochka or your mother?"

"No, no!" Larissa hurried to reassure her. "But I need your help!"

They walked along the Nevsky Prospect and stopped at the little park in front of the Alexandrinsky Drama Theatre. They sat on a bench across from a huge bronze monument to Catherine the Great surrounded by her most trusted men and one woman, Princess Dashkóva, seated in a circle at the Empress's feet. From a distance the monument looked like a medieval town crier's bell, the figure of the Empress representing its handle.

"So, what happened?"

Larissa told her. "I really don't know what they want," she said. "Doctor Kline suggested that if I have someone who knew me well—"

"I'll come with you!" Natasha interrupted. "I'll vouch for you!"

"Would you? Won't it be dangerous for you?"

"Don't you worry; not all communists are eager to arrest and shoot. Most of us want justice, and I'll see to it that you get it!"

The next morning the five members of the Comrades' Court gathered in Commissar Gavrílko's spacious office. Larissa and Natasha sat against the wall, and the Court members' chairs were arranged in a small semi-circle facing a single chair in front of them. Larissa was invited to take that seat.

Commissar Gavrílko introduced Larissa's 'case' to the group. "I have looked extensively through your documentation, Comrade Rezánova, and found something quite unsettling. This court will need you to explain a key omission of information on your application for a job—on several documents over the past few years, including a request for a permit to travel from Odessa to Petrograd." she said icily.

Larissa blanched and then calmed herself. "I don't understand what you mean," she said, trying to keep the tremor from her voice.

"Oh yes, you *do!*" the Commissar said sardonically. "You understand it very well. That is exactly why this little fact is missing from your documents, because you understood the damaging effect it could have had on your application!"

Larissa waited to hear the accusation.

"It's about your father," Gavrílko continued. "You wrote that he was a *soldier*. But we know that he was no ordinary soldier. You failed to mention his rank."

"He was a general," Larissa said without hesitation. "He died *before* the revolution. He had not been in active service for several years due to poor health."

The Commissar was taken by surprise. She had expected Larissa would try to wiggle out of an honest answer or break down in tears. She glared at Larissa.

"Why did you omit that he was a general?"

"I was afraid that I would be denied employment. I was born into a military family. My brother Peter was a cavalry officer, and he was killed in the first year of the war. I have no male relatives left. My father has been dead for nearly ten years, and he had no connection to my profession. Besides, there was only enough space on the line to write one word.

So, I wrote *'soldier'*, which was true. He was a *soldier* and he called himself so."

"Why were you *afraid*, as you say?"

"I had read in *Pravda* about the impending eradication of the *former class*. I was afraid that my *former* background would prevent me from getting a job, and I needed a job badly. As you know I accepted the lowest paying job, even though I am a qualified Operating Room nurse."

"Wasn't your husband also a Tsarist officer?" asked another member of the Comrades' Court. "Wasn't he a pilot?"

"Yes, he was," she replied, a sticky feeling of fear beginning to squeeze her in its coils.

"If the Comrades' Court would allow me to answer the question," Natasha raised her arm like a schoolgirl. "I am Natalia Ivánovna Makarova, member of the Communist Party since 1917, and I knew Lieutenant Rezánov since his cadet years. He was always a liberal-minded young man. Some of you may remember a great hero, a young pilot, who unhooked a live bomb that had stuck in the landing gear of his flying airplane. That pilot was Lieutenant Andrei Rezánov, Larissa's husband! His picture was in newspapers all over the country!"

The ambulance driver nodded. "I remember it! He was very young, wasn't he?" He turned to Larissa.

"Yes, he was twenty-two. We were just married."

"We are not discussing her husband's heroic activities, although I am sure there would be plenty of blatant anti-Soviet activities in *his* past. How well do you know Larissa Rezánova to speak in her defense?" the Commissar asked Natasha.

"I have known her since I was twelve. I lived in their house. My mother worked there, and when I turned sixteen, I joined her in her work …"

"In what capacity did your mother work there and in what capacity did you join her?" The Commissar grinned, sure that she knew the answer.

"We were maids," Natasha replied without hesitation.

"I thought so," the Commissar said smugly. "Were you *ever* invited by your *'friends'* to share a meal with them or to attend their parties?"

"We were *employees*," Natasha said patiently. "Those were different times, Comrades. Employees and employers never mixed, but I learned a lot from her. She even taught me a little French," she smiled at Larissa. "She and her mother wanted me to *'rise to my potential'* as they called it, and because of that I went to nursing school. What is important *now* is to know how well she works and not whether she was born into the nobility. Her *character* is noble," she concluded.

"Bravo, bravo!" the Commissar exclaimed sarcastically. "You should make a fine advocate! Perhaps you can enlighten us about Rezánova's present matrimonial status. I am somewhat puzzled."

Natasha was quick with an answer. "It is a bit complicated and painful."

"We'll be sympathetic," the Commissar said with heavy sarcasm. "But we would like to hear it directly from her." Larissa met her unfriendly stare and thought, "Why does she hate me?"

Larissa said aloud, "I was stranded in Odessa with my daughter during most of the war because the railroads stopped functioning. I was lucky to be employed by Memorial Hospital so my baby and I survived. Andrei did not. I don't know how and where he died. I don't have a grave to cry over, I have no pictures of him. Nothing!" She became emotional and made an effort not to break into tears.

Doctor Kline took over the questioning to give Larissa moral support. "So how did you finally manage to get to Petrograd?"

"That was both painful and shameful for me," Larissa said. "I was in the midst of my grieving, and I suspected that I would be fired from the hospital on account of my *former person* status. I would have died of starvation, as thousands of people had died, or I would have killed myself. But I had my little girl. I knew that I must save her. I was determined to go home, to Petrograd, to be with my mother. An acquaintance of my husband said that he would take me and my daughter to Petrograd if I agreed to travel with him as his wife. I agreed. I thought it would take us a week, but it took a much longer time to travel. We were ambushed by bandits and barely survived. Igor protected us as a good husband and father would, and my daughter called him Papa. She loved him! And he adored her."

"Did you sleep with him?" the cook asked bluntly.

"Yes. Our arrangement was strictly business. I pretended to be his wife, I slept with him and he helped me and my child to get home. We both fulfilled our agreements. He asked that I continue our arrangement by becoming his legal wife, but I could not do it. I was mourning my Andrei, as I still do. So, he deposited us at my mother's and left for his new assignment in the Crimea."

"It is all very *touching* and *noble*," the Commissar said. "And selfish, I may add. Did you ever think of your daughter, who loved this man and called him Papa?"

"She is a very loving child. She understood that her Papa Igor loved her very much but his work was far away. Igor and I parted on friendly terms. We correspond with each other, and he sends little gifts to Ninochka, and she sends him the pictures she draws. He is a good man."

"Then why don't you marry him, for Christ's sake?" exclaimed the cook. "There are very few good men left in Russia, after the war and that cursed Civil War!"

"What is his name? And what is his position that allowed him to travel and have such privileges?"

"His name is Igor Kóshkin and he is a Commissar of a Flight School."

Commissar Gavrilko now understood the child's blabber about two Papas. It all sounded exotic, all those peregrinations of love and sex, of bandits and deaths and the final bittersweet parting. "You favor *flyboys*, don't you?" she said lewdly and looked at her Court expecting them to laugh, but no one did.

"I think we have a good picture of Larissa Rezánova's character," the Commissar said, standing. "Apparently she is capable of doing *anything*, even *prostituting* herself in order to reach her goal." She said to Larissa and Natasha, "You'll be informed of the decision of the Comrades' Court in due time."

Larissa and Natasha stepped into the corridor and closed the door. "Thank you, dear friend, for standing up for me! I hope it won't jeopardize your standing within your own Party!" Larissa said.

"I hope so too, but I don't regret doing it. I did not want this inquiry to become a kangaroo court. But it did, anyway. For some reason that redhead hates your guts! I wonder why?"

"I have no idea ... Yet, she adores Ninochka!"

"What do you know about her?"

"Nothing. It never occurred to me to learn anything about her. Besides, even if I knew something, what good would it be to me against a system where people like me, and perhaps even Ninochka, are the *enemies?*"

"It will change!" Natasha exclaimed. "You'll see, it will change! Ninochka will grow up in a new classless and *just* society!" Natasha's cheeks reddened with excitement, and her eyes sparkled with enthusiasm.

Larissa remained silent.

The next day, Larissa received a dismissal from her job. Commissar Gavrílko personally handed her the Certificate of Dismissal and a few rubles of her two-week salary. She returned to Larissa her Labor card, where her dismissal was explained. Not having yet read the comments on the Labor card, Larissa was grateful to the Commissar: Nínochka was allowed to remain at the Children's Center until she turned six years old.

Larissa stopped at Doctor Kline's office to say goodbye.

"I want you to know that I voted *against* your dismissal," the doctor said. "And as you can see, I refused to sign the dismissal page in your Labor card, but it probably makes no difference. I am sorry! Keep in touch. I am sure that in a little while we can get you a job. I have some connections here and there," she said with tears in her eyes.

"I haven't yet read the dismissal page in my Labor card," Larissa said. "Is it that bad?"

"Yes. Sit down and read it. I'll leave you alone for a few minutes." She left the office.

Larissa opened the Labor card, her hands trembling. The official dismissal was identical to the document form that the Commissar handed to her. It was short, without any explanations. However, the hand-written notes on the next page explaining the reasons and signed by the Commissar and stamped with the official stamp, were the ones that stunned Larissa.

The Commissar wrote that Larissa Rezánova was a deceitful young woman who used sex as her weapon. She was described as an example of a dangerous *former person*, a daughter of a rich general and the wife of a rich pilot. Hers and Andrei's families were described as *nests of poisonous vipers*.

The conclusion of the note was a strong recommendation of denial of future applications for employment.

Under the circumstances of Larissa's life, it was like a death sentence.

96

Lara met Natasha at the University Embankment. "My mother is going to be devastated," she said.

"No, she will be *furious*," Natasha replied.

Natasha was right. Maria Nikoláyevna exploded with indignation. "It's obvious that you have become a marked woman. You can't keep this Labor card!" She took several gulps of water before she continued. "We must destroy it. Immediately!"

"Wait!" Larissa cried. "It is like a passport now. Everybody must carry one. I will be arrested if I don't have one."

"Not if you go to the Militia *at once* and report it stolen along with whatever money you had. The Militia will issue you a temporary identification. When you get a job, you'll get a new Labor card. Be smart!"

"I'll go with you to the Militia and then to the Employment Bureau as your witness," Natasha said.

"You girls stop talking and go *right now!* I'll take care of this cursed Labor card. Go!" She gulped some more water and lit a candle. The timid little fire turned the card into a tiny pile of ashes.

The young women left for the Militia. Maria Nikoláyevna threw herself on her bed. "What *more* do they want from us?" she lamented. "They destroyed our lives, they made us paupers, they killed our men … do they want to humiliate the remainder of us into *nothing* and wipe us off this earth?" She burst into long-suppressed tears.

The Militia officer on duty was sympathetic to Larissa's report of being robbed. "It's getting worse every day," she said. "The other day a band of them threw a matchbox full of *live lice* at a man who refused to give them his overcoat."

"How awful!" Natasha exclaimed.

Larissa sat in front of the desk, barely listening. She feared that the woman would interrogate her about the details of the 'robbery.' But the militiawoman was satisfied with Lara's affidavit and her application for a new identity document. The additional affidavit from Natasha as a Communist Party member guaranteed the validity of the report. The officer proffered Larissa a temporary identification certificate.

"Thank you for your help!" Larissa could barely keep herself from running out of the office.

That evening, they had an unexpected visitor—Doctor Kline. "I hope that you don't mind my visit," the doctor apologized. "I'll come back some other time if it is too late," she said.

"No, no! Come on in! My mother will be delighted!" Larissa led her into the long corridor toward their room. "Mama, we have a visitor! It's Doctor Kline!" she called ahead.

Maria Nikoláyevna flung the door open. "Come in! I've heard so much about you! Welcome, Doctor Kline!"

"Doctor Kline!" Nínochka jumped up from her bed. "How did you know where I live?"

"A little bird told me," the doctor replied, smiling.

"It must be the same little bird who lives in that tree in front of our windows! She knows everything!" Nínochka said seriously.

"Must be. But you'd better get back to bed," the doctor said. "I am glad to meet you, Maria Nikoláyevna." she added. "You're probably curious why I decided to come, so I'll explain."

"Please, do sit down," the old woman said. "A glass of tea?"

"No, thank you," Doctor Kline replied, taking a chair. "I wanted to apologize to you, Larissa Sergéyevna, for what occurred at the hospital. Actually, no apology is enough to explain my shock. Our new leaders demand that we, as a nation, must be respectful of each others' rights for honest work and protect those who are abused. Yet your rights were not respected by the Comrades' Court, and for that I am sorry. However, I may be able to help you. It's a long shot, but I'll talk to some friends and see if there is some way we can arrange for you to meet a very important person in Petrograd's arts community. It could result in part time work, maybe full time work, but I don't want to say too much yet. As I said, it's a long shot. Meanwhile, I think you ought to do some private tutoring of piano students. I can recommend one student already—my grandson, Grisha. He is eleven, and my son thinks he is quite gifted, but he has been without a teacher for almost a year. He lost his teacher during … you know, the purge. So if you are interested, it will give you at least some small income while we wait on the other possibility. My son is a dentist and as a bonus, he would take care of your teeth!" she smiled. "If you agree, you can start tomorrow. We live near the Tróitsky Bridge, on the Petrográdskaya Storoná. So, if you are interested …"

"I am interested," Larissa said, "And grateful!"

"Meanwhile, your granddaughter can stay at our kindergarten," Doctor Kline turned to Maria Nikoláyevna. "The Commissar seems to like Nínochka."

"I am looking forward to meeting that woman with the flaming red hair that our Nínochka so admires!" Maria Nikoláyevna finally smiled.

"Thank you, Doctor Kline, for sticking your neck out in Larissa's defense. I hope that *you* won't suffer the consequences!"

"Let's keep our fingers crossed. For every Commissar Gavrílko there are dozens of decent people, one hopes!" the doctor smiled.

"But who is this very important person whom I might meet?" Larissa asked. She couldn't resist trying to find out more.

The doctor smiled again. "His name is Klimov."

Maria Nikoláyevna and Doctor Kline became friends. They saw each other every day when Maria Nikoláyevna brought Nina to the kindergarten and then picked her up at the end of the day. Sometimes when Doctor Kline was not busy, she invited Maria Nikoláyevna into her office for a glass of tea. It became a moment of pleasure for both of them. They shared their love of French literature. Doctor Kline spoke some schoolgirl French with an atrocious accent and was delighted that Maria Nikoláyevna was fluent in it. They often spoke in French when they were alone. "We mustn't let ourselves forget the language!" Doctor Kline declared.

Commissar Gavrilko churned with anger at their friendship. She eavesdropped on their conversations but, not understanding a word of it, she could do nothing to stop it. Doctor Kline was a distinguished physician with good connections.

While her mother enjoyed her new friendship, Larissa had a tough time. She registered at the Unemployment Bureau and visited it every day, but not a single referral came her way. Once a week she gave piano lessons to Grisha, the grandson of Doctor Kline, and soon acquired another pupil, Rachel, the daughter of another dentist, also a student of Grisha's former teacher.

"It would be nice to have some other doctor," Maria Nikoláyevna joked, "Maybe a pediatrician who could treat our Nínochka free of charge!"

"You don't need to worry, Mama! All doctors' visits and hospitals are now free of charge!" Larissa said. "The private practice of medicine is forbidden. All healthcare is free now!"

"Where did you get *that* information ?"

"I read it in *Pravda*, in the dentist's apartment."

"Why, that's great! These Bolsheviks are finally showing a benevolent human face!" Maria Nikoláyevna exclaimed.

Larissa smiled. "Before long, Mámochka, you'll apply for membership in the Communist Party!"

"That will be the day!" she smirked. "No, I'll never forgive them what they have done to our country and to my family! No free medical service can pay for the destruction of our lives!" She took a deep breath and suddenly dissolved in a flood of bitter tears.

"Mama, Mámochka, what happened? Don't cry! It's good news, Mámochka! Don't cry!" Larissa dropped to her knees in front of her mother's chair, embracing her tightly, but Maria Nikolávevna continued to weep bitterly, as if there was no end to her tears. The good news about Soviet leadership of the country had brought out some new deep feeling that she did not understand. Were the Bolsheviks finally showing positive tangible results of their doctrine? Was the destruction of the old order justified? Were they *right?*

Nínochka, frightened, watched the scene. She had never seen her Bábushka cry. Her mother, yes, she cried often, especially at night when she thought that everyone was asleep, but Babushka?

"Take the towel, darling, and run to the kitchen! Wet it under the faucet and then hurry back. Can you do that?" Larissa said.

Nínochka nodded. She grabbed the towel and rushed into the dark corridor.

"Oh, my God! She'll fall down in the corridor trailing that towel!" Larissa thought.

But the child managed surprisingly well. She asked a neighbor who was washing dishes at the sink for help. "Please help us! My bábushka can't stop crying!"

"What is wrong with your Bábushka? Is she sick?" the neighbor asked, following the child into the corridor.

"I don't know. She cries. She has never cried like that before. Even *I* don't cry that much if I fall down!"

The neighbor, Anna Mikháilovna, the widow of a manager of an atelier of women's high fashion, lived with an adult daughter in a room next to Maria Nikolávevna. She and her daughter were quiet women who seemed to be afraid of their own shadows, who had never expressed any curiosity about Maria Nikolávevna or Larissa or even Nínochka.

This time, Anna Mikháilovna put aside her reticence and offered to help Larissa. Together they partially undressed Maria Nikolávevna, unbuttoned all the buttons and unhooked all the hooks that made it hard for her to breathe, took off her shoes, and placed her on the bed with a

696

cold compress on her head. Nínochka removed her grandmother's shoes and placed them neatly under the bed, lining them up toe to toe.

"I have a small bottle of laudanum," the neighbor said, "perhaps a few drops would help?"

"Oh, yes, thank you!" Larissa exclaimed. "That would be wonderful! I'll get in touch with our friend Doctor Kline, and she will take a good look at my mother. But a little bit of laudanum will certainly help!"

"I am deeply grateful for your help, Anna Mikháilovna," Larissa said once the drops had been administered and Maria Nikoláyevna was quiet.

"Never mind. I've noticed that Maria Nikoláyevna takes Nínochka to school every day. Would you like me to do it in her stead tomorrow?" the neighbor said.

"Yes, Mámochka, please let Auntie Annya take me to school."

Larissa was dumbfounded. "It surely would help if tomorrow you could take her to the kindergarten," she said."Thank you! Are you sure that it won't be an imposition ?"

"It won't!" Nínochka cried happily. "I don't know what it means, but if it is something *bad*, we won't let it happen, shall we Auntie Annya?"

"No, we won't," Anna Mikháilovna laughed. Whether she wanted it or not, she became another recipient of Nínochka's affection. She bade goodbye to Larissa and asked Nínochka's permission to give her a kiss.

"Only on my cheek," the child replied. "They told us at the kindergarten not to kiss anyone and not to *allow* anyone to kiss us. That's how the diseases get spread around. But, Auntie Annya and I, we know each other. We are friends, we even live in the same flat, so we can kiss!" she offered her round cheek to Anna Mikháilovna.

"You are a very smart girl!" the neighbor said, planting a light kiss on her pink cheek.

"I know! Do you want to hear me count to fifty?"

With the help of Nina, Larissa removed Maria Nikoláyevna's stockings. Nínochka's reaction to her grandmother's varicose veins made Larissa smile. "Look, look, Mama, look at all these pretty blue and purple drawings on Bábushka's legs! They are just like the rivers on Yasha's maps! Some of them are so long! Look at that one! It goes... all the way up to ... to Bábushka's private place! They are beautiful! I wish I could get something like that on my legs!" she sighed.

Maria Nikoláyevna opened her eyes and said in a clear voice, as if continuing the conversation, "We should not succumb to their show of goodwill. We must get help from our allies, but meanwhile we should sit tight and wait. The English will come, and everything will be alright again. The English will save us!" She burped loudly.

Nínochka giggled. "Bábushka always said that it is impolite to burp in public!" she said. "But we are not *public*. I'll sit *tight* right here, on Bá-bushka's footstool, and wait!"

She brought out from under the bed a little footstool embroidered with roses and placed it at the foot of the bed. "I can see Bábushka's face from here and watch her. I'll sit here as *tight* as can be, and as *long* as it takes, and I *won't move* until the English come!" she thought. "I want my bábushka to be happy!" She smoothed her dress over her knees, crossed her arms resolutely over her chest, and prepared to wait.

She thought of the marble statues in the park that never moved. "Are they also waiting for the English?" Nina thought.

Her nose began to itch, but she did not move to scratch it.

Larissa watched her, amazed at the child's determination. Then she concentrated on writing fingering for her pupils' next project, Shubert's *Moment Musicale*, which both children were preparing for their school competition. Despite Doctor Kline's optimistic hopes about her grandson's talent, it was Rachel who would probably win the competition, Larissa thought. She was much more talented, showing a real love of music, while Grisha played the piano only to satisfy his family demands.

Nínochka waited. The English were very slow in coming. Her feet were 'falling asleep' but worst of all, she needed to make the *pipí*.

The need became intolerable. Quickly she pulled the night pot out from under the bed and relieved herself. It felt so good! It took only a moment, but the spell was broken.

"It is all my fault ..." Nínochka thought. "The English ... They are not coming."

The English never came.

The summer was gone. Where had it gone? Nínochka stared at the window and the naked tree. The little bird who lived there and knew everything that was going on had probably gone to her winter home in Odessa. Nínochka felt sad. She turned six, and she cried because she was dismissed from the kindergarten. She keenly felt the sudden void in her social life.

"Some children have Papas, some don't. I had *two* of them, but I don't have any … I have never seen my Papa Andrúsha. I know that he was very brave and that he flew his airplane up there in the sky, with the angels. He also looked like me, Bábushka said. My other Papa, Papa Kóshkin, is very big and has a dark moustache. He was a lot of fun on the train, but I have not seen him since he left us at Bábushka's. He sends me presents and sweets, but I would rather have him!"she thought, feeling confused.

Nínochka had heard a conversation between her mother and Bábushka about Kóshkin, Larissa saying that she did not love him. It had cut deeply into her memory and made her ask Larissa why not. Kóshkin was fun! She reminded Larissa about hiding under the berth on the train during the attack. "It was so much fun!"

Her mother did not smile at that memory. "We did not have fun," she said.

"But why don't you *love* him? He is so good! He sends us all kinds of good things to eat! And he loves you and me!" Her mother had no answer to that.

Nínochka felt sad. Was she sad because Papa Kóshkin had left them? Or, was it because her Papa Andrúsha was *never* with them? He was her *real* papa, Bábushka said, but why wasn't he with them now? Her mother had no answer to that either.

That night, when Bábushka turned off the light, Nina cuddled closer to her mother and whispered "Tell me about my *real* papa. Tell me everything about him, tell me about how brave he was!"

And so, Larissa began to tell her daughter stories from the past, sifting through bright gems from her own youth, recalling her courtship with Andrei, and recovering some joy in the retelling.

After a few weeks, Nina could tell the stories herself.

97

The new year arrived, but it brought no changes to their lives. Larissa and her mother decided not to risk recriminations by celebrating Christmas, which was forbidden now.

Larissa still could not find employment through the official Government Employment Bureau, and no meeting had yet been arranged with the mysterious Klimov. Larissa continued to teach piano to some reluctant children, scraping by on very small returns and remaining on the rolls under *'unemployed female, non-worker's food rations.'*

Maria Nikoláyevna was more fortunate. She became friends with their neighbor Anna Mikháilovna, the widow of the manager of the former high fashion atelier *Le Dernier Cri*. Anna Mikháilovna used to be the top seamstress at the atelier. She lived in virtual poverty, surviving on the small salary of her daughter, a typist at a publishing office. Her husband had been arrested as an enemy of the people and had disappeared in some labor camp. By now he was probably dead.

Maria Nikoláyevna suggested to Anna Mikháilovna that they combine their talents in sewing and embroidery and start making custom clothes for the women of the new Soviet upper class. "Isn't the NEP exactly what Lenin created to encourage people to help themselves through private initiative?" she asked rhetorically. "We'll start modestly, the client bringing her own fabric and accessories, and we'll charge a high price for our work to make it exclusive, and exclusivity will make women *drool* for our label!"

"Our label?"

"Yes, of course! We'll create some elegant label and I'll embroider it inside each garment. It will become our *calling card*."

"What a plan! But how can we find our clients?"

"All we need is *one* person, a wife of some well-placed important man. Her new clothes will bring us the customers! All females, be they the peasant babas or Grand Duchesses, love good clothes. It's one of our gender's weaknesses," she winked.

"But do you know any such *well-placed important men?*"

"No. But I do know someone who *might* know such people" She thought of Doctor Kline.

Maria Nikoláyevna desperately tried to break through Larissa's increasing depression. She insisted that Larissa write about her troubles to Igor. "Let him know what happened at the Comrades' Court. He will advise us what to do!"

Larissa took her suggestion and wrote a long letter to Igor describing her problems with getting a job. *"How can I remove that dark spot from my reputation?"*

His reply came back within a week, hidden in the bag of flour in the food package from the American pilots. *"Use the name under which you traveled,"* was his laconic answer. It sounded too lighthearted to her. His method of hiding his message seemed childish. She was annoyed, not thinking that Commissars would be under surveillance like any other citizen.

"You are behaving like a fool!" Maria Nikoláyevna complained. "You take his gifts of food, not asking if he has enough food for himself! He gives you good advice, and you refuse it! Any man would revolt against such neglect, but he *loves* you, Lara, and so he tolerates it! Be thankful to him. Take pride in his achievements. Don't take him for granted."

"Mother is right," Larissa thought. "I have been taking Igor for granted, thinking of him no more than I would think of a loyal *retainer*."

She re-read his letter, ignoring the suggestion of using his name, which repelled her. She switched her attention to the page where Igor wrote that he had finished three terms at the top of the class in *RabFac*, workers educational facility and received an important prize: he was appointed a Commissar for the newly organized university in Vladivostok! He was to continue his education. He asked, almost timidly, whether Larissa would like to join him in Vladivostok. He knew, of course, that she wouldn't.

She put the letter down. She had to admit to herself that she would've liked to see him before he left for such a remote place as Vladivostok! As it was, she hadn't seen him for more than year. ... Being in Vladivostok, he would be even further away ... more than two weeks of travel on the Trans-Siberian railroad.

Kóshkin was determined to become an educated man, a goal he had never thought possible. It was now within his reach. He was well on his way to becoming a *cultured person*, a member of the educated class. He was proud of his advancement in life, but to be *really happy*, he needed more. He yearned for a family.

He entertained himself by re-reading Larissa's letters. He had saved all of them. Reading them in order of their posting, he felt that Larissa's attitude toward him was changing. While in the beginning her letters were dry and cautiously informative, like an article in *Pravda*, they were becoming more intimate, sometimes even *tender*, he thought. Each letter always contained Nina's drawing. Once in a while a note from Maria Nikoláyevna was included. It was always full of good will and practical advice, as if she were *his* mother. He had never had any letters from his mother. She was illiterate.

In her latest letter Larissa wrote about preparations for Nínochka starting school. At the time of her enrollment test when she was seven, Larissa wrote, Nínochka could read and write at a second grade level. They were so proud of her!

And so was Igor. "It is hard to believe that my Nínka is about to enter school!" he thought. "Hell, how I miss them!"

He had been chaste while working and studying in Sevastópol. There was simply not enough time for the demands of the flesh. He fantasized that Larissa might surprise him with a visit or that he would be sent to Petrograd on some official business. But now everything had changed again. Being ordered to go so far from the European part of the country presented new problems. He had to forget about business trips or dreams of a *surprise visit*. However, "*where there are problems, there are also the solutions,*" he thought. He would think of something. He was *educated* now!

On January 21, 1924, Russia was shaken to its foundations once again. Lenin died. It was not known by the general public that he had been in poor health ever since a would-be-assassin had badly wounded him way back in July of 1918. With Lenin's death, a brutal, secret battle for ultimate power sprang up among the top leaders of the Communist Party, but the multitudes of ordinary citizens were unaware of it.

During the first days of mourning all official buildings in the large cities were shrouded with black cloth. Thousands of gigantic portraits of Lenin framed by black bunting appeared on the façades of the buildings. Black and red flags flapped in January snowstorms on lampposts around the country, and black flags waved from the chimneys and smokestacks of the factories as funereal music was broadcast over loudspeakers. All naval ships and locomotives on the railroads sounded a mournful salute. The streetcar drivers and traffic militiamen at city intersections whistled shrilly, and school children were lined up to stand silently at their desks and salute portraits of Lenin.

As the final tribute to the fallen leader, the city of Petrograd was renamed *Leningrad*.

98

A week after the official mourning for Lenin was over, life in the city returned to normal. Theatres resumed their performances, and the music officially broadcast through loudspeakers changed its funereal repertoire to patriotic marches, opening and finishing each day with a rendition of the International.

Larissa and her mother had a surprise visit from Doctor Kline. "I have good news from my friend Vladímir Ivánovich Klimov, who is a senior *repeteur* at the Mariinsky Theatre. Now that the theatres are open, he is in need of an accompanist for his singers," she began. I think Larissa could be exactly who he needs! I told him about you, and he would like to meet you. I know this is short notice, but he can see you tomorrow morning at eleven o'clock, at the theatre. I hope I haven't overstepped my boundaries in my enthusiasm to be of help to both of you, Klimov as well as you!"

"No, no!" Maria Nikoláyevna cried. "We are grateful! Larissa will be there!"

"What about you, Larissa? Are you interested?"

"Oh, yes," she replied without much enthusiasm. "Thank you, Doctor Kline."

Doctor Kline decided not to ask what was bothering Larissa. "Well, I must be going," she said instead.

"Won't you stay for coffee ? We received a tin from the American Red Cross," Maria Nikoláyevna offered.

"No, thank you my dear. Good luck tomorrow!"

"Thank you for your help," Larissa said politely.

"I'll walk you out," Maria Nikoláyevna said, escorting their visitor through the dark corridor. "You must forgive Larissa," she told Doctor Kline in the hall. "She has been terribly depressed ever since her encounter with the Comrades' Court. She can't sleep, she's lost her appetite, and she doesn't even cry for Andrei anymore. She has become listless, almost catatonic …"

"Yes, I noticed. Let's hope that she is able to impress Klimov. He is a dear man and from the same background as you are." She looked at Maria Nikoláyevna.

"I understand. Thank you. Let's hope that your friend likes her. I think if she gets a job, any job, she will be fine, but if she gets a job *in music*, we will be the happiest people in Petrograd!"

"In Leningrad," Doctor Kline corrected her with a smile. "Let's hope!"

It was snowing the next morning.

Larissa left home early, to catch the streetcar that would deliver her to Mariinsky Theatre. On a corner near her home stood an old, deranged beggar woman. She was barefoot, her skeleton-like body covered with rags that looked like potato sacks, her long disheveled white hair hiding her face. She sang *Chanson d'Amour* in perfect French, with her eyes closed, her weak voice quivering. A little saucer of Sévres porcelain was on the ground near the woman's feet, empty.

The pitiful creature deeply disturbed Larissa. She tried to speak to her, in French, but the woman never interrupted her warbling, seemingly unaware of Larissa's presence.

Larissa exited the streetcar and walked briskly toward the left wing of the Mariinsky Theater and its unobtrusive artists' entrance.

"My name is Larissa Rezánova. I have an appointment with Comrade Klimov," Larissa announced to a young man in a military uniform behind a small partition. She felt intimidated. People in Soviet military uniforms ruled her life. She hid her fear behind a nervous smile. Her hands visibly trembled, and she tucked them into her pockets.

"Yes, I know, Comrade Rezánova. We were expecting you." The young man's voice sounded friendly. Larissa felt a wave of relief.

"Go to the second floor. Comrade Klimov's secretary will meet you there and escort you to his office."

"Thank you," Larissa said almost in a whisper.

"Don't mention it," the young man smiled. "Good luck!" he added. Encouraged, Larissa dared to smile back.

"Ah, here you are!" exclaimed a bony, white-haired man in a poorly fitting military uniform. He rose from his elaborately carved chair behind an equally imposing desk and came around to meet her.

"Vladímir Ivánovich?" she asked shyly.

"The one and only! Come in, come in!" he exclaimed jovially. "Do sit down," he indicated a chair at the side of his desk. "Doctor Kline speaks very highly of you."

Larissa liked this warm, older man. She swept the room with her eyes. It was dominated by a grand piano. She noticed the mark—Pleyel. One of her parents' pianos had been a French Pleyel. The walls of the room were lined with waist-tall cabinets above which hung portraits of famous composers. Several marble busts of more composers were dispersed around the room, their gleaming white features stark against the damask-paneled walls. The room smelt a bit musty, but it must have been a handsome room at one time, Larissa thought.

Klimov smiled at her. "Before we start, I must inform you, Larissa Sergéyevna that the position we are offering you is not a permanent one. We have a whole staff of accompanists, but one of our people is … well, quite ill right now. Perhaps, he is even terminal. But if he does pull through, he will return to his position. So, in that case, should we hire you, it will be on a temporary basis. Would that fit your plans?" He observed her closely, knowing that of course she would have no plans. She needed a job; she needed it desperately, under any circumstances. "So, if you don't mind," he continued, "I'll call one of our young singers, who is not yet on our staff, but whom we are 'grooming,' and we'll ask you to play the piano part." He pressed a button on his desk and the elderly woman who had brought Larissa to Klimov's office, entered the room. "Please bring in Fatima Glavuzian."

"Yes, Vladímir Ivánovich," the secretary replied. "Right away."

"May I try the piano?" Larissa asked timidly. "My parents used to have one like yours."

"But of course, of course!" Klimov exclaimed heartily. Larissa noticed that he had a habit of repeating his words. "By all means! By all means!" He lifted the lid over the keyboard and moved a round stool closer to the piano.

Larissa adjusted the height by revolving the seat several turns and ran her fingers over the keys. The piano responded with full sonorous tones even though she played only a couple of arpeggios.

Larissa closed her eyes. "What a beautiful sound," she thought. "Dear God, stay with me," she prayed. She felt calmer now. She was playing the piano again!

Klimov watched her. "She looks radiant," he thought. "She loves music!"

There was a knock and the secretary entered, followed by a young dark-haired slender woman with a stack of music sheets.

"Ah, here you are Fatima! Meet Larissa Sergéyevna!" Klimov exclaimed. The young women shook hands and smiled at one another.

"What would you like to sing?" Klimov asked.

"This." Fatima proffered him a hand-written sheet of music. "It is a beautiful song called 'Lilacs.' I found it in the Conservatory archives."

"Isn't it by Rachmaninoff?" Klimov suddenly looked worried.

"It is."

"In that case, put it away, my girl. Rachmaninoff is one of the composers whose work we do not perform," Klimov said. Larissa saw that he was nervous. "Choose something else, my dear," he said. Both young women knew better than to ask why Rachmaninoff's music was not acceptable anymore. The composer must have been among those who had emigrated from the Soviet Union as Russia was now called.

"How about Tchaikovsky?" asked Fatima.

"Tchaikovsky is fine!"

Fatima handed Lara several loose pages of Tatiana's letter aria from *Eugene Onégin*. Larissa took a deep breath and pressed the keys. The familiar sounds filled the room. Fatima looked at Larissa, waiting for her cue. Larissa met her eyes and nodded her head slightly. Fatima began to sing, "I write to you, what more can I say ..." Her soprano was warm and pure, her diction precise.

The young women were suddenly blended in spirit into one ephemeral being, giving one another something intangible, something exalted, that only music could give to those, who truly love music.

Klimov listened as if enchanted, his eyes closed. It was a long aria. Both women performed perfectly, without a pause for correction or a false note. When they finished, Klimov burst out enthusiastically "Brava! Brava!"

His secretary, full of smiles, joined him in his excitement. "It was beautiful!" she cried.

Fatima and Lara, misty-eyed, still under the spell of the music, embraced silently, both feeling that an invisible bond united them.

"Well, Anna Petrovna, I think, we have found our new accompanist! Yes, I think we have!" Klimov, smiling broadly, announced to his secretary. "Please prepare the necessary documents for Larissa Sergéyevna's temporary employment with our theatre. We don't need to audition her any further. She is obviously well qualified. Well qualified!" he repeated. He turned to the young singer, "Well done, Fatima! Before long, we'll invite you to sing Tatiana on our stage!"

"Thank you, Comrade Klimov!" Fatima's dark Armenian eyes were shining. "Singing at the Mariinsky Theatre has been my dream ever since I was a little girl!" Turning to Larissa she continued, "Thank you also, Larissa Sergéyevna. You were wonderful. I hope to work with you again!"

Larissa blushed. "Thank you. It was a great pleasure to accompany you! You have a beautiful voice."

Fatima embraced Larissa again. "Good luck to you, too!" she whispered in her ear. She collected her music sheets and bid them goodbye.

"Be here next Tuesday at ten in the morning," Klimov said. "I'll introduce you to our artists. My secretary will have the paperwork ready for your employment, and she will arrange the details of your salary and your new ration cards. As you may know, as an employed person and an artist, you are now entitled for workers ration cards. It means, that once in a while you may get some meat or butter!" he winked at her. "Meat and butter! Think of it!"

Larissa let tears of gratitude flow freely down her cheeks. "God bless you, Vladímir Ivánovich."

"Oh-oh! We don't mention God anymore!" he shook his finger at her and laughed. "We don't! See you on Tuesday!

Larissa smiled at the young man in the reception room as she opened the door to leave.

"Congratulations!" he called.

"You know?" she stammered.

"Yes, news travels fast at the theatre. Congratulations!"

It had stopped snowing. The sky was crowded with fast moving clouds of all shades of gray. Once in a while there were even little patches of blue, harbingers of better weather.

Theatre Square looked shiny under the thin layer of snow, footprints crisscrossing it in all directions, making it look as if a white crocheted shawl was thrown over the pavement.

Larissa let the streetcar pass. She did not want to be confined. She wanted to run and skip like a child. She wanted to sing and shout, and she did sing, and she did shout and she did run and skip. She did not even notice that she had crossed the bridge and was near her apartment house, until the sight of the deranged woman sobered her. Larissa slowed down.

The little saucer at the woman's bare feet was covered with snow. Larissa reached into her pocket and gathered the coins that she had not spent on return streetcar fare. She bent down and removed the snow from the saucer. She placed the coins on it. "God bless you," she whispered, looking up at the emaciated face of the old beggar.

The woman remained unaware of Larissa.

Larissa used the time before Tuesday to organizing her 'wardrobe', as she called her one pre-war dress, a skirt, and two blouses. Her mother decided that Larissa's new position justified the purchase of a decent black dress and a pair of black shoes with high heels. "You may be required to accompany a singer at a concert and should be decently dressed," she declared. They consulted with Natasha about the best way to make the purchases using one of the few pieces of jewelry still hidden in Maria Nikoláyevna's vátnik.

"You should try to sell the jewel among the commissars' wives who work at the Housing Authority," Natasha said. "They are the only ones who have any money. And you must buy *good* clothes at some NEP atelier. By the way, Maria Nikoláyevna, I told Dimka about your idea of making some clothes by special order, and he thinks it's great! He said that he would get you a requisitioned sewing machine. I don't know if your neighbor has one, but it won't hurt if you had one of your own."

"Bless you, my girl! With a sewing machine I can teach Larissa how to sew and we can become seamstresses! A noble profession, always in demand!"

Larissa appeared at the Opera Theatre exactly fifteen minutes before the appointed time. She was nervous. "I used to have the same feeling of anticipation when I awaited my Andrúsha," she thought.

Klimov saw her through the open door of his office. "Come in, Larissa Sergéyevna, come in! Today you have two artists. One of them you know, it is Fatima, and another is a wonderful baritone, Nikolái Svirsky, who is already performing at our Theatre in secondary roles. We would like to move him up to the leading roles. You will work with him and Fatima on their duets."

"Are you grooming them for *Eugene Onégin*?" Larissa asked.

"Yes. If Svirsky is as good as we believe he is, we'll have the greatest young operatic lovers since Chaliápin and Brónskaya!"

"I am looking forward to working with them. I already know how marvelous Fatima is. She'll make a great Tatiana! She even *looks* the way Pushkin visualized her!"

"So is Svirsky! Tall, with the bearing of an Imperial Guards officer, God forgive me for mentioning the Guards! He will be a devastating Onégin! And he is young! Only twenty-eight!" Klimov exclaimed ebulliently. "So no *corsets* to hide a fat belly, thank you very much," he added, laughing.

He led Larissa through the labyrinth of corridors behind the great stage, up and down the flights of stairs to a corridor with several doors. Larissa could hear a woman practicing tricky exercises in a high tessitura of coloratura soprano. A few steps further, the sounds of a booming *basso profundo* seemed to shake the door.

Klimov smiled. "I love these sounds of practicing artists. Singers, violinists, trumpet players, no matter who, I love this cacophony of sound!"

"I know what you mean! When I was a girl my parents took me to the opera. I always enjoyed the moments when the orchestra was tuning, waiting for the conductor. Such wonderful chaos, such pleasant anticipation!"

"Well, here we are," Klimov said. "The Rehearsal Room. I think we are the first to arrive." He opened a heavy door with a worn-out padding, and they entered a small, bare room, furnished only with a grand piano, a revolving seat in front of the keyboard, and two tall music stands. Its single narrow window was sealed with tape for the winter, and four hardback chairs were lined up at the wall. Not a picture on the bare walls nor any bright colors were to be found anywhere. It looked more like a monastery cell were it not for the piano.

"Nothing to distract the artists," Klimov said . Larissa nodded. He placed a hefty piano score of *Eugene Onégin* on the piano.

Larissa adjusted the piano stool and let her fingers run freely over several arpeggios and chromatic scales. The piano responded with sonorous deep chords and a bell-like higher register, like a child's laughter.

"What a wonderful instrument!"

"Yes, I know," Klimov agreed. "You don't have a piano anymore, am I right?"

"*Yes,* you are right and *no,* we don't have a piano," she said. "Not anymore." They heard a doorknob turn, and Fatima entered the room accompanied by a tall young man with a cleanly shaved face and shoulder-length hair, his appearance in clear contrast to the current fashion of handlebar moustaches and close-cropped hair. He looked like a French painter from an Impressionist painting.

"Ah, here you are!" Klimov greeted them. Fatima and Larissa embraced one another.

"Allow me to introduce to you our new Onégin!" Klimov said. "Nikolaí Nikolayevich Svirsky."

Larissa proffered Svirsky her hand. "I am Larissa Rezánova."

"*Enchanté!*" Svirsky bowed formally, clicked his heels, and kissed her hand.

"Bravo! Bravo!" Klimov cried, clapping his hands. "I see that Nikolái Nikolayevich is already practicing the role of the high society seducer!"

Larissa smiled awkwardly. "I have heard so much about you! I am looking forward to our collaboration!"

"So do I," he replied, smiling broadly. "I have heard only good things about you, Larissa Sergéyevna."

Klimov said, "Well, good! Now we all know and admire each other. I will leave you now, and you can get to work. I'll be back in two hours when you shall have a break, and we'll have something to eat. Start working! Start working!" Klimov patted Larissa's shoulder as if she were a good little girl and left the room.

Svirsky opened the piano score of the scene where Onégin humiliates Tatiana after reading her passionate love letter. "*The young ladies of our circle must observe the rules of propriety,*" he pontificates. Svirsky made his rich voice sound coldly sarcastic, and Larissa could easily imagine how devastating he would be in the difficult part of a bored Russian aristocrat, a wastrel and seducer.

The two hours passed as ten minutes, all three young artists involved with the passions of the story, not ready to stop when Klimov interrupted their rehearsal.

"I know, I know, you don't want to stop, you are not hungry, you want to continue … I know it all, my dears, and I also know that you must give a bit of rest to your voices and have something to eat. If I were a Commissar I would have barked: *This is an order!*' but since I am not, I just say 'let's go and have some lunch!'" They laughed and followed him to the Artists' Sitting Room.

The room was full of chattering ballet dancers in rehearsal clothes who munched on slices of black bread and cheese, washing it down with weak tea. Several folding tables covered with checkered tablecloths were set up in the room.

One table conspicuously apart was reserved for the opera singers.

"Well, comrades, get your coupons ready. Larissa Sergéyevna, you don't know our routine yet, so let me guide you. Take the coupon that says '*lunch*' and give it to the waitress. Your first month of coupons is prepaid by our office, but later on, you will have to pay for your meals. Do you understand the rules?"

"Yes, Vladímir Ivánovich, they are simple enough."

"Good! Now, let's eat! Bread and cheese! What could be more delicious! And of course, tea with *sugar!*" he exclaimed. The singers and Larissa laughed, but Klimov's enthusiasm was sincere.

The boisterous dancers left, and the big room became quiet.

"I was wondering, Larissa Sergéyevna," Svirsky began. "I used to know a family by the name of Rezánov. Actually, it was in their home that I had met my future benefactress, Alicia Eduárdovna Bolshakóva. It was she who arranged for me to sing for the teachers at the Conservatory, who agreed to accept me as a student. Do you, by any chance, belong to that family? They lived, if I remember, on the Fontánka."

"Yes," she said. "My late husband was Andrei Rezánov, and they did live on the Fontánka. And my mother knew Madame Bolshakóva well. They were friends. She often accompanied Madame Bolshakóva when she was asked to sing at private parties. I heard her only once, in *Carmen,* but many times in private homes. So, she was responsible for your career?"

"Yes. She insisted that I had a natural talent." He did not mention that Alicia Bolshakóva was also his mistress and had paid for his tuition.

"I also remember her as a great mezzo-soprano ..." Fatima said. "Do you know where she is now?"

"No. But I know that her husband, Colonel Bolshakóv, was killed during the Civil War, in the Crimea. I presume that she must have left Russia with Vrángel's troops. She is probably singing somewhere in Europe. She was world famous, as you know."

He turned his attention back to Larissa. "It's quite possible that I met your mother at the Rezánov's house. Was her name Maria Nikoláyevna, by any chance?"

"It still is!" Larissa laughed. "My mother and I live on Vassilievsky Island! I must tell her about meeting you. She will be so pleased!"

"Well! What a wonderful coincidence!" Klimov said with a broad smile. "I love unexpected reunions! It re-kindles my belief that not everything was lost in the war!"

They returned to the rehearsal room for another two hours of practice. This time it was the final duet where Onégin tries to seduce Tatiana to leave her husband. Here Onégin was a different man from the pontificating fool of the previous duet. Here he was all *passion,* ready to sweep Tatiana into his arms. He embraces her victoriously only to be stopped cold with her words: *"But I am given to another, and I'll remain true to him."*

Larissa was impressed by Svirsky as an actor. Being a fabulous singer was already a given, but being able to appear so different in the duets was a revelation to her. It was obvious why Alicia Bolshakóva recognized his huge talent even before he himself was aware of it.

Klimov was delighted. "A week or two of rehearsals and you, my children, will be ready to work with the orchestra! And then, while these two are with the orchestra, you, Larissa Sergéyevna, shall take on another personage—Lensky and his great aria, the one that he sings before Oné-gin kills him. You'll meet our new young tenor who came to us from the provinces. Thus, in the end, you could be proud for being the one who helped our young artists from the very beginning of their careers!"

"I am humbled by working with such outstanding talents. Thank you Vladímir Ivánovich for giving me this opportunity!" she said. "I am really a fortunate woman in getting a job *in music*, the love of my life!"

That night Larissa told her mother about meeting Svirsky. As she expected, Maria Nikoláyevna was delighted. "We must invite him for tea! He used to be your father-in-law's junior aide. General Rezánov was grumpy about losing his aide, but he realized that the young man would be a better artist than a military aide. I don't think that Andrei had ever met him," she added.

"Probably not. I have never heard his name mentioned before."

"Well, anyway, invite him to tea, will you?"

"With pleasure!" Larissa said.

The next day Svirsky surprised Larissa with his own invitation. "I would like to invite you and your mother to hear me in *The Queen of Spades* on Saturday. I sing the part of Yelétsky. I'll have the tickets for you tomorrow. Please do me this honor!"

"Oh, Nikolaí Nikolayevich! What a surprise! We'll be delighted! It has been *years* since either of us has been to the opera!" Larissa exclaimed, her cheeks reddening with pleasure. "And I was just about to invite *you* to visit us on Sunday! My mother remembers you well, and she would love to see you."

"It will be my pleasure!" He kissed her hand.

Fatima arrived and they submerged themselves in the great music.

Larissa could hardly wait to tell her mother about the invitation to the opera. Opera! At the Mariinsky Theatre! She felt like singing. She kept smiling, not caring if the people in the streetcar stared at her. "I am so happy, truly *happy* today" she thought. "Dear God, don't let anything *bad* happen!" she prayed.

She ran up the stairs as if she were still a young girl and fumbled with the keys, hurrying to open the front door. She rushed along the corridor and burst into their room.

Her mother was seated at the sewing machine that Dimka had brought her that morning, but Larissa failed to notice it. "We are going to the opera this Saturday!" she shouted, whirling around the room.

"Wait, wait! What are you talking about? We can't afford going to the opera!"

"But it won't cost us anything!" Larissa exclaimed happily. "Svirsky has invited us to hear him sing in *The Queen of Spades! Píkovaya Dáma!* I am so happy, Mama! Imagine, we'll go to the opera again, after all these years!"

Maria Nikoláyevna finally smiled. "So, your new friend invited us to hear him sing! Yes, it will be exciting. When was the last time that we went to the opera?"

"For me it was in Odessa, for *Carmen*. Remember? We wore the evening gowns that we bought at Julia's store ... Doctor Shubin and his wife were with us. Remember? Andrei was still in the wheelchair, remember?"

"I remember. I also remember *how* we went to the theatre. *In the hospital ambulance!*"

They both laughed. "It was also the last time for me," Maria Nikoláyevna said, "When I came back to Petrograd, the city was in the midst of political disturbances, and I think all the theatres were closed. By the way, did you invite Svirsky to come to tea?"

"Yes. He was pleased. But what can we serve? We have nothing!"

"I'll think of something ... Perhaps Frósya can sell Peter's silver baby spoon and we can buy some *real* cream pastry at the Elyséyev's Gastronomy store! Yes, that's what we'll do!"

"Peter's baby spoon! But you've treasured it so much!"

"It's time to be realistic. One baby spoon is really useless. As for keeping it for memory's sake, well, I don't need items to remind me of my son. I will never forget him. Yes, I'll go to Frósya tomorrow!"

"Am I going to the opera with you?" Nínochka raised her head from the book of Grimm's Fairy Tales. "I've never been to the opera. Is it when people sing instead of talk?"

"Yes," Larissa smiled. "You are too young yet to go to the opera at night. I'll take you there for a matinee, and we'll go to a ballet. I think you'll like it better. Maybe *Swan Lake!*"

"All right." Nínochka turned her attention back to the book. She was becoming a voracious reader.

Neither Larissa nor her mother had clothes suitable for going to the opera. Larissa still had one out-of-style old dress, but Maria Nikoláyevna had not even that. She asked Frósya to lend her a hand-knitted downy Orenburg shawl. Such shawls were admired by the Russophile women flaunting their ethnicity by wearing homespun peasant clothing. The gorgeous shawl easily covered Maria Nikoláyevna shabby cardigan inherited from Ksusha.

With her usual sense of dry humor, she compared her present ritual of dressing for the opera with some years back. Emeralds and diamonds used to encircle her neck and bare shoulders. Long white kid gloves covered her arms, and precious bracelets and rings sparkled on her arms and fingers. Now, she was wearing her maid's old sweater and a shawl borrowed from a peasant cook.

Larissa had the same thoughts but was unable to see any humor in the situation. She put on her old dress with its many buttons. The buttons at least still looked pretty. She painted over the scuffs on her shoes with black paint from Nínochka's paint set and did the same with her mother's shoes." We don't look too bad!" she had finally declared.

"You look *beautiful!*" Nínochka cried. "And look at Bábushka! She looks like a queen in that white shawl!"

"Oh, dear! Don't compare me with a queen or I'll lose my head!" Grandmother sighed, but Nínochka found it funny. "A queen without a head!" she laughed.

Anna Mikháilovna agreed to watch Nina.

"Have a good time at the opera," she said, sounding like a grown-up telling them to behave themselves. "You must tell me later how you enjoyed it!"

They arrived at the theatre in plenty of time. Larissa had a small surprise of her own awaiting her mother. Their seats were in the same tier of boxes as the Imperial Loge, which had become the Government Loge. It was empty now, its entrance cordoned by a velvet rope between two stanchions. The third loge on its right was the one used for invited guests of the actors. Before the revolution, that loge had belonged to several important subscribers, Generals Rezánov and Orlov among them.

"It's *our* loge!" Maria Nikoláyevna whispered in awe. "How did you get it? Oh, my God! *Our loge!*" The knuckles of her hand grabbing the gilded back of the chair turned white.

"It is now designated for special guests," Larissa said, thinking that perhaps it was not such a good idea, after all. Her mother was shaking and fighting tears.

She continued, "Svirsky thought that it would bring back some pleasant memories. He told me that he had been invited several times to join you in that loge along with Alicia Eduárdovna and Colonel Bolshakóv."

"True. But of course, it was before General Rezánov began to suspect that Svirsky was Alicia's lover. He was an extremely handsome young man in those days." Maria Nikoláyevna regained her composure, enjoying the juicy old gossip.

"He is still very handsome," Larissa said and blushed.

They took their seats in the gilded armchairs upholstered in pale blue velvet.

The *grande baroque* décor hadn't changed. The enormous stage still looked impressive. In the pre-war production of *Aida*, it easily accommodated several live horses and a real elephant along with a hundred-voiced chorus and scores of dancers.

The stage was separated from the audience by a heavy velvet curtain with decorative gold swags. It looked untouched by the bloody events of the previous years, although the hammer and sickle emblem had replaced the shield with the Imperial double-headed eagle over the stage.

Larissa looked down at the parterre. It used to be full of military officers in formal attire, all of them with golden epaulettes and aiguillettes and festooned with military decorations, while civilians of high rank wore somber black formal clothes, their white shirts stiff with starch. To Larissa, as a young girl from a distinguished military family, the civilians looked dull as they stood in small clusters during the intermissions, passionately discussing God knows what, looking like a bunch of penguins surrounded by scores of colorful tropical birds.

Women were seldom seated in the parterre. The ladies always occupied the loges. Wearing the latest Parisian fashions, their bare necks and shoulders displaying fortunes in emeralds, diamonds, and rubies. They viewed one another through their bejeweled opera glasses. The younger women, hiding behind their fans, flirted with the young officers in the parterre.

It was all part of the ritual of attending the opera.

The auditorium began to fill in with spectators. While the traditional ambiance of the Opera Theatre was the same, its audience had changed. It was shabby, looking militaristic in the dull khaki tunics worn by the majority of men and women. Some civilians among the audience wore threadbare attire and dirty válenki. There were no children. The difference from the past was in the air as well. The waves of French perfume that used to prevail in the loges and spread throughout the theatre were gone. Now the air stank of mothballs, sweat, dirty boots, and cheap tobacco.

The hall was almost full. The sound of hundreds of voices reached the persistent buzz of a disturbed apiary. Looking down into the orchestra pit, Larissa noted that the musicians were still attired in black tailcoats with white bow ties. However, several women musicians were in the orchestra. "That's interesting," Larissa thought. "I had never seen women engaged by the symphony orchestras! Hurrah for the women!"

The familiar cacophony of tuning was still as exciting to her as when she were a young girl. She looked at her mother, who had a beatific expression on her face, her eyes closed, waiting for the music to lift her out of the mundane world. "She looks happy," Larissa thought. "She is enjoying her happy memories."

There were no other occupants in their loge. Larissa was glad. They would have privacy in their emotional reunion with the past and, perhaps, the acceptance of the present and even a hope for the future.

The lights dimmed. The conductor entered the pit. The musicians stood in greeting to him. Larissa watched the familiar procedure as the conductor turned toward the audience and bowed. It looked as though no one had noticed it, but a few people applauded here and there. The noise in the hall subsided.

The first notes of the overture reverberated through the hall and Larissa relaxed, surrendering to music, feeling unbearably happy.

The *Queen of Spades* was Pushkin's novella adapted by Tchaikovsky to become the famous psychological *dark* opera about compulsive gambling in the eighteenth and nineteenth centuries.

Ghérman, a young officer who had gambled away his inheritance, is obsessed with a legend of *the three cards*. It involves the old Countess, who as a young woman was a favorite at the Court of Louis XVI. According to the legend, the Countess had suddenly become the richest woman in Versailles after a bargain she had made with a stranger: he would let her know the secret of the three cards in exchange for her body.

Ghérman learns that the Countess is still alive. He becomes obsessed with learning her secret.

The Countess has a young orphan girl Liza as her ward and companion. Géhrman decides to get close to the old woman by seducing Liza. He succeeds, and she gives him the key to the house.

Inside the house, Ghérman hears the Countess reminisce about her youth, singing in French a famous aria of regrets. A vivid scene of her disrobing follows, including the removal of a wig and the disclosure that the Countess is now totally bald. The Countess settles in bed, but she cannot sleep: the memories of her success at the French Court invade her mind.

Ghérman suddenly appears before her. He begs her to tell him the secret of the three cards, but the old woman, terrified by him, remains silent. As his pleas turn to threats and Ghérman points his pistol at her, the old woman, still silent, is stricken with apoplexy and dies. Liza watches with horror as Ghérman shouts as an obsessed maniac : "Three cards! Three cards!" and runs out. Liza, dishonored, throws herself into the Nevá River.

Ghérman returns to his barracks and passes out. He has a nightmarish vision of the Countess. Tchaikovsky composed the frightening combination of dark chords suggesting the taps of her cane as she walks toward Ghérman's room. In monotone, she offers him a bargain: "Marry the betrayed girl, and I'll tell you my secret." He promises to do so.

"Three, Seven, Ace," she says and disappears.

Ghérman rushes to the Gaming Club where a drinking and gambling party is in full progress. "Three cards!" he shouts and bids all his money on *"Three."* He wins. He bids his winnings on *"Seven"* and wins again. He should stop now: he is rich! But no, he cannot stop. He wants more! He bids everything on the *"Ace."*

"Your Queen has lost!" the croupier announces, opening the card. It is the grinning old Countess, the Queen of Spades.

Ghérman, in raving madness cries *"Oh, my pitiful lot!"* and collapses.

Larissa and Maria Nikoláyevna watched rapt, swept up in the performance. Svirsky's baritone was velvety, and passionate in his interpretation of the character of Yelétsky, a middle-aged man deeply in love with Liza. The aria was his love declaration to Liza, who reacted to it in confusion, for she was infatuated with the stranger with the burning eyes who pursued her wherever she accompanied her grandmother, the Countess.

Watching Svirsky's seductive confession of love, Larissa felt deep sadness. It was the painful realization that her own life was empty of love and would remain empty in this new, hostile Russia. Yes, Igor loved her, but his love was rough, vulgar, and she did not share it. She yearned for tenderness and romance. "Andrúsha was that way," she thought, unshed tears burning her eyes.

Maria Nikoláyevna intuitively knew what Larissa was thinking. She knew about the loneliness of her daughter, about the lost years of her youth. She was helpless to lighten her suffering. She suspected that because of it Larissa was on the cusp of surrendering herself to Igor's pursuit. While it was understandable, she doubted that it was a good foundation for a happy marriage. She squeezed Larissa's hand in sympathy.

At the intermission there was a knock on the door. Klimov entered their loge.

"Ah, Vladímir Ivánovich!" Larissa jumped up from her chair. "Please meet my mother!"

"Enchanté!" He bent over Maria Nikoláyevna's hand. She actually blushed as if she were a young girl whose hand was kissed for the first time. It had been years since *anyone* had kissed her hand.

"I am delighted to meet you," she said. "It gives me a great pleasure to thank you personally for being so kind to my daughter and giving her an opportunity to be employed. I hope my hand did not smell of onions!" she thought. "Won't you sit down?"

"Thank you, thank you," he said, lowering himself into a gilded chair. "It was our mutual good fortune to come upon each other. We are very happy with Larissa Sergéyevna's work. The singers love her. It looks as though her *temporary* employment status might become a *permanent* one," he said with a smile. "So, how do you like your charge, Nikolái Svirsky?" Klimov asked Larissa. "Isn't he terrific? He will make a marvelous Onégin, don't you think? We are looking ahead, preparing him for a great career."

Yes, Svirsky was perfect. His voice caressed the listeners, and his appearance created the impression of the elegant nobleman Prince Yelétsky. His military posture and bows were not learned and rehearsed. He was *natural*. The spectators apparently thought the same. He was rewarded by thunderous applause.

"As soon as he starts singing Onégin, you'll have to prepare him for Borodin's *Prince Igor*, or even *Borís Godunóv*. Do you think you will enjoy working with him from the start?" Klimov asked.

"Of course!" she exclaimed. "But I would need to use the rehearsal piano at the theatre for my *own* preparation. Will I be allowed?"

"Certainly, my dear, certainly! Actually, I have an idea … no, nothing important," he interrupted himself. "Would you mind if I stay with you for the next act?"

"Of course not! We'll be delighted!" Maria Nikoláyevna said.

He stayed with them for the rest of the opera.

On Sunday, Svirsky arrived at their apartment promptly at five. He carried a bouquet of red roses wrapped in *Pravda* and a small package in colorful wrapping tied with red ribbon. Nínochka, who had run ahead of her mother to open the front door, greeted him with a curtsy, saying politely, as her grandmother had taught her, "I am Nina Rezánova. Welcome to our home!"

Svirsky smiled. "I am delighted to meet you! And I am …"

"I know, you are the singer with a velvet voice! My mother told me about you!"

Larissa, standing behind her, looked embarrassed, but Svirsky laughed. "Well, thank you for the compliment!" he said.

"Let's go to our room. I shall introduce you to my Bábushka!" Nina said like a good hostess. "Follow me."

"I am in your hands, young lady!" he said, bemused.

The three of them reached the room. "Meet my Bábushka! She is called Maria Nikoláyevna!"

"I know. We are old friends!" Svirsky said, passing the roses to the old lady with a small bow. He kissed her hand.

"Nikolaí Nikolayevich! Welcome! After all these years, we meet again, and you sound even better than in those days! You gave us such a great pleasure yesterday! You have become a fine artist! Congratulations!" she embraced him as if they were indeed old friends. "And thank you for the roses. Lara, dear, place them in water."

"And this is for you," Svirsky said, giving Nínochka the bright package.

"Thank you," she curtsied. "What is it?"

"Open it," he said.

She carefully untied the ribbon and took off the pretty paper trying not to tear it, finding a box of chocolates from the Georges Bormann chocolate factory that had reopened under the NEP.

"Chocolates! How did you know that I just *loved chocolates!*" she exclaimed.

"A little ..."

"... bird told you," Nina finished the sentence, "I know. This little bird knows everything! She even knows—"

"Don't you think that you have monopolized our guest long enough?" Maria Nikoláyevna interrupted.

Nínochka subdued her excitement. "I am sorry," she said. "I was just so happy to make a new friend."

"That girl!" The grandmother thought and smiled. "It's alright," she said to her granddaughter. "I am very happy to meet an *old* friend! We'll *share* him, shall we?"

Larissa placed the flowers in a tin can on the table between the two beds. She smiled at their guest. "I ought to apologize for our lack of proper furniture, but then, why should I? It is obviously not our choice!"

Svirsky laughed. "If you knew what *I* have where I live, you would think that your room is a great parlor in the Astoria Hotel! I live in a dormitory and share my room with four other men. I have been promised by the administration of the Opera House to be allocated an individual room as soon as I become a first category soloist. So, a lot is riding on *Eugene Onégin* for me."

"With your voice, you ought to qualify for a furnished apartment!"

"I don't understand what you are talking about," Nínochka said. "If being a good singer means that you can get an apartment, I am a good singer too, and we should get an apartment! Would you like me to sing the snowflake song?"

"Nínochka!" the grandmother raised her voice.

"I will be delighted!" Svirsky said, looking at Maria Nikoláyevna. "Honestly, I would love it!"

"Well, all right. One song. And then let the grown-ups talk!"

Nínochka moved to the empty space before the windows and took a pose. *"We are little white snowflakes,"* she began to sing in a pure voice, not once running off key, every note of the simple melody placed in exactly the right place. She moved gracefully, holding on to the edges of her dress, lowering herself to the floor dramatically in imitation of the snow-flake ready to rest. Following the words of the song that the naughty wind would not let her rest, she whirled around again, repeating the song.

Svirsky was enchanted. "She has perfect pitch!" he thought. "Where did you learn this song and dance? At school?" he asked the child.

"No. My mama taught me. I knew it since I was a little girl!"

"Lara used to sing it when she was that age," Maria Nikoláyevna said. "And I taught it to her when *she* was a little girl."

"We are a family of snowflakes." Nínochka said seriously. "When I grow up and have babies of my own, I'll teach it to my children!"

"She is amazing! She should be taking music lessons!"

"She should, but ..." Grandmother spread her hands in helpless gesture. "If we only had a piano!"

"Yes," he agreed. "I wish I had a piano. I need it, but ..."

Larissa took no part in the conversation. She busied herself with the preparations for the tea, feeling ill at ease, avoiding Svirsky's eyes. "What's the matter with me?" she thought. "I am so glad that he came, and at the same time ... Am I afraid of him?"

Maria Nikoláyevna watched her daughter's strange coolness, and a sudden thought flashed through her mind. "My God! She is in love with Svirsky!"

The conversation continued, turning toward the past. They soon learned that Svirsky's parents were long dead, that he had an older brother who used to be a naval officer but had died during the Russo-Japanese war when Svirsky was a boy. He was raised by his grandparents, who by now were also gone.

"So, you are an orphan!" Nínochka said. "You miss your mother, don't you? I am a half-orphan. It is not as bad as being a full orphan, but I don't like it," she confessed. "I would like to have a father. At school, most of the children have no fathers also. It is because of the war," she explained.

"Yes," he agreed, feeling suddenly uncomfortable.

"We are called the fatherless children," Nina explained.

"Oh, my God! I hope she won't mention Igor!" Larissa thought.

Maria Nikoláyevna thought the same. She tried to intervene, but not fast enough to prevent Nínochka from asking, "Why don't we pretend that my Bábushka is your Mama? We could pretend that you are my Mama's brother! Would you like that?"

An awkward silence descended. Svirsky said after a moment of hesitation, "I don't believe that your Bábushka would like to have such an old son as I am!"

"She told me she would rather welcome to our tent a new husband for my Mama. But we don't even have a tent!" she laughed.

From the corner of her eye Maria Nikoláyevna could see that Larissa's face was red and Svirsky had shifted in his chair, looking uncomfortable.

Maria Nikoláyevna asked a mundane question to defuse the situation. "Were you always interested in opera?"

"Well, I had always loved opera, even as a boy, but I never thought that I would ever sing in the opera myself. Even when I started my studies at the Conservatory I never dreamed that singing would become my career. When your father-in-law, General Rezánov, released me from being his aide-de-camp," he turned to Larissa, "I was *crushed*, thinking that my life was over."

"I did not know that my Dédushka was a *general!*" Nínochka said.

"Don't interrupt!" Maria Nikoláyevna said sternly. She was alarmed. "That child's curiosity is getting dangerous!" she thought.

"Eat your éclair and don't interrupt the grown-ups!" her mother said coldly.

"I am sorry," the child said. She sensed that the mood of the grown-ups had changed. "I think I'll color some pictures in my coloring book. We could send them to Papa Igor!"

"A good idea!" the grandmother said quickly. "You can do it on the window sill!" She placed a pillow on the chair and moved it to the window to raise Nínochka a little higher. "Go to work!" she said, returning to the table.

But the spontaneity of the tea party was gone. Nina's innocent chatter introduced new emotions into their conversation. Larissa was humiliated by Nina's references to her widowhood. Maria Nikoláyevna had premonitions that her daughter was falling in love with the handsome singer, and that Svirsky suddenly suspected he had become prey for the young woman and her mother.

As did many young men in post-war Russia, Svirsky saw every single woman as a predator. "She was already married, that I know," he thought. "But who is Papa Igor? Some lover?"

They continued polite chatter about the theatre and its productions, but by seven o'clock Svirsky was ready to leave. He felt ill at ease with the women, and his original idea of inviting Larissa to the cinema after tea evaporated from his mind. "Let's keep it strictly as a professional relationship," he thought.

At rehearsal the next day, he thanked Larissa for the good time, both agreeing that they should repeat the visit soon, but neither of them suggesting how soon.

99

Maria Nikoláyevna worried about Larissa. She was in love. But was he interested in her? It was hard to say. Was her Larissa to be wounded by a handsome singer? Maria Nikoláyevna had seen the look of confusion cross Svirsky's face at the mention of Papa Igor. Was Larissa now to be denied love by the circumstances of war and the consequences of the following years?

Then—there was Nínochka. The child was charming and smart, but she has become a real nuisance. "We must curtail her participation in adult conversations. We must restrain her curiosity. She must be taught caution. Farewell to innocence!"

And at the bottom of her satchel of worries was Igor. Almost two years had passed since he left, but Igor continued to supply them with food packages and clothing. She was ashamed that they had been demeaning themselves by taking his help without reciprocation. In her mind, she was ready for Larissa to submit to Igor. "Even one-sided marriage is better than none," she thought, trying to convince herself that for the sake of survival and securing Nina's future, it was a necessary solution.

But now everything was changing again! "It had to be expected," Maria Nikoláyevna tried to be fair. "Larissa and Svirsky have everything in common: the same social background, the same type of education ... There is no need to hide from each other who they were. No wonder that they are attracted to one another.

And of course there was music ... "one of the most powerful aphrodisiacs in the world!" A picture of a popular painting suddenly appeared in her mind's eye: a young man with a violin in one hand, passionately kissing a young woman whose hand is still touching piano keys. They had been performing a duet when the music drove them to a sudden outburst of passion. "I would love to have someone like Svirsky as my son-in-law," she thought "but ... is he interested enough in Lara enough to marry her?"

That night when Nínochka was safely asleep, Maria Nikoláyevna faced Larissa. "Are you in love with Svirsky?" she asked bluntly.

Larissa froze. "I admire his talent, and I enjoy working with him," she finally said.

"That is not what I am asking. Are you in love with him?"

Looking down and blushing as if she were still a girl of seventeen," Larissa said, "Yes. I am."

"Is he returning your affection?"

"I don't know. Maybe. He invited me to tea at his residence once, but I declined."

"Why?"

"I just didn't want him to know how I felt about him and ..."

"That was stupid! You prefer to suffer in silence?"

"No, but I thought that after that tea party he might think that we are husband-shopping."

"We are. That is, I am, on your behalf." her mother interrupted. "You would be a most suitable wife for him. And he would even have a ready-made adorable daughter! At least find out if he is interested in you! You are young, and you are beautiful. Let him fall in love with you! Let him fall in love with all three of us!"

"What about Igor?"

"If Svirsky shares your feelings, you break up with Igor. I think that after not seeing you for two years, it shouldn't be too painful for him to give you up! He should know that no studies at some half-baked Communist university would close the gap between the two of you!"

"Oh, Mama, how can you be so cynical! A few months ago you admired him for his ambition!"

"A few months ago I was preparing myself to be his mother-in-law! I had to find some justification for us to step even lower from our ancestral position."

In spite of herself, Larissa laughed. "Mama! This is something new about you that I did not know before: you are an opportunist!"

"Yes, and I am proud of it! If one lives among the wolves ..."

"I know, one must howl like a wolf."

Larissa's life changed drastically once she began to work at the Opera Theatre. She made friends among the artists who began to engage her as an accompanist at their clandestine concerts. Her little black dress and new patent leather shoes were often in use. She was paid a good salary and received first category food rations. To top it all, she was paid after each concert a certain amount of cash, which was becoming more and more reliable as a currency as the country stabilized. Life settled into a familiar, if tenuous, routine.

Late in July, the theatre closed for a major clean up and repairs. The artists were free to concertize at their will. Most of them appeared in privately organized performances, which was lucrative but illegal. Larissa and Svirsky seldom participated, being especially at risk because of their social background.

Klimov worried about them. "There should be some way for them to keep practicing," he thought. "If only any of them had a piano!" Then, an idea that he had dismissed from his mind months before struck him again: there were several unused upright pianos in the storage rooms at the theatre. "Why not lend a piano to Rezánova and have the singers rehearse at her place? Klimov had visited them for tea several times during the year and thought that the room was big enough to accommodate a piano." It was a great idea, he thought.

He asked Larissa if he could visit them that night. He had something important to discuss.

Larissa blanched. "I'll be fired!" she thought in panic. Klimov noticed her distress and hurried to reassure her. "It's nothing bad, don't you worry, my dear! Actually, you might find it very pleasant! Very pleasant!"

"Oh, Vladímir Ivánovich, I have become such a 'scaredy-cat,' as my Scottish friend Veronica used to say! Everything scares me!"

"Me, too. But let's be optimistic and not allow fear to dominate our lives! So, may I come tonight?"

"But of course, Vladímir Ivánovich! We'll be delighted!"

Klimov arrived with a bunch of wildflowers in his arms. "For you, my dear ladies," he said with a ceremonious bow. "Also, I wanted to see a young lady whose name is Nínochka," he said. "I have something special for her! Does anybody know where I can find her?" he asked, pretending to look around.

"I am Nínochka, and I live here," Nina said, stepping forward. "We have met before!"

"That's right, that's right! I didn't recognize you! You've lost your teeth! You must've grown twice as tall since I saw you last time!"

Nínochka giggled. "No I didn't."

"Don't you want to know what I brought you?" Klimov asked.

"Yes. But my Bábushka said that it is impolite to ask."

Klimov chuckled. He reached inside his coat and produced a hand puppet of Petrúshka, the traditional hero of country fairs and puppet shows.

"Petrúshka!" Nina exclaimed in delight. "I always loved Petrúshka! I have a book about his adventures! Thank you, Uncle Volódya!" she kissed him on his bristly cheek.

Klimov smiled. "How old are you?" he asked.

"Seven. I am the youngest girl in my class but I am the best reader the teacher says. But the boys call me baby. I hate boys!"

"Tell them that your Uncle Volódya will punish them!"

"How?"

"Through magic. I will turn them into babies. Instead of school they will be going to the nursery!"

"Can you do it? How?"

"That's enough, Nina," Maria Nikoláyevna said sternly. "Do you remember what I told you about talking too much?"

The child nodded.

Larissa came into the room carrying hot water for tea. She noticed at once the stern expression on her mother's face and Nínochka's petulance. "Alright, my precious, let's get you washed up before getting to bed." Larissa took her by the hand and led her to the kitchen where the tenants performed their morning and night rituals. "Were you chattering too much again?"

"Yes," Nina said sadly. "I just can't help myself!"

Klimov put his teacup back into the saucer. "I have fantasized that you had a piano, Maria Nikoláyevna," he began.

"What a nice fantasy!" she chuckled, "I wish it were true!"

"So, I fantasized that the theatre had lent you an old upright from our storage. It would cost you nothing. Would you like that?"

She was stunned. "I don't know what to say! Of course! I would love it!"

"Consider it done!" He sounded victorious. "It will also be a favor for me and the singers. They could work with your daughter during the time of our renovations at the theatre. Would you allow us to use your home for their rehearsals?"

"What a question! But of course!"

They heard voices in the corridor and Larissa entered holding Nínochka's hand.

"Kiss Vladímir Ivánovich good night and hop to bed," Larissa said, turning back the blanket on the bed that she shared with her daughter.

Nina embraced Klimov and placed a wet kiss on his cheek. "Good night Uncle Volódya! Thank you for Petrúshka! Good night, Bábushka. I promise not to talk so much!"

Klimov took a great risk in arranging his scheme, but he presented it to the Executive Committee of the theatre as a cheap solution for keeping the singers working during the summer interruption. The management agreed, and the upright Diderichs parlor piano was delivered within a week. It had bronze candle holders on each side of the music stand and shiny gilt curlicues that suggested to Maria Nikoláyevna that the instrument was at least fifty years old. She remembered such pianos from her own childhood. It was no Bechstein, but who cared? Its sound was warm and pure, its yellowed ivory keys looked elegant, showing the tiny veins of their origins in Africa. The outer structure of the instrument was obviously touched up with black paint, but it was a beautiful old piano!

Svirsky arrived alone for his first rehearsal. Fatima was ill. He brought along the score of Borodín's epic opera Prince Igor, based on Russia's struggle against the Mongol invaders.

Larissa hadn't seen Svirsky for three weeks since the theatre was closed. He was tanned, and his long hair was shortened to a masculine length. Dressed in white trousers and a white shirt with rolled-up sleeves, he looked athletic, like an English tennis player.

"Well, Larissa Sergéyevna, congratulations! Our old man did it! He schemed for a long time to get you a piano! Fatima and I never thought that he would succeed."

Nínochka monopolized him. "I am so glad that you came back, Uncle Kólya! Mama said that she had never heard anyone singing better than you! She said that God must've loved you to give you such a magnificent voice. She said—"

"Nina!" Larissa raised her voice.

"But it's true! I heard you saying it to Bábushka and then to Doctor Kline!" the child protested.

"It's enough, Nina," Maria Nikoláyevna said sternly, "Let's go to the park while Nikolaí Nikolayevich and Mama work!"

Nínochka wanted to argue, but Maria Nikoláyevna took her by the hand and led her out of the room.

Svirsky laughed. "What an endorsement of my humble talents!"

"There is a saying that God speaks the truth through a child's lips, or something like that," Larissa said quietly.

Svirsky stared at her. "She means it …," he thought. "I was wrong about her! She is not a calculating siren …" he thought. "… Well, thank you," he said, feeling humbled.

"Shall we start?" Larissa said, lifting the keyboard cover.

Svirsky wanted to work on the most important aria in the opera.

Prince Igor, severely wounded in battle, is taken prisoner by the Mongol horde. Tormented by his defeat, he dreams of escape. "No sleep, no rest for my tormented soul," he declares as he thinks of the destruction of Kiev and the fate of his wife. It is a long, difficult aria, with several changes of mood, being mournful at the beginning, then turning tender as he thinks of his wife. And finally, it is heartbreaking as Igor admits the hopelessness of reality.

Larissa opened the score. They read the text together, their heads almost touching, Svirsky crooning the melody in soto voce. "I made some marks on the pages so that you'll understand my interpretation of some particular parts of it," Svirsky said, looking at her long curving eyelashes hiding her eyes as she looked down on the text. "What a perfect face!" he thought, distracted from the score.

"Are you ready?" Larissa asked, noticing that his attention seemed to be somewhere else.

"What? Oh, yes, I am ready."

Larissa struck the first chord.

They worked until Maria Nikoláyevna and Nínochka returned. The child entered the room on tiptoes and sat on the footstool quietly, listening, her face serious. Finally, they finished and looked at one another as if they were a pair of conspirators.

"Well, we did it," Svirsky said, stretching. He winked at Nínochka.

Larissa raised her arms above her head and then moved them slowly down, shaking her wrists as her piano teacher had taught her so many years ago. "Yes. We've made a tiny dent in that monumental aria! When do you want to continue?" she asked.

"Tomorrow? And every day after that, at the same time? Is that possible?"

"Fine with me. Until tomorrow," Larissa replied. Svirsky hoped to be invited to stay a little longer, but Larissa seemed to be not interested in prolonging his visit. He looked at Maria Nikoláyevna hoping that *she* would ask him to stay for a cup of tea, but she was preoccupied with the sewing machine innards spread on a towel over her bed.

728

Larissa went with him to the front door as good manners required. "See you tomorrow," she said.

"I am looking forward to it!"

"I am also looking forward to tomorrow," she said, closing the door.

"She is also looking forward to tomorrow!" he thought, a happy feeling unexpectedly surrounding him like soothing warm water. As if he were still an adolescent boy, Svirsky slid down on the mahogany banister.

"Will Mama marry Uncle Kólya?" Nínochka asked her grandmother.

"Where did you get that idea?" Maria Nikoláyevna exclaimed.

"In my Fairy Tales book. Uncle Kólya sang about his kingdom and how he wished to have a wife. Then he stopped and looked at Mama. They both smiled. But they did not kiss."

"Don't mention this nonsense to Mama. She doesn't like when we talk about her behind her back!"

"I won't, I promise" the child said. "But I like Uncle Kólya. I would like it a lot if he would be my Papa. He can teach me some new songs!"

"Keep it to yourself," Maria Nikoláyevna smiled.

Fatima joined them after two weeks. She had lost weight due to her illness and looked like a stick figure from Nínochka's drawings. It was hard to imagine that such a slip of a girl could have a voice capable of projecting over the orchestra.

The singers wanted to rehearse the duets from *Eugene Onégin* in preparation of their debut in the autumn.

Maria Nikoláyevna listened to them, and a happy feeling overwhelmed her. Somehow the future did not feel so bleak anymore. Many services that were lost with the revolution, such as reliable postal service, were reinstated. Healthcare and education were both free for everyone. Some of the liberal ideas that her late husband had advocated in the privacy of their home were becoming laws of the Soviet government. Food rations were slightly increased. With the return of regular railway service, butter and meat reappeared in the food stores, and warm clothes and household items could be bought once again as various factories resumed the manufacture of ordinary goods. Her own enterprise as a seamstress also showed promise. She acquired two customers through the recommendation of Doctor Kline. Life was definitely becoming sweeter.

Maria Nikoláyevna enjoyed listening to the rehearsal. She watched the young artists closely. "Svirsky is in love with Larissa ... I can see it. She must write to Igor immediately!"

That night she brought her thoughts to Larissa. "I hope Igor won't do anything stupid, like coming to Petrograd, I mean, Leningrad," she corrected herself. "Perhaps you should write him that you have remarried."

"I don't want to lie," Lara said.

Her mother interrupted, "Oh, come on! You are old enough to know when a lie is necessary. It will help Igor to let go of you. Also, I think, you should tell Svirsky about Igor. Nínochka has mentioned him. I am sure Svirsky is curious."

Larissa said nothing, but she knew her mother was right.

The next day Fatima did not come, but Svirsky was punctual as usual, arriving with a bouquet of pink and red carnations. "I couldn't resist them," he said. "I hadn't seen anyone for years selling flowers on the street corner! Just an old woman, with bunches of carnations! It looked so peaceful!"

"It's high time! Perhaps it is a sign that life is getting easier," Maria Nikoláyevna said. "Thank you for the flowers!"

Nínochka examined the bouquet. "May I have a flower for my own?" she asked politely, yet seductively, demonstrating the first traces of a future siren.

"Of course! I hope your babushka won't mind. What color do you like?"

"Pink."

Svirsky took one carnation out of the bouquet and gallantly offered it to the child. "What are you going to do with it?"

"First, I'll admire it, and then I'll draw a picture of it for you. Thank you very much for the flower!" she curtsied.

Larissa watched their exchange, thinking how quickly her daughter had turned into a self-possessed little lady. She no longer needed to be reminded to say "thank you."

Svirsky watched as Nínochka placed the flower into an empty bottle and followed her grandmother to the kitchen to fill the container with water. "What a dear little girl!" he thought.

He was in no mood for the rehearsal. Dutifully he sang a couple of vocal exercises to warm up his voice, but he could not concentrate. He was too preoccupied with Larissa. He said, "Let's quit for a day. Let's go to the islands. The weather is so pleasant. We should take advantage of these last few sunny days before we will be back in the rainy season."

Larissa felt his shy frustration. Getting away from the house would be good. It would give them a chance to talk. "Alright. I'll tell Mother that we won't rehearse today."

They walked slowly, exchanging comments about the weather and the theatre, both saying something just to say something, hovering around the edges of a conversation that both knew was coming.

"Who is Papa Igor?" Svirsky asked suddenly. Larissa was taken aback. She hadn't expected the question put so bluntly. She had hoped to bring up the subject of Igor after she had told him about Andrei and her life in Odessa. However, Svirsky's sudden demand left her without the logical preamble. His attack, and it sounded to her like an attack, left her no choice.

She sighed heavily and replied. "He was the Commissar of my husband's Flight Detachment in the last months of the war. His name was Igor Kóshkin and he was, of course, a communist. My Andrei and he were political enemies even though they respected and even liked one another."

"Kóshkin! I can't imagine Larissa being involved with someone named Kóshkin!" Svirsky thought. "Was that Kóshkin also a pilot?"

"No. He was just the political boss. After the Reds executed my husband, I was left alone with a baby, living in Odessa, working at a large military hospital. I had no proper documents, no money except my small salary and only one or two friends who were in similar dire circumstances." She unfurled the tale for him, not shying away from the desperation of her situation when she agreed to pretend to be Igor's wife and teach Nina to call him Papa. What was I to do?" she asked simply. "I had no other choice."

It sounded plausible enough to Svirsky. "But how far did your role as wife extend? Did you marry him?"

"No."

"How did you pay for his help? Or did he do it for nothing, just out of the goodness of his heart?" he asked with heavy sarcasm.

"He is hostile," she thought. "I had to pay," she said defensively. "He knew who I was, that we were the *former people*. He was kind, but he also knew that I had no way out, so he made his terms clear. I fulfilled my obligations." She did not elaborate. They kept walking without speaking, Larissa staring at the yellow sand on the path.

Svirsky looked at her profile, his heart aching. "He did fulfill his part of the bargain, didn't he?" he finally asked, still avoiding the crucial question.

"Yes. He brought us to Petrograd. What's more, he arranged for us to receive food packages from America. Being a commissar gave him certain privileges. So, I sold myself for my life and my child's life. I had nothing else to offer," she concluded and looked at him boldly. "There!" she thought, " I've said it!"

He averted his eyes.

They continued to walk silently, Svirsky's mind churning with conflicting emotions. One moment he was full of pity, perfectly understanding her hopeless predicament, the next, burning with fury that he had fallen for a woman who had admitted to prostituting herself.

"Where is Kóshkin now?" he finally asked.

"Vladivostok. He brought us to my mother as he promised, and the day after, he had to leave. He tried to convince me to marry him and join him, but I refused because I did not love him and it would be wrong if we married."

It bothered Larissa that Svirsky avoided looking at her. She felt that her confession compromised her in his opinion.

He asked no more questions.

They continued to walk side by side, but she removed her hand from the crook of his arm. He seemed not to notice. They reached the Strelka, and the gray panorama of the Gulf of Finland rippled before them. The Strelka was deserted except for a group of young pioneers in their uniforms of white shirts and dark pants and skirts, all wearing triangular red kerchiefs around their necks. The children listened with great attention to a talk of their adult leader. Larissa caught a few words that they must be thankful to Comrade Lenin for opening the park for all children and not only those of the rich.

Svirsky looked grim. Larissa felt that he was judging her, and it made her angry. "Is he going to despise me for accepting Kóshkin's conditions? If so, I am glad that I told him the truth now rather than later." She smiled awkwardly.

"How can you smile? I am disappointed, Larissa Sergéyevna," he said icily. "Any person of our background should feel insulted by Kóshkin's offer, but you seem not only to accept it, but to find Kóshkin an honorable man!"

Hot blood rushed into Larissa's face. She faced him squarely. "I won't answer to this accusation. Obviously you were never in the situation when your very life and the life of some dear person depended on a quick decision. You have no right to accuse me of being a whore."

His look mixed anger with pain. "I know, I spoke without thinking. I spoke out of jealousy and deep hurt. I was deeply hurt," he repeated. "I never thought that I might learn something so negative about you. I fell in love with you, and I could not conceive that you had made such ... things in your past. I am jealous, yes, but I am mad at myself for feeling that way. I spoke stupidly, like Onégin with Tatiana ..."

"You were playing the role to perfection!" she laughed bitterly, tears filling her eyes. "It's funny!" she said.

"Yes, it is very funny," he replied. They did not talk for the rest of the walk.

Maria Nikoláyevna sensed the tension immediately. Larissa and Svirsky stood far apart and avoided looking at each other. Larissa's eyes were swollen, and Svirsky's mouth was set in a hard line, excluding even a shadow of a smile.

"Won't you sit down, Nikolaí Nikolayevich?' she greeted him with a pleasant smile. "A cup of tea?"

"No, thank you. I am rather in a hurry."

"Shall we rehearse tomorrow?" Larissa asked.

He hesitated with an answer. "If you like ..."

"It's our job. It is not a matter of preference," she said coldly.

"I'll be here tomorrow at the usual time." He bowed to Maria Nikoláyevna as Larissa opened the door. He followed her through the corridor and to the front door.

"Why is Uncle Kólya mad?" Nínochka asked as Larissa returned. "He did not even say hello to me. Did I do something wrong?"

"No, no, dear girl. He had something on his mind, that's all," Larissa replied.

"But he was angry! He did not even look at you!" the child insisted. "And he did not kiss Bábushka's hand! I know he was very angry. I'll ask him tomorrow!"

"You will do no such thing," Maria Nikoláyevna said sternly. "It is very bad manners to ask anyone if they are angry. Do you understand?"

When her bábushka talked about good manners, there was no way Nínochka could disobey. "I understand," she said meekly. "I won't ask."

100

"Well, what happened?" Maria Nikoláyevna asked. "I know that something did not go quite right." It was dark in the room, and Nínochka was long asleep. Maria Nikoláyevna and Larissa were free to indulge themselves in their nightly intimate conversations.

Larissa briefly described the encounter.

"Did he actually admit that he was in love with you? Did he say it?" her mother insisted.

"Yes. He said it casually, as if it was a long known fact. He talked about his disappointment with me, about his hurt, but nothing about his sympathy for my situation. It was all 'I, I, I!' So self-absorbed! I am glad that I found out about it before—"

"Don't rush to the wrong conclusion and condemn him for selfishness!" her mother interrupted. "Remember, you had just shaken him. Look how much he was supposed to absorb in just a few minutes: Kóshkin, an uncouth communist, daring to extort and make love to Svirsky's woman, for he was already thinking of you as his own, and daring to claim Nínochka as his own. All men are selfish when it comes to sharing what they treasure."

She continued, "He was jealous of Kóshkin, who had possessed you through a degrading deal. His pride made him feel hurt. The way I see it, he was too hurt to have control over his feelings!"

"In other words, you agree that he was selfish!" Larissa said. Then, they both laughed "Thank you, Mama. I feel a little better. Tomorrow I shall write to Igor. I'll tell him the truth, enough of it to discourage him from waiting for me to surrender. No matter what happens with Nikolái, I don't want to marry Kóshkin."

"Yes, my dear! But don't give up on Nikolái. Remember, your revelations shocked him. He has not stopped loving you, even though he may hate you right now!"

Svirsky arrived for the rehearsal punctually, but his face was serious and he smiled only when Nínochka greeted him with a kiss. "May I stay here during your rehearsal? I'll be very, very quiet, I promise! I just like to listen to you, Uncle Kólya! I think you have a very good voice, and you can change the sound from very loud to very quiet. I tried to do it, to sing very loudly, but I ended up shouting. I do better with quiet: I can make it almost as quiet as a whisper. But then, the melody escapes me. What do I do wrong?"

Larissa and Maria Nikoláyevna both wished to interrupt her, but Svirsky made a gesture not to. He listened carefully and answered seriously, "It will be easy to do when you are a little older. Meanwhile, after the rehearsal, perhaps I could show you what you can do now, before you grow older. Is that alright with you?"

"Yes," she replied as seriously. "I'll just sit here quietly with my coloring book."

Larissa placed the score on the piano. Maria Nikoláyevna moved her chair to the window and settled down with a silk blouse that she was embroidering for a new client. Svirsky cleared his throat and proceeded with his warm-up exercises. That done, he opened his score and the rehearsal began.

Nínochka kept her promise to be quiet. She listened with great attention at first, forgetting her coloring book, but as Svirsky began to repeat certain sections of the aria again and again, she lost interest and returned to her coloring book.

Larissa could not concentrate on the music. She played mechanically, aching at the thought that perhaps Nikolaí would ask another accompanist to work with him. She made an effort not to think of her love for him. It was too painful …

Suddenly Svirsky stopped in the middle of the aria where Prince Igor thinks of his beloved. He had already repeated this section several times, but he stopped and said, "I think it's no good … I can't concentrate. Let's stop for today." He closed the hard cover of his score with a snap. "So, what is your problem, young lady?" he turned to Nínochka.

"Well, you told me that you would teach me something," she said.

"Yes. You must sing for me. Not the snowflake song, but something else. I am sure you know more songs."

"Yes, I learned a new song not long ago. Mama taught me. It is by the very famous composer Mozart who started composing music when he was only five years old! Imagine that! This song is called 'Sleep, my precious baby, sleep!' It must be sung very softly, because it is a lullaby."

"I understand," he said, his face serious.

Larissa was surprised, but she played the short introduction while Nínochka took her position at the piano, facing Svirsky and her grandmother. She nodded to her mother like a professional singer, and Larissa repeated the introduction.

Nínochka began to sing very softly, filling the room with the charming, innocent melody, her voice pure and clear.

Svirsky felt deeply moved by her performance and the whole atmosphere: mother and child united in music, grandmother peacefully sitting with some handiwork, the room bathed in the sunshine, a picture of domestic bliss. "It all could have been mine!" he suddenly thought.

Larissa also felt the atmosphere of family unity, "It could have been ours ..." she thought.

Maria Nikoláyevna suddenly dropped her work on her lap. She had tears in her eyes. She too, fell under the spell of the sweet aura surrounding the child and the two young people who loved one another but were about to lose each other due to misplaced pride. She was not going to let it happen. She stood up and said in her most authoritarian voice, "We must leave, Nínochka. I forgot that we have an appointment with an elephant at the zoo! Uncle Kólya can talk to you tomorrow. Let's hurry!"

"Oh, the zoo!" The singing was forgotten as Nina grabbed her coat. "I am ready, Bábushka!"

Maria Nikoláyevna, speaking in the same tone of voice, turned to Svirsky and her daughter. "And you, children, tell each other that you are in love with one another. It is ridiculous that you are willing to risk losing one another because of a tragic situation that has already been resolved and ought to be forgotten. You, Nikolaí Nikolayevich, have unpleasant revelations of your own that would shock Larissa. But peace and beauty may still be yours, my dears, starting right now, with this peace and beauty!" She made a wide gesture with her arm. She put her coat and hat on, majestic in her determination. Taking her granddaughter firmly by the hand, she sailed out of the room.

Her mother's interference embarrassed Larissa. She was about to apologize when Svirsky grabbed her and kissed her with a long, rough kiss. For a moment she was stunned, but her own passion made her embrace him in return and seek his mouth. They did not speak. They stood at the piano in a tight embrace, covering one another's faces with little kisses. No words were necessary.

"God bless your mother!" Nikolaí finally exclaimed. "Do you realize that she has saved us from committing the biggest mistake of our lives? I love you, Larissa, and I want to be married to you now. We can ignore the old traditions of a prolonged courtship. We can get on with our lives and get married ... tomorrow, if we wish! And to think that we were on the brink of ..."

"Sh-Sh," Larissa placed her hand across his mouth. He kissed it. "No recriminations! Only happy thoughts!" she said. "Let's go to the park, or to the river. I want to feel free of everything, the walls, the furniture, of everything except this feeling of relief!"

They took a streetcar to Elagin Island Park, sitting on the open platform at the back of the car and holding hands. It was the same park where only yesterday they had wounded each other so deeply. They reached the Grande Alley with its rows of marble statuary. The bushy maple trees were already turning colors, the branches of the trees uniting above the alley to create a leafy ceiling. There was something new which they did not notice the day before: across the alley a large slogan was strung between the trees: "Thank You Comrade Stalin For Our Happy Childhood."

They looked sarcastically at one another. Larissa said, "Speaking of happy childhood, I want to show you something!" A glistening marble statue of a young woman with a bunch of flowers was nestled in the grove. "I want you to take a closer look. It is called 'Flora' but I used to know it as 'Larissa.'"

"Why, it does look like you!" he exclaimed.

"It is me. My father had it made. Our new authorities were decent enough to not destroy everything from the old days. I hold big hopes for our cultural future!"

"So do I. I am happy that classic operas by foreign composers are being translated into Russian. Imagine how many new people, who had never heard an opera before, will be able to enjoy them!"

Larissa nodded. "I understand before Lenin died, he left instructions to his comrades to respect and protect all forms of art as national treasures."

"It's funny," Nikolaí said. "Here we are, talking about Russian culture and operas as if we have been married for a long time, while we have not even slept with one another! It shows that we truly were meant for one another, we fit so neatly!"

They proceeded to the Strelka and sat there watching the placid gray sea and a motionless single sailboat left helpless by the absence of wind. The sea and the sky looked inseparable, like one gray eternity without a horizon.

Larissa placed her head on his shoulder and felt peaceful and safe, as she used to feel with Andrei. "Forgive me, my darling Andrúsha, for falling in love with somebody new," she thought. "I'll never forget you, my angel … But I need somebody to love … And Nínochka needs a father … Forgive me, my love!"

Nikolái noticed that her face turned sad. "Are you alright?" he asked with concern.

She smiled. "I am very, very happy, and I am looking forward to planning our wedding. Since there are no churches anymore, we'll have to go to the marriage registration bureau. I hope my fake documents will present no problems. So far, no one has bothered me."

"I too, have bogus documents. You and I are in the same boat, my love, as the saying goes, but I think we are both safe." He kissed her.

They returned to the flat. Maria Nikolávevna knew immediately that they had reached a happy closure. Nínochka too, felt the sudden closeness between them.

"Are you going to be my father?" she demanded, sounding severe, very much like her grandmother. "Have you proposed marriage to my mother?"

He laughed, feeling somewhat embarrassed. "I did not need to. She read my mind!"

"Oh, no! That doesn't count! You must bend down on one knee to make it official, like in my Fairy Tales book! You must take her hand and say, 'Dear Larissa Sergéyevna, will you marry me please?' And when she says 'yes', you kiss her hand. Then you stand up and kiss her again, but on her lips, making it official."

"Oh, dear!" he exclaimed. "We must make it official!"

He took Larissa by the hand and led her to the windows, the only un-cluttered space in the room. He knelt on one knee and, in the best display of theatrical gallantry, said the prescribed words. When Larissa said 'yes,' he stood and kissed her on the lips. He then turned to Nínochka. "Dear Nínochka, may I marry your mother?"

The child, suddenly shy, replied, "Yes, you may!"

Maria Nikolávevna laughed heartily and clapped her hands. Nikolái opened his arms and Nínochka rushed to him.

"You'll be my Papa forever and ever!" she exclaimed.

"And you will be my daughter forever and ever!" he picked her up and kissed her. "We will be a happy family! All four of us!"

Happy days arrived for Larissa and Nikolái. Upon learning about the engagement, Doctor Kline invited Maria Nikolávevna and Nínochka for a week of 'mushroom hunting in the country.' She was glad that someone had discovered Larissa and fell in love with her. Doctor Kline thought that it would be a good idea for Maria Nikolávevna and Nínochka to disappear for a week. She had a good friend in Luga, also a doctor, who could easily accommodate them.

"Thank you, my friend! That little trip will be beneficial to all of us. Nínochka has never been in the country or seen a mushroom. And of course, the young couple haven't yet made love. I know it's on their minds, but as we both know, there is very little privacy nowadays."

Doctor Kline smiled. "Yes, it must be tough for the young lovers all over the country. I am glad to be of help!"

After rehearsal the next day, Lara settled down to write a letter.

It was going to be a short letter. "No need to go into the details, or be apologetic," she thought.

Dear Igor,

I wanted to write to you for some time but now my life has taken a different and happy course. My job as an accompanist at the Opera House became permanent! I receive all the benefits and rations of a permanently employed artist, including a small pension for being the widow of an ace. Apparently the authorities don't care anymore that Andrei was a White pilot. There is also a small subsidy for Nínochka as the orphan of a hero. All these unexpected rewards and my good salary have made the prospect of decent living a reality. My mother and I are doing really well now and we won't need anymore the food packages from America.

In addition to this change, I met a man, a singer in the opera. We are getting married in a few days. He knows all about you and our arrangement, and even though he was surprised and hurt, he doesn't hold it against me.

So, thank you for all you have done for us, good friend, for all those food packages and warm clothes that you obtained for us, thank you for your love and these years of support without which we could not have survived. You were a good friend, Igor, and I'll be forever thankful to you. I owe you our lives and I'll never forget this!

I wish you good luck and I hope that you'll meet someone who will love and appreciate you. I do hope that we will remain friends. If you choose not to be in touch with me—I'll understand. But if you would like to correspond with me, I'll welcome it!

Good luck to you, dear friend. By now you must have finished your courses at the university. Congratulations!

Your friend,
Larissa Rezánova

She read the letter. It was good, she thought. She sealed it.

That done, she relaxed. She sat at the piano and tried to play some short pieces of Tchaikovsky and Mendelssohn, relying on the physical memory of her fingers, preparing herself for a disappointment. After nearly ten years, it would be a miracle if she still remembered those charming bagatelles. But she did remember them! She sang the melodies in her mind, and her fingers followed almost faultlessly. The old exquisite pleasure of playing, just playing the piano, was hers again!

Svirsky arrived with good news. He had told Klimov about their engagement, and the old man had virtually exploded with good wishes.

"I am a practical man, and my first concern is where you will live. Maria Nikoláyevna's room is good, but it is hardly a proper place for a family of four. I think I have a solution. You are due to have a room allocated to you as an artist of first category. My idea is to have your allocated room and Maria Nikoláyevna's room exchanged for a small flat. You would have to pay a little extra money for it, but I think that with your and Larissa's combined salaries, you'll be able to afford it!"

"That's a great idea!" Svirsky said. "But it would be very difficult to achieve. I don't have the allocated room yet, and who knows how long it will take to obtain it."

"Ah, but that's where we enter the picture! Our theatre commissar and I, that is! We can request a room to be allocated to you immediately since you are working on two leading roles in the new productions. Then, we shall ask for help from Larissa's friend at the Housing Authority. I know that the Housing Authority has a small reserve of exceptional flats in central locations. All will be done through official requests from the Opera Theatre, which carries authority. You'll be living in grand style in no time! I see a great future ahead of the two of you!"

Maria Nikoláyevna and Nínochka left for Luga aboard a commuter train. Nínochka took it upon herself to explain to her grandmother the etiquette of riding in a railroad car. "If you want to make pipi, there is a toilet at the end of each car. It is very uncomfortable and you cannot sit down, because the seat is always dirty. And you cannot go to the toilet when the train stops because everyone will know that someone is making a pipi."

"How would they know that someone is making a pipi?" Maria Nikoláyevna asked, amused.

"Because the pipi will drip to the road through a hole in the toilet. And you cannot drink the water either, Mama says, because it is full of bacterium, that can make you very sick."

"Well, thank you for this valuable information," Maria Nikoláyevna said. "I haven't been on the train for many years!"

"I was on a train for a long time when we were coming to you from Odessa. It was fun! We even had to hide under the bed when some bad people attacked our train! Papa Igor had to shoot his gun! He was my Papa then."

"Don't call him your Papa anymore. Call him Uncle Igor."

Nina looked at her babushka in surprise. "But he and my Mama wanted me to call him Papa! I know I can have only one real Papa, and it was Papa Andrúsha. But now I will have another Papa. I am confused!"

"From now on, Papa Kólya will be your real Papa! And I am sure he won't like it if you call Igor your Papa. So, watch yourself!"

"I'll watch myself. I like him better than Papa Igor. I like when he sings. And Papa Kólya is so handsome! He looks like a Prince from Sleeping Beauty! I am in love with him!"

Maria Nikoláyevna chuckled. "You are too young to be in love. Your Mama is in love."

"That's alright. We both are in love! And you also must be in love with him, so he will have all three women who are in love with him! He will like it!"

"We shall spoil him with so much love!"

"Never! Mama says there is no such thing as too much love!"

Larissa waited for Nikolaí to come back in the afternoon with a few personal items for the week ahead. Her hair was still wet after her visit to the local banya. She let her hair loose as she placed a sweet-smelling ivory soap in a soap dish. She had been saving that gift from the American pilots for Christmas or Easter holidays.

"My first night with Kólya is more important than any holiday," she thought with that sweetly sharp feeling of anticipation in her groin as she changed the sheets on her bed.

It was dark when Nikolaí arrived. Freshly shaved and smelling of eau-de-cologne, he too, had rushed to the public baths after the rehearsal. He brought along a small valise with his nightclothes and other necessities and a bouquet of roses for Larissa. In a straw basket he carried a bottle of Crimean champagne, a small can of Keta Salmon red caviar, and a quarter of a pound of cheddar cheese, spending half of his weekly salary at Eliseyev's Gourmet Emporium.

Larissa opened the door and embraced him. His arms were full, and he couldn't embrace her. As he tried to kiss her in return, he missed and kissed the air instead. They both laughed.

Old Ivan Vassilich, the ombudsman of the apartment, greeted them from the opened door of his room. "Congratulations!" he beamed. "Nínochka told me of your marriage! Mnógy léta! Many years of happiness!"

"Thank you, Ivan Vassilich," Larissa said, preferring not to correct his assumption. "Meet my husband Nikolaí Nikolayevich Svirsky!"

"Delighted!" the old man declared, saluting to Nikolaí like the old soldier he must have been in the days gone by.

"Well, now I'll have to meet your mother's partner in her sewing enterprise, and who else?" Nikolaí laughed.

"My friends Natasha and Dimka. And of course, Doctor Kline. There are others whom you'll meet as the time goes by," Larissa replied, "Meanwhile, kiss me!"

He lifted her off her feet. Kissing her, he lowered her on her bed.

Gently, Nikolaí began to undress her, kissing every new inch of her exposed skin, while she unbuttoned his shirt, kissing his chest, both becoming inflamed by the sight and feel of one another's flesh. What had started so gently soon turned into a passionate assault as they gave themselves to it. It was a fast bout, but they knew that it was only the beginning. They rested, breathing heavily, refusing to separate.

"God!" he finally murmured against her neck. "I am ready to die!"

"Don't!" she whispered hoarsely. "We'll do it again!" They laughed idiotically, clinging to each other. "I love you, Kólya, I do, do love you!"

"I love you Lara, I do, do love you!" He changed his position and stretched out next to her, seeing her nakedness for the first time. "Good Lord, you are so beautiful!" He caressed and kissed her breasts and her shoulders and her chest, slipping to the lower part of her body. He wanted to devour her, to make her body a part of his.

They made love again, this time savoring it. Finally, they realized that they were starved. Larissa put on an ugly robe, the only one she had, while Nikolaí took out of his valise a handsome silk robe, a Christmas gift from Alicia so many years ago.

"We'll get you a new robe, my love," he said. "Meanwhile, put on this pajama coat. I have another set, so we'll get rid of this awful thing!"

"My God, yes! I forgot how it feels to have silk against my skin! I used my last silk nightdress to make dresses for Nínochka when she was two or three years old!"

"We'll wear silks again! You'll see. The artists will be the new aristocracy! And we will be the part of it!"

Larissa donned his pajama jacket, looking like a young girl trying on her father's jacket, her hair loosely plated into a braid.

"You look adorable!" he exclaimed, embracing her.

There was an awkward moment for Nikolaí as he had to make a trip to the communal toilet, but he met no one in the corridor or in the hall. The neighbors, Anna Mikháilovna and her seldom seen daughter and Ivan Vassilich, stayed in their rooms.

Larissa succeeded him at the toilet, coming back to a feast spread on the table.

She laughed as Nikolaí, armed with a Boy Scout knife, struggled with the champagne bottle. Finally uncorked, the warm champagne foamed out of the bottle, wetting the table and the spread food.

"Never mind!" Larissa said cuddling to him. "It is our first meal and nothing is going to spoil it!"

They finally fell asleep at sunrise, their need for one another keeping them awake all night. When they awoke, they tried to rehearse as usual, but they could not concentrate. Nikolaí interrupted their work to kiss and to touch Larissa. He was too happy to work.

"Let's take this week off and just make love and go for long walks! We'll catch up on our work in no time!" Larissa suggested.

Svirsky visited the Eliseyev Gastronomy Emporium again. He bought several cans of sardines and two large cans of Swedish meat balls and a large package of British crackers to have at home. They visited the Conservatory canteen for lunch and dinner, then hurried back home to make love and tell each other about their previous lives.

On the last day of the week Larissa received a letter from Igor. It was far too soon to be an answer to her letter.

"Our letters must have crossed one another," Larissa thought. Nikolaí, seeing the postal mark of Vladivostok, went for a walk to give her some privacy.

It was a short letter, and Larissa could hardly recognize Kóshkin's handwriting: his letters were neatly formed and the words were well spaced—the handwriting of a well-educated person. "Good for you, Igor!" she thought.

Dear Larka,

Finally I am through with schooling, but not with learning! I am a graduate of the University and I shall continue now as a member of the Faculty! I am sure you would be proud of me. My life has changed. I've met a wonderful woman. She is a schoolteacher and we are living together as husband and wife. I won't pursue you with my demands anymore. It's amazing what a long time we haven't seen one another ... I apologize that I have kept bothering you all these years refusing to believe that we could never be happy together. I was an idiot! And you were right!

I hope you are happy living with your mother. I also hope that you'll meet someone whom you could love and that Ninka will grow up a fine Soviet girl.

With my good wishes for all of you,
I remain your friend,

Igor Kóshkin

P.S. I have heard that your friend Commissar Glafíra was arrested some two years ago. Apparently she was an agent of the secret Anti-Soviet group in Odessa. You were lucky to be out of Odessa in the nick of time!!"

"Poor Glafíra!" Larissa thought. The information darkened her relief that Igor was no longer pursuing her. "Poor Glafíra! She must have been denounced to the Cheka ... Poor friend ... She saved my life ..."

Nikolaí returned, entering the room cautiously.

Larissa sighed. "I have some sad news about my friend Glafíra. But there is good news also. Read this!" she proffered him Kóshkin's letter.

He took the letter, and a smile slowly spread over his handsome face. "Marvelous! Good life to the Koshkins in Vladivostok! I'm sorry about your friend, but it is all water under the bridge. She wanted you to be safe, and you are! And you'll honor her memory by living well." He put his arms around her. "We'll live well, my love, you'll see!"

Larissa nodded, but her happiness was dampened by deep sadness. "Poor Glafíra ..."

Nínochka was full of excitement and was eager to tell them about her experiences in the country. "I saw a rabbit in the forest two steps away from me! And I gathered mushrooms in the forest! Doctor Vera Petrovna is my best friend now, and she showed me all the good mushrooms and taught me about the bad ones, the pretty ones, which can kill people! Vera Petrovna has a little dog, *Touzik,* who loved me! Can we have a little dog when we live all together? I'll take care of him, I'll take him for a walk and love him! Can we Papa? Can we?" she begged Nikolaí, who melted with happiness that the little girl has already accepted him as her father.

"Of course, my darling girl you can have a dog, as soon as we get settled," he said, looking at Larissa and her mother with a happy smile, "We'll have a dog and a bird who will talk, and whatever else you would want!" he laughed. "We'll have a happy family!"

"You will be a flower girl at your mother's wedding," Maria Niko-láyevna said.

"When?" The dog was forgotten.

"In a few days," Nikolaí said. "Would you like that?"

"Oh, yes! I would love that!" she clapped her hands. "I'll do a good job, even though I have never done it before!"

That night, Nikolaí went back to the dormitory for his last night there. Larissa and Nínochka cuddled together in the same bed as always, but Nínochka was too excited to sleep.

"Bábushka told me so much about you when you were a little girl, Mama! I wish it was *me!* But she told me almost nothing about *Papa Andrúsha.* Tell me about him, about how he disconnected the bomb from his airplane, tell me how you two met ... I know, you have told me about it before, but I don't remember it. Tell me about my *real Papa!* He was a hero, yes?"

"Yes, he was a *real* hero."

"Tell me about him and the bomb! Tell me how he asked for your hand in marriage! Tell me everything!"

"I have been telling you about it for years!"

"I know, but I like to hear it again, and again! It's even better than a fairy tale, because it was *real!*"

"Well ... All right ... I was about seventeen years old when I *noticed* your father for the first time. I mean, when I noticed him. I knew him all my life, but I suddenly noticed that he was a very good-looking young man ..."

"And you fell in love!"

"Yes ... And I fell in love! Head over heels!"

Nina giggled. "My new Papa Kólya is also very good-looking. Are you head over heels in love again?"

She smiled. "Yes, I am in love again! And I am happy!"

The words of Stalin, the new ruler of Russia, came to Larissa's mind: *"Life became easier, Comrades. Life became happier!"*

"Yes," she thought. "Against all odds, life became easier. And not only for us, but for the whole country! After all the horrors and deprivations, against all odds, life became easier! Life became happier!" she said aloud, smiling in the darkness.

"I am already happy!" Nínochka declared, cuddling closer to her. "I'm very, very, VERY happy!"

Bibliography

Russian Historical Events

Berg, A. Scott. *Wilson*. Putnam, 2013. Print.

Bergamini, John D. *The Tragic Dynasty; a History of the Romanovs*. New York: Putnam, 1969. Print.

Bowet, John. *Moscow and St. Petersburg*. Print.

Bullock, David. *The Russian Civil War, 1918-22*. Oxford: Osprey Pub., 2008. Print.

Cowles, Virginia. *The Romanovs*. New York: Harper & Row, 1971. Print.

Crankshaw, Edward. *The Shadow of the Winter Palace: Russia's Drift to Revolution, 1825-1917*. New York: Viking, 1976. Print.

Farmborough, Florence. *With the Armies of the Tsar: A Nurse at the Russian Front, 1914-18*. New York: Stein and Day, 1975. Print.

Hastings, Max. *Catastrophe: Europe Goes to War 1914*. Print.

Heresch, Elisabeth. *Blood on the Snow: Eyewitness Accounts of the Russian Revolution*. New York: Paragon House, 1990. Print.

Kenez, Peter. *Civil War in South Russia, 1918: The First Year of the Volunteer Army*. Berkeley: U of California, 1971. Print.

Kenez, Peter. *Civil War in South Russia, 1919-1920: The Defeat of the Whites*. Berkeley: Published for the Hoover Institution on War, Revolution, and Peace U of California, 1977. Print.

King, Greg. *The Man Who Killed Rasputin: Prince Youssoupov and the Murder That Helped Bring down the Russian Empire*. Secaucus, NJ: Carol Pub. Group, 1995. Print.

Lincoln, W. Bruce. *Red Victory: A History of the Russian Civil War*. New York: Simon and Schuster, 1989. Print.

Lincoln, W. Bruce. *The Romanovs: Autocrats of All the Russias*. New York: Dial, 1981. Print.

Massie, Robert K. *The Romanovs: The Final Chapter*. New York: Random House, 1995. Print.

Pope, Stephen, and Elizabeth-Anne Wheal. *Dictionary of the First World War*. Havertown: Pen and Sword, 2007. Print.

Rasputina, Mariia Grigorevna and Patte Barham. *Rasputin, the Man behind the Myth, a Personal Memoir.* Englewood Cliffs, NJ: Prentice-Hall, 1977. Print.

Reed, John. *Ten Days That Shook the World.* New York: Vintage, 1960. Print.

Salisbury, Harrison E. *Black Night, White Snow: Russia's Revolutions 1905-1917.* Garden City, NY: Doubleday, 1978. Print.

Service, Robert. *A History of Twentieth-century Russia.* Cambridge, MA: Harvard UP, 1998. Print.

Service, Robert. *Russia: Experiment with a People.* Cambridge, MA: Harvard UP, 2003. Print.

Shoumatoff, Alex. *Russian Blood.* Print.

Smith, Douglas. Former People: The Last Days of the Russian Aristocracy. London: Macmillan, 2012. Print.

Russian WWI Aviation

Blume, August G. *The Russian Military Air Fleet in World War I.* Atglen, PA: Schiffer Military History, 2010. Print.

Durkota, Alan, Thomas Darcey, and Victor Kulikov. *The Imperial Russian Air Service: Famous Pilots & Aircraft of World War One.* Mountain View, CA: Flying Machines, 1995. Print.

Funderburk, Thomas R. *The Fighters: The Men and Machines of the First Air War.* New York: Grosset & Dunlap, 1965. Print.

Guttman, Jon. *Pusher Aces of World War 1.* Oxford: Osprey, 2009. Print.

Guttman, Jon. *SPAD XIII vs. Fokker D VII: Western Front 1918.* Oxford: Osprey, 2009. Print.

Hart, Peter. *Bloody April: Slaughter in the Skies over Arras, 1917.* London: Weidenfeld & Nicolson, 2005. Print.

Holmes, Richard. *Falling Upwards: How the Romantics Took to the Air.* London: HarperPress, 2012. Print.

Holmes, Richard. *Weapon: A Visual History of Arms and Armour.* London: Dorling Kindersley, 2008. Print.

Jackson, Robert and Jim Winchester. *Military Aircraft: 1914 to the Present Day.* Edison, NJ: Chartwell, 2004. Print.

Makanna, Philip and Javier Arango. *Ghosts of the Great War: Aviation in World War One.* San Francisco: Ghosts. Print.

Riaboff, Alexander and Von Hardesty. *Gatchina Days: Reminiscences of a Russian Pilot.* Washington, D.C.: Smithsonian Institution, 1986. Print.

Rickenbacker, Eddie. *Fighting the Flying Circus.* Garden City, NY: Doubleday, 1965. Print.

Rickenbaker, Eddie. *The Flying Circus.* Print.

Sergievski, Boris Vasilevich, Allan Forsyth, and Adam Hochschild. *Airplanes, Women, and Song: Memoirs of a Fighter Ace, Test Pilot, and Adventurer.* Syracuse, NY: Syracuse UP, 1999. Print.

Acknowledgements

I am deeply grateful to many people who have helped me with research about Russian military aviation during the First World War.

I am especially indebted to John Little, Assistant Curator and Research Team Leader at the Seattle Museum of Flight. He supplied me with invaluable information, photographs and maps and guided me through the WWI exhibits and archives.

My pen pal from Russia, Yakov Sapozhnikov obtained for me a vast amount of information directly from Russia, including films, pilot memoirs and rare photographs of vintage airplanes and their equipment. I was pleased that this information arrived in the Russian language.

Charles Brooks, another pen pal, sent me many more detailed photographs of the British and French aircraft used by the Russians, as well as descriptions and specifications of the military equipment.

Asta Aristov, a high school Russian language teacher of my son, allowed me to consult memoirs of her father that gave me another perspective on the Civil War.

Marci Nelson, MD, a beautiful young doctor, helped me to describe the medical problems of my characters, from childbirth to treating open wounds using colonies of maggots.

Another friend, Carolyn Sanders, an equestrienne, gave a lot of help in informing me about the variety of horses and horses' anatomy.

My three editors Kristin Jessup Moore, Celeste Bennett and Adam Finley bravely read hundreds of pages of manuscript, discarding redundancies and modifying the traditional tendencies of Russian writers for detailed descriptions.

Jon McCracken provided important information about the sudden explosion of Russian decadence in literature and music, in visual arts and morals on the cusp of the First World War.

My granddaughter Kyra Alexandra Wayne, a talented young artist, designed the striking cover using the colorful style of WWI public art.

And finally, my son Ronald Wayne, a physician and a pilot who kept after me for years to write a book about my father. He became my in-house authority on dealing with psychological and technical problems of early aviation.

I owe them all my greatest gratitude. Without their help and shared knowledge I would have never been able to undertake such a difficult theme as the First World War, the devastating Civil War and the first few years of Soviet rule.

CPSIA information can be obtained at www.ICGtesting.com
Printed in the USA
LVOW11*0523220216

475889LV00004BB/10/P